WI

M000097149

THE MAIAS

Episodes from Romantic Life

Eça de Queirós

Translated from the Portuguese
with an afterword by Margaret Jull Costa

A NEW DIRECTIONS BOOK

WITHDRAWN

Translation copyright © 2007 by Margaret Jull Costa

All rights reserved. Except for brief passages quoted in a newspaper, magazine,
radio, television, or website review, no part of this book may be reproduced
in any form or by any means, electronic or mechanical,
including photocopying and recording, or by any information storage
and retrieval system, without permission in writing from the Publisher.

Published by arrangement with The Dedalus Press, London.

The translator would like to thank, as always, Maria Manuel Lisboa
and Ben Sherriff for all their help, advice, and support.

Manufactured in the United States of America
New Directions Books are printed on acid-free paper.
First published as a New Directions Paperbook (NDP1080) in 2007
Published simultaneously in Canada by Penguin Books Canada Limited
Design by Erik Rieselbach

Library of Congress Cataloging-in-Publication Data
Queirós, Eça de, 1845–1900.
[Maias. English]
The maias / Eça de Queirós ;
translated from the Portuguese by Margaret Jull Costa.
p. cm.
ISBN 978-0-8112-1649-4 (alk. paper)
I. Costa, Margaret Jull. II. Title.
PQ9261.E3M313 2007
869.3'3—dc22
2007005459

3 5 7 9 10 8 6 4 2

New Directions books are published for James Laughlin
by New Directions Publishing Corporation
80 Eighth Avenue, New York 10011

THE MAIAS

: I :

THE HOUSE IN LISBON to which the Maias moved in the autumn of 1875 was known in Rua de São Francisco de Paula, and in the surrounding area of Janelas Verdes, as the Casa do Ramalhete, the House of the Bouquet of Flowers, or, more simply, as Ramalhete. Despite that fresh green name worthy of some rural retreat, Ramalhete was a large stern house of sober walls, with a line of narrow wrought-iron balconies on the second floor, and, above that, a row of timid little windows sheltering under the eaves, a house which, as befitted a building dating from the reign of Queen Maria I, had the gloomy appearance of an ecclesiastical residence, and indeed, to complete its resemblance to a Jesuit college, it needed only a bell and a cross. The name, Ramalhete, doubtless came from the square panel of decorative tiles placed in the spot intended for a coat of arms that had never materialised, and which depicted a large bunch of sunflowers tied with a ribbon on which one could still just make out the letters and numbers of a date.

For long years, Ramalhete had remained empty; cobwebs appeared on the grilles on the ground-floor windows, and the house slowly took on the grim look of a ruin. In 1858, the Papal Nuncio, Monsignor Buccarini, had visited it with a view to establishing his residence there, seduced by the building's clerical gravity and by the sleepy peace of the neighbourhood: he liked the interior of the house too, with its palatial rooms and coffered ceilings, the walls covered in frescos on which the roses on the garlands and on the cheeks of the little cupids were already fading. However, the Monsignor, accustomed to life as a rich Roman prelate, also wanted a house with a fine garden full of groves of trees and fountains, and Ramalhete, beyond its tiled terrace, boasted only a poor uncultivated plot, abandoned to the weeds, with a cypress, a cedar, a dried-up waterfall, a choked pond, and, in one corner, a marble statue (which the Monsignor immediately identified as Aphrodite) growing ever blacker beneath the encroaching dankness of untamed vegetation. Apart from that, the rent proposed by old Vilaça, the Maia family's administrator, seemed to the Monsignor so extortionate that he asked, with a smile, if Vilaça thought the Church was still living in the age of Pope Leo X. Vilaça retorted that the

1

Portuguese nobility were likewise no longer living in the age of King João V. And so Ramalhete remained empty.

This useless old pile (as Vilaça Junior called it, for he had taken over as the Maias' administrator following the death of his father) only became of use again towards the end of 1870, as a storeroom for the furniture and crockery from the rather more historic family mansion in Benfica, which, after being on the market for some years, had finally been bought by a Brazilian *comendador*. This happened to coincide with the sale of Tojeira, another property belonging to the Maia family, a fact that aroused the curiosity of the few people in Lisbon who remembered the Maias and knew that, for the past twenty years or so, they had been living quietly on their estate, the Quinta de Santa Olávia, on the banks of the River Douro. These few people asked Vilaça if the Maia family were in financial difficulties.

"Oh, they still have a crust of bread to eat," answered Vilaça, smiling, "and butter to spread on it too."

The Maias were an old and never very numerous Beira family, with few relatives and no collateral branches, in fact, they were now down to the last two males, the master of the house, Afonso da Maia, who was an old man, almost a patriarch, older than the century, and his grandson, Carlos, who was studying medicine at Coimbra University. When Afonso had moved to Santa Olávia, the income from the estate was already in excess of fifty thousand *cruzados*, and money had subsequently accrued from savings made during those twenty years of simple country living; there had also been an inheritance from their last surviving relative, Sebastião da Maia, who since 1830 had lived alone in Naples, where he had devoted himself to numismatics: so Vilaça, the administrator, had every reason to smile confidently when he spoke of the Maias and their crust of bread.

Tojeira had been sold on Vilaça's advice, but he had never approved of Afonso's decision to get rid of the house in Benfica merely because its walls had seen so many domestic misfortunes. As Vilaça said, the same thing happened to all walls. Since Ramalhete was now uninhabitable, the Maias had no house in Lisbon, and while Afonso, in his old age, might love the peace and quiet of Santa Olávia, his grandson, a young man with expensive tastes, who spent his holidays in Paris or in London, would not want to bury himself among the steep hills of the Douro Valley once he had graduated. And so it was that, some months before Carlos was due to leave Coimbra, Afonso astonished Vilaça by announcing that he had decided to come and live in Ramalhete! Vilaça immediately drew up a report enumerating the house's many inconveniences, the greatest of which was the vast amount of renovation work that this would involve and the equally vast expense; then, of course, there was the lack of a proper garden, which would, naturally, be deeply felt by anyone forced to abandon Santa Olávia's leafy groves; and, finally, there was the legend, according to which the walls of Ramalhete had always proved fatal to

2

the Maias, although, as he himself admitted sagely, he felt somewhat ashamed even to mention such superstitious nonsense in the age of Voltaire, Guizot, and other liberal-minded philosophers.

Highly amused by this last remark, Afonso replied that while the reasons Vilaça gave were all excellent, he nevertheless preferred to live in a house that had a long family connection, and if renovation work was required, then so be it, there was money enough to pay for it; and the best way to deal with legends and omens was to fling wide the windows and let in the sun.

Afonso had his way, and since it had so far been a dry winter, work began at once, under the direction of a certain Esteves, who was an architect, a politician, and friend of Vilaça's. Esteves enthused Vilaça with his plan for a magnificent staircase flanked by two figures symbolising Portugal's conquests in Guinea and in India. Indeed, he was in the throes of designing a ceramic fountain for the dining room when Carlos arrived unexpectedly in Lisbon accompanied by an architect-cum-decorator from London. After only the briefest of discussions regarding décor and fabric colours, Carlos handed over the four walls of Ramalhete to this Londoner and left him to apply his good taste to creating an interior that would combine comfort with intelligent, sober luxury.

Vilaça bitterly resented this blatant disregard for a Portuguese artist like Esteves, and Esteves went bleating to his political friends that Portugal was a lost cause. Afonso, too, regretted Esteves' dismissal, and even demanded that he should be given the commission to build the new coach houses. The "artist" was just about to accept, when he was appointed to the post of civil governor.

After a year, during which Carlos made frequent visits to Lisbon to collaborate on the work and "to add a few aesthetic touches," all that remained of the old Ramalhete was the grim façade, which, since it constituted the house's physiognomy, Afonso had chosen to retain. And Vilaça was the first to declare that "Jones Bule" (as he called the Englishman), without being too extravagant, had made of Ramalhete "a veritable museum," even incorporating some of the antiques from the mansion in Benfica.

The biggest surprise was the courtyard: once a bare and gloomy place paved with flagstones, now it positively glowed, with its white and red marble tiles, decorative plants, Quimper pots, and two long, carved wooden benches—as solemn as the stalls from a cathedral choir—which Carlos had brought back with him from Spain. Upstairs, in the anteroom, decked out like a shop selling fabrics from the Orient, any sound of footsteps was instantly muffled; it was furnished with divans draped in Persian rugs and with large copper-toned Moorish plates, providing a harmoniously sombre backdrop to the immaculate marble white of a statue—the figure of a young girl, shivering with cold and laughing as she dipped one dainty toe in the water. From here, one passed to a broad corridor, full of the finest pieces from the house in Benfica—Gothic chests, large Indian vases, and ancient devotional paintings. Ramalhete's noblest rooms opened onto this gallery. In the rarely used reception room, decorated entirely in velvet brocades the colour of autumn moss, there was a fine Constable portrait of Afonso's mother-in-law, the Countess de Runa, wearing a plumed tricorn hat and the scarlet riding habit of an English huntswoman, and set against a background of misty countryside. A smaller room to the side, intended as a music room, had an eighteenth-century air about it, with its ornate gilded furniture and gleaming sprigged silks; two faded Gobelin tapestries, in various shades of grey, covered the walls with shepherds and woods.

Opposite was the billiard room, lined with a new kind of leather brought especially from England by Jones Bule, on which silvery storks fluttered, caught in a tangle of bottle-green branches. Next door was the *fumoir*, the most comfortable room in the house, where the ottomans were as large and soft as beds, and the warm, somewhat sombre embrace of the scarlet and black upholstery was offset by the singing colours of the old Dutch faience-ware.

At the end of the corridor lay Afonso's study, furnished like a prelate's chamber in red damasks. Everything in the room—the solid rosewood desk, the low shelves made from carved oak, the sober opulence of the bindings on the books—combined to create an austere air of studious peace, reinforced by a painting attributed to Rubens, a family heirloom, of Christ on the cross, his bare athletic body set against a turbulent fiery sunset. Beside the fire, Carlos had created a little nook for his grandfather with a gold-embroidered Japanese screen, a white bearskin and a venerable old armchair, whose faded silk upholstery still bore the Maia coat of arms.

Afonso had his private rooms on the second floor, off a corridor lined with various family portraits. Carlos, for his part, had chosen to have his quarters in one corner of the house, and these, with their own private entrance and windows overlooking the garden, comprised three interconnecting rooms with the same carpet running through them all; the cushioned chairs and sofas, the silk-lined walls, caused Vilaça to remark that they were more like a dancer's boudoir than a doctor's private apartments!

Once work on the house was completed, it remained empty while Carlos, now a graduate, made a long tour of Europe, and it was only on the eve of his return, in that lovely autumn of 1875, that Afonso finally resolved to leave Santa Olávia and move into Ramalhete. He had not seen Lisbon for twenty-five years and, after only a few brief days, he confessed to Vilaça that he was already longing for the shade of Santa Olávia. But what else could he do? He did not want to live far from his grandson, and Carlos, who fully intended taking up an active career in medicine, had to live in Lisbon. Besides, he did not dislike Ramalhete, even though Carlos, with his enthusiasm for the lavish décor of colder climes, had perhaps overdone the velvet, the tapestries, and the heavy door curtains. He liked the neighbourhood too, liked its air of sweet suburban tranquillity drowsing in the sun. He even liked the little garden. Obviously, it could not compare with the garden at Santa Olávia, but there was, nonetheless, something very pleasant about it, with the sunflowers standing to attention at the bottom of the terrace steps, the cypress and the cedar tree growing old together like two sad friends; and the figure of Aphrodite, who, having recovered the pale tones proper to a garden statue, could easily have come straight from Versailles and the height of the Grand Siècle. And now that there was water in abundance, the little waterfall was a delight, in its niche of shells, with its three large boulders arranged to form a bucolic crag, bringing a touch of melancholy to the far end of the otherwise sunny garden, and creating a sound like that of a weeping domestic naiad, her tears falling drop by drop into the marble basin.

What saddened Afonso at first was the view from the terrace, which would once, no doubt, have been of the sea. The houses built on every side in the last few years had all but blocked that splendid vista. A narrow strip of water and hill between two five-storey buildings, separated by a street, was now the only view to be had from Ramalhete. In the end, though, Afonso managed to find in that, too, a secret charm. It was like a seascape framed in white masonry, suspended from the blue sky opposite the terrace, revealing, in all the infinite varieties of colour and light, fleeting scenes of peaceful river life: the sail of a boat from Trafaria luffing blithely by; a galley in full sail taking advantage of the breeze, serene against the red evening sky; the melancholy of a great steamship setting off, battened down and ready to face the waves, glimpsed one moment and gone the next, as if swallowed by the uncertain sea; or even, for days at a time, in the golden dust of silent noontides, the black hulk of an English battleship. And always, in the distance, there was that fragment of dark green hillside, with a windmill on top, and two white houses at the water's edge, always so expressive—the light glittering and glancing from windows ablaze with sun, or taking on at day's end a pensive air, clothed in a tender sunset pink, almost like the blush on a human face, or again, on rainy days, shivering and sad, so alone, so white, as if naked and at the mercy of the wild weather.

Three sets of French windows connected the terrace and the study, and Afonso quickly became accustomed to spending his days there, in that lovely prelate's chamber, in the cosy fireside nook so lovingly prepared for him by his grandson. Afonso's long residence in England had given him a fondness for quiet hours spent by the hearth. In Santa Olávia, the fires were lit until April, after which they were adorned instead with armfuls of flowers, like a domestic altar; and it was there, in the perfumed freshness, that he still most enjoyed to sit, smoking his pipe and reading Tacitus or his beloved Rabelais.

Afonso, however, was far from being, as he put it, an old sluggard. Winter and summer, he was up at daybreak and out in the garden, having first said his "morning prayers," which took the form of a bracing cold water bath. He had always had a superstitious love of water and used to say that there was nothing better for a man than the taste of water, the sound of water, and the sight of water. What bound him most to Santa Olávia was its abundance of fresh water, in the form of springs, fountains, and the mirror-still surfaces of pools or the cool murmur of streams. Indeed, he attributed to the living vigour of water the fact that he had survived from the beginning of the century with no aches or pains or illnesses, thus keeping up the family's long tradition of rude health—proof against sorrows and the passing years, which had as little effect on him as the passing years and storms had on his oak trees in Santa Olávia.

Afonso was quite short and stocky, with strong square shoulders; and, with his broad face, aquiline nose and ruddy complexion, his close-cropped white hair and long snow-white beard, he had the look, as Carlos put it, of a courageous man from an age of heroes, a Dom Duarte de Meneses perhaps, or an Afonso de Albuquerque. This always made the old man smile, and he would jokingly remind his grandson how deceptive appearances can be!

No, he was no Meneses or Albuquerque, he was merely a good-natured old man who loved his books, the comfort of his armchair, and a game of whist by the fireside. He himself used to say that he was basically selfish, but, in truth, he had never been so profoundly generous as he was in his old age. Part of his income slipped easily through his fingers in acts of tender charity. His heart was touched more than ever by the poor and the weak. In Santa Olávia, the children would run out to him from their doorways, sensing that he was a kind and patient man. Everything that lived seemed deserving of his love; he was the sort who would never stamp on an ant's nest and who took pity on a thirsty plant.

Vilaça was always reminded of descriptions of the patriarchs when he saw Afonso sitting by the fireside, serene and contented, in his worn velvet jacket, with a book in his hand and his old cat curled up at his feet. This vast, plump angora cat, white with ginger markings, had been Afonso's faithful companion ever since the death of Tobias, his superb St. Bernard. Born in Santa Olávia, the cat had been given the name of Bonifácio; then, when he reached the age of love and hunting, he had received the more gallant name of Dom Bonifácio de Calatrava; and now, sleepy and obese, and having clearly achieved the state of repose attained by all ecclesiastical dignitaries, he was known to all as the Reverend Boniface.

Afonso's life, however, had not always flowed by with the easy, clear tranquillity of a lovely summer river. This same old man, whose eyes filled with tenderness whenever he looked at his roses and who sat by his fireside contentedly re-reading Guizot, had, at least in his father's view, once been the fiercest Jacobin in all Portugal! And yet the poor lad's revolutionary fervour had consisted of nothing more than reading Rousseau, Volney, Helvétius and the *Encyclopédie*, setting off a few fireworks in honour of the Constitution, going around wearing a "liberal" hat and a blue cravat, and, in masonic lodges, reciting abominable odes addressed to the Supreme Architect of the Universe. This, however, was quite enough to upset his father. Caetano da Maia was a faithful Portuguese gentleman of the old school, who would cross himself at the mere mention of Robespierre's name, and who, in his devout, feeble brand of aristocratic apathy, harboured only one passionate emotion—a horror and hatred of the Jacobins, to whom he attributed all ills—those of his country as well as his own, from the loss of the colonies to his attacks of gout. In order to root out the Jacobin from Portugal, he had given his heart to that strong Messiah and providential restorer of the nation, the Infante Dom Miguel. And having a Jacobin son seemed to him a trial comparable only to Job's!

At first, in the hope that the boy would mend his ways, he contented himself with shooting him severe glances and addressing him sarcastically as "Citizen"! However, when he learned that his son and heir had been part of a rabble who, during a night of civic celebrations and street illuminations, had thrown stones at the darkened windows of the Austrian envoy and emissary of the Holy Alliance, he decided, then and there, that his son was a new Marat and unleashed upon him the full force of his rage. A particularly virulent attack of gout kept him confined to his armchair at the time and thus prevented him from soundly beating the "mason" with his Indian walking stick, as any good Portuguese father would, and so he decided, instead, to drive him from his house, without an allowance and without his blessing, disowned, as if he were a bastard son, for how could a freemason possibly be of his blood!

His wife's tears caused him to relent, as did the arguments of his wife's sister-in-law, who lived with them in Benfica, a highly educated Irishwoman and a respected tutelary Minerva, who had taught the boy English and adored him as if he were still a little baby. Caetano da Maia confined himself to exiling his son to Santa Olávia, but he did not cease to weep upon the bosom of the priests who came to Benfica and to bemoan the misfortune that had overwhelmed the household. And those saintly men consoled him, telling him that God, the old God, who had seen Dom Afonso Henriques defeat the Moors at Ourique, would never allow a Maia to make a pact with Beelzebub and with the Revolution! And if God the Father did not oblige, Our Lady of Solitude, the household's protecting saint and the boy's sponsor, could always be relied upon to work the necessary miracle.

And the miracle duly occurred. Some months later, the Jacobin, the Marat, returned from Santa Olávia, somewhat contrite and, more than anything, bored to death by the remoteness of the place, where taking tea with Brigadier Sena was rivalled in glumness and tedium only by having to say the rosary with his cousins, the Miss Cunhas. He came to his father to ask for his blessing and a few thousand *cruzados* in order to go to England, that land of bright meadows and golden tresses, of which his Aunt Fanny had so often spoken. His father kissed him tearfully and gave his fervent consent, seeing in all this the evident glorious intercession of Our Lady of Solitude! Even his confessor, Father Jerónimo da Conceição, declared this miracle to be in no way inferior to the vision of Our Lady at Carnaxide.

Afonso set off. It was springtime, and he found England—all in green, with its lavish parks and gardens, its many comforts, the intelligent harmony of its noble customs, its strong, serious-minded people—utterly enchanting. He soon forgot about his hatred of the grumpy priests of the congregation and about the ardent hours spent in the Café dos Remolares reciting Mirabeau, as well as the republic he had hoped to found on classical Voltairean lines, with a triumvirate of Scipios and festivals held in celebration of the Supreme Being. During the 1824 uprising in Portugal, Afonso was to be found at the Epsom races, riding in a gig, wearing a large false nose and uttering fearsome war whoops, utterly indifferent to the fate of his brother masons, who were, at that very moment, being driven along the alleyways of the Bairro Alto in Lisbon by the Infante Dom Miguel mounted on his fine Alter do Chão stallion.

The sudden death of Afonso's father, however, obliged him to return to Lisbon, where he met the Count de Runa's daughter, Dona Maria Eduarda Runa, a lovely, dark-haired girl, albeit rather sickly and delicate. As soon as the period of mourning for his father was over, he married her. They had one son and wanted more; Afonso, full of the fine ideas of a young patriarch, immediately set about improving the house at Benfica, planting trees and preparing shelter and shade for the beloved children who would bring joy to his old age.

Not that he forgot England. Indeed, England was made all the more alluring by Dom Miguel's Lisbon, which seemed to him as unruly as Tunis under Barbary rule: with its crude apostolic conspiracy of friars and coachmen filling taverns and chapels alike; with its fierce, grubby, fanatical populace, who reeled from the Exposition of the Blessed Sacrament to the bull ring, clamouring tumultuously for that prince who so perfectly embodied their own vices and passions.

This spectacle enraged Afonso da Maia, and often, on quiet evenings, among friends, with his small son on his knee, he would give voice to the indignation he felt in his honest soul. He no longer expected, as he had when he was a young man, a Lisbon peopled by such heroes as Cato and Mucius Scaevola. He even accepted the aristocracy's right to maintain its historic privileges, but what he wanted was a worthy intelligent aristocracy, like the Tory aristocracy (which, in his love for England, he greatly idealised), one that would set the moral tone in everything, shaping customs and inspiring literature, living elegantly and speaking well, an exemplar of high ideals and a mirror of patrician manners. What he could not bear was the bestial, sordid world of the Palace of Queluz. However, no sooner had these words been spoken than they flew straight to Queluz. And when the Cortes reassembled, the police raided the Maia house at Benfica "looking for documents and hidden weapons."

Afonso da Maia, with his son in his arms and his trembling wife by his side, watched silently and impassively as rifle butts smashed open drawers and the grimy hands of the bailiff rummaged in the mattress on his bed. The judge found nothing, and, in the pantry, even accepted the offer of a glass of wine and confessed to the administrator that "these were harsh times." From that morning on, the windows of the house remained closed; the main door no longer opened for Dona Maria Eduarda's carriage; and, a few weeks later, with his wife and child, Afonso da Maia left for England and exile.

There, preparing himself for a long stay, he settled, in some style, near Richmond, on the outskirts of London, in a house set in parkland, in the serene and gentle Surrey countryside.

Thanks to the influence of the Count de Runa—a former favourite of Queen Carlota Joaquina and now an uncompromising minister under Dom Miguel—his goods had not been confiscated, and Afonso da Maia was able to live very comfortably indeed.

At first, other liberal emigrés, Palmela and those who sailed from La Coruña in the English ship, the *Belfast*, came to bother and badger him. His upright soul was quick to protest at the separation of castes and hierarchies, which was maintained even on foreign soil among those who had been defeated over the same ideal—the noblemen and high court judges living a life of luxury in London, and the ordinary people and soldiers, after all that they had suffered in Galicia, succumbing to the effects of hunger, vermin, and fever in the hovels of Plymouth. He immediately found himself in conflict with the liberal leaders; he was accused of being a Jacobin and a democrat; and it was at this point that he lost faith in liberalism. He isolated himself then, but still did not close his purse, from which coins continued to flow in their fifties and hundreds. Only when the first expedition left, and the number of emigrés diminished, could he at last breathe freely, and only then, as he put it, did the air of England once again smell sweet to him!

Months later, his mother, who had stayed behind in Benfica, died of a stroke, and Aunt Fanny came to Richmond to complete Afonso's happiness, with her clear judgement, her white curls, and her discreet Minerva-like ways. There he was, then, living out his dream in a fine English house, set amid ancient trees and surrounded by vast pasturelands where pedigree cattle slept or grazed, and feeling that everything around him was healthy, strong, free, and enduring—which was precisely what his heart wanted.

He made friends; he studied England's rich and noble literature; as befitted a nobleman living in England, he took an interest in agriculture, horse breeding, and charitable works, and it pleased him to think that he might stay there forever in that peaceful ordered world.

Afonso sensed, however, that his wife was unhappy. Pensive and sad, she wandered through the rooms, coughing. At night, she would sit by the fire, sighing and saying nothing.

Poor lady! Nostalgia for her homeland, family, and Church was eating away at her. A true *lisboeta*, dark and diminutive, she did not complain, she merely smiled wanly, but, from the moment she had arrived in England, she had felt a secret loathing for that land of heretics and for its barbarous language; she was always cold and swathed in furs, she would gaze out in horror at the grey skies or at the snow on the trees, and her heart was never truly there, but far away in Lisbon, with its churchyards and its sunny streets. Her religious devotion (the devotion of the Runa family!), which had always been strong, grew more intense, strengthened by what she felt to be the prevailing hostility towards "Papists." She was only happy in the evenings, when she could take refuge in the attic rooms with her Portuguese servants and say the rosary with them, kneeling on a mat, savouring, in those mumbled Ave Marias, spoken in a Protestant land, all the charm of a Catholic conspiracy!

Hating, as she did, everything English, she had refused to allow her son, Pedro, to study at the school in Richmond. Afonso's assurances that it was a good, Catholic school were in vain. She would not have it: that particular brand of Catholicism, with no processions, no bonfires on St. John's night, no images of the Stations of the Cross, no monks in the streets, did not seem to her to be a religion at all. She would not abandon her son's soul to heresy, and so she had Father Vasques—her father's chaplain—come over from Lisbon to educate him.

Vasques taught Pedro the Latin declensions and, above all, the catechism, and Afonso da Maia's face would cloud over with sadness whenever he returned from hunting or from the streets of London, from the lively hum of a life freely lived, and heard the dull voice of the priest issuing forth from the classroom, as if out of the depths of darkness:

"Which are the enemies we must fight against all the days of our life?"

And in an even duller voice, the small boy would murmur:

"The enemies which we must fight against all the days of our life are the devil, the world, and the flesh."

Poor little Pedro! The only enemy of his soul was right there, in the form of the obese and none too clean Father Vasques, who belched as he sat slumped in an armchair, his snuff handkerchief on his knee.

Sometimes, Afonso felt so indignant that he would march into the room, interrupt the lesson on doctrine, grab Pedro's hand and carry him off to run around with him beneath the trees by the Thames in an attempt to drive away the heavy gloom of the catechism with the river's broad and generous light. The boy's terrified mother, however, would immediately rush out and wrap the boy up in a large shawl; besides, out of doors, the boy, who had grown accustomed to being mollycoddled by maids and sitting in cosy cushioned corners, was afraid of the wind and the trees; and father and son would end up tramping over the dead leaves in glum silence, the son cowed by the shifting shadows cast by the trees and the father, shoulders bowed, deep in thought, saddened by his son's pusillanimous nature.

Whenever he tried to tear the boy from his mother's enervating embrace or from Father Vasques' deadly catechism, the lady, always delicate in health, would immediately succumb to a fever. And Afonso did not dare to upset the poor invalid, so virtuous and so loving! At such times, he would go and sit with

Aunt Fanny and unburden himself to her; the wise Irishwoman would merely place her spectacles between the pages of the book she was reading—an essay by Addison or a poem by Pope—and sadly shrug her shoulders. What could she do?

Maria Eduarda's cough grew worse, just as her words grew sadder. She spoke now of "her last wish" being to see the sun again! Why did they not go back to Benfica, to their home, now that the Infante Dom Miguel had been exiled and peace restored? Afonso, however, would not agree; he never again wanted to see his drawers smashed open with rifle butts, and he found Dom Pedro's soldiers no more reassuring than Dom Miguel's bailiffs.

At about this time, a great misfortune befell the house: in the cold March weather, Aunt Fanny died of pneumonia, and this loss only made Maria Eduarda's melancholy still blacker, for she, too, had loved Aunt Fanny—for being Irish and a Catholic.

To distract her, Afonso took her off to Italy, to a delightful villa just outside Rome. There she did not lack for sun; it appeared punctually and generously every morning, bathing the terraces and gilding the laurels and the myrtles. And below them, among marble statues, was that precious, holy thing—the Pope!

But the sad lady continued to weep. What she really wanted was Lisbon, her novenas, her local saints, the processions that passed in a slow penitent murmur through the afternoons of sun and dust.

In order to console her, they had to go back to Benfica.

Then began a most unhappy existence. Maria Eduarda became gradually weaker, growing paler by the day, spending whole weeks reclining on a divan, her near-transparent hands resting on the heavy furs she had brought with her from England. Father Vasques took possession of that terrified soul, for whom God was a stern master, and he became the real man of the house. In the corridors, Afonso was constantly bumping into other religious figures, in cape and biretta, old Franciscans, or the occasional scrawny Capuchin on the scrounge; the house took on the musty smell of a sacristy; and from Maria Eduarda's rooms came the incessant sound, slow and mournful, of the litany.

These saintly men ate his food and drank his port in the pantry. The administrator's accounts were full of small pious allowances paid by the lady of the house: one Father Patrício had duped her out of two hundred *cruzados* for two hundred masses to be said for the soul of King José I.

Living surrounded by all this sanctimony aroused in Afonso feelings of rancorous atheism: he wanted all churches and monasteries closed, an axe taken to all images, and for the entire priesthood to be massacred. Whenever he heard the murmur of prayers in the house, he would escape down to the bottom of the garden, sit in the shade of the belvedere and read Voltaire; or he would go and vent his feelings to his old friend, Colonel Sequeira, who lived in a house in Queluz.

By then, Pedro was nearly a grown man. He was, however, as small and nervous as Maria Eduarda, having few of the characteristics and none of the robustness of the Maias; his lovely, dusky, oval face, and his marvellous irresistible eyes, always ready to fill with tears, gave him the appearance of a handsome Arab. He had developed slowly, showing no curiosity about anything, indifferent to toys, animals, flowers, and books. No strong desire ever seemed to trouble that somnolent, passive soul, apart from the occasionally expressed desire to return to Italy. He had taken against Father Vasques, but did not dare disobey him. He was weak-willed in everything; and the continual despondency into which his whole being was plunged resolved itself into occasional crises of black melancholy which would render him, for days on end, silent, pale and listless, leaving him with dark circles under his eyes and looking prematurely aged. Up until then, his one strong, intense feeling had been his love for his mother.

Afonso had wanted to send him to Coimbra, but, at the very idea of being separated from her Pedro, the poor lady had fallen on her knees before Afonso, inarticulate and trembling, and he had, of course, given in at once to those supplicant hands, to the tears streaming down her poor waxen face. The boy remained at Benfica, going for slow rides on his horse, accompanied by a liveried servant, and frequenting Lisbon's taverns, where he had already started drinking gin. There began to emerge in him then a great propensity for falling in love, and, at nineteen, he had his first bastard child.

Afonso da Maia consoled himself with the thought that the boy, despite having been horribly spoiled, did not entirely lack qualities: he was intelligent and healthy enough and, like all the Maias, brave; not long ago, he had soundly whipped three Lisbon louts armed with sticks who had assailed him in the street, calling him "a weed."

When his mother died—after the long, drawn-out death agony of the very devout, grappling with the terrors of going to Hell—Pedro's grief bordered on madness. He had made an hysterical promise, that if she should live, he would sleep for a whole year on the flagstones in the courtyard; and once the coffin was gone, along with the priests, he fell into a state of silent, dull, tearless anguish from which he chose not to emerge, lying face down on his bed like some stubborn penitent. For many months, he remained plunged in sadness, and Afonso da Maia despaired to see this young man, his son and heir, a lugubrious figure in heavy mourning, leave the house each day like a monk to go and visit his mother's tomb.

This period of extreme, morbid grief finally ended and was followed, almost seamlessly, by a period of dissipation and disorder, of banal debauchery, during which Pedro, swept along by a kind of crude romanticism, sought to submerge his longing for his mother in visits to brothels and taverns. However, given the unstable nature of that slightly crazed exuberance, so suddenly and wildly unleashed, it was also quickly spent.

After a year of riotous scenes in the Café Marrare and of derring-do at bull-runnings, after having ridden several horses into the ground and having booed many a performance at the Teatro de São Carlos, the old crises of nervous melancholy began to reappear; the days of glum silence, vast as deserts, returned, and these he spent at home, wandering the rooms, yawning or else lying prostrate beneath a tree in the garden, as if plunged into some well of bitterness. During such crises, he also became very devout; he would read *The Lives of the Saints* and visit the Exposition of the Holy Sacrament. These were the sudden dark nights of the soul which would, at one time, have led weak men to enter monasteries.

All this pained Afonso da Maia deeply; he preferred to hear that Pedro had rolled in from Lisbon in the early hours, exhausted and drunk, than to see him setting off like an old man, his breviary under his arm, heading for the church in Benfica.

And there was a thought now which, despite himself, occasionally came to torment him: he had noticed a strong resemblance between Pedro and one of his wife's grandfathers, a Runa, of whom there was a portrait in Benfica: this extraordinary man, whose name the grown-ups often invoked to frighten the children, had gone mad, and, imagining himself to be Judas, hanged himself from a fig-tree.

All these excesses and crises, however, came to an abrupt end. Pedro da Maia fell in love! It was love Romeo-style, beginning with a fatal dazzling exchange of glances, one of those passions that do sometimes assail a life, laying waste to it like a hurricane, uprooting will, reason, human relationships and hurling them all into the abyss.

One afternoon, while sitting in the Café Marrare, he saw a blue calèche stop opposite, outside Madame Levaillant's door, a calèche occupied by an old man wearing a white hat and by a young blonde woman wrapped in a cashmere shawl.

The old man was short and sturdy with a grey chinstrap beard, the sunburnt face of an old salt and a somewhat awkward air; he leaned heavily on the coachman as he got out of the carriage, as if badly afflicted by rheumatism, then limped into the dressmaker's shop; and the woman turned very slowly and looked for a moment at the café.

Beneath the little roses adorning her black hat, her fair hair, the colour of dark gold, fell in soft waves over her small classical forehead; her marvellous eyes lit up her whole face; the chill air made her marble flesh still paler; and her grave statuesque profile, the noble curve of her shoulders and arms beneath the shawl drawn tight about them, made her seem to Pedro at that moment like some immortal being, too good for this Earth.

He had no idea who she was, but a tall, gaunt young man with a dark moustache and dressed all in black, who was standing next to Pedro, smoking and leaning against the door frame in a pose of utter tedium, noticed his friend's intense interest, saw the burning, troubled gaze with which he followed the calèche as it trotted away up the Chiado, and came over to him, took his arm and said in his slow, gruff voice, his face close to Pedro's:

"Would you like me to tell you her name, Pedro, old chap? Her name, her family connections, with dates and all the principal facts? And will you buy your thirsty friend Alencar a bottle of champagne?"

The champagne duly arrived. And Alencar, having first run his bony fingers through his curly hair and smoothed the points of his moustache, leaned back, tugged at his shirt-cuffs and began:

"One golden autumn afternoon . . ."

"André!" shouted Pedro to the waiter, thumping the marble table top. "Take the champagne away!"

In imitation of the actor Epifânio, Alencar bellowed:

"What? And not quench the burning thirst of my lips?"

All right, the champagne could stay, but friend Alencar must forget that he was the poet of *Voices of the Dawn* and tell him in plain and simple language all about the owners of the blue calèche.

"Very well, my friend, here it is!"

Two years before, at about the time Pedro had lost his mother, the old man, Monforte by name, had, one morning, burst onto Lisbon's streets and into its society in that very calèche and with the same beautiful daughter by his side. No one knew who they were. They had rented the second floor of the Vargas mansion in Arroios, and the girl began frequenting the Teatro de São Carlos, where she had made an immediate impression, the kind of impression, said Alencar, which could easily bring on an aneurism. When she walked across the foyer, male shoulders would bow as if overwhelmed by the glow given off by that magnificent creature, who walked like a goddess, dragging her train behind her, and who, as if every night were a gala night, was always décolleté and resplendent with jewels, even though she was as yet unmarried. Her father never gave her his arm; he would follow behind, his throat in the grip of a huge white cravat worthy of a majordomo and, in the golden light emanating from his daughter, looking even more the sunburnt sailor; indeed, he appeared shrunken, almost cowed, clutching to him opera glasses, libretto, a bag of sweets, a fan, and an umbrella. It was in the box, however, when the light fell on her ivory neck and on her golden hair, that she seemed most truly an incarnation of some Renaissance ideal, a Titian model. The first time Alencar saw her, he had pointed first at her and then at the dark-complexioned ladies in the other boxes, exclaiming:

"Gentlemen, she is like a shiny new gold ducat in a pile of old copper coins from the days of King João VI!"

Magalhães, that vile pirate, had stolen his words and put them in a magazine, but he, Alencar, had said it first!

Inevitably, various young men began to prowl around the mansion in

Arroios, but no window ever opened. The servants, when questioned, said only that the young lady's name was Maria and that the gentleman was called Manuel. A maid finally proved more forthcoming, once her palm had been crossed with silver: the gentleman was very silent, terrified of his daughter, and slept in a hammock; the lady lived in a nest of dark blue silk and spent the day reading novels. This was not enough to satisfy an impatient Lisbon. A slow, painstaking, methodical investigation was set in motion, in which he, Alencar, had taken part.

And the horrors that were uncovered! The father, Monforte, was from the Azores. When he was very young, a knife-fight which left a man dying on a street corner had forced him to flee on board a South American brig. Some time later, the administrator for the Taveira family, a certain Silva, who had known him in the Azores and was in Havana looking into setting up tobacco plantations, came across Monforte (whose real name was Forte) slouching around the port, waiting for a ship to take him to New Orleans. Here there was a blank in Monforte's story. It seemed that he worked for some time as a foreman on a plantation in Virginia, and when he next resurfaced in the bright light of day, he was commanding the brig *Nova Linda* and carrying cargos of slaves to Brazil, Havana, and New Orleans.

He had escaped the English sea patrols and earned a fortune from the skins of Africans, and now that he was rich, a man of reputation and a landowner, he went to the Teatro de São Carlos to hear Corelli sing. In this terrible chronicle, obscure and ill-documented, there were still, as Alencar put it, many gaps.

"And what about the daughter?" asked Pedro, who had listened, grave-faced and pale.

This his friend Alencar did not know. Where had Monforte found such a lovely blonde daughter? Who had the mother been? Where was she? Who had taught the daughter that majestic way of wrapping her cashmere shawl about her?

"Those, my friend, are:

> *mysteries which Lisbon, however it probes,*
> *will never unravel, and which God alone knows!"*

Whatever the truth of the matter, once Lisbon had heard this tale of blood and negro slaves, its enthusiasm for Monforte's daughter rapidly cooled. Really! Juno, it turned out, had a murderer's blood running through her veins; the Titian beauty was the daughter of a slave-trader! The ladies, delighted to be able to pour scorn on a woman so blonde, so beautiful, and with so many jewels, immediately dubbed her "the slaver's daughter," and now, whenever the daughter went to the theatre, Dona Maria da Gama affected to hide her face behind her fan, saying that she thought she could see on the young woman (especially when she wore those lovely rubies) the blood from the knife-thrusts inflicted by her Papa! In short, they slandered her vilely. After that first winter

SILOAM SPRINGS LIBRARY
401 W. UNIVERSITY
SILOAM SPRINGS, AR 72761

in Lisbon, the Monfortes disappeared, and furious rumours made the rounds: they were ruined, the police were after the old man, oh, and a thousand and one other wickednesses. Senhor Monforte, who suffered from rheumatism, was, in fact, calmly, deliciously, taking the waters in the Pyrenees. That was where Melo had met them.

"Oh, so Melo knows them, does he?" exclaimed Pedro.

"Yes, my friend, Melo knows them."

Pedro left the café soon afterwards; and that night, before going home, and despite the cold fine rain that was falling, he spent a whole hour, his imagination all afire, circling the dark, silent Vargas mansion. Two weeks later, when Alencar walked into the Teatro de São Carlos at the end of the first act of *The Barber of Seville*, he was amazed to see Pedro da Maia installed in the Monfortes' box, at the front, next to Maria, and wearing a scarlet camellia in the buttonhole of his tailcoat—identical to the camellias in the bouquet resting on the velvet balustrade.

Maria Monforte had never looked lovelier: she was wearing one of those extravagant theatrical dresses that so offended Lisbon, and which caused the ladies to say that she dressed "like an actress." Her silk dress was the colour of golden wheat; she had two yellow roses and an ear of corn in her hair, and strings of opals around her neck and arms; and these colours, reminiscent of a sunlit field of ripe wheat, blended with the gold of her hair, illuminated her ivory skin, bathed the curves of her statuesque figure, and lent her all the splendour of a Ceres. Behind her could be seen the fair bushy moustache of Melo, who was standing up talking to her father, hidden, as always, in the darkest corner of the box.

Alencar went to the Gamas' box to get a better look at this novel situation. Pedro had returned to his seat and was sitting, arms folded, gazing at Maria. She retained for some time her pose of unfeeling goddess, then, during the duet between Rosina and Lindoro, her deep, blue gaze fell on Pedro gravely and lingeringly. Alencar ran to the Café Marrare, waving his arms in the air, to trumpet the news abroad.

Soon the whole of Lisbon was talking about Pedro da Maia's passion for "the slaver's daughter." He also courted her publicly, in the old-fashioned way, standing on the corner opposite her house, utterly still and pale with ecstasy, his eyes fixed on her window.

He wrote to her twice a day—two letters of six pages each—sprawling poems which he went to the Café Marrare to compose; and everyone there knew for whom they were intended, those closely-written pages which accumulated before him on the tray bearing the gin bottle. If a friend came to the café door to ask for Pedro da Maia, the waiters would reply quite naturally:

"Senhor Dom Pedro? Yes, he's over there, writing to his young lady."

And if the friend came over, Pedro himself would hold out his hand and exclaim joyfully, smiling his beautiful frank smile:

"I'll be with you in a moment, old boy, I'm just writing to Maria!"

Afonso da Maia's oldest friends, who played whist with him in Benfica—especially Vilaça, the Maias' administrator, always eager to guard the dignity of the house—were not slow in bringing him news of Pedro's romance. Afonso had already suspected something of the sort; he had noticed one of the gardeners leaving every day with a large bunch of the best camellias, freshly picked; every morning, early, he would find Pedro's personal manservant walking down the corridor to the young master's room, delightedly sniffing the perfume on an envelope bearing a gold wax seal; and he felt quite relieved that some strong human emotion had dragged his son away from a life of disorder and dissolution, from gambling and from those bouts of motiveless melancholy, when the black breviary would reappear.

However, he did not know the name of the woman involved, nor, indeed, of the Monfortes' existence, but the details his friends revealed to him—the knifing in the Azores, the foreman's whip in Virginia, the *Nova Linda*, the old man's whole sinister history—upset Afonso da Maia greatly.

One night, when Colonel Sequeira, at the whist table, commented that he had seen Maria Monforte and Pedro out riding together, and that "they both looked very handsome, very *distingués*," Afonso, after a silence, said in a bored voice:

"Well, all young men have their mistresses. That's how it is, that's life, and it would be absurd to try to put a stop to such things. But with a father like hers, I must say I find her a bad choice even as a mistress."

Vilaça stopped shuffling the cards, adjusted his gold spectacles, and exclaimed in alarm:

"Mistress? But the young lady is unmarried, sir, and a perfectly decent girl too."

Afonso da Maia was filling his pipe; his hands started to tremble; and turning to Vilaça, he said in a voice that also trembled slightly:

"You surely don't imagine that my son wants to *marry* the creature, do you?"

Vilaça said nothing. And it was Sequeira who murmured:

"No, no, of course not."

And the game continued for a while in silence.

Afonso da Maia, however, began to feel uneasy. Weeks went by without Pedro once dining at Benfica. In the mornings, if Afonso saw him at all, it was only for a moment, when he came down for breakfast, his face aglow, hurriedly pulling on his gloves and asking the servants loudly if his horse was already saddled; then, still standing up, he would take a sip of tea, hastily enquire if Papa wanted anything, smooth his moustache in front of the large Venetian mirror above the fireplace, and immediately, joyfully escape. At other times, he would not leave his room all day; evening would fall and the lights would be turned on, and then his worried father would go up to his room where he would find him stretched out on his bed, his head buried in his arms.

"Whatever's the matter with you?" he would ask.

"I've got a migraine," Pedro would reply in a quiet, hoarse voice.

And Afonso would go back downstairs, feeling indignant and disgusted, seeing in Pedro's cowardly anxiety a letter that had failed to come or perhaps a rose given which was not, later, pinned in the lady's hair.

Sometimes, between rubbers of bridge or chatting over the tea cups, his friends would make disquieting remarks, for these were men who lived in Lisbon and knew all its rumours, while he spent summer and winter in Benfica with his books and roses. The excellent Sequeira, for example, asked why Pedro did not embark on some long educational journey, to Germany or to the Orient. And old Luís Runa, Afonso's cousin, suddenly gave vent, apropos of nothing, to his regret that the days had long since gone when the police commissioner was free to expel from Lisbon anyone he judged to be an undesirable. It was obvious that he was referring to the Monforte woman, whom he clearly considered to be dangerous.

In the summer, Pedro went off to Sintra, and Afonso learned that the Monfortes had rented a house there. Days later, Vilaça arrived in Benfica, looking very worried; the day before, Pedro had come to see him in his office and asked him about the properties he owned and how best to raise money. Vilaça had told him that when he came of age in September, he would receive the inheritance left to him by his mother.

"But I was most unhappy, sir, most unhappy..."

"But why, Vilaça? The boy obviously wants the money to buy presents for his young lady. Love is an expensive business, Vilaça."

"I just hope to God that's all it is, sir, I hope to God it is."

And Afonso da Maia's steadfast confidence in the strength of patrician values, in his son's proud Maia nature, reassured Vilaça.

A few days later, Afonso da Maia saw Maria Monforte for the first time. He had dined at Sequeira's house near Queluz, and they were sitting together on the mirador, drinking their coffee, when a blue calèche drawn by horses in costly trappings appeared on the narrow road below the wall surrounding Sequeira's estate. Maria, holding a scarlet parasol, was wearing a pink dress, the flounced skirt of which almost enveloped Pedro's knees, for Pedro was sitting by her side; the ribbons of her hat, tied in a voluminous bow that covered her chest, were also pink; and among all those rosy tones, her face, grave and pure as a Greek marble sculpture, and lit by two dark blue eyes, looked utterly adorable. The seat opposite was almost entirely filled with packages from the dressmaker, and next to them sat the shrunken figure of Monforte, wearing a large Panama hat and nankeen trousers, with his daughter's cape draped over his arm and a sunshade on his lap. They were riding along in silence and none of them glanced up at the mirador; and the calèche swayed past along the cool green lane, beneath branches that brushed against Maria's parasol. Sequeira paused, his coffee cup to his lips, his eyes staring, and murmured:

"God, she's lovely!"

Afonso did not reply; he looked askance at that scarlet parasol that was now leaning towards Pedro, almost concealing him, almost obscuring him, like a large bloodstain spreading over the calèche as it passed beneath the sad green of the trees.

Autumn passed and an icy winter followed. One morning, Pedro went into the library where his father was sitting reading by the fire; he kissed his father's hand, then, after glancing at a newspaper lying open on a table, he turned brusquely.

"Father," he said, struggling to be clear and decisive, "I've come to ask for your permission to marry a lady called Maria Monforte."

Afonso put his book down on his lap and in a slow, grave voice replied:

"You've never mentioned her to me before, but I understand she is the daughter of a murderer and a slave-trader, and is known by some as 'the slaver's daughter.'"

"Father!"

Afonso got to his feet and stood before him, rigid and inexorable, the very embodiment of domestic honour.

"What else do you have to say to me? You make me blush with shame."

Pedro, who had turned whiter than the handkerchief he was clutching in his hand, exclaimed, trembling, almost sobbing:

"Well, I'm going to marry her, Father, I'm going to!"

He left the room, slamming the door. In the corridor, he called for his valet and, in a loud voice, so that his father would hear, ordered him to pack his bags and take them to the Hotel Europa.

Two days later, Vilaça came to Benfica with tears in his eyes, to report that the young master had got married that morning, and, according to what Sérgio, Monforte's administrator, had told him, had set off with his bride for Italy. Afonso da Maia had just sat down at the lunch table, which had been laid near the fireplace: in the centre of the table, in the blaze from the fire, the leaves were dropping from a bouquet of flowers placed in a Japanese vase; next to Pedro's place lay a copy of the poetry magazine to which he subscribed. Afonso listened, grave-faced and silent, to what Vilaça had to say, all the while slowly unfolding his napkin.

"Have you had lunch, Vilaça?"

Taken aback at such serenity, the administrator stammered:

"Y-yes, sir, I have . . ."

Afonso pointed to the place laid for Pedro and said to the footman:

"You can clear that away, Teixeira. From now on, you need only lay one place at table. Sit down, Vilaça, sit down."

Teixeira, who was still new to the house, removed the young master's place without a flicker of emotion. Vilaça sat down. Everything around was as calm and correct as on other days when he had lunched at Benfica. The footman's steps made no sound on the soft carpet; the flames crackled gaily, glinting gold on the silver dishes; outside, the discreet sun in the blue winter sky made the frost on the bare branches glitter; and by the window, a plebeian parrot, trained by Pedro, continued to hurl insults at the Cabral brothers and their respective ministries.

At last, Afonso got up from the table and stood looking abstractedly out at the garden, at the peacocks on the terrace; then, after leaving the dining room, he took Vilaça's arm and leaned heavily upon it, as if suddenly shaken by the first tremor of old age, and conscious, in his grief, that in Vilaça he had a firm friend. They walked down the corridor in silence. In the library, Afonso sat down in his armchair by the window and began slowly filling his pipe. Vilaça, head bowed, tiptoed past the high shelves, as if visiting a sick room. A flock of sparrows could, for a moment, be heard bickering in the branches of a tall tree that grew by the balcony. Then there was silence, and Afonso da Maia said:

"So, Vilaça, Saldanha's been dismissed by the Palace, has he?"

Vilaça replied vaguely and mechanically:

"He has indeed, sir."

And nothing more was said of Pedro da Maia.

: II :

PEDRO AND MARIA, MEANWHILE, in a storybook state of bliss, travelled slowly down the length of Italy, from city to city, along that Via Sacra which stretches from the flowers and wheatfields of the Lombardy plain to Naples, that languid land of romance, white beneath the blue. They intended to spend the winter there, breathing air that is always warm, by a sea that is always calm, and where the indolent pleasures of married life have a more enduring sweetness. However, one day, in Rome, Maria felt a sudden longing to be in Paris. She found it wearisome to travel so far, bounced about in carriages, merely in order to see Neapolitan *lazzaroni* eating their spaghetti. It would be so much more pleasant to have a cosy little nest in the Champs-Elysées and to enjoy a lovely winter of love there! With Prince Louis Napoleon in power, Paris was safe now. Besides, she was already becoming bored with old classical Italy: all those eternal marble statues, all those Madonnas, were beginning to make her poor head quite dizzy, she said to Pedro, her arms languorously encircling his neck. She yearned for a decent dress shop, for gaslights, for the buzz of the boulevard. And she was afraid of Italy, where everyone was always plotting.

So they went to France.

Paris—still in turmoil, with a faint whiff of gunpowder still lingering in the streets, with every face apparently still warm from the heat of battle—also displeased Maria. At night, she would wake to the strains of the Marseillaise; the policemen, she thought, looked terribly fierce; everything seemed so gloomy; and the duchesses, poor loves, dared not venture into the Bois de Boulogne for fear of the workers, of the insatiable rabble! In the end, however, Pedro and Maria stayed until the spring, in the little blue velvet-upholstered nest she had dreamed of, looking out over the Champs-Elysées.

Then there was talk once more of revolution, of a coup d'état. And Maria's absurd admiration for the new uniforms of the Garde Mobile was making Pedro nervous. When she became pregnant, he longed to take her away from the fascinations of battle-worn Paris and to install her in peaceful, sunny, sleepy Lisbon.

Before leaving, he wrote to his father.

Maria had advised, indeed, almost demanded, that he do so. Afonso da Maia's rejection of her had, at first, driven her to despair. It was not the domestic disunity that troubled her, but the fact that this puritan aristocrat's humiliating "No" underlined all too publicly and brutally her suspect origins! She loathed the old man, and she had hastened the marriage and their triumphant departure for Italy in order to show him that genealogies, a long ancestral line, and family honour were as nothing compared with her bare white arms. However, now that she was about to return to Lisbon where she would give soirées and hold court, a reconciliation had become essential; Pedro's father, living quietly in Benfica, with his stiff, old-fashioned pride, would be a constant reminder, even among all her mirrors and lush interiors, of the brig *Nova Linda* and its cargo of slaves. And she wanted to be seen in Lisbon on the arm of her noble and highly ornamental father-in-law, with his viceroy's beard.

"Say I adore him already," she murmured, as she bent over the writing desk, stroking Pedro's hair. "Tell him that if it's a little boy, I'll give him his name. Write him a nice letter, eh?"

And the letter Pedro sent to his father *was* a nice letter, a very tender letter, for the poor lad loved his father. He spoke with feeling of his hopes that the child would be a boy, of reconciling all their misunderstandings around the cradle of that little Maia-to-be, their first-born and the heir to the Maia name. He described his happiness with all the effusiveness of the indiscreet lover; his account of Maria's kindness, graciousness and cleverness filled two whole pages; and he swore that, within an hour of his arrival, he would come and throw himself at his father's feet.

And indeed, as soon as he disembarked, he drove to Benfica in a carriage, only to find that his father had left for Santa Olávia two days before. Pedro took this as an affront, which left a bitter wound.

A deep gulf opened between father and son. When a daughter was born, Pedro did not tell him, announcing melodramatically to Vilaça that he no longer had a father. She was a lovely baby, chubby, fair and pink, with the Maias' beautiful dark eyes. Contrary to Pedro's wishes, Maria chose not to feed the baby herself, but she adored her madly; she would spend the day kneeling ecstatically by the cradle, running beringed hands over the child's soft skin, devoutly kissing her little feet and the rolls of fat on her thighs, rapturously heaping endearments upon her, dousing her with perfume and adorning her with ribbons and bows.

In her delirious love for her daughter, her anger against Afonso da Maia grew increasingly bitter. She considered that he had affronted both her and the cherub to whom she had given birth. She piled insults on him, called him "the old codger," "the fuzz-ball" . . .

One day, Pedro heard her do so and told her off; she responded sharply, and, confronted by her flushed face, in which her tear-filled blue eyes looked almost black with rage, all he could do was to stammer timidly:

"But he's my father, Maria."

His father! And yet, in full view of the whole of Lisbon, he treated her as if she were a mere concubine! He might be a gentleman, but he had the manners of a peasant. He *was* an old codger and that was all there was to it!

She snatched up her daughter and, holding her close, burst, sobbing, into a litany of complaints:

"No one loves us, my angel! No one loves you! Only your mother! They treat you as if you were a bastard child!"

The baby, shaken about in her mother's arms, began to scream, at which point, Pedro, touched and humbled, ran to them, put his arms about them both, and the matter was concluded with a long kiss.

And he, in his heart, justified her rage as a mother's natural reaction at seeing her little angel scorned. Some of his friends, Alencar and Dom João da Cunha, who had started to visit them in Arroios, also began to make fun of that stubborn antiquated father, sulking in the provinces because none of his daughter-in-law's forefathers had died in the battle of Aljubarrota! After all, what woman in Lisbon could compare with Maria when it came to fashion, grace, and hospitality! For heaven's sake, the world had moved on and left behind it the starchy attitudes of the sixteenth century!

And even Vilaça, when Pedro had shown him the little creature asleep among the lace and linen of her cradle, had been moved to tears, as he so easily was, and had declared, hand on heart, that it really was sheer pigheadedness on the part of Senhor Afonso da Maia!

"Well, all the worse for him, not wanting to see a precious little angel like her!" said Maria, looking at herself in the mirror and adjusting the flowers in her hair. "We don't need him anyway."

And they didn't. In October, when the little girl had her first birthday, there was a great ball in the house in Arroios, where they now lived and which had been expensively refurbished. And the same ladies who had once professed their horror at this "slaver's daughter"—including Dona Maria da Gama, who used to hide behind her fan in order not to see her—all came, as nice as pie and very décolleté, perfectly happy now to kiss her on the cheek and call her "my dear," to admire the garlands of camellias around mirrors that had cost four hundred *mil-réis*, and to enjoy the ices.

And so began a round of lavish parties, which had, according to Alencar— who was now a close friend of the household and one of Madame's courtiers— "just a hint of those very distinguished orgies one reads about in Byron's poetry." They were indeed the liveliest soirées in the whole of Lisbon: a champagne supper would be served at one o'clock; they would play fierce games of monte until late into the night; they would invent tableaux vivants in which Maria would appear, looking superbly beautiful in the classical robes of Helen or in the sombre splendour of Judith's oriental mourning dress. On evenings when only close friends were invited, she would join the men and smoke a perfumed cigarette. Often, in the billiard room, applause would break out when she beat Dom João da Cunha, who was the finest player of his day.

And at all these festivities, which were coloured by the romanticism of the Regenerationist movement, Papa Monforte, in his high white cravat, was a constant presence, silent and shrunken, his hands behind his back, skulking in corners, loitering by windows, only making an appearance in order to snuff out a guttering candle, and never once taking his rapt senile eyes off his daughter.

Maria had never looked lovelier. Motherhood had lent her a more opulent beauty, and she filled and illuminated those high-ceilinged rooms in Arroios with her fair, radiant, Junoesque figure, with the diamonds she wore woven into her hair, the ivory and milk-white of her bare shoulders, and with the rustle of magnificent silks. Wishing, like the ladies of the Renaissance, to have a flower that symbolised her, she chose, quite rightly, the royal tulip, sumptuous and ardent.

People spoke of her extravagance, of underwear and lace worth as much as a piece of land! And she could afford it! Her husband was rich, and she would, without scruple, ruin both him and her father.

Naturally, all of Pedro's friends adored her. Alencar proclaimed himself loudly to be "her knight and her poet." He was always at Arroios now, it was his second home; he would wander the rooms reciting resonant lines of poetry, or else recline on sofas, practising melancholy poses. He was going to dedicate to Maria (and there was nothing more extraordinary than the languorous, plangent tone in which he pronounced that name—MARIA!—with a sombre, fateful look in his eyes), yes, he was going to dedicate to her his long-promised, long-awaited poem *Flower of Martyrdom*! And he would recite lines from it, lines written in the lyrical style of the time:

> *I saw you that night in those splendid halls,*
> *Saw the mad whirl of your golden tresses . . .*

Alencar's passion was entirely innocent, but more than one of Pedro's other close friends, friends of the household, had doubtless stammered out a declaration of love in the blue boudoir where she "received" at three o'clock each afternoon, surrounded by her vases of tulips; her female friends, however, even the most hostile, were quite sure that her favours would never have gone beyond sharing a window seat with someone and perhaps giving them a rose or a long, sweet look over the top of her fan. Pedro, nevertheless, began to have some dark moments of doubt. He was not jealous, but he did sometimes feel suddenly bored with that life of excess and celebration and would be seized with a violent desire to sweep all those men out of the room, all those dear friends crowding so ardently around Maria's bare shoulders.

He would take refuge in a corner, chewing angrily on a cigar, his soul filled with whole hosts of painful nameless things.

Maria was always quick to recognise in her husband's face "these clouds," as she called them. She would run to him and clasp his hands forcefully and boldly in her own.

"What's wrong, my love? You're not angry, are you?"

"No, I'm not angry."

"Look at me then!"

She would press her lovely breast against him; she would run her hands up his arms, from wrists to shoulders, in a slow, passionate caress; then she would look at him prettily and proffer her lips. Pedro would place on them a long kiss and feel entirely consoled.

During all this time, Afonso da Maia did not leave the shade of Santa Olávia, as forgotten as if he were in his tomb. His name was never mentioned in Arroios; the "old codger" was still just as stubborn. Only Pedro occasionally asked Vilaça how "Papa" was feeling. And the agent's words never failed to enrage Maria: Papa was fine; he now had a splendid French cook; Santa Olávia was always full of guests—Sequeira, André da Ega, Dom Diogo Coutinho.

"The old fuzz-ball certainly doesn't stint himself!" she would comment bitterly to her father.

And the former slaver would rub his hands, glad to know that Afonso da Maia was happy in Santa Olávia, for he never ceased to tremble at the idea of one day being confronted in Arroios by that stern, pure nobleman.

However, when Maria had another child, a boy this time, the ensuing peace in Arroios brought back vividly to Pedro's heart the image of his father alone in the gloom of the Douro. Taking advantage of Maria's weak convalescent state, he spoke tentatively to her about a possible reconciliation. And he was overjoyed when Maria, after a moment's consideration, replied:

"Yes, I think it would make me happy to see him here!"

Pedro, thrilled at receiving her unexpected consent, wanted to rush straight to Santa Olávia. She, though, had a better plan. Afonso, according to Vilaça, was soon to visit Benfica; she would go there, unannounced and all in black, taking the little boy with her, throw herself at Afonso's feet and beg his blessing on his grandson! It couldn't fail! It really couldn't! And Pedro saw in this plan the inspiration of motherhood.

To soften his father's heart, Pedro wanted to call the child Afonso, but Maria would not consent to this. She was reading a novel whose hero was the romantic Charles Edward, the last of the Stuarts, and, in love with him and with his adventures and misfortunes, she wanted to give her son his name ... Carlos Eduardo da Maia! Such a name seemed to her to contain a whole destiny of love and heroic deeds.

The baptism had to be delayed when Maria fell ill with tonsillitis. It was only a very mild case, however, and two weeks later, Pedro was able to go hunting on his estate in Tojeira, near Almada. He was supposed to be away for two days. The party had been organised purely for the benefit of an Italian recently arrived in Lisbon, a distinguished young man who had been introduced to him by the secretary of the English legation, and to whom Pedro had taken an immediate liking; he claimed to be the nephew of the prince and princess of Soria and to have been forced to flee Naples where he had plotted against the Bourbons and been condemned to death. Alencar and Dom João Coutinho were to join them, and the party set off in the early hours.

That afternoon, Maria was dining alone in her room when she heard carriages drawing up outside the door and the sound of voices and footsteps on the stairs; almost at once, Pedro burst in on her, pale and trembling:

"Something terrible has happened, Maria!"

"Heavens! What?"

"I've wounded the young man from Naples!"

"But how?"

It had been a stupid accident! As he was jumping over a ditch, his shotgun had gone off, and the Italian had been hit! They hadn't been able to treat him in Tojeira and so they had come straight back to Lisbon. Naturally, he couldn't allow the man he had wounded simply to go back to his hotel and so he had brought him to Arroios, to the green room upstairs and had called the doctor and two nurses to watch over him, and he himself would spend the night at his bedside.

"How is he?"

"Oh, an absolute hero! He smiles and says it's nothing, but he looks as pale as death. He's a wonderful fellow! Oh, this could only happen to me . . . And Alencar was right next to him. If only I'd wounded Alencar, someone I know, a good friend, because then we could have simply laughed it off. But no, it had to be him, a guest!"

At that moment, a carriage rolled into the courtyard.

"That'll be the doctor!"

And Pedro raced off.

He returned shortly afterwards, looking much calmer. Dr. Guedes had almost laughed at such a bagatelle, a bit of shot in the arm, and a few pellets in the back. He had promised the prince that in two weeks he would be back hunting in Tojeira; indeed, the prince was already sitting up, smoking a cigar. A most splendid fellow! He seemed to have hit it off with Papa Monforte as well.

Maria slept badly that night, vaguely excited by the idea of a passionate conspirator-prince, condemned to death and now lying wounded in the room above hers.

Early the next morning—as soon as Pedro had himself gone out to fetch the Italian's luggage from his hotel—Maria sent her French maid, a beautiful girl from Arles, to enquire on her behalf how His Highness was, and "to see what he looked like." The Arlesienne reappeared, eyes shining, and informed her lady, with expansive Provençal gestures, that she had never seen such a handsome man! He was the very image of Our Lord Jesus Christ! Such a throat, as white as marble! He was still dreadfully pale, but had expressed his heartfelt gratitude for Madame Maia's concern; and he had then propped himself up on his pillows to read the newspaper.

After that, Maria seemed to take no further interest in their wounded guest. It was Pedro who was constantly talking to her about him, enthused by the thrilling life led by that conspirator-prince, already sharing in his hatred of the Bourbons and delighted to find that they had so many interests in common, the same love of hunting, horses, and guns. Now, first thing in the morning, still in his dressing-gown and with his pipe in his mouth, he would go up to the prince's room and spend hours chatting and drinking hot toddies—the latter with Dr. Guedes' permission. He even took his friends up there, Alencar and Dom João da Cunha. Maria could hear them laughing above her. Sometimes she would hear someone strumming a guitar. And her father, old Monforte, equally besotted, was also always hanging around the hero's bed.

The maid from Arles was another frequent visitor, bearing lace-edged towels or a sugar bowl no one had asked for, or a vase of flowers to brighten up the room. Maria eventually asked Pedro rather frostily if, as well as all their friends, two nurses, two servants, her father and himself, it was also necessary for her maid to spend every moment of her time in His Highness's room!

It was not, of course, necessary, but Pedro was very tickled by the idea that the maid had fallen in love with the prince. Venus was clearly smiling on him! The prince found her equally attractive: *un très joli brin de femme*, he said.

Maria's lovely face went white with rage. She found all this to be vulgar, impudent, and in the worst possible taste! Pedro had been quite mad to bring into the bosom of their family a foreigner, a fugitive, an adventurer! She was outraged by the sounds of mocking laughter and guitar music that drifted down to her from above—all doubtless encouraged by a great deal of hot grog—for it showed, she felt, a complete lack of consideration for her still weak and nervous convalescent state. As soon as His Highness could manage to get comfortably into a carriage, she wanted him out, and back to the hotel.

"Good Lord, let's not be rash!" said Pedro.

"That's how I feel."

And she was equally severe with the maid from Arles, for that afternoon, Pedro found the girl in the corridor sobbing and dabbing at red eyes with her apron.

A few days later, the prince, fully recovered, decided to go back to his hotel. He had not even seen Maria, but in gratitude for her hospitality, he sent her a magnificent bouquet and, with all the gallantry of a Renaissance artist-prince, placed among the flowers an equally perfumed sonnet in Italian: he compared her to a Syrian noblewoman giving the last water in her pitcher to an Arab knight, lying wounded on the sun-scorched road; he compared her to Dante's Beatrice.

Everyone felt this showed a rare distinction and that it was, as Alencar said, a most Byronic gesture.

A week later, at the party held for Carlos Eduardo's christening, the Italian came too and made a great impression. He was a splendid-looking man, built like an Apollo, with skin as pale as the finest marble; and his short curly beard, his long, wavy, feminine hair with auburn lights, worn parted in the middle like the Nazarene, really did give him the appearance of a handsome Christ, just as the maid had said.

He danced only one quadrille with Maria and, indeed, seemed rather taciturn and proud, but everything about him was fascinating, his bearing, his mysterious life, even his name—Tancredo. Many a female heart beat faster when he stood leaning in a doorway, bestowing on the room the sombre languor of his velvet gaze, with his top hat in one hand and a melancholy look on his face, exuding all the affecting allure of a man condemned to death. In order to examine him more closely, the Marchioness de Alvenga asked Pedro to take her arm and escort her to a nearer viewing-point; there she examined the prince with her gold-rimmed pince-nez as if he were a statue in a museum.

"Oh, he's delicious!" she exclaimed. "A perfect picture! And you're friends, are you, Pedro?"

"My dear lady, we're like brothers-at-arms."

At that same soirée, Vilaça informed Pedro that his father was expected the following day in Benfica. And when Pedro and Maria went up to bed, Pedro spoke to her of their plan to throw themselves at his father's feet. She, however, felt that this would be a mistake and offered him the most unexpected and most sensible of reasons. She had been giving the matter much thought. She realised now that one of the prime causes of Papa's stubborn behaviour— lately she had taken to calling Afonso da Maia "Papa"—was the extravagant life they led in Arroios.

"But, my dear," said Pedro, "it's not as if we're holding orgies here. It's just a few friends."

Of course, of course, but she had decided to start leading a quieter, more domestic existence. Besides, it was better for the children. And she wanted "Papa" to be persuaded of this transformation so that when it came to making peace, it would not only be easier, but also likely to prove more enduring.

"Just wait another two or three months. When he finds out how quietly we live, then I'll invite him here, don't worry. It would be better, too, to make any such overtures when my father has gone to take the waters in the Pyrenees. My poor Papa is terrified of yours. Don't you think that would be better, my love?"

"You're an angel," was Pedro's response, kissing both her hands.

Maria's old manner did appear to be undergoing a change. The soirées stopped. She began spending the evenings in her blue boudoir with just a few close friends. She no longer smoked; she gave up playing billiards; and she dressed all in black with a single flower in her hair, sitting by the gaslight, doing her crochet. And she would discuss classical music with old Cazoti whenever he visited. In imitation of his lady, Alencar also became suitably grave, reciting translations of the German poet Klopstock. They spoke earnestly about politics, Maria being very much on the side of the "regenerationist" government.

And every night, Tancredo would be there too, looking indolent and beautiful, drawing a flower for her to embroider or singing popular Neapolitan songs, accompanying himself on the guitar. Everyone adored him, but none more so than old Monforte, who spent hours, his chin sunk in his high cravat, gazing tenderly at the prince. Then, suddenly, he would get up, cross the room and bend over him, touching him, sniffing him, breathing him in, murmuring in his sailor's French:

"*Ça aller bien . . . Hein? Beaucoup bien . . .*"

And these sudden displays of affection were clearly infectious, for at such moments, Maria would always give her father one of her prettiest smiles or go and kiss him on the forehead.

The day was taken up with serious work. She had started a charitable association, the Blanket Charity, whose aim was to distribute warm clothing and blankets to needy families in the winter; she presided in the living room over the meetings at which its by-laws were drawn up, ringing a little bell in order to call the meeting to order. She also visited the poor and went frequently to church services, all in black, on foot, with a very heavy veil covering her face.

The splendour of her beauty seemed now overlaid by a sweet shadow of grave tenderness: the Goddess was becoming a Madonna; and often, for no apparent reason, she was heard to utter a deep sigh.

At the same time, her passion for her daughter was growing. The child was two by then and utterly adorable. Every evening, she came down for a while to the living room, dressed like a little princess; and Tancredo was constantly exclaiming and going in ecstasies over her. He had made sketches of her in charcoal, crayon, and water-colour; he would kneel before her to kiss her little pink hand, as if she were the holy *bambino*. And Maria, despite Pedro's protests, always slept now with the little girl in her arms.

At the beginning of September, old Monforte left for the Pyrenees. Maria cried and hung about her father's neck, as if he were setting off once more on a ship to Africa.

By suppertime, however, she seemed consoled and radiant, and Pedro spoke again of the postponed reconciliation, for it seemed to him a good moment to go to Benfica and win back that stubborn father of his.

"No, not yet," she said, after thinking for a while, gazing into her glass of Bordeaux wine. "Your father is a kind of saint, and we don't deserve him yet. Let's wait until the winter."

One dreary December day of heavy rain, Afonso da Maia was sitting in his study reading, when the door flew open; he looked up and saw Pedro standing before him. He was muddy and dishevelled, and in his deathly pale face, beneath his wild hair, his eyes had a glint of madness. The old man sat up, terrified. And Pedro, without a word, threw himself into his father's arms and burst into terrible sobs.

"Pedro, my boy, what's happened?"

Perhaps Maria had died. He was filled by a feeling of cruel joy at the idea of seeing his son free of the Monfortes and restored to him, filling up his solitude with two grandchildren—with a whole family to love! And with a trembling voice, he lovingly disengaged himself from Pedro:

"Stop crying, my boy, and tell me what's happened."

Pedro fell back heavily onto the sofa, as a dead body might fall; then, his face suddenly haggard and old, he looked at his father and said in a faint voice, carefully enunciating each word:

"I was away from Lisbon for two days. I came back this morning. Maria has left, taking the little girl with her. She's gone off with a man, an Italian. And here I am!"

Afonso da Maia stood before his son, silent, dumbstruck, like a stone statue; and his handsome face, into which all his blood had rushed, very slowly and gradually filled with rage. He saw, in a flash, the scandal: the whole of Lisbon mocking him, the expressions of condolence, his name dragged through the mud. And it was his own son who, by rejecting his authority and marrying that creature, had tainted the blood of the family and was now covering his name in shame. And there he was, there he *lay*, not screaming or shouting, not even outraged, with none of the violent outbursts one might expect from a betrayed husband! No, he had simply flung himself down on a sofa, crying wretchedly! This enraged Afonso, and he started stiffly, sternly pacing the room, his lips pressed tightly together so as not to utter any of the words of anger and insult crowding his breast. But he was, nevertheless, a father; he could hear the deep pain in that weeping, he could see how those sobs shook the poor unhappy body he had once cradled in his arms. He stood next to Pedro, took his head gravely in his hands and kissed his brow, once, twice, as if he were still a child, restoring to him there and forever all his love and tenderness.

"You were right, Father, you were right," murmured Pedro tearfully.

Then they fell silent. Outside, in a constant clamour, successive sheets of rain lashed the house and garden, and the branches of the trees, caught up in the great winter wind, whispered at the windows.

It was Afonso who broke the silence.

"But where have they gone to, Pedro? Do you know? It's no good just crying."

"I don't know anything," Pedro managed to say. "I only know that she's gone. I left Lisbon on Monday. That same night, she left the house in a carriage, with a suitcase, her jewel box, an Italian maid she'd hired recently, and with our daughter. She told the housekeeper and the boy's nursemaid that she was going to join me. They thought it was odd, but what could they say? When I came back, I found this letter."

It was a grubby piece of paper that had doubtless been read many times since the morning and angrily crumpled up. It contained these words:

It is fate, I am leaving with Tancredo, forget me, I am not worthy of you, and I am taking Maria, because I cannot bear to be parted from her.

"And what about the little boy?" exclaimed Afonso.

Pedro seemed to struggle to remember.

"Oh, he's in the other room with the nursemaid. I brought him with me in the carriage."

Afonso immediately ran out of the room and reappeared shortly afterwards bearing in his arms the baby wrapped in a long, white, fringed cape and wearing a little lace cap. He was chubby, with very dark eyes and lovely rosy cheeks. His whole being seemed to be laughing, as he babbled and brandished a silver bell. With downcast eyes, the nursemaid stood glumly at the door, clutching a small bundle of clothes.

Afonso sat down carefully in his armchair and settled his grandson on his knee. His eyes were alight with tenderness; he seemed to forget his son's agony, and the familial shame; now there was only that small sweet face, wet with drool.

"What's his name?"

"Carlos Eduardo," murmured the nursemaid.

"Carlos Eduardo, eh?"

He sat gazing at him for a long time, as if searching for traces of a family resemblance; then he took hold of the boy's two small red hands—which still kept a firm hold on the bell—and said very gravely as if the child could understand:

"Take a good look at me. I'm your grandfather. And you must love your grandfather."

And at the sound of that powerful voice, the boy did, in fact, open wide his fine eyes, suddenly serious and very focused, but entirely unabashed by Afonso's grizzled beard; then he started fidgeting about until he had managed to free one of his hands and hit Afonso hard on the head with the bell.

The old man beamed at this joyful vigour; he held him for a long time pressed to his broad chest, and planted on his cheek a long, grateful, tender kiss, his first grandfatherly kiss; then, with great care, he returned the child to the nursemaid's arms.

"Off you go. Gertrudes is probably already sorting out a room for you, go and make sure you have everything you need."

He closed the door and went and sat down next to his son, who had not moved from the corner of the sofa, and was still staring fixedly at the floor.

"Now, Pedro, tell me everything. We haven't seen each other for three years."

"For more than three years," murmured Pedro.

He sat up and looked out at the garden, so sad beneath the rain; then he glanced slowly round the library, his eyes lingering for a moment on his own portrait, painted in Rome when he was twelve years old, dressed all in blue velvet and holding a rose in his hand. And he repeated bitterly:

"You were right, Father, you were right."

And gradually, pacing up and down and sighing, he began to speak about the last few years, the winter spent in Paris, their life at Arroios, how the Italian had become a close family friend, his own plans for a reconciliation, and, finally, that vile, shameless letter invoking fate and throwing in his face the other man's name! At first, his one thought had been to pursue them and exact a bloody revenge. However, a glimmer of reason remained. It would be ridiculous. The flight had obviously been planned beforehand, and he couldn't possibly go trawling the inns of Europe in search of his wife. What about complaining to the police and having them arrested? Absurd. That wouldn't prevent her already having slept with the other man. All that was left to him was scorn. She was a pretty woman who had been his mistress for a few years and had now run off with another man. Good riddance! He was left with a motherless son and a besmirched name. But what could he do? He needed to forget, to set off on a long journey, to America perhaps; he would be sure to return stronger and with his heart mended.

He said all these sensible things as he paced slowly up and down, still holding an extinguished cigar between his fingers, talking in a voice that grew calmer as he spoke. Suddenly, however, he stopped in front of his father, gave a short laugh, and said, with a fierce glint in his eyes:

"I've always wanted to go to America, and now is a good opportunity . . . a splendid opportunity, don't you think? I could even become an American citizen, become President, or, of course, die . . . Ha!"

"Yes, yes, all right, my son, let's think about that later," said Afonso, alarmed.

Just then, the dinner bell began to ring slowly at the far end of the corridor.

"You still have dinner early, then," said Pedro. He let out a slow, weary sigh and muttered: "We used to have dinner at seven."

He urged Afonso to eat. There was no reason for his father to miss a meal. He would go upstairs for a while, to the room he had slept in when he was single. His bed was still there, wasn't it? No, he wanted nothing to eat.

"Ask Teixeira to bring me up a glass of gin. Teixeira, poor thing, is still here, I see."

And when his father did not get up out of his chair, he said urgently:

"Go and have dinner, Father, go on, please."

He left the room. His father heard his footsteps on the floor above and the sound of windows being flung open. Only then did he go to the dining room where the servants, whom the nursemaid had doubtless informed of the misfortune, were creeping about on tiptoe, with the same sad slowness as if there had been a death in the house. Afonso sat down alone at the table, but Pedro's place had been laid there once again; winter roses in a Japanese vase dropped their petals; and the old parrot, made restless by the rain, was furiously bobbing up and down on its perch.

Afonso took a spoonful of soup, then drew his armchair closer to the fire, and there he sat, becoming gradually immersed in the melancholy December twilight, staring into the flames, listening to the southwest wind battering the window panes, thinking about all the terrible things invading his peaceful old man's life like a grim unruly throng. However, in the midst of his sorrow, deep as it was, he was aware that somewhere, in one corner of his heart, something very sweet and very new was beating with all the vigour of things reborn, a spring rich in future joys; and his face lit up, and he smiled into the bright flames, seeing again the rosy cheeks beneath the white lace of a baby's cap.

Meanwhile, in the house, the lights had been turned on. With a sudden pang of anxiety, Afonso went up to his son's room; it lay in darkness, as damp and cold as if the rain were falling inside. A tremor ran through the old man, and when he called his son's name, Pedro's voice responded from the blackness of the window; there he was, with the window wide open, sitting on the balcony, staring out at the stormy night and the gloomy rustling of the branches, his face lifted to the wind, the rain, and the wild winter weather.

"There you are, Pedro!" cried Afonso. "The servants will be wanting to prepare the room, come downstairs for a moment. You're soaked, Pedro."

He felt his son's knees and grasped his icy hands. Pedro stood up with a shudder and impatiently drew back from the old man's tender gestures.

"Oh, of course, the room, yes. But the air does me good, you know, it really does."

Teixeira brought some candles and behind him came Pedro's servant, who had just arrived from Arroios, carrying a large travelling bag covered in oilskin. He had left the other luggage downstairs, and the coachman had come too, since neither master nor mistress was at home.

"Don't worry," said Afonso. "Senhor Vilaça will go to Arroios tomorrow and sort everything out."

The servant then tiptoed in and placed the travelling case on the marble top of the chest of drawers; on it stood a few old bottles of toilet water that had once belonged to Pedro; and the candlesticks on the table illumined his large, sad, bachelor bed with the covers turned down.

Gertrudes bustled in with her arms full of bed linen; Teixeira vigorously plumped up pillows and bolsters; the servant from Arroios, still on tiptoe, put down his hat and came to help too. Pedro, meanwhile, like a sleepwalker, had gone back out onto the balcony and had turned his face once more to the rain, drawn to the churning darkness of the garden, which roared like a sea.

Afonso tugged almost roughly at his arm.

"Pedro, come downstairs for a moment. Let them prepare the room!"

Pedro mechanically followed his father down to the library, chewing on the spent cigar he had kept in his hand all this time. He sat away from the lamp, at one end of the sofa, and remained there silent and numb. For a long time, only the slow steps of his father, back and forth in front of the tall shelves, broke the drowsing silence of the room. The flames were dying down in the hearth. The night seemed to have grown still wilder. Caught up by the wind, gusts of rain would suddenly flail the windows, while, with a persistent clamour, it continued to pour in torrents from the roof; then there would be an eerie lull, with only the distant whisper of the wind in the branches; in the silence, the drip-drip of water kept up a slow lament; and then another furious blast of air would whirl about the house, rattling the windows, only to depart once more, uttering mournful whistles.

"It's real English weather tonight," said Afonso, bending down to stir the fire.

But at the word "English" Pedro got abruptly to his feet. He had doubtless been pierced by the idea of Maria, far away, in some strange room, snuggling down in her adulterous bed in the arms of that other man. He clasped his head in his hands for a moment, then went unsteadily over to his father; his voice, however, was quite calm.

"I'm really terribly tired, Father. I'm going to bed. Goodnight. We'll talk again in the morning."

He kissed his father's hand and slowly left the room.

Afonso lingered for a while longer, with a book unread in his hands, as he listened for any noise from above, but everything lay in silence.

Ten o'clock struck. Before going to bed, he went to the room set aside for the nursemaid. Gertrudes, Teixeira, and the servant from Arroios were all standing by the chest of drawers, talking in whispers, in the shadow cast by a book placed in front of the lamp; they all crept away when they heard his footsteps approaching, and the nursemaid continued putting clothes in the drawers. In the vast bed, the boy was sleeping like a weary Baby Jesus, still clutching his bell. Afonso did not dare to kiss him lest he woke him with his rough beard, but he stroked the lace nightshirt, tenderly tucked the bedclothes in against the wall and adjusted the curtain, feeling all his sorrow dissolve in the darkness of the bedroom where his grandson lay sleeping.

"Do you need anything?" he asked the nursemaid, lowering his voice.

"No, sir."

Then, he went noiselessly up to Pedro's room. There was a line of light under the door; he pushed the door open. His son was writing by the light of two candles, with his travelling bag open beside him. He seemed startled to see his father, and in his pale, drawn face, the two dark frown lines between his eyes made his gaze seem harder and brighter.

"I'm writing," he said.

He rubbed his hands together, as if suddenly aware of the coldness of the room, and added:

"I'll need Vilaça to go to Arroios first thing tomorrow morning. The other servants are still there, as well as two of my horses, and there are various other things that need sorting out. I'm writing to him now. He lives at number 32, doesn't he? Teixeira will know. Goodnight, Father, goodnight."

In his own room, next to the library, Afonso could not sleep, gripped by a feeling of oppression and disquiet that made him raise his head from the pillow every few moments to listen; now, the wind had died down and in the silent house Pedro's slow pacing echoed above him.

Day was breaking and Afonso was just dozing off, when a shot rang out in the house. He leapt out of bed and, still in his nightshirt, called for a servant, who appeared immediately, bearing a lantern. From Pedro's room, the door of which was still ajar, came the smell of gunpowder; and at the foot of the bed, Afonso found his dead son, still holding a pistol in his hand, lying face down in a pool of blood that was already soaking into the carpet.

Between the two guttering candles, their flames grown small and pale, Pedro had left a sealed letter bearing these words, written on the envelope in a firm hand: "For Papa."

Two days later, the house at Benfica was closed up. Afonso da Maia, with his grandson and all the servants, left for the house at Santa Olávia.

When, in February, Vilaça accompanied Pedro's body there for burial in the family vault, he could not keep back his tears when he saw that house where he had spent many a happy Christmas. A black baize cloth covered the coat of arms above the main door, and the blackness of that funereal drapery seemed to have leached into the silent façade and into the fine chestnut trees growing in the courtyard; inside, the servants, in heavy mourning, spoke in muted voices; there was not a single flower in any vase; the natural charm of Santa Olávia, the cool babble of running water in pools and fountains, now had the yearning cadence of falling tears. Vilaça found Afonso in the library, the curtains drawn, closing out the lovely winter sunshine; he was slumped in an armchair, his face gaunt beneath his long, white hair, his hands lying thin and idle in his lap.

Vilaça returned to Lisbon and reported that the old man would not last another year.

: III :

BUT THAT YEAR PASSED and others passed too.

One April morning, just before Easter, Vilaça arrived at Santa Olávia.

They had not expected him so early, and since it was the first fine day of that rainy spring, the gentlemen were walking in the garden. The steward, Teixeira, whose hair was turning white, was clearly very pleased indeed to see Vilaça, with whom he occasionally corresponded. He led him into the dining room, where the old housekeeper, Gertrudes, taken by surprise, dropped the pile of napkins she was carrying and threw her arms around his neck.

The French windows stood open, revealing the sunlit terrace and the marble balustrade covered in trailing plants; and Vilaça, as he headed for the steps which led down into the garden, barely recognised Afonso da Maia in the robust, rosy-cheeked, white-bearded old man holding his grandson Carlos by the hand and walking up towards him along the path lined with pomegranate trees.

When Carlos saw Vilaça on the terrace, this stranger all muffled up in a mohair scarf and wearing a top hat, he ran to have a look at him, filled with curiosity, and found himself scooped up into the arms of good old Vilaça, who threw down his parasol and kissed the boy's hair and cheeks, crying:

"Oh, my boy, my dear, dear boy. Aren't you handsome! Haven't you grown!"

"You should have told us you were coming, Vilaça!" exclaimed Afonso da Maia, as he approached with arms spread wide. "We weren't expecting you until next week!"

The two old men embraced, drew apart for a moment, and then, when their eyes met, bright with tears, embraced again.

Beside them, Carlos—grave-faced and slender, his hands plunged in the pockets of his long white flannel knickerbockers, his cap, made of the same material, at a jaunty angle on his lovely dark, curly hair—continued to stare at Vilaça who, with tremulous lip, had taken off his gloves and was wiping away the tears beneath his spectacles.

"And no one there to meet you, not even a servant waiting down below at the river!" Afonso was saying. "But you're here now, and that's what matters. Well, I must say, Vilaça, you're looking very fit!"

"And so are you, sir!" stammered Vilaça, trying to keep his voice from shaking. "You haven't aged at all. Your hair's white, of course, but you still have the face of a young man. I wouldn't have known you! And when I remember how you looked the last time I was here . . . And then there's this lovely flower of a child!"

He was about to clasp Carlos to him again, but the boy eluded him with a pretty laugh, jumped down from the terrace and went and hung from the trapeze that had been set up among the trees and there he stayed, swinging lithely and vigorously back and forth, shouting: "So you're Vilaça!"

Vilaça, his parasol under his arm, gazed at him entranced.

"He's a fine boy! It does one good to see him. And he's like his father too, the same eyes, the Maia eyes, and the same curly hair . . . but he'll turn out to be more of a man, I should think!"

"Oh, yes, he's strong and healthy," said Afonso, smiling and stroking his beard. "And how's your boy Manuel? When's the wedding? Come inside, Vilaça, we've got a lot to talk about."

They had gone into the dining room, where the wood fire in the tiled hearth was burning dully in the fine, generous April light; porcelain and china plates shone on dressers made of lignum vitae; the canaries seemed quite mad with joy. Gertrudes, who had stayed to watch, came over to them, her hands folded on her white apron, and said in fond, familiar tones:

"Isn't it a treat, sir, having this ungrateful wretch back with us in Santa Olávia!"

Her pale, round face, like an old moon, and adorned now with a downy white moustache, glowed with pleasure.

"Oh, Senhor Vilaça, how things have changed! Even the canaries sing. And I would too, if I still could . . ."

And with that she left, suddenly overcome with emotion and close to tears.

Teixeira was waiting, wearing a silent, superior smile that stretched from tip to tip of his high steward's collar.

"You've prepared the blue room for Senhor Vilaça, haven't you?" said Afonso. "The room you usually stay in is occupied by the Viscountess."

Vilaça was quick to ask who this Viscountess was. She was a member of the Runa family, a cousin of Afonso's wife, who, in the days when the poets of Caminha used to sing her praises, had married a minor aristocrat from Galicia, the Viscount de Urigo de la Sierra, who had turned out to be a drunk, a bully, and a wife-beater; later, when she was a poor widow, Afonso had taken her in out of a sense of familial duty, but also in order to have another female presence in Santa Olávia.

Of late, she had been rather unwell . . . but Afonso, glancing at the clock, interrupted his account of her ailments.

"Quick,Vilaça, go and get ready, it's nearly dinnertime."

Vilaça, greatly surprised, looked first at the clock and then at the table set for six, complete with a basket of flowers and bottles of port.

"Do you have your supper in the morning now? I thought it was lunchtime."

"Let me explain. Carlos needs to have a daily regime. By dawn, he's already out in the garden; he has lunch at seven and dines at one o'clock. And I, in order to keep an eye on the boy's manners..."

"Changing your habits at *your* age!" cried Vilaça. "That's what comes of being a grandfather, sir!"

"Nonsense! That's not the reason. It does me good. It really does. Now, hurry up, Vilaça. Carlos doesn't like to be kept waiting. The abbot might be coming too."

"Custódio as well! Oh, wonderful! Well, if you'll excuse me..."

Vilaça had only got as far as the corridor when the steward, eager to talk to him, asked, as he took his parasol and cloak:

"Tell me honestly, Senhor Vilaça, how do you find us?"

"I'm delighted, Teixeira, really delighted. It's a pleasure to visit Santa Olávia now."

And placing a friendly hand on the steward's shoulder and winking a still tearful eye:

"This is the boy's doing. He's brought our master back to life!"

Teixeira gave a respectful laugh. The boy really was the joy of the household.

"Who's that up there?" exclaimed Vilaça, pausing on the stairs, when he heard the mournful sound of a violin being tuned.

"That's Mr. Brown, the boy's English tutor. He's very good, it's a pleasure to hear him; he sometimes plays in the drawing room in the evening, with the judge accompanying him on the concertina. Here's your room, sir."

"Oh, very nice!"

The new furniture stood on a cream carpet scattered with small blue flowers; the varnish gleamed in the light from the two windows; and the cretonne curtains at both window and door were printed with the same bluish flowers and leaves against a light background. This fresh rustic comfort delighted Vilaça.

He immediately went over and felt the cretonne, stroked the marble top of the chest of drawers and tested the solidity of the chairs. Teixeira explained that they had bought the furniture in Oporto. Rather elegant and surprisingly inexpensive too. Vilaça stood on tiptoe to examine two English watercolours representing pedigree cattle lying on the grass in the shade of some romantic ruins. Teixeira studied him, watch in hand.

"You have only ten minutes, sir. The young master doesn't like to be kept waiting."

Only then did Vilaça decide to remove his scarf; then he took off his thick woollen waistcoat; beneath his shirt he had on a red flannel vest, which he wore because of his rheumatism, as well as a few embroidered silk scapulars. Teixeira was undoing the straps on Vilaça's suitcase; at the far end of the corridor, the violin was now attacking "Carnival in Venice"; and outside the closed windows one could sense the clean air, the freshness, the peace of the fields, and all the green of April.

Without his spectacles on and shivering slightly, Vilaça was wiping one corner of a damp towel over his neck and behind his ears and saying:

"So little Carlos doesn't like to be kept waiting, eh? It's easy to see who's in charge here. He's probably horribly spoiled."

Looking very grave and serious, Teixeira soon put Vilaça right. Spoiled? The poor little fellow was ruled with a rod of iron! The things he could tell Senhor Vilaça! When the boy was only five, he was forced to sleep in a room on his own, without so much as a nightlight; every morning, he had to plunge into a tub of cold water, even if it was freezing outside; and many other such barbarities. If he hadn't known how much his master loved the boy, he would have sworn he was trying to kill him. "May God forgive him," Teixeira had sometimes found himself thinking. But no, this, it seemed, was the English way! He was left to run around, fall over, climb trees, get soaking wet, play out in the noonday sun, just like the child of a farm labourer. And the master was so strict about mealtimes! The boy was only allowed to eat certain foods and at certain times! And sometimes he would sit there with wide, tear-filled eyes! Oh, yes, his master was very, very hard on him.

Then Teixeira added:

"Thank God he's turned out strong and healthy, but Gertrudes and I have never approved of the way he's been brought up, oh no."

He glanced again at his watch, attached by a black ribbon to his white waistcoat, and paced slowly about the room; then, picking up Vilaça's frock-coat from the bed, he began helpfully brushing the collar, all the while standing by the dressing table where Vilaça was carefully combing two long strands of hair over his bald head.

"Do you know the first thing the English teacher taught him when he arrived? He taught him to row, sir, like a boatman! Not to mention the trapeze and various other circus tricks. I don't even like to talk about it . . . I mean, I'm the first person to say it, Brown is an excellent person, quiet, clean, and a first-rate musician. But as I'm always telling Gertrudes, he might be fine for an English boy, but he's not suited to teaching a young Portuguese nobleman. Oh, no. You ask Senhora Dona Ana Silveira."

There was a soft knocking at the door, and Teixeira fell silent. A footman entered, gestured to Teixeira, respectfully removed the frock-coat from over his arm, then, still holding it, took up a position by the dressing table where Vilaça, red-faced and flustered, was still battling with the same two rebellious strands of hair.

Teixeira was standing at the door now, watch in hand.

"It's dinnertime. You have two minutes, Senhor Vilaça."

The agent was soon racing after him, buttoning up his jacket as he went down the stairs. Everyone else was already in the living room. By the fire, where the burned-out logs were fading into white ash, Brown was leafing through a copy of *The Times*. Carlos, astride his grandfather's knees, was telling some long story about boys and fights; and next to them was the good abbot Custódio, his snuff handkerchief crumpled and forgotten in his hands, as he listened, open-mouthed, smiling a fond, paternal smile.

"Look who's here, Father," said Afonso.

The abbot turned round and slapped his thigh.

"Well, who would have thought it! It's our Vilaça! And no one said a word! Come here, man!"

Carlos was bouncing up and down on his grandfather's knee, highly amused by the long embrace that brought together the two men's heads—one with two thin strands plastered over a bald patch, the other with a large tonsure surrounded by a white thicket of hair. And when they continued to stand there, hand in hand, in wonderment, studying the lines the years had left on each other's face, Afonso said:

"Vilaça! The Viscountess."

The administrator, however, looked around the room in vain, his eyes wide. Carlos laughed and clapped his hands. Vilaça finally spotted her in a corner—sitting on a little low chair between the sideboard and the window—all dressed in black, timid and still, with her chubby arms resting on her plump waist. Her full soft face, white as paper, and the rolls of fat around her neck, immediately flushed scarlet; she could not find a single word to say to Vilaça, and so she held out to him a pale, pudgy hand, one finger of which was wrapped in a piece of black silk. Then she cooled herself with a great sequinned fan, her breast heaving, her eyes downcast, as if exhausted by the effort.

Two footmen had begun to serve the soup, and Teixeira was waiting, standing to attention behind the high back of Afonso's chair.

But Carlos was still sitting astride his grandfather's knee, eager to finish telling him another story about how Manuel had come at him with a stone in his hand. At first, he thought he'd just make light of it, but then the other two boys had started laughing and so he'd chased them all off.

"And they were older than you, were they?"

"Three big boys, Grandpa, you can ask Tia Pedra. She saw it, she was there. One of them was carrying a sickle."

"All right, all right, we've heard enough now. Come on, dismount, the soup's getting cold. Up you get!"

And with the resplendent air of a contented patriarch, the old man came and sat down at the head of the table, smiling and saying:

"You're getting too heavy to sit on my knee."

Then he noticed Brown and, springing once more to his feet, he introduced Vilaça:

"Senhor Brown, my friend Vilaça. Forgive me, I forgot: it's all the fault of that gentleman at the other end of the table, Carlos the Giant-killer!"

The tutor, tightly buttoned up in his long military frock-coat, marched stiffly round to the other side of the table in order to shake Vilaça vigorously by the hand; then, without a word, he resumed his place, unfolded his napkin, smoothed his formidable moustaches, and announced to Vilaça in heavily accented Portuguese:

"Lovely day . . . glorious!"

"Oh, yes, very nice," replied Vilaça, bowing, intimidated by this athlete of a man.

Naturally, they spoke of the journey from Lisbon, of the excellent service by post-chaise, of the railway line that was about to open. Vilaça had, in fact, come by train as far as Carregado.

"Pretty terrifying, eh?" asked the abbot, pausing with his spoon halfway to his mouth.

The excellent man had never left Resende, and the wide world that lay beyond the darkness of his sacristy and the trees in his garden seemed as frightening to him as if it were another Tower of Babel. Especially the railway, about which everyone talked so much.

"It is a bit alarming," agreed Vilaça. "They can say what they like, but it is alarming."

What mainly frightened the abbot were the inevitable accidents!

Vilaça then reminded him of accidents that had occurred involving the post-chaise. There was that time in Alcobaça, when the whole thing turned over, crushing to death two sisters of charity! Besides, there were dangers everywhere. You could break your leg just walking about in your bedroom.

The abbot liked progress, even believed it to be necessary, but it seemed to him that people nowadays wanted to do everything pellmell. The country wasn't ready for such inventions; what they needed were some decent roads.

"And economic restraint!" said Vilaça, helping himself to the sweet peppers.

"Some Bucelas wine, sir?" a servant murmured over his shoulder.

When his glass was full, Vilaça held it up to the light to admire the rich golden colour, took a sip and winked at Afonso.

"One of ours!"

"A good old wine," said Afonso. "Ask Brown. Delicious, isn't it, Brown?"

"Magnificent!" boomed the tutor enthusiastically.

Then Carlos reached out across the table and demanded to drink some Bucelas too, on the excuse that, since Vilaça was there, it was clearly a special occasion. His grandfather would not allow it; the boy would have his usual one glass of red Colares wine. Carlos folded his arms over the napkin tied around his neck, outraged at such injustice! So he couldn't have a little drop of Bucelas, not even to toast Vilaça! That was a fine way to receive guests. Gertrudes had told him that when Senhor Vilaça came, he would have to wear his new velvet suit in the evening. And now they were telling him that it wasn't a party at all, nor even a reason to drink the good Bucelas wine. He simply didn't understand.

His grandfather, who was delightedly drinking in his grandson's words, suddenly put on a very severe frowning face.

"It seems to me that the gentleman is talking far too much. At the dinner table, it's the grown-ups who talk."

Carlos immediately went back to his plate, murmuring mildly:

"All right,Grandpa, don't get angry. I'll wait until I'm older."

Everyone around the table beamed. Even the Viscountess was delighted and lazily flapped her fan; the abbot turned his ecstatic face to the boy and clutched his hairy hands to his chest, vastly amused; Afonso, meanwhile, was pretending to wipe his beard with his napkin, in order to hide the mingled laughter and astonishment shining in his eyes.

Vilaça, too, was surprised at such vivacity. He wanted to hear more from the boy, and so, setting down his knife and fork, he asked:

"And how are your studies going, Carlos?"

The boy didn't look at him, but lolled nonchalantly in his chair, thrust his hands inside the waistband of his flannel trousers, and replied in a superior tone:

"I can already make Brígida sidestep."

His grandfather could contain himself no longer; he leaned back and burst out laughing.

"Oh, excellent! He can make Brígida sidestep! And it's true, Vilaça, he can. Ask Brown. It's true, isn't it, Brown? The mare's only small, of course, but she's a good horse nonetheless."

"Grandpa," cried Carlos, excited now, "tell Vilaça, go on. Isn't it true that I can drive the dog-cart now?"

Afonso resumed his air of severity.

"I don't deny you can. At least you *might* be able to drive it, if you were allowed to. But kindly don't brag about your exploits. A proper gentleman should be modest, and gentlemen never stick their hands in their trouser waistbands like that either."

Vilaça was cracking his knuckles and preparing his next remark. It was doubtless a great achievement knowing how to ride a horse well, but he had meant to ask how Carlos was getting on with his Phaedrus and his Livy.

"Careful, Vilaça," warned the abbot, waving his fork in the air and wearing a smile that was at once saintly and mischievous. "Don't speak Latin in the presence of our noble friend here. He won't allow it, he thinks it's old-fashioned, but he's the one who's old-fashioned."

"Have some of that fricassee, abbot, go on," said Afonso, "I know it's your favourite, and forget about your Latin."

The abbot gleefully obeyed, but, as he served himself some large pieces of chicken from the rich sauce, he muttered:

"You should start with a little bit of Latin, that's where you should start. It's the basis of everything else."

"No, Latin later!" exclaimed Brown, with a vigorous gesture. "First, strength, strength and muscles!"

And he repeated this twice, shaking his formidable fists:

"First, muscle, muscle!"

Afonso solemnly agreed. Brown was quite right. Latin was a luxury for the erudite. What could be more absurd than starting to teach a child in a dead language about people like Fabius, King of the Sabines, and what happened to the brothers Gracchus, and other such tales from an extinct nation, meanwhile leaving the child ignorant about the rain that falls on him, how the bread he eats is made, and all the many facts about the universe in which he lives.

"Yes, but the classics . . ." began the abbot shyly.

"Classics, my eye! Man's first duty is to live, and to do that he needs to be strong and healthy. That is all a sensible upbringing consists of: creating health, strength and good habits, developing only the animal in the child and making of him a physically superior being. Just as if he had no soul. The soul comes afterwards. The soul is another luxury—a luxury for grown-ups."

The abbot was scratching his head, looking rather startled.

"But a little bit of education is important too," he said. "Don't you agree, Vilaça? You, Senhor Afonso, have more experience of the world than I do, but a little bit of education . . ."

"For a child, education isn't being able to recite *Tityre, tu patulae recubans* . . . it's knowing facts, ideas, and useful things, practical things."

He stopped and, with bright eyes, drew Vilaça's attention to his grandson now chattering away in English to Brown. He was clearly retailing some exploit, some story of fights with other boys, which he recounted with great animation, making punching gestures. The tutor approvingly twirled his moustaches. And at the table, everyone else sat, forks in the air, and, behind them, the footmen, napkins over arms, listened in reverent silence, astonished to hear this little boy speaking English.

"A great gift, a great gift," murmured Vilaça, leaning towards the Viscountess.

The excellent lady blushed and smiled. She looked even plumper like that, hunched in her chair, saying nothing, but eating all the time; and after each sip of Bucelas wine, she would languidly cool herself with her great, black, sequinned fan.

When Teixeira served the port, Afonso proposed a toast to Vilaça. With a friendly murmur, everyone raised their glass. Carlos was about to shout "Hurrah!" but his grandfather, with an admonitory gesture, stopped him; however, in the contented pause that followed, the boy said with great conviction:

"I like Vilaça, Grandpa. He's our friend."

"I am indeed a great friend and have been for many years!" exclaimed Vilaça, so moved that he could barely raise his glass.

Dinner was drawing to a close. Outside, the sun had left the terrace and, beneath the dark blue sky, the garden looked very green in the sweet quiet air. In the grate, all that remained was a little white ash. The lilacs in the vases gave off an intense perfume, which mingled with the smell of crème caramel topped with a little lemon rind; there was the occasional clink of silver as the servants, in their white waistcoats, rearranged cutlery and plates; and the white damask tablecloth gradually disappeared beneath the clutter of dessert, where the golden tones of the port wine glowed among the small glass bowls. The Viscountess, her face aflame, was fanning herself. Father Custódio, the sleeves of whose cassock were shiny with wear, was slowly rolling up his napkin.

Then Afonso, smiling tenderly, made a final toast:

"To Carlos the Giant-killer!"

"To Grandpa!" said the boy, draining his glass.

The boy, with his small dark head, and the old man, with his white-bearded face, toasted each other from either end of the table, while everyone else smiled, touched by this ceremony. Then the abbot, toothpick in mouth, murmured a grace. The Viscountess closed her eyes and put her hands together in prayer. Vilaça, who also had religious beliefs, found it distasteful to see how Carlos simply ignored the grace, leaped out of his chair and threw his arms around his grandfather's neck to whisper in his ear.

"Certainly not!" the old man said. The boy, however, merely tightened his embrace and, in a coaxing voice as gentle as a kiss, murmured still more pressing reasons, until the old man's face softened into indulgent weakness.

"All right, since it's a special occasion," he said at last, vanquished. "But you be careful now."

The boy jumped up and down, clapping his hands, grabbed Vilaça's arms and made him dance around, while he sang a song of his own making:

"It's so nice to see, see, see you . . . I'm going to get Teresa, Teresa, Teresa!"

"His fiancée," said his grandfather, getting up from the table. "Yes, he's already got a girlfriend, Silveira's little girl. We'll have coffee out on the terrace, Teixeira."

Outside, the day looked deliciously inviting, with not a cloud to be seen in a wide sky of the purest and most subtle of blues. At the foot of the terrace, the red geraniums were already out; the still tender leaves on the shrubs, as delicate as lace, seemed to tremble at the slightest breeze; the vague scent of violets wafted to them on the air, mingled with the sweet perfume of wild flowers; the tall fountain sang; and along the garden paths, flanked by low box hedges, the fine sand glistened in the timid, late-spring sunlight, which, farther off, wrapped the green of the garden—slumbering at this siesta hour—in a fresh, golden light.

The three men sat down at the table on the terrace. In the garden, Brown, wearing a tam-o'-shanter at a rakish angle and smoking a large pipe, was pushing the trapeze hard to set Carlos swinging. Then Vilaça asked if they would mind if he looked the other way. He hated watching gymnastics; he knew it was perfectly safe, but it was the same with the circus, all those somersaults and tricks with hoops made him dizzy; he always left with his stomach churning.

"And it does seem somewhat unwise immediately after eating . . ."

"He's only swinging . . . look!"

Vilaça did not move, but kept his face bent over his cup.

The abbot, on the other hand, watched in amazement, mouth open, his saucerful of coffee forgotten in his hand.

"Look at him, Vilaça," repeated Afonso. "It won't hurt you, man."

Vilaça reluctantly turned round. The boy, high in the air, legs braced against the bar of the trapeze, hands gripping the ropes, came swooping down over the terrace, cutting through the air, his hair flying; then he serenely rose up again, into the sunlight, smiling broadly; his shirt and breeches were puffed out in the breeze; and as he came and went, they could see his very dark, very wide eyes shining.

"No, I can't help it, I just don't like it!" said Vilaça. "I find it imprudent!"

Then Afonso applauded, and the abbot cried: "Bravo, bravo." Vilaça turned to join in the applause, but Carlos had vanished; the trapeze swayed slowly to a halt; and Brown, picking up his copy of *The Times*, which he had placed temporarily on the plinth of a bust, wandered off down into the garden in a cloud of pipe smoke.

"A wonderful thing, gymnastics!" exclaimed Afonso, contentedly lighting another cigar.

Vilaça had heard that it greatly weakened the chest. And the abbot, after taking a sip of coffee and licking his lips, uttered his favourite, home-made maxim:

"Your brand of education may make athletes, but it doesn't make Christians. I've said so before."

"You certainly have, abbot!" cried Afonso gaily. "You tell me so every week. Do you know what, Vilaça, the abbot here is always nagging me to teach the boy the catechism. The *catechism!*"

The abbot sat for a moment regarding Afonso, a disconsolate look on his face and his box of snuff open in his hand; the irreligious views of this old nobleman, who owned most of the parish, was one of his greatest sorrows.

"Yes, sir, the catechism, even if you do choose to say it in that mocking tone—the catechism—but I don't want to talk about that now. There are other things. And the reason I say what I say so often, Senhor Afonso da Maia, is out of love for the boy."

And the discussion started up again, as it always did over coffee when the abbot dined at the house.

The good man found it horrifying that a splendid young boy of Carlos' age, the heir to such a large house, with future responsibilities in society, should not know his doctrine. And he told Vilaça the story of Dona Cecília Macedo. This virtuous lady, the scrivener's wife, had passed by the door of the house one day, seen Carlos and, since she was very fond of children, had called him over and asked him to recite the Act of Contrition. And what did the boy reply? That he had never heard of it! Such incidents saddened him. Senhor Afonso da Maia, however, had merely thought it funny and laughed! But now their friend Vilaça was there to tell him that it was no laughing matter. Senhor Afonso da Maia knew a lot about many things and had travelled widely, but this poor priest, who had never even been as far as Oporto, could not be persuaded that true happiness and decent behaviour were possible without the morality of the catechism.

Afonso da Maia replied goodhumouredly:

"So if I handed the boy over to you, abbot, what would you teach him? That he shouldn't pick pockets or tell lies or mistreat his inferiors, because that is against the commandments of God's law and leads straight to Hell, is that right?"

"Well, there's rather more to it than that . . ."

"Yes, but everything you would teach him not to do because it's a sin against God, he already knows he shouldn't do because it's unworthy of a gentleman or, indeed, of any honest man."

"But, sir . . ."

"You see, abbot, that's the main difference. I want the boy to be virtuous out of a love of virtue and honest out of a love of honesty, not out of fear of Old Nick's cauldrons, or because he's tempted by the thought of entering the Kingdom of Heaven."

And getting up, he added with a smile: "But when a day like today arrives after weeks of rain, the real duty of all decent men, abbot, is to go out and breathe the good country air and not sit around here discussing morality. So up you get! And if Vilaça isn't too tired, we can go for a stroll around the estate."

The abbot sighed like a saint forced to witness a blackly impious Beelzebub making off with the finest sheep in the flock; then he gazed into his cup and savoured the last few drops of his coffee.

By the time Afonso da Maia, Vilaça, and the abbot returned from their tour of the parish, it had grown dark, there were lights on in all the rooms, and the Silveiras had arrived, two wealthy sisters from the Quinta da Lagoaça.

Dona Ana Silveira, the elder of the sisters and a spinster, was held to be the talented member of the family, and, in Resende, she was considered a great authority on points of doctrine and etiquette. The widow, Dona Eugénia, contented herself with being an excellent and amiable lady, pleasantly plump, very dark and with long thick eyelashes; she had two children, Teresa—Carlos' "fiancée"—a thin lively girl with hair as black as ink, and Eusèbiozinho—her son and heir—a marvel much talked about in the area.

This remarkable child had revealed, almost from the cradle, an edifying love of old books and of everything to do with knowledge. When he was still at the crawling stage, his one joy was to sit in a corner, on a rug, wrapped in a blanket, leafing through some large tome, with his small, bald, wise man's cranium bent over the large clear letters of the good doctrine; and when he was a little older, he was such a quiet, sensible child that he would spend hours motionless in a chair, dangling his legs and picking his nose: he had no interest in drums or guns, but when they made him a few little notebooks from sheets of paper sewn together, this precocious man of letters, to the astonishment of Mama and Auntie, would spend hours drawing numbers, with his little tongue sticking out.

The family already had his career mapped out for him: he was rich and would be, first, a graduate, and then a judge. Whenever he came to Santa Olávia, Aunt Ana would sit him down at the table, beside the lamp, to look at the pictures in a large, lavish volume: *The Traditions and Costumes of People from Around the World.* That was where he was that evening, dressed, as always, like a Scotsman, with a brilliant red-and-black tartan scarf draped around his neck and pinned to one shoulder with a dragon brooch; in order to preserve the noble air of a Stuart, or of a valiant Walter Scott gentleman, they never removed his beret, which was adorned with a glossy, heroically arching cockerel's feather; and there was no more melancholy sight than his little frowning face, slack and yellow, due to an infestation of threadworms, and his small, perplexed, bluish eyes, entirely devoid of lashes, as if these had been consumed by knowledge, poring gravely over pictures of Sicilian peasants and fierce Montenegran warlords poised on mountain tops, leaning on their rifles.

Next to the sofa where the ladies were sitting was another faithful friend, the public prosecutor, a grave and worthy man who had spent the last five years pondering marriage to the widowed Silveira sister, but who, unable to reach a decision, contented himself instead with buying half a dozen sheets every year and another length of fine Breton cloth to complete the household linen. These purchases were discussed around the fire in the Silveira household, and their modest but inevitable allusions to the two pillowcases he had bought, to the size of the sheets, to the eiderdowns that would keep them warm in January, far from inflaming the magistrate, only made him deeply uneasy. In the days that followed, he would appear preoccupied, as if the prospect of the actual consummation of holy matrimony sent a shudder down his spine, as though it were some great feat to be undertaken, like catching and bringing down a bull or swimming the rapids of the Douro River. Then, for some specious reason, he would postpone the wedding until next St. Michael's day. And feeling relieved and serene, this respectable gentleman, always dressed in black, would continue to accompany the Silveira sisters to teas, church celebrations or funerals, affable, helpful, full of smiles for Dona Eugénia, and desiring no further pleasures than those granted by this safe, paternal familiarity.

As soon as Afonso entered the room, they immediately gave him the bad news: the district judge and his wife could not come because the judge was, again, in too much pain; and the Branco sisters sent their apologies, poor things, but it was seventeen years since the death of their brother Manuel and was, therefore, a day of mourning in their household.

"Well," said Afonso, "Pain, mourning, brother Manuel . . . What about a game of four-handed ombre, then? What do you say, sir?"

The public prosecutor bowed his bald head, murmuring that he was, of course, at his disposal.

"To work, then, to work!" exclaimed the abbot, rubbing his hands, already excited at the prospect of a game.

The players headed for the card room, which was separated from the dining room by a damask door curtain, caught back now to reveal the green table, the circles of light cast by the lampshades, and the fanned decks of cards. A moment later, the public prosecutor returned, smiling broadly and saying that he had decided to leave the three of them to it; and he resumed his position beside Dona Eugénia, crossing his feet under the chair and folding his hands on his chest. The ladies were discussing the judge's "pain." It came on about every three months or so, and the stubborn man resolutely refused to see a doctor. The more drained, withered and sallow-faced he grew, the larger and ruddier his wife Dona Augusta seemed to become. The Viscountess, ensconced plumply at one end of the sofa, her fan open on her chest, told of a similar case she had encountered in Spain: the man dwindled away until he was little more than a skeleton, while his wife became a veritable barrel, though, at first, it had been quite the opposite; someone had even written a poem about it.

"It's all a question of humours," said the public prosecutor gloomily.

Then they talked about the Branco sisters; they recalled the death of Manuel Branco, poor lad, in the flower of his youth! And he had been such a lovely boy! And so sensible! Dona Ana Silveira always remembered, every year, to light a candle for his soul and to say three Our Fathers. The Viscountess, however, seemed terribly upset *not* to have remembered, especially since she had fully intended to do so!

"I very nearly had someone come over and remind you!" exclaimed Dona Ana. "And the sisters do so appreciate it, my dear!"

"There's still time," observed the public prosecutor.

Dona Eugénia indolently formed another stitch on her eternal crocheting, which she was never to be seen without, and said with a sigh:

"We all have our dead to remember."

And in the ensuing silence, another sigh came from the other end of the sofa, from the Viscountess, and doubtless recalling her aristocratic husband from Urigo de la Sierra, she too murmured:

"Yes, we all have our dead to remember."

A drowsiness weighed in the air. In the gilt candelabra on the console tables, the flames from the candles rose up tall and sad. Eusèbiozinho continued cautiously and deftly turning the pages of *The Traditions and Costumes of People from Around the World*. And in the card room, from behind the drawn-back curtain, could be heard the tetchy voice of the abbot, grumbling quietly: "Pass! I've done nothing else all evening."

At this moment, Carlos burst into the room, dragging behind him his "fiancée," Teresa, all flustered and red from playing; and their shouts brought the slumbering sofa back to life.

The betrothed couple had just returned from a picturesque and perilous journey, and Carlos seemed displeased with his fiancée; she had behaved atrociously; when he was driving the post-chaise, she had wanted to sit next to him in the driver's seat . . . well, ladies don't do that!

"And he pushed me off, Auntie!"

"I did not! Honestly, she tells fibs too! It was when we reached the inn. She wanted to go to bed and I didn't. I mean, when you reach your destination, the first thing you do is take care of the horses . . . and the horses were really sweating . . ."

Dona Ana's voice interrupted him, saying very sternly:

"That's quite enough of such nonsense and quite enough jigging about for one day. Sit over there next to the Viscountess, Teresa. Just look at the state of your hair! Whatever can you have been thinking of!"

She hated to see her niece, a delicate girl of ten, playing so roughly with Carlos. The handsome, impetuous boy, equally devoid of doctrine and of sense, absolutely terrified her; through her spinsterish imagination passed an endless stream of ideas and possible outrages he might perpetrate on the girl. At home, when she was getting the child ready before coming to Santa Olávia, she would issue urgent warnings not to go into any dark corners with Carlos and, on no account, to let him fiddle with her clothes! The languorous-eyed little girl would always say: "Yes, Auntie," but as soon as she was in the garden, she would put her arms about her little husband. If they were to be married, why shouldn't they play at house, or have a shop and earn their living from kisses? The rowdy boy, however, was only interested in wars, lining up four chairs in a row and pretending they were a horse, and travelling to lands with the barbarous names Brown had taught him. Slighted and feeling misunderstood, she would call him a ruffian, and he would threaten her with a boxing lesson English-style; and they always ended up quarrelling.

But when she sat down next to the Viscountess, grave-faced and with her hands in her lap, Carlos immediately joined her, slumping against the back of the sofa and swinging his legs.

"Have some manners, boy," Dona Ana said abruptly.

"I'm tired. I've been driving four horses," he retorted insolently, without even looking at her.

Then, suddenly, he pounced on Eusèbiozinho. He wanted to carry him off to Africa to fight savages, and he was already tugging at that fine plaid scarf worthy of a Scottish nobleman, when Eusèbiozinho's terrified Mama rushed to his aid.

"No, no, not with Eusèbiozinho! He's not strong enough for such foolishness. If you don't stop this minute, Carlos, I'll call your grandfather."

Eusèbiozinho, however, after one particularly violent tug from Carlos, had rolled onto the floor, uttering the most terrible screams. There was general tumult and alarm. His trembling mother crouched down beside him, helped him onto his spindly legs and wiped away his great tears, first with her handkerchief, then with kisses, almost in tears herself. Aghast, the public prosecutor picked up the Scottish bonnet and sadly smoothed the lovely cockerel feather. The Viscountess pressed both her hands to her enormous bosom, as if about to be overwhelmed by palpitations.

Eusèbiozinho was then seated lovingly next to his aunt, and the stern lady, her thin face flushed with anger, clutching her closed fan as if it were a weapon, prepared to repel Carlos, who was dancing around the sofa, hands behind his back, laughing and baring his teeth at Eusèbiozinho. Just at that moment, it struck nine o'clock, and the erect figure of Brown appeared in the doorway.

As soon as he saw him, Carlos ran to take refuge behind the Viscountess, crying:

"It's still early, Brown, and today's a special day. Don't make me go to bed!"

Then Afonso da Maia, who had not moved a muscle in response to Eusèbiozinho's piercing howls, said sternly from the other room, from his place at the card table:

"Carlos, be a good boy now, and go to bed."

"Oh, but, Grandpa, it's a special day. Vilaça's here!"

Afonso da Maia put down his cards, strode wordlessly across the room, grabbed the boy by the arm and dragged him down the corridor, while Carlos dug in his heels, resisting and protesting desperately:

"But it's special day, Grandpa. It's not fair! Vilaça might be offended. Oh, Grandpa, please, I'm not even sleepy!"

A door slamming shut silenced his clamour. The ladies were quick to censure such rigidity; it was simply incomprehensible; the grandfather allowed the boy to do all kinds of dreadful things, but refused to allow him to stay up a little bit later than usual to enjoy the party.

"Senhor Afonso, why won't you let the child stay?"

"It's method that matters, method," he muttered as he came back in, still pale from his exertions.

And at the card table, picking up his cards again with tremulous hands, he kept repeating:

"It's method that matters. Children need their sleep."

With her lips pursed into the tight smile she always wore whenever Afonso da Maia mentioned "method," Dona Ana Silveira turned to Vilaça, who had given up his seat at the card table to the public prosecutor and come to join the ladies. Leaning back in her chair and opening her fan, she declared, with heavy irony, that it was doubtless her own lack of intelligence, but she had never quite understood the advantage of "method." It was the English way, they said, and it might work very well in England, but, unless she was very much mistaken, Santa Olávia was in Portugal.

And when Vilaça nodded timidly, a pinch of snuff between his fingers, the sharp-witted old lady unburdened herself to him—in a low voice so that Afonso would not hear. Senhor Vilaça would not, of course, know this, but the family's friends had never approved of the way in which Carlos was being brought up. The presence in the house of Brown, a heretic, a Protestant, as tutor to the Maia family had caused great uneasiness in Resende, especially when Afonso had the saintly abbot Custódio right there, so well-respected and so knowledgeable. *He* would not teach the child the skills of an acrobat; what the boy needed was to be brought up as a nobleman, to prepare him to cut a good figure in Coimbra.

At that point, the abbot, fearing a draft, got up from the card table to close the door curtain; then, since Afonso could no longer hear her, Dona Ana raised her voice:

"It's most upsetting for Custódio, Senhor Vilaça. The boy, poor child, doesn't know a word of doctrine. I must tell you what happened with Dona Cecília Macedo."

Vilaça already knew.

"Ah, you know! Do you remember, Viscountess? Dona Cecília and the Act of Contrition."

The Viscountess sighed, silently raising her eyes to Heaven, somewhere up there beyond the ceiling.

"Dreadful!" went on Dona Ana. "The poor woman was quite distraught by the time she arrived at our house. It shocked me too. Indeed, I dreamed about it three nights in a row."

She stopped speaking for a moment. Vilaça, embarrassed and shy, was fiddling with his snuffbox, his eyes fixed on the carpet. Another languorous wave of somnolence washed over the room: Dona Eugénia, her eyelids drooping, made the occasional limp crochet stitch; Carlos' "fiancée," lying at one end of the sofa, was already asleep, her little mouth open, her lovely dark hair covering her neck.

Dona Ana gave a brief yawn, then returned to her theme:

"And the boy is so backward. He knows a bit of English, of course, but apart from that, nothing. He has no skills whatsoever!"

"But he's so bright, dear lady!" Vilaça cried.

"So they say," replied the intelligent Dona Ana tartly.

And turning to Eusèbiozinho, who had remained by her side as still as if he were a plaster statue, she said:

"Recite that poem for Senhor Vilaça. Go on now, don't be shy! Please, Eusébio, be nice."

But the boy, fearful and dejected, would not leave his aunt's skirts; she had to stand him on his feet and hold him there so that the young prodigy's thin, flaccid legs would not give way; and his Mama promised him that if he recited the poem, he could sleep in her bed that night.

This decided him; he opened his mouth, and in a quavering voice, the slow, lisping recitation came dribbling out, like water from a clogged faucet:

Night, and the sad moon
Breaks through the leaden sky,
Over its lovely face is thrown
a veil, half-grey, half-white ...

He recited the whole poem, without moving, his small hands hanging limply, his dull eyes fixed on his aunt. His mother kept time with her crochet needle, and the Viscountess, a weary smile on her lips, and lulled by his dull rendition, was very slowly closing her eyes.

"Very good! Very good!" cried Vilaça, impressed, when Eusèbiozinho, his temples beaded with sweat, finally reached the end. "What a memory! The boy's a prodigy!"

The servants came in with the tea. The cardplayers had finished their game, and good Custódio, standing, cup in hand, was complaining bitterly at the way in which the other gentlemen had fleeced him.

Since the next day was Sunday, and there was early mass, the ladies left at half past nine. The ever-obliging public prosecutor offered Dona Eugénia his arm; a servant from the estate lit their way with a lantern; and the Silveiras' servant carried Eusèbiozinho, a dark bundle, all swathed in blankets and with a shawl wrapped round his head.

After supper, Vilaça joined Afonso da Maia in the library for a while, for it was there, in English fashion, that Afonso da Maia always drank a brandy and soda before retiring.

The room, with its severe old rosewood bookshelves, drowsed cosily in the soft darkness, with the curtains tightly drawn, a faint glow in the fireplace, and the glass globe of the oil lamp casting a serene light on the table piled with books. Outside, the fountains sang clearly in the silence of the night.

While the footman wheeled a low table bearing the glasses and the bottles of soda water over to Afonso's armchair, Vilaça, his hands in his pockets, remained standing, deep in thought, staring at the embers of the wood burning down into white ash. Then he looked up and said softly, as if apropos of nothing:

"He's certainly a very bright little boy."

"Who? Eusèbiozinho?" asked Afonso, who was making himself comfortable by the fire and happily filling his pipe. "Frankly, Vilaça, I dread having him over here! Carlos can't stand him, and, some months ago, there was the most terrible scene. There'd been a church procession and Eusébio had gone dressed as an angel. The Silveiras, poor things, who are excellent creatures, sent him over here still in his angel's costume to show the Viscountess. Well, we got distracted, and Carlos, who was prowling around, grabbed hold of him, took him up to the attic, and, you won't believe this, Vilaça, he started roughing him up—just because he has a particular dislike of angels. That wasn't the worst of it, though. Imagine our horror when Eusébio came screaming to his Auntie, hair all dishevelled, one wing missing, the other hanging by a thread and dragging at his heels, his crown of roses round his neck, and all the gold braid, tulle and sequins—his whole celestial garment—in tatters! An angel thoroughly plucked and beaten. I thrashed Carlos within an inch of his life!"

He drank half his brandy and soda, then, smoothing his beard with his hand, added with profound satisfaction: "He's a little devil!"

The administrator, perched now on the edge of a chair, gave a mirthless laugh, then again fell silent, looking at Afonso, his hands on his knees, seemingly abstracted and vague. He appeared to be about to say something, hesitated again, cleared his throat, then went back to gazing thoughtfully at the sparks sent up by the burning logs.

Afonso da Maia, meanwhile, his legs stretched out towards the fire, resumed his comments on young Eusébio. He was three or four months older than Carlos, but a Portuguese upbringing had left him pale and puny; even now, he still slept in the maid's bed, never had a bath because they were afraid he might catch cold, and was constantly sheathed in layers of flannel! He spent his days by his aunt's side learning poetry and whole pages from *The Catechism of Perseverance*. One day, Afonso, purely out of curiosity, had opened this little book and found written there "the Sun goes around the Earth (as it did before Galileo) and every day Our Lord gives orders to the Sun about where it should go and where it should stop, etc., etc." And that was their way of preparing the poor boy's soul.

Vilaça gave another silent laugh. Then, with sudden determination, he got up, cracked his knuckles and said:

"Did you know that the Monforte woman has turned up again?"

Without even looking round, still leaning back in his armchair, Afonso asked calmly from his cloud of pipe smoke:

"In Lisbon?"

"No, sir, in Paris. The writer, Alencar, who, as you know, used to spend a lot of time in Arroios, he saw her there . . . He's even visited her house in Paris."

And they both fell silent. It had been years since either of them had mentioned the name of Maria Monforte. At first, when he had retreated to Santa Olávia, Afonso da Maia's ardent desire had been to recover the daughter she had taken with her. At the time, however, no one knew where Maria and her prince had gone, and not even by dint of diplomatic influence or lavish payments to the secret police of Paris, London and Madrid could they find "the beast's lair," as Vilaça used to say at the time. They had both doubtless changed their names, and, given their bohemian natures, they might, who knows, be wandering South America or India or other even more exotic lands. Discouraged by all these futile efforts, and entirely absorbed by the grandson growing up fine and strong by his side and by their constantly growing bond of affection, Afonso da Maia gradually forgot all about Maria Monforte and about his other grandchild, so distant and vague, a child whose name and face he did not even know. And now, suddenly, the Monforte woman had resurfaced in Paris, and his poor Pedro was dead, and the child sleeping now at the far end of the corridor had never even known his mother.

He got up and paced, slow and heavy-footed, about the library, his head bowed. At the desk, by the light of the lamp, Vilaça was going through the papers in his file, one by one.

"And is she in Paris with the Italian?" asked Afonso from the shadowy depths of the room.

Vilaça looked up from his papers and said:

"No, sir, she's with whoever pays her."

And when Afonso silently approached the desk, Vilaça handed him a couple of folded sheets of paper and added:

"These are very serious matters, sir, and I didn't want to trust only to my memory. That's why I asked Alencar, who is an excellent fellow, to set down in a letter everything he'd told me. That way, we at least have a document. I only know what is written here. You can read it, if you'd care to."

Afonso unfolded the two sheets of paper. It was a simple story, which Alencar—the poet of *Voices of the Dawn* and author of *Elvira*—had ornamented with as many flowers and as much gold braid as if it were a chapel on a feast day.

One night, as he left the Maison d'Or, he had seen Maria Monforte jump down from a carriage accompanied by two men in white tie and tails; she and he had recognised each other instantly and had hesitated for a moment, face to face, underneath the gaslight. In the end, she was the one to step boldly forward, smiling and holding out her hand; she asked him to visit her, gave him her address and the name he should ask for: Madame de l'Estorade. And the following morning, in her boudoir, she spoke at length about herself: she had lived for three years in Vienna with Tancredo and with her father, who had joined them later, and who had doubtless skulked in corners there as he had in Arroios, paying for his daughter's clothes and tenderly patting her lover on the shoulder as once he had her husband. Then they had gone to Monaco, and there, according to Alencar, "in a dark drama of passion, the outlines of which she lay before me," the Neapolitan had been killed in a duel. Her father had also died that year, leaving only the remnants of his fortune, a few *contos de réis* and the furniture in the house in Vienna: the old man had ruined himself catering for his daughter's luxurious tastes, their travel expenses, and Tancredo's losses at baccarat. She had then spent some time in London, and had moved from there to Paris with Monsieur de l'Estorade, a gambler and a duellist, who had, in the end, humiliated and abandoned her, leaving her nothing but his name, which he did not need anyway, because he went on to adopt the more sonorous title of Vicomte de Manderville. And thus, poor, beautiful, mad and immoderate, she had plunged into the existence of those women of whom, said Alencar, "pale Marguerite Gautier, that sweet Lady of the Camellias, is the sublime example, the poetic symbol—those women who will be forgiven all because they gave all for love." And the poet concluded: "She is still in the full splendour of her beauty, but the lines and wrinkles will come, and then what will she see around her, but the withered, bloodstained roses of her wedding garland? I left that perfumed boudoir, Vilaça, with my soul cut to shreds! I thought of my poor Pedro lying beneath the moonlight among the roots of the cypress trees. And weary of this cruel life, I went to the Boulevard and called on absinthe to give me an hour of oblivion."

Afonso da Maia threw down the letter, angry not so much at the whole foolish story as at Alencar's awful laboured lyricism.

And he went back to pacing the room, while Vilaça piously picked up the document which he had read and re-read many times, filled with admiration for the sentiment, the style, and the idealism of those pages.

"And what about her daughter?" asked Afonso.

"That I don't know. Alencar wouldn't have mentioned her because he wasn't even aware she'd taken the girl with her. No one in Lisbon was. In the rest of the general scandal that was a detail which went unremarked. I'm of the view that the child must have died. Otherwise, if you follow my reasoning, if the child were alive, the mother could demand what legitimately belongs to the child. She knows the kind of house you live in; there must be days, frequent in the lives of such women, when she lacks money. On the pretext of bringing up her daughter or merely of buying food, she would surely have come to us before now. She has no scruples. The fact that she hasn't must mean that the child is dead. Don't you think so, sir?"

"Possibly," said Afonso.

Then, standing before Vilaça—who was once more staring into the dying embers and cracking his knuckles—he added:

"Possibly. Let's just pretend that *both* of them died and talk no more about it."

The clocks were chiming midnight when the two men went to their beds. And during the rest of Vilaça's visit to Santa Olávia, the name of Maria Monforte was not mentioned again.

On the eve of Vilaça's departure for Lisbon, however, Afonso went up to his room to give him the sugared almonds that Carlos wanted to send to Vilaça Junior, and a tiepin bearing a magnificent sapphire. And while Vilaça, greatly touched, was stammering his thanks, Afonso said:

"Another thing, Vilaça. I've been thinking. I'm going to write to my cousin, André de Noronha, who, as you know, lives in Paris, and ask him to go and see this creature and offer her ten or fifteen *contos* if she'll give me the child, always assuming, of course, that the child is still alive. And I'd like you to ask this Alencar fellow for the woman's address in Paris."

Vilaça did not respond, busy as he was placing the box containing the pin right at the bottom of his suitcase, among his shirts. Then he turned and looked at Afonso, thoughtfully rubbing his chin.

"What do think, Vilaça?"

"It seems risky to me."

And he gave his reasons. The girl would be nearly thirteen. She was almost a woman, with her temperament formed, her character already shaped, and perhaps her habits too. She wouldn't even speak Portuguese. She would miss her mother terribly. Senhor Afonso da Maia would be bringing a stranger into his home.

"You're right, of course, Vilaça, but, then again, the woman is a prostitute and the child is of my blood."

At that moment, Carlos, whose voice had been heard calling down the corridor for his grandfather, burst into the room, his hair wild and his face as red as a pomegranate. Brown had found a baby owl! Carlos wanted his grandfather to come and see it, he'd been looking for him all over the house. It was such a funny creature, very small, very ugly, completely bald and with eyes like a grown man's! And they knew where the nest was too.

"Come quickly, Grandpa, quickly! We've got to put it back in the nest in case the mother bird gets worried. Brown is feeding it some olive oil. Vilaça, you come and see too. Please, Grandpa, hurry! It's got such a comical face! Be quick, the mother bird might notice he's missing!"

Impatient with his grandfather's easy slowness, with his indifference to the mother bird's anxiety, he raced off again, slamming the door.

"What a good-hearted child!" exclaimed Vilaça, touched. "So worried that the mother bird will miss her baby. His mother never missed him! But, as I always said, she has no heart at all!"

Afonso shrugged sadly. When they were already out in the corridor, he paused for a moment and said quietly:

"Oh, I forgot to tell you, Vilaça, Carlos knows that his father killed himself."

Vilaça's eyes grew round with horror, but it was true. Afonso explained how Carlos had come into the library one morning and said to him: "Grandpa, Papa shot himself with a pistol!" Some servant must have told him.

"What did you say?"

"Me? What could I say? I told him it was true. I've done everything that Pedro asked me to do in the few lines he left me. He wanted to be buried in Santa Olávia, and there he is. He didn't want his son to know that his mother ran away, and he'll certainly never find that out from me. He wanted the two portraits of her in Arroios to be destroyed; as you know, I did so. But he never asked me to conceal the manner of his death from the boy, which is why I told him the truth. I said that, in a moment of madness, his Papa had shot himself."

"And what did he say?"

"Well," replied Afonso, smiling, "he asked me who had given him the pistol, and pestered me all morning to let him have a pistol too. And the upshot of the revelation was that I had to send to Oporto for an air-gun."

Then, hearing Carlos down below, still yelling for his grandfather, the two men hurried off to admire the baby owl.

Vilaça left for Lisbon the following day.

Two weeks later, Afonso received a letter which brought him, as well as the address of the Monforte woman, an unexpected revelation. Vilaça had gone back to see the poet Alencar, who, recollecting other incidents from his visit to Madame de l'Estorade, had told him that she had in her boudoir a charming portrait of a child, with dark eyes, jet-black hair and skin as pale as mother-of-pearl. The painting had moved him deeply, not only because it was by a major English artist, but because, from the base of the frame, like a funeral wreath, hung a lovely garland of red and white wax flowers. This was the only painting in the room, and he had asked Madame de l'Estorade if the portrait was real or imagined. She had told him that it was a portrait of her daughter who had died in London.

"So all our doubts are dissipated," Vilaça added. "The poor little angel is in a happier place, a far happier place as far as she's concerned."

Afonso nevertheless wrote to André de Noronha. His reply was some time in coming. When cousin André had finally gone in search of Madame de l'Estorade, she had already left for Germany some weeks before, having sold her furniture and her horses. In the Club Impérial, of which he was a member, a friend, who was familiar with both Madame de l'Estorade and her licentious life in Paris, told him that the mad creature had run away with a certain Catanni, an acrobat in the Cirque d'Hiver encamped in the Champs-Elysées, a magnificent physical specimen, a regular fairground Apollo, over whom all the *cocottes* had been fighting, and who had been carried off by the Monforte woman. She was presumably touring Germany with a horse circus.

In disgust, Afonso da Maia forwarded this letter to Vilaça with no further comment. And the honest Vilaça replied: "You are absolutely right, sir, it is appalling; it would be best to pretend that they had all died and say good riddance to bad rubbish ..." He added, in a postscript: "It seems that the railway line to Oporto will be opening very shortly; with your permission, sir, I and my son will travel up and beg a few days' hospitality from you."

This letter was received on a Sunday in Santa Olávia, at suppertime. Afonso had read the postscript out loud. Everyone was pleased at the thought of seeing good old Vilaça back again so soon; there was even talk of arranging a picnic farther up the river.

However, on Tuesday night, a telegram from Manuel Vilaça arrived, announcing that his father had died that morning of an apoplexy; two days later, further sad details followed. It had happened suddenly, after lunch; Vilaça had felt very breathless and dizzy; he still had strength enough to go to his bedroom and inhale a little ether, but when he returned to the dining room, he was unsteady on his feet and complained that everything looked yellow, then he fell face forwards onto the sofa. His mind, which was about to be extinguished forever, was still running on matters to do with the house he had administered for thirty years: he stammered out some advice to his son about the sale of some cork, but his son could no longer understand him; then he uttered a great sigh and only opened his eyes again to murmur with his last breath these words: "Give my best wishes to Senhor Afonso!"

Afonso da Maia was deeply affected, and in Santa Olávia, even among the servants, Vilaça's death was mourned as a loss to the entire household. One afternoon, the old man was sitting sadly in the library, eyes closed, with a newspaper lying forgotten in his lap, when Carlos, who was sitting nearby, drawing caricatures of faces on a piece of paper, came over, put his arm around his grandfather's neck and, as if divining his grandfather's thoughts, asked if Vilaça would ever come back to see them.

"No, my son, never. We will never see him again."

The boy, encompassed by the old man's knees and arms, was staring down at the carpet and then, as if remembering, he murmured sadly:

"Poor Vilaça. He was always cracking his knuckles. Where have they taken him, Grandpa?"

"To the cemetery, my dear boy, beneath the earth."

Carlos slowly removed himself from his grandfather's embrace and, looking at him very seriously, said:

"Grandpa, why don't you have a nice little stone chapel made for him, with a statue, just like Papa's?"

Touched, the old man drew him closer and kissed him.

"You're absolutely right, my boy. You have a better heart than I have."

And so good old Vilaça had his tomb in the Cemitério dos Prazeres, which had been the one great ambition of his modest existence.

More tranquil years passed over Santa Olávia.

Then, one July morning, in Coimbra, Manuel Vilaça (now administrator of the house) ran up the steps of the Hotel Mondego where Afonso was staying, and, red-faced and sweating, burst into the room ahead of Carlos, crying:

"*Nemine! Nemine!* He's passed, he's passed!"

Carlos had passed his first examination. And what an examination! Teixeira, who had travelled with them from Santa Olávia, ran outside and almost wept as he embraced the boy, who was now taller than him and looking very handsome in his new gown.

Upstairs in the room, Manuel Vilaça, still out of breath and wiping away the beads of sweat, was exclaiming:

"Everyone was astonished, Senhor Afonso! Even the teachers were moved! Such talent! They all agreed he's going to be a great man. What's he going to study, sir?"

Afonso, who was pacing up and down, still trembling with excitement, said with a smile:

"I don't know, Vilaça . . . perhaps both of us will study law."

A beaming Carlos appeared in the doorway, followed by Teixeira and the other footman, who was carrying a bottle of champagne on a tray.

"Come here, you young rascal," said a pale-faced Afonso, opening wide his arms. "You did pretty well, eh? I . . ."

But he could not go on; tears were coursing down his cheeks into his white beard.

: IV :

CARLOS WAS TO STUDY MEDICINE. And, as Dr. Trigueiros used to say, the boy had always shown "a true Aesculapian vocation."

This "vocation" had revealed itself suddenly one day when he discovered in the attic, in the piles of old books, a grubby ancient roll of anatomical drawings; he had spent days cutting them out, then pinning them up on his bedroom wall—livers, looping strings of intestines, sections of heads "with the insides showing." One night, he had even burst triumphantly into the drawing room to show the Silveira sisters and Eusébio a ghastly lithograph of a six-month-old foetus inside its mother's womb. Dona Ana recoiled with a shriek, covering her face with her fan; and the public prosecutor, equally scarlet-cheeked, prudently drew Eusèbiozinho between his knees and shielded the boy's eyes with his hand. However, what shocked the ladies most was Afonso's indulgent attitude.

"What's wrong?" he said, smiling.

"What do you mean 'what's wrong,' sir?" exclaimed Dona Ana. "It's indecent!"

"There's nothing indecent in Nature, my dear lady. Only ignorance is indecent. Leave the child alone. He's curious to know what this poor old machine of ours looks like inside, and nothing could be more worthy of praise."

Dona Ana was fanning herself and breathing hard. Imagine allowing a child to hold such horrors in his hand! She began to see Carlos as a libertine who "already knew about certain things," and felt that she could no longer allow Teresa to play alone with him in the corridors of Santa Olávia.

The more serious-minded of the guests, however, the district judge and even the abbot, while regretting that Carlos had shown so little discretion, agreed that it revealed in the boy a natural bent for medicine.

"If it lasts," Dr. Trigueiros had said with a prophetic gesture, "we can expect great things!"

And it did seem to last.

In Coimbra, where he went to school, Carlos abandoned his textbooks on logic and rhetoric and immersed himself in anatomy: once, during the school holidays, when she was unpacking his cases, Gertrudes fled in horror when she saw a skull grinning wanly out at her from the folds of a jacket; if ever one of the servants fell ill, Carlos would be there, at the patient's bedside, reading up the symptoms in the old medical books he found in the library and making diagnoses to which kindly Dr. Trigueiros would listen respectfully and thoughtfully. In Afonso's presence, he would even refer to the boy as "his talented colleague."

Carlos' unexpected career course (it had always been assumed that he would study law) was viewed with scant approval by the faithful friends of Santa Olávia. The ladies, in particular, regretted that a boy who was growing up to be so handsome and such a good horseman should waste his life prescribing poultices and soiling his hands bleeding patients. One day, the district judge even confessed to doubts that Carlos da Maia was truly serious about becoming "a real doctor."

"Come now!" exclaimed Afonso. "And why shouldn't he be a real doctor? The only reason for choosing a career is in order to practise it with sincerity and ambition, like everyone else. I'm not bringing him up to be an idler, far less a mere amateur; I'm bringing him up to be useful to his country."

"Of course," began the judge with a subtle smile, "but does it not seem to you that there are other equally important and possibly more appropriate ways in which your grandson could be useful?"

"No, I don't," retorted Afonso da Maia. "In a nation whose main occupation is being ill, the most patriotic work one could possibly engage in is that of healing people."

"You have an answer for everything," murmured the judge respectfully.

And what most attracted Carlos to medicine was precisely that "real," practical, useful life: stairs taken two at a time in order to visit patients as part of a busy, burgeoning practice; lives saved with one scalpel cut; nights spent watching at someone's bedside, grappling with death itself, surrounded by the terrified members of a family. Just as, when he was a boy, he had been captivated by the picturesque shapes formed by the viscera, now he was drawn to the militant heroic aspects of medical science.

He enrolled for his university course with genuine enthusiasm. To accommodate him during those long years of quiet study, his grandfather had secured for him a lovely, secluded little house in Celas, as pretty as an English cottage, adorned with green shutters and shaded by cool trees. A friend of Carlos' (one João da Ega) christened it the "Palace of Celas," because of certain luxurious touches rare at the time in Academe: a carpet in the drawing room, morocco leather armchairs, displays of arms and armour, and a liveried valet.

At first, such splendour provoked feelings of veneration in the impoverished aristocrats and suspicion in the democrats; however, when it became known that the owner of all these comforts read Proudhon, Comte, and Herbert Spencer and shared the view that the country as a whole was "a vile rabble," then, even the most rigid of revolutionaries began to visit him at the "Palace of

Celas" as easily as they might visit Trovão, the bohemian poet and committed socialist, whose room was furnished only with a mattress and a Bible.

After a few months, Carlos, who got on well with everyone, had brought together dandies and philosophers, and would often be seen driving along in the company of Serra Torres—a prodigy who had already been promised a post as attaché in Berlin and who always wore white tie and tails in the evening—and the notorious Craveiro, hunched in overcoat and fur hat, pondering his poem *The Death of Satan*.

Beneath its appearance of rural indolence, the Palace of Celas was, in fact, a hotbed of activity. The garden was given over to scientifically-based gymnastics. An old kitchen was transformed into a fencing gallery, for, in that particular group, fencing was deemed to be a social necessity. In the evenings, in the dining room, serious young men played serious whist, and in the drawing room, beneath the crystal chandelier, with *Le Figaro*, *The Times*, and magazines from Paris and London scattered about the tables, Gamacho at the piano played Chopin or Mozart, while the literati sprawled in armchairs; there were noisy passionate debates, in which Democracy, Art, Positivism, Realism, the Papacy, Bismarck, Love, Hugo, and Evolution each had its turn to flame and flicker in the cigarette smoke, as light and vague as the smoke itself. These metaphysical discussions and even revolutionary certainties tasted more exquisite still in the presence of the liveried valet uncorking the beer or serving croquettes.

It was not long, of course, before Carlos' medical books lay unopened on the table. He found Literature and Art, in all its forms, deliciously absorbing. He published sonnets in *The Institute* and an article about the Parthenon; in an improvised studio, he tried his hand at painting in oils; under the influence of Flaubert's *Salammbô*, he wrote historical tales. Apart from that, he went out every afternoon in his carriage. Had he not been so well-known and so wealthy, he would undoubtedly have failed his second year. He trembled to think how upset his grandfather would be; he reined in his intellectual dissipation, immersed himself in his chosen science, and was immediately awarded a B minus. But the poison of dilettantism flowed in his veins, and he was destined, as João da Ega put it, to be one of those literary doctors who invent diseases from which a credulous humanity immediately believes it will die!

His grandfather would occasionally go and spend one or even two weeks at Celas. Initially, his presence, while agreeable to the gentlemen whist-players, disrupted the literary debates. The young men scarcely dared reach out to take a glass of beer, and each "yes, sir" and "no, sir" brought a chill to the room. Gradually, however, when they saw him there, with his pipe and slippers, seated comfortably in his armchair, looking for all the world like a bohemian patriarch, discussing art and literature and recounting anecdotes from his time in England and in Italy, they began to think of him as a white-bearded comrade. They were soon blithely talking about women and debauchery. Even the democrats warmed to this extremely wealthy old aristocrat, who read and admired Michelet. And Afonso enjoyed many a happy hour there, too, seeing his Carlos surrounded by these studious, idealistic, spirited young men.

Carlos spent the long vacation in Lisbon, or else in Paris or London, but at Christmas and Easter, he always went back to Santa Olávia, which his grandfather, more alone now, was lovingly engaged in redecorating. The rooms were hung with superb Arras tapestries and landscapes by Rousseau and Daubigny, and furnished with a few very select pieces. Seen from the windows, the garden had the noble aspect of an English park; sandy paths snaked gracefully across soft lawns; marble statues struck poses in the greenery; and plump pedigree sheep dozed beneath the chestnut trees. But life in this lavish milieu was not as happy as it once had been; immediately after dinner, the Viscountess, who grew fatter by the day, would fall into a heavy sleep; Teixeira had died, and then Gertrudes, both of pleurisy, both during Carnival; and the abbot's kindly face was no longer to be seen at table either, for he lay now beneath a stone cross, among the wallflowers and roses that grew all year round. The district judge and his concertina had been promoted to the court in Oporto; Dona Ana Silveira was too ill even to leave her house; Teresa had grown into an ugly, sallow-complexioned young woman; and Eusèbiozinho, flabby and glum, all trace of his early love of old books and literature long since gone, was about to be married in Régua. Only the public prosecutor, marooned in that backwater, remained the same, slightly balder perhaps, but perennially pleasant and still in love with the phlegmatic Dona Eugénia. And almost every evening, old Dr. Trigueiros would arrive at the door on his white mare to join his friend in idle chatter.

Carlos really only enjoyed these holidays at home when he was accompanied by his best friend, João da Ega, of whom Afonso da Maia had grown very fond, charmed both by the man himself, by his wit and originality, and also by the fact that he was the nephew of his old childhood friend André da Ega, who, many years before, had often stayed at Santa Olávia.

Ega was studying law, but very slowly and deliberately, failing one year, then missing another. His mother, a rich devout widow, lived on an estate near Celorico de Basto with her daughter, another rich devout widow, and had only the vaguest notion of what João had been up to in Coimbra all this time. Her chaplain assured her that all would end well and that the lad would one day be a doctor of law like his father and uncle before him; and this promise sufficed for the good lady, preoccupied above all with her digestive problems and with the well-being of that same chaplain, Father Serafim. She was even rather glad that her son was in Coimbra or, indeed, anywhere far from the estate, because he could not then scandalise people with his irreligious comments and his heretical jokes.

Indeed, it was not only in Celorico de Basto that João da Ega was considered the worst of atheists and the most extreme of radicals ever to appear in human society, but also at the university of Coimbra, which he shocked with his audacious remarks. Flattered by this response, he deliberately exaggerated his loathing for the Divinity and for the social order in general; he called for the massacre of the middle classes, for love to be set free from the fiction of matrimony, for the redistribution of land, and for worship of the Devil. His intellectual efforts in this direction ended up influencing his manners and his physiognomy; with his thin, gaunt figure, his waxed moustache and sharp nose, a square glass monocle fixed in his right eye, he really did look like some kind of satanic revolutionary. Since his arrival at university, he had revived the traditions of the old bohemian way of life; his torn academic gown was darned with white thread; he got drunk on cheap red wine; at night, he would stand on the bridge, with one arm raised, hurling insults at God. And yet, deep down, he was a romantic, always falling in love with fifteen-year-old girls, the daughters of office workers, with whom he would sometimes spend the evening, taking them packets of sweets as a gift. His reputation as a wealthy nobleman made him welcome in many such families.

Carlos made fun of these plebeian idylls, but then he, too, became romantically involved with the wife of a civil servant, a woman from Lisbon, whose main attractions were her graceful doll-like body and her lovely green eyes. She, on the other hand, was beguiled by Carlos' luxurious lifestyle, his groom, and his English horse. They wrote each other letters, and he spent weeks immersed in the harsh, wild poetry of a first adulterous love affair. Unfortunately, the young woman bore the barbarous name Hermengarda, and, when the secret was discovered, Carlos' friends kept calling him "Eurico" after Alexandre Herculano's eponymous hero and even sent letters to him at Celas bearing the hateful name.

One sunny day, Carlos was driving through the marketplace when the civil servant husband passed right by him, holding his little son by the hand. This was the first time Carlos had ever had a close look at Hermengarda's husband. He thought him thin and shabby, but the little boy was chubby and adorable, looking still chubbier on that cold January morning, swathed as he was in a blue woollen garment, tottering along on his poor little legs, purple with cold, and laughing in the bright sun—every bit of him laughing, his eyes, the dimples in his chin, his rosy cheeks. His father was supporting him, and Carlos was impressed by the delight and care with which the man guided his son's uncertain steps. Carlos had been reading Michelet at the time, and his soul was filled by a literary respect for the sanctity of the home. He felt an utter wretch sitting there in his dog-cart, plotting in cold blood the shame and grief of that poor inoffensive father in his worn overcoat. He never again answered Hermengarda's letters, in which she called him "her ideal," and she obviously took her revenge by betraying him, for, ever afterwards, her civil servant husband never passed Carlos without shooting him the most murderous of glances.

But Carlos' "first great romantic stumble," as Ega put it, occurred when, after the holidays, he brought back from Lisbon a magnificent Spanish woman and installed her in a house near Celas. Her name was Encarnación. He hired a carriage for her by the month, along with a white horse, and Encarnación captivated all of Coimbra, as if she were the ghost of the Lady of the Camellias, an exotic flower from some superior civilisation. On the main street, on the road out to Beira, young men, pale with excitement, would stop to see her pass by in her carriage, languid and scornful, revealing one satin shoe and just a flash of silk stocking, with her little white dog on her lap.

The poets of Coimbra University wrote verses in which they referred to Encarnación variously as "the Lily of Israel," "the Dove from the Ark," and "the Morning Cloud." A student of theology, a rough and grimy type from the backwoods of Tras-os-Montes, wanted to marry her, and despite Carlos urging her to accept, she refused; and the student theologian started prowling round Celas, wielding a big knife, wanting to "drink Maia's blood." In the end, Carlos had to drive him away with his walking-stick.

The experience, however, turned Encarnación's head, and she became unbearable, talking endlessly about other passions she had inspired in Madrid and in Lisbon, about how much money Count So-and-so or the Marquis of Such-and-such had given her, about her family's lofty social position, for they were, she claimed, related to the Medinaceli; her green satin shoes were as unpleasant as her strident voice; and whenever she tried to join in their conversations, she would always start by calling the republicans "thieves" and would speak nostalgically of the wit and style of Queen Isabel II, for she was, like all prostitutes, deeply conservative. João da Ega loathed her. And Craveiro declared that he would not go back to Celas as long as that pile of flesh, paid for by the pound like a cow, was still there.

In the end, Baptista, Carlos' famous valet, caught her *in flagrante* with a certain Juca, who played the female roles at the university theatre. At last, Carlos had an excuse! And, suitably remunerated, that relative of the Medinaceli, that "Lily of Israel," that admirer of the Bourbons, was packed off to Lisbon's Rua de S. Roque, her natural element.

In August, following Carlos' graduation ceremony, a jolly party was held at Celas. Afonso came up from Santa Olávia and Vilaça from Lisbon. All evening in the garden, sheaves of rockets rose into the air from among the acacias and the lush shadows; and a shirtsleeved João da Ega, who had finally failed the final exam of his final year, went around tirelessly hanging Venetian lanterns from the branches of the trees and from the swing and placing them around the well to light up the night. A pale and trembling Vilaça made a speech at supper, which was attended by Carlos' teachers, and he was just about to quote from the immortal Castilho when, from beneath the windows, came a roll of drums and a clash of cymbals, and the sound of the university anthem burst forth. A serenade! Ega, red-faced, his gown unbuttoned and his monocle dangling on its string down his back, ran to the balcony and held forth thus:

"Here we have our Maia, Carolus Eduardus ab Maia, setting out on a glorious career, ready to save ailing humanity or, depending on the circumstances, to finish it off entirely! Which far-flung corner of this realm has not yet heard of his genius, his dog-cart, the wretched B minus that still sullies his past, and of this port wine, the contemporary of those great heroes of 1820, which I, as a revolutionary and a drinker, which I, João da Ega, Johanes ab Ega . . ."

The shadowy figures below started cheering. The musicians, along with other students, rushed into the house. Until late into the night, beneath the trees in the garden and in the dining room piled high with plates, the servants scurried to and fro bearing trays of desserts, and there was a ceaseless popping of champagne corks. Vilaça, wiping the sweat from his brow and neck, overwhelmed by the heat, kept saying to whoever would listen, and to himself as well:

"Oh, it's a wonderful thing, a university degree!"

Then Carlos had set off on his grand tour of Europe. A year passed; the autumn of 1875 arrived, and Afonso, installed at last in Ramalhete, was anxiously awaiting his return. Carlos' last letter had been from England, where he was, he said, studying how the English ran their admirable children's hospitals. This was quite true, but he was also spending time in Brighton, betting on the horses at Goodwood, and wandering romantically around the Scottish lochs in the company of a Dutch lady separated from her husband, a venerable judge in the Hague—a certain Madame Rughel, a magnificent creature, as large and white as a Rubens nymph and with hair the colour of burnished gold.

Then boxes had begun to arrive, addressed to Carlos da Maia at Ramalhete, boxes of books, of instruments and apparatus, a whole library and laboratory, which had a dazed Vilaça spending whole mornings traipsing around the Customs sheds.

"My boy has some very ambitious work plans," Afonso would say to his friends.

He had not seen "his boy" for fourteen months, apart from a photograph sent from Milan, in which everyone thought he looked thin and sad. And Afonso's heart was beating fast on that lovely autumn morning, when, from the terrace of Ramalhete, with binoculars in hand, he saw slowly hoving into view, behind the tall building opposite, a great Royal Mail steamship bringing his grandson home once more.

That night, all the old family friends, Sequeira, Dom Diogo Coutinho, and Vilaça, could not get over how well Carlos looked after his journey. What a difference from the photograph he'd sent; he looked so strong, so healthy!

He was, it is true, a fine handsome young man, tall, well-built, and broad-shouldered, with a marble brow beneath his black curls, and with those Maia eyes, the same irresistible eyes as his father, as liquid-black and tender as his father's, but somehow graver too. He wore a full, dark-brown beard, very fine and closely trimmed and slightly pointed at the chin, and this, coupled with the sleek moustache that followed the contours of his mouth, gave him the look of an elegant Renaissance gentleman. His grandfather, whose smiling eyes kept brimming with tears, was almost bursting with pride to see him and to hear him speak so eloquently about his journey: the beautiful days spent in Rome, a fit of ill temper in Prussia, the originality of Moscow, the Dutch landscape . . .

"So what now?" Sequeira asked Carlos, after a moment's silence, as the latter sipped his brandy and soda. "What do you think you'll do now?"

"Now, General?" replied Carlos, smiling and setting down his glass. "After a brief rest, I intend to go on to become a national glory!"

Indeed, the next day, Afonso came down to find him in the billiard room—where all the boxes had been stored—in his shirtsleeves and whistling merrily as he opened and unpacked box after box. On the floor and on the sofas, an entire literature stood pile upon pile; here and there, in the packing straw or where the protective canvas had come unstitched, Afonso caught a gleam of glass, a glint of varnish, the polished metal of some piece of apparatus. He stood in silent wonder at this sumptuous paraphernalia of knowledge.

"And where are you intending to house this museum of yours?"

Carlos had thought of setting up a vast laboratory somewhere nearby, with kilns for chemical experiments, a special room set aside for the study of anatomy and physiology, for his library and his apparatus—in short, a place equipped for methodical study.

As his grandfather listened to this grandiose plan, his eyes lit up.

"Well, don't let any worries about money hold you back, Carlos! We've saved quite a lot at Santa Olávia in recent years."

"Fine words, Grandpa, but try telling Vilaça."

The weeks that followed were completely taken up with these plans. Carlos had returned, filled with a genuine resolve to work: science as a mere ornament of the spirit, as useless to others as the tapestries adorning his bedroom, seemed to him the luxury of the recluse; he wanted to be useful. His ambitions, though, flickered before him, at once intense and vague; at one moment he was planning to set up a large medical practice, at another to write a massive, pioneering work, at still another to conduct physiological experiments, painstaking and revealing . . . He felt inside him, or thought he did, a tumult of energy, but was at a loss to know how or where to channel it. He wanted, as he put it, "to do something really brilliant," and for him, a man of study accustomed to luxury, this meant a mixture of social status and scientific work; a profound rethinking of ideas carried out in the exquisite shelter provided by great wealth; the elevated vagaries of philosophy intermingled with the refinements of sport and good taste; a Claude Bernard who was also a Duc de Morny . . . He was, in short, a dilettante.

Vilaça was consulted about the best place for such a laboratory, and he, greatly flattered, swore tireless diligence. The first thing he needed to know was this: Did Carlos intend setting up a medical practice?

Carlos had not yet decided to work exclusively as a doctor, but he would certainly want to give consultations, even free ones, out of charity and to gain experience. Then Vilaça suggested that the consulting rooms should be separate from the laboratory.

"My reasoning is this: the sight of all that apparatus and machinery and suchlike will only make your patients feel worse."

"You're quite right, Vilaça!" exclaimed Afonso. "As my father always said: never let the ox see the stick."

"Yes, a separate establishment would be best," affirmed Vilaça sagely.

Carlos agreed, and Vilaça soon found a laboratory, a former warehouse, vast and secluded, in a courtyard, near the Largo das Necessidades.

"And as for your consulting rooms, sir, there's no other place for it but the Rossio, actually in the Rossio itself!"

Vilaça's idea was not entirely disinterested. As an enthusiastic follower of the so-called "fusion movement" and a member of the Progressive Party, Vilaça Junior aspired to becoming a city councillor, and on days when he was particularly pleased with himself (for example, when his birthday was given a mention in the *Ilustrado,* or when his references to politics abroad earned him the applause of other party members), it seemed to him that such talents merited him a seat in parliament itself. The idea of a free consulting room in the Rossio, Dr. Maia's consulting room, "*his* Dr. Maia," had immediately struck him as a potentially useful source of influence. And he set about finding one with such energy that, two days later, he had rented the entire second floor of a corner building.

Carlos spared no expense in furnishing it. He would hire a liveried servant, *à la française,* to stand in a hallway furnished with morocco leather benches. The patients' waiting room was a cheerful place with its green, silver-sprigged wallpaper, its plants in Rouen-ware pots, and colourful paintings and plush armchairs arranged around a low table piled with copies of the satirical magazine *Charivari,* and with stereoscopic pictures and albums filled with photographs of half-naked actresses, all intended to eliminate the usual gloomy waiting-room atmosphere; there was even a piano, its lid lifted to reveal its white keys.

Carlos' consulting room next door was simpler, almost austere, all dark-green velvet and rosewood shelves. A few members of the circle of friends beginning to gather around him—Taveira, his contemporary and now neighbour, Cruges, and the Marquis de Souselas, with whom he had travelled round Italy—came to view these marvels. Cruges ran his fingers over the piano keys and declared the instrument appalling; Taveira became immediately absorbed in perusing the photographs of actresses; and the only openly admiring remark came from the Marquis, who, having studied the sofa in the office, an item of furniture worthy of a harem—vast, voluptuous, and soft—tested its springs and said, with a wink:

"Just the thing, eh, Carlos!"

They did not appear to believe in all these preparations, which were, nonetheless, perfectly genuine. Carlos had even advertised his practice in the newspapers; however, when he saw his name in large print cheek by jowl with that of a woman in Boa Hora who did ironing and starching and an advertisement for a guesthouse, he ordered Vilaça to have it withdrawn.

He then turned his attention more to his laboratory which he had decided to install in the warehouse near Necessidades. Every morning, before lunch, he would go and see how work was progressing. Entry to the laboratory was through a large courtyard with a shady well and a climbing plant languishing on an ironwork trellis. Carlos had already decided to transform this area into a small, cool English garden; and he was delighted both with the building's massive main door and with its pointed arch—all that remained of the façade of a small chapel—which provided a worthy entrance to his scientific sanctuary. Inside, however, the work dragged on endlessly; there was always a vague sound of indolent hammering and a cloud of whitish dust; always the same baskets of tools lying on the same layers of shavings! A sad, gawky carpenter seemed to have been there for centuries, planing the same eternal plank with weary languor; and on the roof, in the winter sunshine, the workers, who were supposed to be enlarging the skylight, were constantly whistling some mournful *fado*.

Carlos complained to the foreman Senhor Vicente, who would invariably assure him that "in a couple of days, you'll really start to see a difference." Soft-spoken, clean-shaven, and always very spick and span, he was a jolly middle-aged man, who lived near Ramalhete and was known in the area as a republican. Carlos, as a neighbour, and out of fellow feeling, always shook his hand, and Senhor Vicente, who therefore considered Maia to be "a progressive" and a democrat, would confide his hopes to him. What he wanted was a repetition of what had happened in France in 1793.

"You mean all that bloodshed?" asked Carlos, looking at this democrat's fresh, honest, chubby face.

"No, sir, no, I mean a ship."

"A ship?"

"Yes, sir, a ship chartered by the nation itself, in which they would despatch the king, the royal family, and that whole rabble of ministers, politicians, members of parliament, intriguers, etc., etc."

Carlos would smile and sometimes even argue with him.

"But are you quite sure that as soon as that rabble, as you so rightly call them, sailed over the horizon, all our problems would be solved and we'd live happily ever after?"

No, Senhor Vicente was not that foolish. But once they were rid of that rabble, the country could move forward unencumbered, and then knowledgeable, progressive men could start to govern.

"Do you know what's wrong with us, sir? It's not ill will on the part of those people, it's simply rank ignorance. They don't know what to do; they don't know anything. They're not bad men, they're just blockheads!"

"Yes, well, now about this work, Senhor Vicente," Carlos would say, taking out his watch and giving his foreman a firm handshake, "get a move on, will you. I'm not asking you as a man of property, but as a fellow republican."

"In a couple of days, you'll really start to see a difference, sir," Senhor Vicente would say, removing his hat.

In Ramalhete, punctually at noon, the bell would ring for lunch. Carlos would usually find his grandfather already in the dining room, where he would just have finished reading his newspaper by the fireplace, in which luxuriant hothouse plants took the place of a fire, rendered unnecessary by the sweet, late-autumn warmth.

Elsewhere in the room, on the carved oak sideboards, the old silver cutlery, solid and sober, glinted softly; the oval tapestries on the panelled walls were full of scenes from ancient ballads: medieval hunters releasing a falcon; a lady surrounded by her pages, feeding swans on a lake; a knight, with lowered visor, riding along beside a river; and in contrast to the dark coffered chestnut ceiling, the table glowed with flowers and crystal glasses.

And ever since he had been made a dignitary of the Church, the Reverend Boniface also ate with the gentlemen, seated majestically upon the snow-white table cloth, in the shade of some large floral arrangement. It was there, amid the perfumed roses, that the venerable cat preferred to lap up, with ponderous slowness, his meal of bread soaked in milk, which was served in a Strasbourg porcelain dish. Then he would draw himself into a plump ball of white and gold-flecked fur, arrange the fluffy plume of his tail across his chest and, with eyes closed and whiskers braced, enjoy a gentle afternoon nap.

As Afonso himself confessed, smiling and embarrassed, he was, with age, becoming a demanding gourmet, and he received with critical fastidiousness the works of art produced by the French chef currently employed by him, an irascible gentleman, Monsieur Theodore by name, who was not only a staunch Bonapartist, but bore a striking resemblance to the emperor himself. Lunch at Ramalhete was always a long delicate affair; afterwards, over coffee, they would sit talking; and it would be one or half past one by the time Carlos glanced at his watch and, with a cry of alarm, remembered his consulting room. He would drink a glass of chartreuse and hurriedly light a cigar.

"To work!" he would exclaim.

And his grandfather, slowly filling his pipe, would envy him that occupation, while he stayed behind at home, idling away his days.

"When that wretched laboratory of yours is finally ready, perhaps I'll drop in and try my hand at a bit of chemistry."

"You might turn out to be a great chemist. You've got the makings of one already."

The old man would smile.

"Oh, this old carcass of mine is no good for anything any more, my boy. It's preparing itself for Eternity."

"Do you want anything from town, from Babylon?" asked Carlos, hurriedly buttoning up his driving gloves.

"No, just a good day's work."

"That's most unlikely."

And in the dog-cart drawn by his lovely mare, "Tunante," or in the phaeton that was the talk of Lisbon, Carlos would set off in grand style for the Baixa, to "his work."

His consulting room slept in the lethargic, tepid peace of the thick, dark velvets and in the penumbra created by green silk blinds. In the waiting room, however, the three open windows drank in the light; everything there seemed bright and festive; the armchairs around the table held out friendly, welcoming arms; the white keys on the piano laughed expectantly, with the music for Gounod's songs lying open and waiting; but not a single patient ever appeared. And just like the servant who, with nothing else to do, sat slumped on one of the benches in the hallway, dozing over a newspaper, Carlos would light a cigarette, pick up a magazine and stretch out on the sofa. The prose in which the articles were written, however, seemed to be steeped in the same slow tedium as the office, and it would not be long before he was yawning, and the magazine would fall from his hands.

From the Rossio, the noise of carriages, the errant cries of street hawkers, and the rumble of horse-drawn trams rose keenly up into the thin November air: a soft light, slipping sweetly down from the dark blue sky, gilded the peeling façades, the bare tops of the municipal trees, and the people sitting idly about on benches; and the slow whisper of urban indolence, along with the soft air of a benevolent climate, seemed to seep gradually into that stuffy office, to slither over the heavy velvets, the varnished furniture, and to wrap Carlos in a quiescent torpor. He would sit there, smoking, in that siesta stillness, his head resting on a pillow, absorbed in thoughts which slowly dissolved, vague and tenuous, like the light, tenuous smoke that drifts up from a half-extinguished brazier; until with an effort he would shake off that torpor and begin pacing about the room, taking down a book from the shelves, playing a couple of bars from a waltz on the piano, stretching and yawning, until, at last, staring down at the floral pattern on the carpet, he would finally decide that these two hours spent in his consulting room were utterly ridiculous!

"Is the carriage there?" he would ask the servant.

Then he would hurriedly light another cigar, pull on his gloves, go downstairs, take a long gulp of light and air, pick up the reins and set off, muttering to himself:

"Another wasted day."

*   *   *

71

It was on one such morning, when he was lazing on the sofa with the *Revue des Deux Mondes* open on his lap, that he heard a noise in the hallway and then a familiar, well-loved voice saying from behind the door curtain:

"Is His Royal Highness available for visitors?"

"Ega!" cried Carlos, leaping up from the sofa.

And they fell delightedly into each other's arms and kissed each other on the cheek.

"When did you arrive?"

"This morning. Goodness me!" exclaimed Ega, feeling his chest and shoulders for his square glass monocle, and finally fixing it in his eye. "Goodness me! You look splendid after your sojourn in the Londons of this world, among all those superior civilisations. There's a Renaissance look about you, a kind of Valois air . . . You can't beat a good beard!"

Carlos laughed and embraced him again.

"And where have you come from? Celorico?"

"Celorico? No, from Foz. I'm ill, my boy, ill. There's my liver, my spleen, and all kinds of other damaged viscera. But that's what you get after twelve years of wine and brandy."

Then they talked about Carlos' travels, about Ramalhete, about how long Ega was going to be staying in Lisbon. He had come to settle there for good. From his seat in the stagecoach he had bade farewell forever to the fields of Celorico.

"You can't imagine, my friend, what happened between my mother and myself. After Coimbra, I naturally sounded her out about coming to live in Lisbon—in some comfort, of course, and with a nice fat allowance. Well, she wasn't having it! So I stayed there writing barbed epigrams about Father Serafim and all the Heavenly Host. Then July came, and a veritable epidemic of sore throats broke out, terrible, what you medical fellows call diphtheria, I believe. Mama immediately jumped to the conclusion that it was my presence, the presence of an atheist and a democrat, who neither fasts nor goes to mass, that had offended Our Lord and brought about the plague. My sister agreed. They consulted Father Serafim. And he, who dislikes having me hanging around the house anyway, said that it was just possible that the Lord might be vexed, and my mother came to me, almost on bended knee and with her purse open, begging me to go to Lisbon, to ruin her, just as long as I didn't stay in Celorico calling down upon them the wrath of God. The next day I left for Foz."

"And the epidemic?"

"It immediately abated," said Ega, slowly removing from one thin hand a long, canary-yellow glove.

Carlos was staring at Ega's gloves, at the cashmere gaiters, at his hair which he wore long with a fringe of curls over his forehead, at the satin cravat with the opal tie pin in the shape of a horseshoe! This was a different Ega, a dandified Ega, showy, stylish, artificial, and powdered—and Carlos finally gave voice to the exclamation that had been waiting impatiently on his lips:

"Ega, that really is the most extraordinary coat!"

In the gentle sun of that late Portuguese autumn, Ega, once the bohemian in a tattered student's gown, was wearing a fur coat, a sumptuous fur coat worthy of a Russian prince—made for sledges and snow, long and ample, with Brandenburg fastenings—which wrapped his scrawny neck and his consumptive's wrists in the softest and most luxurious sable.

"Not bad, eh?" he said, getting up and opening it to show off the opulent lining. "I got Strauss to order it for me. One of the benefits of the epidemic."

"How can you bear to wear it?"

"Well, it is a touch heavy, but I've had a bad cold."

He sat down again on the sofa, revealing one highly polished, very pointed shoe, and then, adjusting his monocle, he examined the office.

"And tell me, what have you been up to? You've made a splendid job of all this!"

Carlos told him his plans, explained his lofty ideas regarding work, and the preparations he was making for his laboratory.

"Just a moment, how much has all this cost you?" Ega exclaimed, interrupting him and getting up to feel the velvet curtains and run his hand over the turned wood of the rosewood desk.

"I've no idea. Vilaça will know."

And Ega, his hands plunged in the vast pockets of his fur coat, walked around the office, as if taking an inventory, commenting gravely:

"Yes, velvet lends an air of seriousness. And dark green is the supreme colour, the truly aesthetic colour. It's very expressive, it moves one and makes one think. Oh, and I like this sofa. Made for love."

He proceeded slowly through to the patients' waiting room, and, with his monocle fixed in place, scrutinised the décor.

"Solomon himself couldn't have done it better, Carlos! The paper's really pretty, and I like that cretonne."

He even touched it. Then the silvered leaves of a begonia in a Rouen-ware pot took his eye. He wanted to know the price of everything; and standing at the piano, looking at the music—Gounod's "Songs"—he was filled with tender surprise:

"How odd! Fancy finding this here—the "Barcarolle!" Lovely, isn't it?

> *Dites, la jeune belle,*
> *Où voulez-vous aller?*
> *La voile . . .*

"Sorry, I'm still a bit hoarse . . . It was our song in Foz!"

Another exclamation escaped Carlos' lips, and he stood before Ega, arms crossed:

"You really are quite extraordinary, Ega! In fact, you're a different Ega altogether! And speaking of Foz, who is this Madame Cohen, who was also in Foz, and whom you wrote about in the ecstatic tones of 'The Song of Songs' in letter after letter, or should I say, poem after poem, which followed me around from Berlin to The Hague to London?"

A slight blush reached Ega's cheeks; then, nonchalantly polishing his monocle on his silk scarf, he said:

"She's a Jewess. Hence the Biblical lyricism. She's married to Cohen, you know him I'm sure, he's Director of the National Bank. She and I saw quite a lot of each other. She's charming, but her husband's an oaf. It was just a little seaside flirtation. *Voilà tout.*"

He spoke in short sentences as he strolled about, still blushing and drawing on his cigar.

"But tell me, what do you get up to in Ramalhete? How's your grandfather? Who do you see?"

In Ramalhete, his grandfather played whist with his usual partners. There was that decrepit old lion, Dom Diogo, always with a rose in his buttonhole and still curling his moustaches. Then there was Sequeira, who was getting stouter and redder in the face by the minute, primed for apoplexy. Oh, and Count Steinbroken.

"I don't know him. Is he a refugee? Polish perhaps?"

"No, he's the Finnish ambassador. He wanted to rent some stables from us, but he made this very simple transaction so very complicated, what with the diplomatic niceties, the paperwork, and endless documents requiring the royal seal of Finland, that poor Vilaça couldn't cope and ended up passing him on to my grandfather. My grandfather was equally bewildered by it all and so offered him the use of the stables for nothing. Steinbroken considered this to be a service rendered to the King of Finland, no, to Finland itself, and visited Grandpa in full fig, and with the legation secretary, the consul, and the vice-consul in tow."

"Wonderful!"

"Then Grandpa, of course, invited him to supper, and since the Count is a man of great refinement, a gentleman and an anglophile, a connoisseur of wines and an authority on whist, my grandfather adopted him. And he's now a permanent fixture at Ramalhete."

"Any younger men?"

Taveira often visited, always impeccably dressed, and an employee now of the National Audit Office; there was Cruges, whom Ega did not know, a madman, a maestro, and a pianist with a real spark of genius; then there was the Marquis de Souselas...

"No women?"

"No, certainly not. It's a real bachelors' den. You probably heard about the Viscountess, poor thing."

"Apoplexy, wasn't it?"

"Yes, a brain haemorrhage. Oh, and there's Silveirinha, he's a recent addition."

"That cretin Eusèbiozinho from Resende?"

"The very same. His wife died and he's just come back from Madeira; he himself is still a bit consumptive-looking and in full mourning too. Not exactly fun."

Comfortably seated now in an armchair, and with that air of calm, confident contentment which Carlos had already noticed, Ega slowly tugged at his shirt cuffs and said:

"We need to do something about this life of yours. We must form a club, a kind of well-heeled bohemia, with winter soirées, art, and literature. Do you know Craft?"

"Yes, I think I've heard of him."

Ega made a wide, sweeping gesture. It was essential to know Craft! Craft was simply the best thing in Portugal.

"Isn't he English, a bit of an eccentric?"

Ega shrugged. An eccentric? Well, that was the view of the petit-bourgeoisie in Rua dos Fanqueiros; when confronted by a man of Craft's originality, the only way the natives could explain it was by putting it down to eccentricity. But Craft was an extraordinary fellow. He had just arrived back from Sweden, where he had spent three months with the students of Uppsala. He had been in Foz too. He was an individual of the very first order!

"Isn't he a businessman from Oporto?"

"What do you mean, a businessman from Oporto!" exclaimed Ega, rising to his feet, frowning, enraged by such ignorance. "Craft is the son of a clergyman from the English church in Oporto. It was his uncle, a businessman from Calcutta or Australia or somewhere, a nabob, who left him his fortune. A huge fortune. But he has nothing to do with business, he doesn't know the first thing about it. He gives full rein to his Byronic temperament, that's what he does. He's travelled the whole universe, he collects works of art, he fought as a volunteer in Abyssinia and in Morocco, in short, he *lives*, in the great, strong, heroic sense of the word. You must meet Craft. You'll adore him. You know, you're right, it *is* hot."

He removed the opulent fur coat to reveal that he was in shirtsleeves.

"You mean you're not even wearing a waistcoat!" exclaimed Carlos.

"No, otherwise I really wouldn't be able to stand the heat. I only wear this for moral effect, to impress the natives, but I can't deny it weighs a ton!"

And he immediately reverted to his new idea; as soon as Craft arrived from Oporto, they would get together and organise a club, a decameron of the arts and of dilettantism, men and women, just three or four of the latter to mitigate, by dint of their décolletages, the rigour of the philosophies expounded.

Carlos laughed at Ega's idea. Bring in three women of taste and high fashion as an adornment to a gentlemen's club in Lisbon? This was the sad illusion of a man from Celorico! The Marquis de Souselas had once tried to organise the simplest of social events—a picnic in the country with a group of actresses. The uproar this caused was at once hilarious and typical: one woman didn't have a maid and so wanted to bring with her to the party her aunt and five children; another feared that if she accepted the invitation, her Brazilian protector would take away her monthly allowance; one agreed to come, but, when her lover found out, he beat her up. One had nothing to wear; another demanded money; one even found the invitation insulting. And then the pimps, the boyfriends, and the various young men only complicated matters still further: some demanded to be invited along too, others tried to spoil the party altogether; people took sides, intrigued and plotted, and this most ordinary of outings, a supper with a few actresses, ended with Tarquínio—from the Teatro do Ginásio—getting knifed: "That's Lisbon for you."

"In that case," said Ega, "if there aren't enough women, we'll have to import them, which is what usually happens in Portugal. Here we import everything. Ideas, laws, philosophies, theories, plots, aesthetics, sciences, style, industries, fashions, manners, jokes, everything arrives in crates by steamship. Civilisation comes at a very high price, what with the customs duties one has to pay, and, besides, it's second-hand, it wasn't made for us, and so it's all a bit short in the sleeve. We imagine that we're civilised in just the same way as the blacks in São Tomé imagine that they're gentlemen, or even that they're white, merely because they wear the boss's old tailcoat over their loincloth. We're nothing but a useless lazy rabble. Now where did I put my cigarette case?"

Liberated from the majesty bestowed on him by his fur coat, the old Ega reappeared, holding forth and making large gestures like a Mephistopheles in top form, flinging himself about the room as if he were about to take flight with each vibrant utterance and engaged in a constant battle with his monocle, which kept dropping from his eye and which he was always feeling for on his chest, on his shoulders, in the small of his back, twisting and turning like someone being savaged by wild beasts. Carlos became animated too, the cold room grew warm; they discussed naturalism, Gambetta, nihilism, then, with ferocity and as one man, they laid into Portugal.

At this point, however, the clock beside them struck four; Ega immediately pounced on his fur coat, once more burying himself in it; he twirled the points of his moustache, checked his pose in the mirror, and, armoured behind his fancy frogging, departed with an air of luxury and adventure.

"João," said Carlos, who had followed him out onto the landing and thought he looked absolutely splendid, "where are you staying?"

"At that sanctuary, the Hotel Universal!"

Carlos cursed the Universal; he wanted him to stay at Ramalhete.

"Not convenient, I'm afraid."

"Well, at least come to supper, come and see my grandfather."

"I can't. I'm meeting that wretch Cohen. But I'll be there for lunch tomorrow."

He was already halfway down the stairs when he turned, put his monocle to his eye and called up to Carlos: "Oh, I forgot to tell you, I'm going to publish my book!"

"What! You've finished it?" exclaimed Carlos, amazed.

"It's there in draft form, the broad outline."

Ega's book! He had first started talking about this book during his last two years at Coimbra, describing the plot, revealing chapter titles, quoting sonorous phrases from it in cafés. And his friends already spoke of Ega's book as setting in motion, in form and idea, a literary evolution. In Lisbon (where he came to spend the vacations and where he held suppers at Silva's), the book had been announced as a notable event. Graduates, whether contemporaries or students from other years, had carried the fame of Ega's book from Coimbra and spread it throughout the provinces and islands. Somehow or other, news had even reached Brazil. Aware of the eager expectation surrounding his book, Ega had finally decided to write it.

It was, according to him, a prose epic, using symbolic episodes to describe the great stages of the Universe and of Humanity. It was entitled *Memoirs of an Atom*, and was autobiographical in form. This atom (Ega's atom, as it was, quite seriously, referred to in Coimbra) appeared in the first chapter, still rolling around in the void among those early nebulae; then it got caught up, as a red-hot spark, in the ball of fire that would later become the Earth; it formed part of the first leaf to push up from beneath the still soft crust of the globe. Subsequently, as part of ceaselessly transforming matter, Ega's atom entered the rough physiognomy of the orangutan, the father of Humanity, and went on to live on Plato's lips. It inhabited the grimy sackcloth of saints, glinted on the swords of heroes, pulsated in the hearts of poets. As a drop of water in the Lake of Galilee, it heard Jesus speak at close of evening, when the apostles were hauling in their nets; as a knot in the wood of the tribune at the national Convention, it felt Robespierre's cold hand. It had wandered the vast rings of Saturn; and as one bright petal of a languid, sleepy lily, Earth's dawns had dropped their dews upon it. Having been omnipresent, it was also omniscient. Finding itself, at last, on the nib of Ega's pen, and weary of its journey through Being itself, it was resting and writing its *Memoirs*. Such was Ega's formidable task, of which his admirers in Coimbra would say, thoughtfully and as if awestruck:

"It's a veritable Bible!"

: V :

DESPITE THE LATE HOUR, a game of whist was still going on in Afonso da Maia's study. In its usual corner next to the fireplace, where the flames from the scarlet coals were dying down, the card-table stood in the shelter of a Japanese screen, placed there out of respect for Dom Diogo's bronchitis and his horror of drafts.

This old dandy—who, in better times, the ladies used to call "Delectable Diogo," a gentlemanly bullfighter who had slept in a royal bed—was, in fact, just recovering from one of his coughing fits, a harsh, cavernous, painful cough that shook him as if he were an old ruin, and which he smothered with his handkerchief, his veins all swollen, and purple to the roots of his hair.

But the fit passed. With a still tremulous hand, the decrepit old lion wiped away the tears filling his bloodshot eyes, readjusted the musk rose in the buttonhole of his jacket, took a sip of very weak tea, and said to his partner, Afonso, in a soft, hoarse voice:

"Clubs, was it?"

And once again, there was the sound of playing-cards on green baize, in one of those silences that always followed Dom Diogo's coughing fits. All that could be heard was the wheezing, almost whistling breath of General Sequeira, who was a most unhappy man that night, red-faced and muttering under his breath, driven to despair by his partner,Vilaça.

A delicate tune rang out—the Louis XV clock, blithely and brightly sounding the stroke of midnight; the silvery tones of its minuet chime lingered for a moment, then died away. Silence. The glass shades of the Carcel oil-lamps were draped in red lace, and the filtered light, falling on the red damask walls and chairs, created a soft pink glow, a vaporous cloud in which the slumbering room lay immersed. Here and there, on the sombre oak of the shelves, glowed the gold of Sèvres plates, the pale cream of ivory, and the occasional enamelled tones of some old majolica.

"You're not still hard at it, are you!" exclaimed Carlos, who had pushed aside the door curtain and come into the room, bringing with him the distant click of billiard balls.

Afonso, who was picking up his cards, looked round and asked eagerly:

"How's she doing? Is she quieter now?"

"Yes, she's much better."

"She" was Carlos' first seriously ill patient, a young woman originally from Alsace, who was married to Marcelino the baker and was well-known in the area for her lovely blonde hair, which she always wore in plaits. She had been at death's door with pneumonia, and although she was greatly improved, Carlos would sometimes go over there in the evening, since the bakery was immediately opposite, to see how she was and to calm Marcelino, who sat by her bedside, a cape over his shoulders, choking back loving tears as he scribbled away in his accounts books.

Afonso had taken a keen interest in this case of pneumonia, and was now truly grateful to Marcelino's wife for having allowed herself to be saved by Carlos. He spoke of her in tender tones; he praised her lovely figure, her Alsace neatness, and the prosperity she had brought to the bakery. In preparation for the imminent period of convalescence, he had already sent her six bottles of Château Margaux.

"So she's out of danger, then, is she?" asked Vilaça, dabbling his fingers in his snuff box and affecting more concern than he actually felt.

"Oh, yes, practically bursting with health," said Carlos, who had gone over to the fireside, rubbing his hands and shivering.

It was freezing outside! As night fell, a frost had started forming out of a fine, hard sky filled to overflowing with stars that glittered like sharp steel points; and none of the gentlemen there could ever remember the thermometer plunging so low, except Vilaça, who seemed to recall that the January of 1864 had been even colder.

"Plenty of punch, that's the answer, eh, General!" exclaimed Carlos, playfully patting Sequeira's sturdy shoulders.

"I certainly wouldn't disagree with that," grunted the General, whose gaze was fixed rancorously on a jack of hearts lying on the table.

Carlos, still feeling cold, poked and prodded the coals, provoking a rain of golden sparks from which a larger flame burst forth with a roar, casting a cheery glow over everything around it and tinging with red the bearskin rug on which the plump Reverend Boniface sat, quietly toasting and purring with pleasure.

"Ega must be thrilled," said Carlos, holding his feet to the flames. "He finally has a good reason for wearing that fur coat of his. By the way, have any of you gentlemen seen Ega lately?"

No one answered, caught up as they were in the latest round of play. Dom Diogo's long hand was slowly picking up the cards he had been dealt, then, languidly, in the continuing silence, he put down a club.

"Oh, Diogo, Diogo!" cried Afonso, writhing, as if he were being skewered by a metal spike.

But he said nothing more. The General, eyes flashing, put down his jack; Afonso, deeply distressed, gave up his king of clubs; and Vilaça slammed down an ace. And a noisy debate immediately broke out about Dom Diogo's last move, while Carlos, who'd always found card games tedious, bent down to tickle the Reverend Boniface's soft belly.

"What were you saying, Carlos?" Afonso asked at last, getting up, still angry, to go in search of tobacco for his pipe, his one consolation in defeat. "Oh, yes, Ega. No, nobody's seen him, he's disappeared. He's an ungrateful boy, that João."

Hearing Ega's name, Vilaça stopped shuffling the cards and, looking up, asked, genuinely curious this time:

"Is he really going to set up house here?"

Smiling and lighting his pipe, Afonso replied:

"Yes, set up house, buy a carriage, get a liveried servant, hold literary soirées, publish a poem, you name it!"

"He called in at the office," Vilaça was saying, resuming his shuffling of the cards. "He wanted to know how much your consulting room had cost, the velvet-upholstered furniture, etc. He really liked that green velvet. Since he's a friend of the family, I told him, and even showed him the bills." Then, in answer to a question from Sequeira: "Yes, his mother's got money and I think she gives him quite a bit. But if you ask me, it's politics he's interested in. He's got talent, he's a good speaker, and his father was an enthusiastic member of the Regenerationist Party. Yes, I smell political ambition."

"Well, I smell a woman," said Dom Diogo firmly, emphasising the weight of his words by languidly stroking the curled ends of his white moustaches. "You can see it in his face, you just have to look at him. Yes, I smell a woman."

Carlos smiled, impressed by Dom Diogo's perspicacity, by his acute Balzacian eye; and Sequeira, with the frankness of the old soldier, immediately wanted to know who the Dulcinea in question was. Dom Diogo, though, speaking from the depth of his experience, declared that these were things one never knew and which, indeed, it was preferable not to know. Then, drawing his slow, thin fingers across his cheek, he uttered this lofty, condescending judgement:

"I like Ega, he has something about him, he's very *dégagé.*"

The cards had been dealt, and silence fell around the table. The General, seeing his hand, gave a dull groan, snatched up his cigarette from the ashtray and drew on it furiously.

"I'll leave you gentlemen to your vices and go and see the people in the billiard room," said Carlos. "I left Steinbroken locked in battle with the Marquis and about to lose four *mil-réis.* Shall I leave the punch here?"

No one answered.

Around the billiard table, Carlos encountered the same solemn silence. The Marquis, stretched over the table, one leg in the air, his incipient bald patch gleaming in the harsh light from the porcelain lampshades, was preparing a decisive cannon shot. Cruges, who had bet money on him, had left the sofa and the Turkish hookah and was nervously scratching his curly mop of hair which fell in waves to his jacket collar, as he watched anxiously, eyes narrowed and nose foremost. At the far end of the room hovered the dark figure of Silveirinha, formerly Eusèbiozinho from Santa Olávia, who was also craning forward, his neck swaddled in a widower's black merino cravat, his hands plunged in his pockets, cutting as glum a figure as ever and even more timorous than in the old days, and so funereal-looking that everything about him seemed to complement his heavy mourning, even the black of his hair and the dark lenses of his glasses. The Marquis' partner, Count Steinbroken, was waiting by the billiard table; and in spite of his fear, in spite of the emotion gripping this tight-fisted Northerner, he remained very correct, leaning on his cue, smiling, not for one moment ruffling his very British appearance, for he was the very image of an Englishman, dressed in a rather tight frock-coat, slightly short in the sleeve, and loose check trousers over flat-heeled shoes.

"Hurrah!" Cruges suddenly shouted. "You owe me ten *tostões*, Silveirinha!"

The Marquis, having successfully performed his cannon shot and won the game, cried triumphantly:

"You brought me luck, Carlos!"

Steinbroken immediately lay down his cue and, one by one, slowly lined up along the cushion the four coins he had lost.

But the Marquis, chalk in hand, was demanding another match, hungry for more Finnish gold.

"No, no more! There's no beating you tonight!" said the diplomat in his fluent, heavily accented Portuguese.

The Marquis insisted and stood there before him, his cue resting on his shoulder like a cowherd's staff, his thickset, upright figure towering over the Count. In a powerful voice accustomed to bellowing across fields, he proposed for him various dreadful fates: he wanted to bankrupt him through billiards, to force him to pawn those lovely rings, to see him, ambassador of Finland and representative of a race of powerful kings, scalping tickets outside the theatre in Rua dos Condes!

Everyone laughed, and Steinbroken laughed too, but his laughter was constrained, awkward, and he fixed the Marquis with his cold, bright, pale-blue gaze, in whose myopic depths there was a metallic hardness. He was fond of the Marquis, but he found these familiarities, these impudent jokes, incompatible with his own dignity and with that of Finland. The Marquis, however, who had a heart of gold, had already put his arm about Steinbroken's waist and was saying coaxingly:

"All right, if you don't want to play any more, how about a little song, my friend?"

To this the ambassador gladly agreed, and immediately made himself ready, lightly smoothing his sideburns and the curls of his hair, the colour of faded corn.

All the Steinbrokens, fathers and sons (as he had told Afonso) had fine baritone voices, and this had brought his family a number of social privileges. His father's voice had so captivated the old king, Rudolph III, that he had appointed him head of the royal riding stables, and would keep him for whole nights in his rooms, at the piano, singing Lutheran hymns, school songs, and sagas from Dalecarlia, while he, the taciturn monarch, smoked his pipe and drank, until, saturated with religious feeling and with dark beer, he would lie down on the sofa, sobbing and drooling. Steinbroken himself had spent much of his career at the piano, first as attaché and then as under-secretary. However, once he had been made ambassador, he had abstained from playing, and it was only after he'd read glowing accounts in *Le Figaro* about the waltzes of Prince Artoff, the Russian ambassador in Paris, and the bass voice of Count von Baspt, the Austrian ambassador in London, that he, following these eminent examples, began, now and then, at certain private little soirées, to risk the occasional Finnish tune. He ended up singing at the Palace. And ever since then, he had, with great ceremony and assiduity, exercised his role as "baritone plenipotentiary"—to use Ega's expression. Among gentlemen and with the door curtains discreetly drawn, Steinbroken would happily sing what he called "saucy songs"—"L'amant d'Amanda" or a certain English ballad:

> *On the Serpentine,*
> *Oh, my Caroline . . .*
> *Oh!*

That last "Oh!" was uttered as a sultry, long-drawn-out moan and accompanied by a rather barbaric gesture, expressive, but nonetheless perfectly dignified, although only among men, of course, and with the curtains drawn.

That night, however, the Marquis, who was leading him by the arm to the music room, was calling for one of those Finnish songs, so full of feeling and such a balm to his soul.

"The one that contains all those little words I really like, *frisk, gluzk* . . . You know the one, la-ra-la-la-la!"

"Ah, 'Springtime,'" said the ambassador, smiling.

But before they entered the music room, the Marquis released Steinbroken's arm and beckoned Silveirinha to join him at the far end of the corridor, and there, beneath a sombre painting depicting Mary Magdalene doing penance in the desert and revealing, as she did so, the opulent flesh of a lubricious nymph, he asked almost roughly:

"Come on now, have you reached a decision?"

These negotiations, regarding a pair of horses, had been dragging on for weeks. Silveirinha had a wish to own a carriage, and the Marquis was trying to sell him two white mares, which, he said, were fine enough animals, but he had rather taken against them. He was asking one and a half *contos* for them. Silveirinha had been warned by Sequeira and by Travassos, and by other people who knew about horses, that he was being cheated; the Marquis had his own particular morality when it came to selling livestock, and he loved the idea of hoodwinking someone. Despite these warnings, Silveirinho, cowed by the Marquis' loud voice, robust physique, and ancient title, was finding it very hard to refuse. Nevertheless, he still held back, and that night, scratching his chin, back against the wall, he gave his usual miserly response:

"I'll see, Marquis. One and a half *contos* is a lot of money . . ."

The Marquis raised two threatening arms, like two great wooden beams:

"'Yes' or 'No,' man? How can you refuse two such perfect creatures? Come on, is it 'Yes' or 'No'?"

Eusèbiozinho adjusted his glasses on his nose and mumbled:

"I'll see. It's still a lot of money, you know."

"Perhaps you'd prefer to pay for them in beans! Frankly, you're beginning to get on my nerves."

On the piano, two full chords rang out beneath Cruges' fingers, and the Marquis, who adored music, immediately dropped the business of the horses and tiptoed away. Eusèbiozinho lingered for a while, still pondering, still scratching his chin; then, as Steinbroken sang the first notes, he slipped in, a silent shadow, and stood between the doorframe and the curtain.

Sitting well away from the piano, as was his custom, and leaning back, so that his long hair seemed to rest on his shoulders, Cruges was playing the accompaniment, his eyes fixed on the sheet music of "Finnish Melodies." Beside him, adopting a very erect, almost official pose, a silk handkerchief in one hand, the other pressed to his heart, Steinbroken was singing a jolly song, a kind of triumphant tarantella, in which those mouth-filling words of which the Marquis was so fond, *frisk, slecht, clikst, glukst,* made a sound like pebbles being knocked together. It was "Springtime," the fresh, wild springtime of a mountainous country in the North, when the whole village dances beneath the dark fir trees, when the snow melts into waterfalls, the pale sun casts a velvety light over the moss, and the breeze brings with it the smell of resin. On the low deep notes, the veins in Steinbroken's forehead grew red and swollen. On the high notes, he rose up onto the tips of his toes, as if carried away by the lively rhythm; then he removed his hand from his chest and reached out to his audience, and the lovely jewels on his rings sparkled.

The Marquis, his hands lying limp on his lap, seemed to drink in the song. A tender smile appeared on Carlos' face, as he remembered Madame Rughel who had travelled in Finland and who sometimes used to sing that same spring song when she waxed Flemish and sentimental.

Steinbroken let out a shrill, lonely staccato note, like a voice from on high, and then immediately stepped away from the piano, mopped his brow and neck with his handkerchief, gave a corrective tug to his frock-coat, and thanked Cruges, his accompanist, with a silent handshake.

"Bravo! Bravo!" bawled the Marquis, clapping his two sledgehammer-like hands.

More applause came from the doorway, from the card-players, who had now finished their game. Almost at once, the servants entered, bearing trays of croquettes and sandwiches, offering round St. Emilion or port wine to drink; and on a table, beside the ranks of glasses, the steaming punchbowl gave off a sweet warm aroma of brandy and lemon.

"So, my poor Steinbroken," exclaimed Afonso, coming over and patting him on the back, "you don't mind, then, singing such lovely songs to these bandits who beat you rotten at the billiard table!"

"Oh, they fleeced me good and proper. No, thank you, I'd prefer a glass of port."

"We're today's sacrificial victims," said the General, savouring the smell of his glass of punch.

"Not you as well, General!"

"Yes, they robbed me blind too."

And what did friend Steinbroken think of that morning's news—the fall of MacMahon and the election of Grévy. What pleased him most about the whole affair was the definitive disappearance of that disagreeable man, the Duc de Broglie and his clique. The impertinence of that narrow-minded academician, wanting to impose the opinions of two or three doctrinaire salons on the whole of France, on the whole of a democracy! *The Times* had seen it coming, of course!

"And *Punch*, did you see *Punch*? It was *so* funny."

The ambassador had put down his glass and, cautiously rubbing his hands, he spoke, in a quiet, grave voice, the words he always spoke, the definitive words which he applied to all events notified to him by telegram:

"Very serious, extremely serious."

Then the talk turned to Gambetta, and hearing Afonso predicting the imminent imposition of a dictatorship, the ambassador mysteriously took Sequeira's arm and murmured the supreme words with which he defined all eminent personalities, be they statesmen, poets, travellers, or tenors.

"He's a very strong man, you know, an extremely strong man!"

"The man's a complete rogue!" cried the General, downing his wine with a flourish.

And the three of them left the room, still discussing the Republic, while Cruges continued playing the piano, meandering through Mendelssohn and Chopin, having first devoured a whole plate of croquettes.

The Marquis and Dom Diogo, seated on the same sofa, one sipping his weak invalid's tea and the other sniffing the bouquet of his glass of St. Emilion, were also talking about Gambetta. The Marquis liked him; he was the only one who, during the war, had behaved like a real man; whether he'd had his hand in the coffers or not, he had no idea nor did he care. What mattered was that he had guts! And M. Grévy seemed a serious citizen too, and an excellent choice as head of state.

"A man of the world, would you say?" the old lion asked languidly.

The Marquis had only ever seen him presiding, in very dignified fashion, over the Assembly.

With melancholy disdain in voice, face and eye, Dom Diogo mumbled:

"The only thing I envy that rabble is their health, Marquis!"

The Marquis tried, in a kind, jocular way, to console him. All of these people might appear very strong because they were always dealing with such weighty matters, but they probably all suffered from asthma, gallstones, or gout. Besides, Dom Diogo was a veritable Hercules. "Yes, a Hercules! Your problem is that you tend to mollycoddle yourself too much. Illness is just a bad habit. You've got to fight back. What you need is plenty of exercise and some invigorating cold baths. Basically, you've got a constitution of iron!"

"One that's got badly rusted up," replied Dom Diogo, smiling wearily.

"What do you mean 'rusted up'? If I were a horse or a woman, I'd far rather have you than one of those silly young men tired before their time. They simply don't make men of your calibre any more, Dom Diogo!"

"They don't make much of anything," said Dom Diogo with grave conviction, as if he were the last man left standing amid the ruins of the world.

But it was late, and once he had finished his tea, he was going to fetch his coat and go home. The Marquis lingered a while longer, sitting idly on the sofa and slowly filling his pipe, looking round this room which so delighted him with its Louis XV luxuriance: the floral patterns and the golds, the formal Beauvais armchairs made to accommodate ample hips, the pale tones of the Gobelin tapestries full of elegant shepherdesses, distant views of gardens, ribbons, and woolly lambs—the shadows left behind by lost idylls and glimpsed in the silken weave. At that hour, in the heavy, drowsy atmosphere, beneath the soft warm light from the guttering candles, one sensed the harmony and the air of another century, and the Marquis urged Cruges to play a minuet or a gavotte, something that would evoke Versailles and Marie Antoinette, something that would summon up the gentle cadence of fine manners and the aroma of powdered wigs and skin. Cruges let the notes of a vague melody gradually melt into sighs and die altogether, then he prepared himself, reached out his hands and, pressing down hard on the forte pedal, launched into the national anthem. The Marquis fled.

Vilaça and Eusèbiozinho were out in the corridor, talking, seated on one of the carved oak chests.

"Politicking, are we?" the Marquis asked as he passed.

They both smiled. Vilaça responded good-humouredly:

"Well, someone has to save the country!"

Eusébio also belonged to the Progressive Party and aspired to being a political force in the constituency of Resende, and on the evenings they spent at Ramalhete, the two of them would plot together. At that moment, however, they were discussing the Maias: Vilaça did not hesitate to confide to Eusèbiozinho—as a man of property and close neighbour of Santa Olávia, who had virtually grown up with Carlos—certain things that annoyed him about the household, where his authority appeared to be on the wane; for example, he could not approve of Carlos buying a season ticket for a theatre box.

"What for?" exclaimed the worthy Vilaça, "Whatever for? In order, it seems, never to set foot there, but to spend his evenings here. Take tonight. Apparently the theatre was packed, but did he go? As far as I know, he's been, at most, two or three times. And that box cost him a lot of money. He could have saved himself a small fortune. It's bad economics. What happens is that Ega uses the box, as do Taveira and Cruges. I don't, nor do you, my friend, but then, of course, you're still in mourning."

Eusébio thought bitterly that he could always have sat at the back of the box—had he been invited. And unable to repress a faint smile, he murmured:

"The way they're going, they'll end up in hock."

Such a humiliating expression applied to the Maias, to the house for which he was administrator, shocked Vilaça. In hock! Never.

"No, no, you misunderstand me. There are certain unnecessary expenses but, thank God, the household can cope with them. It's true that every bit of our income gets spent, down to the last penny, and the cheques fly off like autumn leaves, although, up until now, the custom of the house has always been to put money aside, to grow a little nest-egg, to have something in reserve. Now, though, the money is just melting away . . ."

Eusébio mumbled a few words about Carlos' carriages, his nine horses, his English coachman, his grooms, but Vilaça interrupted him:

"But that is exactly as it should be. A family like this has its image to think of, it must always have the very best of everything. It has certain social duties. Take Senhor Afonso. He spends a lot, it's true, he really gets through the money. Not that he spends it on himself, mind, why, I've known that jacket he's wearing now for twenty years; no, he spends it on alms and pensions and loans he'll never get back."

"He's just throwing it away, then."

"Oh, no, I would never criticise him for that. It's the custom of the house; my father used to say that no one left the Maias' door dissatisfied, but a box at the theatre that no one uses, apart from Cruges or Taveira that is . . ."

He stopped talking. Taveira had just that moment appeared at the end of the corridor, with the collar of his ulster coat turned right up, so that only the ends of his pale silk scarf could be seen. Once the footman had helped him out of all his layers, Taveira, in tails and white waistcoat, smoothing his fine moustache still damp with frost, came over to shake the hand of dear Vilaça and his good friend Eusébio; still shivering, he nevertheless declared that he found the cold most elegant and was looking forward to the snow in all its *chic*.

"No, no," said Vilaça, all bonhomie. "I'd rather have our Portuguese sun any day."

And the three of them made their way to the smoking-room where they could hear the voices of the Marquis and Carlos engaged in one of their wise prolix conversations about horses and sport.

"How was it then? How was she?" was the question that greeted Taveira.

However, before reporting back on the début of La Morelli, the new leading lady, Taveira called for something warm to drink. And then, once safely ensconced in an armchair by the fire, stretching out his gleaming shoes to the embers, breathing in the aroma from the punch and drawing on a cigarette, he declared that at least it had not been a total fiasco.

"In my view, she's a complete nonentity, she has no voice, no talent, nothing. But the poor creature was so overwhelmed by it all that we felt sorry for her. People were kind and applauded, and when I went backstage afterwards, she seemed very happy."

"So, Taveira, what's she like?" asked the Marquis.

"Plumpish," said Taveira, placing his words as if they were brushstrokes. "Tall, very white-skinned, good eyes, good teeth."

"And what about her feet?" asked the Marquis, eyes burning, slowly stroking his bald head.

Taveira had not noticed. He was not a great connoisseur of feet.

"Who was there?" asked Carlos, yawning.

"The usual people. Oh, yes, and do you know who's taken the box next to yours? The Gouvarinhos. They were there tonight."

Carlos did not know the Gouvarinhos. The others around him explained: the Count de Gouvarinho was a peer of the realm, a tall man, with spectacles, a bit of a poseur . . . and the Countess was a rather shapely, English-looking woman, with carrot-coloured hair. Carlos still could not place them.

Vilaça knew the Count from the Progressive Club, where he was a pillar of the party. A talented fellow, according to Vilaça. What most astonished him was that, given the financial straits the Count was in, he could afford a season ticket at all. Only three months ago, he'd been taken to court for non-payment of a promissory note for 800 *mil-réis*.

"A fool and a defaulter to boot!" said the Marquis in disgusted tones.

"But their Tuesday soirées are most enjoyable!" commented Taveira, studying one of his silk socks.

Then talk turned to the duel between Azevedo, a journalist who worked for *Opinião*, and Sá Nunes, the author of *King Biscuit*—a highly successful fantasy-cum-farce running at the theatre in Rua dos Condes—and, more recently, minister for the Navy. They had been swapping insults in the papers, calling each other "scoundrel" and "thief," and since the challenge had been issued, ten seemingly interminable days had passed, and all Lisbon waited, in a state of dumb expectation, for blood to be shed. Cruges had heard that Sá Nunes did not want to fight because he was in mourning for an aunt; it was also said that Azevedo had scurried off to the Algarve. The truth, according to Vilaça, was that, in order to forestall the encounter, Azevedo's cousin, the Interior

Minister, had kept the houses of both men under police guard.

"Rogues, the lot of them!" exclaimed the Marquis, making one of his brusque summings-up.

"The minister's quite right really," remarked Vilaça. "These duels can sometimes end very badly indeed."

There was a brief silence. Carlos, who was half-asleep, asked Taveira, through a yawn, if he had seen Ega at the theatre.

"Of course! There he was on duty, at his post, in the Cohens' box, done up to the nines."

"So this business between Ega and Cohen's wife," said the Marquis, "it's quite obvious, is it?"

"Transparent, diaphanous, clear as glass!"

Carlos, who had got to his feet to light a cigarette, hoping it would wake him up, reminded them of Dom Diogo's great maxim: that these were things one never knew and which, indeed, it was preferable not to know! The Marquis, however, weighed in with some ponderous thoughts of his own. He rather liked the fact that Ega "was throwing himself at Madame Cohen," but he saw in it, too, a hint of social revenge because Cohen was both a Jew and a banker. Generally speaking, the Marquis did not like Jews anyway, and there was nothing more offensive to good taste and reason than the race of bankers. He could understand a highwayman, waiting in ambush in the woods; he could accept the communist, risking his life on the barricade; but he really could not stand financiers, with their partners and their companies. He felt, therefore, that destroying the domestic happiness of one of their number was a most worthy enterprise.

"It's a quarter past two!" exclaimed Taveira, glancing at the clock. "And here I am, a public servant, with State duties to attend to at ten o'clock in the morning sharp."

"What exactly do you do at the Audit Office?" asked Carlos. "Gamble? Gossip?"

"We do a little of everything, really, just to pass the time; we even carry out the occasional audit!"

Afonso da Maia had already gone to bed. Sequeira and Steinbroken had left, and Dom Diogo, huddled in his ancient carriage, had also departed to drink one last egg-nog and apply one more poultice, under the solicitous eye of Margarida, his cook and his last lover. The others were not long in leaving Ramalhete either. Taveira, swathed once more in his ulster coat, trotted home to his little house nearby with its lovely garden. The Marquis managed to carry Cruges off with him in his *coupé* so that Cruges could continue making music for him on the organ, until three or four in the morning, sad religious music that would make the Marquis weep, thinking of his lost loves and eating cold chicken and slices of salami. And the widower, Eusèbiozinho, his teeth chattering as he walked along as slowly and gravely as if to his own funeral, was heading for the local brothel where he was "in love" with one of the prostitutes.

Carlos' laboratory was finally ready, and very inviting it was too, with its new floor, freshly tiled kilns, vast marble table, ample horse-hair sofa—on which to rest after making some great discovery—and, all around, on pedestals and shelves, the rich glitter of metal and glass; but the weeks passed, and this wonderful experimental equipment lay virginal and idle in the white glow from the skylight. A servant earned his daily keep by walking indolently around each morning with duster in hand.

Carlos simply did not have time to work in the laboratory; he would—as he joked to his grandfather—allow God a few more weeks to enjoy the exclusive privilege of knowing the secret of all things. Every morning, early, he would do his two hours' fencing with old Randon, then he would visit a few patients in the area, for everyone had heard the now almost legendary news of Marcelina's recovery—as well as about the bottles of Bordeaux Afonso had sent her. Carlos was beginning to acquire a reputation as a doctor. He received patients in his consulting rooms, usually graduates, his contemporaries at university, who, knowing him to be rich and assuming that he would not charge them, would arrive looking sad and sallow and tell him the old, ill-disguised tale of some love affair that had left a fateful mark. He had saved from diphtheria the daughter of a Brazilian who lived on the Aterro and had thus earned his first *libra*, the first that any man in his family had ever earned from his own work. Dr. Barbedo had even invited him to attend an ovariotomy. Finally (and Carlos had not expected to receive such recognition so early), some of his good colleagues, who had grown accustomed to seeing him riding by with his fine English horses and to speaking of him as "the talented young Maia," now, seeing him with the beginnings of a practice, began referring to him instead as "an ass." Carlos was starting to take his career seriously. He had, in the laboriously polished prose of a stylist, written two articles for the *Medical Gazette*, and was considering writing a book for general consumption to be entitled *Medicine Ancient and Modern*. Otherwise, he was as absorbed as ever by his horses, by fine living, and by the acquisition of interesting bric-à-brac. And yet due to that fatal butterfly curiosity of his—which, even when caught up in the most riveting pathological case, would make him turn his head at the mere mention of a statue or a poet—he still felt powerfully drawn to Ega's old idea: the creation of a magazine that would set new standards in taste, politics, and society, one that would, in short, be Lisbon's intellectual engine.

There was, however, no point in reminding Ega of this beautiful plan. He would open one vague eye and say:

"Ah, yes, the magazine. Yes, of course, we really should give that some thought. We'll talk about it. I'll drop round some time."

But he did not "drop round" to Ramalhete or to the consulting room; he was glimpsed occasionally at the Teatro São Carlos, where, when not installed in the Cohens' box, he would invariably take refuge in Carlos' ground-floor box, behind Taveira or Cruges, where he was still in a position to watch Raquel

Cohen—and there he would sit, in silent repose, leaning against the back wall, as if saturated with happiness.

His day (he said) was entirely taken up: he was looking for a house in which to live, and studying how best to furnish it, but it was easy enough to spot him in the Chiado or in Loreto, on the prowl, sniffing around, or else hunched in the back of a hired carriage, galloping off in ostentatious search of adventure.

His dandyism was becoming more extreme: he now sported, with the arrogant boldness of a Beau Brummel, a tailcoat with yellow buttons and a white satin waistcoat; and Carlos, arriving early one morning at the Hotel Universal, found Ega, white with rage, berating a servant because a pair of shoes had not been properly polished. His two constant companions were a friend of Cohen's, Dâmaso Salcede, and a cousin of Raquel's, a beardless young man with hard bright eyes, who always seemed poised to make one an offer of a loan at thirty per cent interest.

Among his friends, in Ramalhete, and especially in Carlos' box at the theatre, Raquel was a frequent topic of discussion, and opinions regarding her differed somewhat. Taveira, lasciviously grinding his teeth, thought her "delicious"; the Marquis felt that the rather "gamey" flesh of a woman of thirty could, on occasions, prove not unappetising; Cruges referred to her as an "insipid snob." In the high society columns of the newspapers, she was "one of our most elegant ladies," and all Lisbon knew her, her gold lorgnette on its gold chain, and her blue calèche with its black horses. She was a tall woman, and very pale, especially in the light; she had a rather delicate constitution, and there was a weariness about her deep-set eyes, indeed, an infinite languor about her whole person, an air of romance and of lilies just past their best; her most beautiful feature was her magnificently dark hair, so thick and wavy that it rebelled against hairpins, and which she artfully allowed to fall almost loose down her back, with just a suggestion of unkempt nakedness. She was, it was said, fond of reading and known for her witty comments. Her constant, pale, listless smile, however, gave her an air of insignificance. Poor Ega adored her.

He had met her in Foz, at the assembly rooms; that same night, drinking beer with his friends, he had called her "a honey-sweet camellia"; days later, he was already toadying up to her husband, and now, Ega the democrat, who had called for the massacre of the middle classes, would often spend hours at a time lying across his bed, sobbing over her.

In Lisbon, from the Grémio to the Casa Havanesa, there was already talk of "Ega's mistress." He, for his part, was trying very hard to keep his happiness safe from prying eyes. While perfectly serious about the complicated precautions this entailed, he also took a romantic delight in mystery, and so always chose the most out-of-the-way places, on the outskirts of the city, in the area near the slaughterhouse, for his furtive meetings with the maid who brought him Raquel's letters. But his every gesture (even the affected way he had of pretending not to look at the clock) revealed the enormous pride he felt in that elegant adultery. He was perfectly aware that his friends knew all about this glorious adventure of his, and were *au fait* with the whole drama, and this was perhaps why, when in the company of Carlos or the others, he never even mentioned her name or betrayed the slightest flicker of emotion.

One night, however, a night lit by a calm white moon, as he and Carlos were walking along together in silence on their way to Ramalhete, Ega, doubtless filled by a sudden inrush of passion, uttered a heartfelt sigh, reached out his arms and declared to the moon in a tremulous voice:

"Oh, laisse-toi donc aimer, oh, l'amour c'est la vie!"

This escaped his lips like the beginning of a confession. Carlos, at his side, said nothing, and simply blew his cigar smoke out into the air.

Ega clearly felt somewhat ridiculous, because he immediately recovered himself and pretended a mere literary interest.

"They can say what they like, but there's no one like old Hugo."

Carlos still said nothing, but recalled Ega's Naturalist outbursts, in which he had inveighed against Victor Hugo, calling him "a spiritualist blabbermouth," "an imitative yokel," "a lyrical old fool" and worse.

But that night, Ega, the great phrase-maker, went on:

"Ah, yes, old Hugo, the heroic champion of the eternal truths. We need a bit of idealism, damn it, because the ideal might one day become reality."

And with this formal recantation he shattered the silence of the streets.

Days later, Carlos was in his consulting room, having just dismissed one of his patients, a certain Viegas, who came to see him every week to give him a detailed account of his dyspepsia, when from behind the waiting room curtain appeared Ega, wearing a blue frock-coat, pearl-grey gloves, and carrying a roll of paper in one hand.

"Are you busy, Doctor?"

"No, you dandy, I was just about to leave."

"Good, I've come to force a little prose on you—a short section from the *Atom*. Sit down and listen."

Ega immediately took a seat himself, pushed aside the papers and books on the desk, unrolled his manuscript, smoothed it flat, tugged at his collar, and Carlos, who had sat down on the edge of the sofa, his hands on his knees, and a look of astonishment on his face, found himself instantly transported from the rumbles of Viegas' intestines to the murmur of the rabble in the Jewish quarter of the old city of Heidelberg.

"Hang on a moment!" he exclaimed. "Let me catch my breath. That isn't the beginning of the book! That isn't Chaos."

Ega leaned back, unbuttoned his frock-coat and he, too, took a deep breath.

"No, it's not the first episode, it's not Chaos. It's the fifteenth century. But in a book like this, you can begin where you like. Besides, it suited me to write this particular episode now, it's called: 'The Hebrew Woman.'"

"Raquel Cohen," thought Carlos.

Ega loosened his collar further and read on, growing increasingly animated, emphasising certain words in order to bring them alive and closing each paragraph with a loud crescendo. After a sombre description of medieval Heidelberg, the famous Atom, "Ega's Atom," turned up lodged in the heart of the splendid Prince Franck, poet, knight, and bastard son of the Emperor Maximilian. And the whole of this heroic heart was beating for the Jewess Esther, marvellous pearl of the East, daughter of the old Rabbi Solomon, who was a great doctor of the Law, persecuted by the theological hatred of the General of the Dominicans.

This was told by the "Atom" in a monologue, as thickly embroidered with images as the Virgin's cloak is with stars, and which was Ega's own declaration of love to Cohen's wife. It was followed by a pantheistic interlude couched in the language of light and eloquent perfumes, in which choirs of flowers and stars burst forth to hymn the beauty, grace, and purity of Esther—and of Raquel—and of her celestial soul. There followed the dark drama of persecution: the flight of the Hebrew family through witch-infested woods and brutish feudal villages; the appearance, at a crossroads, of Prince Franck, come to protect Esther, with spear in hand, on his great steed; the fanatical mob eager to burn the rabbi and his heretical books; then came the battle, and the Prince pierced through by the point of a lance, dying on Esther's breast and she dying with him in a kiss. All this came out in a rush, like a loud unbridled sob; and it was written in the modern style, full of tortured, expressive phrases, with colours laid on thick to make it vivid and alive.

Afterwards, with the vast solemnity of a deep organ note, the "Atom" exclaimed: "And so the hero's heart which I had inhabited, stopped and grew cold; and with the spark of life gone, free once more, I rose up to the stars, carrying with me the pure essence of that immortal love."

"What do you think?" asked Ega, breathless, almost trembling.

Carlos could only say:

"Sensational!"

Then he spoke fulsomely of certain passages: the chorus of the forests, the reading of Ecclesiastes at night in the ruins of the tower of Otho, and certain images of great lyrical power.

Ega, who was, as always, in a hurry, rolled up the manuscript, buttoned up his frock-coat and, with his hat already in his hand, asked:

"So you think it's presentable, then?"

"Are you going to publish it?"

"No, but ..." And he said no more, blushing.

A few days later, Carlos understood everything when he found in the *Gazeta do Chiado* a description of "a reading at the home of Senhor Jacob Cohen, by our friend João da Ega, of one of the most brilliant episodes from his book *The Memoirs of an Atom*." The journalist added his own personal impressions of the soirée: "It is a depiction of the sufferings endured in the days of religious intolerance by those who obey the Law of Israel. What power of imagination! What fluency of style! The effect was quite extraordinary, and when, with the death of his female protagonist, our friend put down the manuscript, we saw tears in the eyes of Lisbon's numerous and estimable Jewish community!"

Ega was furious! That afternoon, he burst into Carlos' consulting room, looking pale and wild-eyed.

"The clods! Those clodhopping journalists! Did you read it? 'Tears in the eyes of Lisbon's numerous and estimable Jewish community!' It makes the whole thing ridiculous. And then that comment about 'fluency of style!' What asses! What idiots!"

Carlos, who was cutting the pages of a book, tried to console him. That was the Portuguese way of talking about works of art. There was no point getting so worked up.

"I could have punched that scribbler in the face!"

"So why didn't you?"

"He's a friend of the Cohens."

And he paced the office like a tiger, muttering insulting comments about the press in general. Finally, irritated by Carlos' indifference, he said:

"What the devil are you reading? *On the Parasitic Nature of Disorders Arising from Impaludism.* What a joke medicine is! Tell me something, though, what's the pricking sensation I get in my arms whenever I go to sleep?"

"Fleas, insects, vermin," murmured Carlos, his eyes on his book.

"Fool!" snorted Ega, snatching up his hat.

"Are you leaving, João?"

"Yes, I have things to do!" And standing in the doorway, brandishing his umbrella at the ceiling and almost weeping with rage: "These stupid journalists are the scum of society!"

Ten minutes later, he reappeared, and in quite another tone of voice, as if speaking of some very serious matter, he said:

"Listen, I forgot to ask you something. Would you like to be introduced to the Gouvarinhos?"

"I don't feel any particular interest in being introduced to them," replied Carlos, looking up, and then after a silence. "But then again I don't feel any particular repugnance either."

"Well," said Ega, "they would like to meet you; the Countess is especially keen. They're intelligent people and enjoyable company. So, it's decided then. I'll come and pick you up at Ramalhete on Tuesday and we'll go 'gouvarinhoing.'"

Carlos sat thinking about Ega's proposal and about the way he had stressed the Countess' keenness to meet him. He remembered now that she was a very close friend of Raquel Cohen and, lately, at the Teatro São Carlos, in the easy neighbourliness of the stage boxes, he had noticed her looking at him. Taveira had gone further and declared that "she'd been making sheep's eyes at him." And Carlos found her highly attractive, with her reddish curls, her pert little nose and those dark, shining eyes that always seemed to be saying a thousand things. She had a wonderful figure, too, and her skin was pale, fine, and so satin-smooth that you could almost feel from afar its softness.

After a glum day of intermittent rain, he had decided to spend the evening doing some proper work by the fire, in the comfort of his dressing-gown. However, after coffee had been served, the Countess' eyes began to wink at him, to "make sheep's eyes at him" from among his cigar smoke, positioning themselves temptingly between him and his night of study, sending a lively, youthful warmth flowing through his veins. It was all the fault of Ega, the Mephistopheles of Celorico!

He got dressed and went to the theatre. Immaculately turned out, wearing a white waistcoat and a black pearl pinned to his shirt, he took his place at the front of the box; however, he saw not reddish curls, but the dark woolly head of a small black boy, a surly twelve-year-old with glossy skin, wearing a broad collar and a jacket with yellow buttons; beside him, another smaller black boy, wearing the same school uniform, was busily poking one white-gloved finger up his nose. Both boys looked at him with wide eyes, the colour of tarnished silver. The person accompanying them, hidden at the back of the box, appeared to have the most appalling cold.

That night there was a benefit performance of *Lucia di Lammermoor*, with the understudy in the lead role. The Cohens had not gone, nor had Ega. A lot of the boxes were empty, revealing their faded red wallpaper in all its sadness. The drizzly night, with a southwest wind blowing, seemed to have seeped into the theatre, infecting it with melancholy and a kind of tepid dampness. Amid the rows of empty chairs sat a solitary woman, dressed in pale satin; Edgardo and Lucia were singing off-key; the gaslights were slumbering; and even the violin bows seemed to be falling asleep over their strings.

"God, this is dreary," said Carlos to his friend Cruges, who was sitting in the dark at the back of the box.

Deep in one of his more splenetic moods, with one elbow hooked over the back of his chair, his fingers plunged in his hair, the whole of him wrapped in layer upon layer of black melancholy, Cruges answered, as if from the depths of a tomb:

"Ghastly."

Carlos stayed out of sheer inertia. And, unable to take his eyes off that small black boy enthroned on the Countess' green rep chair, where the sleeve of his jacket lay on the balustrade in place of the usual lovely white arm, his imagination was, despite himself, drawn to thoughts of her; he remembered the dresses she had worn; and now that he could not see her tight reddish curls— the colour of glowing embers, as if they burned with an inner flame—they had never seemed more alluring. The black boy's thick mat of woolly hair had no parting, only a kind of furrow dug out with scissors. Who were they, these sullen Africans, why were they here?

"Have you noticed that boy's extraordinary hair, Cruges?"

94

From the shadows, Cruges, who had not altered his pose as tumulary statue, grunted an indecipherable monosyllable.

Carlos respected the state of his friend's nerves.

Suddenly, when the chorus hit a more than usually discordant note, Cruges leapt up.

"This is disgraceful! What a company!" he roared, furiously pulling on his overcoat.

Carlos took him in his carriage to Rua das Flores, where Cruges lived with his mother and a sister; and from there until Ramalhete, he bemoaned to himself his lost evening of study.

Carlos' valet, Baptista (known familiarly as "Tista") was waiting for him, reading the newspaper, in the cosy anteroom to "the young master's quarters," its velvet-lined walls hung with equestrian paintings and displays of ancient weaponry, its sofas upholstered in the same cherry-red velvet; even at that late hour, the room was still brightly lit by two globe oil-lamps placed on oak columns carved with twining vine stems.

Carlos had had the same valet since he was eleven years old; he had come with Brown to Santa Olávia, having first served in Lisbon, at the English legation, and had several times accompanied the ambassador, Sir Hercules Morrisson, on trips to London. It was in Coimbra, at the "Palace of Celas," that Baptista had really come into his own. Afonso even used to correspond with him from Santa Olávia. Then he went off travelling with Carlos; they were seasick on the same steamboats, shared the same sandwiches in station buffets; "Tista" became a confidant. He was now a man of fifty, strong and erect, with a fringe of greying beard and an excessively gentlemanly air. Seen in the street, a very upright figure in his overcoat, with a pair of yellow gloves and an Indian cane walking stick, his shoes buffed to a shine, he had all the appearance of a high-ranking civil servant. But he remained as elegant and at ease as when he had learned to waltz and to box in rowdy London dance halls, or when, later on, during the university vacation, he had accompanied Carlos to Lamego and helped him over the wall into the garden belonging to the local tax officer, the one with the very naughty wife.

Carlos went to his study to fetch a book, then came back into the room and stretched out wearily in an armchair. In the opaline light cast by the oil lamps, the turned-down bed revealed, beneath the silk hangings, an almost effeminate luxuriance of Breton linen, lace, and embroidery.

"What's in the evening paper?" he asked, yawning, while Baptista removed his shoes.

"I've read the whole thing, sir, and as far as I can see nothing has happened at all. Things are still quiet in France, but, then again, you never can tell because the Portuguese newspapers always garble any foreign names that crop up."

"They're all idiots, the lot of them. Senhor Ega got quite furious with them today."

Then, while Baptista lovingly prepared him a hot toddy, Carlos, already tucked up in bed, idly opened the book, turned two pages, closed it, picked up a cigarette and lay there, smoking, eyes shut, wrapped in a feeling of immense beatitude. Through the heavy curtains, he could hear the wind buffeting the trees and the rain drenching the windows.

"Do you know the Gouvarinhos, 'Tista?'"

"I know Pimenta, sir, the Count's valet, who also serves at table."

"And what does this Tormenta have to say?" asked Carlos in an indolent voice and after a brief silence.

"Pimenta, sir! Manuel's name is Pimenta. Although Senhor Gouvarinho calls him Romão because he was used to another valet whose name was Romão. And that in itself isn't nice, because everyone has his own name. No, Manuel's name is Pimenta, and Pimenta isn't happy."

And Baptista, once he had placed at Carlos' bedside the tray bearing the hot toddy, the sugar bowl and the cigarettes, told him everything that Pimenta had revealed to him. The Count of Gouvarinho, as well as being both irritating and persnickety, was no gentleman: he had given Romão (or, rather, Pimenta) a light-coloured cheviot-wool suit, but it was so worn and so ink-stained, from his habit of wiping his pen on his shoulder or trouser leg, that Pimenta had thrown the gift away. The Count and his lady wife did not get on well; since Pimenta had been there, they had, on one occasion, argued so ferociously over the supper table that she had grabbed hold of her glass and plate and hurled them to the floor. Any woman would have done the same, because once the Count started harping and carping, he was unbearable. Their arguments were always about money. Old Thompson was fed up with having to keep dipping into the purse.

"And who might this 'old Thompson' be, who's suddenly turned up at this time of night?" asked Carlos who was, despite himself, intrigued.

"Old Thompson is the Countess' father. The Countess was Miss Thompson of the Thompsons of Oporto. Mr. Thompson has recently refused to lend so much as another penny to his son-in-law, and once, again in the time since Pimenta's been there, the Count got so angry that he told his wife that she and her father should remember that they're mere tradespeople and that he had been the one who had made her a Countess; and if you'll forgive my language, sir, the Countess, right there and then, told him that he could send his title to the devil for all she cared. And that sort of thing really isn't Pimenta's style."

Carlos took a sip of his hot toddy. A question hovered on his lips, but he hesitated to ask it. Then it occurred to him that it was childish of him to feel such rigid scruples regarding people who, over supper and in front of the servant, smashed the china and sent the ancestors to the devil. And so he asked:

"And what does Pimenta have to say about the Countess, Baptista? Does she still manage to, um, enjoy herself?"

"No, I don't believe so, sir. But her maid, the Scotswoman, is certainly no better than she should be. And it doesn't look good for the Countess to be so close to her."

A silence fell in the room; the rain beat more loudly on the windowpanes.

"Changing the subject, Baptista, how long is it since I wrote to Madame Rughel?"

Baptista produced an appointments diary from the inside pocket of his tail-coat, went over to the light, placed his glasses on his nose and methodically read out these dates: "1st January, telegram sending best wishes for the New Year to Madame Rughel, Hôtel d'Albe, Champs-Elysées, Paris. 3rd January, telegram received from Madame Rughel, reciprocating greetings, expressing her friendship and announcing her departure for Hamburg. 15th January, letter sent to Madame Rughel, Williamstrasse, Hamburg, Germany. Since then, nothing. So it's five weeks since you wrote to Madame Rughel."

"I must write tomorrow," said Carlos.

Baptista made a note.

Then, from the smoke curling languidly up from his cigarette, Carlos' voice emerged again into the somnolent peace of the room.

"Madame Rughel was *very* pretty, wasn't she, Baptista? Certainly the prettiest woman you've ever seen!"

The old servant returned the diary to his jacket pocket and replied unhesitatingly and with utter confidence:

"Madame Rughel is certainly a fine-looking woman, but the prettiest woman I've ever laid eyes on was, if you'll allow me, sir, the wife of that colonel in the hussars, the one who came to your hotel room in Vienna."

Carlos stubbed out his cigarette on the tray and, sliding down under the bedclothes, filled by a wave of happy memories, he exclaimed from those cosy depths, reverting to the bohemian language of his days in the "Palace of Celas":

"You, Senhor Baptista, have no taste at all! Madame Rughel was a Rubens nymph, sir! Madame Rughel had all the splendour of a Renaissance goddess, sir! Madame Rughel should have slept in the imperial bed of Charles V. Withdraw, sir!"

Baptista tucked in the quilt on the bed more snugly, glanced around the room with a solicitous eye, and, satisfied that everything was neat and ready for sleep, he left, taking with him the oil lamp. Carlos did not fall asleep at once, nor was he thinking about the colonel's wife or about Madame Rughel. The figure that emerged from the curtained shadows around the bed, in a golden glow of tousled reddish hair, was the Count de Gouvarinho's wife—she was not a splendid Renaissance goddess like Madame Rughel, nor, like the colonel's wife, was she the prettiest woman Baptista had ever laid eyes on, but with her pert nose and her large mouth, she shone brighter and better in Carlos' imagination than either of them, and all because he had expected to see her that night and she had not appeared.

On the promised Tuesday, Ega did not come to collect Carlos in order to go "gouvarinhoing." And it was Carlos who, some days later, turned up as if by chance at the Hotel Universal and asked Ega with a smile:

"So, when are we going 'gouvarinhoing,' then?"

That night, at the Teatro São Carlos, in an interval during a perfomance of Meyerbeer's *Les Huguenots*, Ega introduced him to the Count de Gouvarinho in the corridor behind the stage boxes. The count proved most amiable, and was quick to recall that he had, more than once, had the pleasure of driving past the gates of Santa Olávia when he went to visit his old friends, the Tedins, in Entrerios—another fine estate. They spoke then about the Douro and the Beira and compared them with other regions of Portugal. In the Count's opinion, nothing could compare to the Mondego, but he was, of course, understandably biased in its favour, having been born and bred in that fertile valley, and he talked for a while about Formoselha, where he had a house and where his aged ailing mother, the widowed Countess, still lived.

Ega, who had affected to be drinking in the Count's every word, tried to stir up a controversy by propounding, as if it were religious dogma, the superior beauty of "that idyllic paradise," the Minho. As the Count smilingly remarked to Carlos, at the same time fondly patting Ega's shoulder, he merely saw in these comments the rivalry between the two provinces, and a very fertile rivalry it was, he thought.

"For example," he went on, "there's the jealousy between Lisbon and Oporto—that's a genuine duality, as between Hungary and Austria. I often hear people speak of this with regret, but if I had my way, I would encourage it, indeed, if I may use the expression, I would foment it. Where others see only spite and meanness in the struggle between our two great cities, I see signs of progress. I see civilisation!"

He said these things as if he were standing on a pedestal, far above other men, generously bestowing upon those below him the treasures of his intellect, as if they were gifts of inestimable worth. He spoke slowly and deliberately; the lenses of his gold-framed spectacles glittered brightly; and there was about his waxed moustache and his neat goatee something at once pompous and dandified.

Carlos said: "You're absolutely right, Count." Ega said: "You see these things from a loftier perspective, Gouvarinho." The Count crossed his hands under the tails of his coat, and all three men stood there, looking serious.

Then the Count opened the door of his box and Ega disappeared inside. A moment later, Carlos, who was introduced as being from the neighbouring box, was receiving from the Countess a firm handshake, which set a-tinkling the infinite number of silver bracelets and Indian bangles worn over her long, black, twelve-button glove.

The Countess, blushing slightly and a little nervous, immediately reminded Carlos that she had seen him the previous summer in Paris, in the lower room at the Café Anglais; there had been a dreadful old man at the café that night, sitting with two empty bottles in front of him and saying the most dreadful things about M. Gambetta to the people at the next table; someone nearby had protested, but the old man, who, it turns out, was the Duc de Grammont, took not the slightest notice. The Count slowly squeezed his forehead with an almost anguished air: he had no memory of that at all! He then launched into a bitter lament about his lack of memory. And memory was indispensable for someone like him, in public life, but he, alas, had not an atom! For example, he had read (as everyone should) Cesare Cantù's twenty-volume *Universal History*; shut up in his study, absorbed in the work, he had read each volume attentively. But he had forgotten it all—and there he was without a jot of history in his head!

"Do you have a good memory, Senhor Maia?"

"Reasonable."

"It's an invaluable gift."

The Countess had turned towards the stage, covering her face with her fan, apparently embarrassed, as if she felt diminished and sullied by her husband's puerile words. Carlos began talking about the opera. What a handsome Huguenot page Pandolli made! The Countess could not bear Corcelli, the tenor, with his harsh timbre and so fat now that he looked almost comical. But then (put in Carlos) where *were* the good tenors nowadays? The great race of Marios was long gone, men of beauty and inspiration, capable of playing the great lyric roles. And Nicolini was past his best now. This brought them round to the subject of Patti. The Countess adored her, her fairy-like grace and that voice like a shower of gold!

The Countess' eyes shone, apparently saying a thousand things; when she turned her head a certain way, her wavy hair seemed to glow red-gold, and around her, in the warmth of the gaslights and the crowded theatre, there hovered a strong scent of verbena. She was wearing black, with, around her neck, a tight black lace choker *à la Valois*, decorated with two scarlet roses. There was about her whole being a hint of provocation and attack. Standing up, silent and grave, the Count was tapping his thigh with his folded crush-hat.

Act IV had begun; Carlos stood up to leave; and immediately opposite him, in the Cohens' box, he caught sight of Ega, opera glasses raised, observing him and the Countess, and talking to Raquel, who was smiling and fanning herself with a vague and indolent air.

"We receive on Tuesdays," the Countess said to Carlos. And the rest of her words were lost in a murmur and a smile.

The Count accompanied him out of the box into the corridor.

"It's always an honour for me," he was saying as he walked by Carlos' side, "to make the acquaintance of people in this country who are actually worth something. You are one of that number, of which, alas, there are all too few."

Carlos protested, smiling. And the Count, in his slow, deliberate way, went on:

"I'm not flattering you. I never flatter. But I can say such things to you because you belong to the elite. Portugal's misfortune is its lack of personnel. This is a country without personnel. Say you need a bishop. There are none.

Or an economist. There are no economists either. It's the same with everything. Even in the lesser professions. Say you want a good upholsterer, for example. There are none to be found . . ."

The sublime sound of instruments and voices burst forth through the half-open door to his box, cutting short his remarks about the lack of good photographers. He listened, with one hand raised:

"It's 'The Blessing of the Swords,' isn't it? Let's go in and listen. It always does one good to hear it. There's real philosophy in that music. It's a shame, of course, that it harks back to the days of religious intolerance, but nevertheless it contains some genuine philosophy!"

: VI :

THAT MORNING, CARLOS made a surprise visit to Ega's house, the famous Villa Balzac, which Ega, the great fantasist, had been planning and preparing since his arrival back in Lisbon and where he had, at last, installed himself.

Ega had called the house Villa Balzac for the same reason that he had chosen its location—in a distant suburb, in the solitudes of Penha de França—believing that the name of his patron saint, the rural quiet, and the clean air, would all prove favourable to study, to hours spent cultivating art and the ideal. For he was going to shut himself up there, as if in a literary cloister, and finish *Memoirs of an Atom*! Given that the house was a considerable distance from Lisbon, however, he had also taken the precaution of hiring a carriage by the month.

Carlos had some difficulty finding Villa Balzac: it was not, as Ega had told him when he last visited Ramalhete, a quiet, cool, shady little house, smiling among the trees, just past Largo da Graça. One first had to pass Cruz dos Quatro Caminhos, then proceed along a broad road flanked by gardens, down a steep hill, which was, nevertheless, still accessible to carriages, and there, in a corner, surrounded by walls, was a large shabby house with two stone steps up to the front door and new blinds at the windows in a particularly strident shade of scarlet.

On that morning, however, Carlos tugged desperately at the bell-pull, hammered on the door, bawled Ega's name over the garden wall and over the tops of the trees, but all in vain—Villa Balzac remained utterly mute in its rural isolation, as if uninhabited. And yet, it had seemed to Carlos that, just before he knocked, he had heard the popping of champagne corks.

When Ega found out about this attempted visit, he railed against the servants for leaving the house in such a state of abandon, as if it were as louche an abode as that place of orgies, the Tour de Nesle in Paris.

"Come tomorrow, and if no one answers, climb in through a window and set fire to the place, as if it were the Tuileries Palace."

The following day, however, when Carlos arrived, the Villa Balzac was expecting him and in festive mode: at the door "the page," a boy with horribly

101

lascivious features, was standing to attention in his blue jacket with metal buttons and a very stiff white tie; above him, two open windows drank in the country air and the winter sunlight, revealing, inside, some cheap green rep curtains; and at the top of the narrow red-carpeted staircase stood Ega, in a prodigious *robe-de-chambre* made of some sort of damasked fabric from the eighteenth century, a ball gown belonging to one of his grandmothers; bowing low, he exclaimed:

"Welcome, my prince, to the philosopher's humble retreat!"

With an extravagant gesture, he raised the ugly, drab, green door curtain and ushered the "prince" into the drawing room where everything else was equally green: the upholstery on the walnut furniture, the wood-panelled ceiling, the vertical stripes on the wallpaper, the fringed table cloth and the reflection in the round mirror over the sofa.

There was not a single painting, flower, ornament or book, apart from a statue on a pedestal table of Napoleon I, standing atop a globe of the world, in that hero's familiar pose—that of a rather plump man of destiny—in which he conceals one hand behind his back and plunges the other into the depths of his waistcoat. Next to him stood a bottle of champagne, with its gold paper cowl, between two slender glasses.

"What on earth is Napoleon doing here, João?"

"He's a target for my insults," said Ega. "I use him when I rehearse my tirades against tyranny."

He rubbed his hands gleefully. He was in fine and sparkling form that morning. And the first thing he wanted to show Carlos was his bedroom, decorated in red cretonne sprigged with white, and entirely filled and dominated by the bed. The bed appeared to be the *raison d'être*, the very centre of Villa Balzac, and into it Ega had poured all his artistic imagination. It was made of wood, and set low, like a divan, with a high headboard, a lace valance, and, on either side, a luxuriance of scarlet plush rugs; it was draped about with voluminous, red, Indian silk hangings, which gave it the air of a holy tabernacle; and inside, on the headboard, hung a mirror, as if it were a bed in a brothel.

Carlos, very gravely, advised him to remove the mirror. Ega regarded the bed in fond silence, then, running the tip of his tongue over his lips, said:

"I think it's rather chic."

The bedside table was piled high with books: Spencer's *Education* rubbed shoulders with Baudelaire, and John Stuart Mill's *Logic* with Dumas' *The Knight of the Red House*. On the marble-topped sideboard stood another bottle of champagne and two more glasses, and on the somewhat untidy dressing table lay a huge box of face powder, Ega's white shirtfronts and ties, as well as a bundle of hairpins and some curling tongs.

"And where do you work, Ega, where do you produce your great art?"

"There," said Ega gaily, pointing in the direction of the bed.

And he showed Carlos the little study area he had created for himself with a screen placed near the window, a space entirely taken up by a pedestal table on which Carlos was amazed to discover, alongside Ega's fine writing paper, a rhyming dictionary.

And the tour of the house continued.

In the almost bare dining room, with its yellow-painted walls, a pine dresser with glass doors gave melancholy shelter to a cheap service of new china, and from the catch on the window hung an item of clothing, apparently a woman's red dressing-gown.

"It's sober and it's simple," exclaimed Ega, "as befits one who dines daily on a crust of idealism and two forkfuls of philosophy. Now, to the kitchen!"

He opened a door. The cool air from the fields blew in through the open windows, and, outside, one could see the trees in the garden, the soft green of the fields beyond, and, down below, the white houses shining in the sun; a very strong, very freckled young woman brushed the cat from her lap and, still holding the *Jornal de Notícias* in her hand, sprang to her feet. Ega introduced her in jocular tones.

"Senhora Josefa, spinster, of sanguine temperament, and Villa Balzac's culinary artist, not to mention, as one may judge from the newspaper clutched in her hands, an enthusiast for fine literature!"

The woman smiled, unembarrassed, doubtless accustomed to such bohemian familiarity.

"I won't be dining here today, Senhora Josefa," Ega went on in the same tone. "This handsome young man here, Duke of Ramalhete and Prince of Santa Olávia, will be providing his philosopher friend with his daily bread. And since, by the time I return, Senhora Josefa will have surrendered either to innocent sleep or to wakeful licentiousness, I will take the opportunity now of ordering two fine partridges for tomorrow's lunch."

Then, in another voice entirely, and with a look she must have understood, he said:

"Two nice golden-roasted partridges. Cold, of course . . . as usual."

He linked arms with Carlos and they returned to the drawing room.

"Tell me frankly, Carlos, what do you think of Villa Balzac?"

Carlos responded as he had to that passage from Ega's novel about "The Hebrew Woman":

"Sensational!"

He praised its cleanliness, the view from the house and the cool cretonnes. It was perfect as a home for a young man and as a place of work.

"I can't stand knicknacks and bric-à-brac, antique chairs and 'artistic' furniture," said Ega, pacing the room, his hands plunged in the pockets of his prodigious *robe-de-chambre*. "Furniture should be in harmony with the ideas and feelings of the man using it, damn it! I don't think or feel like a gentleman from the sixteenth century, so why surround myself with objects from the period? There's nothing more depressing than seeing a venerable old cabinet from the time of Francis I marooned in the middle of conversations about elections and a rise in the stock market. It has much the same effect on me as seeing a fine hero all got up in his armour, with his visor down and deep beliefs beating in his breast, sitting down at a card table to play a game of ombre. Each century has its own genius and its own attitudes. The nineteenth century conceived Democracy, and its natural attitude is *this* . . ." He collapsed ostentatiously into an armchair and stretched out his thin legs. "An attitude that would be quite impossible while sitting on a thirteenth-century wooden bench, for example. Anyway, it's high time we drank that champagne."

And seeing Carlos eyeing the bottle distrustfully, Ega added:

"Don't worry, it's excellent stuff. Direct from the finest cellar in Epernay. Jacob got it for me."

"Jacob?"

"Jacob Cohen."

He was about to cut the string around the cork when he remembered something and, putting the bottle down again and fixing his monocle to his eye, he said:

"I quite forgot. How did it go the other night at the Gouvarinhos? Unfortunately, I wasn't able to be there."

Carlos told him about the soirée. There had been ten guests distributed between the two drawing rooms, all immersed in a sleepy hum of conversation in the half-light of the oil-lamps. The Count had bored him stiff with politics and with his idiotic admiration for some "great orator," a member of parliament from Mesão Frio, not to mention his endless explanations about educational reform. The Countess, who had a terrible cold, had horrified him by spouting views on England worthy of a common street trader, even though she herself was English. According to her, England was a land without poets, without artists, without ideals, and concerned only with making money. It had all been a frightful bore.

"How ghastly!" murmured Ega in a tone of deep distress.

The cork popped, he filled the glasses in silence, and, after raising them in a silent toast, the two friends drank the champagne that Jacob provided for Ega, and which Ega then enjoyed with Raquel.

Then, standing up, staring down at the carpet and watching the bubbles dying as he swirled the champagne around in his newly filled glass, Ega murmured again in that same sad tone of unexpected disappointment:

"What a shame!"

And then, after another moment:

"I thought you were interested in the Countess."

Carlos admitted that when Ega had first spoken to him about her, he had felt a twinge of attraction for that flame-red hair.

"But now that I've met her, any attraction I felt has vanished."

Ega had sat down again, his glass in his hand, and then, after prolonged study of his silk socks, as scarlet as a prelate's, he said very seriously:

"She's a very beautiful woman, Carlos."

And when Carlos merely shrugged, Ega insisted; she was a woman of intelligence and taste; she was original and bold and with a very piquant hint of the Romantic about her. "And as for her figure, you'll find none better from here to Badajoz!"

"Get thee behind me, O, Mephistopheles of Celorico!"

Tickled by this remark, Ega sang:

> *Je suis Mephisto . . .*
> *Je suis Mephisto . . .*

Carlos continued indolently smoking and talking about the Countess and the almost immediate sense of satiety that had filled him as soon he had exchanged three words with her in her own drawing room. And this wasn't the first time he had experienced these sudden false rushes of desire, which almost always came disguised as love, threatening, at least for a time, to absorb his whole being, but which always ended in tedium and boredom. They were like trails of gunpowder laid on a stone; a spark ignites them and they flare instantly into a flame so fierce that it seems about to consume the entire universe, only to die down at once and leave nothing but a black smudge on the stone. Was his perhaps one of those weak hearts, soft and flaccid, incapable of preserving any true emotion, a heart that allowed deep feelings to slip through the loose weave of its coarse fabric?

"I'm emotionally desiccated," he said, smiling. "I'm sentimentally impotent, like Satan. According to the Fathers of the Church, Satan's one great torment is that he cannot love."

"What a lot of high-sounding guff!" muttered Ega.

What did he mean "guff"? It was the plain, horrible truth! Carlos spent his life watching passions flicker out in his hands like matches. For example, when the wife of that colonel of hussars in Vienna failed to turn up for their first rendezvous, he had sobbed his heart out, buried his head in the pillow and kicked and screamed. And yet two weeks later, he had posted Baptista at the hotel window so that he could make his escape as soon as the poor lady rounded the corner! And with the Dutchwoman, Madame Rughel, it had been even worse. During the first few days, it had been utter madness: he was determined to settle in Holland for good and marry her (once she had got her divorce, that is) and other such foolishness; later, the arms she coiled about his neck, and lovely arms they were, seemed to weigh on him like lead.

"You hypocrite! You still write to the woman!" said Ega.

"That's different. We're friends. Ours is a purely intellectual friendship. Madame Rughel is a woman of great spirit. She's even written a novel, one of those delicate studies of inner lives, rather in the style of Rhoda Broughton: it's called *Faded Roses*. Not that I've actually read it, of course, it's in Dutch."

"*Faded Roses* . . . and in Dutch!" groaned Ega, clutching his head.

Then he went over and planted himself in front of Carlos, his monocle fixed in his eye.

"You really are extraordinary! But your case is a perfectly simple one, it's the old Don Juan syndrome. Don Juan experienced those same alternations between fire and ashes. He was looking for his ideal woman, and looking for her principally, and quite rightly too, among the wives of other men. And once he'd slept with a woman, he would declare that he'd been deceived, that she was not the one for him. He would apologise and leave. He had a thousand and three women in Spain alone. You, like him, are simply a libertine and will end up as tragically as he did—in Hell!"

He downed another glass of champagne and, still pacing the room, went on:

"My dear Carlos, there's no point in any man going around looking for his 'ideal woman.' She'll turn up. We all have our 'ideal woman' and we're bound to meet her one day. Here you are in Cruz dos Quatro Caminhos, while she might be in Peking, but while you're here dirtying my best rep with the polish on your shoes and she's over there praying in some Confucian temple, you are both gradually, irresistibly, inevitably moving towards each other! Oh dear, I'm too eloquent for my own good today, and we've both of us talked a great deal of nonsense. It's high time I got dressed. And while I adorn this carcass of mine, you can prepare a few more phrases about Satan!"

Carlos stayed in the green drawing room, finishing his cigar, while, inside, Ega loudly opened and closed drawers, bawling out Gounod's "Barcarolle" at the top of his tuneless nasal voice. When he finally appeared, in white tie and tails, still putting on his overcoat, his eyes were bright with the champagne he had drunk.

They went downstairs. The page was standing to attention at the front door, beside Carlos' waiting coupé. And Ega was delighted at that tableau created right there outside Villa Balzac—the page's little blue jacket with the yellow metal buttons, the magnificent pair of bay horses whose coats gleamed like satin, the silver of the harnesses, and the majestic, fair-haired, liveried coachman with a flower in his lapel.

"Ah, how pleasant life is," he said.

The carriage set off and, as they were about to turn into Largo da Graça, a hired calèche with the hood down trotted at some speed across their path. Inside was a man in a bowler hat, reading a broadsheet newspaper.

"It's Craft!" cried Ega, leaning out of the window.

The coupé stopped. Ega leapt out onto the road and started running after the calèche, shouting:

"Craft! Craft!"

When, a moment later, Carlos heard two voices approaching, he, too, got out of the coupé and found himself face to face with a short fair-haired man with a fresh complexion and a rather cool demeanour. Beneath his very proper evening wear he had the build of an athlete.

"Carlos, Craft," cried Ega, opting for an introduction of classic simplicity.

The two men smiled and shook hands. Ega insisted on them all going back to Villa Balzac to drink another bottle of champagne in order to celebrate "the Coming of the Just!" Craft declined in his calm placid way; he had just arrived the day before from Oporto and now that he had seen the noble Ega, he would take advantage of being in that somewhat far-flung part of Lisbon to visit old Shelgen, a German friend who lived in Penha de França.

"All right!" exclaimed Ega. "But in order to have a proper conversation and for you two to get to know each other, I want you both to come and dine with me tomorrow at the Hotel Central. Agreed? Perfect. At six o'clock then."

Barely had the coupé set off again than Ega began his usual admiring comments about Craft, for he was thrilled by that chance encounter, which added still more lustre to his happiness. What he loved about Craft was his imperturbable air of the perfect gentleman, for with that same air he would play a game of billiards, ride into battle, lay siege to a woman, or set sail for Patagonia.

"He's one of the best things in Lisbon. You'll love him. And you should see his house in Olivais, he has the most wonderful collection of antiques!"

Then he stopped, and with a frown and a worried look in his eyes, said:

"How the devil did he know about Villa Balzac?"

"You don't exactly make a secret of it, do you?"

"No, but I haven't advertised it in the newspapers either! And Craft only arrived yesterday. He can't yet have seen anyone I might know. It's odd."

"In Lisbon everyone knows everything."

"Vile place!" muttered Ega.

The supper at the Hotel Central was postponed because Ega, carried away by his own idea, had decided, instead, to host a special party in honour of Jacob Cohen.

"I dine at the Cohens so often," he said to Carlos. "I'm there every night and I really should repay some of their hospitality. A supper at the Hotel Central is just the thing. And for moral effect, I'll stick him next to the Marquis and that idiot Steinbroken. Cohen appreciates such people."

The plan, however, had to be changed again: the Marquis had left for Golegã, and poor Steinbroken was suffering with his digestion. Ega considered inviting Cruges or Taveira, but feared Cruges' tangled mop of hair as well as his attacks of melancholy which could so easily ruin a supper. He ended up by inviting two close friends of Cohen's, but then was obliged to exclude Taveira, who had recently quarrelled with one of these gentlemen while visiting the house of "Fat Lola."

With the guest list fixed and the supper arranged for a Monday, Ega had a meeting with the *maître d'hôtel* during which he recommended that there should be plenty of flowers, two pineapples as table decorations, and that one of the dishes on the menu, it didn't matter which, should be *à la Cohen*, his own suggestion being *tomates farcies à la Cohen*.

That evening, at six o'clock, as he was walking down Rua do Alecrim to the Hotel Central, Carlos spotted Craft inside Old Abraão's antique shop.

He went in. The old Jew, who was showing Craft a piece of fake faience-ware, immediately doffed his grimy tasselled cap and bowed low to Carlos, his two hands pressed to his heart.

Then, in an exotic mixture of Portuguese and English, he asked "good Senhor Dom Carlos da Maia," "worthy sir," "beautiful gentleman," if he would be so kind as to examine a little marvel he had reserved especially for him; "the most generous gentleman" had only to turn his head, for the little marvel was there beside him on a chair. It was a portrait of a Spanish woman painted with strong, bold brushstrokes, and her face, set against a striking background of faded pink, was that of an old voluptuary, pockmarked and powdered and oozing vice, with a bestial leer that promised everything.

Carlos nonchalantly offered ten *tostões*. Craft was astonished at such prodigality, and Abraão, amused by "the dear gentlemen's little joke," gave a silent chuckle that opened up, above his grizzled beard, a large mouth containing a solitary tooth. Ten *tostões*! If the painting had been signed by Fortuny, it would be worth ten *contos de réis*. But it did not, alas, bear that blessed name. Even so it was easily worth ten twenty-*mil-réis* notes!

"Ten ropes to hang you with, you soulless Jew!" cried Carlos.

And they stalked out of the shop, leaving the old fraud at the door, bowing low, his hands again pressed to his heart, as he wished the generous gentlemen a thousand happinesses.

"Old Abraão hasn't got a single thing worth having," Carlos said.

"Apart from his daughter," said Craft.

Carlos thought her pretty, but horribly dirty. Then, apropos of Abraão, he asked about Craft's own beautiful collection in Olivais, which Ega, despite his declared disdain for all bric-à-brac, had described as sublime.

Craft shrugged.

"Ega doesn't know what he's talking about. Even in Lisbon, what I have certainly doesn't merit the name 'collection.' It's just a few odds and ends I've picked up by chance, and which, by the way, I'm about to get rid of."

This surprised Carlos. He had understood from Ega that the collection had been a labour of love, accumulated over years, the pride and joy of one man's life.

Craft smiled at this legend. The truth was that he had only become interested in collecting in 1872, when he returned from South America; and he had gradually bought various objects here and there and collected them all together in the house in Olivais, which he had rented on a whim, one sunny April morning when that old ruin of a place, with its little garden, had seemed to him picturesque. Now, however, if he could get rid of what he had, he would devote himself to creating a small, homogeneous collection of eighteenth-century art.

"In Olivais?"

"No, in a house I own near Oporto, right on the river."

They were just entering the courtyard outside the Hotel Central, when a hired coupé, driving in at some speed from Rua do Arsenal, stopped at the door.

A splendid black servant in tailcoat and breeches, his hair already grey, immediately ran to open the door; from inside, a very thin young man with a very black beard handed him a delightful little terrier with long tangled hair, soft as silk and silvery-white in colour; then, stepping down from the carriage, indolent and affected, he offered his hand to a very tall fair woman, wearing a thick dark half-veil that only emphasised her splendid ivory skin. Craft and Carlos stepped back, and she passed them with the sovereign step of a goddess of marvellously beautiful proportions, leaving behind her a kind of glow—the reflection perhaps of her golden hair—and a trail of perfume in the air. She was wearing a close-fitting coat of white Genoese velvet and, for a moment, on the stones of the courtyard, they caught a glimpse of her polished bootees. The young man with her, exquisitely turned out in a suit of English check, was languidly opening a telegram; the black servant followed behind, holding the little dog in his arms. And in the silence, Craft's voice murmured:

"*Très chic.*"

Upstairs, a footman ushered them into a room where Ega was waiting, sitting on a morocco leather sofa and talking to a plump, stocky young man with hair as curled as a provincial bridegroom's and wearing a sky-blue shirtfront and a camellia in his buttonhole. Craft knew him already, and Ega introduced him to Carlos as Senhor Dâmaso Salcede, and then ordered vermouth for everyone since it was, he felt, too late for the literary and satanic refinements of absinthe.

It was a warm, bright, winter's day; the two windows still stood open. Above the river, the afternoon was drawing to a close, in an Elysian peace, without a breath of wind, and with small, high, pink-tinged clouds motionless in the broad sky; the fields and distant hills on the other shore were already disappearing beneath a velvety, violet mist; the water lay smooth and polished as a perfect sheet of new steel; and here and there, in the vast port, huge cargo ships, long foreign steamboats, and two English warships were sleeping, their masts utterly still, as if—overwhelmed by idleness—they had surrendered to the caress of that gentle climate.

"We saw the most splendid-looking woman downstairs," said Craft, taking a seat on the sofa, "with an equally splendid little griffon dog and splendid black servant!"

Senhor Dâmaso Salcede, who had not taken his eyes off Carlos, said immediately: "Oh, I know who you mean. Their name's Castro Gomes. I know

109

them well. I travelled with them from Bordeaux. They're a very chic couple who live in Paris."

Carlos turned round to get a better look at him and asked in a friendly, interested tone:

"Have you just arrived from Bordeaux, then?"

These words seemed to cause Dâmaso as much delight as if he had been given a gift from heaven; he immediately sprang to his feet and, beaming, went over to Carlos.

"I got here a fortnight ago on the *Orinoco*. I was travelling back from Paris, which, if I had my way, is where you'd find me most of the time! I met them in Bordeaux, well, on board ship really. But we were all of us staying at the Hôtel de Nantes. Oh, yes, they're very chic indeed, with a valet, an English governess for the little girl, a *femme de chambre*, and more than twenty trunks . . . *Very* chic! Amazing, really, considering that they're Brazilians, although *she* doesn't have a trace of an accent . . . speaks just like you and me, in fact. He, however, has a very strong accent, but he's still frightfully elegant, don't you think?"

"Vermouth?" the waiter asked, proffering the tray.

"Yes, just a drop to get my appetite going. Are you not having any, Senhor Maia? Oh, yes, I'm off to Paris every chance I get. Now that's what I call a city! Lisbon's nothing but a pig-sty in comparison. You may not believe this, but if I can't visit Paris every year, I start to get quite ill. Ah, the boulevards, eh? Oh, I love it. And I know it like the back of my hand. I've even got an uncle who lives there."

"And what an uncle!" exclaimed Ega, coming over. "He's Gambetta's closest friend and practically rules France. Oh, yes, Dâmaso's uncle rules France."

Dâmaso turned scarlet and looked as if he might burst with pleasure.

"He does have influence, it's true, and he is a close friend of Gambetta; why, they even address each other as *"tu,"* and, indeed, spend most of their time together. And he's not just friends with Gambetta either, there's MacMahon and Rochefort too, and that other man whose name escapes me, well, he's friends with all the republicans really. He can get pretty much whatever he asks for. Surely you know him. He's got a white beard. He was my mother's brother, his name's Guimarães, although in Paris, they call him Monsieur Guimaran."

At this point, the glass door was flung open. Ega exclaimed: "Greetings to the poet!"

And a very tall individual appeared, tightly buttoned up in a black frock-coat, gaunt-faced and hollow-eyed, and with a long, thick, romantic, very grizzled moustache beneath his aquiline nose; he was completely bald on top and the fluffy curls of his remaining fringe of hair fell in an inspired tangle upon his collar; there was about his whole person something antiquated, artificial, and lugubrious.

He silently and unenthusiastically shook hands with Dâmaso, then slowly opened his arms to Craft, saying in a drawling, resonant, theatrical voice:

"There you are, my dear Craft! When did you arrive, my friend? Let me embrace those honest bones, you honest Englishman!"

He did not so much as glance at Carlos. Ega went over and introduced them.

"I don't know if you've met. Carlos da Maia ... Tomás de Alencar, our poet."

So it was he—the illustrious bard of *Voices of the Dawn*, the magnificent stylist of *Elvira*, the dramatist of *The Commander's Secret*. He took two grave steps towards Carlos and held his hand clasped in his for a long time, without saying a word, then, much moved, and in a still more resonant voice, said:

"Sir—for social etiquette requires me to address you as 'sir' —you cannot possibly know the identity of the person now clasping your hand."

Surprised, Carlos muttered: "But I know your name very well ..."

And the other man, eyes staring, lips trembling, said:

"I was the companion and inseparable, nay, intimate friend of Pedro da Maia, my poor valiant Pedro!"

"For God's sake, why don't you fall into each other's arms!" yelled Ega. "Fall into each other's arms and weep, as you're supposed to."

Alencar immediately clutched Carlos to his breast, and when he released him, he once more seized Carlos' hands and shook them, saying with boisterous tenderness:

"So let's have no more of this 'sir' business, shall we? Why, I was practically there at your birth, my boy! You often used to sit on my lap and ruined many a pair of trousers too! Damn it, let me embrace you again!"

Craft was observing these vehement expressions of emotion impassively; Dâmaso seemed impressed; and Ega presented the poet with a glass of vermouth.

"What a performance, Alencar! Good grief, man, have a drink to help you recover from all that emotion!"

Alencar drained the glass in one and declared to his friends that this was not the first time he had seen Carlos. As Carlos rode by in his phaeton, he had often admired him and his beautiful English horses, but he had preferred not to make himself known. He never normally flung his arms around anyone, apart from women that is. He poured himself some more vermouth and, with glass in hand, stood before Carlos and said in heartfelt tones:

"The first time I saw you go by, my boy, was in Pote das Almas! I was in Rodrigues' bookshop poring over some of that old and now-despised literature. I can even remember the book, a volume of the *Eclogues* by our own delightful Rodrigues Lobo, that true poet of Nature, that most Portuguese of nightingales, but now of course entirely ignored, ever since the appearance on the scene of Satanism, Naturalism, Vandalism, and all those other piles of dung that end in 'ism.' At just that moment, you passed by; someone told me who you were, and the book fell from my hand. Can you believe it? I stayed there for a whole hour, just thinking and mulling over the past."

And he knocked back his vermouth. Ega looked impatiently at his watch.

A servant came in and lit the gaslights; the table emerged out of the shadows with a glitter of glass and china and a lush explosion of camellias.

Meanwhile, Alencar (who in the bright light seemed older and more worn) had launched into a long story about how he had been the first to see Carlos after he was born and how he had given him his name.

"Your father, my dear friend Pedro, wanted to call you Afonso after that saint, that man from another era, Afonso da Maia! Your mother, though, had her own ideas and insisted that you should be Carlos. And this was all because of a novel *I* had lent her, for those were the days when one could still safely lend novels to ladies, when novels weren't all pustules and pus. It was a novel about the last of the Stuarts, that fine prince, Charles Edward, with whom you, my boys, are all familiar, and who in Scotland, in the time of Louis XIV . . . but I digress! Your mother, I must tell you, knew her literature and only the very best as well. She consulted me, well, she was always consulting me—in those days I was *someone*—and I remember saying to her . . . I can remember it even though twenty-five years have passed since then, no, what am I saying, twenty-seven. Think of that, boys, twenty-seven years! . . . Anyway, I turned to your mother and I said to her these very words: 'Call him Carlos Eduardo, dear lady, Carlos Eduardo, which is a name made for the title page of a book of poems, for an act of great heroism, and fit to grace the lips of a woman!'"

Dâmaso, who was still staring admiringly at Carlos, gave two loud "Bravos," and Craft tapped his fingers lightly together in quiet applause. Ega, who was nervously prowling about by the door, watch in hand, uttered a lacklustre "Hm, excellent."

Thrilled to have made such an impact, Alencar smiled broadly at everyone, revealing his rotten teeth. He embraced Carlos again and then, hand on heart, cried:

"Great God, boys, I can feel a light shining inside me!"

The door opened, and a very flustered Cohen entered, apologising for being so late, while Ega, who rushed towards him, helped him off with his overcoat. Then he introduced him to Carlos, the only person there who was not already Cohen's close friend. Ringing the electric bell for the waiters, he said:

"The Marquis can't come, I'm afraid, and poor Steinbroken's laid up with gout, the gout of the diplomat, the aristocrat, and the banker . . . the gout from which you, too, will no doubt suffer one day, you rascal!"

Cohen, a short, elegantly dressed man with lovely eyes, and side whiskers so black and glossy they looked as if they had been dipped in varnish, was smiling and removing his gloves and saying that, according to the English, the poor also suffered from gout, and that this, naturally, would be the kind of gout that would afflict him.

Ega, meanwhile, had taken him by the arm and placed him deferentially to his right at table; then he offered him a camellia as a boutonniere; Alencar likewise adorned himself with a flower, and the waiters served the oysters.

Talk turned to a murder that had taken place in the Mouraria district of

Lisbon, a low-life drama that had shocked the whole city: a young woman, wearing only her nightdress, had been found dying in the street, after being stabbed in the stomach by another woman; meanwhile, two thugs had been found attacking each other with knives, leaving a whole street virtually running with blood—a "positive massacre" as Cohen said, smiling and taking a sip of his Bucelas wine.

Dâmaso had the satisfaction of being able to supply more details; he had known the young woman, the one who had knifed her friend, when she was the mistress of the Viscount da Ermidinha. Was she pretty? Oh, yes, and she had the hands of a duchess. And she was a wonderful *fado* singer too. The worst thing was that, even when she was with the Viscount and considered to be chic, she had already shown far too great a liking for drink. But the Viscount, to his credit, had remained on friendly terms with her; he respected her, and even after he was married, used to go and visit her, and had promised her that if she relinquished her singing career, he would set her up in a patisserie near the Cathedral. She had declined his offer, alas. She preferred the louche life of Bairro Alto, with its cheap cafés and its pimps.

Carlos thought that the world of *fado* singers and petty criminals merited a proper study, a novel. This led them onto the subject of Zola's *L'Assommoir* and realism; and Alencar, wiping the drops of soup from his moustache, immediately begged them not to discuss such "lavatorial" literature at the supper table. They were all men of taste, were they not, all men of the world, so, please, no mention of "excrement"!

Poor Alencar! Naturalism, and all those potent, lively books of which thousands of copies were printed and sold; those harsh analyses, taking on the Church, Royalty, Bureaucracy, High Finance, and other sacred topics, brutally dissecting them and then displaying the wounds, as if they were corpses in an anatomy class; that new style of writing, sumptuous and sinuous, capturing *in flagrante* the line and colour and the very pulse of life; all of this (which he, in his confusion, termed "the New Idea"), which had burst in upon and despoiled the cathedral of romanticism, where he had for so many years kept an altar and celebrated mass, had disoriented poor Alencar and become the literary bane of his old age. At first, he had fought back. "In order to erect a permanent dyke against the ignoble tide," as he announced to the Academy as a whole; he wrote two scathing pamphlets, which no one read; the "ignoble tide" spread wider and deeper. Then, as if clambering onto a solid rock, Alencar took refuge in "morality." Was Naturalism, with its alluvium of obscenity, threatening to corrupt social modesty? Very well, then; he, Alencar, would be the paladin of Morality, the gendarme of good manners. And so the poet of *Voices of the Dawn*—who, for twenty years, in songs and odes, had made lewd propositions to all the ladies in Lisbon—the author of *Elvira*—who, in novels and plays, had campaigned on behalf of illicit love, representing conjugal duties as mountains of tedium, depicting all husbands as fat and bestial, and endowing all lovers with the beauty, splendour, and genius of Apollo—this same

Tomás Alencar—who (if one were to believe the autobiographical confessions in *Flower of Martyrdom*) had, amidst velvets and Cyprus wines, himself led a wild existence given over to adultery, sensuality, and orgies—became, instead, austere and incorruptible, a monument to modesty, and began to keep a watchful eye on newspapers, books, and theatres. As soon as he so much as glimpsed the incipient symptoms of realism in a rather too lingering kiss or in too prolonged a show of white petticoat, our Alencar would unleash upon the nation a great cry of alarm; he would take up his pen, and his imprecations recalled (at least, to easily pleased academics) the roaring of an Isaiah. One day, however, Alencar had one of those revelations which can lay low even the strongest of men; the more he denounced a book as immoral, the more copies the book sold! The Universe was, it seemed to him, a most unworthy thing, and the author of *Elvira* fell silent.

Since then, he had kept any expression of rancour to a minimum, to this brief phrase, which he would utter with great disgust:

"Friends, please, no mention of 'excrement'!"

On this night, however, he had the pleasure of finding himself among allies. Craft had no time for naturalism either, for the ugly reality of things and for society laid bare in a book. Art meant idealisation! It should show superior examples of a humanity made perfect, and the most refined ways of living and feeling. Ega, horrified, clutched his hands to his head, when, from the other side of the table, Carlos declared that what most offended him about realism were its scientific pretensions, its much-vaunted aesthetic based on someone else's philosophy, and the unnecessary invocation of Claude Bernard, experimentalism, positivism, John Stuart Mill and Darwin, when all the author was doing was describing a laundress going to bed with a carpenter!

Caught between two fires, Ega thundered forth: the trouble with realism was precisely that it wasn't scientific enough, so that it ended up having to invent plots, create dramas, and lose itself in literary fantasy! The pure form of naturalist art should be the monograph, the clear-eyed study of one character, one vice, one passion, just as if it were a pathological case, stripped of all picturesque detail and all style.

"That's absurd," said Carlos, "characters can only be described through their actions."

"And a work of art," added Craft, "lives only through its form."

Alencar interrupted them, exclaiming that all this philosophising was entirely unnecessary.

"You're wasting good candle wax on some very ripe old corpses, my boys. The only way to criticise realism is to hold your nose! Whenever I see one of these books, I immediately douse myself in eau-de-cologne. But, please, let's not argue about 'excrement.'"

"*Sole normande?*" asked the waiter, approaching with the dish.

Ega was about to launch a counter-attack, but seeing Cohen's smile of bored superiority in response to these literary controversies, he said no more, and, instead, lavished all his attention on him, wanting to know what he thought of the St. Emilion wine, and, once Cohen had been served some *sole normande*, Eça asked with a great show of interest:

"So, Cohen, tell us about this government loan. Is it going to happen or not?"

And he aroused everyone else's curiosity by explaining that the matter of the loan was an extremely grave one. A tremendous operation, a truly historic episode!

Cohen placed a pinch of salt on the side of his plate and replied, with aplomb, that the loan absolutely *had* to go ahead. Loans in Portugal nowadays constituted one of the most regular indispensable sources of revenue, as reliable as taxes. The one concern of all ministries was this—"collecting taxes" and "issuing loans." And so it should continue.

Carlos knew nothing about finances, but it seemed to him that, if things carried on like this, the country would soon be heading—skipping and jumping—into bankruptcy.

"Oh, yes, it's heading straight there at a nice little canter," said Cohen, smiling. "No one has any illusions about that, sir, least of all the Treasury. Bankruptcy is inevitable, as sure as two and two make four."

Ega looked shocked. This was no joke. And everyone listened to Cohen. Ega, after refilling Cohen's glass, leaned his elbows on the table the better to drink in his words.

"Bankruptcy is certain, indeed everything is so disposed towards it," Cohen went on, "that it would be easy for anyone, in two or three years' time, to bring the country to its knees."

Ega begged for "the recipe." Simply this: keep up a constant level of revolutionary activity and, on the eve of a loan being issued, get two hundred or so determined ruffians to attack the police in the city, smash a few gas-lamps and shout "Long live the Republic"; then telegraph the news in nice big letters to the newspapers in Paris, London, and Rio de Janeiro, thus frightening the life out of the stock markets *and* the Brazilians; bankruptcy would then be assured, except, of course, as he pointed out, this was in nobody's interest.

Ega then protested vehemently. What did he mean "in nobody's interest"! Honestly! It was in everyone's interest! Bankruptcy would, of course, be followed by revolution. A country that lives on the interest from unpaid loans is bound to get its come-uppance in the end, and whether on principle or out of pure revenge, the first thing to be done would be to eliminate the monarchy, which represents those unpaid loans, and with it the rabble that supports constitutionalism. Then, once the crisis was over, Portugal, free from the old debt and the old personnel, from that grotesque bunch of idiots . . .

Ega's voice was growing shrill. And Cohen, seeing the men of order who ensured that the banks prospered described as a "grotesque bunch of idiots," placed one hand on his friend's arm and tried to make him see sense. He would be the first to agree that there were plenty of mediocrities and fools among the people who had been in power since 1846, after the unseating of Costa Cabral, but there were also men of great value!

"There's talent and there's valuable experience," he said in the tones of one who knows. "You should at least recognise that, Ega. You always take such extreme views. No, I say again, there's talent in abundance and there's experience too."

And remembering that some of those "idiots" were Cohen's friends, Ega acknowledged that some of them did, indeed, have talent and experience. Alencar, however, was soberly smoothing his moustaches. Lately, he had been tending towards more radical ideas, towards the humanitarian democracy of 1848; seeing romanticism discredited in literature, he instinctively sought refuge in political romanticism, as a parallel place of asylum; he wanted a republic ruled by geniuses, a fraternity of all peoples, a United States of Europe. Besides, he had a long list of complaints against these politicos, people who now had Power, but who had once been his comrades on newspapers, in cafés, and at the gaming table.

"Talent and experience?" he said. "Nonsense. I know them, dear Cohen."

Cohen immediately riposted:

"Oh, no, Alencar! Not you too! It ill behoves you to say such things, to espouse such extremist views. No, sir, I insist, there really are some people of talent and experience."

And confronted by this last sally from Cohen—the respected director of the National Bank, the husband of the divine Raquel, the owner of that hospitable house in Rua do Ferregial where one dined so very well—Alencar reined in his spite and admitted that, yes, of course, there were some people of talent and experience.

Then, having obliged these rebellious spirits—through the influence of his bank, his wife's beautiful eyes, and his excellent cook—to show a little respect for parliamentarians and some reverence for Order, Cohen condescended to say, in the softest of voices, that the country did, he agreed, need reform.

Ega, however, was in incorrigible mood that evening, and uttered a further enormity:

"Portugal doesn't need reform, Cohen, Portugal needs Spain to invade it."

Alencar, who was a patriot of the old school, was scandalised. Cohen was smiling the indulgent smile of the superior man, which showed off his nice white teeth; he saw in this remark merely "another of our Ega's paradoxes." But Ega was serious and went on to explain further. Invasion would not, of course, mean a total loss of independence. Such a stupid fear was worthy only of a stupid society like the First of December Club formed to celebrate the restoration of Portuguese sovereignty in 1640. There had never been an example of six million inhabitants being swallowed up in one gulp by a country of only fifteen million. Besides, no one would allow that lovely Portuguese coastline to fall into the hands of a sea-going military nation like Spain. Not to mention the alliances we would gain in exchange for our colonies, colonies which, anyway, only serve to bail us out in times of crisis, like impoverished heirs pawning the family silver. There was no real danger; if there was an invasion during, say, the course of a European war, we would simply get a tremendous beating, have to pay a large sum in reparation and lose a couple of provinces, and perhaps see Galicia extend as far as the Douro River . . .

"*Poulet aux champignons,*" murmured the waiter, holding the dish for him.

And while he was serving himself, the other guests were asking from all sides how "the country's salvation" could be brought about by such a catastrophe, one that would see Celorico de Basto—noble Celorico, the birthplace of heroes and of Ega's own family—become a Spanish town?

"In the revival of a sense of public spirit and of the Portuguese genius! Battered, humiliated, cowed, beaten, we would have to make a desperate effort to survive. And what a wonderful situation we would find ourselves in! With no monarchy, no rabble of politicians, and no ever-mushrooming debts, because it would all have disappeared; we would be brand-new, as clean and fresh as if we had never been used. And a new history would begin, a different Portugal, a serious intelligent Portugal, strong and decent, eager to study and to think and to create a civilisation like the civilisations of old. Gentlemen, there's nothing like an almighty thrashing to regenerate a nation. O, God of Ourique, send us a Castilian! And you, Cohen, pass me the St. Emilion, will you?"

The invasion now became the subject of animated discussion. They could put up a fine resistance army. Cohen would provide the money. They could buy weapons and artillery from South America, and Craft immediately offered the loan of his collection of sixteenth-century swords. But what about generals? They could always hire some. MacMahon, for example, would be cheap enough.

"Craft and I will organise a guerrilla army," cried Ega.

"At your orders, Colonel!"

"Alencar," Ega continued, "is charged with drumming up patriotic feeling in the provinces with songs and odes!"

And the poet, setting down his glass, made a movement like a lion shaking its mane.

"Mine may be an old carcass, my boy, but it's not just fit for writing odes. I can still hold a rifle and I've got a good enough aim to bring down a few Galicians too. But, boys, boys, the mere idea of such things makes my blood run cold. How can you joke about such matters, when what you're talking about is the land where we were born, for God's sake? It may be in a bad state, but, good God, it's the only one we have; we have no other! This is where we live and where we will die. Damnation, let's talk about something else, let's talk about women!"

He had pushed away his plate, his eyes moist with patriotic fervour.

And in the silence that fell, Dâmaso, absorbed as he was in his near-religious contemplation of Carlos, and who had said nothing since his remarks on the events involving the Viscount's former lover, now cautiously spoke up and said with an air of good sense and delicacy:

"If things ever did reach such a pitch, I mean, if things turned really ugly, I'd take no chances, I'd clear off to Paris."

Ega was so pleased with this remark that he bounced up and down in his chair for sheer glee. There they had it, in Dâmaso's own succinct words, the spontaneous, genuine cry of Portuguese valour! To clear off, to scamper—that, from top to bottom, was what Lisbon society, the constitutional hordes, all thought, from his royal highness down to the most cretinous of penpushers!

"I'm telling you, my friends, a Spanish soldier would only have to cross the frontier for the whole country to run like rabbits; there would be a rout such as has never been seen before!"

There were indignant protests, and Alencar bellowed:

"Down with the traitor!"

Cohen intervened and declared that the Portuguese soldier was valiant in the manner of the Turks—undisciplined, but steadfast. Even Carlos said very gravely:

"No, sir, no one would run away; we would die fighting."

Ega demanded to know why they were all putting on this heroic pose. Were they not aware that this race—after fifty years of constitutionalism, brought up in dark mean buildings, educated in lice-ridden schools, riddled with syphilis, mouldering in musty offices, and only given an airing on Sundays in some dusty park—had lost both muscle and character and was the feeblest and most cowardly race in Europe?

"That's Lisbon, of course," said Craft.

"Lisbon *is* Portugal," bawled Ega. "Outside of Lisbon, there's nothing. The area between the ministries in Praça do Comércio and the parliament in São Bento contains the whole country! It's the most miserable race in Europe!"

He ranted on. And what an army! A regiment, after only two days of marching, had to be admitted en masse into a hospital! At the opening of parliament, he had seen with his own eyes how a Swedish sailor, a sturdy lad from northern climes, had put to flight a whole company of Portuguese soldiers with his bare fists; the soldiers had literally fled, with their cartridge belts joggling; the officer in charge had taken refuge up a staircase, vomiting in sheer terror!

Everyone protested. It wasn't possible. But he had seen it himself! Ah, but perhaps he had seen it only with the lying eyes of the imagination.

"I swear it on my own dear mother's health!" cried Ega, furious.

Then he fell silent again. Cohen had touched him on the arm. Cohen was about to speak.

Cohen wanted only to say that the future belonged to God. It seemed to him certain, however, that the Spanish really were considering invasion, especially if, as seemed likely, they lost Cuba. Everyone in Madrid had spoken to him about this. They were even stockpiling supplies.

"Empty boasts!" muttered Alencar, sombrely twirling his moustache.

"In the Hôtel de París in Madrid," Cohen went on, "I met a judge who told me rather proudly that he had not yet lost all hope of moving to Lisbon; he'd taken a great liking to Lisbon when he came here once for the sea-bathing. And I am of the opinion that a large number of Spaniards are only waiting for that territorial expansion in order to come over here and get jobs for themselves!"

Ega fell into a mock swoon and clutched his hands to his chest. What a masterly stroke! How beautifully observed!

"This man Cohen," he exclaimed to those around him, "what a keen eye, eh? What perspicuity! Eh, Craft? Carlos? Delicious!"

Everyone politely admired Cohen's acuteness of mind. He thanked them, eyes shining, and stroked his side whiskers with a hand upon which glittered a single diamond. At that moment, the waiters were serving a dish of peas in white sauce, murmuring:

"Petits pois à la Cohen?"

À la Cohen? Everyone carefully read their menu. And there it was, the vegetable course: Petits pois à la Cohen. Dâmaso enthusiastically declared that this was "very chic." And with the newly opened champagne, they all raised their glasses in the first toast to Cohen!

They had forgotten about bankruptcy, invasion and Portugal, and the supper ended in high spirits. There were more toasts, ardent and loquacious; Cohen himself, with the smile of someone giving in to a child's caprice, drank to the Revolution and to Anarchy—a complicated toast proposed by Ega, whose eyes were, by now, suspiciously bright. The mauled remains of the dessert were scattered about the table. On Alencar's plate, cigarette ends mingled with bits of chewed pineapple. Dâmaso, leaning towards Carlos, was singing the praises of Carlos' English horses and of his phaeton, which was the loveliest thing in all Lisbon. And immediately after his toast to democracy, Ega, for no apparent reason, started attacking Craft, insulting England, saying that it should be excluded from the company of other thinking nations, and predicting a social revolution that would leave it awash with blood. Craft responded imperturbably, nodding his head and cracking nuts.

The waiters served coffee, and since the guests had already spent three long hours at table, they all stood up, stubbing out their cigarettes and talking with the bright animation bestowed on them by the champagne. The room, with its low ceiling and with its five gaslights, had become unbearably hot, and was filled now with the strong smell of chartreuse and other liqueurs that mingled with the white fog of smoke.

Carlos and Craft, who were suffocating in the heat, went out onto the balcony to get some air; and there—for their common interests and tastes were already beginning to form a bond between them—they resumed the conversation they had begun in Rua do Alecrim about Craft's beautiful collection in Olivais. Craft provided more details: his finest piece was a sixteenth-century Dutch cabinet; apart from that, he had a few bronzes, some faience-ware, and a number of good swords.

Both of them, however, turned round when they heard raised voices around the table, as if some sort of conflict had broken out: Alencar was shaking his great mane of hair and fulminating against "philosophical verbiage"; on the other side of the table, with a glass of cognac in one hand, Ega, looking very pale, but affecting a lofty tranquillity, was declaring that the police should be called in to deal with the lyrical flummery that got published nowadays.

"They're arguing again," Dâmaso told Carlos, coming over to the balcony. "It's all to do with Craveiro. They're both in inspired form."

The argument was, in effect, about modern poetry and, in particular, about Simão Craveiro and his poem *The Death of Satan*. Ega had been earnestly reciting some lines from one particular episode in which the great symbolic skeleton walks down the sunny boulevard, dressed as a cocotte in rustling silks:

> *And between two ribs, in her décolletage,*
> *She wore a posy of roses!*

Alencar, who loathed Craveiro—the man behind the "New Idea," the paladin of Realism—delightedly, mockingly, pointed out that in those two lines alone there was some faulty scansion, some dubious grammar and an image stolen from Baudelaire!

Ega, who had downed two glasses of cognac one after the other, then became very provocative and very personal.

"I know why you say that, Alencar," he said. "And it's not out of any noble motive either. It's because of the epigram he wrote about you:

> *O Alencar of Alenquer*
> *Alight with the joys of Spring...*

"Oh, have you never heard it?" he asked, turning to the others. "It's wonderful, one of the best things Craveiro has written. Have you really never heard it, Carlos? It's sublime, especially this verse:

> *O Alencar of Alenquer*
> *What is it that you seek*
> *In the meadowlands so green?*
> *For you consult not the daisy*
> *Nor pluck the marguerite...*
> *For Alencar of Alenquer*
> *Seeks not flowers in the glade,*
> *Only a fair and willing maid!*

"I can't recall the rest, but it ends with a cry of good sense, which is the only appropriate response to all that foolish lyricism:

> O Alencar of Alenquer
> All you really need
> Is to be soundly thrashed
> Each morning and every lovely eve."

Alencar passed one hand over his deathly pale brow, and with his hollow eyes fixed on Ega, said, in a slow, hoarse voice:

"Let me tell you something, João da Ega, that feeble man's epigrams and silly jokes, and those written by the people who admire him, wash past my feet like so much sewage in a gutter. All I do is roll up my trouser legs. Yes, I roll up my trouser legs, that's what I do, friend Ega. I roll up my trouser legs!"

And he really did roll them up, in a mad delirious gesture, revealing his long underwear.

"Well, next time you come across one of those streams of sewage in the gutter," Ega yelled back at him, "make a point of crouching down and drinking some of it. It might lend a bit of energy and blood to that lyricism of yours!"

Alencar, however, was not listening, he was berating the others and punching the air with his fist.

"If that Craveiro wasn't such a weed, I might amuse myself by kicking him down the street, him and all his pathetic poems, and the excremental nonsense with which he doused poor Satan! And then, after coating him with mud, I would smash his skull in!"

"Skulls aren't that easily smashed," said Ega in a coolly mocking tone.

Alencar turned to him with a terrible look on his face. His eyes were inflamed with rage and cognac; he was trembling all over.

"Oh, yes, I would, João da Ega, I would smash his skull in! I would smash it to smithereens, like this, see, like this!" And he began stamping hard on the floor, shaking the room and making the glasses and the crockery tinkle. "But I prefer not to, my friends. Inside that skull is nothing but excrement, vomit, pus, and green slime, and if I smashed it, because I would, my friends, then all that putrid matter would spill out and infect the whole city, and we'd have cholera, damn it, we'd have the plague!"

Seeing him so worked up, Carlos took his arm to try and calm him down.

"Come on, Alencar, don't be silly. It's not worth it."

Alencar pulled away, panting and unbuttoning his frock-coat, then unleashed one last insult:

"You're right, what's the point in anyone getting angry over Craveiro and his 'New Idea,' when the rascal conveniently forgets that his dirty little sister is a twopenny-halfpenny whore in Marco de Canaveses!"

"That's going too far, you swine," cried Ega, hurling himself on him, fists clenched.

Frightened now, Cohen and Dâmaso grabbed hold of him. Carlos dragged a struggling Alencar over to the safety of the window, where the poet stood, eyes blazing, cravat awry. A chair had fallen over, and the very neat room, with its morocco leather sofas and its camellias was taking on the appearance of a tavern, in which some good-for-nothings were brawling in a cloud of cigarette smoke. Dâmaso, looking very pale, his voice almost gone, kept going from one to the other, saying:

"Gentlemen, really, here in the Hotel Central of all places, the Hotel Central!"

And from Cohen's arms, Ega was shouting hoarsely:

"The swine, the coward! Let me at him, Cohen! He really deserves a beating for that . . . I mean, Dona Ana Craveiro is a saint! The vile slanderer! I'll throttle him!"

Craft, meanwhile, was impassively sipping his chartreuse. He had witnessed other such wrestling matches between rival literatures, which ended with people rolling around on the ground and hurling insults at each other; Alencar's crude comment about Craveiro's sister was merely a standard item in Portugal's repertoire of insults; it left him utterly cold, and he observed it all with a scornful smile. Besides, he knew that a heart-felt reconciliation, with each man embracing the other, would not be long in coming. And so it was. Carlos left the window, and Alencar followed him, hastily buttoning up his frock-coat and looking grave-faced and somewhat sheepish. In one corner of the room, Cohen was speaking in a stern fatherly manner to Ega; then he turned and, raising his hand and his voice, announced that they were all gentlemen there and, as men of talent and of noble heart, the two should embrace.

"Shake the man's hand, Ega, for my sake. Come on, Alencar, do it for me!"

The author of Elvira took a step forward, and the author of Memoirs of an Atom held out his hand; but the first handshake was clumsy and unconvincing. Then Alencar, frank and generous, declared that he wanted nothing to cloud his friendship with Ega. He had gone too far. It was, alas, his hot-blooded nature, which had brought him nothing but grief throughout his life! And he stated out loud, there and then, that Dona Ana Craveiro was a saint. He had met her in Marco de Canaveses, at the Peixotos' house. Dona Ana Craveiro was an impeccable wife and mother. And he acknowledged, from the bottom of his heart, that Craveiro had enormous talent!

He filled a glass with champagne and held it up before Ega, as if it were a chalice before an altar, and said:

"Your health, João!"

Ega responded equally generously:

"Your health, Tomás!"

They embraced. Alencar swore that only the previous evening, at Dona Joaninha Coutinho's house, he had declared that he knew no more dazzling mind than Ega's. Ega averred that no other poems had the lovely lyric vein found in Alencar's work. They embraced once more, clapping each other on the back. They referred to each other as "brothers in art," they spoke of each other as "geniuses."

"Aren't they extraordinary?" Craft said to Carlos in a low voice, then he looked around for his hat. "I find them quite troubling really. I need some fresh air!"

It was getting late, gone eleven o'clock. Still more cognac was drunk. Then Cohen left, taking Ega with him. Dâmaso and Alencar went downstairs with Carlos, who was going to walk home via the Aterro.

At the door of the hotel, the poet paused solemnly for a moment.

"What do you think, boys?" he exclaimed, taking off his hat and fanning his face. "Did I or did I not behave like a gentleman?"

Carlos agreed that he had, indeed, behaved like a gentleman and praised his generosity.

"I can't tell you how much I appreciate you saying that, my boy, because you know what it means to be a gentleman! Off we go to the Aterro then, but first, I must buy some cigars."

"What a strange man!" exclaimed Dâmaso, watching Alencar move off. "Things were getting really ugly in there."

And then immediately, without transition, he began singing Carlos' praises. Carlos could have no idea for how long Dâmaso had wanted to make his acquaintance!

"Oh, please . . ."

"No, it's true. I'm not one for flattery. You can ask Ega. The times I've said to him: 'Carlos da Maia is Lisbon's finest!'"

Carlos looked down, biting back his laughter. Dâmaso said again in earnest tones:

"I mean it, Senhor Maia! I speak as I feel!"

He really did mean it. Ever since Carlos had been living in Lisbon, he had, all unknowing, been the object of that plump, chubby-cheeked young man's profound, unspoken adoration; even the polish on his shoes and the colour of his gloves were, for Dâmaso, reasons to venerate him, as important as any moral principles. He considered Carlos to be the epitome of chic—his beloved chic—a Beau Brummel, a Count d'Orsay, a Duc de Morny, "the kind of marvellous thing one sees only outside of Portugal," as he put it, wide-eyed. That evening, knowing that he would be having supper with Carlos, that he would actually meet Carlos, he had spent two hours in front of the mirror trying on different cravats, and had perfumed himself as if for a rendezvous with a woman, and because of Carlos, he had ordered his coupé to be stationed outside at ten o'clock, with his coachman wearing a flower in his buttonhole.

"So that Brazilian lady is staying here, is she?" asked Carlos, who had taken two steps back to look up at a lighted window on the second floor.

Dâmaso followed his gaze.

"No, she's staying on the other side. They've been here for two weeks now.

They're both of them *very* chic. And she, as you may have noticed, is a very tasty morsel indeed. I made some advances while we were on board ship, and I could tell she liked me! But I've been so terribly busy since I arrived, a supper here, a soirée there, a few little amours, I haven't really had time to visit and so I've merely left my card; but now that it looks as if they're going to stay, I'll certainly be keeping my eye on her. In fact, I might drop by tomorrow. I've got that little tingle down the spine that tells me the time is right ... And if I find myself alone with her, I won't hesitate to plant a kiss on her! Because in my view, I don't know if you would agree, sir, but when it comes to women, my motto is: attack, attack!"

At this point, Alencar returned from his errand, a cigar in his mouth. Dâmaso said his goodbyes, announcing very loudly to his driver, so that Carlos would hear, that he wanted to be taken to Morelli's house, Morelli being the female understudy at the Teatro de São Carlos.

"He's a good fellow, that Dâmaso," Alencar was saying, taking Carlos' arm as they walked along the Aterro. "He's a great friend of the Cohens, and well-liked in society. He's got money too. He's the son of old Silva, the moneylender, who thoroughly fleeced your father, and me too. But he signs himself Salcede now, which may be his mother's name, or else invented. But he's a good lad nonetheless. His father was a real rogue though. I can hear Pedro now saying to him with that noble air of his: 'Silva, you old Jew, I want money and plenty of it!' Oh, they were great days, Carlos, great days, when men were men!"

And as they walked along the dark and gloomy Aterro, with the dim lights from the gas-lamps forming a long funereal line, Alencar talked about the "great days" of his youth and of Pedro's youth; and, as he listened to his lyrical words, Carlos sensed something like a faint, antique perfume emanating from that long-dead world. It was a time when young men still had a little fire in their blood from the various civil wars, a fire they tried to quell by wrecking bars and driving poor tired old coach-horses nearly into the ground on wild rides out to Sintra. For Sintra then was one great bower of love, beneath whose romantic boughs noblewomen would succumb to the embraces of poets. The women were all Elviras, the men all Antonis. There was money in abundance; the court was a joyous place; the witty, literary Regeneration would, they believed, have an ennobling effect on the country as a whole and transform it into the garden of Europe; graduates arrived from Coimbra full of fiery eloquence; ministers of the Crown gave piano recitals; and the same lyric breath filled odes and government bills.

"Lisbon sounds like a far more amusing place than it is now," said Carlos.

"Oh, it was completely different, my boy! You could live then! There was none of this scientific bunk, none of this philosophical verbiage, none of these positivist nonentities that you get nowadays. We had heart, we had spark! Even in the world of politics. I mean, look at the piggery we have now, look at that gaggle of mediocrities. In those days, you would go to the parliament building and feel a buzz of inspiration, of energy! There was a bright light shining in those minds! And then, of course, there were dozens of the most beautiful women . . ."

His shoulders drooped at the thought of that lost world. And he seemed suddenly sadder, with his tangled poet's hair sticking out from beneath the broad brim of his old hat, his worn, ill-fitting frock-coat clinging inelegantly to his ribs.

They walked for a while in silence. Then, in Rua das Janelas Verdes, Alencar wanted to pause to "refresh himself." They went into a small tavern, where the yellow stain of light from an oil-lamp stood out in the subterranean gloom, il-luminating the damp zinc surface of the bar, the bottles on the shelves, and the glum figure of the woman in charge, a scarf tied firmly around her jaw. Alen-car appeared to be a regular customer, for as soon as he learned that Senhora Cândida was suffering from toothache, he descended at once from the roman-tic heights and, in familiar fashion, his elbows resting on the bar, suggested various sovereign remedies. And when Carlos offered to pay for their drinks, Alencar grew angry and slammed down his two-*tostão* coin on the polished zinc, exclaiming nobly:

"I do the honours in the inn, my dear Carlos! Let others pay in palaces, but here in the tavern, it is I who pay!"

At the door, he took Carlos' arm. Then, after they had taken a few slow steps in silence, he stopped again and murmured in a vague, contemplative voice, a voice imbued with the vast solemnity of the night:

"That Raquel Cohen woman is divinely beautiful, my boy! Do you know her?"

"Only by sight."

"Doesn't she remind you of a woman in the Bible? I don't mean one of those viragos, Judith or Delilah, but one of those poetic lilies of the Bible . . . she's positively seraphic!"

She was Alencar's platonic passion, his lady, his Beatrice.

"Did you see the poem I wrote for her, a while ago now, in the *Diário Nacional*?

> *April is here! Be mine!*
> *Said the wind to the rose.*

"Not bad, eh? There's just a suggestion of mischief in that 'April is here! Be mine!' but it's immediately defused, do you see, by 'Said the wind to the rose.' Very clever, I think. But don't go imagining things, don't go thinking I'm set-ting my cap at her. It's enough that she's Cohen's wife, the wife of a friend, a brother. As far as I'm concerned, Raquel, poor love, is like a sister. Oh, but she is divine! Those eyes, my boy, like liquid velvet!"

He took off his hat and fanned his vast forehead with it. Then in a different, rather constrained tone of voice, he added:

"That fellow Ega is a very talented chap. He spends a lot of time at the Co-hens'. Raquel finds him amusing."

Carlos had stopped walking; they were outside Ramalhete. Alencar studied its stern, sleeping, convent-like façade, with not a point of light visible.

"It has a very good feel about it, your house. You go in, my boy; I'll walk on to my own little lair. And whenever you care to, my boy, you'll find me there in 52 Rua do Carvalho, third floor. The building is mine, but I only occupy the third floor. I started out on the first floor, but I've gone up in the world since then. It's the only place, mind, where I *have* gone up in the world."

He made a gesture, as if brushing aside such misfortunes.

"You must come and have supper with me one day. I can't promise you a banquet, but some good soup and a bit of roast meat. When it comes to cooking, my Mateus, a black fellow (and a friend!) who has served me for years now, really knows what he's doing. He cooked many a supper for your father, for my poor Pedro. It was a very happy household then, my boy. I gave bed and board and money to a lot of these rogues I now see go riding by in their hired carriages with a messenger boy behind. But now, when they see me, they turn up their snouts."

"That's just your imagination," said Carlos warmly.

"No, it's not, Carlos," replied the poet gravely, bitterly. "It's not. You know nothing of my life. I have suffered many rebuffs, my boy. And I did not deserve them. My word of honour, I did not deserve them."

He grasped Carlos' arm and said urgently:

"These men you see strutting about nowadays used to get drunk with me. I've lent them money, fed them . . . And now they're ministers, ambassadors, important people, the very Devil. Would they offer you a little piece of the cake they have in their hand? No. Not even to me. And that's hard, Carlos, very hard. It's not as if I wanted them to make me a Count or to give me an embassy somewhere, just a minor job in some ministry office. But not a thing! Anyway, for the moment, I still have enough to buy a little bread and half an ounce of tobacco. That ingratitude of theirs, though, has given me a few white hairs, I can tell you. But I don't want to bore you any further, may God make you as happy as you deserve to be, dear Carlos!"

"Would you like to come in for a moment, Alencar?"

Such generosity touched the poet.

"Thank you, my boy," he said, embracing Carlos. "Thank you very much, because I know that offer comes from the heart. You Maias have always had a lot of heart. Your father did too, a heart as big as a lion's! I want you to know something: you have a true friend in me. These are not mere empty words, either; they, too, come from the heart. Goodnight, my boy. Would you care for a cigar?"

Carlos accepted with alacrity, as if it were a gift from Heaven.

"Then, dear boy, you shall *have* a cigar!" exclaimed Alencar with enthusiasm.

And that cigar given to such a wealthy man, to the owner of Ramalhete, made him, for a moment, return to the days in the Café Marrare when he would hand round his cigar-box with the grand, melancholy air of that Byronic hero Manfred. He enquired as to the quality of the cigar. He himself lit a match. He made sure the cigar was properly alight. Was it a decent cigar? Carlos thought it excellent.

"Well, at least I've given you a good cigar!"

He embraced Carlos once more, and it was striking one o'clock when he, at last, moved off, with a lighter step now, feeling happier with himself, and humming a *fado*.

Up in his room, before going to bed, and while Baptista prepared him some tea, Carlos lay down on a chaise longue, finishing the ghastly cigar Alencar had given him and pondering the strange past summoned up by the old lyric poet.

Poor Alencar was a decent sort. When speaking to him of Pedro, Arroios, and of their friends and lovers of the time, what enormous care he had taken to avoid so much as a mention of the name "Maria Monforte"! More than once, as they walked along the Aterro, he had been on the point of saying: "It's all right, Alencar, you can talk about my mother. I know perfectly well that she ran off with an Italian!"

And his thoughts slowly returned to the almost grotesque way in which he had first found out about the whole sad story, one drunken night in Coimbra. For his grandfather, in keeping with Pedro's last letter, had given him only an expurgated version of the story: a marriage of passion, incompatibilities of character, an amicable separation, the departure of mother and daughter to France, where both had died. Nothing more. And the death of his father had always been presented to him as the sudden climax of a long period of mental instability.

But Ega knew all about it from his uncles. One night, he and Carlos had dined together; Ega was very drunk, and in an access of idealism, he had come up with one of his vast paradoxes, stating that the decadence of the races had its origin in women's chastity, and offering as evidence various bastard sons who were invariably intelligent, brave, and glorious. He, Ega, would be proud if his mother, his own mother, instead of being the devout bourgeois woman she was, saying her rosary by the fireside, had been like Carlos' mother, a free spirit, who for the love of an exile had sacrificed fortune, respect, honour, life! When Carlos heard this, he froze, there in the middle of the bridge, beneath the calm moonlight. But he could not question Ega further, because Ega, by then, was babbling unintelligibly, in the grip of nausea, and was soon in Carlos' arms vomiting copiously. Carlos had to help him back to the house of the Seixas sisters, undress him, endure his tender kisses and his drunken sentimentality, and leave him hugging his pillow, dribbling and muttering that he wished he were a bastard and his mother a strumpet!

Carlos, on the other hand, barely slept all night, tormented by the idea of that mother so different from the one described to him, a woman who had fled into the arms of an exile—who knows, possibly a Pole! Early the next morning, he went into Ega's room to ask him, as an act of friendship, to tell him the whole truth.

Poor Ega! He was feeling dreadful and looking as white as the handkerchief he had tied about his head along with bandages soaked in some sedative solution, and he could not utter a word, poor thing! Carlos sat on the bed, as he had on other occasions when they had talked late into the night, and tried to reassure him. He was not offended, he simply wanted to know the truth. The extraordinary facts about his own parents had been kept from him, damn it, and he wanted to know what they were. There was a story to be told, so let him hear it!

Ega rallied then and stammered out what he knew—what his uncle had told him—about Maria's love for a prince, their elopement together, and the long years of silence that had subsequently surrounded her.

As it happened, the university vacation was just about to start. As soon as he arrived in Santa Olávia, he told his grandfather about Ega's drunkenness, about his wild assertions, about what, between belches, had been revealed to him. His poor grandfather! For a moment, he couldn't even speak, and when he did his voice was as weak and faint as if his heart were dying in his breast. But, detail by detail, he told him the whole wretched tale up until the afternoon when Pedro had come to him, deathly pale and covered in mud, and had fallen into his arms, sobbing his heart out like a little child. And the conclusion of that guilty love, his grandfather had said, had been the death of his mother in Vienna and the death of the little girl, the granddaughter he had never seen, and whom Maria Monforte had carried off with her. And that was all. That domestic shame was now dead and buried, there, in the tomb in Santa Olávia, and in two other distant graves, in some foreign land.

Carlos remembered clearly how, after that melancholy conversation with his grandfather, he had spent the afternoon trying out a new English mare, and how at supper, they had talked only of the mare, whose name was Sultana. And the truth is that, a few days later, he had forgotten about his mother, and he could feel for that tragedy only a vague, almost literary interest. It had all taken place twenty or so years before, in a now more or less vanished world. It was like an historical episode from some old family chronicle, about an ancestor who was killed in the battle of Alcácer-Quibir or a grandmother who had slept in the royal bed. It neither made him weep nor blush. Obviously, he would prefer to feel proud of his mother, as one might of a rare and noble flower of honour, but he could not spend his entire life feeling embittered because of her mistakes; his honour did not depend on the misguided or foolish impulses of her heart. She had sinned and she had died, and that was that. What remained was the image of his father, dying in a pool of blood, in despair at that betrayal. But he had not known his father either; all that remained for him to love of his father and his father's memory was a cold, rather clumsily painted portrait that hung in his dressing-room and which depicted an olive-skinned youth

128

with large eyes, wearing a pair of yellow kidskin gloves and carrying a walking stick. Of his mother, he did not possess so much as a daguerrotype, or even a pencil sketch. His grandfather had told him that she was fair-haired. He knew nothing more. He had not known them; he had not fallen asleep in their arms; he had never received the warmth of their affection. Father and mother were, for him, like the symbols of some conventional religion. Father, mother, and loved ones were all contained in his grandfather.

Baptista had brought him his tea, and he had by now finished Alencar's cigar, but he continued lying on the chaise longue, as if drained of energy by those memories and surrendering now, in a half-sleep, to the fatigue brought on by that long supper. And then, little by little, behind his closed eyelids, a vision arose, took on colour and filled the whole room. The evening was drawing to a close over the river, in a scene of Elysian peace. He could see the broad forecourt of the Hotel Central, where it was still light. A grizzled black manservant was approaching, holding a small dog. A woman was passing, a tall woman with ivory skin, as beautiful as a goddess, wearing a coat made of white Genoese velvet. Next to him, Craft was saying: "*Très chic.*" And he was smiling at the pleasure these images brought him, taking on the shape, the undulating line, and colour of living things.

It was three o'clock by the time he went to bed. And barely had he fallen asleep in the darkness of the silk curtains than another lovely, windless winter's day was drawing to a close, bathed in pink light; the banal hotel forecourt lay before him, still lit by the afternoon sun; the black manservant was there again, carrying the little dog; a woman was passing, wearing a coat made of white Genoese velvet, but she was taller than any human creature, walking upon clouds, with the magnificent air of a Juno mounting up to Olympus; the tips of her gleaming shoes were lost in the blue light, and, behind her, her skirts flapped like flags in the wind. And she kept passing. Craft was saying: "*Très chic.*" Then everything grew confused and there was only Alencar, an Alencar of colossal dimensions, filling the whole sky, obscuring the brilliance of the stars with his black, ill-fitting frock-coat, his moustache fluttering in the whirlwind of passions, as, lifting up his arms, he declared to the void:

April is here! Be mine!

: VII :

IN RAMALHETE, AFTER LUNCH, with the three windows in the study standing open to drink in the warm light of the splendid March day, Afonso da Maia and Craft were playing a game of chess beside the fireplace where no fire now burned, for it was filled instead with potted plants, which gave it the fresh, festive appearance of a domestic altar. On the carpet, in an oblique ray of sunlight, the Reverend Boniface, vast and soft, was quietly taking his siesta.

In a matter of weeks, Craft had become a regular visitor to Ramalhete. Sharing, as they did, similar tastes and ideas, the same enthusiasm for bric-à-brac and antiques, the same passion for fencing, the same spiritual dilettantism, Carlos and he had immediately formed a superficial bond, easy and amicable. Afonso, for his part, had instantly felt the highest esteem for this gentleman from a good English family, the kind of Englishman he so admired—cultivated and physically strong, with a serious demeanour and strict habits, delicate in feeling and correct in thought. They had discovered a mutual interest in Tacitus, Macaulay, and Burke, and even the Lake Poets; Craft was a master at chess; during his many long and arduous journeys his character had acquired the rich solidity of bronze; he was, in Afonso's eyes, "a real man." Craft was an early riser and would leave Olivais on horseback and sometimes surprise the Maias by turning up for lunch, and, if Afonso had had his way, Craft would have dined with them every day as well, and he did almost invariably spend his evenings at Ramalhete, having at last found in Lisbon, as he put it, a place where one could converse in a civilised fashion, comfortably seated and surrounded by ideas.

Carlos rarely left the house. He was working on his book. The flurry of patients, which had given him such hopes of having a busy active career, had dwindled miserably away; all that remained were three patients who lived locally; and he felt now that his carriages, his horses, Ramalhete, and his luxurious tastes, all condemned him irremediably to the life of a dilettante. The keen-eyed Dr. Teodósio had one day said to him quite frankly: "You're too elegant to be a doctor! What female patient could resist flirting with you! And what good bourgeois gentleman is going to trust you with his wife in her bedroom? You would terrify any paterfamilias!" Even the laboratory worked to his disadvantage. His colleagues put it about that Maia, rich, intelligent, and hungry for innovation and modern methods, was carrying out fatal experiments on his patients. His article, published in the *Gazeta Médica*, suggesting that epidemics could be prevented by innoculating patients with the viruses themselves was greeted with derision. They considered him a fantasist. And so he took refuge in his book on medicine ancient and modern, on which he worked in the leisurely manner of a wealthy artist, and which he intended to make the main focus of his intellectual interests for one or two years.

That morning, while, indoors, the game of chess continued in grave silence, out on the terrace, in the shade of an awning, Carlos was sitting sprawled in a vast Indian bamboo chair, finishing his cigar, reading an English magazine, and enjoying the warm caress of the spring breeze which turned the air to velvet and made one yearn for trees and grass.

Beside him, in another bamboo chair, and also smoking a cigar, was Senhor Dâmaso Salcede who was leafing through *Le Figaro*. Legs outstretched, in a posture of familiar indolence, with his friend Carlos by his side, with Afonso's roses before him, and conscious that behind him, through the open windows, lay the rich and noble interior of Ramalhete, the usurer's son was savouring one of the many delicious hours he had recently spent at home with the Maias.

The morning after the supper at the Hotel Central, Senhor Salcede had gone to Ramalhete to leave his cards; these were complicated, showy affairs, with, in one corner, which simulated a turned-down page, a tiny photograph of himself; above his name—DÂMASO CÂNDIDO DE SALCEDE— there was a feathered helmet and beneath his name, his title—COMMANDER OF CHRIST, and at the bottom, his address—Rua de S. Domingos, à Lapa, except that this had been crossed out, and written beside it, in blue ink, was a far more imposing address—GRAND HÔTEL, BOULEVARD DES CAPU- CINES, CHAMBRE NO. 103. He also immediately sought Carlos out in his consulting room and entrusted a card to the servant there. Finally, one afternoon in the Aterro, seeing Carlos walking by, he had pursued him, attached himself to him and managed to accompany him back to Ramalhete.

From the moment they entered the courtyard, he was full of ecstatic exclamations, as if he were visiting a museum, and regardless of whether he was looking at a carpet, a piece of pottery or a painting, he would respond with his favourite expression—"*Very* chic!" Carlos led him into the smoking room, where he accepted a cigar and then, legs nonchalantly crossed, began regaling him with various of his opinions and tastes. He considered Lisbon a paltry place and only really felt at ease in Paris, especially given the absolute dearth of decent female specimens in Lisbon, although Providence had, in fact, been not ungenerous to him in that respect. He, like Carlos, adored bric-à-brac, but there were an awful lot of fakes about, and antique chairs, for example, were most uncomfortable to sit on. He enjoyed reading, and would never be found without a pile of books on his bedside table; lately, he had been working on Daudet, who was apparently terribly chic, but he found him, frankly, rather confusing. As a young man, he used to stay up until four or five in the morning—absolute madness! Now, however, he was a changed man and liked a quiet life, which was not to say, of course, that he didn't occasionally indulge in a little excess, but only on special occasions. He also posed Carlos extremely difficult questions. Did Senhor Maia consider it chic to have an English carriage? Which was more elegant for a young man wanting to spend the summer abroad, Nice or Trouville? When he left, he asked very seriously, very intensely, for the name of Senhor Maia's tailor (always assuming that Senhor Maia did not make a secret of this).

And since that day, he had barely left Carlos' side. If Carlos went to the theatre, Dâmaso would immediately get up from his seat, sometimes right in the middle of some lovely solemn aria, and, stepping on gentlemen's boots and crumpling ladies' dresses, would hurry off, opening his crush-hat with a thwack, to install himself, cheeks flushed, a camellia in his buttonhole, and displaying two enormous ball-shaped cufflinks, beside Carlos in his box. On the one or two occasions when Carlos happened to visit the Grémio, Dâmaso, deaf to the protests of his partners, had immediately abandoned his card game and glued himself to Carlos' side, offering him a glass of maraschino or a cigar, and then following him from room to room like a sheepdog. On one such occasion, Carlos happened to make a trivial joke, and Dâmaso had almost wept with laughter, rolling about on the sofas, clutching his sides, shrieking that he was ready to die laughing. Other members had gathered round, and Dâmaso had repeated the jest to them. Carlos had fled, furious. He came to hate Dâmaso; he responded to him only in monosyllables; he performed dangerous turns in his dog-cart if he caught so much as a distant glimpse of Dâmaso's plump cheeks or roly-poly thigh. All in vain: Dâmaso Cândido de Salcede had got his teeth into him and would not let go.

Then, one day, Taveira turned up at Ramalhete with an extraordinary story to tell. The previous evening, at the Grémio (he had been told this, and had not witnessed it himself), a man, Gomes by name (but no relation to Castro Gomes), who was one of a group of men discussing the Maia family, said in a loud voice that Carlos was an ass! Dâmaso, who was next to him, immersed in reading a magazine, got up, looking very pale, and declared that, since he had the honour to be a friend of Senhor Carlos da Maia, he would smash Senhor Gomes' face in with his walking stick if he ever dared besmirch that gentleman's name again; and Gomes—being a born coward, as well as one of Dâmaso's tenants and very behind with the rent—swallowed this affront with downcast eyes. Afonso da Maia thought this was a wonderful thing to have done, and it was at his request that Carlos had invited Senhor Salcede to dine at Ramalhete.

That had been a quite exquisite day for Dâmaso, an utterly perfect day. Even better, though, was the morning when Carlos, slightly embarrassed and still in bed, had received him in his bedroom, as if they were close friends. Their intimacy dated from that moment; Dâmaso began calling Carlos by his first name. And that same week, he revealed certain useful skills. He went on Carlos' behalf to clear a parcel of clothes through Customs (Vilaça was away in the Alentejo). Then, one day, he arrived when Carlos was copying out an article for the *Gazeta Médica* and offered to do this himself in his own prodigiously fine hand, which was of near lithographic perfection; and from then on, he would spend hours at Carlos' desk, industrious and red-faced, with the tip of his tongue sticking out and his eyes round with concentration, copying out notes, transcribing articles from magazines or other material for the book. Such devotion deserved a more familiar form of address, and Carlos duly began to call him "*tu.*"

Dâmaso, meanwhile, imitated Carlos, showing an anxious attention to detail—from his beard, which he was now beginning to grow, to the style of shoe he wore. He threw himself into collecting antiques. His coupé was always full of archaeological detritus, rusty metal fittings, bits of old brick or tile, the broken handle from a teapot. And if he saw an acquaintance, he would have his driver stop, and would then open the carriage door just a chink—as if allowing privileged access to a tabernacle—and display his treasures.

"What do you think of that? *Very* chic, eh? I'm going to show it to Maia. And look at this! Pure Middle Ages, from the time of Louis XIV. Carlos will be green with envy!"

Life in this bed of roses, however, was not without its longueurs. It was not at all amusing to sit in silence, in an armchair, listening to the endless discussions between Carlos and Craft on art and science. And as he confessed later, he did feel slightly put out when they took him to the laboratory to perform electrical experiments on his body. "They held me down like two demons," he told the Countess de Gouvarinho, "and I've always hated any kind of spiritualism!"

But all of this was more than compensated for when, at night, sitting on a sofa in the Grémio or over tea at a friend's house, he could casually smooth his hair and say:

"I've just spent the most divine day with Maia. We did some fencing, looked for antiques, talked . . . A really *chic* day! Tomorrow I'm doing some work with Maia. We're going to look at bedspreads."

That Sunday, in fact, they were due to go and look at some bedspreads in Lumiar. Carlos had an idea for a boudoir furnished with antique satin bedspreads, embroidered in two particular shades, pearl and soft gold. Old Abraão had been scouring the whole of Lisbon and beyond, and, that morning, had come to Carlos to tell him of two superb finds, "so beautiful, so lovely," in the house of two ladies, Medeiros by name, who were expecting Senhor Maia at two o'clock.

Dâmaso had already coughed three times and ostentatiously looked at his watch, but seeing Carlos comfortably immersed in his magazine, he, too, fell back into a chic, indolent pose, poring over *Le Figaro*. Finally, inside, the Louis XV clock struck two silvery notes.

"Well, what do you think!" exclaimed Dâmaso, slapping his thigh. "Look who's here. Susana, *my* Susana!"

Carlos kept his eyes fixed on the page he was reading.

"Carlos," Dâmaso said, "just listen to this. It's absolutely priceless. This Susana is a girl I knew in Paris. A real romance, it was! She fell in love with me, even tried to poison herself because of me, dreadful really! Well, it says here in *Le Figaro* that she's just made her debut at the Folies Bergères. There's an article about her. Interesting, eh? She was *terribly* chic. They mention here that she had a few affairs, and, of course, they know all about what happened with me. I mean, the whole of Paris knew. Susana, eh! She certainly had damn good legs. But I had the devil's own job getting rid of her!"

"Women!" muttered Carlos, burying himself further in his magazine.

Dâmaso was interminable, torrential, inundatory, when it came to talking about his "conquests," in the firm self-satisfied belief that all women, poor things, were under the spell both of his personality and his dress sense. And in Lisbon, this was, in fact, true. He was rich, well-respected, with a coupé and horses, and so, naturally, all the girls made eyes at him. And in the *demi-monde*, he enjoyed, as he put it, "tremendous prestige." Ever since he was a young man, he had been famous in Lisbon for setting up Spanish women in their own apartments; he had even provided one with a carriage hired out by the month; and this exceptional prodigality had rapidly made him the King João V of the whorehouse. Everyone knew, too, about his relationship with the Viscountess da Gafanha, a scrawny carcass of a woman, powdered and painted, who had been had by every healthy man in the country; she was fifty when Dâmaso's turn came around, and it could not have been much of a pleasure to hold that creaking, lubricious skeleton in his arms, but it was said that, as a young woman, she had graced a royal bed, and that august moustaches had brushed her lips; such high connections fascinated Dâmaso, and he clung to her skirts with such dog-like fidelity that the decrepit creature grew thoroughly sick of him and had to shoo him away by dint of physical force and insults. Then, to his delight, tragedy struck: an actress at the Teatro do Príncipe Real, a veritable mountain of flesh, had fallen in love with him and, on one gin-soaked jealous night, had swallowed a whole box of matches; naturally, a few hours later, she was fine, having vomited copiously all over Dâmaso's waistcoat, while Dâmaso lay weeping by her side—but ever since, this man of love had judged himself to be an *homme fatal*! As he explained to Carlos: given the amount of drama in his life, he almost trembled, yes, trembled, if he so much as looked at a woman.

"The things that went on between Susana and me!" he murmured, after a silence, during which he had been picking bits of dry skin off his lips.

Then, with a sigh, he returned to *Le Figaro*. Silence fell once more upon the terrace. Inside, the chess game continued. Beyond the shade cast by the awning, the sun was growing hot and beating down upon the flagstones and on the white ceramic pots, creating a pale golden glow through which fluttered the season's first butterflies as they flew from carnation to carnation; below, the garden was green and lush, utterly still in the sunlight, with not a branch stirring, cooled by the sound of the bubbling fountain and the liquid glitter of the water in the pool, and enlivened here and there by the red or yellow of the roses and by the flesh-pink of the last camellias. The little patch of river that could be seen between the buildings was the same darkblue as the sky; and between river and sky, the hills formed a thick dark green line, almost black in the heat of the day, with the two windmills immobile on the top and the two small white houses below, so luminous and vibrant that they seemed alive. A sleepy Sunday air of repose lay upon the streets, and from high up came the clear tolling of a bell.

"Ah, I see the Duke of Norfolk is in Paris," Dâmaso said in a knowing tone, crossing his legs. "Now the Duke of Norfolk really *is* chic, isn't he, Carlos?"

Carlos, without looking up, made an ample gesture with his arm as if to express how infinitely chic the Duke was.

Dâmaso put down *Le Figaro* in order to place a cigar in his cigar-holder; then he undid the last buttons of his waistcoat, tugged at his shirt, the better to show off the emblem embroidered on it—an enormous *S* beneath the crown of a count—and then, with half-closed eyes, his lower lip protruding, he sat gravely drawing on his cigar.

"You look very splendid today, Dâmaso," said Carlos, who had also put aside his magazine and was regarding him with a melancholy eye.

Dâmaso blushed with pleasure. He cast a glance at his polished shoes, his flesh-coloured socks, and, turning bulging blue eyes on Carlos, he said:

"Yes, I'm very well, actually, but frightfully *blasé*."

And it was with a truly *blasé* air that he got up to look for the *Gazeta Ilustrada* among the newspapers and cigars on a table nearby, "in order to find out what's going on in Portugal." The first thing he read elicited an exclamation from him.

"Not another debut," commented Carlos.

"No, it's that beast Castro Gomes!"

The *Gazeta Ilustrada* announced: "Senhor Castro Gomes—the Brazilian gentleman to whom we devoted an article on the occasion of the misfortune that befell him in Praça Nova, and of which our correspondent J.T. gave us such a vivid and detailed account—has now recovered and is expected to arrive today at the Hotel Central. Our congratulations to the bold gentleman."

"So the gentleman has recovered, has he?" exclaimed Dâmaso, throwing the paper down. "Fine, then, now is the moment to tell him to his face what I think of him, the wretch!"

"Don't exaggerate," muttered Carlos, who had eagerly snatched up the paper and was re-reading the article.

"Exaggerate!" exclaimed Dâmaso, getting up. "Really! I'd like to see how you would feel if it were you. The man's a beast, a brute!"

And he again told Carlos the story that had so wounded him. Since his arrival from Bordeaux, and as soon as Castro Gomes was installed in the Hotel Central, he had twice been to leave him his card, the last time on the morning after Ega's supper. Well, "His Excellency" had not even deigned to thank him for the visit! Then they had left for Oporto, and it was there, while walking alone in Praça Nova, that Castro Gomes had seen the two horses of a calèche clearly out of control and heard two ladies screaming. Castro Gomes had grabbed the horses' reins and been thrown against some railings, thus dislocating his arm. He had been obliged to stay in Oporto, in his hotel, for five weeks. And Dâmaso (still with his eye on the wife, of course) had sent him two telegrams, one regretting what had happened and the other enquiring as to his recovery. The rude creature had replied to neither!

"No," Dâmaso boomed, pacing the terrace as if mulling over all these various slights, "I'm going to have to teach him a lesson. I don't quite know how yet, but I'll show him. I won't take a snub like that from anyone!"

He opened wide, threatening eyes. Ever since his exploit at the Grémio, when he had reduced a terrified coward to silence, Dâmaso had grown increasingly fierce. The slightest thing would have him talking about "smashing in So-and-so's face."

"Not from anyone!" he repeated, tugging at his waistcoat. "I don't take snubs from anyone!"

At that moment, they heard Ega's brisk tones inside, in the study, and, moments later, he appeared on the terrace, looking very harried and upset.

"Oh, hello, Dâmaso! Carlos, can I have a word with you alone?"

They went down the terrace steps and into the garden, and stopped by two Judas trees in flower.

"Have you got any money?" was Ega's first anxious question.

And he explained the terrible fix he found himself in. He had a bill for ninety *libras* that had to be paid the following day. And then there were the twenty-five *libras* he owed Eusébio, and which Eusébio had demanded back from him in a most insulting letter, and it was this last demand that most troubled Ega.

"I want to pay the swine back and, the next time I see him, stick the letter to his face with spit. And on top of that there's the bill of exchange! And all I have is fifteen *tostões*."

"That's Eusébio for you; he likes things just so. Anyway, what it comes down to is that you need one hundred and fifteen *libras*," said Carlos.

Ega hesitated, blushing. He already owed Carlos quite a sum. He was always turning to his friend for help, as if he were a bottomless pit of money.

"No, eighty will do. I'll pawn my watch and the fur coat, after all, it's not cold any more."

Carlos smiled and went straight up to his room to write a cheque, while Ega carefully chose the prettiest of rosebuds to adorn his frock-coat. Carlos was soon back, holding the cheque, which he had increased to one hundred and twenty *libras* so that Ega would be "covered."

"God bless you!" Ega said, putting the cheque in his pocket and breathing a long sigh of relief.

Then he inveighed against that swine, Eusébio! But he had his revenge already planned. He was going to send him the money all in copper, inside a coal sack, with, for good measure, a dead rat and a note, which would begin: "Vile worm, foul reptile, I hereby throw in your face, or, rather, snout . . . etc., etc."

"I don't know how you can allow that repulsive creature to come here and sit on your chairs and breathe the same air as you!"

It soiled one even to mention Eusébio! He inquired instead about Carlos' work, about the great book. He spoke, too, of his own *Atom*, and, finally, in a different voice, staring hard at Carlos through his monocle, asked:

"Tell me something: why have you not been back to see the Gouvarinhos?"

Carlos had only one reason: he had not enjoyed himself there.

Ega shrugged; this seemed to him an extremely puerile reason.

"You don't understand, do you?" he said. "The woman is madly in love with you. One only has to mention your name and she blushes."

And when Carlos laughed incredulously, Ega very gravely gave his word of honour. Only the previous evening, when they had been talking about Carlos, Ega had observed her. He might not be a Balzac or some other prodigy of observational powers, but he had excellent eyesight, and he had seen in her face and eyes a look of genuine feeling.

"I'm not making it up, dear boy. She likes you, she really does! She's yours for the taking!"

Carlos remarked on the Mephistophelian ease with which Ega urged him to break all kinds of laws, be they religious, moral, social, or domestic.

"Oh, well," said Ega, "if you're going to throw all that tripe about the catechism and the moral code at me, let's say no more about it! If you've caught the mange called virtue and get itchy over the slightest thing, then you're a lost cause. Go and join a Trappist monastery and read Ecclesiastes."

"No," said Carlos, sitting down on a bench among the trees, still under the effects of the idle hours he had spent on the terrace, "my motives are far less noble. The reason I don't go there is because I find Gouvarinho an insufferable bore."

Ega smiled.

"Well, if we were to avoid all the women who had boring husbands . . ."

He sat down next to Carlos and started tracing lines in the sandy earth of the path; then, without looking up, and letting each melancholy word fall, one by one, he said:

"Last night, all night, between ten and one o'clock, I had to listen to the tale of a lawsuit brought against the National Bank!"

It sounded almost like a confidence, a way of unburdening himself of the secret tedium in which, among the Cohens, his artistic temperament was drowning. Carlos was touched.

"My poor Ega! The whole lawsuit?"

"The whole lawsuit! As well as a reading of the report by the general assembly! And I showed great interest and even had opinions on the subject! Life is hell sometimes!"

They went back up to the terrace. Dâmaso was once more sitting in his wicker chair and trimming his nails with a little mother-of-pearl penknife.

"Has a decision been reached, then?" he asked Ega.

"It was decided yesterday. There's to be no *cotillon*."

This was the grand masked ball that the Cohens had been planning to hold for Raquel's birthday. The idea for the party had come from Ega; originally, it was to have had the grand proportions of an artistic gala, a historic resurrection of the balls that were held in the days of Dom Manuel. Then they realised that such a party was impossible in Lisbon and opted for something a little more sober, a simple fancy-dress ball to which people could wear whatever costume they chose.

"Have you decided yet what you're going to wear, Carlos?"

"The classic domino, a simple black hood and cloak, as befits a man of science."

"Well," exclaimed Ega, "if it's science we're talking about, you should go in smoking jacket and slippers! After all, that's where science happens, at home and in slippers. No one ever discovered a law of the universe while wearing a domino. I mean, a domino, really! How uninspired!"

It was precisely what Raquel wanted to avoid at her ball, having everyone turn up in a domino. And Carlos had no excuse. Twenty or thirty *libras* was nothing to him, and with that splendid physique of his, like that of some Renaissance gentleman, he should at the very least adorn the ballroom as a magnificent Francis I.

"That," he added passionately, "is the beauty of a masked ball. Don't you think so, Dâmaso? Everyone makes the most of their appearance. Gouvarinho's wife is a good example. She had a brilliant idea; with her red hair, small nose and plump cheeks, she was born to be Marguerite de Navarre."

"What's all this about Marguerite de Navarre?" asked Afonso da Maia, coming out onto the terrace with Craft.

"Marguerite, the Duchess of Angoulême, the sister of Francis I, the Marguerite of the *Marguerites*, the pearl of the Valois family, the patron saint of the Renaissance, otherwise known as the Countess de Gouvarinho!"

He laughed out loud, then went over and embraced Afonso, explaining that they were discussing the Cohens' ball. And he appealed to him and to Craft regarding Carlos' wretched plan to wear a domino. Wouldn't that great strapping lad, who looked every inch the man of arms, be perfect as a proud Francis I, in the thick of the battle of Marignano?

Afonso looked tenderly at his handsome grandson.

"You may well be right, João, but Francis I, King of France, cannot just step out of a hired carriage and enter a ballroom alone. He needs a whole court—heralds, gentlemen, ladies, jesters, poets—and that would be somewhat difficult to arrange."

Ega bowed. Yes, of course! Now there was an intelligent way of understanding the Cohens' ball!

"And what are you going as?" asked Afonso.

That was a secret. Ega had a theory that one of the charms of such parties was the element of surprise; for example, two men might dine at the Bragança together in normal evening dress, then meet up later that night, one wearing the imperial purple of Charles V and the other bearing the rifle of a Calabrian bandit.

"Well, I'm making no secret of my costume," blustered Dâmaso. "I'm going as a savage."

"Naked?"

"No! I'm going as Nelusko, the slave in *L'Africaine*. What do you think Senhor Afonso? Chic, eh?"

"'Chic' is perhaps not quite the word," said Afonso, smiling. "But 'striking' certainly."

They all wanted to know what Craft was going to wear, but Craft wasn't going as anything at all; he was staying at home in Olivais, in his dressing-gown.

Ega gave a bored, almost angry shrug. Such indifference regarding the Cohens' ball wounded him as if it were a personal slight. He was devoting to this party, not only his time, which included time spent studying in the library, but also the white heat of his imagination; and gradually, the party was taking on in his eyes the importance of a celebration of art that would test the genius of a whole city. People wearing dominos or refusing to come at all seemed to him evidence of a lack of spirit. He cited the example of Gouvarinho; there he was, a busy man, with a position in politics, about to be made a minister, and yet not only was he going to the ball, he had given great thought to his costume; he was going as the Marquis de Pombal!

"He's advertising himself as a potential minister," said Carlos.

"No need to," exclaimed Ega. "He already has all the qualities necessary to become a minister: he's got a good loud voice, he's read Maurice Block, he's heavily in debt, and he's an ass!"

Enjoying the general mirth, he felt suddenly guilty at demolishing a gentleman who'd shown such interest in the Cohens' ball and so added:

"No, he's an excellent fellow really, and has no airs at all! The man's an angel!"

Afonso, smiling paternally, told him off:

"Oh, come now, João, you don't respect anything or anyone."

"Disrespect is a necessary condition of progress, Senhor Afonso. Respect for others is just the beginning of the slippery slope. You start out admiring Gouvarinho, and end up revering the monarch, and before you know it, you've sunk

139

so low you're even worshipping the Almighty! You have to be very careful!"

"Go away, João, go away! You're the Anti-Christ in person!"

Ega was about to respond, for he was in an exuberant mood now, but from inside came the silvery chime of the Louis XV clock, playing its gentle minuet.

"Four o'clock already!" he cried.

Horrified, he checked his own watch, then quickly and silently shook everyone's hand and, in a flash, was gone.

All those present were equally shocked at the lateness of the hour. And the moment to go to Lumiar to see the Medeiros sisters' antique bedspreads had also passed.

"Do you fancy half an hour's fencing, Craft?" asked Carlos.

"All right, and of course it's time for Dâmaso's lesson."

"Ah, yes, my lesson," murmured Dâmaso, with a faint reluctant smile.

The fencing gallery was a room on the ground floor, underneath Carlos' apartments, with barred windows that gave onto the garden where a pale green light filtered through the trees. On misty days, they had to have the gas-lights on. Dâmaso followed behind, at the slow pace of a wary beast.

These fencing lessons—which he himself had requested out of his love of all things chic—were becoming hateful. And that afternoon, as always, as soon as he was encased in the leather plastron and had covered his face with the wire-mesh mask, he began to sweat, and the blood drained from his face. Before him, Craft, foil in hand, seemed cruel and inhuman, with his pale cold eyes and his shoulders like those of a serene Hercules. The two foils clashed, and Dâmaso trembled all over.

"Stand firm!" shouted Carlos.

The unfortunate fellow steadied himself on his chubby legs; Craft's foil flew towards him, vibrating and glinting; Dâmaso staggered back, breathless, his arm limp.

"Stand firm!" Carlos bawled.

Exhausted, Dâmaso lowered his foil.

"It's nerves, that's all, what do you expect! It's because we're not fighting for real; if we were, then you'd see."

The lesson always ended thus, almost as soon as it had begun, and, afterwards, he would sit on a morocco leather bench, fanning himself with his handkerchief, his face as pale as the plaster on the walls.

"I think I'll go home," he said after a while, worn out from all that crossing of swords. "Do you want anything, Carlos?"

"I want you to come to supper tomorrow. The Marquis will be here."

"Oh, how chic! I'll definitely come."

But he didn't come. And when that normally very punctual young man did not appear at Ramalhete for the whole of the rest of that week, one morning Carlos, genuinely worried and imagining that Dâmaso must be dying, went to his house in Lapa. There, however, the servant (a coarse melancholy Galician who, ever since Dâmaso had become friends with the Maias, had been obliged to wear a tailcoat and to squeeze his feet into tight patent leather shoes) assured him that Dâmaso was in excellent health and had even gone out riding. Carlos then went to see Old Abraão, who, like him, had not seen "that beautiful gentleman," Senhor Salcede, for some days. Carlos' curiosity led him to the Grémio, but Senhor Salcede had not been seen recently by any of the staff there either. "He must be enjoying a honeymoon somewhere with some beautiful Andalusian woman," thought Carlos.

He had reached the end of Rua do Alecrim, when he saw Count Steinbroken taking a stroll down to the Aterro, with his carriage following slowly behind. It was only the second time that the diplomat had taken any exercise since his terrible attack of colic. However, not a trace of the illness now remained; he looked very pink-cheeked and blond, very solid in his frock-coat, and with a lovely tea-rose in his buttonhole. He even told Carlos that he was "much much stronger." Nor did he regret his sufferings, for they had given him a chance to realise how many friends he had in Lisbon. He had been most touched. The concern expressed by His Majesty—His Majesty's august concern—had done him more good than "all the drugs in the pharmacy!" Indeed, relations between those two close allies, Portugal and Finland, had never been stronger, or, "if I may put it so," never more intimate, than during his attack of colic!

Then, linking arms with Carlos, he referred warmly to Afonso da Maia's offer of Santa Olávia as a place where he could recuperate in the strong clean air of the Douro. That invitation had touched him *au plus profond de son coeur*. Alas, Santa Olávia was so very far away! He had to make do with Sintra, from where he could visit the embassy once or twice every week. "*C'est ennuyeux, mais...*" Europe was going through one of those moments of crisis in which statesmen and diplomats could not simply go away and enjoy a holiday, however brief. They had to be there in the breach, watching and reporting.

"*C'est très grave,*" he murmured, stopping in his tracks, a look of vague horror filling his blue eyes. "*C'est excessivement grave!*"

He called on Carlos to look around him at Europe. Everything was in total confusion, *un gâchis*. In one place there was the problem of the East, in another that of socialism; and then there was the Pope complicating matters still further. Oh, yes, the situation was *très grave*.

"*Tenez, la France, par exemple... D'abord Gambetta. Oh, je ne dis pas non, il est très fort, il est excessivement fort... Mais... Voilà! C'est très grave...*"

Then there were the radicals, *les nouvelles couches*. The situation really was terribly grave.

"*Tenez, je vais vous dire une chose, entre nous!*"

But Carlos wasn't listening, nor was he smiling any more. Walking very slowly towards them from the far end of the Aterro was a woman whom he recognised at once by her walk—like that of a goddess striding the Earth—by the little silver-haired dog trotting at her side, and by her marvellous body like that of some opulent marble statue, but which vibrated with a warm, pulsating, nervous grace. She was wearing a very simple dark serge outfit, which fitted her perfectly and seemed a natural complement to her person, its very correctness lending her an air of strength and chastity; she was carrying an English parasol, slim and elegant as a walking cane; and as she moved through the luminous evening, along the sad harbour-front of an antiquated city, there was about her whole being a kind of foreign glamour, the bright elegance of superior civilisations. No veil covered her face this time, yet Carlos was still unable to make out the details of her features, for, apart from the splendid ivory of her flesh, all he was aware of were two intensely dark eyes fixed on his. Unconsciously, he made as if to follow her. Steinbroken, who had noticed nothing, was busy finding Bismarck frightening. As she moved off, she seemed to Carlos larger and more beautiful, and yet that false literary image of her as a goddess striding the Earth took deep root in his imagination. Steinbroken, meanwhile, was expressing his horror at the speech made by the Chancellor in the Reichstag. Yes, she really was a goddess. Beneath her hat her chestnut hair, plaited and coiled about her head, was almost blonde in the light; the little dog trotted along beside her, its ears cocked.

"Yes," said Carlos, "Bismarck is very worrying."

Steinbroken, however, had left Bismarck and was now attacking Lord Beaconsfield.

"*Il est très fort . . . Oui, je vous l'accorde, il est excessivement fort . . . Mais voilà . . . Où va-t-il?*"

Carlos looked around at the Cais do Sodré, but it seemed deserted. Steinbroken, before he had fallen ill, had said precisely this to the Minister for Foreign Affairs: Lord Beaconsfield was very strong, but what was he after? What did he want? And His Excellency had shrugged and said he did not know.

"*Eh, oui! Beaconsfield est très fort . . . Vous avez lu son speech chez le lord-maire? Épatant, mon cher, épatant! Mais voilà? Où va-t-il?*"

"Steinbroken, it seems unwise for you to be standing out here catching cold."

"Do you think so?" exclaimed the diplomat, stroking his stomach.

And with that, he delayed not a moment longer. Since Carlos was also going home, Steinbroken offered him a seat in his carriage as far as Ramalhete.

"Come and have supper with us, Steinbroken."

"*Charmé, mon cher, charmé.*"

The carriage set off, and the diplomat, covering his legs and stomach with a large plaid blanket, said:

"Well, young Maia, we've had a most enjoyable walk, but, I must say, I don't find the Aterro terribly interesting."

Not interesting! That afternoon, Carlos had found it the most fascinating place on Earth!

The following day, he was there again, somewhat earlier, and had taken only a few turns among the trees when he saw her. But she was not alone; beside her was the upright figure of her husband, immaculate in an off-white cashmere jacket, a diamond horseshoe pin in his black satin cravat; he was smoking, indolent and languid, and carrying the little dog under his arm. When he passed Carlos, he looked at him in surprise, as if, in the midst of all these barbarians, he had finally found a civilised being, and he made some inaudible comment to her.

Carlos again met her eyes, deep and serious, but she seemed to him less beautiful; she was wearing a more complicated outfit in two tones, blue-grey and cream, and on her broad-brimmed hat, in the English style, fluttered something red, a flower or a feather. That afternoon, she was not a goddess descending from the plump golden clouds gathering in the sky above the sea; she was merely a very pretty foreigner on her way back to her hotel.

He returned to the Aterro three more times, but did not see her again; and then he felt ashamed of himself, humiliated by this romantic fascination which had brought him, as anxious as a lost sheepdog, sniffing his way along the Aterro, from the Rampa de Santos as far as Cais do Sodré, in the hope of catching a glimpse of a pair of dark eyes and a light-brown head of hair which just happened to be passing through Lisbon and which, one of these mornings, a Royal Mail steamship would carry away again.

And to think that he had left his work abandoned on his desk all week, and that every afternoon, before going out, he had spent time in front of the mirror, adjusting his cravat! Ah, wretched, wretched nature . . .

At the end of that week, Carlos was in his consulting room, putting on his gloves, ready to leave, when the servant peered round the door curtain and whispered excitedly:

"There's a lady to see you!"

A very pale little boy with blond curls and all dressed in black velvet appeared, and behind him a woman, also in black, and wearing a veil as thick and tight-fitting as a mask.

"Oh, I've come too late," she said, hesitating at the door. "You were just about to leave."

Carlos immediately recognised the Countess de Gouvarinho.

"Countess!"

He removed newspapers and brochures from the divan; for a moment, as if undecided, she studied that soft, ample seat worthy of a seraglio, then perched lightly on the edge with her little boy beside her.

"I've brought you a patient," she said, still without lifting her veil, as if speaking from the depths of the black clothes disguising her. "I didn't ask you to call because it's nothing really serious and I had to come this way today anyway. Besides, my little boy is such a nervous child; the moment he sees a doctor arrive, he thinks he's going to die. Coming to see you like this, though, it's just as if we were making a visit. And you're not afraid now, are you, Charlie?"

The little boy said nothing; standing quietly at his mother's side, a delicate, fragile figure with angelic shoulder-length curls, he was gazing at Carlos with large sad eyes.

Almost tenderly, Carlos asked:

"And what seems to be the matter with him?"

Some days ago, he had had a rash on his neck. And then she had noticed a swollen gland behind his ear. This had worried her. She herself was very strong and came from good healthy stock, which had produced many athletes as well as many relatives who had lived to a grand old age. However, hereditary anaemia ran in her husband's family, the Gouvarinhos. For all his solid appearance, even the Count suffered from it. And she, fearing that the debilitating influence of Lisbon might not suit Charlie, had vague plans to take him to the country for a while, to Formoselha, where his grandmother lived.

Carlos, shifting his chair slightly forward, reached out his arms to Charlie.

"Come here, my little friend, and let's have a look at you. What beautiful hair he has, Countess!"

She smiled. And Charlie, very serious and polite, and showing no sign of that horror of doctors his mother had mentioned, came at once, carefully unbuttoned his broad collar and, standing almost between Carlos' knees, bent his neck, soft and white as a lily.

Carlos could see only a small pink mark, already fading, and there was no sign at all of any swelling; then a slight redness rose to his cheeks, he glanced quickly up at the Countess, as if understanding everything and seeking from her an admission of the feeling that lay behind the childish pretext that had brought her there, all dressed in black and masked by veils.

She, however, remained impenetrable, sitting on the edge of the divan, her hands folded, attentive, as if awaiting his verdict like any other anxious mother.

Carlos buttoned up the little boy's collar and said:

"There's absolutely nothing wrong, Countess."

Then he went on to ask her a few questions about Charlie's diet and general fitness. The Countess complained in mournful tones that the boy was not being brought up in the more energetic, virile way she would have liked, but his father was opposed to what he called "the English aberration" of cold water, exercise in the open air, and gymnastics.

"Cold water and gymnastics," said Carlos, smiling, "do have a better reputation than they deserve. Is he your only child, Countess?"

"He is, and as an only child, he gets very spoiled," she said, stroking the boy's fair hair.

Carlos assured her that, despite Charlie's delicate nervous appearance, there was no reason for her to worry about him, nor was there any need to exile him to the fresh air of Formoselha. Then, for a moment, they both fell silent.

"You've no idea what a relief that is," she said at last, getting up and adjusting her veil. "Besides, it's a real pleasure to come here—there's not so much as a whiff of illness or even medicine. You've really made this very nice indeed," she added, taking a long look at the velvet furnishings.

"That's precisely the problem," said Carlos, laughing. "It inspires no respect for my science at all. I'm thinking of changing it completely and installing a stuffed crocodile, a stuffed owl or two, a few retorts, a skeleton, and piles of large books."

"Like Faust's cell."

"Exactly, like Faust's cell."

"You need a Mephistopheles," she said gaily, with a twinkle that shone through the thick veil.

"No, what I need is a Marguerite!"

The Countess shrugged prettily, as if discreetly doubting such an idea; then she took Charlie's hand and walked slowly towards the door, once again adjusting her veil.

"Since you've shown such an interest in my décor," said Carlos, wanting to detain her there, "let me show you the other room too."

He drew back the curtain. She went in, murmuring a few words of approval regarding the cool cretonnes and the pale harmonious colours; the piano, though, made her smile.

"Do your patients dance quadrilles?"

"My patients, Countess," he replied slowly, "are not sufficiently numerous to form a quadrille. I rarely even have two here together for a waltz. The piano is simply there to cheer people up; it's like an unspoken promise of good health, future soirées, and lovely arias from *Il Trovatore*, at home with the family."

"Most ingenious," she said, strolling familiarly about the room, with Charlie clinging to her skirts.

And Carlos, walking along next to her, said:

"You have no idea just how ingenious I can be!"

"You told me so the other day. What was it you said? Oh, yes, that you were very inventive when it came to hating."

"But far more so when it comes to love," he said, laughing.

She did not respond; she had stopped next to the piano; she leafed through the sheet music scattered about, then played a couple of notes.

"It sounds like a cowbell!"

"Please, Countess!"

She continued her investigation and went over to examine an oil painting, a copy of a Landseer—a large friendly St. Bernard dog asleep with its head on its paws. Almost brushing against her dress now, Carlos could smell the delicate verbena perfume, of which she always used rather too much; and in contrast to her black clothes, her skin seemed lighter and softer, as alluring as satin.

"Awful," she muttered, turning round. "But Ega tells me that there are some lovely paintings in Ramalhete. He particularly mentioned a Greuze and a Rubens. It's a shame one cannot see such marvels."

Carlos regretted, too, that the bachelor existence he led with his grandfather

145

did not allow them to receive ladies. Ramalhete was beginning to take on the melancholy air of a monastery. If things continued like this for many more months, without the warm rustle of a dress or the scent of a woman, grass would begin to grow up through the carpets.

"That," he added gravely, "is why I'm going to force my grandfather to remarry."

The Countess laughed, and her small pretty teeth gleamed white behind her veil.

"I'm glad to find you in such a cheerful mood," she said.

"It's all a question of diet. Are you not cheerful?"

She shrugged, not knowing what to say. With the tip of her parasol she tapped one of her patent leather shoes, which stood out dark against the pale carpet, and then, eyes lowered, allowing her words to emerge in an intimate confiding tone, she said softly:

"People tell me I'm not, that I'm sad, that I suffer from spleen."

Carlos' gaze had followed hers and alighted on the patent leather shoe which so delicately shod her long, slender foot. Charlie was amusing himself tinkling the piano keys, and Carlos said in a low voice:

"Your problem is bad diet. You need treatment, a further personal consultation. I might well have much to tell you . . ."

She interrupted him, looking sharply up at him with eyes in which he saw a flash of tenderness and triumph: "No, come and tell me over tea one day, at five o'clock. Charlie!"

The boy ran to her at once and clung to her arm.

Carlos, accompanying her downstairs to the street, apologised for the ugliness of the stone steps.

"I'll order it all to be carpeted for when you next do me the honour of consulting me."

She said jokingly, all smiles:

"No, no, you promised us all perfect health, and I sincerely hope you don't expect me to come and take tea with *you*."

"Ah, Countess, when I start to hope, I never set any bounds to my hopes."

She stopped, still holding her little boy by the hand, and she looked at him, as if amazed and charmed by his grandiose self-confidence.

"You're that confident, are you?"

"Yes, I'm that confident, Countess!"

They were standing on the last step, before the bright clamour of the street.

"Hail a cab for me, will you?"

A coachman responded at once to Carlos' wave and drove up with a carriage.

"And now," she said, smiling, "tell him to take me to Graça Church."

"Are you going to kiss the feet of our Lord of the Stations of the Cross?"

She blushed slightly and murmured:

"I have my devotions."

Then she jumped lightly into the carriage, leaving behind Charlie, who Carlos lifted paternally up in his arms and placed beside her.

"May God keep you and watch over you, Countess."

She thanked him with a look and a nod, both of which were as sweet as caresses.

Carlos went back upstairs and without removing his hat remained there, rolling a cigarette and pacing up and down in that ever-deserted, ever-chilly room, where she had now left a little of her warmth and her perfume.

He very much liked that boldness of hers—coming to his consulting room in secret, almost masked in that elaborate black outfit, inventing a swollen gland on Charlie's perfectly healthy neck, purely in order to see him and to tie a quick, tight knot in the fragile thread of their relationship which he had so negligently allowed to fall and break.

Ega had not been imagining things this time: she was offering him her lovely body as blatantly as if she had undressed. Ah, if only she were a woman of flighty easy feelings, what a lovely flower to pluck, to smell and then throw away! But, as Baptista said, the Countess had never "enjoyed herself." And what he did not want was to become involved in some jealous passion, one of those turbulent affairs with a woman in her thirties, from which, afterwards, it would be very hard to disentangle oneself. In her arms, his heart would grow silent; and as soon as that first curiosity had been satisfied, the tedium of undesired kisses would begin, the dreariness of pleasure served up cold. Worse, he would have to become a household friend and have the Count clap him on the back, have to listen to him droning dully on about political doctrine. He found all of this truly alarming. And yet he had liked that boldness of hers! There was something romantic, unusual, piquant about it. And she would most certainly have a delectable body. In his imagination, he undressed her, became lost in her satiny curves, about which he had sensed something at once mature and virginal. And he again felt tempted, just as he had on those initial occasions when he had seen her at the theatre, when he had seen those warm reddish curls.

He left, and had gone only a few steps along Rua Nova do Almada when he spotted Dâmaso bowling along in a coupé; he called to Carlos, had the carriage stop, then stuck his flushed and radiant face out of the window.

"I haven't been able to come and see you," he exclaimed, grasping Carlos' hand as soon as he approached and shaking it enthusiastically. "I've been in a positive frenzy of activity! I'll tell you all about it! It's the most divine romance. But I'll tell you about it later. Mind the wheel now. Off you go, Calção!"

The horses galloped off, and Dâmaso, still leaning out of the window, waving, yelled into the clamorous street:

"The most divine romance, and *so* chic!"

A few days later, in the billiard room at Ramalhete, Craft, who had just beaten the Marquis, put down his cue and, lighting his pipe, asked:

"Any news of our Dâmaso? Have you found any explanation for his most regrettable disappearance?"

Carlos told how he had met him, red-faced and triumphant, announcing from the window of his coupé, right in the middle of Rua Nova do Almada, the news of a "divine romance"!

"Oh, yes, I know," said Taveira.

"How do you know?" exclaimed Carlos.

Taveira had seen him the night before, in a large hired landau, with a most splendidly elegant woman, a foreigner apparently.

"No!" cried Carlos. "And did she have a little griffon dog with her?"

"Exactly, a little silver-haired griffon. Who are they?"

"And a thin young man with a very black beard and a rather English look?"

"Indeed! Very properly turned out and with something of the sportsman about him. What sort of people are they?"

"Brazilian, I believe."

It was, of course, Castro Gomes and his wife. Carlos was astonished. Only two weeks earlier on the terrace, Dâmaso, with clenched fists, had been fulminating against them both for the way they had, in his view, "snubbed" him. He was about to ask Taveira for more details, but the voice of the Marquis emerged from the depths of the armchair in which he was sitting, wanting to know Carlos' views on that morning's great event in the *Gazeta Ilustrada*. In the *Gazeta Ilustrada*? Carlos knew nothing about it, he hadn't read a newspaper all day.

"Don't any of you say a word!" cried the Marquis. "It'll be a surprise. Have you got a copy here? Have one brought in!"

Taveira tugged the bell pull, and when the servant arrived bearing the newspaper, he grabbed it, intending to read it out loud.

"No, let him see the picture first," bawled the Marquis, getting to his feet.

"No, first the article!" exclaimed Taveira, holding the newspaper behind his back.

But then he gave in, and held the paper in front of Carlos' eyes, holding it wide open, as if it were an unfurled shroud. Carlos immediately recognised the face of Cohen. And the prose around it—framing that dark face with its still darker side whiskers—filled six columns and was written in an ornate lyrical style, praising to the skies Cohen's domestic virtues, his financial genius, his witty sayings, his furniture; there was even a paragraph alluding to the imminent party, to Cohen's great masked ball. And all of this was signed by J. da Ega—João da Ega!

"How ridiculous!" cried Carlos, disgusted, throwing the paper down on the billiard table.

"It's more than ridiculous," remarked Craft, "it shows a complete lack of moral sense."

The Marquis protested. He liked the article. He thought it both brilliant and base, and besides, who, in Lisbon, cared about moral sense?

"You see, Craft, you don't know Lisbon. Everyone finds this perfectly natural. He's a close friend of the household and so he celebrates its master and mistress. He admires the wife and flatters the husband. It fits perfectly with the local logic. It will be a huge success, you'll see. And it's beautifully written."

He picked up the newspaper from the billiard table and read out loud the passage on Madame Cohen's pink boudoir: "There," wrote Ega, "one breathes in the perfume of something intimate and chaste, as if the whole rose-pink décor gave off the very aroma of a rose!"

"I mean that's beautiful by anyone's standards!" exclaimed the Marquis. "That young man is very talented. I only wish I had his talent!"

"None of that takes away from the fact," repeated Craft, puffing tranquilly on his pipe, "that it shows an extraordinary lack of moral sense."

"It's pure unadulterated madness!" said Cruges, uncurling himself from one corner of a sofa in order to let fall these weighty syllables.

The Marquis turned on him.

"And what would you know about it, maestro? The article is sublime. More than that, it's shrewd too."

Cruges, too lazy to argue, silently moved to the other end of the sofa, where he curled himself up again.

And then the Marquis, springing to his feet and gesticulating, appealed to Carlos to explain what Craft meant by "moral sense."

Carlos, who was pacing impatiently up and down the room, did not reply; instead, he took Taveira's arm and led him into the corridor.

"Tell me something. Where did you see Dâmaso with these people and where were they going?"

"They were heading down the Chiado, the day before yesterday, at two o'clock. I'm sure they were going to Sintra. There was a suitcase in the landau itself and there was a servant behind them in a coupé with another larger trunk. It all reeked of a trip to Sintra. And the woman is just divine! What clothes, what presence, what chic! She's a real Venus! However did he meet her?"

"In Bordeaux, on a steamship or something."

"What I liked were the airs he gave himself as they drove down the Chiado! A little bow to the right, a little bow to the left and then leaning tenderly towards the woman to whisper something, as if to announce to everyone: 'She's mine!'"

"The fool!" exclaimed Carlos, stamping his foot.

"A fool you say," said Taveira. "A decent civilised woman arrives in Lisbon, and he's the one who meets her and he's the one going to Sintra with her. Some fool! Anyway, who cares, let's go and have a game of dominoes."

Taveira had recently introduced dominoes to Ramalhete, and furious games were sometimes played there now, especially when the Marquis was present. For it was Taveira's ambition to beat the Marquis.

First, however, the Marquis had to cease his gesticulations and abandon the long reasoned argument with which he was tormenting Craft, who, from the depths of his armchair, pipe in hand, was responding only in sleepy monosyllables. The Marquis was still going on about Ega's article, about how to define "moral sense." He had already mentioned God and Garibaldi and even his own famous gundog Finório and now he was defining conscience, which, according to him, was merely a fear of the police. Had Craft ever actually known anyone express genuine remorse? No, apart from in melodramas at the Teatro da Rua dos Condes.

"The truth is, Craft," he concluded, giving in to Taveira, who was dragging him over to the games table, "conscience is merely a matter of upbringing. It's something you acquire, like good manners. Suffering in silence because you've betrayed a friend is something you learn, just as you learn not to pick your nose in public. It's all a matter of upbringing. Otherwise, conscience is just the fear of prison or of the big stick. Oh, so you want me to beat you at dominoes like I did last Saturday, do you? In that case, I'm all yours."

Carlos, who had been re-reading Ega's article, also went over to the table. They were all sitting down, shuffling the tiles, when Steinbroken appeared at the door, erect and resplendent, with his corn-gold hair, tailcoat, and medals, and with the Grand Cross pinned to his white waistcoat. He had dined at the Palace and had come to complete his soirée, *en famille*, at Ramalhete.

The Marquis, who had not seen him since his famous attack of colic, left the game of dominoes, ran over and noisily embraced him, and then, without even giving him time to sit down or shake hands with the others, begged him to sing one of his lovely Finnish songs, just one, of the kind that warmed his heart!

"Just the 'Ballad,' Steinbroken. I haven't got much time either, because they're waiting to start the game. Just the 'Ballad'! Go on, Cruges, into the other room with you and play the piano!"

The diplomat smiled, claiming to be tired, for he had already made delightful music for His Majesty at the Palace. However, he had never been able to resist the Marquis' playful manner, and so off they went to the music room, arm in arm, followed eventually by Cruges, who took an eternity to uncurl himself from his corner of the sofa. Moments later, drifting in through the half-drawn curtains at the door, the diplomat's lovely baritone voice, along with a sighing piano accompaniment, was filling all the rooms with the sweet swaying melancholy of the "Ballad," with the lyrics, which the Marquis so adored, translated into French, speaking of the sad mists of the North, of icy lakes and golden-haired fairies.

Taveira and Carlos, meanwhile, had launched into a game of dominoes, with one *tostão* per point. Carlos was not in the mood for dominoes that night, and he played distractedly, occasionally humming along to some of the sadder bits of the "Ballad"; then, when Taveira had only one tile left, and Carlos had to keep drawing interminably on the tiles that remained in the boneyard, he turned to Craft to ask if the Hotel Lawrence in Sintra was open all year.

"Dâmaso's little trip to Sintra really got to you, didn't it?" grumbled Taveira impatiently. "Come on, play!"

Carlos said nothing, but limply placed one tile on the table.

"Domino!" cried Taveira.

And in triumph, bouncing up and down in his chair, he counted the sixty-eight points by which Carlos was losing.

At that moment, the Marquis came in, and reacted indignantly to Taveira's victory.

"Our turn now," he exclaimed, grabbing a chair. "Carlos, let me give this thief the drubbing he deserves. Then the three of us can play. How do you want it, Taveira? Two *tostões* a point? Ah, only one. Right, now I'll show you. Come on, put down that double-six, you wretch."

Carlos sat for a moment longer, watching the game, holding an extinguished cigarette between his fingers and wearing the same distracted air; suddenly, he appeared to come to a decision; he crossed the corridor and went into the music room. Steinbroken had gone to the study to see Afonso da Maia and observe the game of whist, and Cruges, between the two candles placed on the piano, sat on alone, gazing absently up at the ceiling, wistfully improvising.

"What do you say, Cruges," Carlos said, "to a little trip out to Sintra tomorrow?"

The piano fell silent, the pianist looked up, startled. Carlos did not even give him time to respond.

"Of course you'd like to go. A trip to Sintra would do you nothing but good. I'll be outside your house tomorrow morning with the break. And make sure you put a fresh shirt in your suitcase, just in case we decide to spend the night there. At eight o'clock on the dot, all right? And not a word to any of the others."

Carlos went back into the other room and stood watching the game of dominoes. There was a prolonged silence. The Marquis and Taveira were slowly, wordlessly moving the tiles, each with an air of deep unspoken rancour. On the green cloth of the billiard table, a little clump of white balls was sleeping beneath the light cast by the porcelain lampshades. The vague sorrowful sound of the piano occasionally drifted in. And Craft, his arm hanging limply from his armchair, was dozing beatifically.

: VIII :

THE FOLLOWING MORNING, at eight o'clock sharp, Carlos drew up in Rua das Flores, outside Cruges' familiar front door. However, the footman he sent to ring the bell of the third-floor apartment returned with the puzzling news that Senhor Cruges no longer lived there. Where the devil did he live then? The maid had said that he now lived in Rua de São Francisco, four doors along from the Grémio. In a moment of despair, Carlos considered going to Sintra alone. Then he set off for Rua de São Francisco, cursing the ever vague, ever secretive Cruges for having moved without telling him! It was so typical—Carlos, for example, knew nothing about his past, about his inner life, his affections, or his habits. The Marquis had simply arrived with him at Ramalhete one night, whispering to Carlos that he had brought him a genius. And Cruges had immediately charmed them all with his modest manner and his marvellous piano-playing, and everyone at Ramalhete began to address him as "maestro," to speak of him as a genius, and to declare that Chopin had never written anything to compare with Cruges' "Meditation on Autumn." And no one knew anything more about him. It was only through Dâmaso that Carlos had found out Cruges' address and the fact that he lived with his mother, who was a still relatively youthful widow and the owner of several buildings in the Baixa.

Carlos had to wait a quarter of an hour outside the house in Rua de São Francisco. First, a maid, her head bare, made a furtive appearance at the bottom of the stairs, took one look at the break and the liveried servants and immediately fled upstairs again. Then, a shirt-sleeved manservant arrived, bringing the master's suitcase and travelling rug. Finally, the maestro himself came running, almost stumbling down the stairs, a silk scarf in one hand, an umbrella under his arm, and fumbling with his overcoat buttons.

As he came bounding down the last few steps, a shrill female voice called from up above: "Don't forget the cheese pastries!"

And with that, Cruges clambered hurriedly into the seat beside Carlos, grumbling that he had been so worried about having to get up early that he'd barely slept at all.

"What's the idea of moving without telling anyone?" exclaimed Carlos, who, seeing that Cruges was shivering, arranged some of his own rug over the maestro's knees.

"This is one of our houses too," he said simply.

"Oh, well, that would be the reason then," murmured Carlos with an amused shrug.

They set off.

It was a very fresh morning, all blue and clear, not a cloud in the sky, and with a gentle sun that did not really warm, but which cast bright bars of golden light onto the streets and the façades of the houses. Lisbon was slowly waking up; women from the countryside were still going from door to door carrying their great baskets of vegetables; shopkeepers were languidly sweeping the bit of pavement outside their shops; and the faint, distant tolling of a bell calling people to mass was slowly dying on the soft air.

Cruges, having arranged his scarf and buttoned up his gloves, took a long look at the splendid pair of bay horses, whose coats gleamed like satin beneath the silvery glitter of the harness, at the liveried servants, each with a flower in his buttonhole, at the perfect rolling harmony of all that luxury, in which his overcoat stood out like a stain; but what impressed him most was Carlos' resplendent appearance, his bright eyes, his healthy colour and beautiful smile, and the vibrant, luminous quality which, despite the simple brown check jacket he was wearing and the bourgeois, cushioned seat of the break, gave him the energetic look of a jovial hero, setting out in his war chariot. Cruges sensed an adventure, and immediately asked the question that had been on his lips since the previous night.

"Tell me frankly, just between you and me, why this sudden desire to go to Sintra?"

Carlos made a joke of it. Would Cruges swear on Mozart's melodious soul and on Bach's fugues never to reveal the secret? Right, then, his idea was to visit Sintra, to breathe the air of Sintra and to spend the day in Sintra. But, please, he must promise to tell no one!

And he added, laughing:

"Just enjoy yourself, you won't regret it."

No, Cruges did not regret it. He was really excited to be going, for he had always loved Sintra. He had no very clear recollection of it, however, only a vague memory of large rocks and springs of flowing water. And, finally, he confessed that he had not been to Sintra since he was nine years old.

What, he didn't know Sintra? Then they must stay there and visit all the classic places of pilgrimage, walk up to Pena, drink water from the Fonte dos Amores, take a boat to Várzea . . .

"The place I would really like to visit is Seteais, with all that fresh butter."

"Oh, yes, there's plenty of butter," said Carlos. "And donkeys too, lots of donkeys. It's a veritable eclogue!"

They were driving along the Benfica road, past the overgrown walls of gardens, past gloomy mansions with broken windows and inns each adorned with a packet of cigarettes dangling at the door from a piece of string; and everything—the smallest tree, the tiniest scrap of grass with poppies, a fleeting distant glimpse of green hill—delighted Cruges. It had been so long since he had seen the countryside!

Gradually, the sun rose higher. The maestro removed his vast scarf. Then he was so hot that he took off his overcoat and declared that he was starving.

Fortunately, they were just driving into Porcalhota.

His greatest wish would have been to taste some of their famous rabbit stew, but since it was still somewhat early for that particular delicacy, he decided, after much thought, to have a generous plateful of eggs and chorizo sausage. It was something he had not eaten for many years and it would make him feel as if he really were in the countryside again. When the owner of the inn, with an air of importance and as if he were doing them an enormous favour, placed the vast dish on the bare wooden table, Cruges rubbed his hands, finding it all delightfully rustic.

"Life in Lisbon is so unhealthy!" he said, heaping his plate with eggs and sausage. "Aren't you having anything?"

To keep him company, Carlos ordered a cup of coffee.

Cruges, who was busily devouring his food, suddenly said, with his mouth full: "The Rhine must be magnificent too!"

Carlos stared at him in amazement and laughed. What did the Rhine have to do with anything? The maestro explained that ever since they had left Lisbon, he had been filled with thoughts of travel and landscapes; he longed to see the great snow-topped mountains and the rivers one reads about in books. His ideal would be to explore Germany on foot, a knapsack on his back—the sacred homeland of his gods, Beethoven, Mozart, Wagner.

"Wouldn't you rather go to Italy?" asked Carlos, lighting a cigar.

Cruges pulled a scornful face and uttered one of his sybilline phrases: "Nothing but folk dances!"

Then Carlos spoke of a plan to go to Italy in the winter with Ega. Visiting Italy was, for Ega, a form of intellectual cleansing; he needed the placid majesty of marble statues to calm that riotous, overexcited, peninsular imagination of his.

"What he needs is a good whipping," snarled Cruges.

And he took up the main topic of the previous evening, the famous article in the *Gazeta*. He found it, as he put it, utterly stupid and thought it revealed an unseemly obsequiousness. What upset him most was that Ega, with all his talent, all his spark and verve, did nothing.

"No one does anything," said Carlos, yawning and stretching. "You, for example, what do you do?"

Cruges, after a silence, shrugged and muttered:

"Even if I wrote a good opera, who would put it on?"

"And if Ega wrote a fine book, who would read it?"

The maestro concluded: "This country is simply impossible. I think I'll have a coffee too."

The horses had rested by then, so Cruges paid the bill and they left. Shortly afterwards, they were driving across the empty, apparently unending heath. On either side, as far as the eye could see, the land was dark and sad, and high above them, in all that solitude, the endless blue sky seemed equally sad. The horses' hooves kept up a steady trot, beating monotonously on the road. There was no other sound; occasionally a bird would cut through the air, flying fast, fleeing that bleak wasteland. Inside the break, one of the servants was sleeping; Cruges, heavy with eggs and sausage, was staring vaguely and glumly at the horses' lustrous rumps.

Carlos, meanwhile, was pondering the reason that was taking him to Sintra. And he did not really know why he was going there; but it had been two weeks since he had seen that woman who seemed to walk the Earth like a goddess and since he had met the intense darkness of those two eyes that had fixed on his; now that he imagined her to be in Sintra, he was hurrying there too. He expected nothing and desired nothing. He did not know if he would see her or if she would already have left, but he was going there, and it was enough of a pleasure, as he drove along that road, simply to think of her with those sweet feelings in his heart, and to drive into the town under the shade of Sintra's lovely trees. It was always possible that, in a while, in the old Hotel Lawrence, he would meet her suddenly in the corridor, perhaps brush against her dress, perhaps hear her voice. If she was there, she would doubtless appear in the dining room, a room he knew so well, and which he was already longing to see again, with its cheap muslin curtains, inelegant little bunches of flowers on the table, and its two large antique brass candelabra. She would enter, with the beautiful bright air of a blonde Diana; good old Dâmaso would introduce his friend Maia; those dark eyes, which he had seen in the distance like two stars, would rest for a moment longer on his; and she would, in English fashion, hold out her hand to him.

"At last!" exclaimed Cruges, with a sigh of relief and already breathing more easily.

They were approaching the first houses in Sintra; there was already some greenery growing alongside the road, and they could feel on their faces the first strong cool breeze from the hills.

The break drove in under the trees of Ramalhão, and as they entered the peace of that vast arboreal shade, they were gradually wrapped about by the slow soothing whisper of leaves and the vague, diffuse murmur of running water. The walls were covered in ivy and moss; through the foliage flashed long arrows of light. A subtle, velvety breeze was blowing, redolent of new green growth; here and there, on the darkest branches, birds twittered and sang; and on that simple stretch of road, all dappled with sunlight, one could already feel the religious solemnity of the dense woods to come, the distant coolness of natural springs, the melancholy that falls from the high rocks, and the noble repose of summer mansions. Cruges was taking long voluptuous lungfuls of air.

"Where is the Hotel Lawrence? In the hills?" he asked, suddenly thinking he might spend a whole month in that paradise.

"We're not going to the Lawrence," Carlos said, emerging abruptly from his silence and urging on the horses. "We'll go to the Nunes, we'll be more comfortable there!"

The idea had come to him suddenly, as soon as they had passed the first houses in São Pedro and the break had begun to roll along these roads where he might, at any moment, meet her. He had been gripped by a shyness mingled with just a touch of pride, the fear that, even if she failed to recognise him, it might be both indelicate and indiscreet of him to be following her to Sintra and installing himself under the same roof and taking a seat at the same table. There was something else too: he could not bear the idea of being introduced to her by Dâmaso; he could just see him, plump-cheeked and attired for the country, making a slight bow and showing off "his friend Maia" and addressing him as "*tu*," then affecting an equally close friendship with her and eyeing her flirtatiously. That would be intolerable.

"We'll go to the Nunes, the food is better there!"

Cruges did not reply, silent, spellbound, receiving a sense of almost religious awe from the sombre splendour of the trees, from the rocky outcrops of the hills glimpsed up above, amid the clouds, from the perfumes which he drank delightedly in, and from the gentle babble of water rushing down to the valleys.

Only when he saw the Paço Real did he open his mouth to speak:

"Oh, yes, what style!"

And it was the royal palace that pleased him most, that vast silent palace, towerless and unadorned, seated like a patriarch among the houses of the town, with the beautiful Manueline windows that give it a noble royal face, with the valley down below, leafy and cool, and, above, the two colossal twisted chimneys, which sum it all up, as if the palace were nothing but a giant kitchen built to cope with the gluttonous appetite of a king who consumes a whole kingdom daily.

And as soon as the break stopped at the door of the Hotel Nunes, he went and stole another timid look, from a distance, as if fearing a brusque reprimand from one of the palace guards.

Carlos, meanwhile, jumping down from the driver's seat, discreetly questioned the doorman who had come out to carry their luggage.

"Do you know Senhor Dâmaso Salcede? Do you know if he's in Sintra?"

The servant knew him very well. Only yesterday morning, he had seen him going into the billiard hall opposite in the company of a gentleman with a very dark beard. He must be staying at the Hotel Lawrence, because Senhor Dâmaso only stayed at the Nunes when he was with young ladies or in celebratory mode.

"Right, then, you'd better find us two rooms!" exclaimed Carlos, as happy as a child, certain now that "she" was in Sintra. "And a private room, just for us, where we can have some lunch."

Cruges, who had joined him, protested, and said that he would prefer to eat in the ordinary dining room, which so often gave one the opportunity to meet genuine eccentrics.

"Fine," said Carlos, laughing and rubbing his hands. "Serve lunch in the dining room, or in the square itself if you like. And lots of fresh butter for Senhor Cruges!"

The coachman drove off in the break, and the servant walked ahead, carrying one suitcase under each arm. Thrilled to be in Sintra, Cruges raced up the stairs, whistling; draped over his shoulders was the travelling-rug, from which he dared not be separated because it had been lent to him by his Mama. And as soon as he reached the door of the dining room, he stopped, threw up his arms in surprise and shouted:

"Eusèbiozinho!"

Carlos ran to join him and stared in astonishment. It really was Eusèbiozinho, the widower, just finishing his lunch, in the company of two young Spanish women.

He was seated at the head of the table, as if presiding over the meal, surrounded by the remnants of crème caramel and some plates of fruit; he looked sallow and dishevelled and was still dressed in heavy mourning, with the long ribbon from his black spectacles looped over one ear, and a round patch of black taffeta on his neck, doubtless concealing some burst pimple.

One of the Spanish women was large and swarthy, with a pockmarked face; the other was very thin, with kindly eyes and a feverishly high colour which no amount of powder could disguise. Both were dressed in black satin and both were smoking cigarettes. And in the bright light and cool air coming in through the window, they seemed even more worn and lacklustre, still sticky from their warm damp beds and giving off a frowsty bedroom smell. The last member of this rabble was a man, short and fat, with no neck, sitting with his back to the door, his head bent over his plate, and sucking noisily at half an orange.

For a moment, Eusèbiozinho froze, his fork poised in the air; then he rose, napkin in hand, and came over to offer his friends a limp handshake, immediately muttering some complicated excuse: his doctor had recommended a change of air, his friend there had come with him and insisted on bringing the two young women. All hunched and shrivelled at Carlos' side, he had never looked more funereal or more vulgar than when mumbling these hypocritical words.

"And quite right too, Eusèbiozinho," said Carlos at last, clapping him on the back. "Lisbon's ghastly just now, and love is a very sweet thing."

Eusèbiozinho continued to invent excuses for his presence there. Then the very thin Spanish woman, who was smoking and sitting back from the table with her legs crossed, asked loudly if Cruges was no longer speaking to her. Cruges looked at her for a moment, then, with open arms, walked over to greet his friend Lola. And that corner of the table was immediately filled with the rapid babble of Spanish and an energetic shaking of hands: "*Hombre, ¡que no se le ha visto, que me he acordado de ti!*" and "*¡Caramba, que reguapa estás!*" Then Lola, putting on a rather affected air, introduced the other woman, "*la señorita Concha.*"

Impressed by such familiarity, the fat man, who, until then, had barely looked up from his food, decided to pay more attention to Eusèbiozinho's friends; he crossed his knife and fork on his plate, wiped his mouth, brow, and neck with his napkin, painstakingly placed on his nose a large lorgnette with very thick lenses, and then, with unabashed impudence, raised his broad, flabby, sallow face and gave first Cruges and then Carlos a long appraising look.

Eusèbiozinho introduced his friend Palma, and his friend, hearing Carlos da Maia's celebrated name, was immediately eager to show this gentleman that he, too, was a gentleman. He flung down his napkin, pushed back his chair, and, proffering Carlos one limp, nail-bitten hand, gestured to what remained of dessert and exclaimed:

"Sir, if you would care to join us, please do! After all, that's why we all come to Sintra, isn't it, to get up an appetite and to fill our bellies."

Carlos thanked him and made as if to withdraw, but Cruges, who was still exchanging bantering remarks with Lola, made his own introduction from the other side of the table:

"Carlos, I'd like you to meet the lovely Lola, an old friend of mine, and Señorita Concha, to whom I have just had the pleasure of being introduced."

Carlos respectfully greeted both ladies.

The burly Concha muttered a brusque "*Buenos días.*" She did not appear to be in the best of moods: heavy with lunch, half-asleep and silent, elbows resting on the table, thick-lashed eyes half-closed, when not drawing on her cigarette she was picking her teeth. Lola, however, was delightful and, very much the lady, she got to her feet and offered Carlos her small damp hand. Then, taking up her cigarette again, and adjusting her gold bracelets, she declared, with a flirtatious look, that she had known about Carlos for a long time.

"Weren't you with Encarnación?"

Yes, Carlos had had that honour. And what had become of the lovely Encarnación?

Lola gave a sly smile and nudged Cruges with her elbow. She found it hard to believe that Carlos did not know what had become of Encarnación. In the end, she explained that their mutual friend was now with Saldanha.

"But not the Duke de Saldanha!" cried Palma, who was still standing, his tobacco pouch open on the table while he rolled himself a fat cigarette.

Lola, very tartly replied that he might not be a duke, but that he was, nevertheless, "*un chico muy decente.*"

"Is he now?" said Palma slowly, his cigarette in his mouth and taking a flint out of his pocket. "Well, I'll have you know that about three weeks ago—if that—I slapped him twice around the face. Ask Gaspar, he was there. It was in the Café Montanha. I slapped him so hard his hat ended up in the middle of the street. I'm sure you know Saldanha, Senhor Maia. You must, he's got a very nice little horse and carriage."

Carlos made a gesture, indicating that he did not, in fact, know Saldanha, and he was once again saying goodbye and bowing to the ladies, when Cruges detained him for a moment longer, while he satisfied his curiosity; he wanted to know which of these young women was "our friend Eusébio's wife."

Hearing his name taken thus in vain, the widower was roused to anger, and, without looking up from the orange he was peeling, he retorted morosely that he was simply there on a visit and had no wife and that both girls belonged to his friend Palma.

Barely had he spoken these words than Concha, who had been leaning back in her chair digesting her lunch, suddenly sat bolt upright, thumped the edge of the table and, with flashing eyes, challenged Eusébio to repeat what he had just said! She challenged him to say it again, to say that he was ashamed of her and of having brought her to Sintra. Eusébio, who had turned quite pale, tried to make a joke of it and to pat her hand, but she would have none of it and started calling him every name under the sun, interspersing each insult with a loud thump on the table, her mouth contorted with rage, and with two bright spots of red on her plump dark cheeks. Lola, embarrassed, tugged at her arm, but Concha pushed her away, and further excited by the strident tones of her own voice, she poured out all her bile, called him a pig, a miser, and generally wiped the floor with him.

Palma, in great distress, was leaning across the table and exclaiming anxiously:

"Concha, listen! Listen to me, Concha! I can explain."

Suddenly, she sprang to her feet, her chair clattered to the floor, and she flounced out of the room, the long satin train of her dress whisking angrily across the parquet, and from within they heard the sound of a door slamming. On the floor lay a torn scrap of her lace mantilla.

The waiter, who had entered through the other door, bearing the coffee pot, paused, inquisitive eyes alert, sensing scandal; then, in a silent, business-like manner, he walked round the table, serving each person coffee.

For a moment, no one spoke. However, as soon as the waiter had left, Lola and Palma, both very agitated, but moderating their voices, rounded on Eusèbiozinho! He had behaved very badly indeed. That wasn't the behaviour of a gentleman! He had brought the girl to Sintra and he should treat her with due respect, not deny her, just like that, in front of everyone.

"*¡Esto no se hace,*" Lolita was saying, standing up now, gesticulating, eyes shining and addressing Carlos, "*ha sido una cosa muy fea!*"

And when Cruges, with a smile, regretted having been the involuntary cause of this catastrophe, she told him in a low voice that Concha always was a bit of a termagant, hadn't wanted to come to Sintra anyway, and had been in a terrible mood all morning. But, nevertheless, what Eusébio had done was unspeakable!

Poor Eusébio, head bowed, ears ablaze, was desolately stirring his coffee; his eyes remained invisible behind his dark glasses, but he gave an audible sob. Palma then put down his cup, licked his lips, and standing in the middle of the room, face gleaming, waistcoat unbuttoned, sagely summed up the whole unpleasant affair.

"Forgive me for saying so, Silveirinha, but all this stems from the fact that you simply do not know how to treat Spanish women!"

At these cruel words, the widower crumbled. The spoon fell from his fingers. He stood up and went over to Carlos and Cruges, as if seeking refuge in them, wanting the warmth of their friendship, in order to unburden himself; and these heartfelt words escaped his lips: "You see how it is, my friends, you come to a place like this to enjoy a little poetry and this is how it ends!"

Carlos patted him sadly on the shoulder.

"That's life, Eusèbiozinho."

Cruges stroked his back.

"Pleasures are so unreliable, Silveirinha."

Palma took a more practical approach and declared that they must sort things out. Had they come to Sintra in order to quarrel and sulk? No, they had not! What they wanted during these few days away was harmony, good humour, and pleasure—not tantrums! If that was what they had wanted, it would have been cheaper to stay in Lisbon.

He went over to Lola and lovingly stroked her face.

"Go on, Lola, go and see Concha and tell her not to be so silly, tell her to come and have her coffee. Go on, you know how to handle her. Tell her to do it for my sake!"

Lola lingered for a moment while she selected two good oranges, then smoothed her hair in the mirror, picked up the train of her dress and left the room, throwing Carlos a look and a little smile as she passed him.

No sooner were they alone than Palma turned to Eusébio and gave him some very sage advice on the best way to treat Spanish women. You had to treat them kindly, that was why they liked Portuguese men, because Spanish men were so rough with them. He wasn't saying, of course, that, in certain cases, a good slap or even a couple of whacks with a walking stick might not come in handy. Did his friends there happen to know when it was right to resort to such methods? Whenever a girl turned nasty and got too uppity. All it took was a short sharp beating, and you'd have her eating out of your hand. But afterwards, you had to be the soul of kindness and politeness again, just as if you were dealing with a Frenchwoman.

160

"Believe me, Silveira, I have experience. Senhor Maia here will tell you whether it's true or not, after all, he, too, has had experience of Spanish women and knows how to handle them!"

And these words were spoken with such fervour and such respect that Cruges burst out laughing, which made Carlos laugh too.

Rather shocked, Senhor Palma adjusted his glasses and looked at them.

"It's no laughing matter, gentlemen. You don't imagine I'm joking, do you? I first had dealings with Spanish women when I was fifteen. No, don't laugh, it's true. When it comes to tackling Spanish women, I'm your man! Not that it's easy, mind! You have to have a knack for it. Alexandre Herculano may write beautiful essays in the most elegant of styles, but bring him face to face with a couple of Spanish girls and then see how he fares! He wouldn't last a minute!"

Eusèbiozinho, meanwhile, had gone over to the door a couple of times to listen. A great silence had fallen over the whole hotel, and Lola had not returned. Then Palma advised him to take a bold step.

"Go on in there, Silveira, go into the room, walk straight up to her . . ."

"And give her a sound beating?" asked Cruges in a mock-serious tone, poking fun at Palma.

"A beating! No, kneel down and ask her forgiveness. That, in this case, is what you must do. And as a pretext, Silveira, you can take her a cup of coffee."

Eusèbiozinho shot his friends a dumb anxious look. But his heart had already decided, and a moment later, pale and shaken, clutching the scrap of lace mantilla in one hand and a cup of coffee in the other, he was walking slowly down the corridor to beg Concha's forgiveness.

Carlos and Cruges followed him out of the room without saying goodbye to Senhor Palma, who, equally indifferent, had already settled down at the table again to make himself a nice hot toddy.

It was two o'clock when Carlos and Cruges finally left the hotel to walk to Seteais, the idea of which had so attracted Cruges. In the square, outside the empty silent shops, stray dogs were sleeping in the sun; through the bars of the jail, prisoners were begging for alms. Filthy, ragged children hung around the street corners, and the best houses still had their windows closed, continuing their winter sleep among the already green trees. Now and then, there was a glimpse of the hills above the town—looking like ramparts above the rocky outcrops—or else, high up, the solitary Palácio da Pena. And April touched everything with the sweetness of its luminous, velvet air.

Carlos slowed his step outside the Hotel Lawrence and pointed it out to Cruges.

"It looks very nice," said Cruges. "But it was worth going to the Nunes just to see that splendid bit of theatre. So Senhor Carlos da Maia has experience of Spanish women, does he?"

Carlos did not reply, his eyes were fixed on the hotel's grey façade, where a pair of serge bootees were drying on the sill of the one open window. At the door, two silent Englishmen in knickerbockers were smoking their pipes; and two men with donkeys for hire, sitting opposite them on a stone bench, kept their eyes trained on them, smiling and watching, like beasts waiting to pounce on their prey.

Carlos was about to move on, when he seemed to hear, emerging from the silence of the hotel, the distant melancholy sound of a flute, and he stopped in his tracks, going over his memories, for he was almost certain that Dâmaso had told him that, on board ship, Castro Gomes used to play the flute.

Beside him, much moved, Cruges exclaimed: "Ah, this is sublime!"

He had stopped by the railings, from which he had a view of the whole valley. And from there he was looking out, enraptured, over the lush vastness of dense forest, of which one could see only the trees' round tops, which clothed the steep slopes the way moss clothes a wall, and which, at that distance, in the bright sunlight, really did look as smooth and soft as a great expanse of dark moss. And in those dark-green depths, beneath the ancient shade, the intriguing white façade of a house nestled amid the foliage with an air of noble repose. For a moment, he was filled by an artist's dream—to live there with a woman, a piano, and a Newfoundland dog.

The thing that most enchanted him, though, was the air. He opened wide his arms and filled his lungs with deep, delicious drafts.

"What air! It's so good for you! It really brings you back to life!"

To enjoy it at his leisure, he sat down on a stretch of low wall, opposite a high, railinged terrace, where old trees cast their shade over garden benches and road alike, reaching out cool leafy branches full of singing birds. And when Carlos showed him his watch and how the time available for visiting the royal palace, Pena, and Sintra's many other beauties was slipping by, Cruges declared that he would prefer to stay there, listening to the water, than go and see a lot of old monuments.

"Sintra isn't just old stones and Gothic architecture. Sintra is this, a little water, a little moss. This is paradise!"

And waxing loquacious in his contentment, he added, repeating his earlier mocking comment:

"As I'm sure you know, Senhor Maia, you who have so much experience of Spanish women!"

"Oh, please, spare me, and have a little respect for Nature," muttered Carlos, who was pensively tracing lines in the dust with his walking stick.

They fell silent. Cruges was now admiring the garden that could be seen down below from the wall on which they were sitting—a thick nest of greenery, of bushes, flowers, and trees growing in the close prodigality of a wild wood, leaving only enough space for a small round pond, whose still, cold surface, scattered with one or two waterlilies, looked green beneath the shade of that profusion of leaves and branches. Here and there, in the lovely disorder of foliage, they caught glimpses of certain bourgeois touches, a curve in a path—

narrow as a ribbon—which gleamed in the sun, or the predictable paleness of a statue. In other corners of that rich man's garden, exposed to view, there were plants more suited to a hothouse, aloes and cacti, and the arching arm of a monkey-puzzle tree, reaching up into the dark needles of wild pines and the fronds of a palm tree, with its sad air of a plant in exile, alongside the light perfumed boughs of pink-flowering Judas trees. At intervals, there were white clumps of marguerites, discreet and graceful, or, fluttering around a solitary rose, butterflies in pairs.

"What a shame this doesn't belong to an artist!" murmured Cruges. "Only an artist would truly be able to love these flowers, these trees, these murmurings."

Carlos smiled. Artists, he said, were only interested in the effects of line and colour in nature; but in order to feel concern for the well-being of a tulip, to ensure that a carnation was not going thirsty, to feel sad when the frost scorched the first buds on the acacias, you had to be a bourgeois, a bourgeois who, every morning, would step out into his garden wearing an old hat and bearing a watering-can, and who would see in those trees and plants another silent family for which he was also responsible.

Cruges, who had been listening distractedly, exclaimed:

"I mustn't forget those cheese pastries!"

The sound of carriage-wheels interrupted them, and an open calèche appeared, trotting along the road from Seteais. Carlos started to his feet, convinced it was "her" and certain that he was about to see her lovely eyes shine and blaze like two stars. The calèche passed by, carrying an ancient man with a patriarchal beard, and an old Englishwoman with her lap full of flowers and wearing a blue veil that floated in the breeze. Immediately behind them, almost lost in the dust stirred up by the carriage, there appeared a tall man, all in black, wearing a large Panama hat over his eyes, and walking along thoughtfully, his hands behind his back. Cruges was the first to recognise the man's long romantic moustache:

"Look, it's Alencar, the great Alencar!"

For a moment, the poet stood stock-still in the middle of the road, his arms spread wide in a gesture of amazement. Then, with noisy effusion, he clasped Carlos to his bosom and kissed Cruges on the cheek, for he had known Cruges since he was a child; Cruges was like a son to him. Now this was a surprise he would not exchange for a dukedom! What a joy to see them! But what the devil were they doing there?

However, he did not wait for an answer, he immediately told his own story. He had been afflicted by one of his sore throats and had had a touch of fever, and Melo, good old Melo, had recommended a change of air. Now, for him, good air meant only one thing—Sintra: because there, it was not only your lungs that breathed more easily, it was your heart too. And so he had arrived there the previous evening on the omnibus.

"And where are you staying, Alencar?" asked Carlos.

"Where do you think, my boy, at the Lawrence, of course. Poor Senhora Lawrence! She's getting on a bit now, but she's always been a good friend to me, almost a sister really! And what about you, where are you off to with those flowers in your lapels?"

"To Seteais. I'm going to show our maestro here Seteais."

Then he would go to Seteais too! There was nothing to do up there but breathe good air and think. He had spent all morning there, wandering about, hanging dreams on the branches of the trees. But he wasn't going to let them out of his sight now; it was positively his duty to show the maestro around Seteais.

"It's like a second home to me! There isn't a tree there that I don't know. I don't want to start spouting poetry at you, but do you remember a little thing I wrote about Seteais and which even had a bit of success?

> *How many moons have I seen there?*
> *How many sweet April morns?*
> *And how many sighs have I sighed there?*
> *Not seven, but a thousand and more!*

As you see, my boys, I have good reason to know Seteais, that place of the 'Seven Sighs,' very well indeed."

The poet sighed deeply, and for a moment all three of them were silent.

"Tell me something, Alencar?" Carlos said quietly, stopping and clutching the poet's arm. "Is Dâmaso staying at the Lawrence?"

Alencar had not seen Dâmaso, but the truth of the matter was that, last night, when he had arrived, he had gone straight to bed, exhausted, and his sole companions at lunch that day had been two young English fellows. The only other living creature he had seen had been a little pedigree dog, barking in the corridor.

"And where are you boys staying?"

"At the Nunes."

Then Alencar stopped again and, regarding Carlos tenderly, said:

"I'm so glad you managed to drag our maestro up here, my boy! The times I've told the wretch to get on that omnibus and come and spend a couple of days in Sintra. But no one can make him stop hammering away at that piano! But you know, if you want to make music or to compose, to understand a Mozart or a Chopin, you need to have seen this, to have heard this gentle murmuring, this melody played by the leaves."

He lowered his voice and pointed at the maestro, who was walking ahead of them, entranced:

"He has a great deal of talent, a great sense of melody! I used to carry him on my shoulders, you know. And his mother is a very fine woman indeed."

"Look at this," cried Cruges, who had stopped and was waiting for them. "This is sublime."

It was a short stretch of road, enclosed by two old ivy-covered walls and shaded by large trees interlacing their branches to form a leafy, lacy awning open to the light; on the ground trembled patches of sunlight, and in the coolness and silence, an invisible stream of water rushed away, singing.

"If you want the sublime, Cruges," exclaimed Alencar, "you need to climb up into the hills. There you have space, there you have clouds, there you have art."

"I'm not so sure," muttered the maestro. "I think I prefer this."

His timid nature doubtless did prefer these humble corners, made up of a little cool foliage and a stretch of mossy wall, places of quietness and shade, where the thoughts of the indolent can find greater comfort.

"Besides, my boy," Alencar went on, "everything in Sintra is divine. There isn't a single corner that is not a poem. Just look at this little blue flower, for example."

And, very tenderly, he plucked it.

"Come on," said Carlos impatiently, for now, after the poet's mention of the little pedigree dog, he was even more convinced that "she" was staying at the Hotel Lawrence and that he was about to meet her at any moment.

However, when they reached Seteais, Cruges was disappointed by the vast courtyard overgrown with grass and by the dirty, neglected house beyond, with its broken windows, and which still displayed its great coat of arms above a grandiose arch silhouetted against the sky. As a child, his impression of Seteais had been of a picturesque pile of rocks, overlooking the deep valley; and he had a vague memory, too, of moonlight and guitars, but what he was seeing now was such a disappointment.

"Life's full of disappointments," said Carlos. "Let's go on!"

And he walked briskly across the courtyard, while the maestro, who was growing more animated by the minute, repeated the joke of the day:

"Well, *you* should know, you who have so much experience of Spanish women!"

Alencar, who had fallen back to light a cigarette, pricked up his ears and wanted to know what this comment about Spanish women meant. Cruges described to him their encounter with Eusèbiozinho at the Nunes and Concha's furious outburst.

They were walking along one of the side avenues—green and cool and filled, like a leafy cloister, by an almost religious peace. The courtyard was deserted; the grass covering it grew freely, starred with yellow laxleaf shining in the sun and with tiny white daisies. Not a leaf moved, and through the fine branches the sun threw shafts of golden light. The blue sky, drenched in luminous silence, seemed to have withdrawn to some infinite distance; and all one could hear, from time to time, monotonous and slow, was the voice of the cuckoo in the chestnut trees.

The whole house—with its rusty railings facing the road, its stone rosettes eaten away by the rain, its heavy rococo coat of arms, its windows full of cobwebs, its broken roof tiles—seemed voluntarily to be allowing itself to die in that green solitude, as if it had grown tired of life since the last graceful tricorn hat and sword had departed, and since the hems of the last crinoline dresses had brushed those lawns. Cruges was now describing to Alencar the figure of Eusèbiozinho, coffee cup in hand, going to beg forgiveness from Concha; and the poet, still wearing his large Panama hat, kept stooping to pick wild flowers.

When they had passed under the arch, they found Carlos sitting on one of the stone benches, pensively smoking a cigarette. The house cast the shadow of its sad walls on that particular part of the courtyard, where a cool expansive air rose up from the valley; and from somewhere below they could hear the sad babble of a fountain. Alencar sat down beside his friend and began speaking with distaste of Eusèbiozinho. That was one mistake he had never made, taking prostitutes with him to Sintra or, indeed, anywhere, but far less Sintra! He had always felt, as everyone should, a profound respect for these trees and a love for the shade they cast.

"And that man Palma," he added, "is an old fraud. I know him. He used to run a kind of newspaper, and I boxed his ears once in Rua do Alecrim. It was an odd story. Let me tell you about it, Carlos. The swine! When I think about it now . . . That vile little ball of putrid matter! That fat little sausage of pus!"

He got up and nervously smoothed his moustaches, excited by the memory of that now dead dispute, all the while heaping vile names on Palma, in the grip of one of those hot-blooded moods that were his downfall.

Cruges, meanwhile, leaning on the balustrade, was gazing out at the farmland stretching out beneath him, a fertile, well-tended plain, divided up into squares of pale green and dark green that reminded him of the patchwork cloth covering his desk in his bedroom at home. The white ribbons of roads snaked through the fields; here and there, a house gleamed white amid the thick trees; and every so often, in that land of abundant water, a line of small elms revealed the presence of a cool stream that ran glittering through the grass. Beyond, lay the straight line of the sea, grown blurred and tenuous in the bluish mist; and above, the great curve of lustrous blue, like an exquisite piece of enamel, with only one tiny scrap of cloud, high up, that had been left there by mistake, and which, adrift in the light, had curled up and gone to sleep.

"It was disgusting!" Alencar exclaimed as he reached the dramatic conclusion of his story. "I was really disgusted! I threw my walking stick down at his feet, folded my arms and I said to him: 'You can take the walking-stick, you coward, all I need are my bare hands!'"

"I mustn't forget those cheese pastries!" muttered Cruges to himself, moving away from the balustrade.

Carlos had got up too, looking at his watch, but, before leaving Seteais, Cruges wanted to explore the other terrace, and no sooner had he mounted the two stone steps than he uttered a triumphant cry:

"What did I tell you? There they are! And yet both of you denied it!"

They joined him before a pile of huge rocks, worn smooth by use, and which now looked rather like seats left there long ago in order to give the terrace the wild, poetic grace of virgin forest. Didn't he tell them so? He knew there were rocks in Seteais!

"I had such a clear recollection of them! It's called the Penedo da Saudade, isn't it, Alencar?"

The poet did not respond. Standing before the rocks, arms folded, he had a mournful smile on his face; a sombre motionless figure in his black suit, his Panama hat pulled down over his eyes, he slowly and sadly surveyed the view.

Then, in the silence, he spoke in a yearning, desolate voice:

"Do you remember, dear boys, in *Flower of Martyrdom*, one of the best poems of mine in that collection, one with a fairly free rhyme scheme, called 'August 6th'? Perhaps you don't . . . Well, I'm going to recite it to you."

Mechanically, he drew a white handkerchief from his pocket and held it loosely in his hand, drawing Carlos to him and beckoning Cruges to join him; then he dropped his voice to an awed whisper and spoke the lines with a suppressed ardour, stressing each syllable, with all the ephemeral passion of the too-highly-strung:

> *You came! I clasped you to my breast.*
> *All around us, darkest night!*
> *No lace hangings adorned our nest,*
> *No embroidered sheets our berth,*
> *For our bed was hardest granite . . .*
> *Far off in the distance, a strummed guitar*
> *Played arpeggios sad and plangent . . .*
> *(You see I have not forgot!)*
> *And beneath love's bright flame*
> *The cold hard rock grew warm.*

He stood for a moment, his eyes drinking in the sight of those white rocks; he gestured sadly towards them and murmured:

"It was here."

And he moved off, head bowed beneath his large Panama hat, his white handkerchief still in his hand. Cruges, impressed by such romantic outpourings, stayed gazing at the rocks as if at an historic site. Carlos was smiling. However, as they left that corner of the terrace, they came upon the poet, hunched near the arch, fastening his long johns.

Alencar immediately straightened up, all emotion gone, and revealing his bad teeth in a friendly smile, exclaimed, pointing towards the arch:

"Now, Cruges, my boy, regard that sublime canvas."

Cruges stood openmouthed. Through the archway, he saw a marvellous picture, as if framed in stone, aglow in the splendid afternoon light, an almost fantastical composition, like the illustration of some beautiful legend of chivalry and love. In the foreground was the deserted, grass-grown courtyard, scattered with yellow flowers; farther off, the closed ranks of ancient trees, with ivy twining about their trunks, formed a wall of glossy greenery along the railings, and—emerging abruptly out of that luxuriant line of sun-baked trees, in the full splendour of the day, and standing out sharply against the backdrop of bright blue sky—rose the airy tops of the hills, crowned by the solitary and romantic Palácio da Pena, with its shady garden at its feet, its slender tower dreaming in the air, and its cupolas glinting in the sun as if made of gold.

Cruges thought it a painting worthy of Gustave Doré. Alencar came out with some beautiful phrase about the Arabic imagination. Carlos was impatiently urging them on.

Cruges, greatly impressed, was now eager to climb up to Pena. Alencar would join them with pleasure. Pena was for him another nest of memories. Nest? He should say, rather, cemetery. Carlos hesitated, standing by the railings. Would "she" be at Pena? He looked at the road, looked at the trees, as if he could divine from the footsteps in the dust or from the movement of the leaves, the direction taken by those steps he was following. At last, he had an idea.

"Let's go to the Hotel Lawrence first. And then, if we still want to go up to Pena, we can always hire some donkeys."

And he wouldn't even listen to Alencar, who was talking about Colares and visiting his friend Carvalhosa there; he set off briskly to the hotel, while the poet again adjusted the fly on his long johns, and Cruges, full of bucolic fervour, was busy decorating his hat with ivy leaves.

Opposite the Lawrence, the two men with their donkeys, having failed to tempt the Englishmen, were lazing in the sun, each smoking a cigarette.

"Do you happen to know," asked Carlos, "if a family staying in this hotel has been up to Pena today?"

One of the men made a wild guess and, snatching off his hat, said:

"Yes, sir, they went up there a little while ago, and I have my donkey here ready and waiting to take you too, sir!"

But the other, more honest man disagreed; the people who had gone up to Pena were staying at the Nunes.

"The family you're talking about, sir, have just gone down to the palace."

"A tall woman?"

"Yes, sir."

"And a man with a dark beard?"

"Yes, sir."

"And a little dog?"

"Yes, sir."

"Do you know Senhor Dâmaso Salcede?"

"No, sir. Is he the one who takes the photographs?"

"No, he doesn't take photographs. Here you are."

And he handed the two men a five-*tostão* coin and rejoined the others, saying that it really was getting rather late to go all the way up to Pena.

"Now what you *must* see, Cruges, is the royal palace. That really does have both originality and style! Isn't that right, Alencar?"

"I would say, my boys," began the author of *Elvira*, "that historically speaking ..."

"And I've still got to buy those cheese pastries," muttered Cruges.

"Exactly!" cried Carlos. "There are still the cheese pastries to buy; there's no time to lose! We'd better go!"

Leaving the other two men still undecided, he strode off to the palace and in just four long strides, he was there. And from the square he saw, coming out of the main door, past the sentinel, the famous family staying at the Hotel Lawrence, along with their little pedigree dog. The man did, indeed, have a black beard and white canvas shoes; and beside him stood a vast matron, wearing a small lace cape and bits of gold jewellery round her neck and on her bosom, and carrying a little woolly dog in her arms. They were both grumbling irritably about something to each other—in Spanish.

Carlos stood staring at the couple with the melancholy look of someone contemplating the shattered fragments of a once lovely marble statue. He did not wait for the others, nor did he want them to find him. He hurried to the Lawrence by a different route, hungry for certainty, and there, the servant who greeted him told him that Senhor Salcede and Senhor and Senhora Castro Gomes had left the previous evening for Mafra.

"And from there?"

The servant had heard Senhor Dâmaso saying that from there they would be returning to Lisbon.

"Right," said Carlos, throwing his hat down on the table, "bring me a glass of brandy and a little water."

Sintra seemed to him suddenly an unbearably sad and empty place. He had no desire now to go back to the palace, he didn't even want to leave that spot; and pulling off his gloves and walking round the dining table, where the flowers from the previous evening were beginning to fade, he felt a desperate urge to gallop back to Lisbon, to run to the Hotel Central and force his way into her room, just to feast his eyes on her! For what irritated him now was that in the tiny city of Lisbon, where people lived elbow to elbow, he could not find the woman he was so urgently seeking! He had spent two weeks sniffing around the Aterro like a stray dog; he had traipsed, like some ridiculous pilgrim, from theatre to theatre; one Sunday morning he had even done a circuit of all the church masses! But he had not seen her again. Now, knowing that she was in Sintra, he had flown there and once more had failed to see her. She had happened to pass him one day, as lovely as a goddess lost on the Aterro, she had chanced to let drop into his soul one of those dark-eyed looks, and then she had disappeared, evaporated, as if she really had ascended into Heaven, to remain, for ever more, invisible and supernatural; and there he was, with that gaze lodged in his heart, unsettling his whole being and silently directing his inner life, his thoughts, desires and curiosities—and all because of a delightful stranger, of whom he knew nothing except that she was tall and fair and owned a griffon dog. That's how it is with shooting stars! They are no different in essence, nor do they contain more light than other stars, but precisely because they are so fleeting and so evanescent, they appear to give off a more divine light, and the dazzle they leave behind in our eyes is more troubling and more enduring. He had not seen her again. Others had seen her. Taveira had. In the Grémio, he had even heard a corporal in the lancers talking about her and asking who she was, because he came across her every day. Yes, the corporal came across her every day. He, however, never saw her and so could not rest easy.

The servant brought him his brandy. And Carlos, carefully preparing his drink, talked to him, speaking for a moment about the two young Englishmen and about the plump Spanish woman. Then, overcoming his feelings of shyness, but almost blushing as he spoke, his questions interspersed by long silences, he asked him about Senhor and Senhora Castro Gomes. And each answer seemed to him a precious acquisition. The lady was a very early riser, said the servant. By seven o'clock, she had bathed and dressed and would then go out on her own. Senhor Castro Gomes, who slept in a separate room, never stirred before midday; and, at night, he lingered at the dining table for hours, smoking cigarettes and sipping brandy and water. He and Senhor Dâmaso would play dominoes. The lady had masses of flowers in her room, and they had intended to stay until Sunday, but she had been the one to hasten their departure.

"Ah," said Carlos, after a silence, "so it was the lady who hastened their departure?"

"Yes, sir, she was worried about her little girl whom she had left behind in Lisbon. Would you care for some more brandy, sir?"

Carlos waved him away and went out to sit on the terrace. Without so much as a leaf trembling, evening was falling, calm and radiant, filled with golden light and exuding a kind of vast serenity that pierced the soul. Had she not been so impatient to see her daughter—doubtless some small fair child left alone with the nursemaid—he would have found her there on that very terrace, also watching the evening fall. The dazzling goddess, it seemed, was also a good mother, and this only lent her a still deeper charm; and the thought that her lovely marble form could be shaken by such a tender human anxiety made him love her all the more. She would be in Lisbon now, and he imagined her, magnificent and white-skinned, in a lace peignoir, her hair hastily curled, lifting up her baby in her splendid Junoesque arms and talking to it and laughing a golden laugh. She seemed to him adorable in that pose, and his whole heart flew to her. Ah, if only he had the right to be by her side in those moments of intimacy, to be close, close enough to smell her perfumed skin, and to smile, too, at the baby. And gradually a romance began to take shape in his soul, a

170

brilliant, utterly absurd romance: a passionate wind, stronger than any human law, would violently catch them up and bind their two destinies together, his and hers; then what a divine existence would be theirs, hidden away in a sunny flowery nest, in some remote corner of Italy. And he was filled by all kinds of delicious ideas about love, devotion, and sacrifice, while his gaze grew distant, absent, absorbed in the religious solemnity of that lovely evening. A marvellous pale-gold colour was rising up from the sea and mounting the sky to transform the blue into an uncertain shade of gentle, swooning, opaline white; and each tree was tinged with a delicate, languid, golden tint. Every sound became as soft as a lost sigh. Nothing moved, as if all were frozen in the immobility of ecstasy. And the houses, turned to the west, with one or more windows aflame with light, the round tops of the crowded trees rushing in a thick flock down the mountain to the valley, everything, as it watched the dying sun sink slowly into the sea, seemed caught in grave, melancholy meditation.

"Is that you up there, Carlos?"

From down below, in the street, came Alencar's deep voice. Carlos appeared at the balustrade.

"What the devil are you doing, dear boy?" exclaimed Alencar, gaily waving his Panama hat. "We waited for you in the royal 'hovel.' We even went to the Nunes. In fact, we were just about to go to the prison to look for you!"

And the poet laughed out loud at his own joke, while Cruges, beside him, his hands behind his back, stood looking up at the terrace, yawning disconsolately.

"I came for a little 'refreshment,' as you would call it, to have some brandy. I was thirsty."

Brandy? That was just the treat poor Alencar had been longing for all afternoon, ever since Seteais. And he immediately bounded up the steps to the terrace, calling to his friend, Senhora Lawrence, the owner of the hotel, to send up half a bottle of brandy.

"So you visited the palace, then, Cruges?" Carlos asked the maestro, when, dragging his feet, he finally joined them. "Well, in that case, I think all that remains for us to do is to have dinner and leave."

Cruges agreed. He had returned from the palace apparently drained of energy, exhausted by that vast historic mansion, by the monotonous voice of the guide showing them His Majesty's bed, the curtains in Her Majesty the Queen's bedroom, "far superior to those at Mafra," and His Royal Highness's bootjack; and he had brought with him a little of the melancholy that always hangs, like an atmosphere, about all royal residences.

And as evening fell, Sintra's natural beauty was, he said, beginning to depress him.

They agreed to dine there, at the Lawrence, to avoid the ugly spectacle of Palma and the ladies, and to ask for the break to be brought to the hotel door: they would depart as soon as the moon rose. Alencar would take advantage of their departure to return to Lisbon with them.

"And just to complete the party," he exclaimed, wiping the brandy off his moustache, "while you go to the Hotel Nunes to pay your bill and to give orders for the break to be brought round, I'll go down to the kitchen and have a word with the cook and make you a dish of *bacalhau à Alencar*, my own recipe. Then you'll see what *bacalhau* ought to taste like! Others may write better poetry, but no one makes a better *bacalhau*!"

As they walked across the square, Cruges was praying that they did not meet Eusèbiozinho again. However, as soon as they set foot on the steps up to the hotel, they could hear their rowdy chatter. They were in the drawing room, with harmony restored and Concha contentedly sitting at a table playing cards. Palma, armed with a bottle of gin, was playing for money with Eusèbiozinho, while the two Spanish women, cigarette in mouth, were having a languid game of bisque.

Eusèbiozinho, looking deathly pale, was losing. In the kitty, which had started with only two crowns, there was already the glint of gold coins. Palma was winning, talking loudly and planting the occasional wet kiss on his beloved. At the same time, though, he was also pretending to be the gentleman and talking about letting his opponent have his revenge and how he was prepared to stay up until dawn if necessary.

"Aren't you gentlemen tempted to join us? We're just killing time really. In Sintra anything will do. Jack! You've lost another king! That's a *libra* plus fifteen *tostões* you owe me, Silveira!"

Carlos, followed by the footman, had walked past without saying a word, just at the moment when a furious and suspicious Eusèbiozinho was peering through his dark glasses at the pack, trying to find out if all the kings were actually there.

Palma took no offence and slowly spread the cards. After all, they were among friends! His Spanish sweetheart was greatly scandalised, however, and defended her man's honour: was he accusing her Palma of palming the king? Concha, on the other hand, was more concerned about her dear widower's money and suggested that perhaps the king had got lost. The kings, however, were all there.

Palma tossed back another tot of gin and started majestically shuffling the cards.

"So you're not tempted then, sir?" he said to Cruges.

Cruges had, in fact, stopped by the table, clinking his money in his pocket, unable to resist, his eyes on the cards and on the gold in the kitty. An ace decided him. With one nervous hand, he slipped a *libra* underneath it, betting five *tostões*. He lost straight away. When Carlos came down with a servant carrying the luggage, Cruges, having committed his one *libra*, was already in too deep, his eyes ablaze and his hair dishevelled.

"Not you as well," Carlos said severely.

"I'll be right down," grunted Cruges.

In a hurry now, he bet all his money on a three beating a king. A difficult trick, as Palma said, and he began dealing the cards with painful slowness, very carefully putting one down and then another. He put down a card and let out a curse. It was a two, and Eusèbiozinho had lost again. Palma gave a little sigh of relief, covered the deck with both hands and directed the glittering lenses of his glasses at Cruges.

"You still want to bet the whole *libra*?"

"Yes."

Palma sighed again, anxiously this time, and, looking paler now, he turned the cards over very quickly.

"A king!" he cried, grabbing the money.

It was the king of spades; his Spanish love applauded, and Cruges left, feeling furious.

At the Hotel Lawrence, supper went on until eight o'clock, and the lights had to be lit. Alencar talked all the time. With life's disappointments and literary rivalries temporarily forgotten, he was in excellent form: he told stories about the old days in Sintra, about his famous visit to Paris, saucy anecdotes regarding women he had known, and intimate titbits about the years of the Regeneration. And he did all this at the top of his voice, addressing them loudly as "boys" and "lads," making wild gestures that made the flames of the candles tremble, and, all the while, downing glasses of Colares wine. On the other side of the table, the two Englishmen, very correct in their black tailcoats and their white carnations, were taken aback by this show of disorderly Latin exuberance and affected an air half of embarrassment and half of disdain.

The *bacalhau* was a triumph, and the poet was so pleased that he wished Ega could have been there!

"I have always wanted him to try this *bacalhau*! Since he doesn't appreciate my poetry, he might at least enjoy my cooking, because this *bacalhau* really is a work of art! The other day, I made it for the Cohens, and Raquel, poor dear, came over to me and embraced me, because you see, boys, poetry and cooking are sister arts! Just look at Alexandre Dumas. You'll say that Dumas isn't a poet, but what about d'Artagnan? D'Artagnan is a poem—he's all fire and fantasy and inspiration and dream and rapture! So, you see, he *is* a poet. You'll have to come and have supper with me one day, and Ega must come too. I'll cook you a dish of partridges *à l'espagnole* that will have castanets growing out of your finger-tips! Oh, I like Ega, I really do! All this business about realism and romanticism is a lot of nonsense. A lily is as natural as a bedbug. If some prefer the stench of the gutter, fine, open up the public sewers. I prefer a dusting of powder on a soft white breast; I'll take the breast, you can do what you like. What you need is heart. And Ega has it. And he has fire and audacity and style in plenty. That's all you need, so let's drink to Ega's health!"

Then he put down his glass, smoothed his moustache and said in a low voice:

"And if those two Englishmen don't stop gawping at me, I'll smash this glass in their face, and we'll unleash a storm here that will show Great Britain just what we Portuguese poets are made of!"

But there was no storm; Great Britain remained in ignorance of just what Portuguese poets are made of, and supper concluded with a quiet cup of coffee. It was nine o'clock and the moon was up when Carlos climbed onto the driver's seat of the break.

Alencar, swathed in a cape worthy of a village priest, was carrying a bunch of roses, and, having stowed his Panama hat in his bag, had donned instead an otter-skin cap. Cruges, heavy with supper and with his spirits slowly sinking, huddled silently in one corner of the break, his coat collar turned right up and with his Mama's travelling-rug over his knees. They set off. Sintra lay sleeping beneath the moonlight.

For some time, the break rolled on in silence, in the beauty of the night. Here and there, along the road, lay pools of warm, sparkling light. The pale, mute façades of houses emerged from the trees with an air of romantic melancholy. Murmuring streams vanished into the shadows, and whenever the break passed a wall overgrown with trees, the air filled with perfume. Alencar had lit his pipe and was gazing up at the moon.

As they passed the houses of São Pedro and joined the sad silent road, Cruges stirred and coughed and, looking up at the moon as well, said softly from his many layers of clothing:

"Alencar, recite something for us."

The poet agreed with alacrity, even though one of the servants was there with them, inside the break. But on such an enchanted moonlit night, what could he possibly recite? All poetry seemed dull in comparison with the moon. Then he explained that he would tell a very true and very sad story. In his great cape, he went over to sit next to Cruges, tapped out his pipe and, after stroking his moustache for a while, he began in a simple, familiar tone:

> *Once upon a time in an ancient garden*
> *With no ornate statues or exotic flowers,*
> *Only simple box hedges and lavender bowers,*
> *Carnations and roses and . . .*

"Oh, damn!" cried Cruges, flinging off his blanket with a yell that silenced the poet, startled the footman and made Carlos turn round in the driver's seat.

The break stopped, they all stared at him, and in the vast silence of the plain, which lay bathed in peaceful moonlight, a distraught Cruges exclaimed:

"I forgot to buy the cheese pastries!"

: IX :

AT THE END OF A WEEK of sweet luminous weather, the day of the Cohens' famous soirée dawned sad and misty. When, at an early hour, Carlos opened his window and looked out at the garden, he saw a low heavy sky, like grubby cotton wool: the damp trees seemed to be shivering; in the distance, the river looked murky; and in the limp air there was just a breath of wind from the warm southwest. He had decided not to go out, and, wrapped in his vast blue velvet dressing-gown, which made him look rather like a noble Renaissance artist-prince, he had been seated at his desk since nine o'clock, trying to work; but, despite two cups of coffee and endless cigarettes, his brain that morning, like the sky outside, remained drowned in mists. He sometimes had dreadful days like this; he thought himself "a complete dolt," and the pile of torn-up, screwed-up sheets of paper that accumulated on the carpet at his feet left him feeling like the mere ruin of a man.

It was a real relief, a truce in that battle with rebellious ideas, when Baptista announced Vilaça, who had come to discuss with him the sale of some land in the Alentejo which was part of his inheritance.

"A little deal," said the administrator, placing on one corner of the desk his hat and in it a roll of papers, "which will place in your pocket more than two *contos de réis*. Not a bad little gift, first thing in the morning."

Carlos yawned and stretched his arms, knitting his fingers together behind his head.

"I could certainly do with two *contos de réis*, but I would much prefer a little clarity of thought. I'm feeling so stupid today."

Vilaça looked at him mischievously for a moment.

"Do you mean to say that you would rather write a fine piece of prose than receive nearly five hundred *libras*? Well, there's no accounting for tastes. It would be nice if you turned out to be an Herculano or a Garrett, but two *contos de réis* are two *contos de réis*. They're worth a pamphlet any time. Anyway, this is the deal . . ."

He explained it all to him hurriedly, without sitting down, while Carlos, arms folded, was thinking what a frightful tie-pin Vilaça was wearing (a coral

175

monkey eating a golden pear) and through his mental fog he could just make out that "the deal" had something to do with a certain Viscount de Torral and some pigs. When Vilaça set the papers before him, Carlos put his signature to them with all the vim of a dying man.

"So, are you staying for lunch, Vilaça?" he said, seeing the administrator putting his roll of papers under his arm.

"That's very kind of you, sir, but I have a meeting with our friend Eusébio. We're going to the Ministry of the Interior; he's hoping for some preferment, well, what he really wants is to be given the Order of the Conception, but the powers-that-be are rather less than happy with him."

"Surely not," murmured Carlos respectfully, failing to suppress a yawn. "Fancy the government being unhappy with Eusèbiozinho."

"He didn't perform very well during the elections. Some days ago, the Interior Minister said to me: 'Eusébio's a nice enough fellow, but devious.' Oh, yes, Cruges mentioned to me that you bumped into Eusébio in Sintra the other day."

"Indeed, and he was hard at work earning his Order of the Conception."

When Vilaça left, Carlos slowly took up his pen again and remained for a moment, staring at the half-filled page, scratching his beard and feeling uninspired and sterile. Then Afonso da Maia came in, still with his hat on, just back from his morning constitutional and bearing a letter addressed to Carlos, which he had found mixed up with his correspondence. Apart from that, he had been hoping to find Vilaça there.

"He was here, but he had to rush off to sort out some kind of commendation for Eusèbiozinho," said Carlos, opening the letter.

And he was surprised to find on the piece of paper—impregnated with the same verbena perfume as that worn by the Countess de Gouvarinho—a supper invitation from the Count for the following Saturday, couched in such carefully chosen terms of affection that it verged almost on the poetic; he even made some jocular comment about friendship and Descartes' *atomes crochus*. Carlos burst out laughing and told his grandfather that it was a letter from a peer of the realm, inviting him to supper and quoting Descartes into the bargain.

"They're capable of anything, these people," muttered Afonso.

And glancing with a smile at the manuscripts scattered about the desk, he added:

"So you're managing to get some work done, then?"

Carlos shrugged.

"If you can call it work. Look at the floor, look at all the rejects! When it's a question of taking notes, collating documents, gathering material, I'm fine, but when it comes to giving those ideas and observations some kind of shape and symmetry, giving them colour, bringing them to life, I'm lost!"

"A very peninsular preoccupation, my boy," said Afonso, sitting down by the desk, his broad-brimmed hat in his hand. "Don't let it get a grip on you! I was saying exactly this to Craft the other day, and he agreed. We Portuguese will never be men of ideas because of our passion for form. We're all obsessed with turning a fine phrase, seeing it shine and hearing it sing. If we have to falsify or exaggerate an idea or even leave it incomplete in order to make a phrase read more beautifully, we, poor wretches, wouldn't hesitate. The thought may have been lost, but the beautiful phrase has been saved."

"It's a matter of temperament," said Carlos. "There are inferior beings to whom the sound of an adjective is more important than the exact working of a system—and I'm one of those monsters."

"Oh, no, you're not a rhetorician, are you?"

"Who isn't? Perhaps style has a disciplining effect on thought. As you yourself know, in poetry, it's often the need for a rhyme that produces the most original image. And who can say, perhaps the effort of finding the right cadence for a phrase might sometimes shed a new and unexpected light on an idea. Long live the beautiful phrase!"

"Senhor Ega," announced Baptista, drawing aside the door curtain, just as the lunch bell rang out.

"Speaking of beautiful phrases," said Afonso, laughing.

"What's all this about phrases?" asked Ega, who burst into the room looking disoriented, unshaven, and with his overcoat collar turned up. "Fancy meeting you here at this hour, Senhor Afonso da Maia! How are you, sir? Carlos, I need you to get me out of a scrape. Do you, by any chance, have a sword I can use?"

And in response to Carlos' look of astonishment, he added impatiently:

"Yes, man, a sword! I'm not going to impale anyone; I'm perfectly at peace with the whole of humanity. It's for tonight, for my costume."

That fool Matos had only given him his costume for the ball the previous night, and Ega had been horrified to find that instead of an artistic sword, he had given him a guard's sabre! He had felt tempted to run him through with it. He went racing over to see Old Abraão, but he only had court swords, as cheap and pretentious as the Court itself. Then he had thought of Craft and his collection, indeed, he had just come from there; but they were all great iron things, scimitars that weighed a ton, broadswords with which those brutes, the British, had conquered India, but nothing that was of any use to him. Then he had remembered Ramalhete's antique panoplies of arms.

"You must have what I need: a long, slender sword, with a guard made of filigreed steel and lined with scarlet velvet. And definitely no cross-guard!"

Afonso, immediately taking a paternal interest in Ega's problem, mentioned that there were some Spanish swords in the corridor, high up on the wall.

"High up, in the corridor?" exclaimed Ega, already drawing back the curtain.

His haste was in vain, for he failed to find them. They were not on display, but still in the trunks that had been brought from Benfica.

"I'll go, you wretch, I'll go," said Carlos, getting reluctantly to his feet. "But they don't have scabbards."

Ega was cast down, but Afonso came up with an idea to save him.

"Just have a simple scabbard made out of black velvet. It would only take an hour. And have strips of scarlet velvet sewn around it."

"Splendid!" cried Ega. "Ah, what it is to have taste!"

And as soon as Carlos had left the room, Ega railed against Matos.

"Can you imagine, a municipal guard's sabre! And he's the man who makes all the costumes for the theatres! A complete idiot! But then that's the way it is in this ridiculous country!"

"My dear Ega, you're surely not going to make the whole of Portugal, the State, and its seven million inhabitants responsible for Matos' behaviour?"

"Yes, I am," exclaimed Ega, striding up and down the room, his hands in his overcoat pockets. "Yes, it's all of a piece. The costumier who sends a municipal guard's sabre along with a fourteenth-century outfit; a minister who, apropos of taxes, quotes from Lamartine's *Méditations poétiques*; and the man of letters, that supreme fool . . ."

But he stopped when he saw the sword Carlos had in his hand, a sixteenth-century foil, well-tempered, fine and supple, with a guard as fine as lace, and the illustrious name of its maker, Francisco Rui of Toledo, engraved on the blade.

He immediately wrapped it up in newspaper, hurriedly declined the offer of lunch, shook them both vigorously by the hand, pulled on his hat and was just about to dash off, when Afonso's voice stopped him.

"Listen here, João," said the old man gaily, "that sword belongs to our family and has, as far as I know, never been used ingloriously. Mind what you do with it!"

Ega turned at the door and, clutching to his breast the sword wrapped up in a copy of the *Jornal do Comércio*, he exclaimed:

"I will not draw it unjustly, nor will I return it to its scabbard dishonoured. *Au revoir!*"

"Ah the energy of youth!" murmured Afonso. "He's certainly happy, our João! Go and get changed, my dear, they've already rung the first bell for lunch!"

Carlos lingered a while longer to re-read the Count's elaborate letter, and he was just about to summon Baptista in order to get dressed for lunch, when downstairs, at the private entrance to his rooms, the electric bell began to ring violently. Anxious footsteps came echoing down the hallway, and Dâmaso appeared, panting, eyes wide and face ablaze. And without giving Carlos time to express surprise at seeing him back in Ramalhete, he threw up his arms and cried:

"Thank God you're here! I need you to come and see a patient—now. I'll explain on the way. It's that Brazilian family. But, please, for the love of God, come quickly."

Carlos had leapt to his feet, looking very pale:

"Is it her?"

"No, it's the little girl, she's deathly ill apparently. But get dressed, Carlos, get dressed! It's all my responsibility!"

"She's just a baby, isn't she?"

"What do you mean 'a baby'? No, she's nearly six. Come on!"

Carlos, already in his shirtsleeves, was holding out his foot to Baptista who, down on one knee, and in equal haste, almost tore the buttons off the boot. And Dâmaso, still with his hat on, paced up and down, exaggerating his impatience, bursting with self-importance.

"The scrapes one gets oneself in! And, of course, I feel responsible. I was making my usual morning visit, only to find that they had left for Queluz."

Carlos turned round, still pulling on his frock-coat.

"So . . ."

"No, *they've* gone to Queluz, but the little girl stayed behind with the governess. She complained of a pain after lunch. The governess wanted to call an English doctor because she only speaks English. The hotel sent for Dr. Smith, but he never came. And the little girl appeared to be dying. Fortunately, at that point, *I* arrived and thought of you. I was damned lucky to find you in!"

And he added, looking out at the garden.

"Fancy going to Queluz on a day like this! They won't have much fun there! Are you ready? I've got the coupé downstairs. Leave your gloves, you look fine without them!"

"Tell my grandfather not to wait for me for lunch," Carlos shouted up to Baptista from the bottom of the stairs.

In the coupé, a huge bouquet of flowers almost filled the whole seat.

"They were for her," said Dâmaso, placing it on his knees. "She's mad about flowers."

As soon as the coupé set off, Carlos closed the window and asked the question that had been burning on his lips ever since Dâmaso's sudden arrival.

"I thought you wanted to punch Castro Gomes in the face."

Dâmaso immediately and triumphantly told him everything. It had all been a mistake! Castro Gomes had explained it like the true gentleman he was. If he hadn't, then Dâmaso would definitely have punched him in the face. He didn't take snubs from anyone! No one! But this is what had happened: the visiting cards he had left for him still showed his address at the Grand Hotel in Paris, and Castro Gomes, assuming that this was where he lived, had, in accordance with the address provided, sent his cards there! Odd, eh? Rather stupid really. And the lack of response to his telegrams had been Madame's fault, an oversight during a most upsetting period when her husband had dislocated his shoulder. They had apologised most humbly. And now they were intimate friends, and he went there almost every day.

"A real romance, but I'll tell you about that later."

The coupé had stopped outside the door of the Hotel Central. Dâmaso jumped out and ran over to the doorman.

"Did you send the telegram, António?"

"Yes, sir, it's on its way."

"Of course," he was saying to Carlos as he bounded up the steps, "I immediately sent a telegram to their hotel in Queluz. I don't want to take on any more responsibility than I have to."

In the corridor, outside the office, a waiter was passing, with a napkin over his arm.

"How's the little girl?" Dâmaso cried.

The waiter shrugged in incomprehension.

But Dâmaso was already marching, panting, up the next flight of stairs, booming:

"This way, Carlos. I know this place like the back of my hand! Number 26!"

He flung open the door of room 26. A maid, who was standing at the window, turned round.

"Ah, *bonjour*, Melanie!" exclaimed Dâmaso in his extraordinary French. Was the child better? *L'enfant était meilleur?* He had brought the doctor with him, Dr. Maia.

Melanie, a skinny freckle-faced girl, said that *mademoiselle* was feeling more comfortable now and that she would go and tell Miss Sara, the governess, that they were there. She ran a duster over the marble top of a console table, straightened the books that were lying there, and left, darting a burning glance at Carlos as she did so.

It was a spacious room, with furniture upholstered in blue rep; a large mirror hung above the gilt console table between the two windows; the larger table in the middle of the room was covered with newspapers, cigar boxes, and French novels by Capendu; on a chair beside it was some embroidery work, rolled up.

"She's such a slattern, that Melanie," muttered Dâmaso, shutting the window and struggling with the catch. "Leaving everything open like this! Honestly!"

"The gentleman appears to be a Bonapartist," said Carlos, seeing numerous copies of *Pays* on the table.

"Oh, we have the most terrible arguments," exclaimed Dâmaso, "which I always win hands down. He's a good enough fellow, but not exactly deep."

Melanie returned and asked *Monsieur le Docteur* to come into the dressing-room for a moment. And there, after picking up a towel from the floor and shooting Carlos another saucy look, she informed him that Miss Sara would join him at once and then tiptoed out. In the drawing room, Dâmaso's voice could be heard reminding Melanie of her responsibilities and declaring that he was *très affligé*.

Carlos remained alone in the intimacy of that dressing-room, which had not yet been tidied. Two huge magnificent trunks, clearly belonging to *Madame*, with locks and corners made of polished steel, stood open: the lovely wine-red silk train of a dress spilled forth from one, and the other afforded a glimpse of delicate white underwear, a whole refined, secret world of lace and batiste, all bright as snow, worn soft by use and exuding a delicious scent. Over a chair cascaded a pile of silk stockings of every shade, plain, embroidered, lacework, and so light that the slightest breeze would carry them off; and on the floor stood a line of patent-leather shoes, all in the same elongated, low-heeled style, with broad ribbon laces. In one corner was a padded basket in pink silk, in which the little dog doubtless travelled.

But what drew Carlos' eye most was a sofa on which lay, sleeves outspread, like two welcoming arms, the white Genoese velvet jacket she had been wearing when he had seen her for the first time, stepping out of her carriage at the door of the hotel. The white satin lining contained no padding at all, so perfect must be the body that wore it; and lying like that on the sofa, in that life-like attitude, in that half-naked, unbuttoned state, with just the vague suggestion of two full breasts, and with those arms outstretched in surrender, the very fabric seemed to exhale a human warmth and to contain the shape of an amorous body, swooning in the silence of a bedroom. Carlos was aware of his heart beating. All those intimate garments exuded a strong, indefinable scent of jasmine, *maréchale*, and tanglewood, which seemed to touch his cheek like a soft caressing breeze.

He looked away and went over to the window, which had only a view of the shabby façade of the Hotel Shneid. When he turned round, Miss Sara was there before him, all dressed in black and looking very flushed; she was a small, pleasant, chubby person, with the air of a plump, well-fed pigeon, with kindly eyes and a virginal forehead beneath her fair, straight hair. She stammered out some words in French, of which Carlos understood only *docteur*.

"Yes, I'm the doctor," he said.

The excellent Englishwoman's face lit up. Oh, it was so good to find someone she could talk to at last! The little girl was much better, but the doctor would relieve her of such a weight of responsibility!

She drew back the door curtain and ushered him into a room where all the windows were closed and he could just make out the shape of a large bed and the glint of glass on a dressing table. He asked why the room was so dark.

Miss Sara had thought that it would be good for the little girl and help her to fall asleep. And she had brought her into her mother's room because it was larger and airier.

Carlos asked her to open the curtains, and when the bright light poured in and he saw the girl lying on the bed, with the bed-curtains drawn back, he could not contain his surprise and admiration.

"What a beautiful child!"

And he stood for a moment, looking at her, as rapt as an artist, thinking that the softest and loveliest of whites in the most skilful combination of light could never equal the ivory paleness of that marvellous skin; and this adorable whiteness was set off by the child's thick, lustrous, intensely black hair caught up beneath a lace cap. Her two large eyes, of a deep liquid blue, seemed at that moment even larger and wider as they looked gravely up at him.

She was leaning back against a large pillow, not moving, still frightened by the pain she had experienced, looking small and lost in that vast bed, and clutching in her arms a huge elaborately dressed doll with curly hair and with the same very wide blue eyes.

Carlos took the child's hand and kissed it, asking if her doll was also ill.

"Cricri had a pain too," she replied very seriously, never taking her magnificent eyes off him. "I don't have a pain now though."

She did, in fact, look as fresh as a flower; her little tongue was nice and pink, and she was eager to have something to eat.

Carlos reassured Miss Sara. Yes, she could see now that *mademoiselle* was better. It was just that she had been frightened to find herself all alone, without the child's mother there; it was such a responsibility. That is why she had put her to bed. If she were an English child, she would have taken her out for a walk, but these foreign children, so weak, so delicate . . . And the Englishwoman's plump lips revealed a compassionate disdain for these inferior, degenerate races.

"But her Mama is not ill?"

No, *Madame* was very strong. The gentleman, however, seemed weaker.

"And what's *your* name, my little friend?" Carlos asked, sitting down on the bed.

"This is Cricri," said the child, introducing the doll again, "and my name is Rosa, although Papa says I'm Rosicler."

"Rosicler? Really?" said Carlos, smiling at this name straight out of some chivalric novel, and redolent of tournaments and fairy-tale woods.

Then, as if simply gleaning the kind of information a doctor might need, he asked Miss Sara if the child had perhaps reacted badly to the change of climate. They usually lived in Paris, didn't they?

Yes, they spent the winter in Paris, in Parc Monceaux; in summer they went to an estate in Turennes, near Tours, where they stayed until the beginning of the hunting season; and they always spent a month in Dieppe. At least that is how it had been for the last three years, since she had been with *Madame*.

While the Englishwoman was talking, Rosa, with her doll in her arms, kept staring gravely at Carlos, as if in amazement. He smiled at her now and then and stroked her little hand. Her mother's eyes were dark; her father's were small and jet-black; so from whom had she inherited those marvellous blue eyes, so intense, liquid, and sweet?

His visit as a doctor had come to an end, and he got up to write a prescription for a sedative. While the Englishwoman was carefully preparing a piece of paper and trying out the pen, he briefly examined the room. In that banal hotel bedroom, certain delicately elegant touches revealed a woman of taste and luxury: there were large floral arrangements on the dresser and on the table; the pillowcases and the sheets were not from the hotel, but her own, made from fine Breton linen edged with lace and bearing bold embroidered monograms in two colours. A length of Tarna cashmere disguised the hideous faded rep of the armchair.

When he had written the prescription, Carlos noticed various richly bound books on the table, novels and English poetry: looking strangely out of place was a pamphlet entitled *Manual for the Interpretation of Dreams*. And on the dressing table, among ivory-backed brushes, crystal bottles, and fine tortoise-shell combs, there was another peculiar object, an enormous gilt silver powder box with, encrusted in the lid, a magnificent sapphire surrounded by a circle of tiny diamonds, a gaudy jewel worthy of a *cocotte*, which struck a boldly dissonant note of vulgar splendour.

Carlos went back to the bedside and asked Rosicler for a kiss; she immediately offered him her fresh rosebud mouth; he did not, however, dare to kiss her mouth while she lay there in her mother's great bed, and so he merely planted a kiss on her forehead.

"When are you coming again?" she asked, grasping the sleeve of his coat.

"There's no need for me to come back, my dear. You're better and so is Cricri."

"But I want my lunch. Tell Sara that I can have my lunch now. And Cricri too."

"Yes, of course, you can both have something to eat now."

He made his recommendations to the governess and then, taking the little girl's hand, said:

"Goodbye, then, my pretty Rosicler, since that is your name."

And not wishing to treat the doll with any less formality, he shook her hand as well.

This appeared to charm Rosa even more. Miss Sara was at her side, a smile dimpling her cheeks.

It wasn't necessary, Carlos reminded her, to keep the girl in bed, nor to be overly protective of her.

"No, sir!"

And should the pain return, however slight, they should call for him at once.

"Yes, sir!"

And he left his card with his address on it.

"Thank you, sir!"

When he went back into the drawing room, Dâmaso, who had been leafing through a newspaper, sprang to his feet like a wild beast whose cage door had just been flung open.

"I thought you were never coming out! What on earth were you doing in there! I nearly died of boredom."

Carlos, drawing on his gloves, smiled and said nothing.

"So, is it anything bad?"

"No, she has nothing wrong with her at all. But she has lovely eyes and an extraordinary name."

"Oh, yes, Rosicler," muttered Dâmaso, bad-temperedly picking up his hat. "Pretty ridiculous, don't you think?"

The French maid reappeared in order to open the drawing room door, again shooting Carlos a bright ardent look. Dâmaso told her to be sure to tell her master and mistress that he, Dâmaso, had fetched a doctor immediately, and that he would be back that night with a little surprise and to find out if they had enjoyed Queluz—*s'ils avaient aimé Queluz.*

Then, as they passed the office, he put his head round the door to tell the bookkeeper that the little girl was better and that there was no need to worry.

The bookkeeper smiled and bowed.

"Shall I take you home?" Dâmaso asked Carlos rather grumpily, as he opened the door of his carriage.

Carlos preferred to walk.

"Walk with me for a while, Dâmaso; after all, you have nothing to do now."

Dâmaso hesitated, looking up at the ominous sky, at the clouds heavy with rain. Carlos took his arm and affectionately tugged at it, joking with him.

"Now that I have you here, you wretch, you libertine, I want to hear all about this romance. You told me there was a romance, and now I won't let you go. You're mine. Come on, what *is* this romance of yours? I know you only ever have the very finest of romances, so out with it!"

Gradually, Dâmaso began to smile, his fat cheeks grew red with pleasure.

"Well, no, I certainly have no complaints on that score," he said, bursting with pride.

"Did you go to Sintra with them?"

"I did, but it was terribly dull. The 'romance' is something else entirely."

He detached his arm from Carlos' grip, signalled to the coachman to follow them and, as they walked along the Aterro, he regaled Carlos with the tale of his "romance."

"The thing is the husband is going back to Brazil in a few days' time to deal with business there. And she's staying behind. She's going to wait for him here with the maids and the little girl for two or three months. She says they've already been looking for a furnished house because she doesn't want to stay on in the hotel. And there I am, a close family friend, the only person she knows, on the inside! Do you see?"

"Perfectly," said Carlos, irritably throwing down his cigar. "And, of course, the poor creature is already in love with you! You have, as usual, behind her husband's back, bestowed passionate kisses on her! The wretched woman has doubtless already got the box of matches ready for when you leave her later on!"

Dâmaso turned pale.

"Now don't you start in with your cutting remarks and your innuendos. I haven't kissed her because I haven't had the chance. But what I can tell you is this—she's mine!"

"About time too!" exclaimed Carlos, unable to control his irritation and almost throwing the words at him as if lashing him with a whip. "About time too! The women you've been with before have been the lowest of the low, mere bawdy-house riff-raff. At least, you're progressing. I like my friends to lead a decent orderly love-life. And don't behave as you usually do! Don't go boasting about it in the Grémio or the Casa Havanesa!"

This time Dâmaso drew back in anger, unable to understand why Carlos was being so aggressive. White-faced, he managed, at last, to stammer out: "You may know a lot about medicine and antiques, but when it comes to women and how to behave, I certainly don't need any lessons from you."

Carlos looked at him, feeling a terrible desire to hit him. Then, suddenly, he sensed how inoffensive and insignificant this soft chubby-cheeked Dâmaso was, and, feeling ashamed of his own spiteful feelings, he took Dâmaso's arm again and said gently:

"Dâmaso, you misunderstand me. I didn't mean to make you angry. It's for your own good. I was simply afraid that you, being your reckless, bold, passionate self, might spoil this beautiful adventure through some indiscretion."

Dâmaso's anger was immediately assuaged and he smilingly allowed his friend to take his arm again, convinced that Carlos' one desire was for him to have a chic mistress. He hadn't been angry, he never got angry with his friends. He understood that Carlos had only said what he said out of friendship. "But you can be very sharp-tongued sometimes— a habit you've picked up from Ega."

He reassured Carlos. He wouldn't "spoil things" by any recklessness. He had it all worked out. He had more than enough experience of such things. He had Melanie eating out of his hand already; why, he'd given her two *libras*.

"Besides, this is a serious business. Madame Gomes knows my uncle, she's known him since she was a child; they even call each other 'tu.'"

"Which uncle?"

"My Uncle Joaquim, Joaquim Guimarães, Monsieur de Guimaran, the one who lives in Paris and is a friend of Gambetta."

"Ah, yes, the communist."

"He's no communist—he has his own carriage!"

He suddenly remembered something else, a point of dress about which he wanted to consult Carlos.

"I'm having supper with them tomorrow, and two other Brazilians are going as well, friends of his who arrived a few days ago and who will be leaving on the same boat. One of them is *very* chic, from the Brazilian embassy in London. So it's going to be a formal do. Castro Gomes hasn't said anything to me about what to wear, but what do you think, should I wear tails?"

"Yes, full evening dress and a rose in your button-hole."

Dâmaso looked at him thoughtfully.

"I was thinking of wearing the Order of Christ."

"The Order of Christ . . . Yes, why not? Hang it round your neck and stick a rose in your button-hole."

"You don't think that would be too much, do you, Carlos?"

"No, it would suit you."

Dâmaso ordered the carriage that had been following them to stop, and as he shook Carlos' hand, he said:

"Have you had any further thoughts on what you're wearing to the Cohens' costume ball or is it still to be the domino? My slave outfit has turned out brilliantly. I'm going to show it to my Brazilian lady tonight. I'll go into the hotel wrapped in a big cloak and burst in on them in the drawing room, dressed as Nelusko the slave and singing:

> *Alerta, marinari,*
> *Il vento cangia . . .*

"*Very* chic!" And he added in English: "Goodbye!"

At ten o'clock, Carlos was getting dressed for the Cohens' ball. Outside, the night had grown dark, with great gusts of wind and sheets of rain that battered the garden. There in the dressing-room a vague aroma of soap and good cigars floated in the warm air. On two Indian rosewood chests of drawers, inlaid with ivory, two old bronze candelabra proffered bunches of lit candles, which cast a golden light on the brown silk of the walls. The black satin domino costume with its large pale-blue bow had already been laid out on the armchair next to the tall cheval-glass.

Baptista, holding Carlos' tailcoat, was waiting until Carlos had finished sipping his cup of black tea, which he was drinking standing up, in shirtsleeves and white tie. Suddenly, the electric bell again rang out loudly, urgently.

"Perhaps it's another surprise," murmured Carlos. "It's been a day of surprises."

Baptista smiled and was just about to put down the tailcoat in order to go and open the door, when the bell sounded again, this time with wild impatience.

Gripped by curiosity, Carlos went out into the hallway. In the half-light of the oil lamps, further tempered by the cherry-red velvets, he watched as the front door opened, letting in a cold blast of night air, and saw a lanky scarlet figure slip lithely in, accompanied by a faint clank of metal. Then, bobbing up the stairs, came two black cockerel feathers and a fluttering scarlet cloak—and there was Ega, standing before him dressed as Mephistopheles!

Carlos barely had time to say "Bravo," before the look on Ega's face silenced him. Despite those elements of his disguise that rendered him almost unrecognisable—the diabolical eyebrows, the wildly exaggerated moustache—Carlos could see how distressed Ega was from his bloodshot eyes and ashen face. He gestured to Carlos and hurried into the dressing-room. Baptista discreetly withdrew, drawing the curtain closed behind him.

They were alone, and Ega, desperately wringing his hands, said in a faint, hoarse voice:

"Do you know what's happened to me, Carlos?"

But he could say no more, choked with sobs, trembling all over; and Carlos, watching his every move, turned pale and trembled too.

"I went early to the Cohens' house," Ega managed at last to stammer out, "just as we had arranged. When I went into the drawing room, two or three people were already there. Cohen came straight over to me and said: 'Out in the street with you, you scoundrel. Out in the street with you. If you don't leave, I'll kick you out myself, with these people here as witnesses!' And Carlos, I . . ."

Anger once more drowned his voice, and he stood for a while biting his lips, choking back sobs, his eyes bright with tears.

When his words returned, it was in a savage explosion:

"I want to fight a duel with the wretch, at five paces, and put a bullet through his heart!"

Further strangulated sounds emerged from his throat; then, stamping his feet and punching the air, he screamed out, again and again, as if drawing strength from the sheer volume of his own voice:

"I'll kill him! I'll kill him! I'll kill him!"

Beside himself with rage and forgetting all about Carlos, he started furiously pacing the room, his cloak thrown back and his loosely buckled sword banging against his scarlet shins.

"So he knows everything," murmured Carlos.

"Of course he knows everything," exclaimed Ega, continuing his wild pacing and gesticulating. "I don't know how he found out, but he did, and that's bad enough, but, worse, the man threw me out. I'll put a bullet in him! I swear on the soul of my own father, I'll pierce his heart! Tomorrow morning, I want you to go there with Craft . . . and the conditions are these: pistols at fifteen paces!"

Carlos, who had once more recovered his calm, finished his cup of tea and said very simply:

"My dear Ega, you can't challenge Cohen to a duel."

Ega stood stock-still, his eyes still flashing with anger, an anger which was lent a theatrical, comical ferocity by the hideous crêpe eyebrows and by the two bobbing cockerel feathers in his cap.

"I can't challenge him to a duel?"

"No."

"So ejecting me from his house . . ."

"He had every right to do so."

"Every right? With witnesses there?"

"Weren't there witnesses to you being his wife's lover?"

Ega stared at Carlos for a moment, as if stunned. Then he made a grand dismissive gesture:

"It has nothing to do with his wife! His wife wasn't even mentioned! As far as I'm concerned, it's a question of honour. I want to challenge him to a duel, to kill him."

Carlos shrugged.

"You don't know what you're saying. There's only one thing to do: you must stay home tomorrow and wait and see if he challenges you."

"Who, Cohen?" exclaimed Ega. "He's a coward and a swine! I'll either kill him or scar his face with a whip. *Him* challenge *me*! Him! You're mad."

And breathing hard, grinding his teeth, and repeatedly pushing back his cloak, he resumed his furious pacing from the mirror to the window, making the tall flames of the candles flicker.

Carlos said nothing, standing by the table, slowly refilling his cup with tea. He was beginning to feel that none of this was very serious or very dignified, neither the husband's threats to kick Ega out of the house nor Ega's melodramatic ravings, and he even found it hard not to smile at the sight of this scrawny Mephistopheles filling the room with the bright scarlet of his velvet cloak and speaking furiously of honour and death, and wearing fake eyebrows and a leather purse at his belt.

"Let's go and talk to Craft about it!" exclaimed Ega, who, having arrived at this decision, abruptly ceased his pacing. "I want to know what Craft has to say. I've got a cab downstairs, we'll be there in an instant!"

"What," asked Carlos, looking at his watch, "go to his house in Olivais now?"

"If you are truly my friend, Carlos . . ."

Without summoning Baptista, Carlos immediately finished getting dressed.

Ega, meanwhile, was pouring himself some tea and adding a little rum to it, still so upset he could barely hold the bottle. Then, with a great sigh, he lit a cigarette. Carlos had gone into the bathroom next door, which was lit by a strong gaslight that whistled as it burned. Outside, the monotonous rain continued to fall, the water from the gutters spilling out onto the soft earth of the garden.

"Do you think the cab will make it?" Carlos called out.

"Yes, it's Canhoto's."

He noticed the domino and picked it up to examine the rich satin and the lovely pale-blue bow. Then, realising that he was standing in front of the large cheval-glass, he fixed his monocle in his eye, stepped back a little, and took a long look at himself, ending up by placing one hand on his hip and resting the other elegantly on the hilt of his sword.

"I look pretty good, don't you think, Carlos?"

"You look splendid," replied Carlos from the other room. "It's a shame it all came to nothing. Who was she going as?"

"Marguerite."

"And him?"

"That idiot? As a bedouin."

And he remained standing at the mirror, admiring his slender figure, the feathers in his cap, his pointed velvet shoes, and the glittering point of the sword that lifted his cloak at the back to form a knightly fold.

"So," said Carlos, as he emerged from the bathroom, drying his hands, "you have no idea what happened, what he might have said to his wife, what kind of scandal there might be."

"No, no idea at all," said Ega, calmer now. "When I went into the first drawing room, there he was dressed as a bedouin; there was another man there, too, dressed as a bear, and a lady as something else, a Tyrolean I think. He came over to me and said: 'Out in the street with you!' and that's all I know. If the swine has found out, he won't want to spoil the party and so he won't have said anything yet to Raquel. Afterwards, though, all hell will break loose!"

He raised his hands to heaven, murmuring:

"It's just *awful!*"

He resumed his pacing; then, screwing up his face, he said in quite a different voice:

"I don't know what the devil Godefroy gave me to glue these eyebrows on with, but they itch like the devil!"

"Take them off."

Still standing before the mirror, Ega seemed reluctant to spoil his fierce, Satanic appearance, but, in the end, he tore the eyebrows off and, at the same time, removed his tight feathered cap, which was making his head unbearably hot. Then Carlos suggested that, before going to Craft's house, he should also take off the cloak and sword and borrow one of his overcoats. Ega gave one last, long, silent look at his fine, infernal outfit and, with a deep sigh, started unbuckling his sword-belt. The overcoat proved to be too large and too long, and he had to roll the sleeves up slightly. Then Carlos placed a Scottish cap on his head. Thus attired, with his red devil's shins sticking out beneath the overcoat, the scarlet Charles IX ruff protruding above the collar, and that old Scottish cap on his head, Ega, alas, looked like a somewhat down-at-the-heels Satan, to whom a charitable gentleman had kindly donated his oldest set of clothes.

Baptista, grave and discreet, lit the way. Ega, as he passed him, murmured:

"Things are looking bad, Baptista, very bad indeed."

The old servant gave a sad shrug as if to say that nothing in the world was looking particularly good.

Out in the dark street, the horses were waiting patiently, their heads bowed beneath the rain. When offered a tip of one *libra*, Canhoto loudly urged them into action, and the old cab thundered down the street at a gallop, trailing water.

Occasionally, they would pass a private coupé, and the waterproof coats of the footmen would gleam white in the lantern light. Then came the thought of the party which would, by now, be in full resplendent swing—Marguerite, unaware of everything, waltzing in the arms of other men, wondering anxiously where he was; the supper afterwards, the champagne, the brilliant things he would have said—all these lost delights pierced poor Ega's heart and caused him to mutter bitter curses. Carlos was silently smoking, his mind on the Hotel Central.

After Santa Apolónia, the seemingly endless road began, exposed to the raw river air. Neither of them said a word, each in his corner, shivering in the chill wind that blew in through the cracks in the carriage. Carlos could not rid his mind of the image of that white velvet jacket, with its outspread sleeves, like two welcoming arms.

It took more than an hour to reach the house; the drenched coachman tugged at the bell pull by the gate, and the sound echoed lugubriously through the dark, village silence. A dog barked furiously, and other more distant barks responded; and Carlos and Ega still had to wait quite a while before a sleepy grumbling servant appeared, bearing a lantern. An avenue of acacias led up to the house; Ega cursed at having to sully his beautiful velvet shoes on the muddy path.

Surprised by all the noise, Craft came to meet them in the corridor in his dressing-gown and with the *Revue des Deux Mondes* under his arm. He realised at once that some disaster had occurred. Without a word, he led them to his study, which was entirely furnished with bright cretonnes and warmed and cheered by a good coal fire. Both men headed straight for the fire.

Ega immediately launched into an account of what had happened, while Craft, who showed neither surprise nor indignation, went about methodically preparing three hot toddies of brandy and lemon. Carlos, sitting beside the fire, was warming his feet, and Craft, once he had heard Ega out, made himself comfortable in his armchair on the other side of the hearth, his pipe in his mouth.

"So," exclaimed Ega, standing up and folding his arms, "what do you advise me to do?"

"The only thing you can do," said Craft, "is to stay at home tomorrow and wait for him to send you his seconds, which I'm sure he won't. However, if you are challenged, you must either allow yourself to be wounded or killed."

"Exactly what I said," murmured Carlos, taking a sip of his hot toddy.

Astonished, Ega stared at them both in turn. Then he let out a flood of garbled thoughts, complaining that he had no friends. There he was, facing the biggest crisis of his life, and his friends from childhood and from university, far from offering support, solidarity and loyalty *à tort et à travers*, were abandoning him, and appeared to wish him either dead or to expose him to still further humiliations. He grew emotional, and his eyes became red and tearful. And if one of them attempted to interrupt him with some word of common sense, he stamped his foot and stubbornly insisted that what he wanted was to challenge Cohen and to kill him and to have his revenge. He had been insulted. That was all that mattered. There had been no mention of Cohen's wife. He was the one who should be sending seconds, in order to cleanse his honour. There had been other people in the room when he was insulted—a bear and a woman in a Tyrolean costume. And he certainly had no intention of allowing himself to be pierced by a bullet! He had more right to live than Cohen, who was a bourgeois and a money-lender, whereas *he* was a man of letters, an artist! He had a head full of books and ideas and other splendid things. He owed it to Portugal and to civilisation to stay alive. If he did go off into the country it would be to practise his marksmanship and to shoot Cohen then and there, like the vile beast he was.

"But," he cried, exhausted at last, and collapsing onto a sofa, "it would seem that I have no friends!"

Craft was silently sipping his brandy.

It was Carlos who stood up, looking grave and austere. Ega had no right to doubt his friendship. When had he ever let him down? But he must stop engaging in these puerile theatrics. The fact was that Cohen had found out that he was having an affair with his wife. Therefore, he was perfectly within his rights to kill him or to hand him over to the courts or, indeed, to kick him out of his drawing room.

"Or worse still," said Craft, "send you the lady in question with a note saying 'Keep her.'"

"Exactly!" Carlos went on. "Instead, all he has done is to forbid you from entering his house, rather rudely, it's true, but by doing so, he has made it clear that he wants nothing more violent or more dramatic. It was, therefore, a very moderate reaction. And yet you still insist that you want to challenge him to a duel?"

Ega rebelled again, leapt to his feet and strutted about the room, minus his overcoat now, looking dishevelled and even more fantastical in his simple scarlet tunic, muddy velvet shoes, and long stork's legs clothed in red silk tights. He insisted that it had nothing to do with the wife! That was not it.

Carlos then got angry with him.

"So why the devil did he throw you out of his house? Don't talk nonsense, man! We're only telling you what anyone with any common sense would tell you. And it's sad how very hard it is for you to see that. Let's not beat about the bush here: you betrayed your friend! You publicly declared your friendship for Cohen. You betrayed him and you have to accept the law: if he wants to kill you, you have to die. If he chooses to do nothing, then likewise you must do nothing. If he wants to walk the streets calling you a scoundrel, you must simply bow your head and accept that you are indeed a scoundrel."

"You mean that I must simply swallow the insult?"

His two friends put it to him that his Satanic garb was clearly curbing his ability to judge things by mere worldly criteria, and that it was bordering on crass stupidity for Ega to speak of insults.

Ega, once more prostrate on the sofa, clutching his head, said at last:

"I just don't know any more. You're probably right. I feel like a complete fool. Tell me, then, what should I do?"

191

"Is your cab still waiting for you?" Craft asked calmly.

Carlos had told the coachman to unharness the exhausted horses and let them rest.

"Excellent! Right, my dear Ega, there is something else you must do before your possible demise tomorrow, and that is to have supper. I was just about to dine, and, for reasons too complicated to explain, I happen to have some cold turkey in the house, and there's sure to be a bottle of Burgundy around somewhere."

Shortly afterwards, they were all seated at the table in Craft's beautiful dining room, which had always so enchanted Carlos, with its oval tapestries depicting solitary woodland scenes, its severe Persian faience-ware, and its highly original fireplace flanked by two black Nubian figures with sparkling crystal eyes. Carlos, who declared himself to be famished, was already carving the turkey, while Craft was reverently uncorking two bottles of his finest Chambertin in order to comfort Mephistopheles.

Mephistopheles, still red-eyed and in a sombre mood, pushed away his plate and refused a glass, although he did subsequently condescend to take a sip of the Chambertin.

"When you arrived," Craft was saying, as he picked up his knife and fork, "I was reading a very interesting article about the decline of Protestantism in England."

"What's that over there, in that tin?" asked Ega glumly.

It was pâté de foie-gras. Mephistopheles dully took a truffle from a dish.

"Very good this Chambertin of yours," he sighed.

"Come on, eat and drink with a bit of gusto," cried Craft. "Don't romanticise your situation. Your problem is that you're hungry. All the ideas you've expressed tonight are simply a consequence of a lack of food."

Ega agreed that this was probably the case. What with all his excitement over his Satanic outfit, he had had no dinner, assuming that he would eat a hearty supper in the other man's house. Yes, it was true, he was hungry! And the foie-gras *was* excellent.

He was soon digging into slices of turkey, a large portion of tongue, two servings of ham, and other good English fare of the kind that Craft always had in his house. And Ega alone drank almost a whole bottle of Chambertin.

The footman had gone to prepare the coffee, and they, meanwhile, discussed Cohen's likely attitude to his wife. What would he do? Perhaps he would forgive her. Ega rejected the idea. The man was too vain and definitely the type to bear a grudge. And since she was a Jewess, he could hardly despatch her to a convent.

"Perhaps he'll kill her," said Craft quite seriously.

Ega, his eyes aglow now with Burgundy wine, declared tragically that, in that case, he would enter a monastery. The other two men teased him mercilessly. Which monastery would he choose? None really seemed exactly made for Ega!

He was too thin to be a Dominican, too talkative to be a Trappist, too lascivious to be a Jesuit, and too ignorant to be a Benedictine. An order would have to be created especially for him. Craft suggested the Order of the Holy Joker!

"You have no heart, you two," exclaimed Ega, filling a large glass with more wine. "You don't understand. I adored that woman!"

Then he started talking about Raquel, and he doubtless enjoyed the finest moments of that whole passionate affair right there, because he could, without scruple, burnish his lover's halo and bathe in the milky sea of vainglorious confidences. He began by describing how he had first met her in Foz. Craft—eager to learn and not missing a word—had meanwhile got up to open a bottle of champagne. Ega spoke then of their outings to Cantareira; the still hesitant, entirely platonic letters they had exchanged, concealed between the pages of the books they had lent each other, and in which she had signed herself "Violeta de Parma"; their first kiss, and the best, snatched behind a door while her husband ran upstairs to fetch him some special cigars; their rendez-vous in Oporto, in the Cemitério do Repouso, ardently holding hands in the shade of the cypresses, making plans among the gravestones for future voluptuous meetings.

"Fascinating!" said Craft.

At that point, Ega had to stop talking because the servant came in with the coffee. While the cups were being filled and Craft went in search of a box of cigars, Ega, by now looking very pale and pinched, finished off the bottle of champagne.

The footman left, drawing the tapestry curtain closed, and then Ega, a glass of brandy beside him, resumed his confidences, telling of the return to Lisbon, to Villa Balzac, of the delicious mornings they had spent there in the warmth of that bower.

He broke off, his eyes grown dark, fists pressed for a moment to his head. Then he added further details, the lewd nicknames she gave him, a particular black silk bedspread on which she glowed like veined marble. His eyes filled with tears, and he swore he would die!

"If you only knew what a body she had!" he cried suddenly. "What a body! And her breasts . . ."

"We don't want to know," said Carlos. "Be quiet! You're drunk, you wretch!"

Ega got up, tensing his legs and leaning against the table.

Drunk? Him? Really! He was incapable of getting drunk. He had done his best, tried everything, even turpentine, and he had never once got drunk. He couldn't.

"Look, I'll drink that whole bottle and it won't have the slightest effect. I can discuss philosophy if you like. Shall I tell you what I think about Darwin? The man's a fool. There, that's what I think. Now give me that bottle."

Craft refused and, for a moment, Ega stood there swaying and staring at him, ashen-faced.

"You either give me that bottle . . . you either give me that bottle or I'll put a bullet through your heart. No, you're not worth a bullet. I'll box your ears instead."

Suddenly, his eyes closed and he collapsed like a dead weight back into his chair and slid from there onto the floor.

"Out for the count!" said Craft casually.

He rang the bell for the footman and together they picked up João da Ega. As they carried him to the guest room and took off his Satanic outfit, Ega never ceased to sob and plant wet kisses on Carlos' hands, stammering:

"My little Raquel! Racaquê, my little Raquel. Do you love your baby boy?"

When Carlos left in the cab for Lisbon, it was no longer raining, and as dawn was breaking, a cold wind was sweeping the sky clear of clouds.

The next day, at ten o'clock, Carlos returned to Olivais. Finding Craft still asleep, he went straight up to Ega's room. The windows stood open, and a broad ray of sunlight was gilding the bed; surrounded by that halo of light, Ega was lying on his side, snoring, his knees drawn up, his nose buried in the sheets.

When Carlos shook him, poor João opened one sad eye and quickly raised himself up on his elbow, startled to find himself in that room, with its green damask curtains and a portrait of a much-powdered lady smiling at him from her gilt frame. Assailed by memories of the previous evening, he immediately slithered down in the bed again, pulling the sheets up to his chin; and his greenish suddenly much older face expressed his displeasure at having to leave those soft covers and the comfortable peace of that house to return to Lisbon and confront all kinds of bitter things.

"Is it cold out?" he asked glumly.

"No, it's a gorgeous day. But come on, get up! If someone should go to your house on behalf of Cohen, they might think you've run away."

Ega jumped out of bed and, stunned and dishevelled, went in search of his clothes, barking his bare shins on the furniture as he did so. He found only Satan's tunic. They called for the servant, who brought a pair of Craft's trousers. Ega quickly pulled them on and, without bothering to wash or shave, his overcoat collar turned up, once more donned the Scottish hat. Then, turning to Carlos with a tragic air, he said:

"Right, let's go."

Craft, who had now got up, accompanied them to the gate, where Carlos' coupé was waiting. Along the avenue of acacias, which had seemed so dark in last night's rain, birds were now singing. The garden, fresh and rain-washed, was green in the sunlight. Craft's huge Newfoundland dog bounded after them.

"Does your head hurt, Ega?"

"No," replied Ega, buttoning up his overcoat. "I wasn't drunk last night, I was merely in a state of debility."

As he got into the coupé, he announced as if it were a great philosophical profundity: "That's what happens when one drinks fine wine. I'm as good as new!"

Craft said to send him a telegram if there was any news. And with that, he closed the carriage door, and the coupé set off.

During the morning, no telegram arrived at Craft's house; and when Craft turned up at Villa Balzac, where Carlos' carriage was waiting at the door, it was already dark, and two candles were burning in the sad green drawing room. Carlos, stretched out on the sofa, was dozing, a book open on his stomach; and Ega, looking very pale, was pacing up and down, all dressed in black, with a rose in his button-hole. They had spent the whole tedious day in that room, waiting for Cohen's seconds to arrive.

"Didn't I tell you? Nothing's going to happen. How could it?" murmured Craft.

But Ega, tormented by dark thoughts, feared that Cohen might have murdered his wife. Craft's sceptical smile outraged him. Who knew Cohen better than Ega? Beneath that bourgeois exterior, Cohen was a monster. He'd seen him kill a cat once, merely in order to shed a little blood.

"I have a terrible sense of foreboding," he said in a frightened, tremulous voice.

At precisely that moment, the door bell rang. Ega woke Carlos and herded his two friends into his bedroom. Craft again assured him that, at that late hour, it could not possibly be Cohen's seconds. But Ega wanted to be alone in the drawing room and there he stood, very pale and stiff, his frock-coat tightly buttoned, his eyes fixed on the door.

"What a bore!" said Carlos, feeling his way around the darkened room.

Craft lit the stub of a candle he had found on the dressing table. It shed a lugubrious light upon the surrounding disorder: a nightshirt lay on the floor; in one corner stood a bathtub full of soapy water; but, in the middle, the vast bed, draped in its red silk curtains, retained its usual temple-like majesty.

They were silent for a moment. Craft, in a spirit of investigation, was methodically examining the contents of the dressing table: a bunch of hair pins, a garter with a broken clasp and a bunch of faded violets. Then he went over to the marble-topped chest of drawers; there he found a plate containing chicken bones and, beside it, half a sheet of paper on which there was some writing in pencil, full of emendations and crossings-out, doubtless some literary work of Ega's. Craft found all this very interesting.

Meanwhile, from the drawing room came subtle, intimate whispers. Carlos, who was listening, thought he could hear a woman's soft voice. Impatient, he went into the kitchen. The maid was sitting idly at the table, resting her head on her hand and staring into space; the page-boy, sprawled in a chair, was smoking a cigarette.

"Who came in just now?" asked Carlos.

"Senhor Cohen's maid," said the boy, hiding the cigarette behind his back.

Carlos went back into the bedroom, announcing:

"It's his confidante. It looks like things are going to end amicably."

"How else did you expect them to end?" said Craft. "Cohen has his bank, his business deals, his bills of exchange, his credit, his respectability, a whole array of things for which any scandal is absolute anathema. And that is what always brings husbands to their senses. Besides, he's done enough to satisfy his honour by offering, literally, to kick him out of his house."

At that moment, there was a noise from the drawing room, and Ega flung open the door.

"Absolutely nothing is going to happen," he exclaimed. "He gave her a bit of a beating, and they leave tomorrow for England!"

Carlos looked at Craft, who was nodding his head as if, to his wholehearted approval, he were seeing all his predictions come true.

"A bit of a beating," hissed Ega, his eyes glinting. "And then they made up. They will continue to be a model household! The cane purifies everything. What scoundrels!"

He was furious. Just then, he hated Raquel, unable to forgive his idol for allowing herself to be beaten into submission. He knew Cohen's walking stick, an Indian cane, its handle the carved head of a greyhound. And that cane had thrashed the flesh he had so passionately clasped! Leaving purple bruises where his lips had provoked pink blushes! And "they had made up." Thus the most important romance of his life reached its banal and insignificant end! He'd prefer to hear that she'd been killed, rather than just beaten. But no, she had taken her beating and then lain down with her husband, and he, doubtless regretting what he had done, would have spoken sweetly to her and, still in his long johns, would himself have applied arnica to her bruises. That's what it came down to in the end—arnica!

"Come in here, Senhora Adélia," he called into the drawing room, "come in here! We're all friends. We've done with secrecy and with modesty too! That's what friends are for. There may be three of us, but we are as one. You have before you the great mystery of the Holy Trinity. Sit down, Senhora Adélia, sit down. Don't stand on ceremony. You can tell these gentlemen everything. Senhora Adélia saw it all, saw the beating."

Senhora Adélia, a short, plump young woman with pretty eyes and wearing a hat with red flowers on it, bustled in from the drawing room saying, no, no, she hadn't actually seen the beating. Senhor Ega had misunderstood. She had merely heard it.

"This is how it was, gentlemen. I'd stayed up, of course, until the end of the dance, and by then, I can tell you, I could barely stand. It was already getting light by the time the master, still dressed as an Arab, went up to his room with the mistress. I stayed in the kitchen with Domingos, waiting for them to ring for us. And all of a sudden, we heard these screams! I was terrified. I thought it must be thieves. We ran up there, Domingos and me, but the bedroom door was locked, and they were in there together, at the far end of the room by the sounds of it. I even peered through the keyhole, but I couldn't see anything. I could hear slaps and thuds and thwacks from the cane, though, oh, I could hear that perfectly—that and the screaming. I said straight off to Domingos: 'They're having an argument; he must have found out!' Then, just as suddenly, complete silence! We went back to the kitchen, and shortly afterwards, Senhor Cohen appeared, in shirtsleeves, his hair all over the place, to say that we could go to bed, that they didn't need anything and that he would talk to us tomorrow. Well, there they stayed for the rest of the night, and in the morning, they seemed to be the best of friends. I didn't so much as lay eyes on my mistress, but, as soon as he got up, Senhor Cohen came into the kitchen, settled up with me and put me out in the street; the rude devil even threatened me with the police. It was Domingos who told me, when I went with a porter to fetch my trunk, I mean, told me that Senhor Cohen was leaving with my mistress for England. Anyway, a nice way to behave. My stomach's been churned up all day."

Senhora Adélia sighed and sat staring at the floor in silence. Ega, arms folded, was looking at his friends, bitterness etched on his face. What did they think of that, eh? A beating! If a coward like Cohen didn't deserve a bullet through the heart, he didn't know who did! But she was just as bad, letting him beat her, rather than running away, and then to end up sleeping with him in the same bed! They were scum, both of them!

"And do you have any idea how he found out?" Craft asked Senhora Adélia.

"That's what so astonishing!" cried Ega, clutching his hands to his head.

Yes, astonishing! No letter had been intercepted, because they no longer wrote to each other. She couldn't have been seen on one of her visits to Villa Balzac because these had been organised with the most subtle and impenetrable skill. In order to get there, she had never been so indiscreet as to use her own carriage. She had never come in through the front door. The servants had never seen her and had no clue as to the identity of the lady who visited him. He had taken such care, and now it was all ruined!

"Strange, very strange," muttered Craft.

There was a silence. Senhora Adélia finally made herself comfortable on a chair, with her bundle of clothes on her lap.

"Do you know what I think, Senhor Ega," she said, after some thought, "I think it happened in her sleep. It's not the first time. She must have talked about you in her sleep, and Senhor Cohen must have heard her, felt suspicious enough to spy on her and then found out about the whole business . . . because I happen to know that she does talk in her sleep."

Ega planted himself in front of Senhora Adélia, eyes flashing, and looked her up and down, from her flowered hat to the hem of her skirt.

"How can he possibly have heard her? They have separate rooms. I know they do!"

Senhora Adélia lowered her eyes and stroked the round bundle of clothes with her black-gloved fingers, and then, more softly, said:

"No, they don't, sir. My mistress would never allow such an arrangement. She loves her husband very much and gets really jealous."

There was an awkward, embarrassed silence. On the dressing table, the candle stub was burning low, giving off a lugubrious light. And Ega, who had tried to affect a nonchalant smile and a shrug, was walking slowly and sadly about the room, furiously, tremulously, twirling one end of his moustache. Then Carlos, irritated and thoroughly fed up with the whole episode—which had been going on now since the previous night, and which seemed to be plunging them into ever murkier waters—declared that it was time to call a halt. It was eight o'clock and he wanted his supper.

"Yes, let's go and have some supper," murmured Ega, looking confused and crestfallen.

He suddenly beckoned to Senhora Adélia, led her back into the drawing room and closed the door.

"Aren't you bored with all this, Craft?" exclaimed Carlos, in despair.

"No, I find it fascinating."

They waited another ten minutes. Suddenly the candle went out. A furious Carlos called for the page. The boy was just coming in, bearing a filthy oil lamp, when Ega, more composed now, returned from the drawing room. It was all over. Senhora Adélia had left.

"Let's go and have supper," he said. "But where, at this hour?"

Then he himself suggested André's in the Chiado. Downstairs, Craft's carriage waited alongside Carlos' coupé. The two carriages set off. Villa Balzac was left behind them, dark, silent and, thenceforth, redundant.

They had to wait a long time at André's in a gloomy room decorated with wallpaper speckled with little gold stars, cheap cotton curtains with blue rep valances and two noisy gaslights. Slumped on a dilapidated, ill-sprung sofa, Ega had closed his eyes, apparently exhausted. Carlos was studying the engravings on the wall, all of which depicted Spanish women: one leaving a church; another jumping over a puddle; another, eyes lowered, listening to advice from a priest. Craft was already sitting at the table, resting his head on his hands, leafing through the *Diário da Manhã*, which the waiter had given them to help pass the time.

Ega gave the sofa a sudden thump, and the sofa uttered a mournful creak.

"What I still don't understand," he cried, "is how the wretch found out!"

"Senhora Adélia's hypothesis seems plausible," said Craft, looking up from his newspaper. "Whether asleep or awake, the poor lady was obviously indiscreet. Or perhaps he received an anonymous letter. Or perhaps it was merely chance. The fact is he became suspicious, kept a watchful eye on her and caught her out."

Ega had stood up:

"I didn't want to say anything to you while Adélia was there, because she wasn't entirely au fait with all the arrangements, but the house opposite mine, on the other side of the lane, do you know the one I mean, the house with the big garden? Well, an aunt of the Count de Gouvarinho lives there, Dona Maria Lima, a most respectable person. Raquel used to go and see her now and then. They're close friends, but then Dona Maria Lima is close friends with everyone. Anyway, Raquel would leave by a little door in the garden wall, walk across the lane, and find herself at the door to my house, the side door, the door that leads to the bathroom. So you see, the servants never even caught so much as a glimpse of her. When she came to lunch with me, lunch would already be laid in my room, and the doors closed. Even if someone did see her, she was just a woman wearing a black veil walking across from Dona Maria's house. How could the man have found out? More than that, she used to change into another hat in the other house and put on a waterproof."

Craft congratulated him:

"Brilliant. It's like something out of a play by Scribe."

"And so," said Carlos, smiling, "this respectable noblewoman . . ."

"Dona Maria, poor thing. As I said, she's an excellent old lady, who is received everywhere, but since she's rather hard up, she does these little favours . . . sometimes even in her own house."

"Does she charge much for these services?" Craft asked calmly, eager to learn as much as he could from this affair.

"No, poor thing," said Ega. "People just slip her five *libras* from time to time."

The waiter came in carrying a dish of prawns, and the three friends silently took their places at the table.

After supper, Carlos and Ega decided to go back to Ramalhete. Ega was intending to sleep there, fearing, in his current state of nerves, the solitude of Villa Balzac. They set off, cigars lit, in the open calèche, in the warm, starry night.

Fortunately, everyone at Ramalhete had either gone to their own homes or to bed; Ega, who was exhausted, could retire immediately to his room, a guest room on the second floor, where there was a fine old rosewood bed. As soon as the servant had left him, Ega went over to the dressing table, where the lights were lit, and removed from around his neck, from beneath his shirt, a gold locket. Inside was a photograph of Raquel: his intention now was to burn it and to throw the ashes of that passion into the slop-pail. However, when he opened the locket, the lovely smiling face, beneath the oval glass, seemed to gaze at him with such sadness in those languid velvet eyes. The photograph showed only her head and just a suggestion of décolletage, and Ega's memories once more explored that décolletage, seeing again her throat and neck, her extraordinary satin-soft skin, the little mole above her left breast . . . He felt the taste of her kisses on his lips again, and once more felt in his soul something like an echo of the weary sighs she would utter in his arms. And she was leaving; he would never again see her! The desolate bitterness of that "never again" overwhelmed him, and with his face buried in the pillow, the poor democrat, the great phrase-maker, sobbed long into the dark secret night.

That whole week was painful for Ega. The very next day, Dâmaso turned up at Ramalhete, and from him they learned of the rumours filling Lisbon. People at the Grémio, in the Chiado—everywhere—knew that he had been thrown out of the Cohens' house. The bear and the Tyrolean shepherdess who had witnessed the scene had enthusiastically bruited it abroad. Some even said that Cohen had actually kicked him. Friends of the Cohens, especially Alencar, fervently defended Senhora Dona Raquel's innocence. Alencar stated in public that Ega, a mere inexperienced provincial and a village Lothario, had taken the amiable smiles of a society lady as evidence of passion and had written Dona Raquel a letter bordering on the obscene, which she, poor thing, bathed in tears, had then shown to her husband.

"So they're giving me a rough time, are they, Dâmaso?" murmured Ega, who, sitting in Carlos' study, wrapped in an old ulster and huddled in an armchair, was listening to Dâmaso with a wan weary air.

Dâmaso agreed that they were indeed giving him a rough time.

Ega was not surprised. He had enemies in Lisbon. Not everyone had yet forgiven him for that fur coat. They found his sarcastic wit offensive. And it was disagreeable to many people that a man of his fire-brand nature should have a rich mother and be financially independent.

The following Saturday, Carlos, on his return from supper at the house of the Count and Countess de Gouvarinho—which had been excellent—told Ega about a conversation he had had with the Countess. She had spoken to him very frankly, almost man to man, about Ega's disaster. She had been very upset, not just for Raquel, poor thing, who was her friend, but for Ega, whom she greatly admired—such a brilliant, interesting man, and who emerged from the whole affair badly besmirched! Cohen was telling everyone (he had said so to the Count), that he had threatened to kick Ega out of his house for having written a lewd letter to his wife. Those who, like the Count, were not in the know, believed it and shook their heads in horror; and those who were in the know, those who had spent the last six months smirking at Ega's close friendship with the Cohens, pretended to believe it too and clenched their fists in indignation. Ega was an object of hatred. And the little Lisbon world that spent its life going to and fro between the Grémio and the Casa Havanesa was thoroughly enjoying itself "burying" Ega.

Ega did, in fact, feel that he was being "buried." And that night, he declared to Carlos that he had decided to retreat to his mother's house for a year so as to finish his *Memoirs of an Atom*, return in triumph to Lisbon once his book had been published, and thus crush all these mediocrities. Carlos said nothing to puncture this bright hope.

However, when, before his departure, Ega attempted to put his financial and domestic affairs in order, he found himself faced by the most appalling situation. He owed money to everyone, from the upholsterer to the baker, and three bills of exchange were about to fall due; if he left those debts unpaid, if he let them go barking down the street, so to speak, that would only add to the gossip about the Cohen affair, and he would become, as well as the lover who had been kicked out of a house, a rogue pursued by creditors! What could he do except turn to Carlos? Carlos, in order to sort everything out, lent him two *contos de réis*.

Then, when Ega had dismissed all the servants from Villa Balzac, further complications arose. The mother of the page turned up at Ramalhete some days later, and, in the most insolent manner, declared that her son had disappeared. And it was true: the famous page-boy, under the corrupting influence of the cook, had vanished with her into the alleyways of the Mouraria district and embarked upon a diverting career as a criminal.

Ega refused even to hear the matron's demands. What the devil did he have to do with such sordid matters?

Then the cook's lover made his own alarming intervention. He was a policeman, a pillar of order, and he let it be understood that it would be easy for him to prove that "unnatural things" had gone on in the Villa Balzac, and that the page-boy had not been employed solely to serve at table. Sick to death of the whole business, Ega gave in to blackmail and paid the policeman five *libras*. When, that night—a sad, rainy night—Carlos and Craft accompanied him to Santa Apolónia station in a carriage, he said these words to them, a sad summation of a romantic love affair:

"I feel as if my soul had fallen into a latrine! What I need is an inner bath!"

When Afonso da Maia found out about Ega's misfortunes, he said to Carlos sadly:

"A bad beginning, my boy, a very bad beginning indeed!"

And that night, when he came back from the station, Carlos was pondering those words, and repeating them to himself: "A bad beginning!" And Ega was not the only one; he, too, had had a bad beginning. And perhaps that's why his grandfather's words had been tinged with such sadness. Bad beginnings! Ega had arrived from Celorico just six months ago, swathed in his vast fur coat, ready to dazzle Lisbon with his *Memoirs of an Atom*, to hold sway over it with the new magazine he was planning to set up; he was to be a beacon, a force to be reckoned with, and a thousand other things. And now, debt-ridden and an object of ridicule, he was scuttling back to Celorico, his tail between his legs. A bad beginning! He, for his part, had arrived in Lisbon full of ambitious plans for his work, armed as if for a battle: there was his practice, his laboratory, his pioneering book, and a thousand other bold projects. And what had he achieved? Two articles for a journal, a dozen or so prescriptions, and that melancholy chapter on "Medicine among the Greeks." A bad beginning, indeed!

No, life did not seem very promising to him at that moment as he paced up and down the billiard room with his hands in his pockets, while friends chatted in the next room and the southwest wind moaned outside the windows. Poor Ega! How wretched he would be feeling, huddled in the corner of his train compartment! And his other friends there that night were no happier. Craft and the Marquis had just begun a gloomy, disconsolate conversation about life. What was the point of being alive, Craft was saying, if one were not a Livingstone or a Bismarck? And the Marquis, with a philosophical air, believed that the world was becoming brutish and stupid. Then Taveira arrived with a horrible story about a colleague whose son had fallen down the stairs and broken his neck, just as his wife was dying of pleurisy. Cruges muttered something or other about suicide. The words lingered mournfully in the air. Every now and then, in an instinctive response to the surrounding gloom, Carlos went round the room turning up the oil lamps.

However, moments later, when Dâmaso arrived and told him that Castro Gomes was in bed unwell, everything around him in the room seemed suddenly aglow.

"Naturally," Dâmaso said, "since you attended their little girl, they'll be sure to send for you."

The next day, Carlos did not leave the house, but waited, incandescent with impatience, for a message to come. No message came. And two days later, as he was walking down to the Aterro, the first person he saw was Castro Gomes riding along Rua das Janelas Verdes in an open carriage, with his wife by his side and the little dog in his lap.

She passed by without seeing him. Then Carlos decided to put an end to this torment and to ask Dâmaso to introduce him to Castro Gomes before the latter departed for Brazil. He could bear it no longer, he needed to hear her voice, to see precisely what her eyes were saying when interrogated more closely.

However, all that week, without quite knowing how, he found himself in the company of the Gouvarinhos. It started with a chance meeting with the Count, who linked arms with him and marched him off to his office in Rua de São Marçal, sat him down in an armchair and read him an article he had written for the *Jornal do Comércio* about the state of Portugal's political parties; then he invited him to supper. The following afternoon, they organised a game of croquet, and Carlos took part in that too. And, standing at a window that looked onto the garden, he had a brief, intimate moment with the Countess during which he told her, laughing, how enchanted he had been by the colour of her hair the first time he had seen her. That same night she mentioned a book by Tennyson which she had not read; Carlos offered her a copy and took it to her the following morning. He found her alone, all dressed in white, and he and she were laughing and already instinctively lowering their voices, their two chairs shifting gradually closer together, when the footman announced Senhora Dona Maria da Cunha. How extraordinary! Fancy Dona Maria da

Cunha visiting at that hour! Carlos, however, was very fond of Dona Maria, a kindly, amusing old lady, always ready to forgive the sins of others, having herself been a great sinner when she was young and pretty. Dona Maria was also a great talker and seemed to have a lot to say to the Countess in particular; and so Carlos left them, promising to return one afternoon to have tea and talk about Tennyson.

On the afternoon when he was getting dressed to go there, Dâmaso, irritated beyond belief, came into his room to bring him some news. That madman Castro Gomes had changed his mind about leaving for Brazil! He was now intending to stay there, in the Hotel Central, until the middle of summer. So all Dâmaso's plans were ruined.

Carlos immediately considered asking Dâmaso to introduce him to Castro Gomes, but, as in Sintra, without quite knowing why, the idea of Dâmaso introducing him to Castro Gomes' wife filled him with repugnance. And he continued dressing in silence.

Dâmaso, meanwhile, was cursing his bad luck.

"And she was there for the taking; given the opportunity, she was mine! But what can I do now, damn it?"

He went on to complain about Castro Gomes, who was, in short, quite mad. And the man's life was a complete mystery. What the devil was he doing in Lisbon? There was clearly some financial difficulty. And he and his wife didn't get on at all well. The previous evening, they had obviously had a row of some sort. When Dâmaso had arrived, he had found her looking pale and red-eyed and Castro Gomes furiously pacing the room, tugging at his beard. They were clearly upset and only uttered a word about every fifteen minutes.

"Do you know," he exclaimed, "I've a good mind to send them both to the devil!"

He complained about her too. She was so changeable, sometimes charming and sometimes chilly, and just occasionally, he would say something perfectly natural, the usual kind of remark one makes in society, and she would burst out laughing. It was enough to annoy anyone. They were, to put it bluntly, most peculiar.

"Anyway, where are you off to?" he asked, with an angry sigh, seeing Carlos putting on his hat.

Carlos was going to take tea with the Countess de Gouvarinho.

"I'll tell you what, I'll come with you, shall I? I have nothing else to do."

Carlos hesitated for a moment, then said:

"Yes, why not, you'd be doing me a favour actually."

It was a beautiful afternoon. Carlos drove his dog-cart.

"It's been such an age since we went for a ride like this together," Dâmaso said.

"You've been too caught up with your foreign friends!"

Dâmaso sighed again and said nothing more. Then, when they reached the

Gouvarinhos' house, and he learned that the Countess had other visitors, Dâmaso suddenly resolved not to go in. No, he was feeling too out of spirits, he wouldn't have anything to say.

"Oh, and there's something else I meant to tell you," he exclaimed, keeping Carlos waiting at the Countess' front door. "Yesterday, Castro Gomes asked me how much he owed you for visiting the little girl. I told him that you'd made the visit as a favour to me. Anyway, he said he'd have to leave you his card. So it looks very likely that you'll meet them too."

Carlos would not have to rely on Dâmaso for an introduction!

"Come and see us one night, Dâmaso. How about supper tomorrow?" cried Carlos, suddenly radiant, shaking his friend warmly by the hand.

When he went into the drawing room, the footman had just served tea. The room, decorated in severe green and gold paper and hung with family portraits in heavy frames, gave onto two balconies that looked out onto the leafy garden. There were baskets of flowers on the various tables. On the sofa, two ladies in hats and both dressed in black were talking over their cups of tea. When the Countess held out her hand to Carlos, she turned the same pink as the padded silk chair in which she was sitting, next to a tall wooden lamp-stand. With a smile, she immediately remarked upon the radiant look on Carlos' face. Had he met with some good fortune? Carlos smiled too and said that it was impossible to enter that room looking anything other than radiant. Then he asked after the Count.

The Count had not yet returned, detained, no doubt, at the Upper Chamber of Peers, where they were debating a bill on the reform of state education.

One of the ladies in black hoped most devoutly that they would give children less to study. The poor things were becoming virtually buried under the sheer number of subjects and all those things to memorise; her little boy, João, for example, looked so pale and wan that she sometimes felt like letting him remain entirely ignorant of everything. The other lady placed her cup on the console table beside her and, dabbing at her lips with her lace handkerchief, said that her greatest complaint concerned the examiners. It was nothing short of scandalous the demands they made on children and the questions they posed merely in order to fail them anyway. They had asked her little boy the most stupid and trivial of questions, for example, what was soap and why was it possible to wash with soap?

The other lady and the Countess both pressed their hands to their bosom in consternation. And Carlos amiably agreed that it was, indeed, an abomination. Her husband—went on the lady in black—had felt so desperate about the whole business that, on meeting the examiner in the Chiado, he had threatened to thrash him with his walking stick. This had been imprudent, of course, but then the examiner had been positively wicked! The only worthwhile subject was the study of languages. It seemed arrant nonsense to torture a child with botany, astronomy, and physics. Why bother? These were matters quite useless in society. Her little boy was now being given lessons in chemistry. How absurd! As his father said, he didn't want his son to grow up to become a pharmacist!

After a silence, the two ladies got to their feet at the same time; there was a murmur of kisses and a rustle of silks.

Carlos remained alone with the Countess, who had returned to her pink seat.

She immediately asked after Ega.

"The poor man's gone off to Celorico."

She protested, with a pretty laugh, at that ugly expression "gone off to Celorico." No, she would not have it. Poor Ega! He deserved a better funeral oration than that! Celorico provided a terrible ending to a romance.

"It does indeed," exclaimed Carlos, laughing too, "it would be far more romantic to be able to say: 'He's gone off to Jerusalem!'"

At that moment, the servant announced a visitor's name, and Teles da Gama, a close friend of the family, entered the room. When he learned that the Count was probably still battling over the reform of education, he clutched his head in his hands as if bemoaning such a terrible waste of time and said that he would not stay. No, not even a cup of the Countess' excellent tea would tempt him. The truth was that he had fallen so far from the grace of God and had so entirely lost any sense of the beautiful, that he had dropped by not to see the Countess, but to talk to the Count. The Countess pouted prettily like an offended princess and asked Carlos if such rough rustic sincerity did not make him long for the polished manners of the Ancien Régime. And Teles da Gama, swaying slightly back and forth, and with a laugh that revealed magnificent teeth, declared himself a democrat and a creature of Nature. Then, as he was leaving and shaking his friend Carlos by the hand, he asked when the Prince of Santa Olávia would finally do him the honour of coming to dine with him. The Countess was most indignant. Really, this was too much! Handing out invitations in her drawing room, in her presence—a man who made so much fuss about his German cook and who had never so much as offered her a plate of sauerkraut!

Teles da Gama, still laughing and swaying, swore that he was in the process of having his dining room decorated in order to give such a party for the Countess that it would be set down in the annals of history! But with Carlos it was different; they would dine together in the kitchen, plates on their laps. And with that he left, still swaying and laughing and showing his magnificent teeth, even when he had reached the door.

"He's such an amusing fellow, Gama, don't you think?" said the Countess.

"Very," said Carlos.

Then the Countess looked at the clock. It was half past five; at that hour she no longer received visitors, but they could, nonetheless, talk for a while, like good friends. A slow silence ensued during which their eyes met. Then

Carlos asked after Charlie, his charming patient. The boy wasn't very well, he had a slight cough which he had caught while out in Passeio da Estrela. The child was always such a worry! Then she fell silent, staring blankly at the carpet, languidly moving her fan; that afternoon, she was wearing a particularly elaborate dress in an autumnal shade of yellow and made of such thick silk that the slightest movement produced a rustle as of dry leaves.

"Hasn't the weather been wonderful!" she exclaimed suddenly, as if waking up.

"Wonderful!" said Carlos. "A few days ago, I was in Sintra, and you can't imagine . . . it was absolutely idyllic."

He immediately regretted this remark, reproaching himself for having mentioned his visit to Sintra in that room.

The Countess, however, appeared not to have heard him. She had got to her feet and was talking about some songs she had received from England that morning, the new season's novelties. Then she sat down at the piano, ran her fingers over the keys and asked Carlos if he knew a song called "The Pale Star." No, he didn't, but then all English songs were alike, they always struck the same sorrowful romantic tone. They were songs suited to young women really, songs set in a melancholy park, beside a gently flowing stream, and there was always a kiss exchanged beneath the chestnut trees.

The Countess read the words of "The Pale Star" out loud, and they were exactly as he'd said, a tiny star of love twinkling in the twilight, a pale lake, a timid kiss under the trees.

"You see, it's always the same," said Carlos, "and, of course, always equally delightful."

But the Countess had thrown the music down, finding it stupid. She started nervously searching through the other sheet music, her eyes growing increasingly sombre. In order to break the silence, Carlos praised her lovely flowers!

"Ah, let me give you a rose!" she exclaimed, abandoning her music.

The flower she wanted to give him was in the next room, in her boudoir. Carlos followed the long train of her dress, which shimmered gold, like autumn leaves in sunlight. The room was papered in blue, and furnished with a lovely eighteenth-century dressing table and mirror and, on a stout oak pedestal, a clay bust of the Count, in oratorical mode: brow lofty, cravat rumpled, lips parted in passionate speech.

The Countess chose a flower with two leaves and she herself placed it in the buttonhole of his frock-coat. Carlos was aware of her verbena perfume, of the warmth emanating from her agitated bosom. She struggled to fix the flower in place with clumsy trembling fingers, which seemed to cling and linger on the cloth of his coat.

"*Voilà!*" she said at last, very softly. "There you are, my handsome knight of the Red Rose. And there's no need to thank me!"

Irresistibly, almost unaware of what he was doing, Carlos found his lips pressed to hers. Her silk dress brushed against him, rustling gently in his arms, and she leaned her head back, her face white as wax, her eyes softly closed. With her limp body clasped in his arms, he took a step forward, but his knee collided with a low sofa, which rolled away from him. The silk train of her dress became tangled about his feet, and Carlos stumbled after the sofa, which only fled still further off, until it, at last, bumped against the pedestal on which the Count raised his inspired brow heavenwards. A long sigh died on the air amid the murmur of crumpling silk.

A moment later, they were both on their feet: Carlos, standing next to the bust, was smoothing his beard and looking embarrassed and already somewhat repentant; she was standing before the Louis XV mirror, tremulously tidying her hair. Suddenly, they heard the Count's voice in the hallway. She turned abruptly, ran to Carlos and, taking his face in her long bejewelled hands, planted two passionate kisses on his hair and his eyes. Then she sat down nonchalantly on the sofa, and when the Count entered, followed by a bald old gentleman who was blowing his nose on a vast Indian silk handkerchief, she was talking about Sintra and laughing loudly.

When he saw Carlos in the boudoir, the Count seemed pleasantly surprised and stood for a long time warmly shaking his hand and telling him that he had been thinking about him only that morning, in the Chamber.

"And why are you so late?" chided the Countess, laughing, suddenly all movement, animation and charm, and immediately taking charge of the old gentleman.

"Our Count spoke!" said the old man, his eyes still bright with enthusiasm.

"You spoke?" she exclaimed, turning towards the Count with a captivating show of interest.

Yes, he had spoken—not that he had intended to! However, when he had heard Torres Valente (a man of letters, but a madman with no common sense at all), when he had heard him say that gymnastics should be made compulsory in schools, he had risen to his feet, but his friend Maia should not go thinking that he had made a speech.

"Oh, really!" exclaimed the old man, waving his handkerchief. "It was one of the best speeches I've ever heard in the Chamber, really first-rate!"

The Count modestly demurred. No, he had merely contributed a few words of good sense and sound principles. He had simply asked his illustrious friend, Senhor Torres Valente, if, in his opinion, our children, our heirs, were destined to be clowns!

"It was so witty, Countess!" exclaimed the old gentleman. "I only wish you had been there to hear it. And the way he said it, with such panache!"

The Count smiled and turned to thank the old gentleman. Yes, that is what he had said. And in response to further remarks by Torres Valente, who did not want our schools and colleges to be "entirely imbued with the catechism," he had turned the full might of his verbal wrath on him.

"It was quite frightening!" exclaimed the old gentleman hoarsely, preparing his handkerchief in order to blow his nose again.

"Yes, frightening," said the Count. "I turned to him and said: 'Does the worthy peer believe that this country will ever regain its place at the head of civilisation if, in our schools and colleges, in all our educational establishments, we, the legislators, with impious hand, replace the crucifix with the trapeze.'"

"Sublime," mumbled the old gentleman, trumpeting loudly into his handkerchief.

Getting to his feet, Carlos praised the Count's delicious irony.

And when Carlos said goodbye, the Count, not content with merely shaking his hand, put his arm around his waist, calling him "my dear Maia." Her eyes still moist, her face still pale, the Countess was smiling and languidly fanning herself as she reclined against the sofa cushions, underneath the bust of her husband still raising his inspired brow heavenwards.

: X :

THREE WEEKS LATER, one sultry afternoon, beneath a gloomy sky heavy with thunder, when a few large drops of rain were just beginning to fall, Carlos was getting out of a hired coupé, which had pulled slowly to a halt on the corner of Rua da Patriarcal, its green blinds mysteriously drawn. Two male passers-by had smirked at him, as if catching him creeping self-consciously out of some low, suspicious door. And in fact, the old cab, with its yellow wheels, had served as a verbena-scented bower of love for the two hours in which Carlos had been riding around in it, along the Queluz road, with the Countess de Gouvarinho.

The Countess had got out in Largo das Amoreiras, and Carlos had taken advantage of the quiet Rua da Patriarcal in order to dismiss the decrepit old carriage with its hard seats, in which, for the last hour, legs numb, he had been suffocating in the heat, not daring to lower the windows, and feeling wearied and irritated by the yards of crumpled silk and by the interminable kisses which the Countess kept planting on his beard.

During those three weeks, they had been meeting in Rua de Santa Isabel, in a house belonging to the Countess' aunt, who had gone to Oporto with her maid, leaving the Countess with the key to the house and the care of her cat. This kindly aunt, a little old lady called Miss Jones, was a saint and a militant apostle of the Anglican church with a missionary zeal for spreading the Word; every month, she made a proselytising trip into the provinces, distributing Bibles, rescuing souls from Catholic darkness, and purifying (as she put it) the Papist slough. The sweet sad smell of spinsterish devotion lingered even on the stairs, and on the landing hung a large poster, with a poem in gold letters interlaced with purple lilies, exhorting all those who entered to persevere in the ways of the Lord! When Carlos first went in, he had stumbled over a pile of Bibles. Indeed, the bedroom was a veritable nest of Bibles; there were small towers of them on various bits of furniture, others spilled out from old hat-boxes or were jumbled up with pairs of galoshes or had fallen into the hip bath, and all were of exactly the same format, bound in the same scowling, aggressive black leather as if buckled into armour for battle! The walls glowed, lined with cards printed in coloured lettering, radiating austere verses from the Bible, stern moral advice, cries from the psalms, and bold threats of hell-fire. And in the middle of all this Anglican religiosity, at the head of a small iron bedstead, stiff and virginal, stood two almost empty bottles of brandy and gin. Carlos finished off the sainted lady's gin, and her hard bed was left as turbulent and disorderly as a battlefield.

Then the Countess began to have doubts about a neighbour, Senhora Borges, who was a regular visitor to her aunt's house and the widow of the Gouvarinhos' former administrator. On one occasion, they were lying on Miss Jones' chaste bed, languidly smoking cigarettes, when they heard three thunderous blows on the door that echoed round the house. The poor Countess nearly fainted, and Carlos ran to the window just in time to see a man moving off, carrying a plaster statue in one hand and, in his other hand, a basket containing more of the same. The Countess, however, was convinced that Senhora Borges must have told the Italian seller of religious images to pound on the door in that way, each knock a sign, a warning shot from Morality. Thereafter, she had preferred not to return to her aunt's saintly cot-bed. And that afternoon, since they had no other hiding-place, they had found shelter for their love inside that hired carriage.

However, Carlos was coming away from that meeting enervated, drained, and feeling already inside him the beginnings of the first bored yawns. It was only three weeks since those verbena-scented arms had flung themselves about his neck, and now, as he walked along São Pedro de Alcântara, beneath the light drizzle falling on the avenue of trees, he was wondering how he could free himself from her tenacity, her ardour, her weight. For the Countess was becoming quite absurd in her eager, audacious determination to invade his whole life and to occupy the largest, deepest space in it, as if the first kiss they had exchanged had not only briefly united their lips, but had joined their destinies for ever. That afternoon, resting her head on his chest, her eyes filled with imploring tenderness, she had again uttered the words: "If you wanted to, we could be so happy! What a wonderful life we could have, just the two of us!" The Countess, of course, had conceived the extravagant idea of running away with him, of living out an eternal dream of lyrical love in some corner of the world, as far away as possible from Rua de São Marçal! "If you wanted to!" No! Devil take it, he did *not* want to run away with the Countess de Gouvarinho!

And that was not all, there were demands and tantrums, the unrestrained explosions of a jealous temperament; on more than one occasion, in just those few short weeks, for no reason at all, she had become hysterical, talked of dying, and had dissolved into tears. Ah, but those tears did add a kind of voluptuousness, made the satin skin of her neck and throat seem still softer! What worried him were certain expressions that flashed across her face, certain sharp excitable looks, which revealed that the passion lit in the nerves of that 33-year-old woman had burned her to the depths of her being. True, this love affair contributed further to the luxury of his life, added a new perfume, but its very charm lay in its remaining easy, serene, and never more than skin-deep. If, for any reason, she came to him again with tear-filled eyes, wringing her hands, speaking of dying, and saying that she wanted to run away with him—then it would be goodbye! Everything would be ruined, and the Countess, with her verbena scent, her flame-coloured hair, and her tears would become a mere nuisance!

The drizzle had stopped, and a patch of rain-washed blue sky appeared among the clouds. Carlos was walking down Rua de São Roque when he met the Marquis, who was gloomily leaving a sweetshop, with a packet in his hands and his neck swathed in a vast white silk scarf.

"Whatever's wrong? Have you caught a cold?" asked Carlos.

"Oh, everything's wrong," said the Marquis, walking along beside him with all the slow languor of a dying man. "I went to bed late. I'm tired. I feel like I've got a weight on my chest. Catarrh. Pains in my side. Dreadful. I've just bought some throat lozenges."

"Don't be silly, man! What you need is some roast beef and a bottle of Burgundy. Isn't it your night to dine at Ramalhete? Craft will be there, and so will Dâmaso. Now that it's stopped raining, let's take a brisk walk down Rua do Alecrim, and then along the Aterro, and by the time we get to Ramalhete, you'll be cured."

The poor Marquis shrugged. He had only to feel slightly unwell, to experience a pain or a shiver, and he immediately considered himself, as he put it, "done for." His world began to crumble, he became gripped by Catholic fears and anxious thoughts about Eternity. On days like this, he would closet himself with his chaplain, with whom, as often as not, he would end up playing draughts.

"Anyway," he said, cautiously doffing his hat as he passed by the open door of the Church of the Martyrs, "let me just drop in at the Grémio first. I want to write a note to Manuela telling her not to expect me tonight."

Then, distracted and melancholy, he asked for news of that libertine Ega. "That libertine Ega" was in Celorico, at his mother's house, listening to Father Seraphim's belches, and, so he said, seeking refuge in great art: he was writing a five-act play which was to be called *The Mudhole*, his revenge on Lisbon.

"The worst thing," muttered the Marquis, after a pause and burying himself still deeper in his scarf, "would be if I still felt like this on Sunday for the races!"

"What!" cried Carlos. "Do you mean they now allow races on a Sunday?"

The Marquis explained, as they walked down the Chiado, that the races had been moved forward at the request of Clifford, the great horse-breeder from Córdoba, who was supposed to be bringing two of his English horses. It was a little humiliating to have to depend on Clifford, but he was, when all's said and done, a gentleman, and with his thoroughbred horses and his English jockeys he constituted the sole reason for taking the Belém racecourse seriously at all.

Without Clifford it would be a complete farce, with just a few old nags fit only for the knacker's yard.

"Don't you know Clifford? A fine fellow! He's a bit of a poseur, perhaps, but pure gold."

They had reached the courtyard of the Grémio, and the Marquis held out his arm to Carlos.

"Feel that pulse!"

"Your pulse is excellent. Go and break the bad news to Manuela. I'll wait for you here."

So the races were to be on Sunday, in five days' time. And "she" would be there, he would finally meet her. During these three weeks, he had seen her twice: on one occasion, he had been standing talking to Taveira at the door of the Hotel Central, and she had appeared on one of the balconies, in a hat, drawing on a long, black glove; the second time, only a few days ago, on a rainy afternoon, she had drawn up outside Mourão's in the Chiado in a hired carriage, and had waited outside while the footman delivered a package in the form of a small chest tied up with red tape. On both occasions, she had seen him and fixed her eyes on him for a moment, and it had seemed to Carlos that, the second time, her eyes had rested on his for longer, as if abandoning themselves to looking, as if growing softer and more tender as they gazed into his. It was perhaps an illusion, but, in his impatience to meet her, it was this that finally persuaded him to realise an old (albeit disagreeable) idea of his— that of having Dâmaso introduce him to her husband. Poor Dâmaso was at first greatly upset by this request, and with the air of a dog defending its bone, he immediately reminded Carlos of Castro Gomes' deplorable behaviour, for the latter had still not carried out his announced intention three weeks before of leaving his card at Ramalhete. Carlos dismissed such formalities between men, besides, Castro Gomes seemed to him to be a man of taste, a sporting man; it was not every day in Lisbon that one met someone who knew how to tie his cravat correctly; and it would be pleasant, for Dâmaso too, were they all to get together from time to time, with Craft and the Marquis, to smoke a cigar and discuss horses. This decided Dâmaso, who finally suggested taking Carlos with him to the Hotel Central one afternoon. Carlos, however, did not want to go into the hotel, hat in hand, behind Dâmaso. They had determined instead to wait for the horse-races, which Castro Gomes had expressed a wish to attend.

"In the weighing-in enclosure," Dâmaso said, "that would be the really chic place to make the introductions. Oh, yes, that positively oozes chic."

"Let's just hope it doesn't rain on Sunday," murmured Carlos when the Marquis emerged from the club, looking still gloomier and with his scarf wrapped still more tightly about his neck.

They continued down the street, in the direction of Ferregial. Farther along the street from the Grémio, at the kerb, stood a hired coupé with a white-gloved footman waiting by the door. Carlos glanced casually at the carriage, and saw, looking out of the window, a child's face of exquisite paleness smiling at him, a beautiful smile that dimpled her cheeks. He recognized her at once. It was Rosa, Rosicler; and not content with merely smiling, her sweet blue eyes fixed upon him, she reached out one small hand and waved enthusiastically. Beside her in the black-lined carriage, he saw a statuesque figure, a suggestion of abundant golden hair. Carlos immediately took off his hat, so flustered that he almost stumbled. "She" nodded slightly, and something luminous, a vague thrill of excitement, crossed her face. And, very fleetingly, it was as if from both mother and daughter he had received a sweet emanation of warmth and sympathy.

"Goodness, is she yours?" asked the Marquis, who had noticed Madame Gomes' expression.

Carlos blushed.

"No, she's a Brazilian lady. I attended her little girl once when she was ill."

"Well, that's what I call gratitude!" rumbled the Marquis from inside the many folds of his scarf.

Walking in silence along the Ferregial, Carlos was turning over in his mind an idea that had come to him suddenly, when he received that warm look. Why shouldn't Dâmaso take Castro Gomes to Olivais one morning to see Craft's collection? He would be there too, Craft would open a bottle of champagne, and they would discuss antiques. Then, naturally, he would invite Castro Gomes to lunch at Ramalhete and show him the large Rubens and his antique Indian bedspreads. Then a sense of camaraderie would already exist even before the races; they would be on a more friendly footing.

On the Aterro, fearing the chill breeze from the river, the Marquis suggested they take a cab, and they rode on to Ramalhete without a word. The Marquis was anxiously feeling his throat. Carlos was painstakingly analysing to himself that slow nod, that gaze, that fleeting blush . . . Perhaps she hadn't before realised who he was. For after her enthusiastic wave, Rosa, still smiling, had turned to her mother and would doubtless have told her that he was the doctor who had made her and her doll better. And then the lovely colour that had suffused her face took on a deeper meaning—it was like a happy surprise, a feeling of chaste embarrassment, knowing that the man she had noticed before for other reasons entirely had already, in a way, been admitted into the privacy of her home, had kissed her daughter and even sat on the edge of her bed.

Then he began rearranging the planned visit to Olivais, making it longer and more elaborate. Why shouldn't she be invited to see Craft's collection of curios too? What a delightful afternoon that would be, a real party, an idyll! Craft would have a delicate lunch served on his finest Wedgewood china. Carlos would sit next to her at the table, then they would walk round the garden, which would already be in flower, or they could take tea in the Japanese pavilion, with its walls lined with rugs. What he most wanted, however, was to stroll with her through Craft's two drawing rooms and for them to linger together before some beautiful faience-ware or a rare piece of furniture, and to feel the sympathy of their hearts rise like a perfume from their concordant tastes. He had never known her look lovelier than that afternoon, inside the dark-lined coupé, where the pure white of her profile shone more brightly. Her gloves had glowed palely on the lap of her black dress, and about her hat had curled the tip of a snowy feather.

The cab had stopped outside Ramalhete, and Carlos and the Marquis were soon standing among the silent tapestries of the hall.

"How does she know Cruges?" the Marquis asked suddenly in a suspicious tone, removing his scarf.

Carlos looked at him, as if he had just woken up.

"Who? That lady? How does she know Cruges? Of course, you're right! That was Cruges' house! The carriage was outside Cruges' door! Perhaps she was visiting someone who lives on another floor."

"No one else lives there," said the Marquis, walking down the corridor. "At any rate, she's a damn fine specimen."

Carlos found this expression odious.

From the corridor, Dâmaso's petulant voice could be heard issuing forth from Afonso's study, speaking loudly about "handicaps" and "dead heats." They found him there discoursing about horse-racing with all the conviction and authority of a member of the Jockey Club. Afonso, sitting in his old arm-chair with the Reverend Boniface on his lap, was listening to him, smiling and courteous. Craft was ensconced in one corner of the sofa, leafing through a book.

Dâmaso immediately appealed to the Marquis for his support. Wasn't it true, as he had been telling Senhor Afonso da Maia, that these races were going to be the finest ever held in Lisbon? Eight horses were entered for the Grand National Prize alone—which was worth some six hundred *mil-réis*! And Clifford was bringing Mist.

"Oh, yes, and Marquis, you've got to be at the Jockey Club on Friday night so that we can finish drawing up the handicap."

The Marquis had dragged a chair over to where Afonso was sitting in order to tell him all about his various ailments; however, when Dâmaso interposed himself between them, still talking about Mist, and deciding that Mist was most definitely chic and wanting to bet five *libras* on Mist against the field, the Marquis, rather annoyed, turned to Dâmaso and informed him that he was giving himself foolish airs. Bet on Mist! Any true patriot should bet on the horses bred by the Viscount de Darque, the sole Portuguese breeder present!

"Isn't that so, Senhor Afonso da Maia?"

The old man smiled and stroked the cat.

"It would perhaps be a truer act of patriotism," he said, "to put on a good bullfight rather than a horse-race."

Dâmaso clutched his head. A bullfight! Senhor Afonso da Maia preferred bulls to horse-races? He, who was practically an Englishman?

"I'm from Beira, Senhor Salcede, from Beira, and proud of it. The only reason I lived in England was because my king, as he then was, threw me out of my own country. But, yes, I do have a certain Portuguese weakness for bullfights. Every race has its national sport, and ours is bullfighting—with plenty of sunshine, a holiday atmosphere, cool water to drink and fireworks. Do you know what the advantage of the bullfight is, Senhor Salcede? It's a great place to learn strength and courage and skill. There's no more important institution in Portugal than that of amateur bullfighting. And believe you me, if, in this current pathetic generation, there are still a few boys in Lisbon with some muscle, a good straight back, and able to deliver a decent punch, it's all down to bulls and amateur bullfighting."

The Marquis applauded warmly. That was telling him! There you had the philosophy of the bull ring! Bullfighting really did provide a wonderful physical training! And yet some imbeciles were talking about abolishing bullfights! The fools would put an end to Portuguese courage entirely!

"We don't have the games of skill that other countries have," he exclaimed, striding about the room and gesticulating, his ailments entirely forgotten. "We don't have cricket or football or running, like the English; we don't have the kind of gymnastics they practise in France; we don't have military service, which is what makes Germany so strong. We don't have anything that can give a young man a bit of fibre. All we have is bullfighting. Take away the bullfight, and we'll be left with nothing but a lot of spineless nonentities mincing along the Chiado! Don't you agree, Craft?"

From his corner of the sofa, where Carlos had joined him for a quiet chat, Craft replied resolutely:

"Bullfighting? Of course! In Portugal it should be the same as education is in other countries—free and compulsory."

Dâmaso, meanwhile, was earnestly assuring Afonso that he, too, loved bullfighting. When it came to patriotism, there was no one more patriotic than he. Horse-racing, though, had a different kind of chic. What about the Bois de Boulogne on a Grand Prix day? It took your breath away!

"Do you know what I think is a shame," he cried, turning suddenly to Carlos. "It's the fact that you don't have a four-in-hand, a mail-coach. We could all go together then—now that *would* be chic!"

Carlos thought to himself that it was indeed a shame not to have a four-in-hand, but he said, jokingly, that he felt it would be more in keeping with the Jockey Club's headquarters in the Travessa da Conceição for them all to go in an omnibus.

Dâmaso turned back to Afonso with a despairing gesture.

"There you have it, Senhor Afonso da Maia! That is why Portugal never does anything right! Because no one wants to make the effort to ensure that things turn out well. It's just impossible. I believe that every person should contribute in some way to the civilisation of their country."

"Well spoken, Senhor Salcede!" cried Afonso. "You have said a great and noble thing!"

"It's true, isn't it?" declared Dâmaso triumphantly, bursting with pride. "I, for example . . ."

"You?" came the cry from every side. "What have *you* done for civilisation?"

"I've ordered a white frock-coat for the day of the races and I'll be wearing a blue veil on my hat!"

A footman came in bearing a tray with a letter for Afonso. The old man, still smiling at Dâmaso's ideas about civilisation, put on his spectacles and read the first few lines; all hilarity died on his face, and he immediately got to his feet, having first deposited Boniface's large bulk on the cat's personal cushion.

"That's what taste means, that's what real discernment is," Dâmaso was exclaiming, standing before Carlos, waving his arms about, as Afonso pushed aside the damask curtain at the door. "Your grandfather, for example, simply *oozes* chic!"

"Forget about my chic grandfather for a moment. Come here, I want to ask you something."

He opened one of the doors that gave onto the terrace and led Dâmaso outside, rapidly outlining his plan for a visit to Olivais, and the delightful afternoon they could spend there with Monsieur and Madame Castro Gomes. He had already spoken about it to Craft, who had agreed at once and thought it a splendid idea; he would, he said, fill the house with flowers. Now all that remained was for friend Dâmaso to be so kind as to issue the invitation.

"Goodness!" murmured Dâmaso warily. "You really are desperate to meet her, aren't you?"

In the end, though, he agreed that it would be terribly chic! And he saw it as a good opportunity for himself as well. While Carlos and Craft were showing Castro Gomes around and talking to him about horses, he would head off into the garden with her . . . and who knew what might happen?

"I'll talk to them about it tomorrow. I'm sure they'll accept. She adores bric-à-brac."

"And come and tell me if they accept or not."

"I will. You'll like her. She's read a lot and knows about literature. Sometimes, when she's talking, even I'm left behind . . ."

The Marquis came over to summon them inside, impatient to draw the door curtain, once more preoccupied with the health of his throat. And before supper he wanted to go to Carlos' room to gargle with salt water.

"There's the sturdy Portuguese for you," exclaimed Carlos, cheerily linking arms with him.

"My throat is, if you like, my Achilles' heel," the Marquis said, detaching himself from Carlos and eyeing him fiercely. "Yours is your emotions. Craft's is his respectability. And Dâmaso's is his stupidity. Portugal's other name should be Achilles & Co."

Laughing, Carlos led him down the corridor. And as they entered the hall, they came across Afonso talking to a woman dressed in heavy mourning; she was kissing his hand, almost kneeling, barely able to speak for tears. And beside her was another woman, her eyes also bathed in tears, who was cradling a tiny baby wrapped in a shawl; the baby was crying softly and appeared to be ill. Carlos stopped, embarrassed; the Marquis instinctively put his hand in his pocket. Afonso, surprised thus in his charitable work, immediately hurried the two women down the stairs, and they went off, huddled together, still heaping blessings on him and quietly sobbing. He turned to Carlos and said, almost apologetically and in a still shaken voice:

"These endless requests for help ... But this was a very sad case. And the worst of it is that however much you give, it's never enough. The world's a very badly run place, Marquis."

"Very badly run indeed, Senhor Afonso da Maia," replied the Marquis, touched by his friend's generosity.

The following Sunday, at around two o'clock, Carlos, in an eight-spring phaeton—with Craft, who had decided to install himself at Ramalhete for the two days of racing—stopped at the end of Largo de Belém, just at the moment when some fireworks were being set off beside the race-course. One of the servants got out in order to buy Craft a ticket to the weighing-in enclosure from a hastily constructed wooden booth put up the day before, and run by a small man with a large, grizzled beard.

The day was already hot, the sky dark blue, with one of those glittering holiday suns that scorches the cobblestones, gilds the dull, dusty air, draws a mirror-like sparkle from windows and bathes the whole city in a white, monotonous, implacable dazzle, which, in the slow hours of summer, somehow saddens and wearies the soul. In the bright scalding silence of Largo dos Jerónimos, an omnibus was waiting, its horses unharnessed, outside the church door. A workman carrying a child in his arms and, by his side, his wife wearing a sprigged shawl were strolling along, gazing open-mouthed at the road and the river, enjoying their Sunday of leisure. A boy was disconsolately trying to sell programmes for the races, but no one was buying. The water-seller, having no customers, had sat down in the shade with her pitcher and was delousing her little boy. Four heavy-set municipal guards on horseback were slowly patrolling this deserted place. And in the distance, endless joyful rockets exploded and died in the hot air.

Meanwhile, the footman was still leaning over the counter of the ticket booth, unable to get change for a *libra*. Craft had to get down from the seat and go there himself to negotiate, while Carlos, impatient, flicked the whip at the horses' haunches—as glossy as brown satin—and took a brief nervous turn about the square. He had driven from Ramalhete in the same irritable mood, without uttering a word. That whole week, ever since the evening when he had arranged the visit to Olivais with Dâmaso, had proved most unsatisfactory. Dâmaso had disappeared, without letting him know Castro Gomes' response. He, out of pride, had not bothered to track Dâmaso down. The days had passed emptily; the jolly idyll in Olivais had not taken place; he had still not met Madame Gomes; he had not seen her again either, nor did he expect to see her at the races. And that holiday Sunday, the bright sun, the people in the street, wearing their Sunday-best cashmeres and silks, all filled him with melancholy and malaise.

A hired calèche passed by, with two men wearing flowers in their buttonholes and drawing on their gloves, then a dog-cart, driven by a fat man in dark glasses, almost collided with the archway. Craft at last returned with his ticket, after having been told off by the man with the prophet's beard.

Beyond the arch, the air was filled with suffocating dust. Women leaned from windows, looking out from beneath their sunshades. More mounted guards were blocking the road.

At the entrance to the hippodrome—an opening made in the wall of a small adjoining garden—the phaeton had to stop behind the dog-cart driven by the fat man, who, in turn, could go no farther because the gateway was filled by the hired calèche in which one of the two men with flowers in their buttonholes was furiously arguing with a policeman. They wanted him to call Senhor Savedra! Senhor Savedra, a member of the Jockey Club, had told him that he could get in without having to pay for the carriage! He had told him this only yesterday, when they met at Azevedo's pharmacy. Would he please call Senhor Savedra! The policeman, embarrassed, kept waving his arms about. And the man, taking off his gloves, was just on the point of opening the carriage door to get out and punch the man, when a municipal guard, mounted on a great charger, raised his fist, shouted and swore at the fat man and forced the calèche to withdraw. Another municipal guard intervened equally brutally. Two terrified ladies, snatching up the hems of their dresses, fled into a doorway. And drifting above all the hubbub and the dust came the strains of *La Traviata* played on a hurdy-gurdy.

The phaeton drove in behind the dog-cart, where the fat man, incandescent with rage, kept looking back, scarlet-faced, still swearing that he would give the municipal guard "what for."

"So very delicately arranged," murmured Craft.

The hippodrome rose before them on the gentle slope of a hill, seeming, after the hot dusty street and the harsh chalky glare, cooler and more spacious, with its grass already wilting slightly in the June sun and with the occasional bright red poppy. A languid soothing breeze blew in from the river.

In the middle, as if lost in that large, green, sunlit space, a tight knot of people and a few carriages formed a small dark mass from which the pastel shades of parasols, the glint of a lantern, or a coachman's white coat stood out in sharp contrast. Beyond, on either side of the royal box—lined with the kind of red baize normally reserved for the tops of office desks—were the two public grandstands, which looked as if they had been hastily cobbled together like the wooden stands at a fair. In the one on the left, still empty and as yet unpainted, light shone through the cracks between the planks. In the one on the right, which had been given a quick lick of pale-blue paint, there was a line of ladies, almost all of whom were dressed in black, leaning on the balustrade, while others were seated here and there on the lower rows; the rest of the stand looked sad and deserted, and the whitish tone of the wood muted the bright tones of the rare summer dress. The gentle breeze occasionally caught the blue pennants on the top of the two masts. A great silence descended from the glittering sky.

In the area around the stands, closed off by a picket fence, there were more infantrymen, their bayonets flashing in the sunlight. Carlos recognised the glum man at the entrance taking the tickets, and who was wearing a vast, white, starched waistcoat that reached down to his knees, as the servant he employed at his laboratory.

They had only gone a few steps when they met Taveira at the entrance to the bar, where he was treating himself to a beer. He was wearing a little posy of yellow carnations in his buttonhole and white gaiters, determined to enjoy the whole event. He had already seen Mist, Clifford's filly, and had decided to bet on her. What a fine head she had, and such splendid legs!

"I was really taken with her! Besides, today isn't just any day, and we need to set the tone. I'm betting three *mil-réis*. What about you, Craft?"

"Yes, possibly later. Let's have a look around first."

In the sloping enclosure between the grandstand and the track, there were only men from the Grémio, from various ministries, and from the Casa Havanesa; most were dressed casually in light-coloured jackets and bowler hats; others, more stylishly attired in frock-coats and with a pair of binoculars slung around their neck, seemed awkward, almost as if they were embarrassed to look so chic. Men talked quietly, walking slowly over the grass, taking short puffs on their cigarettes. Here and there, the occasional solitary individual, hands behind his back, stood languidly eyeing the ladies. Two Brazilians standing next to Carlos were complaining about the price of the tickets, and finding the whole business "damnably dull."

The track opposite, with its trampled grass, was empty and guarded by soldiers; and on the far side, by the rope cordon, knots of people by the carriages were not saying a word, as if in the grip of a grim indolence, under the weight of the June sun. A burly lad, with a mournful voice, was selling cool water. In the background, the broad blue Tejo River, as blue as the sky, gave off a glitter of finely powdered light.

The Viscount de Darque, who had the placid air of a fair-skinned gentleman inclining to fat, came over and shook hands with Carlos and Craft. And as soon as they mentioned his horses (Rabino, the favourite, and another one), he shrugged and closed his eyes like a man prepared to make a sacrifice. What could he do, the boys had wanted to enter them, but it would be another four years before he could come up with a really decent horse worthy of wearing his colours. Besides, he wasn't breeding horses to run at this wretched Belém track, he wasn't that much of a patriot; no, his aim was to go to Spain and beat the Spanish breeder Caldillo.

"Anyway, we'll see. Give me a light, will you? It's all pretty dire, don't you think? For heaven's sake, if you're going to have a proper horse-race you need *cocottes* and champagne, not grim faces and cold water, it just won't work!"

At this point, one of the race stewards, a beardless young man, his face red as a poppy and sweating under the white hat which he wore pushed back on his head, came to fetch Darque, who was needed urgently at the weighing-in enclosure to sort out some minor problem.

"I'm just a dictionary," said Darque, giving another resigned shrug. "Every now and then, these gentlemen from the Jockey Club come and leaf through me. You should see the state of me, Maia, once the race is over—I'll have to be entirely rebound!"

And off he went, laughing at his own joke, propelled along by the steward, who was clapping him familiarly on the back and complimenting him on how well turned out he was.

"Let's go and have a look at the women," Carlos said.

They slowly walked the length of the grandstand. There, leaning on the balustrade, in a long silent line, staring vaguely out as if viewing a procession from a window, were all the ladies who might merit a mention in the society columns of the newspapers or be seen in the boxes at the Teatro de São Carlos or at the Gouvarinhos' Tuesday soirées. Most were wearing the kind of sober outfit appropriate for going to mass. Here and there, one of those large, feathered, Gainsborough-style hats, which were just beginning to be worn, cast a still deeper shadow over a small dark-complexioned face. And, in the frank afternoon light, in the fresh air of that bare hill, their dull, powdered complexions all seemed faded, worn, and flaccid.

Carlos greeted Taveira's two fair-skinned scrawny sisters, both of them correctly dressed in checks, then the Viscountess de Alvim, shiny-faced and pallid, her black bodice aglitter with beads, and the Viscountess' dear inseparable friend, Joaninha Vilar, who was growing plumper by the day and had an ever sweeter look in her long-lashed eyes. After them came the Pedroso sisters, from a family of bankers, both dressed in bright colours and taking a lively interest in the races; one had the programme in her hand and the other was standing up, studying the track through her binoculars. Beside them, chatting to Steinbroken, was the Countess de Soutal, looking somewhat dishevelled and concerned that she might have mud on her skirts. On an isolated row of seats, Vilaça sat in silence alongside two ladies in black.

The Countess de Gouvarinho had not yet arrived, nor had the woman for whom Carlos' eyes were restlessly, hopelessly searching.

"A garden of faded camellias," said Taveira, repeating one of Ega's phrases.

Carlos, meanwhile, had gone to speak to his old friend Dona Maria da Cunha, who had, for some moments, been trying to beckon him over with a look, with her fan, and with her maternal smile. She was the only woman who had dared to descend from the windowed retreat of the grandstand and sit with the men below; but, as she put it, she could not bear the tedium of being up there on show, as if she were waiting for a Holy Week procession to come by. And, still beautiful despite her greying hair, she appeared to be the only person who was enjoying herself, perfectly at ease, with her feet resting on a chair, her binoculars in her lap, receiving greetings from all sides and addressing all the young men as "my boy." She introduced Carlos to the relative who was with her, a Spanish lady who would have been pretty were it not for the dark circles under her eyes, extending almost as far as her cheeks. As soon as Carlos sat down beside her, Dona Maria immediately asked after "that adventurer Ega." The adventurer, said Carlos, was in Celorico, composing a play called *The Mudhole*, which was to be his revenge on Lisbon.

"Does Cohen feature?" she asked, laughing.

"We all do, Senhora Dona Maria. We're all in the mud together."

At that moment, from behind the enclosure, came a lethargic clatter of drums and cymbals, then the National Anthem, intermingled with the voice of an official and the thud of rifle-butts. Flanked by gold epaulettes, the King appeared in the royal box, smiling and wearing a velvet jacket and a white hat. A few of his subjects bowed very slightly; the Spanish lady took Dona Maria's binoculars from her lap and very coolly examined the King. Dona Maria thought the music ridiculous and said that it made the races sound like some sort of fairground. And how absurd to play the National Anthem as if they were at a parade!

"Especially that peculiarly ghastly example," said Carlos. "Have you ever heard Ega's definition, his theory of national anthems. It's priceless!"

"Ah, Ega!" she said smiling, charmed already.

"Ega says that the national anthem is the musical definition of a nation's character. The rhythm of a country's national anthem is, he says, the moral rhythm of the nation. This is what Ega had to say about the various anthems. The "Marseillaise" marches forth like an unsheathed sword. "God save the Queen" advances, dragging a royal train . . ."

"And ours?"

"Ours minces along in a tailcoat."

Dona Maria was still laughing when the Spanish lady, sitting down again and calmly replacing the binoculars in Dona Maria's lap, murmured:

"He has the face of a good man."

"Who? The King?" Dona Maria and Carlos both exclaimed. "Oh, excellent!"

Somewhere a bell was rung, the sound fading on the air. And on the indicator board there appeared the numbers of the two horses—number 1 and number 4—who would be in the first race for a prize that would be awarded "in kind." Dona Maria wanted to know their names, eager to bet and win five *tostões* from Carlos. When Carlos got up to fetch a programme for her, she touched his arm and said:

"That's all right, my boy. Here comes Alencar with the programme. Just look at him. Can you think of anyone else these days who combines that air of sentiment and poetry?"

In pearl-grey gloves and looking younger in a new suit of pale cheviot wool, Alencar was strolling along, his ticket tucked in his buttonhole, fanning himself with his programme and smiling from afar at his good friend Dona Maria. When he reached her side, he doffed his hat—his hair was neatly combed that day and slicked down with a little oil—and, with great gallantry, raised her hand to his lips.

Dona Maria had been one of his lovely contemporaries. They had danced many a passionate mazurka together in the salons of Arroios. She addressed him as "*tu*" and he always called her either "my dear friend" or "my dear Maria."

"Let me see the names of those horses, Alencar. Sit down here and keep me company."

He pulled up a chair, amused at her sudden interest in the races. As long as he had known her, she had been an enthusiastic follower of bullfighting! The names of the horses were Jupiter and The Scotsman.

"No, I don't like either of those names. I won't bet. So what do *you* think of all this, Alencar? Our Lisbon appears to be coming out of its shell."

Alencar put his hat down on a chair and, running one hand over his broad bardic brow, he agreed that the whole thing had a courtly whiff about it, a real air of elegance. And there was the marvellous Tejo River down below, not to mention the importance of improving the stock of Portuguese race-horses. "Isn't that so, Carlos? You know about horses, and, being a master of all sports, you're bound to know more about it than I, about the importance of breeding, I mean . . ."

"Yes, yes, of course, breeding is most important," said Carlos vaguely, looking up again at the grandstand.

It was nearly three o'clock; "she" would certainly not be coming now, and it seemed that the Countess de Gouvarinho had not arrived either. A great wave of lassitude washed over him. Responding with a nod to a sweet smile from Joaninha Vilar in the stands, he considered going back to Ramalhete and concluding the day quietly, in his dressing-gown, reading a book, far from all this tedium.

However, ladies were still continuing to arrive. Little Sá Videira, the daughter of a wealthy shoe-merchant, entered on her brother's arm, looking like a small petulant doll, rather irritated with everything and talking very loudly in

English. Then came the Bavarian ambassador's wife, Baroness von Craben, dressed to the nines, with the broad face of a Roman matron, her skin covered in bright red blotches, her vast body bursting out of a blue-and-white-striped grosgrain dress; behind her skipped the charming, diminutive Baron, wearing a large straw hat.

Dona Maria da Cunha stood up to talk to them and, for a moment, one could hear only the Baroness' voice, like the high-pitched gobble of a turkey, saying of everything: *c'est charmant, c'est très beau*. The Baron, hopping from foot to foot and giggling, found it all *ravissant*. Confronted by these foreigners who had not even bothered to greet him, Alencar polished his pose as a major national figure by twirling his moustache ends and holding his bare forehead still higher.

When the Baron and Baroness continued on to the grandstand, and Dona Maria had sat down again, the poet indignantly declared that he loathed Germans! The superior way she had looked at him, at *him*, that barrel of a woman, so fat her seams were positively straining. The insolent whale!

Dona Maria was smiling and looking at him sympathetically. Then, turning suddenly to the Spanish lady, she said:

"Concha, allow me to introduce you to Dom Tomás de Alencar, our great lyric poet."

At that moment, some of the keener young men, those who had binoculars round their neck, rushed over to the rope edging the track. Two horses galloped serenely past, almost neck and neck, beneath the frenzied whipping of two jockeys with large moustaches. A loud voice announced that The Scotsman had won. Others declared that the winner had been Jupiter. And in the ensuing limp, anticlimactic silence, the notes of the "Madame Angot" waltz, played by the piccolos in the band, floated more brightly on the air. Some of the men had remained with their backs to the track, smoking and looking at the grandstand, where the ladies still leaned on the balustrade, "waiting for the Holy Week procession to pass." A gentleman next to Carlos summarised his impressions by saying that "the whole thing was a fraud."

And when Carlos got up to go in search of Dâmaso, Alencar, chatting animatedly now to the Spanish lady, was speaking of Seville, of *malagueñas*, and the poet Espronceda's "heart."

What Carlos wanted now was to find Dâmaso and ask him why the visit to Olivais had not happened, and then go home to Ramalhete where he could hide the strange mixture of childish melancholy and irritability that was wrapping about him like a mist, making him hate the voices that spoke to him, the rat-a-tat-tat of the music, even the calm beauty of the afternoon. However, as he went round the corner of the grandstand, he bumped into Craft, who stopped him and introduced him to a sturdy fair-haired fellow with whom he was engaged in sprightly conversation. It was the famous Clifford, the great sportsman from Córdoba. Men stood around, gaping at this Englishman, who was a legend in Lisbon—an owner of race-horses, a friend of the King of Spain, and the very embodiment of chic. He cut a relaxed, albeit slightly affected figure, dressed in a simple blue flannel jacket, as if he were in the country, and laughing with Craft about their schooldays together at Rugby. He asked amiably if he and Carlos had not met before, nearly a year ago, in Madrid, at a supper in Pancho Calderón's house. Indeed, they had! They shook hands again, more warmly this time, and Craft proposed watering the flower of that friendship with a bottle of cheap champagne. The amazement of the onlookers grew still more.

The bar was situated beneath the bare boards of the grandstand, with no proper floor, no decoration, not even a flower. At the back was a shelf filled with bottles and plates of cakes. Behind the bar, two exhausted, grubby waiters were making sandwiches and pressing them into shape with hands sticky with beer.

When Carlos and his two friends went in, they noticed, next to one of the metal posts underpinning the grandstand seats, an animated group of men with champagne glasses in hand—the Marquis, the Viscount de Darque, Taveira, a pale young man with a dark beard who had a red starter's flag rolled up under his arm, and the beardless steward, his white hat pushed still farther back on his head, his face scarlet and his collar sodden with sweat. He was the one buying the champagne, and as soon as he saw Clifford come in, he rushed over to him, holding his glass up high, and making the beams tremble with his booming voice.

"Let's drink to our friend Clifford! The Peninsular's premier sportsman and one of the boys! Hip, hip, hooray!"

Glasses were raised amid a clamor of hurrahs, in which the starter's vibrant, enthusiastic voice was the loudest. Clifford, slowly pulling off his gloves, thanked them with a smile, while the Marquis, drawing Carlos to one side, quickly introduced him to the steward, his cousin, Pedro Vargas.

"Delighted to meet you."

"No, please, I was the one who was mad to meet you," exclaimed the steward. "All of us sportsmen should know each other, because this is the true brotherhood here, and the rest is nothing but a rabble!"

And he immediately raised his glass in the air again, and bellowed so loudly that his face grew still redder:

"Let's drink to the health of Carlos da Maia, Portugal's most elegant man and a first-rate hand at the reins! Hip, hip, hooray!"

And again it was the starter's voice that gave the most vibrant and enthusiastic hurrah.

A clerk appeared at the entrance to the bar and summoned the steward. Vargas threw a *libra* coin down on the counter and rushed off, shouting back to everyone, his eyes ablaze:

"That's it, enjoy yourselves, boys! Keep drinking! And you down there,

Senhor Manuel, bring some more ice. People here are drinking warm champagne. Go on, off you go! Quickly!"

While a bottle of champagne was being uncorked for Craft, Carlos was inviting Clifford to dinner that night at Ramalhete. Clifford accepted, taking a sip of champagne, and saying that he thought it an excellent idea for them to continue the tradition of dining together whenever they met.

"Hello!" cried Craft. "What's the General doing here?"

The others all turned round. It was indeed Sequeira, his face beet-red, his body squeezed into a short frock-coat that made him look even stockier than usual, his white hat down over his eyes, and a large walking-stick underneath his arm.

He accepted a glass of champagne and was delighted to meet Senhor Clifford.

"And what do you think of this dull affair?" he exclaimed, turning to Carlos.

He himself was thrilled, of course, jumping for joy. These insipid races, with no horses and no jockeys, with half a dozen yawning spectators, had convinced him that there would be no further attempt to hold a race ever again, and that the Jockey Club would finally go bust—and a good thing too! People would be liberated from an entertainment which did not suit the country's habits. Horse-races were for betting. Had anyone placed a bet? No! So what was the point? In England and France, they would place bets. There, horse-racing was a game, just like roulette or cards. They even had bankers for the purpose, known as bookmakers. There was no comparison.

And when the Marquis, setting down his glass and hoping to calm the General, mentioned the importance of breeding and of supplying horses for the cavalry, the General straightened his back and replied indignantly:

"What *are* you talking about? Are you saying that there's some connection between thoroughbred race-horses and the horses supplied to the cavalry? That would be a fine thing, an army full of race-horses! In the army, you don't want the horse that can run the fastest, you want the horse with most stamina! Anything else is pure nonsense. Race-horses are freaks really! They're like an ox with two heads. Pure nonsense! In France, they even give them champagne to drink. Imagine that!"

And his shoulders shook furiously every time he spoke. Then he gulped down his champagne in one, said again what a pleasure it had been to meet Senhor Clifford, turned on his heel and departed, still indignant and still clutching his walking-stick under his arm, the point of the stick quivering as if eager to give someone a good thrashing.

Craft was smiling and patting Clifford on the back.

"You see how it is; we Portuguese dislike both novelty and sport, apart from bullfighting, that is."

"Quite right too," said Clifford very seriously, straightening his collar. "Why, only a few days ago, I was at the King of Spain's estate and he was telling me . . ."

Suddenly, outside, there was the sound of scuffling and startled voices shouting: "Order!" A lady, who happened to be passing by with her little boy, took refuge in the bar, looking pale with fear. A policeman ran past.

A fight had broken out!

Carlos and the others hurried outside and saw, beside the royal box, a group of men, among them the gesticulating figure of Vargas. Excited, inquisitive boys emerged from the weighing-in enclosure and crowded round on tiptoe; other men came running from the carriage enclosure, jumping over the rope around the track, despite police efforts to hold them back, and soon the group had become a tumultuous mass of top hats and pale suits pressed up against the steps of the royal box, watched calmly by one of the king's adjutants, bare-headed and resplendent in gold braid and aiguelettes.

Carlos, pushing his way through, finally managed to spot, in the middle of the mêlée, the man who had ridden Jupiter in the first race, still in his boots, with a pale grey coat over his jockey's shirt, beside himself with rage and hurling insults at Mendonça, the track referee, who stood there, stunned and wide-eyed, unable to say a word. The jockey's friends kept tugging at him, telling him that he should lodge a formal protest. But he, white-faced and trembling, stamped his foot and said that he didn't give a damn about lodging a protest! He had been cheated of the race! The only protest these people would understand was a good whipping! There was nothing at this race-track but favouritism and double-dealing!

Some very grave-faced men were shocked at such rudeness.

"How dare you, sir!"

Others took the jockey's part; on either side, fierce arguments were breaking out. A man in grey yelled that Mendonça had decided for Pinheiro, who was riding The Scotsman, because he was a friend of his; another gentleman with binoculars slung around his neck found such an allegation monstrous; and the two men, face to face, fists clenched, began furiously calling each other "scum" and "scoundrel!"

Throughout all this, a stocky little man, wearing a broad, spotted collar, kept trying to interrupt, waving his arms about and exclaiming in hoarse, supplicant tones:

"Please, gentlemen, please ... One moment ... I have experience of such matters ... I'm ..."

Then Vargas' great voice boomed forth like a bellowing bull. He stood before the jockey, hatless, face ablaze, and told him that he did not deserve to be there with decent folk! When a gentleman doubts the referee's decision, he lodges a protest! Only a knave and a crook like him, who should never have been allowed to join the Jockey Club in the first place, would dare to denounce them all as thieves! The jockey, held in check by his friends and stretching out his scrawny neck as if to bite Vargas, spat out a vile name. Then, pushing the people around him out of the way in order to make a space, Vargas rolled up his sleeves and bawled:

"Say that again, go on, say that again!"

The crowd immediately stirred into life, bumping against the boards of the royal box, milling around, with cries of "Order!" and "Enough!"; hats were waved in the air and there was the dull thud of punches.

Above the hubbub could be heard furious police whistles; ladies, catching up their skirts, escaped across the track, frantically looking for their carriages; and the thick breath of gross disorder wafted over the hippodrome, cracking the thin veneer of civilisation and artificially imposed decorum.

Carlos found himself next to the Marquis, who was looking pale and exclaiming:

"This is incredible, just incredible!"

Carlos, on the other hand, found it all rather picturesque.

"What do you mean 'picturesque,' man! It's shameful in front of all these foreigners!"

Meanwhile, the crowd was slowly dispersing, obeying the advice of the officer of the municipal guard, a small but determined fellow, who was standing on tiptoe and telling all those around him, in the voice of an orator, to be sensible and to behave like gentlemen. Supported by a friend, the jockey in the pale grey overcoat moved off, limping and with blood dripping from his nose; and the steward and his entourage proceeded triumphantly down to the track, the steward now collarless and shoving his crumpled hat into a briefcase. The band was playing the march from *Le Prophète*, while the unfortunate track referee, Mendonça, arms hanging limp by his side, leaned against the royal box, looking lost and shaken, and repeating:

"Why did this have to happen to me? Why me?"

The Marquis, in a group that had been joined by Clifford, Craft, and Taveira, continued to inveigh against Portugal.

"Now are you convinced? Haven't I always said as much? This is a country fit only for picnics and funfairs. Horse-races, like many of the other civilised pastimes they enjoy abroad, require, first and foremost, an educated public. Basically, we're nothing but thugs! What we like is cheap wine, a bit of guitar music, a good brawl, and plenty of back-slapping bonhomie afterwards! That's how it is!"

Beside him, Clifford, who had maintained his gentlemanly poise throughout the hurlyburly, bit back a smile, kindly assuring him that such conflicts happened everywhere, although, he seemed, in fact, to find it all most undignified. He was even said to be considering withdrawing his horse Mist. And quite right too, thought some. It was humiliating for a thoroughbred like that to have to race in a hippodrome where there was neither order nor decency, where, at any moment, knives might be drawn.

"Listen," said Carlos, taking Taveira to one side, "you haven't seen that wretch Dâmaso anywhere, have you? I've been looking for him now for an hour."

"He was over there a while ago, in the carriage enclosure, with Josefina do Salazar. He's in the most extraordinary get-up—a white frock-coat and a veil on his hat!"

But when, shortly afterwards, Carlos tried to make his way across to the enclosure, the track was closed off. The race for the Grand National Prize was about to be run. The numbers were up on the indicator board, and the sound of a bell was already fading on the air. One of Darque's horses, Rabino, with his jockey in scarlet and white, was being led down by a groom and accompanied by Darque himself; a few men stopped to examine the horse's legs, looking very serious and affecting to know about things equine. Carlos, too, paused for a moment to admire the horse: it was a lovely dark chestnut, light and nervous, but with a narrow chest.

Then, when he turned round, he caught sight of the Countess de Gouvarinho, who had doubtless just arrived and was standing talking to Dona Maria da Cunha. She was wearing a simple, close-fitting English-style outfit in cream cashmere, to which her long, black musketeer's gloves stood out in bold contrast; her black hat was enveloped by the delicate folds of a white veil, which she wore wrapped about her head, concealing half her face, and giving her an oriental air which did not sit well with her pert nose and fiery red hair. All around, though, men were staring at her as if she were a painting.

When she saw Carlos, the Countess could not suppress a smile that lit up her eyes and face. She instinctively took one step towards him and for a moment they were alone, speaking in low voices, while Dona Maria watched, smiling benevolently, prepared to bestow on them her maternal blessing.

"I nearly didn't come," said the Countess, who appeared rather nervous. "Gastão has been so unpleasant today. And, of course, tomorrow I have to go to Oporto."

"To Oporto?"

"Papa wants me to come; it's his birthday. He's getting on a bit now, poor love, and he wrote me such a sad letter. He hasn't seen me for two years."

"Is the Count going?"

"No."

And the Countess—having smiled at the Bavarian ambassador, who greeted her as he came skipping past—looked deep into Carlos' eyes and said:

"I wanted to ask you something."

"What?"

"To come with me."

At that precise moment, Teles da Gama joined them, programme and pencil in hand:

"Do you want to enter a really big sweepstake, Maia? Fifteen tickets, ten *tostões* each. Over there by the grandstand, they're betting like mad. The fight did everyone good, I think, got the blood moving, woke 'em up. Would you like to enter too, Countess?"

The Countess said that she did, and so Teles da Gama wrote down her name and shot off. Then Steinbroken came over, a flower in his buttonhole and wearing a white hat, a ruby horseshoe pin in his cravat, and looking somehow blonder, more elegant, more English, on that solemn day of official sport.

"*Ah, comme vous êtes belle, comtesse! Voilà une toilette merveilleuse, n'est-ce pas, Maia? Est-ce que nous n'allons pas parier quelque chose?*"

The Countess, despite her annoyance at not being able to talk to Carlos, still managed a smile and said regretfully that she had already staked a whole fortune. However, she was sure she could afford five *tostões* on Finland's horse. Which one had he chosen?

"*Ah, je ne sais pas, je ne connais pas les chevaux . . . D'abord, quand on parie . . .*"

Somewhat impatient now, she suggested he choose Vladimiro. Then she had to greet the other Finn, Steinbroken's secretary, a slow, languid, fair-haired young man, who bowed silently before her, allowing his gold monocle to slip from one pale vague eye. Almost immediately, Taveira rushed excitedly up to them to announce that Clifford had withdrawn Mist.

Seeing the Countess thus besieged, Carlos moved slowly away. Indeed, Dona Maria's gaze, which had not left him, was beckoning him now, more brightly and more warmly. When he reached her side, she tugged at his sleeve and made him bend down so that she could whisper delightedly in his ear:

"Doesn't she look stylish today?"

"Who?"

Dona Maria shrugged impatiently.

"What do you mean 'who'? Who do you think? You know perfectly well who I mean. The Countess. She's looks wonderful."

"Yes, indeed, very stylish," said Carlos coolly.

Standing there at Dona Maria's side, slowly getting out a cigarette, he was, almost indignantly, pondering the Countess' words. Go with her to Oporto! He saw in that bold demand the same impertinent desire to organise his time, his movements, his life! He felt an urge to go over and tell her "No," coldly, roughly, rudely, for no reason, with no explanation.

Silently accompanied by Steinbroken's tall thin secretary, she was coming slowly towards him, and the bright gaze she bestowed on him only irritated him all the more, sensing, as he did, in her serene glow, in her calm smile, her utter confidence that he would submit.

And she was quite confident. As soon as the Finn had moved languidly off, and with Dona Maria still there beside them, she set out for him, in English, the charming plan she had conceived, meanwhile pointing at the track as if she were discussing Darque's horses. Instead of leaving for Oporto on Tuesday, she would leave on Monday night, travelling in a reserved compartment accompanied by her Scottish maid and confidante. Carlos would take the same train. In Santarém, they would both get off and spend the night in the hotel there. The following day, she would travel on to Oporto and he would return to Lisbon.

Carlos looked at her with wide surprised eyes, lost for words. He had not expected such madness. He had assumed that she would want him to stay hidden away at the Hotel Francfort in Oporto, for romantic trips to Foz or furtive visits to some hovel in Aguardente. But the idea of spending a night in a hotel in Santarém!

He pulled an angry, incredulous face. On a train on which one was constantly meeting people one knew, how could she even think of getting out with him at Santarém station, taking his arm in wifely fashion and going off to a hotel? She, however, had thought of everything. No one would recognise her because she would be wearing a voluminous waterproof and a wig.

"A wig?!"

"Ssh, here's Gastão!" she hissed.

The Count had come up behind him and put his arm fondly round his waist. He, of course, wanted to know his friend Maia's opinion of the races. There was a good atmosphere, eh? And some lovely outfits, even a certain style about it all. There was, at least, nothing to be ashamed of. It only proved what he had always said, that all the finer points of civilisation could easily be adapted to life in Portugal.

"Our moral soil, Maia, like our physical soil, is a most fertile one!"

The Countess had rejoined Dona Maria. And Teles da Gama, passing by again, caught up in the noisy business of organising his sweepstake, summoned Carlos to the grandstand so that he could draw his ticket and bet with the ladies.

"Gouvarinho, you come too!" he exclaimed. "We need to get a bit of excitement going here, it's our patriotic duty!"

And the Count agreed, on patriotic grounds.

"It's an excellent thing," he said, linking arms with Carlos, "to encourage these elegant diversions. As I said once in the Upper Chamber: luxury is essentially conservative."

Up above, in a corner, in a group of ladies, they found the excitement they were seeking—an almost scandalous excitement in that otherwise silent grandstand, whose denizens still looked as if they were waiting for some Holy Week procession to pass. The Viscountess de Alvim was hastily folding up the sweepstake tickets; and the diminutive, blue-eyed wife of the Russian delegation secretary, already carried away with it all and frantically scribbling in her programme, was desperately, distractedly laying bets of five *tostões*. The thinner of the two Pinheiro sisters, wearing a light dress in a sprigged Pompadour fabric, which formed into hollows beneath her bony clavicles, was loftily offering opinions on the horses in English, while Taveira, eyes shining in the midst of all those skirts, was speaking of bankrupting the ladies, of living entirely at their expense. And all the men, elbowing each other in their eagerness, wanted to place a bet with plump, languid Joaninha Vilar, who, leaning against the grandstand balustrade, was smiling, her head back, her eyelashes drooping, apparently offering her delightfully full bosom to all those hands reaching greedily out to her.

Teles da Gama, meanwhile, was organising this happy chaos. The tickets had all been folded, and now they needed a hat. The gentlemen all affected an excessive devotion to their hats, not wishing to entrust them to the nervous hands of the ladies; one young man, in heavy mourning, went still further, clutching the brim of his hat with both hands and screaming his dissent.

Growing impatient, the Russian delegation secretary's little wife ended up offering her son's sailor hat—the fat child having been left on one side like a bundle of clothes. Joaninha Vilar passed round the hat containing the tickets, laughing and lazily shaking them up, while Steinbroken's secretary, as if performing some solemn duty, gravely collected the coins, which fell with a silvery tinkle into his large hat. The draw was the best part. Since there were only four horses in the race and fifteen entries, eleven of the tickets in the draw were terrifying blanks. They were all hoping to pick number 3, Rabino, Darque's horse and the favourite for the National. Each anxious little hand that lingered too long in the bottom of the sailor hat, rummaging around, feeling the bits of paper, provoked a lot of playful indignation and exaggerated laughter.

"You're spending far too much time choosing, Viscountess! And since you were the one who folded them up, you probably know which is which. A little probity, please, Viscountess!"

"Oh, mon Dieu, j'ai Minhoto, cette rosse!"

"Je vous l'achète, madame!"

"Senhora Dona Maria Pinheiro, you've got two numbers!"

"Ah, je suis perdue . . . Blanc!"

"Me too! We must do another sweepstake. Let's do another one!"

"Yes! Yes! Another sweepstake!"

Meanwhile, higher up, occupying a whole row as if it were a throne, the enormous Baroness von Craben had got to her feet, grasping her ticket. She had drawn Rabino and, affecting in a superior manner not to comprehend her good fortune, was asking who or what Rabino was. When the Count de Gouvarinho solemnly explained to her the importance of Rabino, and that Rabino was very nearly a national treasure, she revealed her large teeth, and condescendingly grunted from behind her double chins: "Charmant." Everyone envied her; and the great whale deposited herself once more on her throne, fanning herself majestically.

There was a moment of surprise: while they had been busily drawing tickets, the horses had set off and were now galloping past the grandstand. Everyone stood up, binoculars in hand. The starter was still on the track, with the red flag lowered, and the horses' hindquarters, gleaming in the light, were disappearing round the bend, beneath the jockeys' shirts puffed out by the breeze.

The roar of voices ceased, and in the silence, the lovely afternoon seemed to spread out around them, softer and calmer. In the dustless air, without the shimmer created by the sun's strongest rays, everything took on a delicate clarity: opposite the grandstand, on the hill, the grass had turned a warm gold; among the carriages, there was the odd gleam of glass on a lantern or of metal on a harness, and the occasional top-hatted figure perched on the driver's seat stood out darkly; the horses, looking smaller now, raced along the green track, clearly silhouetted against the light. Farther off, the white-washed houses were tinged a watery shade of pink, and the distant horizon, aglow with the golds of sunset and the glassy glitter of the river, was dissolving into a luminous mist, in which the blue hills looked almost transparent, as if made of some fine and precious substance.

"It's Rabino!" cried a man standing on a step behind Carlos.

The scarlet and white colours of Darque were, indeed, in front. The other two horses were neck and neck, and bringing up the rear, in a sleepy gallop, was Vladimiro, Darque's other horse, a light bay, almost blond in the light.

Then the wife of the Russian delegation secretary clapped her hands and called out to Carlos, who had drawn Vladimiro in the sweepstake. She had drawn Minhoto, a melancholy nag belonging to Manuel Godinho; and they had made a complicated bet on the two horses involving gloves and bags of almonds. She had already tried to catch Carlos' attention with her pretty blue eyes, and now she was tapping his arm with her fan and saying in mock-triumph:

"*Ah, vous avez perdu, vous avez perdu! Mais c'est un vieux cheval de fiacre, votre Vladimiro!*"

A cab-horse! Vladimiro was Darque's best animal! He might one day be Portugal's one glory, just as Gladiator had been the one glory of France. He might even replace the national poet, Camões!

"*Ah, vous plaisantez . . .*"

No, Carlos was not joking. He was even prepared to bet everything on Vladimiro.

"You're going to bet on Vladimiro?" cried Teles da Gama, turning round sharply.

Carlos, purely to amuse himself and without really knowing why, declared that he was placing his money on Vladimiro. There was general surprise; then everyone wanted to bet, to take advantage of a rich man's whim, backing an inexperienced three-quarter-blood, which even Darque described as a "nag."

He smilingly accepted, even raising his voice and declaring that Vladimiro would beat the whole field. And from all sides, they called to him, eager for plunder.

"*Monsieur de Maia, dix tostons.*"

"*Parfaitement, Madame.*"

"How about half a *libra*, Maia?"

"Fine."

"Me too, Maia! Me too! Two *mil réis*!"

"Senhor Maia, I'll bet ten *tostões.*"

"With the greatest of pleasure, dear lady."

In the distance, the horses were coming round the bend and up the hill. Rabino was already out of sight, and Vladimiro, in what looked like a weary gallop, was alone on the track. A voice rose up, claiming that Vladimiro had gone lame. Then Carlos, who was still backing Vladimiro against the rest of the field, felt somone tugging gently at his sleeve; he turned round; it was Steinbroken's secretary, sidling subtly up to take part in this assault on Maia's purse and proposing a wager of two sovereigns in his name and in that of his superior, as the Legation's and, indeed, the kingdom of Finland's collective bet.

"C'est fait, monsieur!" cried Carlos, laughing.

Now he was beginning to enjoy himself. He had only caught a glimpse of Vladimiro, but he had liked the horse's light head and broad, deep chest. However, he was betting mainly in order to enliven that part of the grandstand and to see the greedy gleam in the women's self-interested eyes. Teles da Gama, beside him, approved wholeheartedly, finding such an attitude both patriotic and chic.

"It's Minhoto!" Taveira yelled suddenly.

On the bend, there had been a change in the running order. Rabino had lost ground, struggling up the hill, panting. And now it was Minhoto, Manuel Godinho's obscure little horse, who had surged forward, determinedly eating up the track, admirably ridden by a Spanish jockey. And immediately behind came the scarlet and white colours of Darque; at first, it seemed that it was still Rabino, but an oblique ray of light revealed, instead, the lustrous tones of a light bay horse and, with great surprise, they saw that it was Vladimiro! The race was between him and Minhoto.

Godinho's friends rushed towards the track, bawling "Minhoto! Minhoto!" and waving their hats in the air.

And all around Carlos, those who had bet against Vladimiro were also cheering on Minhoto, standing on tiptoe by the grandstand balustrade and stretching out their arms to him, urging him on:

"Come on, Minhoto! That's it! Stay with it, boy! Well done! Minhoto! Minhoto!"

The Russian woman, all excited and hoping to win, was clapping her hands. Even the vast Baroness von Craben had got to her feet, dominating the grandstand and filling it with her blue-and-white-striped grosgrain, while, beside her, the Count de Gouvarinho, also standing, was smiling, his patriotic heart aglow, seeing in those waving hats and in those jockeys racing along, the bright light of civilisation.

Suddenly, down below, at the foot of the grandstand, from among the boys surrounding Darque, a cry went up:

"Vladimiro! Vladimiro!"

In a last desperate bid, the horse had drawn level with Minhoto, and they were now racing for the finish, neck and neck—their light-coloured coats gleaming and their eyes bulging—beneath the lashes raining down on them from their riders.

Teles da Gama, forgetting all about his own bet, which had been on his friend Darque's other horse, also started shouting for Vladimiro. The Russian woman, pale and excited, was on the steps, leaning on Carlos' shoulder, urging on Minhoto, giving little shrieks and occasionally tapping him sharply with her fan. The excitement in that part of the grandstand spread to the enclosure, where they could see a line of men standing by the rope beside the track, waving their arms about. On the opposite side, a line of pale faces were fixed in a look of brief anxiety. Some ladies were standing up in their carriages, and two gentlemen came racing over the hill to see the finish, hanging onto their hats as they ran. Here and there, isolated cries of "Vladimiro!" "Vladimiro!" were heard.

With the sound of dully thundering hooves, the horses approached, creating a breeze as they ran.

"Minhoto! Minhoto!"

"Vladimiro! Vladimiro!"

They were nearly there. The English jockey, all afire now, seemed to lift Vladimiro—who, with lustrous neck outstretched, looked as if he were about to escape from between his rider's legs—and with one last triumphant flick of the whip, he drove Vladimiro over the line, two heads in front of a foam-flecked Minhoto.

All around Carlos, gloom descended; there was a long weary sigh. They had all lost; he had swept the board, won all the bets, got away with everything. What luck! An Italian attaché, the sweepstake treasurer, turned pale when he had to surrender the handkerchief full of coins; and from every side, small hands sheathed in pearl grey or chestnut brown sulkily tossed in their lost bets, a rain of coins which Carlos laughingly collected in his hat.

"*Ah, monsieur,*" exclaimed the vast Baroness von Craben angrily, "*méfiez-vous. Vous connaissez le proverbe: heureux au jeu . . .* Lucky at cards . . ."

"Alas, I do, Madame!" said Carlos resignedly, holding out his hat to her.

Then a subtle finger touched his arm. It was Steinbroken's slow silent secretary, who was bringing him his money and that of his superior, the wager placed by the kingdom of Finland.

"How much have you won?" cried Teles da Gama, amazed.

Carlos had no idea. There was gold glinting now in the bottom of his hat. Teles counted it, his eyes bright.

"You've won twelve *libras*!" he said in astonishment, looking at Carlos with renewed respect.

Twelve *libras*! News of this sum spread all around in tones of amazement. Twelve *libras*! Down below, Darque's friends were still waving their hats and cheering. However, a feeling of glum indifference, of slow tedium, soon began to weigh on them again. Yawning and looking exhausted, the boys plumped themselves down in their chairs. The equally lacklustre band was now playing plangent tunes from *Norma*.

Carlos, meanwhile, was standing on a step in the grandstand, scanning the carriage enclosure with his binoculars, in the hope of finding Dâmaso. People were beginning to disperse over the hill. In their calèches, the ladies had resumed their pose of melancholy immobility, hands folded on their laps. Here and there, the occasional inelegant dog-cart would trot across the grass. Concha and Carmen, Eusèbiozinho's two Spanish women, were seated in a victoria, each holding a scarlet parasol. And a group of men, hands behind their back, were gawping at the kind of four-in-hand made fashionable by the Duke d'Aumont: sitting in it were the members of a morose family, along with a wetnurse wearing a peasant's headscarf and suckling a baby swathed in an elaborate lace shawl. Two shrill-voiced boys were selling cold water.

Carlos was just leaving the grandstand, having failed to find Dâmaso, when he bumped right into him as he was coming up the steps, face scarlet, and wearing his famous white frock-coat.

"Where the devil have you been?"

Dâmaso grabbed his arm and stood on tiptoe to whisper in his ear that he had been with the most divine woman, Josefina do Salazar. *Very* chic and beautifully dressed! He thought he might have found himself a woman!

"You Sardanapalus, you!"

"One does one's best. Come back up into the grandstand with me. I haven't had a chat yet with anyone who's anyone in high society. And I'm absolutely furious. People made fun of my blue veil. This truly is a country of idiots. They made fun of me! 'Mind the sun doesn't ruin your complexion!' they said. 'Where do you live, sweetheart?' they said. The rabble! I had to take the veil off in the end. I'm quite determined now to appear at any other races stark naked! I mean it! This country is a blot on civilisation. Aren't you coming? No? I'll see you later, then."

Carlos stopped him.

"Wait, I need to speak to you. What happened to the visit to Olivais? You never said another word about it. We had arranged that you would invite Castro Gomes, that you'd come and give us his reply. You never came and didn't even bother to send a note. Craft was waiting. Anyway, it was damnably rude of you, the behaviour of a savage."

Dâmaso threw up his hands. Carlos obviously had not heard the great news. He hadn't returned to Ramalhete, as agreed, because Castro Gomes couldn't come to Olivais. He was leaving for Brazil. Indeed, he had left already, on Wednesday. It was the most extraordinary thing. He went there to issue the invitation, and His Excellency announced that he was very sorry, but he was leaving the next day for Rio. He had his luggage packed, had rented a house for his wife for three months, and had his ticket in his pocket. It had all happened very suddenly, from one day to the next. He was definitely a bit touched, that fellow Castro Gomes.

"And so off he went," Dâmaso exclaimed, turning to greet the Viscountess de Alvim and Joaninha Vilar, who were leaving the grandstand. "Off he went, and she's now installed in the new house. I went to call on her yesterday, but she wasn't at home. Do you know what worries me? That initially, because of the neighbours and with her being alone, she might not want me to go there too often. What do you think?"

"Possibly. And where does she live?"

Dâmaso quickly explained where Madame lived. It was odd, really, that she should be living in the same building as Cruges! Cruges' mother had, for years now, been renting out the first floor as a furnished apartment. Last winter, Bertonni, the tenor, had stayed there with his family. It was a delightful place; Castro Gomes had been very clever.

"And, of course, it's terribly handy for me, being just down the road from the Grémio. Aren't you going back up to the grandstand to chat with the fillies? I'll see you later then. La Gouvarinho is looking terribly chic today . . . and simply crying out for a man, if you ask me! Goodbye."

Standing opposite Carlos, the Countess—who was with Dona Maria and her group of friends, a group that had just been joined by the Viscountess de Alvim and Joaninha Vilar—kept shooting him insistent, anxious glances and torturing her large black fan. He did not, however, obey at once, remaining where he was, at the bottom of the grandstand steps, absentmindedly lighting a cigarette, feeling troubled by Dâmaso's words, which had left a luminous furrow in his soul. Now that he knew she was alone in Lisbon, he felt very close to her, able at any moment to step across the threshold of her home and climb the same steps she had climbed. His imagination was already alight with the possibility of a chance encounter, a brief exchange of words—tiny things, subtle as threads, but through which their destinies might begin to mesh. He was immediately seized by the puerile temptation to go there that very afternoon, that very moment, and, as a friend of Cruges, enjoy the right to walk up that same staircase, stop outside her front door, and overhear a voice, the notes of a piano, or some other sound emanating from her life.

The Countess still had not taken her eyes off him. Finally, he walked irritably over to her; she immediately stood up, left the group of other women and, as they strolled about on the grass, she again talked about the trip to Santarém. Carlos abruptly declared the whole idea foolish.

"Why?"

Why?! Because of the danger and the discomfort, because it was ridiculous. As a woman, she was inevitably prone to such picturesque flights of romantic fancy, but it fell to him, as a man, to show some common sense.

She bit her lip and blushed scarlet. She saw no common sense in his words at all, only coldness. When she was prepared to risk so much, the least he could do was to put up with the discomforts of an inn for one night.

"That's not the point!"

What was the point, then? Was he afraid? It was no more dangerous than those visits to her aunt's house. No one could possibly recognise her when swathed in a waterproof, with her hair a different colour and concealed beneath all kinds of veils. They would arrive at night, go straight to their room, which they would not thereafter leave, and be served only by her Scottish maid. The following day, she would continue her journey to Oporto on the night train, and that would be that. In her insistence, in her vehement active passion, she appeared to take the role of the man, the seducer, tempting him, inflaming him, while he was more like the woman, hesitant and frightened. And that is what Carlos felt. His prolonged resistance to that invitation to a night of love was threatening to become grotesque; at the same time, the voluptuous warmth emanating from her breast, rising and falling beside him and because of him, was gradually weakening his resolve. At last, he looked at her, and as if his desire were suddenly rekindled by the brief flame burning in her dark, liquid, eager eyes, promising him a thousand things, he said, somewhat pale-faced:

"All right, then. Tomorrow night, at the station."

At that moment, laughter and mocking exclamations broke out all around them: a solitary horse was galloping nonchalantly across the finishing line, as if trotting down an avenue in Campo Grande on a Sunday afternoon. People were wondering what kind of race would be run for one horse only, when, in the distance, as if emerging from the golden glow of the sun as it set over the river, a poor white nag came into view, forcing itself onward, breathing hard, making one last painful effort, beneath the frantic lashes of a jockey in purple and black. When the horse finally arrived, the other jockey had already ridden slowly back from the finish line and was talking with friends by the trackside.

Everyone was laughing. And thus the King's Prize reached its absurd end.

There was still the Consolation Prize race, but all that earlier and entirely fictitious interest in horses had disappeared. In the calm radiant beauty of the evening, some ladies, copying the Viscountess de Alvim, had gone down to the weighing-in enclosure, weary of the immobility of the grandstand. More chairs were put out; groups formed here and there on the trampled grass, enlivened by the occasional pale dress or by a bright feather on a hat; and men talked and smoked as familiarly if they were in someone's salon in winter. The group surrounding Dona Maria and the Viscountess de Alvim were planning a great picnic in Queluz. Alencar and the Count de Gouvarinho were discussing educational reform. The ghastly Baroness von Craben, among various diplomats and young men with binoculars round their necks, was, from the depths of her double chin, holding forth about Daudet, who was, in her opinion, *très agréable*. And when Carlos finally took his leave, the enclosure on the cool breezy hill, with the races forgotten, was increasingly taking on the air of a soirée, with a murmur of voices, a flutter of fans, and, in the background, the band playing a waltz by Strauss.

Carlos, after looking everywhere for Craft, found him in the bar with Darque and others, drinking more champagne.

"I have to go back into Lisbon," he said, "which means taking the phaeton. I'm very rudely going to have to abandon you here, I'm afraid. You'll have to make your own way back to Ramalhete."

"I'll take him," cried Vargas, whose cravat, by now, was all awry. "I'll take him in my dog-cart. I'll look after him. Leave him with me. Do you need a receipt? Let's drink to the health of Craft, my favourite Englishman. Hooray!"

"Hip hip hooray!"

Shortly afterwards, Carlos, trotting along in his phaeton, was turning into Rua de São Francisco. He was in a strange, delicious state of agitation brought on by the certainty that she was alone now in Cruges' house: the last look she had given him seemed to go ahead of him, calling to him; and a turbulent stirring of nameless hopes drew his soul up into the blue.

When he stopped at the door, someone was slowly closing the blinds at her windows. The silent street was already filling with evening shadows. He threw the reins to the coachman and crossed the courtyard. He had never visited Cruges before, never been up those stairs, and he felt a shudder of horror at the sight of those cold, carpetless, stone steps and those bare, grimy walls, pale and sad in the oncoming dark. He stopped on the first landing. That was where she lived. And he stood looking, with ingenuous awe, at the three blue-painted doors; the central door was blocked by a long wicker bench, and by the door on the right hung the bell-pull with a huge ball on the end. Not a sound came from within, and that heavy silence, along with the sight of the blinds he had seen being closed, seemed to surround the people who lived there in impenetrable solitude. Despondency washed over him. What if, without her husband there, she were about to begin a reclusive solitary life? What if his eyes never met hers again?

He went slowly up to Cruges' apartment and hardly knew what he could possibly say to the maestro to explain this strange, unaccountable visit. It was a relief when the little maid came to tell him that Master Vitorino had gone out.

Down below, Carlos took up the reins again and slowly drove the phaeton as far as the Largo da Biblioteca. Then he drove slowly back. Now, behind the white blinds, there was a vague glow. He gazed up as if at a star.

He went back to Ramalhete. Craft, covered in dust, was just stepping down from a hired cab. For a moment, they stood at the door, while Craft, fumbling for change to give the coachman, was telling Carlos about the final race. In the Consolation Prize race, one of the two horsemen had fallen almost at the finish line, but had not been injured; and, finally, as they were about to leave, Vargas, who was on his third bottle of champagne, had punched one of the waiters at the bar.

"And so," said Craft, handing over his change to the coachman, "the races at least fulfilled that old Shakespearian principle: all's well that ends well."

"A punch," said Carlos, laughing, "certainly makes an excellent full stop."

In the courtyard, the old doorman was waiting, his hat off, with a letter for Carlos in his hand. A man had brought it only moments before.

It was a large envelope, sealed with a crest, and it was written in a woman's hand, an English hand. Carlos opened it at once and, as soon as he read the first line, he made a gesture of such joyful surprise and his face lit up with such intense happiness, that Craft, beside him, asked, smiling:

"A love affair perhaps, or an inheritance?"

Blushing, Carlos put the letter in his pocket and muttered:

"No, no, it's only a note from a patient . . ."

It may have been only a patient and only a note, but it began thus: "Madame Castro Gomes presents her respects to Senhor Carlos da Maia and asks if he would be so kind . . ." Then, in a few brief words, she asked him to come the following morning, as early as possible, because a member of the household was unwell.

"Right, I'm going to get dressed," said Craft. "Supper at half past seven, eh?"

"Yes, supper," replied Carlos nonsensically, his face wreathed in ecstatic smiles.

He ran to his rooms, and standing by the window, without even taking off his hat, he read the note again and then again, gazing, enraptured, at the writing, voluptuously sniffing the scented paper.

It was dated that very day, in the afternoon. So, when he had passed by her door, she had already written it, her thoughts had already lingered on him, even if only during the time it took her to write the simple letters of his name. She was not the person who was ill. And if it had been Rosa, she would not have referred coolly to "a member of the household." It was perhaps the splendid negro servant with the grizzled hair. Perhaps it was Miss Sara, blessings be upon her, who wanted a doctor who understood English. Anyway, someone was ill in bed, a bed to which she herself would lead him, through the inner corridors of that house which, only moments before, had felt sealed off and eternally impenetrable! And then this wonderful note, this delicious request to go to her house—now that she knew who he was and had seen Rosa gaily waving to him—took on a profound and troubling significance.

If she had chosen not to understand or to accept the distant love which his eyes had so clearly offered her, in those fleeting moments when they met hers, she could have called another doctor, another practice, a stranger. But no, her gaze had answered his, and she was opening her door to him. And this idea aroused in him a feeling of inexpressible gratitude, a wild, overwhelming impulse to fall at her feet, to kiss the hem of her dress, devoutly, eternally, never wanting anything more, never asking anything more.

When Craft came down shortly afterwards, looking fresh and clean and starched and correct, he found Carlos, still covered in the dust from the road, his hat still on his head, pacing about the room, in a state of radiant agitation.

"You're positively glowing, man!" said Craft, stopping in front of him, his hands in his pocket, and studying him for an instant from the height of his resplendent collar. "You're on fire! You look as if you had a halo round your head! Something very, very good must have happened to you!"

Carlos stretched and smiled. Then he looked at Craft for a moment in silence, shrugged and murmured:

"The thing is, Craft, we never know whether what happens to us is, ultimately, good or bad."

"Ordinarily speaking, it's bad," said Craft tartly, going over to the mirror to tie his white cravat still more correctly.

: XI :

THE FOLLOWING MORNING, CARLOS, who had risen early, walked from Ramalhete to Rua de São Francisco, to Madame Gomes' house. On the landing, where the faint glow from the skylight died away in the shadows, an old lady in headscarf and black shawl was waiting, seated glumly on one end of the wicker bench. The open front door revealed an ugly corridor wall, lined with yellow paper. Inside, a clock was listlessly striking ten.

"Have you already knocked?" asked Carlos, raising his hat.

From the depths of the shadow cast by her headscarf, the old lady murmured in a weary, ailing voice:

"Yes, sir, they've been kind enough to talk to me already, sir. The butler, Senhor Domingos, won't be long..."

Carlos waited, pacing slowly up and down the landing. From the second floor came the happy sound of children playing; up above, Cruges' manservant was vigorously scrubbing the steps, loudly whistling a *fado*. One long minute dragged by, then another, seemingly endless. From the darkness of her headscarf, the old woman uttered a small defeated sigh. Somewhere in the background, a canary burst into song; and then Carlos, growing impatient, gave the bell-pull a tug.

Immediately, a manservant with ginger sideburns and very correctly buttoned up in a flannel jacket, came running out, bearing a dish covered with a napkin; and when he saw Carlos, he was so taken aback that he stood swaying in the doorway, and spilled a little of the gravy onto the floor.

"Oh, sir, please come in. I'm so sorry. If you wouldn't mind waiting just one moment, I'll open up the drawing room. Here you are, Senhora Augusta, here you are, and be careful that no more is spilled. My mistress says she'll send over some port wine soon. I'm so sorry, Senhor Carlos. This way, sir."

He drew back a red rep door curtain and ushered Carlos into a spacious, high-ceilinged room lined with blue-sprigged wallpaper and which had two balconies that looked out onto Rua de São Francisco; hurriedly raising the two white blinds, he asked Carlos if he had perhaps forgotten him. And when he turned round, smiling and hastily rolling down his shirtsleeves, Carlos recognised him by his ginger whiskers. It was Domingos, an excellent valet who had

241

worked at Ramalhete during the early winter months, but who had left after squabbles of a patriotic and jealous nature with the French chef.

"I couldn't see you clearly before, Domingos," Carlos said. "It was rather dark out on the landing, but, yes, of course, I remember you. So this is where you're working now, is it? And are you happy here?"

"Yes, sir, very happy. And Senhor Cruges, of course, lives upstairs."

"Yes, I know."

"Would you mind waiting for just one moment while I go and tell Senhora Dona Maria Eduarda that you're here."

Maria Eduarda! It was the first time Carlos had heard her name, and it seemed to him perfectly suited to her serene beauty. Maria Eduarda, Carlos Eduardo. Even their names were similar. Perhaps this presaged the meeting of their two destinies!

Domingos, meanwhile, standing at the door, with one hand holding back the curtain, had stopped to tell him in a confiding tone and with a smile:

"It's the English governess who's ill."

"Ah, so it's the governess."

"Yes, sir, she's had a bit of a fever since yesterday and a tight feeling in her chest."

"Ah!"

Domingos drew the curtain a little farther back, but seemed in no hurry to leave; then he looked at Carlos admiringly and said:

"And is your grandfather well, sir?"

"Yes, Domingos, he is, thank you."

"He's a fine gentleman, sir. There's not another man like him in the whole of Lisbon!"

"Thank you, Domingos, thank you."

When Domingos finally left, Carlos slowly took off his gloves and made a slow, inquisitive tour of the room. The floor had been newly carpeted. By the door was an old grand piano, covered with a cream-coloured cloth; on a shelf beside it, piled high with scores and sheet music and illustrated magazines, rested a Japanese vase in which three beautiful white lilies were fading; all the chairs were upholstered in the same red rep; and at the foot of the sofa lay an old tiger-skin. As in the Hotel Central, the summary furnishings of a rented house had been overlaid with touches of comfort and taste: new cretonne curtains that matched the blue wallpaper had replaced the usual muslin variety; a small Moorish chest of drawers, which Carlos remembered having seen only days before in old Abraão's shop, had been brought in to relieve the bareness of one of the walls; the plush cloth on an oval table in the centre was laden with beautifully bound volumes, albums, two bronze Japanese goblets, a Dresden flower basket, and other delicate objets d'art which clearly did not belong to Cruges' mother. And floating above the general order of things and marking them all with a particular charm hung the same indefinable perfume that Carlos had noticed in the rooms at the Hotel Central and in which the dominant note was jasmine.

What Carlos liked most was a lovely screen in raw linen embroidered with bouquets of flowers, and which stood by the window, creating a sheltered, cosy corner. Next to it was a low chair in scarlet satin, a large pouffe, a sewing table, which looked as if the woman working there had just that moment abandoned what she was doing, covered as it was with various fashion magazines, a roll of embroidery, and balls of coloured wool overflowing from a small wicker basket. And there, curled comfortably up on the soft seat of the chair, was the little griffon dog that had so often passed through Carlos' dreams, trotting lightly along the Aterro, following some radiant female figure or else nestling sleepily on a soft lap.

"*Bonjour, mademoiselle,*" he said softly, hoping to gain the dog's sympathy.

The dog sat up, ears pricked, staring at this stranger through its ruffled fur with two lovely, suspicious, jet-black eyes possessed of an almost human penetration. For a moment, Carlos was afraid it might start barking, but, instead, the dog surrendered itself to him and rolled over on the chair, legs in the air, shamelessly exposing its belly to be caressed. Carlos was just about to approach in order to pat and stroke it, when he heard a light step on the carpet. He turned and saw Maria Eduarda before him.

It was like an unexpected apparition, and he bowed low not so much in order to greet her as to disguise the wave of blood he felt burning his face. Tall and pale, in a simple close-fitting dress of black serge, with a neat, rather mannish little collar, and with a rosebud and its two green leaves pinned to her breast, she sat down next to the oval table and took out a small lace handkerchief. In response to her smiling gesture, Carlos perched awkwardly on the edge of the sofa. And after a moment's silence, which seemed to him profound and almost solemn, Maria Eduarda spoke in a voice that was slow and rich, with a caressing, golden tone.

Through his ecstatic mist, Carlos vaguely understood that she was thanking him for the trouble he had taken over Rosa; and, whenever his gaze lingered on her for a moment longer, he immediately discovered some fresh enchantment, some new perfection. Her thick hair, which formed a gentle wave above her brow, was not blonde, as he had thought when he saw her in the sunlight, but, rather, it mingled two rich shades of brown. In the great dark light of her eyes there was something at once very grave and very sweet. In an easy gesture, she sometimes folded her hands on her knees when she spoke. And through the close-fitting serge sleeves, which ended in a white cuff, he could sense the beauty, the whiteness, the softness, almost the warmth of her arms.

She had fallen silent. Carlos, when he spoke, again felt the blood burning his face. And despite Domingos having already explained to him that the governess was the patient, in his agitation all he could think of to ask was this one timid question:

"It's not your daughter who is ill again, is it, Senhora?"

"Oh, no, thank goodness!"

And Maria Eduarda told him exactly what Domingos had told him earlier, that the English governess had been feeling unwell for the last two days, with breathing difficulties, a cough and a touch of fever.

"We thought, at first, that it was a slight cold, but yesterday afternoon she was worse, and I'm anxious now that you should see her."

She got up and went over to the enormous bell-pull that hung beside the piano. Her hair, from behind, drawn up onto the top of her head, left a few delicately curling, downy, golden threads on the milk-white nape of her neck. Set among the cheap furniture, beneath the drab ceiling of dingy stucco, her whole person seemed to Carlos more radiant, to possess a nobler, almost inaccessible beauty; and it occurred to him that now he would never dare to look at her as frankly as he had, and with such patent adoration, as when he had encountered her in the street.

"What a lovely little dog you have, Senhora," he said, when Maria Eduarda sat down again, and he spoke these simple words, smiling as he did so, with a certain tenderness.

She smiled too, a pretty smile that dimpled her chin and lent a more delicate sweetness to her grave features. She gaily clapped her hands and called to the dog:

"You're being complimented, Niniche, come and say thank you!"

Niniche appeared from behind the screen, yawning. Carlos thought Niniche a lovely name. Oddly enough, he had once had a little Italian greyhound called Niniche.

At that moment, the maid came in, the same thin, freckled girl with the insolent gaze whom Carlos had met at the Hotel Central.

"Melanie will show you to Miss Sara's room," Maria Eduarda said. "I won't come with you because she's so timid and so worried about being a nuisance, that, if I'm there, she could easily deny everything and swear she has nothing wrong with her at all."

"Of course, of course," said Carlos, smiling and finding everything utterly enchanting.

And it seemed to him that something in her eyes, something keen and sweet, shone more brightly then and flowed towards him.

With hat in hand, walking confidently along that private corridor and noticing various small details of domestic life, Carlos felt the joy almost of possession. Through a half-open door, he glimpsed a bathtub and, hanging beside it, large Turkish bathrobes. On a table, farther on, bottles of mineral water, from Saint-Galmier and from Vals, were lined up as if they had just been removed from their crates. From all these simple, unremarkable things he deduced evidence of a life tastefully lived.

Melanie drew back a linen curtain and showed him into a cool bright room;

there he found poor Miss Sara sitting up in a narrow iron bedstead, with a blue silk ribbon round her neck and her hair brushed as smoothly and neatly as if she were about to go to Sunday service at a Presbyterian chapel. On the bedside table, her English newspapers lay scrupulously folded, next to a glass containing two lovely roses; and everything in the room had the strict glow of order about it, from the portraits of the British royal family displayed on the lace cloth covering the chest of drawers to the gleaming boots sorted and arranged in ranks along a pine shelf.

As soon as Carlos sat down, her cheeks flushed scarlet with embarrassment and, coughing feebly, she declared that there was really nothing wrong with her at all. It was her mistress, so kind and so concerned about her health, who had forced her to stay in bed. It was dreadful sitting there, idle and useless, especially now that Madame was so alone, in a house with no garden. Where was the little girl to play? Who would go out with her? Madame was virtually a prisoner!

Carlos reassured her and took her pulse. Then, when he got up in order to listen to her chest, the poor lady blushed with shame and clutched the bed-clothes more closely to her, asking if that were really necessary. He assured her it was. He found her right lung slightly congested, and while he covered her up again, he asked her a few questions about her family. She told him she was from York, the daughter of a clergyman, and that she had fourteen siblings; her brothers were all in New Zealand and as strong as athletes, every one of them. She had been the runt of the family, so much so that when her father saw that, at seventeen, she weighed no more than eight stone, he had immediately taught her Latin so that she could at least find work as a governess.

There was no history in her family of lung disease, then? She smiled. No, never! Her mother was still alive, and her father had died at a great old age after being kicked by a horse.

Standing up now and with hat in hand, Carlos continued to observe her thoughtfully. Then, for no reason, she became upset, and her little eyes filled with tears. And when she heard him say that she must remain confined to her bed and to her room for another two weeks, she grew still more upset, and two small timid tears almost escaped her eyelashes. Carlos patted her hand paternally.

"Thank you, sir," she murmured, quite overcome.

Back in the sitting room, Carlos found Maria Eduarda sitting at the table making a flower arrangement, with a large basket of flowers beside her on a chair, and her lap full of carnations. A lovely ray of sunlight fell across the carpet and died at her feet; Niniche was lying there, gleaming, as if her coat were made entirely of silver threads. In the street, underneath the windows, in the bright morning sun, a hurdy-gurdy was playing the "Madame Angot" waltz. From upstairs came the sound of children running about and playing.

"How is she?" she cried, turning round, a bunch of carnations in her hand.

Carlos reassured her by saying that Miss Sara had a mild case of bronchitis and a slight fever. She merely needed to rest and to be well looked after.

"Of course. And she probably needs some medicine too, I should think."

She placed the remaining carnations in the basket and went over to an Indian rosewood desk that stood between the windows. She herself found the paper on which he could write the prescription and carefully fitted the pen with a new nib. Carlos found these attentions as troubling as caresses.

"Really, Senhora," he murmured, "a pencil would do."

When he sat down, his eyes lingered with tender curiosity on those familiar objects upon which her gentle hands had rested—an agate seal lying on an old accounts book, an ivory knife bearing a silver monogram, next to a little Saxe vase containing various hand-stamps; and there was, in everything, a bright order that perfectly matched her own pure profile. Out in the street, the hurdy-gurdy had stopped playing, and upstairs the children were no longer racketing about. And while he was slowly writing, he was aware of her trying to walk more lightly across the carpet and to make less noise moving the vases around.

"What lovely flowers you have, Senhora!" he said, turning round, while he distractedly blotted the prescription dry.

Standing up by the Moorish chest of drawers, where she had placed a yellow vase, she was busy arranging some foliage around two roses.

"They make a room seem fresher somehow," she said. "But, you know, I imagined that Lisbon would have far prettier flowers than these. I've found nothing to compare with the flowers in France. Don't you agree?"

He did not reply at once, absorbed in watching her, thinking how sweet it would be to stay eternally in that room of red rep furniture, full of light and silence, and watch her arranging green leaves around stem roses!

"There are some beautiful flowers in Sintra," he murmured at last.

"Oh, Sintra is delightful!" she said, without looking up. "It's worth visiting Portugal purely to see Sintra."

At that moment, there was a rustling sound as the curtain was pushed aside, and Rosa, carrying her doll, ran into the room; she was all in white, apart from her black silk stockings and the long wave of dark hair that bobbed against her back. When she saw Carlos, she stopped abruptly and looked at him with wide amazed eyes, clutching Cricri—who was dressed only in her chemise—more tightly in her arms.

"Don't you recognise the gentleman?" her mother asked as she took up her seat again beside her basket of flowers.

Rosa was starting to smile now, and her little face blushed prettily. Dressed all in white and black, like a swallow, she had a rare charm, with her delicate figure, her light grace, her large blue eyes and a womanly blush on her cheek. When Carlos held out his hand to renew an old acquaintance, she stood on tiptoe and blithely offered him her lips, fresh as a rosebud. Carlos dared do no more than lightly pat her head.

He went to shake hands with his old friend Cricri, but Rosa suddenly remembered what had brought her there.

"It's Cricri's *robe-de-chambre*, Mama, I can't find it and so I haven't been able to dress her yet. Do *you* know where it is?"

"Untidy creature!" murmured her mother, looking at Rosa with a slow, fond smile. "Cricri has her own chest of drawers and her own wardrobe, so she has no excuse for losing things. Isn't that so, Senhor Maia?"

He, still with the prescription in his hand, was smiling too, without saying a word, absorbed in the tender intimacy in which he felt himself so sweetly immersed.

The little girl went over to her mother and pressed against her arm, saying in a slow, languid, wheedling voice:

"Oh, tell me. Don't be so mean. Go on, where's Cricri's *robe-de-chambre*, tell me, please, Mama."

Maria Eduarda, with the tips of her fingers, retied the little white silk bow securing the child's hair. She said more seriously then:

"All right, be quiet now. You know perfectly well that I'm not the one who looks after Cricri's things. You should be tidier. Go and ask Melanie."

And, equally seriously, Rosa obeyed at once, saying to Carlos as she passed, with an aristocratic air:

"*Bonjour, Monsieur.*"

"She's charming," he murmured.

Maria Eduarda smiled. She had finished arranging the carnations and immediately turned to Carlos, who had put the prescription down on the table and, making himself comfortable in an armchair, began giving instructions on the kind of food Miss Sara should be eating and the spoonfuls of codeine syrup she should take every three hours.

"Poor Sara!" she said. "It's odd, you know, I had a feeling, almost a certainty, that she would fall ill in Portugal."

"She'll come to hate Portugal then."

"Oh, she loathes it already! It's too hot and smelly, the people are hideous . . . oh, and she goes in fear of being insulted in the street . . . In short, she's miserable and can't wait to leave."

Carlos laughed at these Anglo-Saxon antipathies, although Miss Sara was perhaps right in many ways.

"And are you enjoying Portugal, Senhora?"

She gave an indecisive shrug.

"Yes, but then I should. It's my country, after all."

Her country? And he had assumed she was Brazilian!

"No, no, I'm Portuguese."

And, for a moment, there was silence. She had picked up from the table a large black fan painted with red flowers, which she slowly opened. And, without knowing why, Carlos felt a new sweetness pierce his heart. Then she spoke of the voyage, which had been most agreeable; she loved being at sea; and the morning they arrived in Lisbon had been quite divine, with a deep blue sky and an equally blue sea, and, already, the balmy air of a warm climate. But then, as soon as they disembarked, everything had been most disagreeable. The rooms they had been given at the Hotel Central had proved most unsuitable. Niniche had terrified them all one night with a bad bout of indigestion. And then there was the accident in Oporto.

"Ah, yes," said Carlos, "your husband, in Praça Nova."

She looked surprised. How did he know about that? Ah, of course, Dâmaso must have told him.

"You're close friends, I understand."

After a slight hesitation, which she understood, Carlos murmured:

"Yes . . . Dâmaso comes to Ramalhete quite often, but I've only known him for a few months."

She opened her eyes wide in amazement.

"Dâmaso? But he told me you had known each other since you were children, that you were related."

Carlos shrugged and smiled.

"It's a nice story . . . and if it makes him happy . . ."

She, too, smiled and shrugged.

"And you, Senhora," Carlos went on, not wanting to say anything more about Dâmaso, "what do you think of Lisbon?"

She liked it enormously, she found the blue and white of a southern city very pretty. But there were so few comforts! Life there had an air about it which she had not yet been able to put her finger on—she wasn't sure if it was simplicity or poverty.

"It's simplicity, Senhora, the simplicity of the savage."

She laughed.

"I wouldn't go that far, but I suppose in a way the Portuguese are like the Greeks—content to sit eating an olive and gazing up at the lovely blue sky."

This seemed to Carlos an utterly adorable remark, and his heart melted further.

Maria Eduarda's main complaint was the quality of the houses, so lacking in comfort, so devoid of taste, so neglected. The one she was living in now was making her quite wretched. The kitchen was appalling; none of the doors closed properly; and there were some paintings of boats and hills on the dining room wall that positively ruined her appetite.

"Apart from that," she said, "it's just dreadful not having a garden where the little one can run around and play."

"It isn't easy to find a big house like this that also has a garden," said Carlos.

He glanced at the walls, at the dingy stucco ceiling, and he suddenly thought of Craft's house, with its view of the river, fresh air and cool avenues of acacias.

Fortunately, Maria Eduarda was only renting it by the month and was thinking of spending the rest of her time in Portugal by the sea.

"Besides," she said, "that was what my doctor in Paris, Dr. Chaplain, advised me to do."

Dr. Chaplain? Carlos knew Dr. Chaplain very well. He had attended lectures by him and even visited him at his home in Les Maisonettes, near St-Germain. He was a great teacher and a very fine man!

"And he's so kind-hearted!" she said with a bright smile, her eyes shining.

And that common feeling seemed suddenly to bring them subtly closer; each of them at that moment adored Dr. Chaplain; and they continued talking about him for some time, enjoying, through this slight affection for an old doctor, a nascent harmony of hearts.

Good old Dr. Chaplain! He had such a kindly, noble face! And he always used to wear that little silk cap . . . and a big flower in his buttonhole. He was, quite simply, the greatest practitioner to have emerged from the generation of Armand Trousseau.

"And Madame Chaplain," added Carlos, "is an equally delightful person, don't you think?"

Maria Eduarda, however, had not met Madame Chaplain.

In the next room, the listless clock had begun striking eleven. Carlos got up, bringing to an end this brief, delicious, unforgettable visit.

She proffered her hand, and a little blood once more rushed to his face when he touched that soft cool skin. He asked her to give his compliments to Mademoiselle Rosa. Then, at the door, as he lifted the curtain, he turned again to say one last goodbye and to receive the soft gaze with which she followed him.

"We'll see you tomorrow, then!" she exclaimed suddenly, smiling her lovely smile.

"Yes, of course!"

Domingos was already out on the landing, in his tailcoat, looking cheerful and with his hair now carefully combed.

"Is it anything serious, sir?"

"No, Domingos, nothing serious. And I'm very pleased to have seen you again."

"So am I, sir. We'll see you tomorrow, then, sir."

"Yes, tomorrow."

Niniche came out onto the landing as well. Carlos bent down affectionately to stroke her and said, beaming:

"See you tomorrow, Niniche!"

Tomorrow! As he walked back to Ramalhete, this was the one distinct idea he could fix upon in the luminous mist drowning his soul. The day was finished for him now, but once the long hours had passed, and the long night was over, he would once more enter that room decorated in cheap red rep, where she would be waiting for him, wearing the same serge dress, still arranging those green leaves around the same stem roses.

As he crossed the Aterro, amid the summer dust and the clatter of carriages, what he could see was that room, newly carpeted, cool, bright, and silent; occasionally, something she had said would sing in his memory, in that golden-toned voice of hers; or the stones in her rings as she stroked Niniche would glitter before his eyes. Now that he knew the delicate grace of her smile, she seemed still prettier; she was all taste and intelligence; and the old lady at the door, the invalid to whom she was sending some port, was evidence of her kindness. What delighted him most was that he would no longer have to go sniffing around the city, like a lost sheepdog, in search of her dark eyes; now he had only to go up a few steps, and the door of her house would open to him; and suddenly everything in his life seemed easy, balanced, free of all doubts and anxieties.

In his room at Ramalhete, Baptista handed him a letter.

"The Scottish woman brought it shortly after you had gone out, sir."

It was from the Countess de Gouvarinho! Half a sheet of paper on which she had written in pencil, in English, the two words: "All right." Carlos angrily screwed it up! The Countess! Caught up in the radiant tumult of his heart, he had barely given her a thought since yesterday. And, in a few hours' time, they were supposed to catch the night train for Santarém, in order to make secret love at some inn! He had promised he would be there; she would already be prepared, wearing some ghastly wig and that all-enveloping waterproof; everything was "all right." At that moment, she seemed to him ridiculous, despicable, stupid. It was as clear as day now that he would not go, that he would never go, never! But he still had to be at Santa Apolónia station to mumble some clumsy excuse, witness her disappointment and watch her eyes brimming with tears. What a bore! He loathed her.

When he joined the lunch table, Craft and Afonso were already there, speaking—coincidentally—about the Count de Gouvarinho and the earnest articles which he continued to publish in the *Jornal do Comércio*.

"What a stupid sot the man is," hissed Carlos and heaped upon the husband's political writings all the rage he felt for the wife's amorous importunings.

Afonso and Craft looked at him, astonished at such violence. And Craft criticised him for his ingratitude, given that the poor unfortunate statesman's enthusiasm for Carlos was unequalled anywhere on Earth.

"You have no idea, sir. It's a religion. It verges on idolatry."

Carlos shrugged impatiently. And Afonso, already well disposed towards a man who could admire his grandson so prodigally, said kindly:

"Poor man, I imagine he's quite inoffensive."

Craft applauded Afonso.

"'Inoffensive!' Admirable! 'Inoffensive' applied to a statesman, a peer, a minister and a legislator is absolutely spot on! For that is precisely what he is, 'inoffensive'! That's what they all are."

"Chablis, sir?" murmured the valet.

"No, thank you, I'll have tea."

And he added:

"That champagne we drank yesterday at the races, for purely patriotic reasons of course, just about finished me off. I'll have to drink nothing but milk for a week."

Then talk returned to the subject of the races, to Carlos' winnings, to Clifford, and to Dâmaso's blue veil.

"Now one person who *was* well turned-out was the Countess de Gouvarinho," said Craft, stirring his tea. "That creamy white dress with touches of black suited her admirably. The perfect outfit for the races. *C'était un oeillet blanc panaché de noir* . . . Didn't you think so, Carlos?"

"Hm," grunted Carlos, "she looked all right, I suppose."

That Gouvarinho woman again! It seemed to him he would never have another conversation in his life in which her name didn't crop up, and that there would be no road in his life which she didn't block! And he decided there and then not to see her again, to write her a short, polite note, refusing to go to Santarém and offering no excuses.

However, back in his room, smoking a cigarette and with the sheet of paper before him, he could only come up with words that were either puerile or brutal. He did not even feel sufficient warmth towards her to use the banal "My dear." He even felt for her a kind of vague physical revulsion; a whole night of that heavy verbena perfume of hers would be unbearable, and he remembered that the skin on her neck, which once he had thought like satin, was a cloying yellowish colour where the line of face powder ended. He decided not to write to her. He would go to Santa Apolónia and, just as the train was leaving, he would run to the window and offer her some garbled excuse; he wouldn't give her time for whining or recrimination; a quick handshake and goodbye, forever.

That night, when the time came to go to the station, what a sacrifice it was to have to tear himself away from the comforts of his armchair and his cigar. He climbed angrily into the coupé, cursing that afternoon in her blue boudoir where, all because of a rose and a particularly becoming dress, the colour of autumn leaves, he had found himself lying on a sofa with her in his arms.

When he reached Santa Apolónia, there were still two minutes to go before the express train was due to leave. He rushed to the end of the ticket hall, almost empty at that hour, to buy a platform ticket, and there he waited for what seemed an eternity, watching as the two slow, indolent hands on the other side of the window laboriously counted out his change.

At last, he rushed into the waiting room, where he collided with Dâmaso, who was wearing a broad-brimmed hat and had a travelling bag slung over his shoulder. Dâmaso, overcome with emotion, grasped his hands:

"Oh, you shouldn't have! But how did you know I was leaving?"

Carlos did not disillusion him, muttering something about having bumped into Taveira who had told him the news . . .

"It was absolutely the last thing I was expecting!" exclaimed Dâmaso. "There I was this morning, all snug in bed, and a telegram arrives. I was furious, I mean, you can imagine how I felt, getting a shock like that."

It was then that Carlos noticed Dâmaso was in heavy mourning, wearing a black band around his hat, black gloves, black gaiters, and a black border on his handkerchief. He said awkwardly:

"Taveira told me that you were leaving, but he didn't say anything more. Has some member of your family died?"

"My uncle Guimarães."

"The communist, the one in Paris?"

"No, his brother, the eldest brother, the one from Penafiel. Wait there, will you, while I go over to the café and get my flask filled with brandy. I was so upset, I forgot my brandy."

Harried passengers were still arriving, wearing dust-coats and carrying hatboxes. Porters were slowly wheeling their luggage along. A portly gentleman in an embroidered cap leaned out of a carriage window, where a cluster of polite friends were standing on the platform, maintaining a respectful silence. In one corner of the carriage, a woman wearing a veil was quietly sobbing.

Spotting a carriage bearing a "Reserved" sign, Carlos assumed the Countess must be in there. However, a guard bustled angrily forward, as if Carlos were about to profane a temple. What did he want? What was he doing there? Didn't he know the carriage had been reserved for Senhor Carneiro?

"No, I didn't."

"Well, you should have asked, then," muttered the guard, still agitated.

Carlos ran up to other carriages, where people were piling in, breathless and anxious, surrounded by packages; in one carriage, two men were exchanging insults over some dispute about seats; in another, farther on, a child was sitting on a nursemaid's lap, kicking and screaming.

"Who the devil are you looking for?" cried Dâmaso cheerily, coming up behind him and slipping an arm around his waist.

"No one. I thought I saw the Marquis."

Dâmaso immediately began complaining bitterly about the tedium of having to go to Penafiel.

"And just when I really need to be in Lisbon. Because I've had damnedly good luck with the ladies lately, I really have!"

A bell rang. Dâmaso embraced Carlos tenderly, then jumped into his carriage, pulled on a silk cap and, leaning out of the window, continued his confidences. What annoyed him most was leaving that nice little set-up in Rua de São Francisco. It really was a damned nuisance! Especially now that it was all going so well, with the husband in Brazil and her there, easily to hand, just a step or two away from the Grémio!

Distracted, Carlos was barely listening to him, staring instead at the huge glass face of the station clock. Suddenly, Dâmaso, still at the window, gave a start of surprise.

"Look, it's the Gouvarinhos!"

Carlos was equally startled. The Count, wearing a pale overcoat and a bowler hat suitable for travelling, was walking unhurriedly along, as befitted a director of the railway company, chatting to some high station official, all in gold braid, who was carrying His Excellency's cardboard hat-box. And the Countess, wearing a superb light brown foulard dust-coat and a grey veil that covered both hat and face, followed behind, accompanied by her Scottish maid and carrying a bunch of roses.

Carlos ran over to them in amazement.

"What are you doing here, Maia?"

"Are you off on a trip somewhere, Count?"

Yes, he was. He had decided to accompany the Countess to Oporto for her father's birthday celebration. It had been a last-minute decision, and they had very nearly missed the train.

"So we'll have the great pleasure of your company on the journey, will we, Maia? Is that right?"

Carlos explained rapidly that he had only come to the station in order to say goodbye to poor Dâmaso, who was travelling to Penafiel after the death of his uncle.

Leaning out of the window, poor Dâmaso was gravely, funereally waving two black-gloved hands at the Countess. And the good Count simply had to go over and shake his hand and offer him his condolences.

Alone for a brief moment with the Countess, Carlos said only:

"What a bore!"

"The wretched man!" she exclaimed between clenched teeth and shooting her husband a furious glance through her veil. "Everything was so perfectly arranged and then, at the last moment, he insists on coming too!"

Carlos accompanied them to their reserved compartment, in a carriage that was being added especially for His Excellency the Count. The Countess took the corner seat next to the door. And when the Count, in a tone of acid politeness, advised her to sit facing the engine instead, she could not contain her intense irritation, and angrily flung down her bunch of roses and settled herself still more deliberately in her chosen seat; a hard, angry look passed between them. Carlos, embarrassed, asked:

"Will you be away for long?"

The Count replied with a smile, disguising his ill humour:

"Yes, two weeks or so, a little holiday."

"Three days at the very most," she retorted in a cold voice that cut like a knife.

The Count, purple with rage, did not respond.

All the doors were now closed and silence fell on the platform. Then the engine's whistle pierced the air, and, with a squeal as the brakes were released, the long train began to move, with people still leaning from the windows, holding out their hands to be clasped one last time. Here and there a white handkerchief fluttered. The Countess gave Carlos a look that was as sweet as a kiss. Dâmaso asked him to send his best regards to all at Ramalhete. The lit windows of the mail van slid past, and with one final penetrating whistle, the train plunged into the night.

Alone in the coupé on the way back to the Baixa, Carlos felt a sense of triumphant joy at the departure of the Countess and at Dâmaso's unexpected journey. It was like a providential scattering of all importunate presences, creating a kind of delightful, complicit solitude around Rua de São Francisco.

On Cais de Sodré he left the carriage and proceeded on foot along Ferregial, then past her windows on Rua de São Francisco. He could see only a faint strip of light between the half-closed shutters, but that was enough. He could now imagine precisely the quiet evening she would be spending in the large red-upholstered room. He knew the titles of the books she was reading and the music that was on the piano, and that morning he had seen her arranging the flowers that would, at this very moment, be perfuming the room. Would her thoughts alight for an instant upon him? Of course, the fact that someone was ill in the house would oblige her to remember when to administer the medicine, the instructions he had given, and the sound of his voice; and when she spoke to Miss Sara, she would be sure to mention his name. He walked up and down the street twice, before making his slow way home beneath the starry sky, savouring the sweetness of that great love.

Then every day, for weeks, he enjoyed that delicious, splendid, perfect hour when he visited "the Englishwoman."

He would leap out of bed, singing like a canary, and launch into his day as if into some triumphal march. The post would arrive and it invariably brought him a letter from the Countess, three sheets of paper from which some small, fading flower would always fall. He left the flower where it fell on the carpet, and he would have been hard pressed to say what information was contained in the letter's long, tortuous lines. He gleaned vaguely that, three days after she arrived in Oporto, her father, old Mr. Thompson, had had an attack of apoplexy. She was there now in the role of nurse. Then, taking two or three particularly lovely flowers from the garden and wrapping them in silk paper, he would set out for Rua de São Francisco, always in his coupé, for the weather had changed, the days passing gloomily, full of rain and a constant south-west wind.

At the door, Domingos would welcome him with an ever more affectionate smile. Niniche would come bounding gleefully out to meet him and he would scoop the dog up in his arms and kiss her. He would stand for a moment in the living-room, greeting with his eyes the furniture, the flowers, and the bright orderliness of all things; he would go over and see what music she had been playing that morning, or the book she had left unfinished, the ivory paper knife placed between the pages.

Then she would enter the room. Each day, her smile and her golden voice when she said "Good morning" had a new and more penetrating charm for Carlos. She usually wore a dark, simple dress; a *fichu* of fine antique lace or a belt with a jewel-encrusted buckle would occasionally enliven her sober, almost severe attire, which seemed very beautiful to Carlos, almost an expression of her soul.

They would start by talking about Miss Sara and about the wild, wet weather which was so unfavourable to Miss Sara's state of health. Still standing, Maria Eduarda would continue talking, now and then adjusting the position of a book or moving a chair that was not quite straight; she had the restless habit of constantly trying to restore things to symmetry; and, as she passed, she would mechanically run the magnificent lace of her handkerchief over already perfectly dusted surfaces.

She always went with him now to Miss Sara's room. Along the yellow corridor, walking by her side, Carlos would be troubled by the caress of that intimate jasmine-tinged perfume, which seemed to emerge from the movement of her skirts. She would sometimes casually push open the door of a room which was furnished only with an old sofa; that was where Rosa played and where Cricri's clothes and carriages and kitchen were kept. They would find Rosa dressing the doll or engaged in deep conversation with her; or else, sitting very still at one end of the sofa, her little feet crossed at the ankle, lost in wonderment at some picture book open on her lap. She would run over to them then and offer her little mouth to Carlos to be kissed; and her whole person had the freshness of some lovely flower.

In the governess' room, Maria Eduarda would sit at the foot of the white bed; and poor Miss Sara, embarrassed and coughing, and checking at every instant that her throat was still modestly covered by her silk shawl, would declare that she was fine. Carlos would joke with her, telling her that in that awful winter weather, bed was the best place to be, especially if one was well looked after, had a few romantic novels to read and enjoyed a delicious Portuguese diet. She would look gratefully at Madame and sigh. Then she would murmur:

"Oh, yes, I'm very comfortable here."

And her eyes would fill with tears.

When they went back into the living-room, even after the very first of these visits, Maria Eduarda had sat down on her scarlet chair and, still chatting to Carlos, simply taken up her embroidery again, as if she were in the familiar presence of an old friend. With what deep happiness he would watch her unroll that embroidery canvas! It would, in time, be a pheasant with brilliant plumage, but so far she had embroidered only the branch of the apple tree on which it was perched, a fresh spring branch covered in tiny white flowers, as in an orchard in Normandy.

Carlos, positioned next to the lovely Indian rosewood desk, occupied the oldest and most comfortable of the red-upholstered armchairs, whose springs creaked slightly. Between them lay the sewing table with copies of *Illustration française* or some fashion magazine; sometimes, he would fall silent for a moment, looking at the fashion plates, while Maria Eduarda's lovely hands, glittering with jewels, drew the woollen threads through the canvas. Niniche would lie dozing at her feet, occasionally looking up at them through the long hair falling over her dark, grave, beautiful eyes. And on those grim, wet days, with chill winds blowing outside and the sound of dripping rain, that corner by the window had a fond, intimate air, filled as it was with the slow peace of her embroidery work, with their calm, friendly voices and, now and then, with an easy silence.

Yet they never spoke of anything personal. They would talk about Paris and its charms, of London, where she had spent four gloomy winter months, about Italy, which she dreamed of visiting, about books and art. Her preferred novelist was Dickens; she liked Feuillet rather less because he covered everything, even broken hearts, with a dusting of face powder. She had been educated in a strict convent in Tours, but had nevertheless read Michelet and Renan. Indeed, she was not a practising Catholic; she was attracted only by the gracious, artistic aspects of worship, the music, the lights, or the lovely *mois de Marie* in France, when the sweet flowers of May were out. She had a very straightforward, very healthy way of thinking, with an underlying tenderness that inclined her to all those who suffered or were weak. That is why she liked the idea of a republic, because it seemed to her to be the regime that cared most for the humble. Carlos laughed and declared that she was clearly a socialist.

"Socialist, legitimist, Orléanist," she said, "I don't mind, as long as people don't go hungry!"

But was that possible? Even Jesus, who had such fine aspirations, had said that the poor would be always with us.

"Jesus lived a long time ago, and he didn't know everything. We know more now, people are better informed. We need to build a different society and quickly too, one in which poverty does not exist. In London sometimes, during all that snow, I saw children in doorways, shivering and crying with hunger. It was terrible! And in Paris too. People only see the boulevards, but there is so much poverty, so much need."

Her lovely eyes almost filled with tears. And each word brought with it all the complex kindnesses of her soul, just as a single breeze can bring with it all the perfumes of a garden.

Carlos was delighted when Maria involved him in her charitable work, asking him to visit the sister of her ironing woman, who had rheumatism, and the son of Senhora Augusta, the old lady on the landing, who had tuberculosis. Carlos carried out these commissions as fervently as if they were religious acts. These merciful acts of hers reminded him of his grandfather. Like Afonso, she found the suffering of animals deeply distressing. One day, she had returned from the Praça da Figueira, filled almost with ideas of revenge, having seen on the poulterers' stalls baskets crammed with chickens and rabbits who suffered for days on end the torments of confinement and the pain of hunger. Carlos took this fine rage with him to Ramalhete and passionately berated the Marquis, who was a member of the Society for the Protection of Animals. The Marquis, equally indignant, vowed that justice would be done, and even spoke of imprisonment and deportation to the coast of Africa for the perpetrators. And Carlos, much moved, reflected upon the broad, far-reaching influence that a just heart can have, even if that heart lives the most isolated of lives.

One afternoon, they talked about Dâmaso. She found him unbearable, with his insolence, his bulging eyes, and his idiotic questions. Do you think Nice elegant, Senhora? Senhora, do you prefer the chapel of St. John the Baptist or Notre Dame?

"And the way he insists on talking about people I don't know! The Senhora Countess de Gouvarinho and the Senhora Countess de Gouvarinho's tea parties, and the Senhora Countess de Gouvarinho's box at the theatre, and how very fond the Senhora Countess de Gouvarinho is of him . . . And so on for hours! I was afraid sometimes I might fall asleep."

Carlos blushed scarlet. Why, of all people, had she mentioned the Countess? He was reassured by her bright, easy laughter. She clearly didn't even know who the Countess de Gouvarinho was. However, in order to rid the conversation of that name, he began to speak of M. Guimarães, Dâmaso's famous uncle and friend of Gambetta, who had such influence in the Republic.

"Dâmaso told me that you know his uncle well."

She looked up, momentarily embarrassed.

"Monsieur Guimarães? Yes, I do know him well. We've seen rather less of him lately, but he was a great friend of Mama's."

And then, after a brief silence, once again pulling on the long woollen embroidery thread, she smiled faintly and said:

"Poor Guimarães! His influence on the Republic, I'm afraid, is confined to translating articles from Spanish and Italian newspapers for *Rappel*, because that's how he makes his living. He may well be a friend of Gambetta's, I don't know—Gambetta does have some extraordinary friends—but Guimarães, as well as being a good and honest man, is also a grotesque, a kind of Republican fool. And he's so poor! If Dâmaso, who is rich, had any decency or any fellow feeling, he wouldn't allow him to live so wretchedly."

"What about his uncle's carriages and the luxurious lifestyle Dâmaso is always boasting of?"

She shrugged and said nothing; and Carlos felt for Dâmaso a terrible disgust.

Gradually, their conversations took on a more intimate intensity. She asked Carlos how old he was, and he told her about his grandfather. And during those sweet hours, while she silently continued her tapestry work, he talked to her about his past life, his plans for his career, his friends, and his travels. Now she knew all about the countryside surrounding Santa Olávia, about the Reverend Boniface and about Ega's eccentricities. One day, she asked Carlos to explain in detail the idea behind his book *Medicine Ancient and Modern*. She warmly approved of him describing the great doctors of the past, those benefactors of humanity. Why did people only glorify warriors and the strong? The saving of a child's life seemed to her far more beautiful than the battle of Austerlitz. These words were uttered with such simplicity and without her even looking up from her work, and yet they dropped into Carlos' heart and lay there for a long time, pulsating and bright.

He had spoken freely to her about his life, but he as yet knew nothing about her past, not even where she had been born, not even the street where she lived in Paris. He had never heard her so much as murmur her husband's name, or speak of a friend or of some happy family event. In France, where she lived, she seemed to have neither interests nor home; she really did seem to be the goddess he had dreamed of, with no previous connections with the Earth, a goddess who had stepped off her cloud of gold in order to encounter there, in that rented apartment in the Rua de São Francisco, her first human emotion.

During the very first week of Carlos' visits, they had spoken of affections. She sincerely believed that there could be such a thing as pure, disinterested friendship between a man and a woman, based on the loving meeting of two sensitive souls. Carlos swore that he, too, had faith in such beautiful unions of minds—full of respect and reason—as long as they were mingled with just a touch of tenderness. This lent a special charm to such relationships and in no way diminished their sincerity. And with these somewhat vague words, exchanged over the embroidery wools and with many warm smiles, it had become subtly established that there would, between them, only ever be such feelings, chaste, virtuous, gentle, and free from anguish.

What did Carlos care? As long as he could spend that hour sitting in his usual armchair, watching her embroider and talking about interesting things, or things made interesting by her personal grace; as long as he could see her slightly flushed face bend, with the slow attraction of a caress, over the flowers he brought her; as long as his soul could be warmed by the certainty that her thoughts would continue to follow him sweetly throughout his day as soon as he left the adored red-upholstered room, his heart was totally, splendidly satisfied.

It did not even occur to him to think that this ideal friendship, with its entirely chaste intentions, was the surest road to deceive her gently into his ardent male arms. He was so dazzled to find himself suddenly admitted into the intimacy of a home he had thought to be impenetrable that his desires were disappearing; when he was far from her, those desires were still bold enough to go so far as to hope for a kiss or a fleeting, finger-tip caress, but as soon as he walked through her front door and felt the calm ray of her dark eyes, he was overcome by feelings of devotion and judged it a brute outrage so much as to brush the folds of her dress.

This was, without a doubt, the sweetest and most delicate period of his life. He felt, with a touching freshness, a thousand fine new qualities within himself. He had never imagined that such happiness could be had from looking up at the clear night sky and seeing the stars, or going out into the garden in the morning and choosing the fullest, finest rose. His heart wore a constant smile, which his lips repeated. The Marquis thought he looked besotted and beatific.

Sometimes, walking up and down in his room, he wondered to himself where this great love would lead him. He did not know. Before him lay the three months that she would be in Lisbon and during which only he would occupy the old armchair beside her embroidery work. Her husband was far away, separated from her by leagues of uncertain sea. He himself was rich and the world was large.

He still had great ideas as regards his own work, wanting his days to be filled only by noble hours, and for the hours not devoted to the pure happiness of love to be given over to the passionate joys of study. He went to the laboratory, added a few lines to his book, but before his daily visit to Rua de São Francisco, he could not discipline his restless mind, which was in a constant tumult of hopes, and when he returned from there, he would spend the rest of the day going over everything she had said or that he had said in reply, her every gesture, the grace of a particular smile . . . Then he would smoke cigarettes and read poetry.

Every night, in Afonso's study, a game of whist was played. The Marquis did battle over dominoes with Taveira, both of them immersed in the same vice and playing with a growing rancour that even led them to trade insults. Since the horse-races, Steinbroken's secretary had also started coming to Ramalhete, but he was a useless addition, for he could not, like his superior, sing Finnish ballads; he merely sat slumped in an armchair in his tailcoat, with his monocle in his eye, bouncing one crossed leg up and down and silently stroking his long, sad moustaches.

The friend Carlos most liked to see walk into the room was Cruges, who came from Rua de São Francisco and brought with him something of the same air that Maria Eduarda breathed. The maestro knew that Carlos went to the building every day to see the English governess and often, quite innocently, unaware of the deep interest with which Carlos listened to him, he would give him the latest news about his neighbour.

"She was playing Mendelssohn today, with great skill and expression too. There's genuine energy there. And she understands her Chopin."

If Cruges did not come to Ramalhete, Carlos would go to his house to fetch him. They would visit the Grémio together and smoke cigars in some isolated room, and Cruges would talk about his neighbour whom he judged to be "a real *grande dame.*"

There they almost always met the Count de Gouvarinho, who had come to see (as he put it, positively sparkling with irony) what plots were being hatched "in the land of Gambetta." He seemed to have grown younger lately, more relaxed, and a bright optimism glinted in the lenses of his spectacles, on his lofty brow. Carlos asked after the Countess. She was still in Oporto being the dutiful daughter.

"And your father-in-law?"

The Count would bow his radiant face and murmur in a tone of grave resignation:

"In a very bad way."

One afternoon, Carlos was talking to Maria Eduarda and stroking Niniche, who had come to sit on his lap, when her footman, Romão, discreetly peered around the curtain and, with an embarrassed, knowing air, whispered:

"It's Senhor Dâmaso!"

She looked at him, surprised and almost scandalised by his manner.

"Well, show him in!"

And Dâmaso burst into the room, still dressed in heavy mourning, a flower in his buttonhole, and looking plump, friendly and familiar, with his hat in his hand and carrying, dangling from a string, a large brown paper parcel. However, when he saw Carlos comfortably installed there with the dog on his lap, he stopped in his tracks, goggle-eyed, as if stunned. Finally, he put down his parcel, greeted Maria Eduarda with near indifference, then, turning to Carlos, with arms spread wide, his astonishment overflowed into noisy effusiveness:

"Fancy seeing you here, man! This *is* a surprise! Who would have thought it! This was the very last thing I would have expected."

Maria Eduarda, distressed by such bellowing, hastily bade him sit down, interrupted her embroidery and asked how he was after his journey.

"Perfect, Senhora! A little tired, but that's only natural. I've come straight from Penafiel. As you see," and he indicated his dark clothes, "I have suffered a recent bereavement."

Maria Eduarda muttered some vague, cold words of condolence. Dâmaso stared down at the carpet. He had returned from the provinces rosy-cheeked and brimming with rude health; he had also trimmed his beard (which, for months, he had been growing in imitation of Carlos) and his face looked somehow fatter and shinier. His chubby thighs were almost bursting out of his black wool trousers.

"So," asked Maria Eduarda, "will you be with us for some time now?"

He dragged his chair a little closer to hers and, with his smile restored, said:

"Wild horses wouldn't drag me away from Lisbon now. Someone could die for all I care, I mean, obviously, I would hate anyone actually to die, what I mean is that it would take a hell of a lot to shift me!"

Carlos continued quietly stroking Niniche. There was a brief silence. Maria

Eduarda took up her embroidery again. And Dâmaso, after smiling, coughing and twirling his moustache, reached out a hand to stroke Niniche where she sat on Carlos' lap. The dog, however, which had been eyeing him distrustfully for some moments, started to its feet and began barking furiously.

"*C'est moi, Niniche!*" Dâmaso said, pushing his chair further back. "*C'est moi, amie . . . Alors, Niniche.*"

Maria Eduarda had to speak severely to Niniche. The dog snuggled down once more on Carlos' lap, but with one eye trained on Dâmaso and keeping up a constant angry growling.

"She's forgotten who I am," he said dully. "Most odd."

"She knows exactly who you are," said Maria Eduarda gravely. "I don't know what you've done to her, Senhor Dâmaso, but she loathes you. It's the same every time."

Dâmaso, scarlet-faced, spluttered:

"Really, Senhora! What did I ever do to her? I've always been very kind."

Then, he could contain himself no longer and spoke ironically, bitterly, about Mademoiselle Niniche's "new friends." There she was in another's arms, while he, her old friend, was cast aside.

Carlos laughed.

"How can you accuse her of ingratitude, Dâmaso, when, according to Senhora Dona Maria Eduarda, she's always hated you."

"Always," exclaimed Maria Eduarda.

Dâmaso was smiling too, albeit rather wanly. Then, taking out a black-edged handkerchief, he dabbed at his lips and even dried the sweat on his neck, and reminded Maria Eduarda that she had let him down on the day of the races. He had waited all afternoon for her.

"It was the day before my husband's departure," she said.

"Ah, yes, of course, your husband. And how is Senhor Castro Gomes? Have you received any news?"

"No," she replied, her head bent over her embroidery.

Dâmaso fulfilled his other social duties. He asked after Mademoiselle Rosa, then after Cricri. One must not forget Cricri.

"Well, Senhora," he went on, borne along on a sudden wave of loquacity, "it was your loss, because the races were quite splendid. We haven't seen each other since the races, have we, Carlos? Oh, no, that's right, you were there at the station. It was all terribly chic, don't you think? Of one thing you can be sure, Senhora, there isn't a prettier race-track anywhere, with that delicious view out over the estuary. You can even see the ships coming in. Isn't that right, Carlos?"

"Yes," said Carlos, smiling. "I mean it's not, properly speaking, a race-track. And there are not, properly speaking, any racehorses . . . or any jockeys. And there isn't, properly speaking, any betting either . . . nor any real racing public . . ."

Maria Eduarda was laughing gaily.

"So what is there, then?"

"A lovely view of the ships coming down the river, Senhora."

Dâmaso protested, his ears red. That really was most unfair. The races had been excellent. It was just the same there as anywhere else, the same rules and everything.

"Even in the weighing-in enclosure," he added very seriously, "they spoke only English."

He said again that the races had been *very* chic. Then he ran out of things to say about the races and told them, instead, about Penafiel, where it had rained constantly, so much so that he had been obliged to stay indoors with nothing to do but read.

"Such a bore! I mean if there had at least been some women one could talk to, but the only women around were hideous. And I don't go for laundresses or barefoot girls myself, they're not my type at all. Some men like them, but I can assure you, Senhora, that I can't even bear to be around them."

Carlos blushed, but Maria Eduarda appeared not to have heard, as she busily counted her stitches.

Suddenly Dâmaso remembered that he had a present for Senhora Dona Maria Eduarda, but she mustn't go thinking it was anything extravagant. It was really a present for Mademoiselle Rosa.

"All right, no more mysteries. Do you know what it is? It's over there in that little brown paper parcel. Six little boxes of cakes from Aveiro. They're very famous, these cakes, even abroad; you can buy them elsewhere, but only the ones from Aveiro have real chic. Ask Carlos. It's true, isn't it, Carlos, it's a delicacy that's known even outside Portugal?"

"Of course," muttered Carlos, "of course."

He had put Niniche down on the floor, then got up to fetch his hat.

"Are you going already?" asked Maria Eduarda, with a smile intended solely for him. "We'll see you tomorrow, then!"

And she immediately turned to Dâmaso, expecting him to get up too. He, however, remained where he was, looking distinctly permanent and part of the family, his legs casually crossed. Carlos merely raised his hand to him in farewell.

"*Au revoir*," said Dâmaso. "Give everyone at Ramalhete my best wishes. I'll drop by some time."

Carlos went down the stairs, fuming.

There the imbecile stayed, rudely imposing his presence on her, so obtuse he did not even notice her annoyance, her icily abrupt manner. And why was he staying? What further crass and coarsely worded banalities had he yet to unleash, sitting there with his legs crossed? And suddenly he remembered what Dâmaso had said to him on the night of Ega's supper party, at the door of the Hotel Central, regarding Maria Eduarda, and women in general, that his motto was "attack, attack." What if that over-excited and brutish idiot should attempt some outrage? It was a ridiculous thought perhaps, but it nevertheless caused him to wait downstairs in the courtyard, his ears cocked for any noises upstairs, full of fierce ideas of waiting there for Dâmaso and forbidding him ever to climb those stairs again, and, at the slightest hint of impudence from him, of smashing his skull, right there on the flagstones.

Then, hearing the door upstairs open, he hurriedly left, afraid that he might be caught eavesdropping. Dâmaso's coupé was outside in the street. Carlos was filled by an intense desire to know just how long Dâmaso would stay with Maria Eduarda. He ran to the Grémio and barely had time to fling open a window there, when he saw Dâmaso leave the building, jump into his coupé and slam the door: he had the clear air of a man rejected, and Carlos felt a sudden sympathy for that grotesque figure.

After supper that night, alone in his room, Carlos was sitting in his armchair, smoking and re-reading the letter from Ega he had received that morning, when Dâmaso appeared. And standing there in the doorway, without even putting down his hat, he exclaimed with the same mixture of alarm and surprise he had shown that morning:

"All right, so how come I found you there today with that Brazilian woman, tell me that! How on earth did you meet her? How?"

Still leaning back in his chair, his hands folded over Ega's letter which still lay on his lap, and feeling now full of bonhomie, Carlos said in a tone of gentle, paternal reprimand:

"Fancy exposing a lady to your lubricious views on the laundresses of Penafiel!"

"What do you mean? I know perfectly well what I can and cannot expose!" exclaimed Dâmaso, red-faced. "Come on, tell me. Damn it, I reckon I have a right to know. How did you meet her?"

Carlos, imperturbable, closed his eyes as if trying to remember and then, slowly and solemnly, as if reciting a poem, began:

"One warm Spring afternoon, when the sun was setting amid clouds of gold, an exhausted messenger arrived and grasped the Ramalhete bell-pull. In his hand, he held a letter bearing an heraldic seal, and the expression on his face . . ."

Dâmaso, angry now, threw his hat down on the table.

"It seems to me that the decent thing would be to stop all this mystification!"

"Mystification? You're the one who's being obtuse, Dâmaso. You go into a house where a person has been gravely ill for a month and you're amazed, dumbstruck, to find a doctor there! Who did you expect to find? A photographer?"

"What gravely ill person?"

Carlos told him briefly about the governess' bout of bronchitis, while Dâmaso, sitting on the edge of the sofa, chewing on his unlit cigar, eyed him distrustfully.

"And how did she know where you lived?"

"How does one know where the King lives, or where the customshouse is, or where in the sky to find the evening star, or where Troy once stood? One learns these things in primary school."

Poor Dâmaso strode furiously up and down the room, his hands in his pockets.

"She's got Romão working for her now; he used to work for me," he murmured, after a silence. "I recommended him to her. She's often guided by my advice."

"Yes, he's been working there for a few days, but only while Domingos is away visiting his village. She intends to dismiss him, though. The man's an imbecile, and you've taught him some very bad manners."

Dâmaso plumped himself down on the sofa and confessed that, when he had gone into the room and seen Carlos installed there with the little dog on his lap, he had been furious. Now that he knew about the governess' illness, however, all was explained. When left alone with her, he had even thought about asking her, but had feared it might be indelicate and, besides, she was in a bad mood.

Then he added, lighting a cigar:

"But as soon as you left, her mood lightened, and she seemed more at ease. We laughed a lot. In fact, I stayed for almost two hours; it was nearly five when I left. By the way, did she ever mention me to you?"

"No. She's a person of good taste, and, since she knows that we know each other, she would never dare to speak ill of you in my presence."

Dâmaso stared at him, wide-eyed:

"Why would she not have spoken well of me, instead?"

"Oh, she's got far too much common sense for that!"

Then springing to his feet, Carlos went over and put his arm around Dâmaso's waist, patting and stroking him, and asking about the inheritance he would get from his uncle and about the mistresses, journeys, and thoroughbred horses he was planning to spend his millions on.

Dâmaso responded coldly and sulkily to these fond caresses, eyeing Carlos warily.

"You know," he said, "I have a feeling you're going to turn out to be yet another scoundrel. One can't trust anyone!"

"Everything in this world, Dâmaso, is mere appearance and deceit!"

They walked into the billiard room to play a conciliatory game. And gradually, under the spell that Ramalhete always worked upon him, in the midst of all that sombre luxury, Dâmaso grew calmer and more cheerful, once again enjoying his closeness to Carlos and addressing him familiarly as "my dear fellow."

He asked after Senhor Afonso da Maia. He wanted to know if the Marquis had been there lately. And what had become of Ega, the great Ega?"

"I had a letter from him" said Carlos. "He's coming to Lisbon, indeed, he should arrive on Saturday."

Dâmaso was astonished.

"How very odd! I met the Cohens today. They arrived from Southampton two days ago. Is it my shot?"

He played and missed the red ball.

"No, it's true, I bumped into them today and spoke to them briefly. Raquel looks better, plumper. She was wearing an English outfit with white and pink bits on it. Terribly chic, she looked rather like a strawberry! So Ega is coming back, is he? Well, it looks like we're in for more scandal then!"

: XII :

AND SO IT WAS, on Saturday, when Carlos returned home from his visit to Rua de São Francisco, that he found Ega waiting for him in his room; he was wearing a pale cheviot wool suit and had let his hair grow long.

"No fuss, please," he cried, "I'm in Lisbon incognito."

And once they had embraced, he declared that he had only returned to Lisbon for a few days in order to eat well and talk well. And he was counting on Carlos to supply both commodities, there, in Ramalhete.

"Have you got a room for me? I'm at the Hotel Espanhol at the moment, but I haven't even opened my suitcase. A little corner somewhere, with a good pine table, large enough for me to write some sublime literary work?"

Of course! There was the room upstairs where he had stayed after leaving Villa Balzac, and which was more sumptuously decorated now, with a lovely Renaissance bed and a copy of Velázquez's "Topers."

"The perfect lair for an artist! Velázquez is, after all, one of the holy fathers of Naturalism. Now guess who was travelling in the train with me? The Countess de Gouvarinho. Her father has been at death's door apparently, but he's recovered now, and the Count had just been to fetch her. She looked rather thin to me, but she still has that same ardent air. Oh, and she talked about you constantly."

"Really," murmured Carlos.

Ega, with his monocle in his eye and his hands in his pockets, was studying Carlos.

"Yes, it's true. She talked constantly, irresistibly, immoderately about you! You never told me what happened between you, but I assume you followed my advice. Lovely body, eh? And how is she in bed?"

Carlos blushed and told him not to be so vulgar, and swore that he had never had anything more than a superficial relationship with the Countess. He went there occasionally for tea, and when he was out for a stroll along the Chiado, he would, as everyone did, end up talking to the Count on the corner of Loreto and discussing the appalling state of public life. And that was all.

"You're lying, you libertine!" Ega said. "Not that it matters, I'll discover all on Monday anyway, with my Balzacian eye . . . you see, we're having supper there."

"We? Who's we?"

"Us. Me and you. You and me. The Countess issued the invitation while we were on the train. And the Count, as befits an individual of his species, immediately said that we had to have 'our Maia' there too. His Maia and her Maia! A most holy alliance. A perfect arrangement."

Carlos looked at him sternly.

"You've returned from Celorico in a most obscene mood, Ega."

"That's the effect being in the bosom of the Mother Church has on one."

But Carlos had news for Ega too, news which should make him tremble. Ega, however, already knew about the arrival of the Cohens. He had read about it that morning, in the society column in *Gazeta Ilustrada*. It had said only that they were returning from a trip abroad.

"And what was your response to that?" asked Carlos, laughing.

Ega merely shrugged.

"Simply that there would be one more cuckold in the city."

And when Carlos accused him again of having brought a filthy tongue back with him from Celorico, Ega, blushing, perhaps slightly repentant, launched into more critical reflections, stating that it was a social necessity to call things by their proper name.What use, otherwise, was the great Naturalist movement? If vice continued unabated, it was because an indulgent, romantic society gave it names that embellished and idealised it. Why should a woman scruple to roll about in the conjugal sheets with a third party if the world insisted on referring to it sentimentally as "a romance" and if poets sang of it in golden verses?

"Speaking of which, how's your play *The Mudhole* coming on?" asked Carlos, who had gone into the bathroom for a moment.

"Oh, I abandoned it," said Ega. "It was too full of venom. Besides, it forced me to steep myself once more in corrupt Lisbon life, to plunge again into the human sewer, which I found, frankly, too distressing."

He stopped in front of the long mirror and gave a discontented glance at his pale coat and scuffed boots.

"I need to smarten myself up again. Poole has doubtless sent you a summer suit already. I should like to examine the latest designs despatched to you from high civilisation. There's no denying it, I look damnably commonplace."

He brushed his moustache and continued addressing Carlos, who was still in the bathroom.

"What I need now is to immerse myself in the world of the imagination. I'm going to have another go at my *Memoirs of an Atom*. Yes, under Velázquez's gaze, a vast quantity of major artistic work will be done in that room you're giving me. I really should go and say hello to old Afonso, since he's providing me with bread and roof and mattress."

They went to find Afonso da Maia in his study, where he was sitting in his usual armchair, with, on his lap, an old volume of *Illustration française*, which he was poring over in the company of a bright-eyed little boy with dark curly hair. The old man was delighted to learn that Ega would, for a while, be enlivening Ramalhete with his fine flights of fancy.

"I'm afraid I've run out of fancy, sir!"

"All right, then, illumine our house with your clear reason instead," said the old man, laughing. "We're in great need of both."

Then he introduced him to the little boy, Senhor Manuelinho, a delightful child who lived nearby, the son of Vicente, the builder. Manuelinho sometimes came to alleviate Afonso's solitude, and they would leaf through picture books together and hold philosophical conversations. He was, at that very moment, having a hard time trying to explain to the child just why General Canrobert (a picture of whom, seated elegantly atop his horse, they had just been admiring) was not currently languishing in prison, given that he had issued orders for so many people to be killed in various battles.

"It's obvious," exclaimed the little boy, very bright and confident, hands clasped behind his back. "If he gave the order for people to be killed, then he should be locked up in prison!"

"There, friend Ega!" said Afonso, laughing. "How would you respond to such fine logic? Look, my dear, now that these two graduates from Coimbra are here, I'm going to discuss the matter further with them. You go and play with the toys over there on the table, and then it'll be time for you to go in to Joaninha for your tea."

Carlos, helping the little boy settle himself at the table with a large picture book, was thinking how much his grandfather, who adored children, would love to meet Rosa!

Afonso, meanwhile, was also asking Ega about his play. What! Abandoned already? When would João stop making these incomplete sketches of masterpieces? Ega blamed the country and its indifference to art. What original spirit would not shrivel up and die finding itself surrounded by these dense bourgeois masses, lethargic and crass, who scorned intelligence and were incapable of appreciating a noble idea or a well-turned phrase? "It's not worth it, sir. In this country, in the midst of this prodigious national imbecility, any man of sense and taste should restrict himself to tending his vegetable plot. Look at Herculano, who abandoned history for the countryside."

"Fine, then," said Afonso, "tend your vegetables. That would at least contribute to the public good, but you don't even do that."

Carlos, looking very serious, supported Ega.

"He's right, planting vegetables is the only thing one can do in Portugal— until, that is, the revolution comes, and some of those strong, original, energetic elements currently buried down below finally come to the surface. And if it turns out that there is nothing buried down there, then let's voluntarily surrender our status as a nation, lacking, as we do, the necessary elements to be one, and become instead a fertile, stupid Spanish province, and plant more vegetables!"

Afonso listened sadly to his grandson's words, in which he sensed a kind of decomposition of the will, a mere glorification of Carlos' own inertia. He ended by saying:

"Then why don't you two do something to bring about that revolution? Why, for God's sake, don't you do something, anything?"

"Carlos is doing his best," exclaimed Ega, laughing. "He parades his person, his clothes, his phaeton, and thereby educates the taste of others!"

The Louis XV clock interrupted them, reminding Ega that he must, before supper, go and fetch his suitcase from the Hotel Espanhol. Outside, in the corridor, he confessed to Carlos that, before going to the hotel, he wanted first to visit Fillon, the photographer, to have them take a decent portrait of him.

"A portrait?"

"A surprise that must be despatched to Celorico in three days' time, for the birthday of a dear little creature, who was a great balm to me during my exile."

"Oh, Ega!"

"It's awful, I know, but what can one do? She's the daughter of Father Correia, and recognised as such, as well as being married to a rich landowner in the area, a vile reactionary. So, as you see, I am striking a double blow at Religion and Property."

"Oh, well, in that case . . ."

"We must not shirk our great democratic duties, my friend!"

The following Monday, it was drizzling when Carlos and Ega, in the closed coupé, set off to go to supper at the Gouvarinhos. Since the Countess' return, Carlos had seen her only once, at her house, and it had been a most disagreeable, awkward half hour, punctuated by the occasional cold kiss and by endless recriminations. She had complained about his letters, so few and so peremptory. They could not agree on their plans for the summer, since she had to go to Sintra, where they had already rented a house, and Carlos declared it his duty to accompany his grandfather to Santa Olávia. The Countess found him distracted, and he found her demanding. And then she had sat for a moment on his knee, and that light, delicate body had felt to Carlos like an oppressive bronze weight.

Finally, the Countess had extracted a promise from him to meet her on that Monday morning, at the house of her aunt, who was away in Santarém, for the Countess still took a perverse, subtle pleasure in holding him in her naked arms on the very days when she would later receive him formally in her drawing room. Carlos, however, had failed to keep that appointment, and now, as he drove towards her house, he already felt irritated at the prospect of the many complaints of which he would be the object during muttered conversations with her at window-seats, and the many foolish lies he would have to mumble back.

Suddenly Ega, who was silently smoking, buttoned up in his summer overcoat, tapped Carlos' knee and, half-smiling, half-serious, said:

"Tell me something, unless it's a sacrosanct secret, of course. Who is this Brazilian woman with whom you spend all your mornings now?"

For a moment, Carlos was stunned and merely stared at Ega.

"Who told you?"

"Dâmaso told me or, rather, roared it at me, because when I met him at the Grémio, he told me about it through gritted teeth, meanwhile thumping the sofa and looking positively apoplectic."

"Told you what?"

"Everything. That he'd introduced you to a Brazilian woman he'd had his eye on for a while, and that you, taking advantage of his absence, had slipped in there and now scarcely left her side."

"That's a complete lie!" exclaimed Carlos angrily.

And Ega, still smiling, said:

"So what is the truth, as old Pilate asked the so-called Christ?"

"There is a lady, whom Dâmaso imagined, as he does with all women, to be head over heels in love with him, and when that lady's English governess fell ill with bronchitis, she asked me to treat her. The governess has still not recovered, and I'm still going there every day to see her. And Madame Gomes—for that is the lady's name, who, by the way, turns out not to be Brazilian at all—finds Dâmaso as unbearable as everyone else does and has shut her door to him. That is the truth, and I may just have to box Dâmaso's ears for him!"

Ega merely murmured:

"So that is how history is written. I'll never trust a historian again!"

They rode the rest of the way to the Gouvarinhos' house in silence, Carlos still seething with rage at Dâmaso. The gentle, benign shadow in which his love lay sheltered had been torn asunder by that imbecile! Maria Eduarda's name had been spoken in the Grémio, and what Dâmaso had told to Ega would be repeated to others, in the Casa Havanesa, at Silva's restaurant, even in brothels perhaps; and thus the supreme interest of his life would, from then on, be constantly troubled, spoiled, and soiled by Dâmaso's base tittle-tattling!

"It would appear that there are other guests here tonight," said Ega, as they entered the hallway and saw, on the couch, a grey overcoat and some ladies' cloaks.

Waiting for them in the little room at the end, known as "the room of the bust," was the Countess, dressed all in black, with, about her neck, a velvet ribbon adorned with three diamond-studded stars. A basket of splendid flowers almost filled the table, which was otherwise taken up with English novels and a copy of the *Revue des Deux Mondes* with an ivory paperknife still between its pages. As well as good Dona Maria da Cunha and the Viscountess de Alvim, there was another lady, whom neither Carlos nor Ega knew, a fat woman, dressed entirely in scarlet, and a tall, grave, gaunt-faced man, with a sparse beard and wearing the Order of the Conception, who was standing talking quietly to the Count, his hands behind his back.

The Countess, slightly flushed, extended to Carlos a limp, angry hand, reserving her smiles for Ega. The Count immediately led his "dear Maia" off to introduce him to his friend, Senhor Sousa Neto. Senhor Sousa Neto had already had the pleasure of hearing all about Carlos da Maia, as a distinguished doctor and a credit to the University. That, said the Count, was the advantage of living in Lisbon: everyone was known by their reputation, which allowed one to make a more accurate judgement of people's characters. In Paris, for example, this was impossible, which explained why there was so much immorality, so much lax behaviour.

"You never know who you're inviting into your house."

Ega was lounging on the divan, revealing the small embroidered stars on his socks and regaling the Countess and Dona Maria, seated on either side of him, with tales of his exile in Celorico, where he had passed the time composing sermons for the abbot, which the abbot would later read out in church. The sermons were, in fact, revolutionary statements in mystical form, which the dear good man uttered with great fervour, thumping the pulpit. The lady in scarlet, sitting opposite them, her hands in her lap, listened to Ega with a look of horror on her face.

"I thought you would have left for Sintra by now," Carlos said to the Baroness, sitting down next to her. "You're usually the first to go."

"How can you possibly expect me to set off to Sintra in weather like this?"

"Yes, you're right, it's absolutely vile."

"And what's new in Lisbon?" she asked, slowly opening her great black fan.

"I don't think anything new has happened in Lisbon, dear lady, since King João VI died."

"There's your friend Ega, for example."

"True, there's Ega. How do you find him, Baroness?"

She did not even bother to lower her voice when she said:

"Since I've never liked him and have always thought him terribly affected, I can't really say."

"How very uncharitable of you, Baroness!"

The footman announced supper. The Countess took Carlos' arm and, as they crossed the drawing room, amid the soft murmur of voices and the slow rustle of silk, she managed to say sharply:

"I waited for half an hour, but then I realised, of course, that you must have been detained by that Brazilian woman."

In the somewhat sombre dining room lined with wine-red wallpaper and made darker still by two gloomy landscape paintings, the oval table, surrounded by carved oak chairs, stood out white and fresh, adorned by a splendid basket of roses flanked by two gilt candelabra. Carlos sat to the Countess' right, with, next to him, Dona Maria da Cunha, who seemed somehow older that evening and whose smile had a certain weary edge to it.

"What have you been up to lately? No one's seen hide nor hair of you," she said, unfolding her napkin.

"Oh, here and there, Senhora."

Opposite Carlos, Senhor Sousa Neto, who had three large coral buttons in his shirtfront, was remarking to the Countess, as he stirred his soup, that on her trip to Oporto, she must have noticed great changes in the streets and buildings. The Countess, alas, had barely been out during her stay in the city. The Count, however, spoke admiringly of the progress being made. He went on to list examples: he praised the view from the Crystal Palace; he spoke of the fecund antagonism that exists between Lisbon and Oporto and compared it, yet again, with the rivalry between Austria and Hungary. And while he dropped these grave, weighty, superior pronouncements as if from on high, the Baroness and the lady in scarlet, on either side of him, were engaged in a conversation about the Salesian Convent.

Carlos, meanwhile, silently eating his soup, was pondering the Countess' words. So she, too, knew about his friendship with "the Brazilian woman." It was clear, then, that Dâmaso's clumsy, defamatory tittle-tattle had spread. And by the time the servant offered him some Sauternes, he had decided that he would give Dâmaso a sound beating.

Suddenly, he heard his own name. From the end of the table, a slow, sing-song voice was saying:

"Senhor Maia must know. Senhor Maia has been there."

Carlos quickly set down his glass. It was the lady in scarlet who was speaking to him, smiling and revealing pretty white teeth beneath the kind of dark fuzz on her upper lip that besets so many pale forty-year-old women. No one had introduced her to him, and he had no idea who she was. He smiled back and asked:

"Where is that, Senhora?"

"In Russia."

"In Russia? No, Senhora, I've never been to Russia."

She seemed slightly disappointed.

"Oh, I was told ... I don't know who told me now, but it was a person who should have known."

The Count, on the other side of the table, explained kindly that their friend Maia had been to Holland.

"A land of great prosperity, Holland! And in no way inferior to ours. I even met a Dutchman once who was really very learned."

Absent-mindedly tearing off a piece of bread, the Countess lowered her eyes, suddenly more serious, more withdrawn, as if Carlos' voice, rising up so tranquilly beside her, had rekindled all her grievances. After taking a slow sip of his Sauternes, he turned to her quite naturally and cheerfully and said:

"You see, Countess! It had never even occurred to me to go to Russia, and there are an infinite number of other things that people say and which are equally untrue. And if one makes an ironic allusion to them, no one understands either the allusion or the irony."

The Countess did not reply at once, first giving a silent order with her eyes to the footman. Then, with a wan smile, she said:

"Behind everything that people say there is always some hard fact, or a fragment of a fact, which *is* true. And that is enough, at least for me."

"Then you have the credulity of a child. You obviously believe all the fairy-tales you hear . . ."

The Count interrupted him, wanting to know his opinion on a book written by an Englishman, Major Bratt, who had travelled across Africa and had the most perfidious and unpleasant things to say about Portugal. The Count saw in these comments only envy, the envy all nations felt for Portugal because of the size of its colonies and its vast influence in Africa.

"Of course," the Count went on, "we don't have England's millions or its navy, but we have other great glories: Prince Henry, for example, was a remarkable man, and the taking of Ormuz a masterpiece of strategy. And I, who know a little about colonial systems, can say that there are no colonies with more potential for wealth, or with more belief in progress or, indeed, more liberal than ours. Don't you agree, Maia?"

"Yes, possibly. There's a lot of truth in that."

Ega, apart from occasionally fixing his monocle to his eye and smiling at the Baroness, had, until then, been rather silent, but he now gaily announced his opposition to all explorations of Africa and to all other such missions to various parts of the globe. Why didn't they just leave the black man in peace with his idols? What harm did the existence of savages do to the order of things? On the contrary, they gave the Universe a deliciously picturesque quality! This French, bourgeois mania for reducing all regions and all races to the same type of civilisation would turn the world into the most abominably boring place. Tourists would end up making enormous sacrifices and spending vast amounts of money in order to travel to Timbuktoo, only to find it full of black men in top hats reading *O Jornal dos Debates*.

The Count gave a superior smile. And good Dona Maria, emerging from her slight lowness of spirits, fanned herself, and said to Carlos:

"Ah, Ega! Always so witty, always so chic!"

Then Sousa Neto, gravely setting down his spoon, asked Ega this very earnest question:

"Am I to understand, then, that you are in favour of slavery, sir?"

Ega told Senhor Sousa Neto firmly that, yes, he was all for slavery. The discomforts of life, according to him, had begun with the liberation of the blacks. Only someone who was seriously feared could be seriously obeyed. This was why nowadays no one could ever get their shoes properly polished, their rice properly cooked, their stairs properly cleaned, because there were no longer any black servants whom one had the legal right to whip. There had been only two civilisations in which mankind had been able to live in reasonable comfort: the Roman civilisation and the civilisation peculiar to the planters in New Orleans. Why? Because absolute slavery, with power over life and death, had existed in both those civilisations.

For a moment, Senhor Sousa Neto seemed totally disoriented. Then he wiped his lips with his napkin, steeled himself, and turned to Ega.

"So you, an intelligent man, living in this day and age, do not believe in progress?"

"I do not, sir."

The Count intervened gently and with a smile:

"Our Ega is simply creating a paradox, and quite right too, because he comes up with some truly brilliant ones."

Jambon aux épinards was being served. For a moment, the talk turned to paradoxes. According to the Count, another creator of brilliant and near-unsustainable paradoxes was Barros, the minister of state.

"A man of great talent," Sousa Neto muttered respectfully.

"Oh, yes, magnificent," said the Count.

But he was talking now not of Barros' talent as a parliamentarian or as a statesman. He was referring to his social skills, to his *esprit*.

"In fact, just last winter we heard him come out with the most brilliant paradox. It was at Senhora Dona Maria's house, I believe. Can you remember, Senhora? Oh, really, my memory! Teresa, can you remember Barros' paradox? Oh, dear God, what *was* it about? Anyway, it was a paradox that was particularly difficult to sustain. My memory, really! Surely *you* remember, Teresa?"

The Countess did not remember. And while the Count sat, his hand pressed to his forehead, trying desperately to plumb the depths of his memory, the lady in scarlet returned to the subject of blacks and black servants, and one particular black cook who had worked for an aunt of hers, Aunt Vilar. Then she complained bitterly about modern-day servants; ever since Joaninha had died, Joaninha, who had been with her for fifteen years, she just didn't know what to do, she had been quite sick about it, nothing but disasters. In six months, she had seen four new faces. And what slovenly, uppity, immoral creatures they were! She suppressed a sigh, then, biting disconsolately into a piece of bread, said:

"Do you still have Vicenta, Baroness?"

"How could I not? Yes, Vicenta is still there, or, rather, Senhora Dona Vicenta, if you please."

The other woman gazed at her for a moment, envying her happiness.

"Is it Vicenta who does your hair?"

It was Vicenta who did her hair. She was getting on a bit now, poor thing, but she was still as stubborn as ever. Her current mania was for learning French. She knew the verbs already. It was hilarious listening to Vicenta saying *j'aime, tu aimes* ...

"I see you're having her learn the essential verbs first," said Ega.

It was, agreed the Baroness, *the* essential verb, not that it would do Vicenta much good at her age!

"Ah!" cried the Count, almost dropping his knife and fork. "Now I remember!"

He had finally remembered Barros' superb paradox. Barros said that the more you teach dogs—no, that wasn't it!

"Honestly, my wretched memory! It was about dogs, though. Absolutely brilliant, philosophical almost."

This mention of dogs reminded the Baroness of the Countess' greyhound Tommy, and so she enquired after his health. She hadn't seen brave Tommy for so long. The Countess didn't even want to talk about Tommy, the poor love. He had started to get these awful things growing in his ears. She had sent him to the Institute and there he had died.

"This galantine is delicious," said Dona Maria da Cunha, leaning towards Carlos.

"Yes, it is."

And the Baroness, on the other side of the table, also declared the galantine to be perfection. The Countess glanced at the footman, indicating that he should serve more galantine, then she responded to Senhor Sousa Neto, who, apropos of dogs, was speaking to her about the Society for the Protection of Animals. Senhor Sousa Neto approved of it and considered it a sign of progress. Indeed, according to him, it would not be a bad idea if the government were to give it a subsidy.

"It seems to be doing very well and it deserves a subsidy, it really does. I've studied the matter, and of all the societies that have been founded lately, in imitation, naturally, of societies abroad, such as the Geographical Society and others, the Society for the Protection of Animals certainly strikes me as one of the most useful."

He turned to Ega, who was sitting beside him:

"Are you a member?"

"Of the Society for the Protection of Animals? No, sir, I'm one of those being protected. I belong to the other one, to the Geographical Society."

The Baroness gave a merry laugh. And the Count looked extremely serious; he himself belonged to the Geographical Society and considered it a pillar of the State; he believed in its civilising mission and detested such irreverence. However, the Countess and Carlos had also laughed, and, suddenly, the coldness that had kept them sitting side by side in reserved silence, in feigned solemnity, seemed to dissipate in that exchange of laughter, in the shining glance of two gazes irresistibly meeting. The champagne had been served, and the Countess' face was already slightly flushed. Her foot—how she did not know—touched Carlos' foot; they smiled again, and since the rest of the table was talking about the classical concerts to be held at Price's Circus, Carlos asked her quietly, in a gently scolding tone:

"What's all this nonsense about the Brazilian woman? Who told you that?"

She confessed at once that it had been Dâmaso. He had come to tell her about Carlos' enthusiasm for the lady and how Carlos spent whole mornings there, every day, at the same hour. Dâmaso had made her think there was some sort of liaison going on.

Carlos shrugged. How could she possibly believe anything that Dâmaso said? She should know by now that he was a gossip and a fool.

"It's true, I do go to that lady's house—and she isn't Brazilian, by the way, she's as Portuguese as I am—but the reason I go there is because she has a governess who is very ill with bronchitis, and I'm her doctor. In fact, Dâmaso was the one who first summoned me there in my capacity as physician."

A smile spread over the Countess' face, and a light that came from the sweet relief she felt in her heart.

"But Dâmaso said she was very pretty!"

Yes, she was pretty, but what of that? As a doctor, one could hardly demand a certificate of ugliness before entering a patient's house, in a vain attempt to remain true to and avoid upsetting those to whom one was attached by bonds of affections!

"But what is she doing here?"

"She's waiting for her husband, who has gone off on business to Brazil and will be back shortly. They're very distinguished people and, I believe, very rich. Besides, they'll be leaving Lisbon soon, and that's about all I know. My visits are purely medical. I've merely talked to her a little about Paris and London and about her impressions of Portugal."

The Countess drank deep of these delicious words, transfixed by the loving gaze that accompanied them; and her foot pressed harder against Carlos' foot in passionate reconciliation, with all the force she would have liked to put into an embrace, were she able to embrace him there and then.

The lady in scarlet, meanwhile, had taken up the subject of Russia again. What most alarmed her was that the country was so expensive, and all that dynamite was terribly dangerous, and a weak constitution was bound to suffer with so much snow in the streets. And only then did Carlos realise that she was the wife of Sousa Neto, and that she was talking about a son of theirs, their only son, who had been given the post of under-secretary at the embassy in St. Petersburg.

"Do you know him?" Dona Maria whispered into Carlos' ear, shielded by her fan. "He's unbelievably stupid. He doesn't even know French! Otherwise, I suppose, he's no worse than any of the others, because the number of dolts, dullards, and nincumpoops who represent us overseas is enough to make one weep. Don't you think so? This really is a most unfortunate country."

"Worse, dear lady, much worse than that, it is what the Spanish call *cursi*—pretentious."

They had finished their dessert. Dona Maria gave the Countess a weary smile; the lady in scarlet had, in readiness, fallen silent, and had even moved her chair back a little; then the ladies left the table just as Ega, still on the subject of Russia, had concluded a story he had heard from a Pole, proving beyond doubt that the Tsar was an idiot.

"A liberal, though, and quite progressive," the Count murmured, already on his feet.

Once alone, the men lit their cigars, and the footman served coffee. Then Senhor Sousa Neto, with his cup in his hand, went over to Carlos to say again what a pleasure it was to make his acquaintance.

"Years ago, I had the pleasure of meeting your father too . . . yes, Senhor Pedro da Maia. I was just beginning my career in public life then. And how is your grandfather, he's well, I hope?"

"Yes, sir, he is, thank you."

"A most respectable gentleman. Your father was—well—he was what people call 'an elegant man.' I had the pleasure of knowing your mother too . . ."

But he stopped, embarrassed, and raised his cup to his lips. Then, slowly, he turned so as to be able to hear Ega, who was standing beside him, discussing women with the Count. The subject was the wife of the secretary at the Russian legation, with whom he had found the Count talking that very morning in Largo do Calhariz. Ega found her delicious, with her small, nervy, curvaceous body, and her large blue eyes. And the Count, who also admired her, praised most of all her wit and education. These qualities, according to Ega, spoiled her, for the first duty of a woman was to be beautiful, and the second, to be stupid. The Count declared exuberantly that he himself disliked blue-stockings; yes, a woman's place was definitely beside the cradle and not in the library.

"On the other hand, it's a good thing if a lady can speak about pleasant subjects, about an article in a magazine, or the publication of a book. Not, of course, when it is a book by a Guizot or a Jules Simon, but when it's a Feuillet, or . . . In short, a lady should be accomplished. Don't you agree, Neto?"

Neto murmured gravely:

"Yes, a lady, especially when she is young, should boast a few accomplishments."

Ega protested vehemently. A woman with accomplishments, especially of the literary variety, with opinions on Thiers or Zola, was a monster, a freak, and would be better off joining a circus and jumping through hoops astride a horse. A woman should have only two accomplishments: she should be good in the kitchen and good in bed. "I'm sure you will recall what Proudhon had to say on the subject, Senhor Sousa Neto."

"I can't remember the exact words, but . . ."

"But you know your Proudhon, nonetheless."

Sousa Neto, who was not enjoying this interrogation, said brusquely that Proudhon was, of course, a writer of great renown.

Ega, however, insisted, with perfidious impertinence:

"But you will have read, as we all have, Proudhon's great pages on love?"

Senhor Neto, by now red-faced, put his cup down on the table. He made an attempt to be sarcastic, to crush that overly bold and overly literary young man.

"I did not know," he said with an infinitely superior smile, "that the philosopher had written on such indelicate matters."

Ega threw his hands up in consternation.

"Oh, Senhor Sousa Neto! Do you, a family man, really think love an indelicate matter?"

Senhor Neto grew angry. Very erect and very dignified, and speaking from the lofty heights of his considerable bureaucratic position, he said:

"It is my custom, Senhor Ega, never to enter into arguments and always to respect other people's opinions, even when they are absurd."

And he almost turned his back on Ega, addressing Carlos instead, enquiring in a still slightly tremulous voice, if he was planning to remain in Portugal for some time. Then, for a moment, as they were finishing their cigars, they discussed travel. Senhor Neto regretted that his many duties did not allow him to tour Europe. As a boy, that had been his ideal, but now, with so many public obligations, he felt unable to leave his desk. And so there he was, never even having visited Badajoz on the Spanish border.

"And which did you like best, Paris or London?"

Carlos really did not know, nor could he compare them. They were two such different cities, two such original civilisations.

"I suppose in London," remarked Sousa Neto, "there is coal everywhere."

Yes, said Carlos, smiling, there was quite a lot of coal, especially in stoves when it was cold.

Senhor Sousa Neto murmured:

"And I suppose it is almost always cold there, being such a northerly climate."

He stood for a moment drawing on his cigar, his eyes closed. Then he made this wise and profound observation:

"They're basically a practical people, very practical."

"Yes, very," said Carlos vaguely, taking a step towards the drawing room, where he could hear the Baroness' musical laughter.

"And tell me something else," Senhor Sousa Neto went on, full of interest and intelligent curiosity. "In England, do they have the same very pleasing literature we have here, writers of serials and important poets?"

Carlos placed the stub of his cigar in the ashtray and replied shamelessly:

"No, no, there's none of that."

"I thought as much," said Sousa Neto. "They're all businessmen over there, I suppose."

They went into the drawing room. It was Ega who was making the Baroness laugh, sitting in front of her and talking again about Celorico, describing a soirée there, adding all kinds of picaresque details about the local worthies and about an abbot who had killed a man and who sang sentimental *fados*, accompanying himself on the piano. The lady in scarlet, on the sofa next to them, her hands lying limply in her lap, sat listening in amazement to Ega in full flow, just as she might have watched the tricks of a clown. Dona Maria, at the table, was leafing wearily through a magazine, and seeing Carlos come in and look round for the Countess, she called him over and told him quietly that the Countess had gone to see Charlie, her little boy.

"Ah, yes," said Carlos, sitting down beside her, "how is the little fellow?"

"Apparently, he's had a cold today and is slightly out of sorts."

"You seem a little out of sorts yourself, Senhora."

"It's the weather. I'm at an age when one's good humour or lack of it depends entirely on the weather. At your age, of course, it depends on other things. And speaking of other things, has Cohen's wife arrived back in Lisbon as well?"

"She has," said Carlos, "but not 'as well.' 'As well' would suggest that it had been arranged, but it really is pure coincidence that she and Ega both arrived back in Lisbon today. Besides, that's ancient history, like the loves of Helen and Paris."

At that moment, the Countess came into the room, looking slightly flushed, and with her large black fan open. Without sitting down, and addressing mainly Senhor Sousa Neto's wife, she complained that Charlie was still not well. He was so hot, so restless. She was almost afraid it might be measles. Then turning brightly to Carlos, she said with a smile:

"I feel dreadful about asking, but if you wouldn't mind popping in to see him for a moment. It's awful, I know, asking you to examine a patient just after supper, but ..."

"Of course, Countess!" he exclaimed, already on his feet.

He followed her. In a small room to the side, the Count and Senhor Sousa Neto were sitting on a sofa, talking and smoking.

"I'm just taking Senhor Maia to see Charlie."

The Count, uncomprehending, made to get up from the sofa. But, by then, she had left the room. Carlos silently followed her long, black silk train through the deserted, gaslit billiard room, adorned with portraits of four powdered, grim-faced ladies from the Gouvarinho family. Next door, behind a heavy green curtain, was a study, with an old armchair, a few books in a glass-fronted cabinet, and a desk on which stood an oil-lamp with a pink lace shade. And there, brusquely, she stopped and threw her arms around Carlos' neck; her lips fastened on his in a full, urgent, penetrating kiss that ended with a swooning sob. He felt her lovely body tremble and slide from his arms as her knees gave way.

"Tomorrow, at my aunt's house, at eleven," she murmured, when she was able to speak again.

"All right."

Detaching herself from his embrace, she stood for a moment with her hands over her eyes, waiting for it to pass, that sweet vertigo, which had turned her pale as wax. Then, tired and smiling, she said:

"I must be mad. Let's go and see Charlie."

The little boy's room was at the end of the corridor. And there, in a small iron bedstead, next to the maid's much larger one, Charlie lay sleeping, serene and cool, with one small arm hanging limply over the edge of the bed, and his pretty golden curls spread on the pillow like the halo of an angel. Carlos merely felt his pulse; and the Scottish maid, who had brought a light from the chest of drawers, said, smiling calmly:

"He's been really well these last few days."

They left the room. In the study, before going through into the billiard room, the Countess, her hand on the curtain, once more offered Carlos her insatiable lips. He snatched the briefest of kisses. And, as they passed through the smaller room, where Sousa Neto and the Count were still deep in grave conversation, she said to her husband:

"Charlie's sleeping. Senhor Maia thought he looked fine."

The Count affectionately patted Carlos' shoulder, and, for a moment, the Countess stood there, chatting, taking advantage of the kindly semi-darkness to recover herself before venturing into the bright light of the drawing room. Then, still on the subject of health, she invited Senhor Sousa Neto to a game of billiards; but Senhor Neto, being from Coimbra, from the University, had never played. And she was about to ask Ega instead, when Teles da Gama came in, just back from Price's Circus, and immediately behind him came Steinbroken. The rest of the evening was spent in the salon, around the piano. Steinbroken sang songs from Finland, and Teles da Gama played some *fados*.

Carlos and Ega were the last to leave, after drinking a brandy and soda, of which the Countess also partook, like the strong Englishwoman she was. And downstairs, in the courtyard, as he was buttoning up his overcoat, Carlos was at last able to ask the question he had been burning to ask all night:

"Ega, who is that man, Sousa Neto, who asked me if there was any literature in England?"

Ega stared at him in amazement.

"Didn't you guess? Didn't you instantly know? Didn't you realise at once who in this country would be capable of asking such a question?"

"No, I didn't. There are so many possible candidates."

Ega triumphantly declared:

"Why, he's a high-up official in a large State Department!"

"Which department?"

"*Which* department! Why, which would it be—Education, of course!"

The following afternoon, at five o'clock, Carlos, who had lingered too long with the Countess, detained by her interminable kisses, positively flew in his coupé from her aunt's house to Rua de São Francisco, glancing all the while at his watch, afraid that Maria Eduarda might have gone out on that lovely, bright, cool summer's day. There was, indeed, a hired carriage at the door, and Carlos bounded up the stairs, furious with the Countess, and with himself for being so weak, so passive, as to allow himself to be imprisoned again by those demanding arms, arms that weighed ever more heavily upon him and which no longer excited him in the least.

"Madame has just arrived," said Domingos, who had returned from his village three days before and had not ceased smiling at him since.

Sitting on the sofa, still with her hat on, and pulling off her gloves, she welcomed him, her cheeks slightly pink, and fondly scolded him:

"I waited for more than half an hour before going out! Such ingratitude! I thought you had abandoned us!"

"Why? Has Miss Sara got worse?"

She looked at him in mock horror. Miss Sara, indeed! Miss Sara was continuing to progress very nicely, but it was no longer the visits of the doctor they looked forward to, but those of their friend, and their friend had let them down.

Troubled, Carlos did not respond, but turned to Rosa, who was sitting at the table leafing through a new picture book; and all the tenderness and infinite gratitude which was filling his heart, and which he dared not show the mother, he poured into the loving caress he bestowed on the daughter.

"They're stories Mama bought for me just now," Rosa said, serious and engrossed in her book. "I'll tell them to you later. They're stories about animals."

Maria Eduarda had got up, slowly untying the ribbons on her hat.

"Would you like to have a cup of tea with us? I've been dying for one. Isn't it a lovely day? Rosa, stay here and tell Senhor Maia about our walk while I go and take my hat off."

Alone with Rosa, Carlos sat down beside her, drawing her away from the book and taking both her hands in his.

"We went for a walk in Passeio da Estrela," she said. "But Mama didn't want to stay long because she was afraid you might come!"

Carlos kissed each of Rosa's little hands.

"And what did you do there?" he asked, after giving a gentle, irrepressible sigh of happiness.

"I ran around and there were some little ducklings too . . ."

"Were they very pretty?"

She shrugged:

"No, no great shakes."

No great shakes! Who had taught her such an expression?

Rosa smiled. Domingos. And Domingos said other things, too, funny things . . . He said that Melanie was a tart. Domingos made her laugh.

Carlos told her that a pretty girl wearing pretty clothes shouldn't say such words. That was how dirty people in rags talk.

"Domingos isn't dirty and he doesn't wear rags," said Rosa gravely.

Then suddenly, seized by another idea, she clapped her hands and jumped up and down between his knees, her face shining.

"And he brought me some crickets from the market! Domingos brought me some crickets! Niniche is frightened of crickets, you know. It's incredible, isn't it? She gets ever so scared!"

Then she paused for a moment, looking at Carlos, and added very seriously: "It's Mama's fault because she spoils her. It's a shame really."

Maria Eduarda came in, still smoothing her wavy hair, and, hearing Rosa talking about her spoiling someone, wanted to know who it was she spoiled. Niniche? Ah, poor Niniche, she had had to tell her off that very morning.

Then Rosa burst out laughing, again clapping her hands.

"Do you know how Mama punishes her?" she exclaimed, tugging at Carlos' sleeve. "She puts on a deep voice and says to her in English: 'Bad dog! Dreadful dog!'"

She was delightful like that, imitating her mother's severe tones, wagging one threatening finger at Niniche. Poor Niniche, imagining that she was being told off again, crawled away in shame under the sofa. Rosa had to kneel down on the tiger-skin rug and reassure Niniche that she had only been copying Mama. Niniche wasn't a bad dog or a dreadful dog, she assured her, holding the dog in her arms.

"Go and give her some water, she must be thirsty," said Maria Eduarda, going over to her red chair. "And tell Domingos to bring us some tea."

Rosa and Niniche raced off together. Carlos went and sat down by the window in his usual armchair. But, for the first time since their friendship had begun, there was an awkward silence between them. Then, as she absentmindedly unrolled her tapestry work, she complained about the heat; and Carlos still said nothing, as if for him, on that day, charm and meaning were to be found only in a certain word that was there on the tip of his tongue, but which his tongue did not dare to speak, and even though it so filled his heart he almost feared it might give him away.

"It doesn't look as if it will ever be finished that tapestry of yours," he said at last, impatient to see her serenely selecting different wools.

With the canvas spread out on her knees, she replied, without looking up:

"Why should I ever finish it? The real pleasure is in doing it, don't you think? A stitch today, another stitch tomorrow, it becomes almost a companion. Why should one always want to get to the end of things?"

A shadow crossed Carlos' face. He sensed in these insignificant words about her tapestry work a discouraging allusion to his love—the love which had been filling his heart just as the wool was covering the canvas—the work of the same white hands. Did she want to keep him there, like that piece of tapestry, always growing and always incomplete, stored away in her sewing basket as a salve for her solitude?

Then he said with some feeling:

"No, that's not true. There are some things that only exist when they are complete and which only then give the happiness one hoped to gain from them."

"That's a very complicated idea," she said, blushing, "and very subtle too."

"Would you like me to put it more plainly?"

At that moment, Domingos, drew back the curtain and announced that Senhor Dâmaso was there.

Maria Eduarda made a brusque, impatient gesture.

"Tell him I'm not receiving!"

Outside, in the silence, they heard the door slam. And Carlos felt uneasy, thinking that Dâmaso would surely have seen his coupé downstairs in the street. Oh, dear God! What mean, rancorous rumours he would spread now, after such a humiliation! It even felt to him then that Dâmaso's existence was incompatible with the tranquillity of his love.

"That's another disadvantage of living here," Maria Eduarda said. "Being right next to that place, the Grémio, and only a few steps from the Chiado, one is far too vulnerable to importunate callers. I have to repel this assault on my front door almost every day now. It's intolerable."

Then, taken by a sudden idea, she threw her tapestry work into the sewing basket and, folding her hands on her lap, said:

"There's something I've been meaning to ask you. Would it be possible for me to find a little house somewhere, a cottage, where I could spend the summer months? It would be so good for Rosa! But I don't know anyone, I don't know who to ask."

Carlos immediately thought of Craft's lovely house in Olivais, as he had once before, when she had expressed a desire to go to the country. Indeed, recently, Craft had spoken again, more definitely this time, about his old plan to sell the house and get rid of his collection. What a marvellous house it would be for her, both artistic and rural, so perfectly suited to her tastes. He succumbed to an irresistible temptation.

"I do know of a house actually. It's in a lovely spot and is exactly what you want."

"Is it for rent?"

Carlos did not hesitate.

"I'm sure that could be arranged."

"Oh, it would be like a dream come true!"

These words decided him, since it would be cruel and mean to arouse such hopes in her and then not do his utmost to realise them.

Domingos had come in bearing the tea tray. And while he was setting it down on a small table by the window in front of Maria Eduarda, Carlos, getting up and pacing about the room, was thinking that he must immediately start negotiations with Craft to buy his collection and rent the house from him for a year, then offer Maria Eduarda the use of it for the summer months.

And he did not consider, at that moment, what difficulties might arise, or how much it would cost. He imagined only her joy as she strolled with Rosa among the beautiful trees in the garden. And how much grander and more beautiful Maria Eduarda would look among all that severe, noble Renaissance furniture!

"More sugar?" she asked.

"No, that's perfect, thank you."

He had returned to his old armchair and, taking from her the ordinary china cup with a simple blue border, he remembered Craft's magnificent Wedgwood tea service, in gold and flame-red. The poor woman! She had such delicate tastes and yet there she was buried among all that cheap rep upholstery, soiling her graceful hands on Mother Cruges' vulgar crockery!

"And where is the house?" asked Maria Eduarda.

It was, he explained, in Olivais, very close to Lisbon, about an hour's carriage ride away. He described to her exactly where it was, adding, with his eyes fixed on hers and with an uneasy smile:

"I'm preparing wood for my own funeral pyre here, because, if you do move there, once the summer heat arrives, when shall I ever see you again?"

She seemed surprised.

"But why should that be a problem, when you have horses and carriages and very little to do?"

So she thought it perfectly natural that he should continue to visit them in Olivais! And it seemed to him then impossible to give up the charm of that friendship, so generously offered, a friendship that would doubtless be all the sweeter in that village solitude. By the time he had finished his cup of tea, it was as if the Olivais house, with its furniture and its trees, were already his—already hers. And he spent a delicious moment describing to her the quiet garden, the entrance along an avenue of acacias, the wonderful dining room with two windows that opened onto a view of the river.

She listened to him, enthralled.

"It's exactly the house I've dreamed of!" she said. "Now I'm going to be on tenterhooks, hoping that it won't all come to nothing. When do you think you'll be able to let me know?"

Carlos looked at his watch. It was too late to drive out to Olivais now, but tomorrow morning, early, he would go and speak to his friend, the owner of the house.

"I'm putting you to an awful lot of trouble," she said. "How can I ever thank you?"

She fell silent, and her lovely eyes gazed for a moment into his, in a look almost of surrender, revealing, irresistibly, a little of the secret locked in her heart.

He murmured:

"However much I did for you, I would feel well rewarded if you'd simply look at me like that again."

The blood rushed into Maria Eduarda's face.

"Don't say that."

"Why do I even need to say it? You know perfectly well that I adore you!"

She sprang to her feet, so did he, and they stood there silently, full of anxious yearning, their gaze lost in each other's gaze, as if some great change had taken place in the Universe, and they were waiting, expectantly, for a supreme decision to be made regarding their destinies. She was the one to speak first, falteringly, almost fainting, holding out to him tremulous, troubled hands as if to keep him at bay.

"Listen! You know how I feel about you, but listen . . . before it's too late, there is something I must tell you . . ."

Carlos saw her trembling, saw how pale she was, but he did not listen, did not understand. He felt only, in one dazzling instant, that the love which had, until then, been imprisoned inside his heart had burst triumphantly forth and, in striking her heart, through the seemingly obdurate marble of her breast, had sparked an identical flame. He saw only that she was shaking; he saw only that she loved him. And, with all the impressive gravity of an act of possession, he slowly took hold of her hands, which she abandoned to him, suddenly submissive, vanquished, her strength all gone. And he slowly kissed each hand, her palms and her fingers, murmuring:

"My love, my love, my love!"

Maria Eduarda had gradually sunk back into her chair, and, while still not withdrawing her hands, but raising to him passionate, tear-filled eyes, she managed to utter, more feebly now, one final plea:

"There's something I must tell you!"

Carlos was already kneeling at her feet.

"I know what it is!" he cried ardently, his face close to hers, not allowing her to say any more, certain that he knew what she was thinking. "There's no need to say it, I know what you mean. It's what I have thought so often myself—a love like ours imposes quite different conditions from other ordinary loves, and that when I say that I love you, it is as if I were asking you to be my wife before God."

She drew back and looked at him, perplexed, as if she did not understand. And Carlos went on, more softly now, still holding her hands, filling her with the same emotion that was making him tremble too.

"Whenever I've thought about you, it was always with the hope of our one day having a life of our own, far from here, far from everyone, having broken all our present ties, placing our love above all the usual human fictions, and going off to be happy in some other corner of the world, alone and forever. We would take Rosa, of course, I know you could never be parted from her. And we would live there alone, just the three of us, a charmed life."

"Dear God! You mean run away together?" she said, shocked.

Carlos had got to his feet.

"What else can we do? What else can we do that would be worthy of our love?"

Maria Eduarda did not respond or move; she merely sat looking up at him, her face as pale as wax. And little by little, an idea, unexpected and troubling, seemed to rise within her, stirring her whole being. Her eyes grew large and bright and eager with longing.

Carlos was about to say more, but the light sound of footsteps crossing the carpet stopped him. It was Domingos who had come to collect the tea tray; and for what seemed an interminable moment, those two beings, shaken by an ardent whirlwind of passion, were separated by the homely figure of a servant removing their empty cups. Maria Eduarda took refuge behind the cretonne curtains, her face pressed against the window pane. Carlos went and sat on the sofa and leafed through a magazine, his hands trembling. He was not thinking of anything, he did not even know where he was. The previous day, indeed, only a few minutes before, he had been talking to her and addressing her formally as "Senhora." Then there had been that look, and now they would have to run away together, and she had become the most important object in his life, his heart's secret wife.

"Do you need anything else, Senhora?" asked Domingos.

Without turning round, Maria Eduarda replied:

"No."

Domingos left and the door closed. Then she crossed the room and went over to Carlos, who was waiting for her on the sofa, his arms outstretched. And it was as if she were obeying the pure impulse of her love, all doubts gone. However, she hesitated once more before that passion which was about to take over her whole being, and said almost sadly:

"But you know so little about me! You know too little about me for us even to think about going away together, breaking with everything and everyone, choosing a path from which there would be no turning back."

Carlos took her hands and gently pulled her down to sit beside him.

"I know enough to adore you and want nothing else in life!"

For a moment, Maria Eduarda sat there thinking, as if she had withdrawn into the very depths of her heart, listening to its last gnawing anxieties. Then she gave a long sigh.

"Let it be so, then, let it be so. There was something I wanted to tell you, but it doesn't matter. It's better this way!"

What else could they do, asked Carlos radiantly. It was the only dignified, serious solution. And nothing could stop them; they loved each other and trusted each other absolutely; he was rich and the world was large . . .

And she said again, more firmly, determined now, and as if that resolution were taking ever deeper root in her soul, penetrating it entirely and forever. "Let it be so! It's better this way!"

They remained silent for a moment, staring passionately at each other.

"Tell me at least that you're happy, my love," murmured Carlos.

She threw her arms around his neck, and their lips met in a deep, infinite kiss, so ecstatic as to be almost immaterial. Then Maria Eduarda slowly opened her eyes and said very softly:

"Go now, leave me."

He picked up his hat and left.

The following day, Craft, who had not visited Ramalhete for a week, was walking in his garden before lunch, when Carlos appeared. They shook hands and spoke briefly about Ega and the return of the Cohens. Then Carlos, making a sweeping gesture that took in the garden, the house and the whole horizon, asked with a laugh:

"How would you like to sell me all this, Craft?"

Craft replied, without so much as blinking or taking his hands out of his pockets: "*A la disposición de usted.* I'm at your disposal, sir."

And they closed the deal there and then, strolling along a little box-lined path past the flowering geraniums.

Craft gave over to Carlos all his furniture, antique and modern, for 2,500 *libras*, to be paid in instalments; he only kept back a few rare pieces from the reign of Louis XV, which would form part of the new, more homogeneous collection he was planning, which would consist solely of objects from the eighteenth century. And since Carlos did not have space at Ramalhete for this enormous accumulation of antiques, Craft rented him the house and the garden at Olivais for a year.

Then they went in to lunch. Carlos did not for an instant think about the vast expense he was incurring merely in order to offer a summer residence, for two brief months, to someone who would have been quite content with a simple cottage surrounded by a few trees. On the contrary! As he walked through Craft's rooms, with the eyes now of an owner, he found it all rather poky and was immediately thinking of changes that could be made and small tasteful touches that could be added here and there.

With what joy he left Olivais and ran to Rua de São Francisco to tell Maria Eduarda that he had definitely managed to rent that lovely house in the country for her! Rosa, who had seen him from the balcony getting out of his carriage, came to meet him on the landing; he lifted her up in his arms and entered the room in triumph. And he could not contain himself, and gave "the great news" to the little girl, announcing that she would have two cows, and a goat, and flowers and trees where she could put up a swing.

"Where is it?" exclaimed Rosa, her lovely eyes shining, and her little face wreathed in smiles: "Tell me where it is!"

"Far from here. You have to go there in a carriage. You can see the boats passing by on the river. And you go in through a big door where there's a guard-dog watching."

Maria Eduarda came in, carrying Niniche.

"Mama, Mama!" cried Rosa, running towards her and tugging at her dress. "He says I'm going to have two goats and a swing. Is it true? Tell me, go on, where is it? Tell me. Are we going there now?"

Maria and Carlos shook hands and exchanged a long silent look. Carlos told her of his trip to Olivais. The owner was prepared to rent it out, straight away, in a week's time. And thus she found herself the tenant of a picturesque, wonderfully salubrious home, furnished in fine style.

Maria Eduarda seemed surprised, almost suspicious.

"I'll need to take bed-linen with me, table cloths."

"There's everything you need there," exclaimed Carlos gaily. "Well, almost everything. It's just like a fairy tale. The lights are on, the vases are full of flowers. All you have to do is get in a carriage and go."

"There's just one thing I need to know, how much is this paradise going to cost me?"

Carlos turned red. He had not foreseen that she would speak of money and would want to pay for the house she was to live in. He decided to confess everything. He told her that, for almost a year now, Craft had been wanting to get rid of his collection and rent the house out; he and his grandfather had often thought of acquiring a large part of the furniture and the china in order to finish furnishing Ramalhete and to add to the décor in Santa Olávia; and he had decided to make that purchase when he had seen the happy chance of being able to offer her such a gracious and comfortable residence for part of the summer.

"Rosa, go inside," said Maria Eduarda, after a moment's silence. "Miss Sara is waiting for you."

Then, looking at Carlos very seriously, she said: "So if I had expressed no desire to live in the country, you would not have made this purchase."

"No, I would have made the purchase anyway and rented the house for six months or a year. After all, where else could I store all of Craft's things? I would not perhaps have bought the bed-linen and tableware, the furniture for the servants' rooms, etc."

And he added, laughing: "Now if you want to recompense me for this in some way, I'm sure we can discuss details . . ."

She lowered her eyes and thought for a while before replying.

"Yes, but in a few days' time, your grandfather and your friends will find out that I'm going to move into that house . . . and they are sure to think that you bought it for me to live in."

Carlos tried to look into her eyes, but she remained pensive, eyes lowered. And it troubled him to see her recoil from that absolute communion of interests in which he wished to involve her, as the wife of his heart. "So you don't approve of what I've done? Be honest now . . ."

"How could I not approve of everything you do and of everything that comes from you, but . . ."

He snatched up her hands, sensing victory:

"There are no 'buts.' My grandfather and my friends will know that I have a house in the country, which I will not be using for the moment, and that I have rented it out to a lady. If you like, we can use the services of my administrator. My dear friend, it would be wonderful if our love could take place outside of this world, far from all eyes, safe from all suspicions, but that's impossible! There will always be someone who knows something, even if it's only the coachman who takes me to your house every day or the servant who opens the door to me. There will always be someone who notices an exchange of glances or guesses where one has come from at a particular hour. The gods arranged these things better: they had a cloud to wrap about themselves to become invisible. We, fortunately, are not gods."

She smiled.

"So many words to convert the converted!"

And harmony was restored with a long kiss.

Afonso da Maia fully approved of the purchase of Craft's collection. "It's a real asset," he said to Vilaça, "and it means we can fill Santa Olávia and Ramalhete with fine art."

Ega, however, was furious. Annoyed at not being consulted about this secret transaction, he went so far as to refer to it as an "act of madness." What irritated him more than anything was seeing, in this unexpected acquisition of a house in the country, another symptom of the deep dark secret which he sensed in Carlos' life; he had been living at Ramalhete for two whole weeks now and Carlos had still not confided in him! Ever since their youthful friendship in Coimbra, in Paços de Celas, he had been Carlos' secular confessor, and even when Carlos had gone off travelling, he always sent Ega a "report" of the most trifling encounter in a hotel. He knew all about the affair with the Countess de Gouvarinho, which Carlos had, at first, tried to conceal behind a delicate veil of mystery; he had even read her letters and been to her aunt's house.

But he knew nothing of this other secret, and felt positively outraged. Every morning, he would see Carlos setting off for Rua de São Francisco, bearing flowers; he would see him come back, as he put it, "oozing ecstasy"; he noticed Carlos' blissful silences and that indefinable air, at once serious and frivolous, smiling and superior, of a man who feels profoundly loved. And he knew nothing.

A few days later, when they were alone and discussing plans for the summer, Carlos spoke enthusiastically about Olivais, mentioning some of the precious items in Craft's collection, the quiet and peace of the house, the clear view over the Tejo. For a handful of *libras*, he really had bought himself a little piece of Paradise.

This was at night, in Carlos' room, quite late. And Ega, who was pacing about with his hands in the pockets of his dressing gown, shrugged impatiently, bored with hearing Carlos eternally singing the praises of Craft's little house.

"Your idea of Paradise," he exclaimed, "seems to me worthy of an upholsterer in Rua Augusta! For nature, a few rows of cabbages, for decoration, the old cretonne in the study, faded from one too many washings. A bedroom as gloomy as a church chapel. A drawing room as cluttered as a junk-dealer's warehouse and where it is impossible even to hold a decent conversation. Apart from the Dutch dresser and the odd plate, it's just a pile of archaelogical rubbish. God, how I loathe bric-à-brac!"

From his armchair, Carlos remarked calmly and as if pondering what Ega had said: "Yes, that cretonne really is ghastly, but I'm going to have it all redone and make the place more habitable."

Ega stopped his pacing and, with his glittering monocle trained on Carlos, asked:

"Habitable? Are you planning to have guests?"

"Yes, I'm going to rent it out."

"Rent it out! To whom?"

And Carlos' silence, as he sat exhaling the smoke from his cigarette and gazing up at the ceiling, infuriated Ega. He bowed very low and said sarcastically:

"Oh, forgive me, I should never have asked such a vulgar question. It was the behaviour of someone trying to force a locked drawer. I realise that revealing the identity of one's tenants is always one of those delicate secrets of sentiment and honour which one should not even brush with the wing of one's imagination. It was most rude of me, coarse and rude!"

Carlos remained silent. He understood Ega's feelings and felt something like remorse for his own stiff reserve. However, he was constrained by a kind of modesty, which prevented him from so much as mentioning Maria Eduarda's name. He had always told Ega about his love affairs, and those confidences had given him perhaps more real pleasure than the affairs themselves. This, though, was not an "affair." His love was mingled with a near religious feeling, and, like all true devotees, he found it repugnant to discuss his faith. Yet, at the same time, he was tempted to talk about "her" to Ega, and thus to make the divine, confused emotions filling his heart come alive and become, in a way, visible to his own eyes, by giving them the shape and substance of words. Besides, Ega was sure to find out everything sooner or later from the idle gossip of others. It would be better to tell him now, brother to brother. Nevertheless, he still hesitated and lit another cigarette. Ega had meanwhile taken up his candlestick and was slowly and sulkily lighting it with a taper.

"Don't be silly, don't go to bed just yet, sit down," said Carlos.

And then he told him everything in minute, prolix detail, from their first encounter at the entrance to the Hotel Central on the night of the supper Ega had given for Cohen.

Ega listened to him, without saying a word, slumped on the sofa. He had assumed it would be a minor romance, of the kind that is born and dies be tween a kiss and a yawn; and now, simply by the way in which Carlos spoke of that great love, he realised that this was something profound, absorbing and eternal, which would, for good or ill, and forever after, be Carlos' inalterable destiny. He had imagined a pretty, empty-headed Brazilian woman, who had acquired a veneer of culture in Paris, who, with her husband far away in Brazil and a handsome young man by her side on the sofa, was simply and cheerfully giving in to what circumstances had offered her; and yet here was a creature full of character, full of passion, capable of sacrifice and of heroism. As always happened when confronted by genuine emotion, Ega's wit shrivelled up, and he had no clever remarks to make; and when Carlos stopped speaking, Ega could ask only the rather foolish question:

"So you're determined to run off with her, then?"

"No, not run off with her, but, yes, I am determined to go and live with her somewhere far from here!"

Ega sat for a moment staring at Carlos as if at some prodigious monster, then he murmured:

"Extraordinary!"

But what else could they do? In three months' time, Castro Gomes would probably be arriving back from Brazil. Neither she nor Carlos could ever accept one of those situations in which the woman belonged both to the husband and the lover at different times. Only one dignified, decent solution was left to them—to flee.

After a silence, Ega said pensively:

"The husband might not be too pleased to lose, at one fell swoop, wife, daughter and dog."

Carlos stood up and took a few steps about the room. Yes, he, too, had thought about that. But he felt no remorse, were it even possible to feel such a thing in the absolute egotism of passion. He did not know Castro Gomes himself, but he had a sense of the kind of man he was and could imagine what he was like from what Dâmaso had told him and from a few conversations with Miss Sara. Castro Gomes was not a serious husband: he was a dandy, a fop, *un gommeux*, a man who liked sport and *les cocottes*. He had married a beautiful woman, sated his passion for her, and resumed his life of clubs and actresses. One had only to look at him, to observe his clothes and his manners, to see his utter triviality.

"What's he like as a man?" asked Ega.

"A dark, elegant-looking Brazilian, flashy, the kind of foreigner you'd find in the Café de la Paix. When this all happens, he may well feel a touch of wounded vanity, but his is the kind of heart that will find easy consolation at the Folies Bergères."

Ega said nothing, but he thought that a clubbable man like that—even one capable of finding consolation at the Folies Bergères—while he might not care much about his wife, might still love his daughter very much indeed. Then another idea occurred to him and he said:

"What about your grandfather?"

Carlos shrugged.

"For me to be profoundly happy, my grandfather will have to suffer a little, just as I would have to be wretched for the rest of my life if I wanted to spare him this unhappiness. That's how the world is, Ega. On this point, I'm not prepared to make sacrifices."

Ega slowly rubbed his hands together, staring down at the floor and repeating the same word, the only one that came to mind in the face of such vehemence:

"Extraordinary!"

: XIII :

CARLOS, HAVING LUNCHED EARLY, had already put on his hat and was about to leave in the coupé, when Baptista came to tell him that Ega wished to speak to him about a matter of great seriousness and had asked him to wait for a moment. Senhor Ega was shaving.

Carlos immediately thought it must be something to do with Madame Cohen. She had arrived in Lisbon two weeks earlier, but Ega had not yet seen her and spoke of her only rarely. Carlos sensed, however, that he was nervous and uneasy. Every morning, when the post arrived and brought only a newspaper or letters from Celorico, poor Ega seemed disappointed. At night, he would visit two or even three theatres, but, at the beginning of summer, they were already almost empty; and when he returned home he would meet only with further misery when the servants informed him that no letter had come for him. Ega had clearly not resigned himself to losing Raquel and still longed to see her; and the wounding thought still gnawed at him that she had given him no indication that any nostalgia for past joys lingered in her heart. The previous evening, Ega had arrived at suppertime, looking distraught. He had passed Cohen in Rua do Ouro, and "the scoundrel" had given Ega an impudent look and shaken his cane at him; Ega swore that if "that scoundrel" dared to so much as glance his way again, he would tear the man to pieces, pitilessly and publicly, on a street corner in the Baixa.

In the hall, the clock was striking ten. Carlos, impatient to leave, was about to go up to Ega's room. At that moment, however, the post arrived, bringing a copy of the *Revue des Deux Mondes* and a letter for Carlos. It was from the Countess. Carlos had just finished reading it when Ega appeared, wearing a jacket, but still in his slippers.

"I have something very serious to tell you."

"Read this first," said Carlos, handing him the Countess' letter.

The Countess, in bitter tones, complained that Carlos had now missed two of their rendez-vous at her aunt's house and had not even taken the trouble to write her a note explaining why; she thought this behaviour both cruel and insulting; and she was writing to beg him, "in the name of all the sacrifices she had made for him," to meet her at Rua de São Marçal, at midday on Sunday, so that they could clear things up once and for all before she left for Sintra.

"An excellent opportunity to break it off!" exclaimed Ega, as he handed the letter back to Carlos, having first breathed in the perfume from the paper. "You don't go and you don't reply. She leaves for Sintra and you for Santa Olávia, you never see each other again, and thus ends the romance. It ends as all great things do, like the Roman Empire or like the Rhine, imperceptibly, by a process of dispersal."

"That's precisely what I'm going to do!" said Carlos, pulling on his gloves. "The woman is a pest!"

"And shameless to boot! I mean, fancy using the word 'sacrifices'! She forces you to meet her at her aunt's house twice a week, commits all kinds of excesses there—drinking champagne, smoking cigarettes, experiencing heavenly bliss itself—and then, eyes downcast, refers to these things as 'sacrifices'! The woman deserves to be whipped!"

Carlos shrugged resignedly, as if one could expect nothing from the world, or from Countesses, but confusion and bad faith.

"What was it you wanted to talk to me about?"

Ega adopted an appropriately serious air. He slowly took a cigarette from his cigarette case and equally slowly buttoned up his jacket.

"You haven't seen anything of Dâmaso, then?"

"No, he's never been back," said Carlos. "I think he's sulking. Whenever I see him in the distance, though, I give him a friendly wave."

"Well, you should be shaking your stick at him instead. Dâmaso is going around talking about you and about that lady, your friend. He calls you a 'rogue' and her far worse things. It's the old story; he says that he introduced you to her, that you then wheedled your way into her affections, and since the lady's main concern is money, and since you are richer than he is, she has shown him the door. You see how he's slandering you! And this is being talked about in the Grémio, in the Casa Havanesa, with crude details too, always involving money. It's quite appalling. You must put a stop to it."

Carlos, who had turned very pale, said simply and gravely:

"Justice will be done."

He angrily left the house. It seemed to him that this vile insinuation about "money" could be punished only by death. And for a moment, as he grasped the handle of the coupé door, he even considered going straight to Dâmaso's house and exacting a brutal revenge.

But it was nearly eleven o'clock, and he had to go to Olivais. The next day, Saturday—the most beautiful of all days and for his heart the most solemn— Maria Eduarda would at last visit Craft's house, and they had arranged to spend the long, hot afternoon there together, alone, with no servants, in that solitary house hidden away among the trees. He had hesitated and trembled when he suggested this, but she had agreed at once, smiling, as if it were the most natural thing in the world. That morning, he had sent two servants to Olivais to air and dust the rooms and fill the whole place with flowers. He was going there now, like a devotee, to ensure that the shrine to his goddess had been suitably adorned. And it was while he was immersed in all these delightful preoccupations, when he was so fully and completely happy, that Dâmaso's grubby gossip came to trouble him again, dulling the lustre of his love.

He spent the whole of the journey to Olivais pondering vague acts of violence annihilating Dâmaso. There would be no peace for his love as long as that villain continued to make sordid remarks about it on every street corner. He would have to insult him in such a way and so publicly that Dâmaso would never dare to show his wretched chubby face in Lisbon again. When the coupé stopped outside the gate at Olivais, Carlos had decided to give Dâmaso a sound thrashing with his cane one afternoon in the Chiado, in full view of everyone.

Later, though, driving back from Olivais, he felt calmer. He had walked the lovely avenue of acacias that her feet would tread the following morning; he had gazed long upon the bed that would be her bed: lavish and raised up on a platform, surrounded by curtains made of gold brocatelle, and with all the grave splendour of a pagan altar. In a few hours' time, they would be alone there in that silent house, cut off from the world; then, all summer, their love could live secluded in that cool village retreat; and three months later, they would be far away, in Italy, beside the clear waters of a lake, among the flowers of Isola Bela. Compared with such voluptuous pleasures, what did plump, vulgar Dâmaso matter to him, filling the billiard rooms at the Grémio with his loud slangy comments. By the time Carlos reached Rua de São Francisco, he had decided that, if and when he did see Dâmaso, he would continue to greet him with a cheery wave.

Maria Eduarda had gone to Belém with Rosa, but had left him a note, asking him to come that night *pour faire un bout de causerie*. Carlos went slowly down the stairs, putting the slip of paper away in his wallet, as if it were a sweet relic; and he stepped out onto the street just as Alencar, all in black, was emerging slowly and pensively from the street opposite, the Travessa da Parreirinha. When he saw Carlos, he stood there, his arms flung wide; then suddenly, as if remembering something, he glanced up at the second-floor windows.

They had not seen each other since the races, and the poet embraced Carlos effusively. Then he spoke at length about himself. He had been in Sintra again, in Colares with his old friend Carvalhosa; and how often he had thought of the wonderful day he had spent with Carlos and Cruges in Seteais! Sintra had been divinely beautiful, but he'd had a bit of a cold. And despite the wise and erudite company of Carvalhosa, and despite the great musical gifts of Carvalhosa's wife, Julinha (who was like a sister to him), he had grown bored. He must be getting old.

"You do seem a little downcast," said Carlos. "You've lost your customary golden glow."

The poet shrugged.

"The gospels put it very clearly ... or is it the Old Testament, no, it's St. Paul ... St. Paul or perhaps St. Augustine. Anyway, it doesn't matter who it was who said it, but one of those holy books declares that this world is but a vale of tears."

"In which people laugh a great deal," said Carlos brightly.

The poet gave another shrug. Tears or laughter, what did it matter? It was all feeling, it was all living! He had said as much the night before at the Cohens.

And suddenly, stopping in the middle of the street, clasping Carlos' arm, he said: "Speaking of the Cohens, tell me something, my boy, in all frankness. You're a close friend of Ega's and, damn it, no one admires the lad's talent more than I do, but really, do you approve of him turning up again in Lisbon as soon as he found out about the Cohens' return, after all that's happened?"

Carlos assured the poet that Ega had only learned of the Cohens' arrival from the *Gazeta Ilustrada* a few hours after he himself had arrived in Lisbon. Besides, if people between whom there had been bitter fallings-out were incapable of living together in the same city, human societies would disintegrate.

Alencar did not respond, but continued to walk along beside Carlos, head bowed. Then he stopped again, frowning.

"There's another thing I wanted to ask you. Have you and Dâmaso had some kind of quarrel? I only ask because the other day, at the Cohens', he was making the most extraordinary claims and insinuations. I told him straight out: 'Dâmaso,' I said, 'Carlos da Maia, son of Pedro da Maia, is like a brother to me.' And Dâmaso fell silent, because he knows me and knows that in matters of loyalty and the heart, I am not to be trifled with."

Carlos said only:

"No, there's been no quarrel that I know of. I haven't even seen Dâmaso."

"It's true you know," Alencar went on, taking Carlos' arm, "I often thought of you while I was in Sintra. I even wrote a short little thing, which didn't turn out too badly at all, and I dedicated it to you. A simple sonnet, a landscape, a portrait of Sintra at sunset. I wanted to show those 'New Idea' people that, when necessary, we, too, can chisel out a bit of modern, realist verse. One moment, and I'll recite it to you, if I can remember it, that is. It's called: 'On the way to the Convento dos Capuchos.'"

They had stopped on the corner outside the Hotel Seixas, and the poet was just clearing his throat to begin his recitation when Ega suddenly appeared, coming up the hill, dressed as if for the country, with a lovely white rose in the buttonhole of his blue flannel jacket.

Alencar and he had not met since the Cohens' fateful soirée. And just as Ega still bore the poet a deep grudge, assuming him to be the inventor of that perfidious story about the "obscene letter," Alencar hated Ega because of his certainty that he had been the secret lover and beloved of his divine Raquel. Both men turned pale, and the handshake they exchanged was icy and reluctant; and the three of them stood in silence while a nervous Ega took an eternity to light his cigar from Carlos' match. But Ega, amidst a cloud of cigar smoke, was the first to speak, affecting an amiable superiority.

"You're looking very well, Alencar!"

The poet was equally amiable and equally haughty, smoothing his moustaches and saying:

"Oh, I'm not too bad. And what are you up to? When are you going to publish those *Memoirs*, my boy?"

"I'm waiting for the country to learn how to read."

"Well, you're in for a long wait. Ask your friend the Count de Gouvarinho to hurry things along, now that he's in charge of state education. Look, there he is, as earnest and empty as a column in the government gazette."

Alencar was pointing with his stick at the other side of the road, where the Count was walking very slowly along, talking to Cohen; and beside them, in white hat and white waistcoat, Dâmaso was looking around him, like a smiling, jubilant, rather paunchy conquistador surveying his domain. That plump, smug air of confident triumph irritated Carlos, and when Dâmaso stopped opposite him, on the other pavement, with his back to him, laughing ostentatiously at something the Count had said, Carlos could no longer contain himself and crossed the road.

The encounter was brief and cruel: he shook the Count's hand, bowed curtly to Cohen, and without even bothering to lower his voice, addressed Dâmaso coldly.

"Listen. If you continue to talk about me and about people of my acquaintance in the unseemly way in which you *have* been talking, I'll box your ears."

The Count intervened and placed himself between them.

"Maia, please, not here in the Chiado."

"Oh, don't worry, Gouvarinho," said Carlos, grave and serene. "I'm merely issuing this imbecile here with a warning."

"I . . . I don't want any trouble," stammered Dâmaso, ashen-faced, backing into a tobacconist's shop.

And Carlos calmly returned to his friends, having once again bowed to Cohen and shaken the Count's hand.

He looked only slightly pale; Ega was far more upset, for it seemed to him that there had been something intolerably provocative about the way in which Cohen had looked at him. Only Alencar remained oblivious, still discoursing on things literary, explaining to Ega what concessions could safely be made to Naturalism.

"I was just saying to Ega here that when it comes to landscape, one must imitate reality. One cannot describe a chestnut tree *a priori*, as one would a soul. And that is what I was trying to put into practice in the sonnet about Sintra that I dedicated to you, Carlos. Given that it's a landscape, it is, inevitably, realistic. I'll recite it to you now. I was just about to do so, when you appeared, Ega. You don't mind, do you?"

Mind? Not in the least, indeed, in order to hear the sonnet better, they withdrew into the much quieter Rua de São Francisco. There, taking one slow step at a time, the poet recited his eclogue in a soft murmur. It was in Sintra, at sunset; an Englishwoman, her hair loose, and dressed all in white, is riding on a donkey along a path that enjoys a view over the whole valley; the birds are singing sweetly, butterflies are fluttering about the honeysuckle; then the Englishwoman stops, dismounts, and looks up, entranced, at the sky, the trees, the quiet houses, and there, in the last three lines, came the "realistic note" of which Alencar was so proud.

> She looks at the sleeping flower, at the clouds above as they pass,
> While the smoke from the chimneys rises up to the heavens,
> And beside her, the donkey pensively crops the grass.

"There you have it, that note, that trace of naturalism. 'And beside her, the donkey pensively crops the grass.' That's the reality, the pensive donkey. For there is nothing in the world more pensive than a donkey. And it is these small things in Nature that one must notice. So you see, it is possible to be realistic, without tipping over into obscenity. What do you think of my little sonnet, eh?"

They both praised it lavishly—Carlos thinking regretfully that he had not completed Dâmaso's humiliation by beating him soundly with his stick; Ega thinking that, one of these afternoons in the Chiado, he would definitely have to slap Cohen's face. Since they were walking back to Ramalhete, Alencar, his gloom now dispersed, accompanied them along the Aterro. He talked constantly, describing his plan to write an historical novel, in which he wanted to depict the great figure of Afonso de Albuquerque, but from a more human, more intimate perspective. Afonso de Albuquerque in love; Afonso de Albuquerque alone at night, at the stern of his galleon, watching Ormuz burn, and kissing the petals of a dried flower, sobbing as he did so. Alencar found this sublime.

After supper, Carlos was getting dressed in order to go to Rua de São Francisco when Baptista came to tell him that Senhor Teles da Gama wished to speak to him urgently. Not wishing to receive him, there, in his shirtsleeves, Carlos asked him to wait in the scarlet and black study. He entered that room a moment later to find Teles da Gama admiring the exquisite examples of Dutch faience-ware.

"You've made this room really lovely," Teles da Gama exclaimed. "I adore porcelain. I must come back another time and spend more time looking at it all in the daylight. But today I'm in a hurry, for I've come on a mission. You can guess what it is, I'm sure."

Carlos could not.

And Teles da Gama, taking a step back, said with a gravity belied by his smile:

"I have come here to ask, on Dâmaso's behalf, if you intended to insult him when you spoke to him as you did today. That is all. My mission is merely that: to ask if your intention was to insult."

Carlos looked at him gravely:

"What! Did I intend to insult Dâmaso when I threatened to box his ears? Not at all. My sole intention was to box his ears!"

Teles da Gama bowed low.

"Exactly what I said to Dâmaso: that you clearly had no other intention. Anyway, my mission is at an end. You really have made this room lovely. Is that large plate there majolica?"

"No, it's an example of old Nevers. Have a closer look . . . it shows Thetis carrying Achilles' shield. It's a splendid piece and very rare. And have you seen this Delftware with the two yellow tulips. Absolutely charming!"

Teles da Gama looked slowly round at all these treasures, then picked up his hat from where he had left it on the sofa.

"Very lovely indeed! So your intention, then, was just to box his ears, but you had absolutely no intention of insulting him?"

"That's right, no intention of insulting him, but every intention of boxing his ears. Would you like a cigar?"

"No, thank you."

"A glass of cognac?"

"No. I never touch wine or spirits. Goodbye, then, my dear Maia."

"Goodbye, Teles."

The next day, on a brilliant July morning, Carlos, holding a bunch of keys, jumped out of his coupé beside the gate to Craft's house. Maria Eduarda was to arrive at ten o'clock, alone, in her hired carriage. The gardener, who had been given two days off, had gone to Vila Franca; there were not as yet any other servants in the house; the windows were closed. And the street and road were enveloped in one of those grave, airy, rural silences, in which one can hear only the sleepy buzz of horseflies.

Immediately beyond the gate lay a cool avenue of sweet-smelling acacias. To one side, through the trees, could be seen the pavilion with its red-painted wooden roof, a whim of Craft's, and which he had furnished in Japanese style. And beyond that stood the house, newly whitewashed, with balconied windows, green blinds, and a little front door in the middle, up three steps flanked by blue ceramic pots full of carnations.

It was a pleasure to Carlos, with a now unnecessary caution, merely to slip the key into the lock of that discreet dwelling. He opened the windows, and the bright light flooding in seemed to bring with it a far rarer sweetness and a greater joy than on other days, as if specially prepared by the good Lord to illumine the gladness of his heart. He went straight to the dining room to make sure that, on the table, already set for lunch, the flowers he had left the day before were still fresh. Then he went back to the coupé and took out the ice-chest he had brought from Lisbon, wrapped in flannel and bedded in sawdust. On the road, which had been silent up until then, a local girl rode past on her mare.

As soon as he had found a place for the ice, he heard the slow sound of a carriage aproaching. He went into the cretonne-lined study that opened onto the corridor and remained there, watching the door, out of sight of the coachman. A moment later, he saw Maria Eduarda come walking down the acacia avenue, tall and beautiful, dressed in black, and wearing a half-veil, as dense as a mask. Her little feet came up the three stone steps. He heard her anxious voice asking softly:

"*Êtes-vous là?*"

He showed himself, and they stood for an instant at the study door, passionately clasping hands, rendered dumb by emotion and amazement.

"What a beautiful morning!" she said at last, laughing, her face flushed.

"Yes, a beautiful morning, beautiful!" repeated Carlos, watching her, entranced.

With a sense of delicious weariness, Maria Eduarda sat down on a chair by the door, allowing the tumult in her heart to quiet down.

"Oh, it's very comfortable, really charming," she said, looking slowly round at the cretonne furnishings in the study, at the Turkish divan covered by a Bursa silk throw and at the glass-fronted cabinet full of books. "Yes, I will feel totally at home here."

"But I haven't even thanked you for coming," murmured Carlos, still gazing at her. "I haven't even kissed your hand."

Maria Eduarda began removing her veil and then her gloves, talking all the while about the journey. It had seemed so long and tiring. But what did it matter? Once she was settled into that cool little nest, she would never go back to Lisbon!

She threw her hat onto the divan and stood up, aglow with happiness.

"Let's have a look around the house. I'm longing to see all your friend's marvels! Is his name really 'Craft?' 'Craft' means energy!"

"But I haven't even kissed your hand!" said Carlos, smiling and supplicant.

She offered him her lips, and he folded her in his arms.

And Carlos, slowly kissing her eyes and hair, told her how happy he was and how he felt that she was much more "his" between the four walls of that house and in that garden, which sealed them off from the rest of the world.

Serious and grave, she allowed herself to be kissed.

"Is this real? Is it really real?"

Was it real? Carlos uttered an almost melancholy sigh.

"What can I say? I can only repeat those worn words of Hamlet's: 'Doubt that the sun doth move; doubt truth to be a liar; but never doubt I love.'"

Maria Eduarda, somewhat troubled, pulled slowly away from him.

"Let's go and see the house."

They began on the upper floor. The stairs were dark and ugly, but the rooms above were cheerful, with new rugs and pastel wallpaper, and views out over the river and the fields.

"Your room, of course," said Carlos, "will be downstairs, among all the fine furniture, but Rosa and Miss Sara would be splendidly at home here, don't you think?"

She walked through the rooms, attentive and observant, carefully assessing the size of wardrobes and testing the springiness of mattresses, eager to ensure that the people in her charge would be comfortably lodged. Occasionally, she even demanded some alteration. And it really was as if the man following her, loving and radiant, were merely some aged landlord.

"The room with two windows at the end of the corridor would be best for Rosa, but she can't possibly sleep in that vast rosewood bed."

"We'll change it!"

"Yes, it could be changed. And she needs a big room to play in when it's too hot to be outside. If it wasn't for that partition wall between the two small rooms . . ."

"We'll knock it down!"

He was gleefully rubbing his hands, perfectly prepared to have the whole house rebuilt; and in order to ensure the most perfect comfort for her people, she accepted all his suggested modifications.

They went down to the dining room. And confronted by the famous carved oak fireplace, flanked, in the manner of caryatids, by the two black Nubian figures with their glittering glass eyes, Maria Eduarda began to find Craft's taste eccentric, almost exotic. Carlos agreed that Craft did not perhaps have the correct taste of an Athenian. He was an Anglo-Saxon touched by the rays of the southern sun, but there was a great deal of talent in his eccentricity.

"Oh, but the view is wonderful!" she exclaimed, going over to the window.

By the balcony stood a clump of marguerites and beside that a vanilla plant perfumed the air. Beyond lay a carpet of rather long grass, already yellowing slightly in the July heat; and between two large shade trees stood a broad cork bench for whiling away the lazy siesta hours. A line of dense bushes seemed to close off the garden on that side, like a hedge. The hill sloped away to other smaller gardens, hidden houses and a factory chimney; and off in the distance, the river Tejo was a sparkling vitreous blue, silent and sun-filled, stretching as far as the hills on the other side, which were also blue in the shimmering brilliance of the summer sky.

"It's beautiful," she said.

"It's a paradise. Didn't I tell you? We must give the house a name. What shall we call it? Villa Marie? No. Château Rose? No, that's no good either! It sounds like a wine! It would be best to baptise it once and for all with the name we always used to call it. We used to call it the Toca—the Lair."

Maria Eduarda found the name most original. They should have it painted in red letters above the door.

"Yes, with, as our coat of arms, an animal in its lair," said Carlos, laughing. "A very selfish animal, very pleased with his happiness and his home, bearing the motto: 'Leave me alone!'"

But she had stopped, a lovely smile of surprise on her face, by the table ready laid and full of bowls of fruit, and with two chairs drawn up to it and wine glasses glinting among the flowers.

"It's like the wedding at Cana!"

And Carlos' eyes shone.

"Yes—our wedding!"

Maria Eduarda blushed deeply and looked away to pick first a strawberry and then a rose.

"What about a drop of champagne?" cried Carlos. "With ice perhaps? Because we have ice, we have everything. We lack for nothing, not even God's blessing. Go on, have a little drop of champagne!"

She accepted; they drank from the same glass; and again their lips met in a passionate kiss.

Carlos lit a cigarette, and they continued their tour of the house. She very much liked the tiled, English-style kitchen. In the corridor, she paused in front of a display of bullfighting paraphernalia—the black head of a bull, swords and banderillas, red silk capes that fell in smooth, elegant folds, and a yellow poster advertising a *corrida*, bearing the name Lagartijo. She thought all this enchanting, like a warm ray of festive Spanish sun.

However, when Carlos showed her the room that was to be hers, she found its air of strident, sensual luxury most disagreeable. The bedroom itself received its light from a larger room lined with tapestries whose fading woollen threads depicted the loves of Venus and Mars; a heavy wrought-iron Renaissance lamp was suspended above the arched doorway connecting the two rooms; and at that time of day, filled with sunlight, the bedroom glowed like the inside of a profaned temple, transformed into the lascivious inner sanctum of a seraglio. Walls and ceiling were lined with marigold-yellow brocade; a velvet rug in the same rich tones formed a surface of bright gold across which the naked, ardent feet of an amorous goddess might run, and the four-poster bed—raised up on a platform, with its yellow satin coverlet embroidered with golden flowers and with its solemn curtains in an equally yellow brocatelle— filled the whole bedroom, splendid and severe, a bed built for the large, voluptuous pleasures of some tragic passion from the days of Lucretia or Romeo. And it was there that Craft, peaceful and alone, a silk scarf tied about his head, snored away his seven hours of rest each night.

Maria Eduarda disliked these gaudy yellows, and was then shocked to notice a dark old painting looming blackly out of all that gold: one could discern only a decapitated head, livid and frozen in its own blood, on a copper dish. Even more eccentric was the enormous stuffed owl, perched in one corner on an oak column, its two round, baleful eyes fixed, in an air of sinister meditation, on that couch of love. Maria Eduarda thought it would be impossible to enjoy sweet dreams in such a room.

Carlos immediately grabbed the column and the owl and threw them out into the corridor, and suggested replacing the yellow brocade with cheerful pink satin.

"No, no, I'll get used to all these golds, but that picture, with the head and the blood is just dreadful!"

"On closer examination," said Carlos, "I believe it's our old friend John the Baptist."

To undo this gloomy impression, he led her into the main room, where Craft kept most of his treasures. Maria Eduarda, however, still unhappy, thought it had the cold, cluttered air of a museum.

"It's the sort of room you might visit in passing, but you certainly couldn't sit in here, talking."

"But this is just the raw material," exclaimed Carlos. "With all this you could make a really delightful drawing room. What else are our decorative talents for? Look at that armoire, what a centrepiece! A real gem!"

Filling almost the whole of the back wall, the famous armoire, Craft's "*pièce de résistance*," a carved wooden cabinet, splendid and sombre, dating from the age of the Hanseatic League, did have a kind of architectural majesty; at its base, four warriors, armed like Mars, flanked the doors, each of which depicted, in bas-relief, either the tents of an encampment or the assault on a city; the upper section was guarded at its four corners by the evangelists, Matthew, Mark, Luke, and John, stiff figures swathed in the usual wind-ruffled garments that always seem caught up in some prophetic gale; the cornice was crowned with an agricultural trophy comprising sheaves of wheat, scythes, bunches of grapes, and plough handles; and, on either side, in the shade of these emblems of work and abundance, leaned two fauns playing their panpipes in bucolic defiance of both heroes and saints.

"What do you think?" said Carlos. "What a piece of furniture, eh? It's a whole Renaissance poem, fauns and apostles, wars and georgics. What could one put inside such an armoire? If I had any letters from you, this is where I would deposit them, as if on a high altar."

She did not reply, smiling and wandering slowly among these things of the past, things possessed of a cold beauty, exhaling the vague sadness of a now defunct luxury: fine furniture from the Italian Renaissance, like marble palaces, inlaid with cornelian and agate, which lent a soft, jewel-like sheen to the black of ebony or to the satin of the pinker woods; wedding chests, as big as trunks, painted in purples and golds with the delicacy of miniatures, which once stored gifts from popes and princes; stately Spanish cabinets, adorned with burnished metal and red velvet, and with mysterious, chapel-like interiors, full of niches and tortoiseshell cloisters. Here and there, on the dark-green walls, there glowed a satin coverlet all embroidered with golden flowers and birds; elsewhere the severe tones of a fragment from an Oriental rug bearing verses from the Koran were juxtaposed with the gentle pastoral of a minuet danced in Cythera on the silk of an open fan.

Maria Eduarda had to sit down wearily on a Louis XV armchair of noble, ample proportions, intended for the majesty of hoop-skirts and upholstered with Beauvais tapestries, which still seemed to exhale a faint smell of rice powder.

Seeing María's amazement, Carlos was triumphant. Did she still consider it an extravagance, this purchase made in a moment of enthusiasm?

"No, there are some wonderful things here; it's just that I'm not sure I would dare to live a quiet, rural life in the midst of all these rarities."

"Oh, don't say that," exclaimed Carlos, laughing, "or I'll set fire to the whole lot!"

What pleased her most was the lovely faience-ware, a whole immortal, fragile art arranged on the marble tops of console tables. One in particular attracted her, a splendid Persian bowl bearing an unusual design, a line of black cypresses, each one sheltering a brightly coloured flower, which made one think of long sadnesses interspersed with brief smiles. Then there were the magnificent majolicas, in strident, clashing tones, full of famous personages, Charles V crossing the river Elbe, Alexander crowning Roxanne; the lovely grave naïveté of Nevers pottery; the Marseilles-ware on which a huge red rose opened as voluptuously as a nakedness revealed; the Derbyware with its golden lacework against the dark blue of a tropical sky; the Wedgewood, milky-white and pink, with the shifting colours of a shell seen under water . . .

"Just one more thing," cried Carlos, seeing that she was about to sit down again, "we have to greet the tutelary genius of the house!"

In the middle of the room, on a broad pedestal, sat a bronze Japanese idol, an ugly god, naked, bare, obese, goitered, cheerful, and wreathed in smiles, with a victorious belly—distended from a bout of indigestion brought on by consuming the whole universe—and two thin, drooping legs, as flaccid as the flesh of a dead foetus. And this monster was mounted triumphantly on a fabulous beast with human feet that bowed its submissive neck, betraying in its snout and its narrowed eyes all the unspoken resentment of its humiliation.

"And to think," said Carlos, "that entire generations came to kneel before this extraordinary creature, to pray to him, to kiss his navel, to offer him money, and to die for him."

"Isn't it more deserving of praise," said Maria Eduarda, "to love a monster?"

"Perhaps that's why you don't consider my love for you particularly praise-worthy."

They sat down by the window, on a long, low divan covered with cushions and surrounded by a white silk screen that created a snug corner of modern comfort among all those other luxurious objects from the past; and when she complained a little of the heat, Carlos opened the window. There was another large clump of marguerites outside that balcony too, and beyond it, in an old stone pot on the lawn, grew a cactus with a scarlet flower, and a walnut tree cast its own fine, cool shadow.

Maria Eduarda went over and leaned out of the window; Carlos followed her; and they stayed there together, silent, profoundly happy and filled by the sweetness of that solitude. A bird sang softly on the branch of the tree, then fell silent. She asked the name of a village they could see gleaming white in the sun on the distant blue hill. Carlos could not remember. Then, playfully, he plucked a marguerite in order to ask: "*Elle m'aime un peu, beaucoup . . .*" She snatched it from his hands.

"Why do you need to ask the flowers?"

"Because you still haven't told me as clearly and as absolutely as I want you to."

He put his arms around her waist, and they smiled at each other. Then Carlos, his eyes fixed on hers, said softly and imploringly: "We haven't yet seen the bathroom."

Maria Eduarda allowed herself to be led by him, his arm about her waist, through the drawing room, then across the room of tapestries, where Mars and Venus were still making love in the woods. The bathroom was off to one side and had a tiled floor, enlivened by an old red rug from Caramania. With his arms still around her, he placed on her neck a long slow kiss. She abandoned herself to him still more, her eyes closed, heavy and vanquished. They made their way into the warm, golden bedroom; Carlos, as he passed, unfastened the curtains covering the arched doorway, so that the room became steeped in the pale blonde light sifting in through the thin silk; and for an instant, Carlos and Maria Eduarda, finally alone, stood without touching, as if holding their breath, overwhelmed by the abundance of their happiness.

"Oh, that ghastly head!" she murmured.

Carlos pulled the coverlet off the bed and draped it over the sinister painting. Then all sound was extinguished, and among the trees, in the July heat, the house slept a long, long siesta.

Afonso da Maia's birthday fell on the following day, Sunday. Almost all of the friends of the house had dined at Ramalhete and drunk their coffee in Afonso's study, where the windows stood open. The night was warm and starry and utterly serene. Craft, Sequeira, and Taveira were strolling on the terrace, smoking. Sitting at one end of a sofa, Cruges was listening earnestly to Steinbroken, who was gravely telling him about the progress being made in Finnish music. And around Afonso, who was lounging, pipe in hand, in his old armchair, the talk was all of a visit to the country.

Over supper, Afonso had announced his intention of going to visit the ancient trees of Santa Olávia around the middle of the month; and a grand pilgrimage of friends to the banks of the Douro had immediately been arranged. Craft and Sequeira would be going with Afonso. The Marquis had promised to visit in August "in the melodious company," as he put it, of his friend Steinbroken. Dom Diogo was unsure, fearing the long journey and the damp of the countryside. And now they were trying to persuade Ega to go too, with Carlos, when Carlos had finally finished putting together the material for his book, which would keep him in Lisbon, "chained to his desk." But Ega was resisting. The country, he said, was fine for savages. Man, as he became more civilised, tended to withdraw from Nature; and progress, the Paradise on earth foreseen by Idealists, Ega conceived as a vast city covering the whole globe, made up entirely of houses and of stone, with here and there a small sacred wood planted with rosebushes, where people could go and pick posies to perfume the altar of Justice.

"And where would we get corn? Where would we get nice juicy fruit? Where would we get our vegetables?" asked Vilaça, smiling mischievously.

Did Vilaça really imagine, retorted Ega, that in a few centuries' time, we would still be eating vegetables? The vegetable habit was merely a remnant of man's coarse animality. In time, a truly civilised being would eat only artificial products, out of bottles and in pill form, manufactured in the state's own laboratories.

"The countryside," said Dom Diogo, gravely smoothing his moustaches, "does have some advantages for society: picnics, for example, donkey-rides, and games of croquet. Without the countryside there can be no society."

"Yes," snorted Ega, "as a kind of drawing room with a few trees in it, the countryside is just about acceptable."

Leaning back in an armchair, languidly smoking, Carlos was smiling to himself. He had been like that all through supper, smiling benignly at everyone, with an air of luminosity about him, a delicious lassitude. The Marquis, who, having spoken to him twice and been met with the same radiant abstractedness, finally lost his temper:

"Oh, for God's sake, man, speak, say something! You have the most extraordinary look about you today, like some over-pious churchgoer who has just swallowed the Host!"

Everyone turned their sympathetic attention on Carlos. Vilaça thought he had a better colour and looked happier; Dom Diogo, with the air of one who knows and sensing that a woman was involved, envied him his youth and vigour. And Afonso, refilling his pipe, merely gazed fondly at his grandson.

Carlos immediately stood up, anxious to escape this affectionate scrutiny.

"You're right," he said, stretching slightly, "I have felt rather languid and lethargic today. It's the onset of summer. But I need to buck myself up a bit. Do you fancy a game of billiards, Marquis?"

"Of course, if that will bring you back to life."

They left, and Ega followed. As soon as they were out in the corridor, the Marquis stopped, as if remembering something, and asked point-blank if Ega had any news of the Cohens. Had they met? Was it all over? For the Marquis, who was the soul of loyalty, there were no secrets. Ega told him that the romance had ended, and now Cohen, when they passed in the street, prudently lowered his eyes.

"I only ask," said the Marquis, "because I've seen Madame Cohen twice now."

"Where?" Ega exclaimed urgently.

"At Price's Circus, and always in the company of Dâmaso. The last time I

306

saw her was this week. And there she was with Dâmaso, and they seemed very friendly indeed, talking nineteen to the dozen. He came and sat with me for a while later on, but always with one eye on her. And she, with that very affected look of hers, kept her lorgnette trained on him the whole time. There was no doubt about it, there's definitely something going on between them. Poor old Cohen is doomed."

Ega turned pale and nervously fiddled with his moustache, then said:

"Dâmaso is a close friend of theirs, but he might be trying it on, that wouldn't surprise me in the least. Well, all I can say is, they deserve each other."

In the billiard room, while Carlos and the Marquis played a rather lacklustre game, Ega, very agitated, kept pacing up and down, chewing on his now extinguished cigar. He suddenly stopped in front of the Marquis and, with eyes flashing, said:

"When was the last time you saw that vile daughter of Israel at Price's Circus?"

"On Tuesday, I believe."

Ega resumed his sombre pacing.

At that moment, Baptista appeared at the door of the billiard room and, with the most subtle of glances, silently beckoned to Carlos. Carlos went over to him, surprised.

"There's a coachman at the door, sir," murmured Baptista. "He says he has a lady in his carriage who wishes to speak to you."

"What lady?"

Baptista shrugged. Carlos, still holding his cue, looked at him, terrified. A lady! It must be Maria Eduarda. Good God, what could have happened for her to come in a hired carriage to Ramalhete at past nine o'clock at night?

He sent Baptista to fetch him a hat, and in his frock-coat, without even bothering with an overcoat, he went to the door in a state of great anxiety. In the hall he met Eusèbiozinho, who had just arrived and was carefully wiping the dust from his boots with a handkerchief. Carlos didn't even speak to him. He ran out to the silent, mysterious, terrifying coupé which had drawn up outside the private entrance to his rooms.

He opened the cab door. From the depths of the old carriage, a black shape, its face covered by a lace mantilla, leaned earnestly forward and stammered: "It'll only take a moment. I need to speak to you!"

What a relief! It was the Countess! Carlos did not bother to rein in his anger and indignation.

"What the devil is all this about? What do you want?"

He went to slam the door shut, but she, in desperation, pushed it open again; and she did not hold back, but had her say right there in front of the coachman, who was quietly adjusting a buckle on the harness.

"What do I want? I want to know why you treat me like this? It will only take a moment. Get in! I need to talk!"

Carlos jumped into the carriage, furious.

"Take a turn down to the Aterro," he shouted to the coachman, "slowly!"

The ancient carriage set off down the hill, and, for a moment, in the darkness, each recoiling from the other on the narrow seat, they exchanged the same abrupt, angry words, above the noise of the rattling windows.

"What rank foolishness, what madness!"

"And whose fault is it, whose fault is it?"

Then, on the Rampa de Santos, the coupé rolled more quietly over the smooth paved surface. Carlos, then, regretting his earlier harshness, turned to her and almost in his old affectionate tone, gently reproved her for such imprudence. Wouldn't it have been better to write?

"What for?" she exclaimed. "Only to receive no reply? To have you ignore it, as if I were some importunate beggar asking you for alms!"

Feeling hot and uncomfortable, she removed the mantilla. As the coupé travelled noiselessly along beside the river, Carlos could hear her agitated, anxious breathing. But he said nothing, nor did he move, gripped by a terrible unease, glimpsing vaguely through the fogged window the sad shadow of the sleeping river and the blurred rigging of the *faluas*—the ferry boats that crossed the Tejo. The horses seemed to be falling asleep; and her complaints tumbled out, profound, biting, bitter.

"I ask you to come to Santa Isabel, and you don't come ... I write to you, and you don't reply ... I ask to have a frank talk with you, you don't turn up ... Nothing, not a note, not a word, not a sign ... Nothing but brutal, cruel contempt. I know I should never have come, but I had to! I wanted to know what I had done to you. What *is* going on? What have I done?"

Carlos was aware of her eyes, glittering beneath a mist of repressed tears, pleading and eager for him to look at her. Lacking the courage even to do that, he could only mutter painfully:

"Really, my dear ... Things speak for themselves, explanations are hardly necessary."

"But they are! I need to know if this is just some passing mood, if you're simply annoyed with me about something, or if it's final, the end!"

He shifted awkwardly in his seat, unable to find a gentle, even affectionate way of telling her that all his desire for her had died. Finally, he said that, no, he wasn't annoyed with her. His feelings had always been more elevated than that, and he would hardly be so frivolous as to sulk.

"So it's the end, then?"

"No, not that either. It's not an absolute break, not a permanent break, no."

"So you *are* annoyed with me. But why?"

Carlos did not reply. In despair, she shook his arm.

"Say something! Say something, for the love of God! Don't be such a coward, at least have the courage to tell me what it is!"

Yes, she was right. It *was* cowardice on his part; it was undignified to blunder on like that, hidden in the shadows, stammering out wretched lies. He tried to be clear, to be strong.

"I simply felt that our relationship should change ..."

Again he hesitated. Conscious of the agonies the trembling woman beside him was going through, the truth faded on his lips.

"I mean that it should change in the sense that we might be able to transform a passionate caprice, which could never last, into a pleasant, nobler form of friendship ..."

And gradually, above the gentle rumble of the wheels, his words became easy, clever, persuasive. Where would this relationship lead? Only to the usual denouement, when, one day, everything was discovered, and their fine romance collapsed in scandal and shame; or else, after long years of meetings in secret, their relationship would take on, instead, the banality of a quasi-conjugal union, bereft of spark or interest. It was clear, moreover, that if they continued meeting here, in Sintra, or in other places, Lisbon's narrow, inquisitive, gossip-ridden society would soon notice their fondness for each other. And was there anything worse, for anyone with pride and delicacy of soul, than a love affair about which the whole world knows, even the city's coachmen? No, there was not. Good sense, good taste even, indicated the need for a separation. Later on, she would be grateful to him. True, this first interruption of a very pleasant habit would be painful, and he himself was certainly not enjoying it, but that is why he had not had the courage to write to her. However, they must be strong and not see each other, at least for a few months. Then, gradually, what had started as a frail whim, filled with anxieties, would become a good friendship, solid and enduring.

He stopped talking, and, in the silence, he was aware that she was softly weeping, hunched in one corner of the carriage, like a wretched, half-dead thing, her veil clasped to her.

It was almost unbearable. She was not sobbing loudly, but gently, a slow weeping that seemed as if it would never end. And all Carlos could find to say were the trite, insipid words: "This is madness, madness!"

They were passing along by the houses opposite the gasworks. A tram passed, all lit up, carrying various ladies wearing light-coloured outfits. On that starry summer night, people were out strolling beneath the trees. She continued to cry.

That slow, sad, continual lament began to tug at his emotions, and, at the same time, he almost hated her for not holding back those endless tears lacerating his heart. And there he had been in his armchair in Ramalhete, feeling so easy and relaxed, smiling at everything around him and enjoying a delicious state of lassitude!

He took her hand to try and calm her, pitying her, but impatient too.

"Really, there's no need for this. It's absurd. It's for your own good."

She stirred slightly, wiped her eyes and blew her nose mournfully, all the while still sobbing. Then, suddenly, in a fit of passion, she threw her arms about his neck, clinging desperately to him, crushing him to her breast.

"Oh, don't leave me, my love, don't leave me! If you only knew . . . You're the only joy I have in my life . . . I'll die, I'll kill myself. What did I do to you? No one knows about our love. And what if they did! I would sacrifice everything for you, life, honour, everything!"

She was making his face wet with what remained of her tears, and he let himself succumb to the feeling of that warm, uncorseted, seemingly naked body climbing onto his lap and cleaving to him, in a furious desire to possess him again, with greedy, frantic kisses that took his breath away . . . Suddenly, the carriage stopped, and, for a moment, they remained like that, Carlos motionless, and she pressed against him, panting.

The carriage still did not move. Carlos freed one arm, wound down the window, and saw that they were outside Ramalhete. The man, obeying the orders he had been given, had taken a slow turn along the Aterro, come up the hill and returned to the house. Carlos was tempted momentarily to get out and put an end to that long torment there and then, but this seemed horribly cruel. In desperation, hating her, he shouted up to the coachman:

"Once more down to the Aterro, and keep moving!"

The carriage turned wearily round in the narrow street and set off again; once more the cobblestones made the windows rattle; once more, more slowly this time, they went down the Rampa de Santos.

She had resumed her kisses, but they had lost the flame which, for an instant, had rendered them almost irresistible. Now Carlos felt only fatigue, an infinite desire to go back to his room, to the repose from which she had wrenched him in order to torture him with these recriminations, this tearful passion. And suddenly, while the Countess was babbling idiotically and still hanging about his neck, he saw surfacing in his soul, bright and resplendent, the image of Maria Eduarda, who, at that hour, would be spending a quiet evening in her red-upholstered drawing room, trusting in him, thinking of him, remembering the pleasures and joys of the previous day, when the Toca—the Lair—full of their love, slept white among the trees. He felt only disgust for the Countess then, and, brutally, pitilessly, pushed her away from him, into the other corner of the carriage.

"Stop it! This is absurd. Our relationship is over. We have nothing more to say to each other!"

She sat for a moment as if stunned. Then she shuddered, gave a brief, nervous laugh, and started frantically pushing him away too, bruising his arm.

"Fine then, go, leave me! Go to that other woman, the Brazilian! I know her. She's nothing but an adventuress with a bankrupt husband, and she needs someone to pay her dressmakers' bills!"

He turned on her with clenched fists, as if he were about to beat her with them; and in the dark carriage, with its faint smell of verbena, the eyes of both, even though they could not see each other, flashed with hatred. Carlos beat furiously on the window. The carriage did not stop. And the Countess, on the other side, was desperately trying to open her window, hurting her fingers in the process.

"Get out!" she said breathlessly. "I can't bear to be here by your side! I can't bear it! Driver! Driver!"

The rackety old carriage stopped. Carlos jumped out, slammed the door shut and without a word, without even tipping his hat, turned and strode back to Ramalhete, still trembling and full of vengeful ideas, in the peace of the starry night.

: XIV :

IT WAS A SATURDAY when Afonso da Maia left for Santa Olávia. Earlier that same day, Maria Eduarda, who had chosen it as being particularly auspicious, had moved into Olivais. And Carlos, returning from Santa Apolónia station, where he had gone with Ega to see his grandfather off, was saying cheerfully:

"So here we are left all alone to roast in this 'city of marble' and of rubbish."

"Rather that," retorted Ega, "than have to walk around in white shoes in the dust of Sintra, thinking deep thoughts."

However, when Carlos returned to Ramalhete on Sunday evening, Baptista announced that Senhor Ega had just that moment departed for Sintra, taking with him only a few books and some hair-brushes wrapped in newspaper. Senhor Ega had written Carlos a letter and announced to Baptista: "I'm going out to pasture."

The letter, written in pencil on a large sheet of coarse paper, read as follows:

I was suddenly assailed, my friend, along with a horror of the dusty air of Lisbon, by an infinite longing for Nature and for greenery. The little that still remains of the animal in my ultra-civilised being urgently needs to roll around on the grass, to imbibe water from streams and fall asleep perched among the branches of a chestnut tree. Please have the ever-solicitous Baptista send on to me tomorrow, by omnibus, the suitcase with which I did not wish to overburden Mulato's carriage. I will only be away for a few days. Time enough to converse a while with the Absolute, high up in the Convento dos Capuchos, and to see what the forget-me-nots are doing near the dear little Fountain of Lovers.

"Pedant!" snorted Carlos, angry that Ega should have so ungratefully abandoned him to solitude.

And throwing down the letter, he said:

"Baptista, Senhor Ega says that we should send him a box of cigars, 'Imperiales,' he says. Send him some 'Flor de Cuba' instead, 'Imperiales' are positively poisonous. The wretch doesn't know the first thing about cigars!"

After supper, Carlos skimmed *Le Figaro*, leafed through a volume by Byron, played a solitary game of billiards, whistled a few *malagueñas* on the terrace, and ended up going out and heading aimlessly off in the direction of the Aterro. Ramalhete, silent and dull and open to the heat of the night, made him feel sad. Walking along, smoking, he unwittingly found himself in Rua de São Francisco. Maria Eduarda's windows were also open and dark. He went up to Cruges' apartment. He was not at home.

Still cursing Ega, he went into the Grémio. He met Taveira, who was standing with his overcoat draped over his shoulders and reading the latest news. There was nothing much of note happening in old Europe, a few nihilists had been hanged, that was all; and he, Taveira, was off to Price's Circus.

"Come with me, Carlos! There's this very pretty woman who gets into a tank of water with snakes and crocodiles! I adore women who perform with animals. This one's a bit difficult, mind, because she's got a pimp, but I've written to her a couple of times, and she gives me the eye from inside the tank."

He dragged Carlos along with him, and as they walked down the Chiado, he immediately asked if he had received news of Dâmaso. Had he seen that "prince among men" recently? Well, he was going around telling everyone that after the incident in the Chiado, Maia had sent him, via a friend, the most humble and cowardly of excuses. God, he was a terrible man! He had the appearance, interior, and nature of a rubber ball! However hard you threw him at the ground, he would always bounce triumphantly back.

"He's a treacherous creature, and you need to watch him like a hawk."

Carlos shrugged and laughed.

"No, really," said Taveira very seriously. "I know my Dâmaso. When he and I had that fight in Lola Gorda's house, he behaved like a complete coward at the time, but afterwards he made things very awkward for me indeed. He's capable of anything. The night before last, I was dining at Silva's, and he came and sat next to me for a while and immediately started making insinuations about you and issuing threats too."

"Threats? What kind of threats?"

"He says you fancy yourself as a swordsman and a daredevil, but that you're about to meet someone who will teach you a lesson, that a monumental scandal is brewing, and that he wouldn't be surprised if you were found quite soon with a bullet in your head."

"A bullet?"

"That's what he said. You laugh, but I know him. If I were you, I'd go to Dâmaso and say: 'My dear Dâmaso, my prince, I would like you to know that, from now on, whenever anything in the least unpleasant happens to me, I will come here and break one of your ribs—be warned!'"

They had reached Price's Circus. It was filled to bursting with a jolly, gaping, Sunday crowd, right up to the benches at the back where young men in shirt-sleeves sat drinking from litre bottles of wine; loud, coarse guffaws greeted the antics of the clown, his face daubed in red and white, as he touched the little feet of a young woman on horseback and then licked his fingers, rolling

313

his eyes, as if he could taste honey. Mounted on a broad golden saddle-blanket, atop a white horse champing at the bit, the scrawny grave-faced girl, with flowers in her hair, was led slowly round the ring by a groom; and the foolish drooling clown followed, his hands pressed to his heart, like a besotted pleading suitor, languidly swaying his hips inside a vast pair of spangled pantaloons. One of the other members of the company, wearing gold-striped trousers, was pushing him away, as if he were jealous; and the clown fell backwards onto his bottom with a great crash that provoked the laughter of the children and a drum roll from the orchestra. The heat was suffocating, and the cigar smoke that rose constantly into the air created a kind of mist around the long, tremulous gas jets. Carlos could not bear it and left at once.

"At least wait to see the lady with the crocodiles," Taveira shouted after him.

"No, I can't, the stink in here will kill me."

At the door, however, he ran into the open arms of Alencar, who was just arriving in the company of a tall, elderly, white-bearded gentleman, dressed in heavy mourning. The poet was astonished to see Carlos there. He had assumed that he would be in Santa Olávia! He had seen news to this effect in the papers.

"No," said Carlos, "my grandfather left for Santa Olávia yesterday. I'm not yet in the mood to go and commune with Nature."

Alencar laughed, slightly flushed, a tipsy glint in his sunken eyes. Beside him, the ancient, bearded gentleman was gravely drawing on his black gloves.

"With me it's quite the contrary," exclaimed the poet. "I could do with a good dose of pantheism—ah, fair Nature, the fields, the woods! So I might spoil myself with a little trip to Sintra next week. The Cohens are there. They've rented a very pretty little house, just opposite the Hotel Vítor."

The Cohens! Now Carlos understood Ega's sudden departure and his "longing for greenery."

"Listen," the poet said to him confidentially, tugging at his sleeve. "Do you know my friend here? He knew your father well, oh, the fun we had together... He wasn't anyone important, just a hirer-out of horses, but you know, in Portugal, especially in those days, things were very easy-going, and noblemen happily befriended muleteers. Now that I think of it, you must know him! He's Dâmaso's uncle!"

Carlos could not recall him.

"Guimarães, the uncle in Paris!"

"Oh, the communist!"

"Yes, he's a great republican, a man of humanitarian ideals, a friend of Gambetta, and he writes for *Rappel*. A most interesting man! He's here to see about some land he's inherited from his brother, that other uncle of Dâmaso's who died a few months ago. And he'll be staying for a while, I think. We dined together tonight, imbibed a little alcohol, and even talked about your father. Shall I introduce you?"

Carlos hesitated. Perhaps it would be better on another more private occasion, when they could smoke a quiet cigar together and talk about the past.

"Excellent. You'll like him. He knows his Victor Hugo and loathes the priesthood. A man of large ideas!"

The poet warmly clasped Carlos' two hands. Senhor Guimarães slightly raised his crêpe-swathed hat.

All the way back to Ramalhete, Carlos thought about his father and the past, so suddenly recalled and strangely sumoned up by the presence of that patriarch, that former hirer-out of horses, and with whom his father had had such fun. And this brought with it another idea, a persistent, tormenting one which, during recent days, had nagged at him, causing a sombre shudder of pain and sorrow to trouble his otherwise radiant happiness. Carlos was thinking about his grandfather.

Maria Eduarda and he had decided that they would leave for Italy at the end of October. In his most recent letter from Brazil, Castro Gomes had drily and pretentiously announced that he would "appear in Lisbon, along with the elegantly cold weather, about the middle of November," and so it was important that, by that date, they should be far away in the green beauties of Isola Bela, taking refuge in their love, which would protect them from the world like the walls of a cloister. All this seemed easy enough, and his heart deemed it almost legitimate, and something that brought glory to his life. There was, however, one sticking point—his grandfather.

Yes, his grandfather! He was leaving with Maria, embarking on the great adventure of his life, but, in doing so, he would be destroying forever Afonso's happiness and the noble peace that had brought such contentment to his old age. His grandfather was a man from another era, austere and pure, one of those strong souls who never weaken, and in Carlos' frank, virile, dramatic solution to indomitable feelings of love, he would see only libertinism. It meant nothing to him, the natural marriage of two souls, above and beyond all legal fictions; and he would never understand the subtle emotional ideology with which they, like all transgressors, tried to colour their errors. For Afonso, he would merely be a man taking another man's wife, stealing another man's daughter, scattering a family, destroying a home, and choosing to be stuck ever after in the mud of an illicit liaison: all the subtleties of passion, however fine, however strong, would burst like soap bubbles on the four fundamental ideas of Duty, Justice, Society, and Family—as hard as blocks of marble—on which he had based his life for almost a century. It would have for him all the horror of some ever-recurring fate! His son's wife had run away with a man, leaving behind her a corpse; his grandson was now running away too, and taking someone else's family with him; the history of his household would thus become a series of repeated adulteries, elopements, dispersals, each one provoked by the brutish goad of the flesh! All the hopes Afonso had placed in him would come to nothing, would lie dead in the mire! He would become, in his grandfather's anguished imagination, a permanent fugitive, a nonentity, having cut all the roots that bound him to his native land, having abandoned the work that would have elevated him in his own country—and instead seeking refuge in temporary hotels, speaking foreign tongues, surrounded by an equivocal family that would grow up around him like weeds around a ruin. A dark, implacable, and ever-present torment would consume his poor grandfather's final years! But what could he do? He had said as much to Ega. Life is like that. He was not hero or saint enough to make such a sacrifice. And, besides, what would lie at the root of his grandfather's sorrows? Pure prejudice, of course. And his happiness had rights too, rights that had their basis in Nature itself!

He reached the end of the Aterro. The silent river melted into the darkness. "The other man" would soon be sailing into that port from Brazil, a man who, in his letters, did not even think to send his love to his daughter! If only he would never return! If only some providential wave would carry him off. Everything then would be so easy, so perfect, so clear! What use to the world was that desiccated creature anyway? It would be like an empty sack slipping into the sea! Ah, if only he would die! And Carlos drifted off, enraptured, into a vision in which the image of Maria Eduarda called to him, waited for him, free, serene, smiling, and dressed in mourning.

When Carlos returned to his rooms at Ramalhete, Baptista, seeing him sink into his armchair with a weary, disconsolate sigh, said, with an amused little cough, as he turned up the oil-lamp:

"Without Senhor Ega here, it does all seem rather lonely."

"Yes, lonely and sad," muttered Carlos. "We need to shake off this gloom. As I told you, though, we might well go travelling this winter."

He had, it seemed, mentioned nothing of the sort to Baptista.

"Yes, we're going to Italy. Do you fancy going back there?"

Baptista considered the idea.

"I didn't manage to see the Pope last time, and I would rather like to see him before I die."

"I'm sure that can be arranged. You shall see the Pope."

After a silence, Baptista asked, with a glance in the mirror:

"One would have to wear a tailcoat to see the Pope, I suppose."

"Yes, I'd recommend a tailcoat. What you should wear, for such occasions, is the decoration of the Order of Christ. I'll see if I can get you one."

Baptista stood for a moment in amazement. Then, scarlet with embarrassment, he turned and said:

"That's very kind of you, sir. A lot of people have that decoration, some of whom perhaps deserve it rather less than I do. They say even barbers . . ."

"You're quite right," said Carlos gravely. "How stupid of me! What I need to get you is the Order of the Conception."

Now, every morning, Carlos travelled the dusty road to Olivais. In order to save his own horses from the heat, he went in the cab belonging to Mulato,

Ega's favourite coachman, who would put his horses in the old stables at the Toca and while away the hours visiting the local taverns until Carlos chose to return to Ramalhete.

Normally, after lunch, Maria Eduarda, hearing the carriage approaching along the silent road, would come to wait for Carlos at the door of the house, at the top of the steps, which were adorned with plant pots and shaded by a cool, pink awning. She always wore light-coloured dresses now; sometimes, in the old Spanish style, she wore a flower in her hair; the fresh, bracing country air had brought a warmer colour to the matte ivory of her face, and thus, simple and radiant, in the sun and the greenery, she dazzled Carlos each day with an unexpected and ever-growing charm. As he closed the gate, which creaked on its hinges, Carlos immediately felt himself wrapped in "an extraordinary feeling of moral ease" as he put it, in which his whole being moved more easily, more fluidly, with a permanent sense of harmony and sweetness. His first kiss, however, was always for Rosa, who ran down the avenue of acacias to meet him, her long wave of dark hair bobbing behind her, and with Niniche beside her, jumping and barking for joy. He would pick Rosa up. Maria Eduarda would smile at them from beneath the pink awning. Everything around them was luminous, peaceful, and somehow familiar.

Inside, the house now had a more delicate feel about it. The main drawing room had lost its stiff, museum air and no longer exuded the vague sadness of long-dead luxury; the flowers that Maria Eduarda placed in vases, a newspaper put down and forgotten, the wool she used in her tapestry work, the rustle of her cool dresses, had already imbued with a subtle, vital warmth and ease even the most straight-backed of Charles V cabinets with their burnished metal trimmings, and it was there that they would sit talking until it was time for Rosa's lessons.

At that hour, Miss Sara would appear, looking reserved and serious, always in black and with a silver horseshoe brooch fastening her rather mannish collar. The roses in her doll-like cheeks had returned, and she displayed a more than usual virginal shyness in the way she bowed her head—with its primly parted hair—and lowered her eyelids, her plump bosom imprisoned inside the severe bodice of her dress. She appeared very happy with the slow, quiet life of the village, although the dark groves of olive trees did not seem to her like the countryside. "It's so dry, so harsh," she would say, feeling an indefinable longing for England's moist green landscape, and for its vague, grey, misty skies.

The clock struck two, and in the room upstairs, Rosa's long lessons would begin. Carlos and Maria would then take refuge in the more secluded privacy of the Japanese pavilion, a folly that Craft—who loved Japan—had had built near the avenue of acacias, thus taking advantage of the shade and bucolic solitude of two old chestnut trees. Maria had grown fond of the place, and referred to it as her "thinking room." Made entirely of wood, it had just one small round window and a pointed Japanese roof against which the branches of the trees brushed, a roof so light that through it, in moments of silence, one could sometimes hear the birds chirruping. Craft had covered the floor with fine Indian rugs, and the whole was soberly decorated with a lacquered table and a few pieces of Japanese pottery; the ceiling was concealed behind a coverlet of yellow silk, which hung in festoons from the four corners like the canopy of some exotic tent; and the pavilion seemed to have been constructed solely in order to house a low, soft divan, more suited to the languors of a seraglio—deep enough to accommodate any amount of dreaming and broad enough for every kind of idleness.

They would enter the pavilion, Carlos carrying some book he had chosen in the presence of Miss Sara, and Maria Eduarda some embroidery or sewing to do. However, embroidery and book were immediately flung to the floor, and lips and arms met in a passionate, impetuous embrace. She would sit slowly down on the divan, and Carlos would kneel on a cushion, trembling and impatient after their enforced reserve in front of Rosa and Sara, and there he would stay, his arms about her waist, stammering out a thousand childish, ardent words in between the long kisses that left them both weak, their eyes closed in swooning sweetness. She wanted to know what he had done during the long, long night they had spent apart. And Carlos had nothing to recount except that he had thought about her and dreamed about her. Then a silence fell; above the light roof, the sparrows chirruped and the doves cooed; and Niniche, who always accompanied Carlos and Maria Eduarda, followed their murmurings and their silences from where she lay, curled up in one corner, one black, glittering eye peering suspiciously out from beneath her silvery locks.

Outside, on those hot, windless days, the parched garden, dusty green, slept beneath the motionless trees, beneath the weight of the sun. From the white house, through the closed shutters, came only the sleepy sound of the scales Rosa was playing on the piano. And in the pavilion, too, a replete, satisfied silence reigned, broken only by the occasional sweet, exhausted sigh from the silk cushions on the divan, or the sound of some unusually prolonged and ardent kiss. Niniche was the one who would drag them from that pleasurable torpor, having grown bored with her enforced stillness and with being shut up in all that hot wood and that sleepy atmosphere filled by now with an elusive, jasmine-tinged perfume.

Slowly, drawing her hands across her face, Maria Eduarda would get up, only to fall once more at Carlos' feet in an expression of sheer gratitude. Dear God, how difficult the moment of separation was for her! Why did it have to be like this? Given that they were husband and wife, it seemed so unnatural for her to spend all night on her own there, longing for him, and for him to sleep alone at Ramalhete without her caresses. And they lingered on, in a kind of dumb ecstasy, in which their moist eyes continued, in mutual gazing, the unsated kisses that had died on their weary lips. It was Niniche who would finally force them to leave, trotting impatiently from the door to the divan, growling and even threatening to bark.

Often, when they returned to the house, Maria Eduarda was seized by an anxiety. What would Miss Sara think of that long silent siesta of theirs, spent cloistered inside the pavilion, with the one window shut? Melanie, who had served Maria Eduarda since she was a girl, was a confidante; kindly, foolish Domingos would never say a word. But Miss Sara? Maria Eduarda smilingly confessed to Carlos that she felt slightly humiliated when, afterwards at the table, she met the Englishwoman's candid eyes beneath her smooth, virginal, neatly parted hair. Needless to say, if the good Miss Sara ever had the audacity to pass some muttered remark or ever so slightly to wrinkle her brow, she would immediately receive her ticket for the first Royal Mail boat back to Southampton! Rosa wouldn't mind, since she felt no affection for her. But Miss Sara was such a serious young woman and so admired her mistress! She would not like to lose the admiration of such a serious young lady. In the end, they decided that they would dismiss Miss Sara, royally paid, and replace her, later, in Italy, with a German governess, for whom they *would* be husband and wife, "*Monsieur et Madame.*"

Gradually, however, the desire for a more intimate, more complete happiness grew inside them. Those brief hours on the divan, with the birds singing above them, with the sun-filled garden and everything around them awake and alive, were no longer enough for them; they yearned for the larger contentment of a whole night, when their arms could entwine without the obstruction of clothes, and when everything else—fields, people, light—was all asleep. And nothing could be easier! The room of tapestries that led into Maria Eduarda's room opened onto the garden through some French windows; the governess and the servants went up to their rooms at ten o'clock; the house would be sound asleep; Carlos had a key to the gate; and the one dog, Niniche, was the loyal confidante of their kisses.

Maria Eduarda wanted that night as ardently as he did. One evening, at dusk, returning from a cool walk across the fields together, they both tried the duplicate key—which Carlos had already promised to have gilded—and he was surprised to notice that the old gate, which used to creak so abominably, now moved on its hinges in oiled silence.

He came that same night, having left Mulato and his calèche in the village, so that he could be driven back at dawn, Mulato being a very discreet —and very well-paid—coachman. Not a single star shone in the heavy, sultry sky, and above the river there was the occasional silent flash of lightning. Keeping unnecessarily close to the wall, Carlos, with the long-desired moment of possession so nearly within reach, was filled by a kind of anxious melancholy which almost made him feel like turning back. He was practically trembling as he opened the gate and, after taking only a few steps, he stopped when he heard Niniche's furious barking. Then silence fell again, and in the corner window that gave onto the garden, a comforting light appeared. He found Maria Eduarda, wearing a lace peignoir and standing by the French windows, almost suffocating Niniche in her arms to keep her from growling. Despite Maria Eduarda's nervous state and her impatience to have him by her side, she did not want to go in at once, and so they stayed for a moment sitting on the steps, together with Niniche, who had calmed down now and kept licking Carlos. Everything around them was like an infinite ink stain; only in the distance, lost and faint, did the occasional tremulous light on the mast of a ship emerge out of the gloom. Maria, sitting close to Carlos, as if seeking refuge in him, gave a long sigh, and her eyes peered anxiously into that silent blackness, where the familiar trees and the whole garden seemed to be losing reality, as they vanished and dissolved into the shadows.

"Why don't we leave for Italy now?" she asked suddenly, taking Carlos' hand in hers. "If that's what we're going to do anyway, why not now? Then we wouldn't have to put up with all these secrets, all these worries."

"What worries, my love? We're as safe here as in Italy or in China. But we can leave sooner if that's what you want. Just name a day!"

She did not respond, laying her head gently on his shoulder. He went on, more hesitantly:

"Of course, as you know, I would have to go to Santa Olávia first, to see my grandfather."

Maria Eduarda's eyes were once more staring into the darkness, as if she were receiving from it some premonition of a future in which everything would be equally confused and dark.

"You have Santa Olávia, you have your grandfather, you have your friends . . . I have no one!"

Carlos held her to him, touched by her words.

"How can you say to me that you have no one! But I won't speak of injustice or even of ingratitude. It's simply nerves, and what the English might call 'an inexact use of terminology.'"

She remained nestled against Carlos, as if too weak to move.

"I don't know why, but I'd like to die."

A long flash of lightning lit up the river. Maria was afraid, and so they went inside to the bedroom. The light from the candles in the candelabra, striking the yellow damasks and satins, filled the warm faintly perfumed air with the ardent splendour of a temple; and the linen and lace of the bedclothes, already drawn back, lent the chaste whiteness of fresh snow to all that amorous, flame-coloured luxury. Outside, over towards the river, a slow peal of thunder rumbled across the sky. But Maria could not hear it now, folded in Carlos' arms. She had never desired him, never adored him so ardently! Her urgent kisses seemed to go beyond his flesh, to pierce him through, as if wanting to absorb both will and soul, and all night, among the radiant brocades, with her hair loose, and divine in her nakedness, she really did seem to him like the goddess he had always imagined, bearing him away at last, clasped to her immortal bosom, and hovering with him high above on clouds of gold, in a celebration of love.

When he left at dawn, it was raining. He found Mulato asleep in a tavern, dead drunk. He had to bundle him into the carriage and then—wrapped in a blanket lent to him by the innkeeper—drive back to Ramalhete himself, drenched and singing and splendidly happy.

Some days later, when he was walking with Maria Eduarda near the Toca, Carlos noticed a cottage by the roadside, with a "To Let" sign in the window; it immediately occurred to him to rent it, in order to avoid that unpleasant dawn departure with a drunk and sleepy Mulato wrecking his cab by driving too fast over the potholed road back to Lisbon. They visited it and found a large room, which, once furnished with carpet and curtains, could be turned into a comfortable refuge. He rented it on the spot, and Baptista arrived the following day in a cart with various bits of furniture to adorn the new nest. Maria said almost sadly:

"Not another house!"

"This one," promised Carlos laughing, "will be the last one! No, the next to last! We still have another one to come, *our* house, the real one, far away, who knows where."

They began meeting every night. Smoking his cigar, Carlos would leave the Toca punctually at half past nine, and Domingos would go on ahead with a lantern, to close the gate behind him and remove the key. Carlos would then walk slowly back to his "cabin" where he was served by the son of Ramalhete's gardener. There was a loose rug on the old floor and, apart from that and the bed, there was only a table, two wicker chairs, and a sofa upholstered in a striped fabric; and Carlos whiled away the hours that separated him from Maria by writing to Santa Olávia and, above all, to Ega, who was still in Sintra.

He had received two letters from him, in which Dâmaso was almost his sole topic. Dâmaso turned up everywhere with Madame Cohen; Dâmaso had made a fool of himself in a donkey-race; Dâmaso had worn a veil on his hat while visiting Seteais; Dâmaso was a filthy swine; Dâmaso, sitting outside the Hotel Vítor, legs crossed, had mentioned Madame Cohen familiarly as "Raquel"; it was one's public moral duty to give Dâmaso a real thrashing! Carlos shrugged, finding such jealousy unworthy of Ega's heart. And to feel jealous over her, over that pretentious daughter of Israel, that craven, indolent woman, who had let herself be beaten with a cane by her own husband! "If," he wrote to Ega, "she really has passed from you to Dâmaso, then you must act just as you would if your cigar had fallen in the mud; you can't possibly pick it up and continue smoking it yourself; you should, therefore, simply allow the urchin who did pick it up to smoke it in peace; getting angry with the urchin or the cigar is quite simply imbecilic." Normally, though, when he replied, he wrote to Ega only of Olivais, the walks he took with Maria Eduarda, her conversation, her charm, her many superior qualities . . . He had almost nothing to say to his grandfather; in the ten or so lines he addressed to him, he would describe the heat, tell him not to overdo things, send greetings to his guests and messages from Vilaça, whom he never saw, even though he was in Lisbon.

When he had no letters to write, he would lie on the sofa with a book, his eyes fixed on the hands of the clock. At midnight, he would throw on a cloak and arm himself with a big stick. His footsteps, alone in the silence of the fields, rang out with all the melancholy of secrecy and guilt.

On one of these very hot nights, Carlos, worn out, fell asleep on the sofa, and only woke with a start when the clock on the wall was striking two. He was in despair! He would miss his night of love! And Maria Eduarda was sure to be waiting for him, worried and imagining all kinds of disasters! He took up his stick and set off, running, down the road. Then, easing open the garden gate, it occurred to him that Maria Eduarda might have gone to sleep; Niniche might bark; and so he trod more cautiously, more lightly, as he walked along the avenue of acacias. And suddenly, beside him, beneath the trees, in the grass, he heard a man's heavy breathing, intermingled with the sound of kisses. He froze, and his first impulse was to give these two animals, coiled upon the grass, vilely soiling his love's poetic retreat, a sound beating with his stick. In the darkness, however, he caught a glimpse of white skirt, and a swooning voice moaned: "Yes, yes!" It was the Englishwoman!

Good heavens, it was her, Miss Sara! Stunned, Carlos crept away, slipped out of the garden gate, gently closed it behind him and walked along the road a little, where he could hide by the wall, beneath the shadows cast by the branches of a beech tree. He was trembling with indignation. He must tell Maria Eduarda of this outrage at once! He could not allow Maria Eduarda to let that tainted woman remain by Rosa's side a moment longer, besmirching the innocence of her angel. Such calculated, methodical hypocrisy was horrifying. And she had never shown so much as a hint of such proclivities; why, only days before, he had seen the creature avert her eyes from an engraving in *Illustration française*—a shepherd and shepherdess in a bucolic grove, exchanging a chaste kiss! And now there she was lying on the grass, moaning!

On the dark road, near the gate, a cigarette glowed. A strong, heavily-built man passed by, a blanket about his shoulders. He looked like a farm labourer. Miss Sara had certainly not shown much taste! She, so clean and correct, with her primly parted hair, had been happy to accept anyone, however rough and dirty, as long as he was male. And for months, she had kept them in the dark about these two completely separate existences of hers! By day, the stern virgin, quick to blush, and with a copy of the Bible in her sewing basket, and by night, when the little girl was sleeping, and all her serious duties were over, the saint became a bitch in heat, who would put a shawl about her shoulders and lie down on the grass with whoever happened by. He couldn't wait to tell Ega!

He went back down the road, slowly opened the gate, and once again, made his way as quietly as he could along the avenue of acacias. Now he was uncertain whether to tell Maria Eduarda about this "outrage" or not. He could not help thinking that Maria was, after all, waiting for him with the sheets drawn back, in the silence of the sleeping house, and that he, too, was a surreptitious visitor, just like the man in the blanket. Obviously, it was quite different, the immeasurable difference between the divine and the bestial . . . And yet he feared wounding Maria Eduarda's scrupulous feelings by showing, in parallel to their own tender love-making amid the gold brocades, this other, ruder love—as secret and illegitimate as hers—and reducing it all to a mere tumble on the grass. It would be like showing her a reflection of her own guilt, slightly blurred and far cruder, but similar in outline, horribly similar. No, he would say nothing. And what of Rosa? In her dealings with Rosa, the woman would continue to be, as usual, the hard-working puritan, grave and orderly.

There was still a light shining in the French window; he threw a little loose earth at the glass, then tapped gently. Maria Eduarda appeared, half-asleep, pulling on her dressing-gown and tidying her loosened hair.

"Why are you so late?"

Carlos kissed her heavy, drowsy eyelids.

"I was reading and I very foolishly fell asleep. Then, when I arrived, I thought I heard footsteps in the garden and had a prowl around. It was just my imagination, though; there wasn't a soul to be seen."

"We should get a guard-dog," she murmured, yawning.

Sitting on the edge of the bed, her arms limp and heavy by her side, she smiled at her own laziness.

"Are you really so weary, my love? Would you like me to leave?"

She pulled him towards her warm perfumed breast.

"*Je veux que tu m'aimes beaucoup, beaucoup, et longtemps.*"

The next day, Carlos did not go to Lisbon, but appeared early at the Toca. Melanie, who was tidying the pavilion, told him that Madame, who was tired, had just had her cup of hot chocolate in bed. He went into the drawing room; opposite the open window, on the cork bench outside, Miss Sara was sitting in the shade of the trees, sewing.

"Good morning," Carlos said, going over to the window, curious to observe her reaction.

"Good morning, sir," she replied with a modest, timid air.

Carlos said how hot it was. Miss Sara found the heat quite bearable at that hour and the view of the river down below was most refreshing.

Last night in particular, insisted Carlos, lighting a cigarette, had been particularly sultry. He had hardly been able to sleep at all. Had she?

No, she had slept straight through. Carlos asked if she had had pleasant dreams.

"Oh yes, sir."

Oh yes! Only now she did not moan that "yes," she spoke it with modestly downcast eyes. And she looked so proper, so neatly ironed, as fresh as if she had never known a man! It really was extraordinary! And Carlos, with a twirl of his moustaches, thought that she must have very full white breasts.

Thus the summer passed in Olivais. At the beginning of September, Carlos received a letter from his grandfather informing him that Craft would be arriving in Lisbon on Saturday at the Hotel Central; and he went there early that same morning to hear all the news from Santa Olávia. He found Craft standing at a mirror, shaving. At one end of the sofa, Eusèbiozinho, who had arrived the night before from Sintra and was also staying at the hotel, was silently cleaning his nails with a penknife and was still dressed in heavy mourning.

Craft had found Santa Olávia enchanting. He could not comprehend how a sturdy countryman like Afonso could bear Rua de São Francisco de Paula and the cramped little garden at Ramalhete. He had had a wonderful time! Afonso, who was bursting with health, had lavished upon him a hospitality reminiscent of Abraham and the Bible. Sequeira had been in fine form too, eating so much that, after supper, he was good for nothing but to sit slumped and groaning in an armchair. He had met old Travassos there, who could never speak of his dear colleague Carlos' talent without his eyes filling with tears. And the Marquis had been equally splendid, embracing all the minor nobility of the area as if they were his cousins, and falling hopelessly in love with a boatman's wife. Otherwise, there had been superb suppers, a few rabbit-shoots, a fiesta, girls dancing outside the church, guitar music galore, corn to be husked—in short, it had been a perfect Portuguese idyll.

"But we'll talk about Santa Olávia properly later," said Craft, going back into his bedroom to shampoo his hair.

"And what about you?" Carlos asked, turning to Eusèbiozinho. "What's the news from Sintra? How's Ega?"

Eusèbiozinho sat up straight, put away his penknife and adjusted his glasses.

"Oh, he's installed at the Hotel Vítor, as witty as ever, of course—oh, and he's bought himself a donkey! And Dâmaso's there too, but I didn't see much of him, he spends all his time with the Cohens. So it's not been too bad, but fairly hot."

"Did you go there with that same prostitute, with Lola?"

Eusèbiozinho turned scarlet. Please! He had been staying as a respectable guest at the Hotel Vítor. Palma, however, had turned up there with a Portuguese girl. He owned a newspaper now, *The Devil's Trumpet.*

"*The Trumpet?*"

"Yes, *The Devil's Trumpet,*" said Eusèbiozinho. "It's a newspaper of jokes and gossip. It used to be known as *The Whistle,* but now Palma's taken it over and he's going to make it bigger and spice it up a bit."

"Meaning, I suppose," said Carlos, "that it will be just as vile and greasy as Palma himself."

Craft reappeared, drying his hair. And while he was dressing, he spoke of the tempting journey he had been planning while at Santa Olávia. Now that he no longer had the Toca and since his house near Oporto required a great deal of work, he was going to spend the winter in Egypt, travelling up the Nile, in spiritual communion with the ancient Pharaohs. Then he might move on to Baghdad to see the Euphrates and the ruined sites of Babylonia.

"Ah, that's why I saw that book on the table," cried Carlos, "about Nineveh and Babylonia. Gosh, so you like that kind of thing, do you? I have a horror of dead nations and civilisations. I'm only interested in Life."

"That's because you're a sensualist," said Craft. "And speaking of sensuality and Babylonia, do you want to join me for lunch at the Bragança? I'm meeting a fellow Englishman there, my man from the mines. But we have to go via Rua do Ouro, because I want first to drop in at the hovel my administrator inhabits. Anyway, we'd better go; it's midday already!"

They left Eusèbiozinho downstairs in the foyer, again adjusting his lugubrious dark-tinted glasses as he peered at the latest news telegrams. And as soon as they left the hotel, Craft linked arms with Carlos and told him that the serious thing he had to tell him about Santa Olávia was his grandfather's evident and profound displeasure at Carlos' failure, all summer, to make even the briefest of visits.

"Your grandfather didn't say anything to me about it, but I could tell he was terribly hurt. And there's really no excuse. It's only a few hours' away. Damn it, man, you know how he adores you. *Est modus in rebus.*"

"I know," murmured Carlos, "I should have gone. But what do you expect, my friend? Anyway, enough is enough, I must make the effort. Perhaps I'll go there next week with Ega."

"Yes, do, your grandfather would be so thrilled. Stay a few weeks."

"*Est modus in rebus.* I might manage a few days."

The agent's "hovel" was opposite a pawnshop. Carlos waited outside and was strolling slowly up and down past the shops, when he suddenly spotted Melanie coming out of the pawnshop accompanied by a matronly figure wearing a purple hat. Surprised, he crossed the road. She turned bright red, as if she had been caught out, and did not even give him time to ask what she was doing there; she immediately stammered out some excuse about Madame having given her permission to come into Lisbon and how she was visiting a friend of hers. An old calèche, drawn by two white horses, was stationed just outside. Melanie hurriedly jumped in, and the broken-down old carriage clattered off in the direction of Terreiro do Paço.

Astonished, Carlos watched her disappear. And Craft, who had returned and was watching too, recognised the old rattletrap as belonging to Torto in Olivais, and which he himself had used sometimes when he came "to disport himself in Lisbon."

"Was it someone from the Toca?" he asked.

"A maid," said Carlos, still troubled by Melanie's strange embarrassment.

And they had only gone a few steps, when Carlos stopped, lowered his voice and said:

"Listen, Craft, did Eusèbiozinho say anything to you about me?"

Craft admitted that as soon as Eusèbiozinho had entered the room, he had immediately begun making insinuations about Carlos' mysterious life in Olivais.

"But I shut him up," added Craft, "by telling him that I was so lacking in curiosity that I had never even wanted to read a history of Rome. Anyway, you *must* go to Santa Olávia."

Carlos spoke to Maria Eduarda that same night about the visit he owed his grandfather. She, grave-faced, told him that he must, of course, go, and regretted that she had kept him there so selfishly and for so long, far from the other people who loved him.

"But, my love, you won't be away for long, will you?"

"For two or three days at the most. And I'll bring my grandfather back with me. He's not doing anything there, and I'm not prepared to make another visit later on."

Maria Eduarda threw her arms about his neck and shyly, quietly, told him of her one great wish . . . which was to see Ramalhete! She wanted to see his rooms, the garden and all the other places where he had so often thought of her and despaired, believing her to be distant and unattainable.

"Would you like that? Although, it would have to be before your grandfather comes back. Can I?"

"I think it's a wonderful idea! There's just one danger. I might never let you leave again and keep you prisoner in my cave and eat you up."

"Oh, I wish you would!"

They arranged that she would go and dine at Ramalhete on the day of Carlos' departure for Santa Olávia. Later that night, the coupé would drop him at Santa Apolónia, and she would continue on to Olivais.

The visit took place that Saturday. Carlos arrived at Ramalhete very early, and his heart was beating with all the delicious excitement of a first meeting when he heard Maria Eduarda's carriage stop outside and heard her dark clothes brush against the cherry-red velvet that lined the discreet stairs up to his rooms. The kiss they exchanged in the hallway had the tender depths of a first kiss.

She went straight over to the dressing table to remove her hat and to tidy her hair. He continued to kiss her, his arms about her waist, and, cheek to cheek, they smiled at themselves in the mirror, captivated by their own shining youth. Then, impatient, curious, she walked through the rooms, scrutinising everything, even the bathroom; she read the titles of the books, sniffed at bottles of cologne, drew back the silk curtains around his bed. On a Louis XV chest of drawers was a silver salver full of photos that Carlos had forgotten to hide: the wife of the colonel of hussars in a riding outfit, Madame Rughel in a very low-cut dress, and still others. With a sad smile, she plunged her hands into this profusion of mementos. Carlos, laughing, begged her not to look at "his heart's mistakes."

"Why not?" Maria Eduarda asked seriously. She knew he had not descended from the clouds, pure as a seraph. There were always photographs in a man's past. Besides, she was sure that he had never loved these other women as he loved her.

"It's almost a profanation to speak of 'love' in relation to such chance affairs," murmured Carlos. "They are merely rooms in an inn where one sleeps only once."

Maria Eduarda, meanwhile, was studying the photograph of the colonel's wife. She looked very pretty! Was she French?

"No, from Vienna. The wife of one of my administrators, a businessman. They were quiet people; they lived in the country..."

"Ah, Viennese. They say that the women of Vienna have great charm."

Carlos took the photograph from her hand. Why talk about other women? There was only one woman in the whole wide world, and he was holding her now pressed to his heart.

They went on to explore the rest of the house, as far as the terrace. She particularly liked Afonso's study, with its damasks more suited to a prelate's chamber, its stern air of studious peace.

"I don't know why," she said softly, looking slowly round at the book-laden shelves and at the crucifix, "I don't know why, but your grandfather frightens me."

Carlos laughed. What nonsense! If his grandfather were to meet her, he would treat her with good, old-fashioned gallantry. His grandfather was a saint! And a fine-looking gentleman!

"Did he ever have any great passions?"

"I don't know, possibly. Although I think my grandfather has always been a puritan."

They went down into the garden, which she also liked for its quiet, unpretentious air and for the sweet sad rhythms of the little waterfall. They sat for a moment underneath the old cedar, at a rustic stone table carved with some now faded letters and an ancient date; the chirruping of the birds in the trees seemed to Maria Eduarda sweeter than that of any birds she had ever heard; and she picked some flowers to take with her as a relic.

They even went, just as they were, bareheaded, to see the stables; the doorkeeper stood with his hat in his hand, open-mouthed at the sight of this lady—so beautiful, so fair-skinned—the first he had ever known to enter Ramalhete! Maria Eduarda patted the horses, and paid particular attention to "Tunante" in gratitude for the many times he had brought Carlos to see her in Rua de São Francisco. Carlos saw in all these simple gestures the incomparable grace of a perfect wife.

They went back up Carlos' private stairs, which Maria Eduarda found "mysterious," lined with all that thick cherry-red velvet like the inside of a chest, and which muffled the sound of her skirts. Carlos swore that no other dress had ever passed through these doors, except once, when Ega had appeared, got up as a fishwife.

Then he left her in the room for a moment, to give orders to Baptista; when he returned, he found her sitting on the sofa, looking so cast down and so dispirited, that he grasped her hands anxiously.

"What is it, my love? Are you ill?"

She gave him a long look, her eyes shining with tears.

"I was just thinking of you leaving this lovely house, all your comforts, your peace, your friends, for my sake. It's so sad, it seems so wrong!"

Carlos knelt by her side, smiling at her scruples, telling her not to be silly, and kissing away her tears as they rolled down her cheeks. Did she really think she was worth less than the waterfall in the garden and a few old rugs?

"I'm only sorry that I'm sacrificing so little for you, my dear Maria, when you are sacrificing so much!"

She gave a wry shrug.

"Me!"

She ran her fingers through his hair and drew him gently to her, saying softly, as if talking to her own heart, quieting its doubts and uncertainties:

"No, you're right, nothing else matters in the world except our love, nothing! If our love is true and deep, nothing else really matters."

Her voice died away beneath Carlos' kisses, as he led her, still held in his embrace, to the bed, where so often he had yearned for her, as for an intangible goddess.

At five o'clock, they decided to have supper. The table had been set in the small room which Carlos had once wanted to hang with pearl and marigold-yellow satins. He had not yet done so, and the walls preserved their dark green paper. Carlos, however, had recently placed a portrait of his father there, a rather mediocre work, depicting a pale young man with large eyes, who was wearing chamois leather gloves and holding a riding crop.

Baptista served them, already dressed in his travelling clothes. The small round table resembled a basket of flowers; the champagne was cooling in the silver bucket; and, on the sideboard, the rice pudding bore Maria Eduarda's initials.

Such sweet touches made her smile tenderly. Then she noticed the portrait of Pedro da Maia and was intrigued; she sat contemplating the sad, faded face, which time had turned almost white, and in which his great, dark, languid eyes, the eyes of an Arab, seemed still sadder.

"Who is he?"

"He's my father."

She examined the painting more closely, holding up a candle to it. She could see no family resemblance. And while Carlos was uncorking, with due veneration, a bottle of old Chambertin, she turned to him very seriously and said:

"Do you know who you do resemble sometimes? It's extraordinary, but it's true. You look like my mother!"

Carlos laughed, delighted by a resemblance that not only drew them closer together, but that flattered him too.

"You're right to be flattered," she said, "Mama was very beautiful. Yes, there's something about your forehead and your nose ... but it's more to do with certain expressions, a particular smile, and the way you have, sometimes, of staring into space, lost in thought. I've often thought that."

Baptista came in carrying a Japanese tureen. And Carlos cheerily announced a supper *à la portugaise*. Monsieur Antoine, the French chef, had gone off to Santa Olávia with Afonso. Micaela, the household's other cook, had stayed behind, and Carlos thought her magnificent, for she kept up the tradition of convent cooking from the days of King João V.

"So to start with, my dear Maria, you have chicken soup, as eaten in the licentious convent of Odivelas, in the cell of that sweetest of sinners, Sister Paula, on nights of mystical union."

The supper was delightful. Whenever Baptista withdrew, they would clasp hands over the flowers. Carlos had never found her more beautiful, more perfect; her eyes seemed to radiate a still greater tenderness; in the simple rose adorning her bosom, he saw evidence of her exquisite good taste. And they were both filled by the same desire, to stay there forever in that young man's room, eating Portuguese suppers in the style of King João V and served by Baptista in his travelling coat.

"I'm almost tempted to miss that train!" Carlos said, as if asking for her approval.

"No, you must go. We mustn't be selfish. But be sure to send me a long telegram every day, because, as my Mama used to say, telegrams were invented solely for lovers who are far apart."

Then Carlos made some joke about his resemblance to her mother, and, bending down to stir the champagne bottle about in the ice bucket, he said:

"It's odd you've never mentioned it before, but then you've never talked to me about your mother."

Maria Eduarda's cheeks grew pink. She had never spoken about her mother because the subject had never arisen.

"Besides, there's nothing very interesting to tell," she added. "Mama was from Madeira, she had no fortune of her own, she got married ..."

"Did she marry in Paris?"

"No, she got married in Madeira to an Austrian who had gone there with his brother, who had tuberculosis. He was a very distinguished gentleman. He saw Mama, who was extremely pretty, they fell in love, *et voilà*."

She said all this without looking up from her plate, slowly slicing through a chicken wing.

"Aha," exclaimed Carlos, "if your father was Austrian, my love, then that makes you Austrian too, which might mean that you are one of those Viennese women who, according to you, have such great charm."

Yes, perhaps, in the eyes of the law, she was Austrian, but she had never known her father, and had always lived with her mother and spoken Portuguese, and, indeed, considered herself to be Portuguese. She had never even been to Austria and knew not a word of German.

"Did you have any brothers or sisters?"

"Yes, I had a little sister, who died when she was very young. But I can't remember her. I have a portrait of her in Paris . . . *so* pretty!"

At that moment, downstairs in the street, they heard a carriage approaching at a fast trot and coming to a sudden halt outside. Surprised, Carlos ran over to the window, clutching his napkin.

"It's Ega!" he cried. "The wretch must just have arrived back from Sintra."

Maria got anxiously to her feet. For an instant, they stood looking at each other, uncertain what to do. But Ega was like a brother to Carlos. He had been waiting for Ega to return from Sintra in order to take him to the Toca. It was better that the meeting should take place here, now, in a spontaneous, open, simple way.

"Baptista!" Carlos called, without further hesitation. "Tell Senhor Ega that I'm having supper and show him in."

Maria Eduarda had sat down, her face scarlet, quickly adjusting the pins in her hair, still slightly dishevelled, having been arranged somewhat hurriedly.

The door opened, and Ega stood in the doorway, startled and intimidated, wearing a white hat and carrying a white sunshade and a brown paper parcel in his hand.

"Maria Eduarda," said Carlos, "let me introduce you, at last, to my great friend Ega."

And to Ega he said simply:

"Maria Eduarda."

Ega hurried to put down the parcel in order to shake the hand that Maria Eduarda, blushing and smiling, was holding out to him. However, the brown paper parcel, only loosely tied together, came undone, and a fresh supply of special Sintra cheese pastries tumbled out onto the floral rug and promptly crumbled into nothing. All their embarrassment dissolved into happy laughter, as Ega stood, arms spread wide, desolately regarding the ruins of dessert.

"Have you dined already?" asked Carlos.

He had not. And he had already spotted on the table that national speciality, *ovos moles*, sweet soft eggs, a sight which delighted him, weary as he was of the awful cuisine at the Hotel Vítor. What ghastly food! Miserable dishes translated from French into Portuguese slang like the plays that were put on at the Teatro Ginásio.

"Dig in, then!" exclaimed Carlos. "Quick, Baptista! Bring back the chicken soup! We still have time. You know I'm going to Santa Olávia today, don't you?"

Of course he knew; he had received his letter, which is why he had come. But he couldn't dine like that, all covered in the dust from the road and wearing that bucolic jacket.

"Tell them to keep the chicken soup warm for me, Baptista! Tell them to keep everything, because I'm as hungry as an Arcadian shepherd!"

Baptista had served coffee. The lady's carriage, which would take them to Santa Apolónia, was already waiting at the door with the luggage. But Ega wanted to talk, he assured them that they had plenty of time and, to prove it, took out his watch, which had stopped. Then he declared that in the countryside one told the time by the sun, like the flowers and the birds.

"Are you staying in Lisbon?" asked Maria Eduarda.

"No, Senhora, only long enough to fulfil my duties as a citizen by walking up and down the Chiado a couple of times. Then I'm going straight back to the grass. Sintra is starting to get interesting, now that no one's there. Sintra, in the summer, full of the bourgeoisie, is like an idyll bespattered with grease stains."

Baptista was offering Carlos a glass of chartreuse and saying that he really should not delay unless, of course, he wanted to miss the train. Maria Eduarda immediately left the room to fetch her hat. And the two friends sat alone for a moment in silence while Carlos slowly lit a cigar.

"How long will you be away?" asked Ega at last.

"Three or four days. But don't you go back to Sintra until I return; we need to keep in contact. What the devil have you been up to there?"

Ega shrugged.

"I have drunk in the pure air, picked small flowers, and occasionally murmured: 'How lovely all this is!' etc."

Then, elbows on the table, spearing an olive with a toothpick, he added:

"Otherwise, nothing. Dâmaso is still there! Always at Madame Cohen's side, as I told you. It's as plain as day that there's nothing between them, it's just intended as an irritant to me. He's a real swine, that Dâmaso! The first excuse I get, I'll throttle him."

He tugged hard at his shirt cuffs, with an angry look on his sunburnt face.

"Naturally, I still talk to him, shake hands with him, call him 'my friend Dâmaso' and all that, but the first excuse I get ... The animal ought to be put down. It's a moral duty, a question of public hygiene and good taste, to do away with that ball of human slime."

"Who else was there?" asked Carlos.

"Who are you interested in? The Countess de Gouvarinho, but I only saw her once. She doesn't go out much, poor thing, now that she's in mourning."

"In mourning?"

"For you."

He fell silent. Maria Eduarda came in, with her veil down, and buttoning up her gloves. Then Carlos, with a resigned sigh, held out his arms to Baptista so that he could put on his light travelling jacket. Ega helped, asking him to send a filial embrace to Afonso and best wishes to plump Sequeira.

He went downstairs with them, still without his hat, and closed the carriage door for them, promising Maria Eduarda that he would visit the Toca as soon as Carlos returned from the rugged landscape of the Douro.

"Don't go back to Sintra until I return!" Carlos told him. "Micaela will take care of you!"

"All right, all right," said Ega. "Have a good journey. And meanwhile, Senhora, I remain your humble servant, and I will see you in Olivais."

The coupé set off. Ega went up to his room where another servant was preparing his bath. In the deserted dining room, among the flowers and the remnants of supper, the solitary candles continued to burn, highlighting, in the dark portrait, Pedro da Maia's pallor and the melancholy look in his eyes.

The following Saturday, at around two o'clock, Carlos and Ega, still at the lunch table, were finishing their cigars and talking about Santa Olávia. Carlos had arrived back in Lisbon at dawn, alone. His grandfather had decided to stay on in Santa Olávia with his ancient trees until the end of what was proving to be an exceptionally sunny, warm autumn.

Carlos had found him looking strong and cheerful, despite having been obliged by a touch of rheumatism to abandon his beloved cold-water baths. His grandfather's robust good health had been a salve to Carlos' heart, and his departure with Maria Eduarda for Italy in October seemed to him easier, less cruel. Besides, he had thought of a trick, as he was telling Ega, by which he could realise the supreme desire of his life without hurting his grandfather, without troubling the peace of his old age. It was simple enough, consisting, as it did, in him setting off on his own for Madrid, at the start of a "study trip" for which he had already primed his grandfather while he was in Santa Olávia. Maria Eduarda would stay on at the Toca for a month, after which time, she would take the steamboat to Bordeaux, where Carlos would meet her, and they could then set off for a happy, romantic existence perfumed by the flowers of Italy. In spring, he would return to Lisbon, leaving Maria Eduarda installed in their love-nest; and then, little by little, he would tell his grandfather about that relationship, to which he was bound by honour, and which would involve spending long months in another land that had now become the country of his heart. What could his grandfather do but accept the romance, whose less unpleasant aspects he would not see, a romance that would have the advantages of distance and the attenuating mist of passion. For Afonso, it would be merely a vague love affair about which he knew nothing and which had Italy as a backdrop. He might regret the fact that it took his grandson far away from him each year, and each year, he would console himself by thinking that such human idylls rarely last. Carlos was counting, too, on the generosity and benevolence that soften even the most rigid of souls when they are only a few steps from the grave. In short, he thought his plan an excellent one, and Ega heartily approved of it.

Then, more cheerfully, they talked about where he and Maria Eduarda should live out their love. Carlos still clung to the romantic notion of a cottage on the shores of a lake. Ega, however, disapproved of lakes. Looking out every day on the same smooth blue expanse of water seemed to him dangerous for the durability of such a passion. Living in the constant stillness of one unchanging landscape, two solitary lovers, he said—unless, of course, they were keen botanists or anglers—would find themselves forced to live exclusively on their desire for each other, and to draw from that desire all their ideas, sensations, occupations, jokes, and silences. And not even the most steadfast of feelings could withstand that! Two lovers, whose sole profession is to love each other, should seek out a city, a vast, chaotic, creative city, where, during the day, the man could enjoy clubs, conversation, museums, ideas and the smiles of other women, while the woman would have streets, shops, theatres and the attentions of other men; in that way, when they got together in the evening, not having spent the endless day merely observing each other and themselves, but, rather, bringing with them the strong vibration of the life they had lived that day, they would find a new and genuine charm in their cosy solitude and a constantly renewed savour in their repeated kisses.

"Now," Ega went on, standing up, "if I were to run away with a woman, I certainly wouldn't choose a lake, or Switzerland, or the mountains of Sicily, I would choose Paris, the Boulevard des Italiens, just around the corner from the Vaudeville, with a view from my window of the larger life, a step away from *Le Figaro*, from the Louvre, from philosophy and witty conversation. Anyway, there you have my doctrine! And here we have our friend Baptista with the post."

It was not the post, merely a card that Baptista was bringing in on a salver, and Baptista was clearly so troubled that he announced, unbidden, that "there was a man outside in the courtyard, in a carriage, waiting."

Carlos looked at the card and turned terribly pale. He sat there, as if stunned, turning it slowly around in his trembling fingers. Then, without saying a word, he threw it across the table to Ega.

"Good God," muttered Ega, astonished.

It was Castro Gomes!

Carlos sprang determinedly to his feet.

"Show him into the main drawing room!"

Baptista indicated the flannel jacket that Carlos had worn for lunch and asked discreetly if he would prefer to wear a frock-coat.

"Yes, bring me one now."

When they were alone, Ega and Carlos exchanged an anxious glance.

"Well, it's obviously not a challenge," said Ega nervously.

Carlos did not respond. He was examining the card again; the man was called Joaquim Álvares de Castro Gomes; underneath his name were the pencilled words "Hotel Bragança." Baptista returned with a frock-coat, and Carlos, slowly putting it on and buttoning it up, left the room without saying another word to Ega, who was standing by the table, foolishly wiping his hands on his napkin.

In the main drawing room, which was decorated with brocades in an autumnal shade of moss-green, Castro Gomes, one knee resting on the edge of the sofa, was scrutinising the splendid Constable portrait of the Countess de Runa, strong and beautiful in her red velvet riding habit. At the sound of Carlos' footsteps crossing the carpet, he turned, his white hat in his hand, smiling and apologising for staring so familiarly at that superb Constable. With a stiff gesture, Carlos, still very pale, motioned to him to take a seat. Bowing and smiling, Castro Gomes sat slowly down on the sofa. He wore a rosebud in the buttonhole of his very close-fitting frock-coat; his patent leather shoes gleamed beneath his linen gaiters; he had a gaunt, tanned face and a pointed black beard; his hair was growing thin along the parting; and even when he smiled he had an air of weary indifference.

"I have a fine Constable of my own in Paris," he said in a nonchalant drawl, his rolled *r*'s softened by his Brazilian accent. "But it's only a small landscape with two figures in it. He's not a painter I like that much, to be honest, but he lends tone to a collection. One has to have a Constable."

Carlos, sitting opposite him on a chair, his fists tightly clenched on his knees, was as still as a statue. And confronted by the other man's affable manner, an anguishing, lacerating idea crossed his mind, lending an irrepressible gleam of anger to his wide eyes which did not leave the other man for a moment—the idea that Castro Gomes might have arrived, disembarked, and gone straight to Olivais, where he had spent the night! He was, after all, her husband, he was young, he would have clasped her in his arms—*her*! And now there he was, with a flower in his buttonhole, coolly discussing Constable! Carlos' one desire, just then, was that the man should insult him.

Meanwhile, Castro Gomes amiably apologised for coming to his house like this, even though they had never met, and without, at the very least, leaving a note requesting an interview.

"The reason that brings me here, however, is so urgent that I arrived from Rio de Janeiro or, rather, from Lazareto, at ten o'clock this morning and came straight here! And tonight, if I can, I will be leaving for Madrid."

An infinite relief filled Carlos' heart. So he had not yet seen Maria Eduarda, nor had those dry lips touched hers! And he emerged at last from his statuesque immobility and attentively moved his chair closer.

Castro Gomes, having put down his hat, had produced from the inside pocket of his frock-coat a wallet bearing a large gold monogram, and he slowly went through the papers in the wallet, looking for a letter. Then, with the letter in his hand, he said very calmly:

"Just before I was about to leave Rio de Janeiro, I received this anonymous note. But don't go imagining that it was this letter that brought me so swiftly back across the Atlantic. That would be absurd. And I would like to assure you, too, that the letter's contents are a matter of complete indifference to me. Here you are. Will you read it, or shall I read it out to you?"

Carlos said in a constrained murmur:

"You read it."

Castro Gomes unfolded the piece of paper and turned it round and round in his fingers for a moment.

"As you see, it is an anonymous letter in all its horrid glory: cheap, blue, lined paper; vulgar writing; vulgar ink; vulgar smell; an entirely odious document. And this is what the writer has to say:

As a man who has had the honour of shaking your hand, sir—an honour I could well have dispensed with, frankly, anyway—*who has had the honour of shaking your hand and who appreciates your gentlemanly qualities, I feel it is my duty to warn you that your wife, in the full gaze of all Lisbon, has become the lover of a very well-known young man, Carlos Eduardo da Maia, who lives in a house in Janelas Verdes called Ramalhete. This "hero," who is very rich, has bought a house in Olivais for the express purpose of installing your wife in it, and he goes there every day, sometimes staying, to the general scandal of the neighbourhood, until dawn. Your honoured name, sir, is being dragged through the mud of Lisbon.*

"That is all the letter says, and I would only add, because I know it to be true, that everything he says is exact in every detail. You, Carlos da Maia, are, to the public knowledge of all Lisbon, the lover of this lady."

Carlos stood up very calmly. And opening his arms in acceptance of all his responsibilities, he said:

"I therefore have nothing to say to you, sir, except that I am at your disposal!"

A fleeting wave of colour enlivened Castro Gomes' sallow complexion. He slowly folded up the letter and, with equal slowness, put it back in his wallet. Then, smiling coldly, he said:

"Forgive me, but you know as well as I do, sir, that if this situation were to have a violent solution, I would not have come to your house in person to read you this letter. The case is entirely different."

Carlos fell back into his chair in amazement. The slow, mellifluous voice was becoming unbearable to him. A vague horror of what might come from those lips, which smiled with impertinent politeness, was almost making his poor heart burst. He felt a brutal desire to scream at this visitor: Either stop talking or kill me! If neither, then simply leave the room, where your presence is futile or indecent!

The other man smoothed his moustache and proceeded slowly, choosing his words with care and precision.

"The fact is this, sir. There are people in Lisbon who do not know me, but who do know that somewhere, at this hour, in Paris or in Brazil or in Hell itself, there exists a certain Castro Gomes who has a pretty wife, and that the wife of this Castro Gomes fellow has a lover in Lisbon. This is unpleasant, especially since it is not true. And you will understand, sir, that I prefer not to be burdened any longer than is necessary with the reputation of an 'unhappy husband,' given that I do not deserve it and cannot legally have it. That is why

I have come here to speak to you frankly, gentleman to gentleman, and to tell you, as it is my intention to tell others, that the lady is not my wife."

For a moment, Castro Gomes waited for Carlos to speak, but the latter remained dumb, only his eyes glittering anxiously in the dreadful pallor of his otherwise impenetrable face. Finally, with an effort, he bowed his head slightly, as if placidly accepting that revelation, which rendered all other words between them unnecessary and vain.

Castro Gomes shrugged with languid resignation, like someone who attributes everything to the malice of the Fates.

"It is merely one of life's little absurdities. You see how it is, I'm sure. It's an old, old story. I've been living with this lady for three years now, and when, last winter, I had to travel to Brazil, I brought her to Lisbon with me simply in order not to have to travel alone. We went to the Hotel Central. As you will perfectly well understand, I did not confide in the manager of the establishment. The lady arrived with me, slept with me, and was, therefore, as far as the hotel was concerned, my wife. She remained at the Hotel Central as Castro Gomes' wife; she later rented a house in Rua de São Francisco as Castro Gomes' wife; and, finally, it was as Castro Gomes' wife that she took a lover. She has passed herself off as Castro Gomes' wife even in circumstances that have proved particularly disagreeable to Castro Gomes. And who can blame her! There she was in possession of an excellent social position and an unspotted name, and it would have taken a more than average love of truth for her, as soon as she met someone else, to declare that both social position and name were only borrowed and that she was a mere Nobody—not a wife, but a mistress. And let's be fair, she wasn't morally obliged to give such explanations to the shopkeeper from whom she bought her butter or to the matron who rented her the house, nor, I think, to anyone, except perhaps to a paterfamilias who wanted to introduce her to his daughter, fresh out of a convent. Indeed, I am not a little to blame; in relatively delicate situations, I allowed her to use my name. For example, she used the name of Castro Gomes when she took on the English governess. The English are so very particular, especially that governess—such a serious girl. Anyway, this is all now water under the bridge. What matters is that I should officially remove from her the name that I lent her, and leave her with her own name, that of Madame MacGren."

Carlos got to his feet, ashen-faced. And with his hands gripping the back of the chair so hard that he almost tore the fabric, he said:

"I take it that is all?"

Castro Gomes bit his lip slightly at this brutal dismissal.

"Yes, that is all," he said, picking up his hat and getting very slowly to his feet. "I should just mention, so that you do not get any wrong ideas, that the lady is not some young girl whom I seduced and to whom I am refusing reparation. The child is not my daughter. I have known the mother for only three years. She came from the arms of some other man and passed into mine. I can say, without insult, that she was merely a woman for whose services I paid."

With those last words, he completed Carlos' humiliation. He was deliciously revenged. Carlos said nothing, but brusquely drew aside the door curtain. Faced with this new act of rudeness, which now revealed only mortification, Castro Gomes conducted himself with perfect aplomb; he bowed and smiled and murmured:

"I leave tonight for Madrid and take with me the regret that we only came to know each other under such disagreeable circumstances . . . disagreeable, that is, for me."

His light easy footsteps vanished into the hallway, with its rugs and wall-hangings. Then, below, a door banged shut, and a carriage rumbled off down the street.

Carlos was slumped in a chair by the door, his head in his hands. And of all the words that Castro Gomes had spoken, and which still echoed around him, mellifluous and slow, all that remained to him was the confused sense of something very beautiful and lofty and resplendent having suddenly fallen and shattered in the mud, leaving him horribly spattered. He was not in pain; his whole being simply stood aghast at this obscene end to a divine dream. He had passionately joined his soul to another noble and perfect soul, high up somewhere among clouds of gold; and suddenly a voice full of rolled *r*'s had passed over them like a breeze, and their two souls were hurled into a muddy puddle where they flailed and fought; and he found himself with a woman in his arms whom he did not know, and whose name was MacGren.

MacGren! She was Madame MacGren!

He got to his feet, fists clenched, and, with a feeling of terrible revulsion, his pride reared up at the ingenuousness of months spent timidly, tremulously, yearningly following that woman as if she were a star, a woman whose easy, naked body any man in Paris with a thousand francs in his pocket could have enjoyed on a sofa. It was too awful! And he remembered now, with a hot rush of shame, the almost religious feeling with which he used to enter the red rep interior of her apartment in Rua de São Francisco; the tender charm with which he would watch those hands, which he judged to be the purest hands on Earth, drawing the woollen threads through the canvas of her tapestry work, as if she were a modest, hard-working mother living quite apart from the world; the spiritual veneration that had kept him from so much as brushing the hem of her garment, which was, for him, like Our Lady's tunic whose stiff folds not even the roughest and most bestial of men would have dared besmirch, however slightly! What a fool he had been! What an imbecile! And all that time she must have been smiling to herself at this simple-minded provincial from the Douro! He felt ashamed now of the loving bouquets of flowers he had brought her, ashamed of having treated her so respectfully!

And it would have been so easy, from the first day he saw her in the Aterro, to have realised that the goddess who seemed to have descended from the clouds was none other than the Brazilian's mistress! But no, his absurd, romantic passion had placed between his eyes and all those flagrant and revealing facts one of those golden mists that makes even the most rugged of black mountains glitter and glow like a precious stone! Why else had she chosen to invite into the privacy of her home as her doctor the same man who had stared at her in the street, his face aflame with desire? Why, during their many long conversations, on those mornings in Rua de São Francisco, had she never talked about Paris, about her friends and about her home there? Why is it that, after two months, with no preparation, with none of those progressive proofs of love that grow and blossom like a flower, she had simply and eagerly abandoned herself to him as soon as he uttered the first "I love you"? Why had she accepted that furnished house as easily as she had accepted the flowers he brought her? And there were other tiny details too, which would not have escaped even the most innocent of men: enormous jewels, which revealed the vulgar luxury of a *cocotte*; the book on her bedside table, *Manual for the Interpretation of Dreams*; her overly familiar relationship with Melanie . . . And now even the ardour of her kisses seemed to him to have less to do with sincerity and passion than with a knowledge of the voluptuous arts! Fortunately, though, it was all over! The woman he had loved, along with all her seductive qualities, was dissolving in the air like a radiant, lubricious dream from which the Brazilian had so kindly woken him! This woman was merely Madame MacGren. His love, from the moment he saw her, had been like the very blood in his veins, and it was oozing away now through this incurable wound inflicted on his pride, a wound that would never heal!

Ega, still pale, appeared at the door.

"What happened?"

Carlos' anger exploded.

"The most extraordinary thing, Ega, the most abject, obscene thing!"

"Did the man ask you for money?"

"No, worse than that!"

Pacing furiously up and down, Carlos told Ega everything, holding nothing back, using the same crude words the other man had used, words, which, once repeated and rekindled by his own lips, revealed to him still more reasons to feel humiliated and sickened.

"Has anything more horrible ever happened to anyone?" he exclaimed at last, abruptly ceasing his pacing, violently folding his arms and standing before Ega, who was sitting slumped on the sofa in a state of shock. "Can you imagine a more sordid state of affairs? Or a more ludicrous one? It's enough to make your heart break or, indeed, to make you burst out laughing. Priceless! The little man, with a flower in his buttonhole, sitting right there on that sofa where you are now, saying very sweetly: 'Look, that woman isn't my wife, she's just someone I paid for her services.' Can you believe it? The man pays her. How much is a kiss? A hundred francs. All right, here's a hundred francs. It's just incredible!"

And he resumed his wild pacing, going over in his mind what had happened, still repeating Castro Gomes' words, which he distorted and made still more brutal.

"What do you think, Ega? Say something. What would you do? It's awful, isn't it?"

Ega, who was pensively polishing the lens of his monocle, hesitated at first, then declared that, looked at from a superior point of view—the view of men of their time and "their world"—the situation really gave no reason for anger or even sorrow.

"Then you have understood nothing!" cried Carlos. "You haven't grasped my position at all!"

No, no, Ega understood perfectly well that it was dreadful for a man on the point of lovingly joining destinies with a woman to learn that others had previously enjoyed her favours for so much a night. But this, in fact, simplified and eased matters. What had been a complicated drama became, instead, a pleasant diversion. Carlos, of course, was relieved of any feelings of remorse for having broken up a family; he no longer had to exile himself to some flowery corner of Italy in order to conceal his errors; he was no longer bound forever by honour to a woman to whom he might not always feel bound by love. All of these things, damn it, were advantages!

"And what about her dignity?" exclaimed Carlos.

Yes, but the diminution to her dignity and purity was not really that great, given that, before Castro Gomes' visit, she was already a woman running away from her husband, which, not to be too harsh, is neither a very pure nor a very dignified thing to do. Such a humiliation was, of course, galling, but no more so than that of a man who owns a Madonna which he contemplates with religious awe, believing it to be by Raphael, only to discover one day that the divine work was painted in Bahia by some fellow called Castro Gomes! However, it seemed to Ega, that the result, both private and social, was this: Carlos, up until then, had been having a highly problematic affair with a beautiful woman, and now he could have an entirely unproblematic affair with the same beautiful woman.

"Now what you should do, my dear Carlos . . ."

"What I'm going to do is write her a letter and enclose a cheque in payment for the two months I've been sleeping with her."

"Ah, romantic brutalism! It's already been done in *The Lady of the Camellias*. You are, I fear, failing to see the nuances of the matter in a reasoned and philosophical light."

Carlos broke in impatiently:

"Look, Ega, let's talk no more about it! I'm too upset right now. I'll see you later. You'll be dining at home, I assume. Fine, then, I'll see you later."

He was about to leave, slamming the door, when Ega, his calm restored and getting slowly up from the sofa, said:

"The little man has gone there now."

Carlos spun round, his eyes flashing:

"What, to Olivais? To see her?"

Yes, he had ordered the carriage to take him to Craft's house. Ega, eager to see this Senhor Castro Gomes, had hidden in the door-keeper's hut. And he had watched him come downstairs, lighting a cigar. He really was one of those *rastaquouères*, flashy foreigners, coarse, hard fellows, who, in poor, long-suffering Paris, turn up at the Café de la Paix at two o'clock in the morning to drink their *groseille*. And it was the door-keeper who had told him that the man seemed in excellent spirits and had ordered the coachman to take him to Olivais.

Carlos seemed distraught:

"All this is disgusting! Perhaps the two of them will reach some agreement. I feel as you did some time ago. I feel as though my soul has fallen into a latrine and I need an inner bath!"

Ega said in a melancholy murmur:

"The need for moral baths is becoming so frequent that there really should be an establishment in the city that provides them."

In his room, Carlos was pacing up and down before the desk where the sheet of white paper on which he was going to write to Maria Eduarda already bore that day's date followed by a "Dear Madam" which he had struggled to write in a firm, serene hand, and then stopped, not knowing what else to say. He was still determined to send her a cheque for two hundred *libras*, an outrageously generous payment for the two months he had spent in her bed. But he wanted also to compose two icy, impassive lines that would wound her more deeply than the money, and all he could come up with were phrases expressive of great anger, but which revealed an equally great love.

He stared at the blank sheet, and the banal phrase "Dear Madam" filled him with a piercing longing for the woman who, only the night before, he had still been addressing as "My adored one," for the woman whose name was still not MacGren, who was perfect, and who had been dazzled and overwhelmed by an indomitable passion that defied all reason. And his love for that Maria Eduarda, the noble, tender lover, who had been transformed into Madame MacGren, the false kept woman, was now infinitely greater and all the more desperate because it could never be fulfilled, like the love one might feel for a dead woman, beating all the more ardently when confronted by the coldness of the grave. Ah, if only she could emerge once more, clean and clear, from the mud into which she had plunged, and be once more Maria Eduarda working away at her chaste embroidery! With what delicate love he would surround her in order to make up to her for the marital love she had ceased to deserve! With what veneration he would treat her in order to compensate for the respect which the affected, superficial world had withdrawn from her! For she

340

had all the qualities that command love and respect—she had beauty, grace, intelligence, happiness, motherhood, kindness, incomparably good taste . . . and yet despite all these strong, sweet qualities, she was a mere adventuress!

But why? Why? Why had she entered upon this prolonged deception, woven day by day, lying about everything, from the modesty she feigned to the name she used.

He clutched his head and found life unbearable. If she was lying, where then was the truth? If she was betraying him, with those clear eyes of hers, then the universe might well be one vast unspoken betrayal. It was like placing a bunch of roses in a vase and finding that they stink of the plague! Like walking upon the cool grass and finding that it conceals a swamp! But why, why had she lied? If, on that very first day when he, tremulous and devoted, had observed her bent over her embroidery as one might observe some holy act, if she had told him then that she was not the wife of Senhor Castro Gomes, but only Senhor Castro Gomes' mistress, would his passion for her have been any less intense, less profound? It was not the priest's stole at the marriage ceremony that gave beauty to her body or value to her caresses. So why the dark and shameful lie, which now made him imagine her very kisses, her very sighs to be deceptions too! And with that whole long invented history, she would have led him to leave his country and give his whole life for a body for which others would have given only a handful of *libras*. And for the sake of that woman, paid for by the hour like a hired cab, he had been intending to sour his grandfather's old age, cause irreparable damage to his own future and restrict his own male freedom of movement!

But why? Why that banal farce, familiar from every comic opera: the *cocotte* pretending to be a lady? Why had she done it, why the honest words, the pure profile, the maternal sweetness? Solely for money? No. Castro Gomes was richer than he was and could far more easily satisfy her worldly appetite for fine dresses and carriages. Did she sense that Castro Gomes was about to abandon her and so wanted to have, ready and waiting, another rich purse by her side? In that case, it would have been simpler by far to have said to him: "I'm free, I love you, take me as freely as I give myself to you." No. There was something secret, tortuous, impenetrable in all this, and he would have given anything to know what it was!

And then, very gradually, a desire began to grow in him to go to Olivais. No, it would not be enough for him to avenge himself arrogantly by throwing in her lap a cheque accompanied by an insolent letter! What he needed, for his own complete peace of mind, was to wrench from the depths of that murky soul the secret that lay behind the whole grotesque farce. Only this would calm his terrible torment. He wanted to go to the Toca once more and see what this woman, now called MacGren, was like and to hear what she had to say. He would not go there full of anger and recriminations, but calm and smiling, and purely to have her tell him the reason for that laborious, futile lie, purely so that he could ask her serenely: "My dear lady, what was the purpose of all this trickery?" And then watch her weep. Yes, he felt a kind of loving desire to see her cry. The agony he had felt in the moss-green drawing room, as he listened to that other man's drawling voice, he wanted to see repeated in her breast, that breast upon which he had slept so sweetly, oblivious to everything, and which was beautiful, so divinely beautiful!

He gave an abrupt, determined tug on the bell pull. Baptista appeared, carefully buttoned-up in his frock-coat, and with a resolute air, as if armed and ready to be useful in what he sensed was a crisis.

"Baptista, go to the Hotel Central and ask if Senhor Castro Gomes has returned! No, go and stand at the entrance to the hotel and wait until you see that man arrive, the man who was here just now. No, it's best to ask! Anyway, find out whether that man has returned or is in the hotel. And as soon as you are sure of this, jump in a cab and come straight back here as fast as you can. And make sure he's a reliable driver, because I want him to take me to Olivais afterwards."

As soon as he had issued this order, he felt calmer. It was an immense relief not to have to write the letter, not to have to find the appropriately acerbic, lacerating words. He slowly tore up the sheet of paper. Then he wrote a cheque for two hundred *libras*, made out "To the bearer." He would take it to her himself. He would not hurl it dramatically into her lap. He would leave it on a table, in an envelope addressed to Madame MacGren. He was suddenly filled with compassion for her. He could see her now, opening the envelope with two large, slow, silent tears running down her cheeks. And his eyes grew wet with tears too.

At that moment, Ega, from the other side of the door, asked if he was disturbing him.

"No, come in," Carlos cried.

And he continued his silent pacing, his hands in his pockets; Ega, equally silent, went over to the window and looked out at the garden.

"I need to write to my grandfather to tell him I've arrived safely," Carlos muttered at last, stopping by the desk.

"Give him my regards."

Carlos sat down and languidly took up his pen, only to throw it down again almost at once; he interlaced his hands behind his head, leaned back in the chair and closed his eyes, as if exhausted.

"One thing seems certain to me," Ega suddenly said from his place at the window. "The person who wrote that anonymous letter to Castro Gomes was Dâmaso."

Carlos looked at him:

"Do you think so? Yes, perhaps you're right. After all, who else could it have been?"

"There is no one else, my friend. It was Dâmaso!"

Carlos remembered then what Taveira had told him, about Dâmaso's mysterious allusions to a scandal that was brewing and about him ending up with a bullet in his head. Dâmaso, therefore, had been sure that the Brazilian would return and that a duel would follow.

"The vile creature should be put down!" exclaimed Ega, suddenly furious. "There can be no security and no peace in our lives as long as the wretch remains alive!"

Carlos did not respond. And Ega raged on, horribly pale now, giving voice to days and days of accumulated loathing:

"*I* can't kill him because I have no reason to, but if I had a reason, if, for example, he were to address some insolent remark to me, give me a bold look, then, that would be that, I would squash him as if he were an insect. But you must do something, things can't go on like this, they can't! Blood needs to be spilled. I mean, how despicable, an anonymous letter! Our peace and happiness are exposed to constant attack by Senhor Dâmaso. It can't go on like this. I just wish I had some real pretext, but you do, so make the most of it and crush him!"

Carlos shrugged vaguely.

"He certainly deserves a good beating, but he only turned traitor on me because of my relationship with this lady, and since that is now a closed case, everything to do with it is also over. *Parce sepultis*. And he was, after all, right when he said she was an adventuress."

He thumped the desk with his fist and got up, smiling a bitter smile, as if amused by the infinite tedium of it all.

"Yes, Senhor Dâmaso Salcede was right!"

At this thought, all his rage stirred into angry life again. He glanced at his watch. He could not wait to see her, to insult her!

"Have you written the letter?" asked Ega.

"No, I'm going there myself."

For a moment, Ega looked shocked. Then he started silently pacing again, staring at the carpet.

It was growing dark when Baptista returned. He had seen Senhor Castro Gomes arrive at the hotel and order his luggage to be taken in, and the cab, to take Carlos to Olivais, was waiting for him downstairs.

"Right, goodbye, then," said Carlos, looking frantically around for a pair of gloves.

"Aren't you having any supper?"

"No."

Shortly afterwards, he was travelling along the road to Olivais. The gaslamps had been lit. Shifting restlessly about on the narrow seat, nervously lighting cigarettes which he then did not smoke, he was filled with dread at the prospect of that difficult, painful meeting. He did not even know how to address her, whether he should call her "Madam," or, with lofty indifference,

"My dear friend." And at the same time, he felt for her an ill-defined compassion, which mitigated his anger. He could imagine already how she would react to his chilly demeanour, she would turn pale and tremble, her eyes would brim with tears. And the very tears which he had longed to see filled him only with unease and sorrow, now that he was so close to seeing them shed. For a moment, he even considered turning back. It would, after all, be much more dignified to write a few arrogant words, rudely shaking her off forever. He might not give her the cheque—a wealthy man's brutal insult. She might be a liar, but she was also a woman, nervous and fanciful, and who did perhaps feel for him a disinterested love. A letter, though, would be more dignified. And now the words that he should have written to her came to him, incisive and precise—while he may have been ready to give up his life to a woman who had surrendered herself to him "for love," he was determined not to waste even his moments of leisure on a woman who had given in to him "for purely professional purposes." That would be simpler, more clear-cut. And it would mean that he would not have to see her or bear the torment of her explanations or her tears.

Then he was gripped by doubt. He beat on the windows to make the driver stop, so that he could reflect for an instant, more calmly, without the rattle of the wheels. The driver did not hear him; the sound of the horses' hooves, trotting along the dark road, continued. And Carlos let himself be carried onwards, again uncertain what to do. Then, as he recognised the places—obscured now by shadows—which he had passed so often with a joyful heart, when his love was in fullest bloom, he experienced a new wave of anger, directed less at Maria Eduarda herself and more at the "lie" which she had created, and which had wrecked the one great happiness of his life. It was that "lie" which he hated now, imagining it as something material and tangible, like a great, ugly, iron-grey weight, crushing his heart. If it were not for that one tiny unforgettable "thing" that lay between them, like an indestructible block of granite, he would open his arms to her again, if not with the same utter belief, at least with the same ardour! What did it matter whether she was the other man's wife or merely his mistress? Just because a priest had not mumbled his blessing over the kisses given to her by that other man, was her skin more sullied by them or less fresh? But there was still the "lie," the initial "lie," spoken on the first day he went to Rua de São Francisco, and which, like bad yeast, had been corrupting everything ever since: sweet conversations, silences, walks, siestas in the heat of the garden, murmured kisses lost among those golden curtains ... Everything was stained and contaminated by that first "lie" which she had uttered with a smile on her lips and looking at him with her calm limpid eyes.

He felt as if he were suffocating, and as he was struggling to lower the window, which was missing its strap, the carriage suddenly stopped in the middle of the empty road. He opened the door. A woman with a shawl over her head was talking to the driver.

"Melanie!"

"Oh, Monsieur!"

Carlos quickly jumped out. They were very close to the house, just around the corner, where the wall curved beneath the beech tree, opposite the hedge of aloes protecting the olive groves. Carlos shouted to the driver to continue on and wait for him at the gate. And he remained there, in the dark, with Melanie huddled in her shawl.

What was she doing there? Melanie appeared distraught; she explained that she had come looking for a carriage because her mistress wanted to go to Lisbon, to Ramalhete. She had thought the carriage was empty.

She wrung her hands in relief and gratitude. She was so glad, so very glad that he had come. Her mistress was beside herself; she had eaten no supper and could not stop crying. Senhor Castro Gomes had arrived there unexpectedly. Her mistress, poor love, kept saying that she wanted to die!

Then, keeping close to the wall, Carlos questioned Melanie. How had Castro Gomes seemed to her? What had he said? How had he behaved when he left? Melanie had heard nothing. Senhor Castro Gomes and her mistress had talked alone in the Japanese pavilion. But she had seen him saying goodbye to Madame, and he had seemed completely calm and friendly, even laughing and joking about Niniche. Her mistress, however, had looked deathly pale, and when he left, she had been close to fainting.

They were near the gate now. Carlos drew back, breathing hard, his hat in his hand. Now all his pride was consumed by the urgency of his need to know. He had to know! And so he asked more questions and confided to Melanie the painful secrets of his love. "*Dites toujours, Melanie, dites!*" Did her mistress know that Castro Gomes had been with him at Ramalhete and confessed everything?

Of course she knew, that was why she was crying, said Melanie. She had always told her mistress that it would be best to tell the truth. She was her mistress' great friend, she had served her since she was a young girl, and had even been there at Rosa's birth . . . And she had told her, there in Olivais as well, that the truth was best.

Carlos bowed his head in the darkness of the wall. Melanie "had told her"! This meant that she and her maid had cosily discussed the "lie" in which his life was so entangled! The revelations vouchsafed to him by Melanie, who was sighing now, her shawl almost covering her face, demolished the last fragments of that dream which he had raised up so high among clouds of gold. Nothing remained. It lay in pieces in the filthy mud.

For a moment, his heart weary, he considered going straight back to Lisbon. But *she* was on the other side of that dark wall, lost in tears, wishing to die. And slowly he again started walking towards the gate.

Liberated now from any resistance previously put up by his pride, he asked Melanie more probing questions. Why had Maria Eduarda not told him the truth?

Melanie shrugged. She didn't know; not even her mistress knew! She had been staying at the Hotel Central as Madame Gomes; she had rented the house in Rua de São Francisco as Madame Gomes; she had received him as Madame Gomes, and she had simply let things drift, not even thinking about it, talking to him, falling in love with him, and, finally, coming to live in Olivais. And by then it was too late; caught up in the lie, and fearful of what might happen if she told him, she had not dared to confess.

But, exclaimed Carlos, had it never occurred to her that he was bound to find out one day.

"*Je ne sais pas, Monsieur, je ne sais pas,*" she murmured, almost in tears herself.

There were other discrepancies too. Was she not expecting Gomes to return? Did she not assume he would be back? Did she never speak of him?

"*Oh, non, Monsieur, non!*"

Ever since Carlos had started visiting Rua de São Francisco every day, Madame had considered any connection she had with Senhor Castro Gomes to have been severed. She never talked about him and did not want anyone else to talk about him. Before, the little girl always used to call Senhor Castro Gomes *petit ami*. Now she did not call him anything. She had been told that there was no *petit ami*.

"She still wrote to him though," said Carlos, "I know she wrote to him."

Yes, Melanie believed that Maria Eduarda had written to him, but the letters contained no expressions of affection. Indeed, her mistress was so scrupulous that, since she had come to live in Olivais, she had not spent one penny of the money sent to her by Senhor Castro Gomes. The letters of credit had remained untouched, and she had handed them over to him that evening. Didn't he remember meeting her one morning outside the pawnshop? Well, she had gone there, with a French friend, to pawn a diamond bracelet for her mistress. Her mistress was now living on her jewels; others were already in pawn.

Carlos stopped, deeply touched. But then why had she lied?

"*Je ne sais pas,*" said Melanie, "*je ne sais pas . . . Mais elle vous aime bien, allez!*"

They had reached the gate. The carriage was waiting. At the end of the avenue of acacias, the door of the house stood open, letting the pale sad light from the corridor spill out into the darkness. Carlos thought he saw Maria Eduarda, in a dark cloak and with her hat on, cross that one bright patch. She had probably heard the carriage arrive. What a torment of impatience she must be feeling!

"Go and tell her that I'm here, Melanie, go on!" murmured Carlos.

The girl ran ahead of him, and he, walking slowly along beneath the acacias, could feel, in the sombre silence, the wild beating of his heart. He went up the three stone steps, which already seemed to him to belong to a house he did not know. Inside, the corridor was empty, apart from the Moorish lamp illuminating the display of bull-fighting paraphernalia. He waited there. Melanie, carrying her shawl in her hand, came to tell him that her mistress was in the tapestry room.

Carlos entered.

She was standing there, waiting, still in her cloak, terribly pale, her whole soul concentrated in eyes that glittered with tears. She ran to him, clasped his hands, unable to speak, sobbing and trembling.

Greatly agitated, Carlos could find only these sadly foolish words to say:

"I don't know why you're crying, there's no need to cry."

At last, she managed to stammer:

"Please, for the love of God, listen to me! Don't say anything, let me explain. I was on my way, I had sent Melanie to find a carriage, I was coming to see you. I simply never had the courage to tell you. I was wrong, it was very wrong of me . . . But listen, don't say anything yet, forgive me, it wasn't my fault!"

She was again overwhelmed by sobbing. She collapsed onto the sofa, weeping uncontrollably, her whole body shaken by sobs, her hair, only loosely tied up, falling about her shoulders.

Carlos stood before her, unmoving. His heart seemed frozen in surprise and doubt, lacking the strength to unburden itself to her. Now he felt only how base and brutal it would be to leave her that cheque, which he had there in his wallet and which filled him with shame. She looked up, her face all wet with tears; then, making a great effort, she said:

"Listen! I don't even know where to begin. There are so many things, so many! Don't go, sit down, listen!"

Carlos slowly pulled up a chair.

"No, here, next to me. To give me courage. Please, I beg you, have pity on me, at least do me that kindness."

He gave in to the look of humble, heart-rending supplication in her tear-filled eyes, and, feeling infinitely sad, sat down as far as away as possible at the other end of the sofa. Then very quietly, her voice hoarse from crying, without even meeting his gaze, as if she were in the confessional, Maria Eduarda began talking about her past, tentatively, hesitantly, incoherently, in between the sobs that still occasionally overwhelmed her and the feelings of bitter shame that caused her to bury her face in her hands in distress.

It was not her fault, it was not! He should have asked that man who knew everything about her life. It had been her mother's fault. It was terrible to say so, but it had been because of her mother that she had met and run away with the first man, the other man, an Irishman. And she had lived with him for four years, as his faithful wife, living the quietest of domestic lives. And he had been going to marry her, but he was killed in the war with the Germans, in the battle of St-Privat. And she had been left alone with Rosa, an ailing mother, no money, and with nothing more left to sell. At first, she had tried to work. In London, she had offered herself as a piano teacher, but in vain. For two days, they had no fire and only salt fish to eat, and it was terrible to see Rosa, her poor child, going hungry! Your own child going hungry! He couldn't imagine what that was like! In the end, thanks to the charity of a friend, they had been repatriated to Paris. And there she had met Castro Gomes. He was an awful man, but what else could she have done! She was lost . . .

She slowly slid down from the sofa and fell at Carlos' feet. And he remained motionless, dumb, his heart torn apart by opposing and equally painful emotions: a tremulous compassion for all the miseries she had endured—a mother's suffering, her attempts to find work, hunger, all of which made her somehow more worthy of love; but also revulsion to learn for the first time of this other man, this Irishman, and which made her, in his eyes, even more soiled and debased.

She continued talking about Castro Gomes. She had lived chastely with him for three years, never once straying, without so much as a wayward thought. Her one wish was to stay quietly at home. He was the one who forced her to go out to suppers and late-night parties.

Carlos, in torments, could not bear to hear any more. He pushed away her hands, which sought his. He wanted to escape, he wanted it all to be over!

"Oh, no, no, please don't push me away," she cried, clinging to him anxiously. "I know I deserve nothing. I know I'm a poor worthless wretch. I simply didn't have the courage, my love! You're a man, you don't understand these things. Look at me, why don't you look at me? Just for a moment, no, don't turn away, have pity on me."

No, he didn't want to look at her. He feared those tears, that face so full of pain. In response to the warmth of the breast rising and falling against his knees, all the emotions he was feeling—pride, spite, dignity, jealousy—began to waver. Then, unwittingly, unwillingly, his hands clasped hers. She immediately covered his fingers, his sleeves even, with impetuous kisses, and implored him, from the depths of her misery, for one instant of mercy.

"Oh, say that you forgive me! You're so good! Just one word . . . Say only that you don't hate me, and then I'll let you go . . . But say it first . . . Look at me as you used to, just once!"

And now it was her lips seeking his. The weakness into which Carlos could feel his whole being slowly sinking filled him with rage, against himself and against her. He shook her roughly and cried:

"Why didn't you tell me, why didn't you tell me? Why this long lie? I would have loved you anyway. So why did you lie?"

He again pushed her away, and she fell prostrate on the floor. And, standing over her, he unleashed on her this desperate complaint:

"It's your lie that separates us, that's all! Your horrible lie!"

She gradually managed to get to her feet, barely able to stand, all colour drained from her face.

"I tried to tell you," she murmured softly, utterly exhausted, her arms hanging limp by her sides. "I did try to tell you. Don't you remember, that day when you arrived late, and I talked to you about renting a house in the country, which was the first time you told me you loved me? I said at once: 'There's something I must tell you.' But you wouldn't let me finish. You imagined I was going to say that I wanted to be yours alone and to go away with you. And you said then that we must leave with Rosa and be happy in some other corner of the world. Don't you remember? And that was the first time I was tempted, tempted to say nothing, simply to let things happen, and then, much later, years later, when I had proved to you what a good wife I was, worthy of your esteem, to confess everything and say: 'Now, if you like, send me away.' Oh, I know it was wrong, but I was tempted and I didn't resist. If you hadn't mentioned running away together, I would have told you everything, but the moment you said that, I had a vision of another life, of, oh, I don't know, of a great hope. And, of course, it was a way of postponing that dreadful confession! I don't know how else to explain it other than to say that it was as if Heaven opened before me, and I could see myself living with you in a house of our own. I was tempted! And it would have been awful, at that moment when you loved me so much, to say to you: 'No, don't do all those things for me, I'm nothing but a poor wretch who doesn't even have a husband.' What can I say? I couldn't bear the thought of losing your respect. It was so good to feel so loved. What I did was wrong, very wrong ... but now, there it is, I'm lost and it's all over!"

She hurled herself to the floor, like a vanquished, dying creature, burying her face in the sofa. And Carlos, walking slowly to the other end of the room, then returning brusquely to her side, could only repeat the same recriminatory words, "the lie, the lie"—that stubborn lie, day after day. As answer he received her sobs.

"Why didn't you at least tell me afterwards, here in Olivais, when you knew that you were everything to me?"

She raised her head wearily.

"Why do you think? I was afraid your love for me would change, that you would start behaving differently. I could imagine you treating me disrespectfully. I could imagine you coming into the house without bothering to take off your hat, no longer caring about Rosa, insisting on paying the household expenses. And I couldn't bear the thought of that, and so I kept postponing the moment. I would say: 'Not today, just one more day of happiness, I'll tell him tomorrow.' And so it went on. Oh, I don't know, it's just too horrible."

There was a silence. And Carlos heard Niniche outside, whining softly, pitifully, wanting to come in. He opened the door. The dog ran in and jumped onto the sofa, where Maria Eduarda was still kneeling at one end, sobbing; the dog, troubled, tried to lick her hands, then stationed herself at her side, as if guarding her, watching distrustfully with bright, jet-black eyes as Carlos resumed his sombre pacing.

A longer, sadder sigh from Maria Eduarda made him stop. He stood for a moment observing her pain and humiliation. Greatly shaken, his lips trembling, he murmured:

"Even if I could forgive you, how would I ever be able to believe you again? This horrible lie will always be there between us! I would never have a single day of trust and peace."

"That was the only thing I lied to you about, and I did it out of love for you," she said gravely, from the depths of her prostration.

"No, you lied about everything. It was all false, your marriage, your name, your whole life. I would never be able to believe you again. How could I, when I'm not even sure I believe the motive behind your tears now?"

Indignation made her draw herself up, straight and proud. Her eyes, suddenly dry of tears, glittered, wide and angry, in the marble whiteness of her face.

"What do you mean? That my tears have some ulterior motive, that my pleas to you are false? That I'm pretending all this just to keep you here, so as not to lose you, to be sure I have another man, now that I've been abandoned?"

He stammered:

"No, no, that's not what I meant!"

"And what about me?" she exclaimed, walking imperiously over to him, suddenly magnificent and with the light of truth in her face. "What about me? Why should I believe in the grand passion you once swore for me? What was it you loved in me? Tell me! Was it the fact that I belonged to another man, was it my name, the chic of having an adulterous affair, my clothes perhaps? Or was it me, my body, my soul and my love for you? Look at me! I'm still the same person! These arms are the same, this breast is the same! Only one thing is different, my passion for you. That, alas, has grown greater, oh, infinitely greater."

"If only that were true!" cried Carlos, wringing his hands.

In an instant, Maria Eduarda was at his feet, her arms flung wide.

"I swear to you on the soul of my daughter, on Rosa's soul! I love you, I adore you, madly, absurdly, until death!"

Carlos was trembling. His whole being was drawn to her; he felt an irresistible impulse to let himself fall upon the breast of the woman who lay sobbing at his feet, even if it were an abyss into which he was hurling his whole life. However, again the chill idea of the "lie" passed through his mind. And he drew back, desperately clutching his head in his hands, recoiling from that tiny indestructible thing that refused to go away, and which interposed itself like an iron bar between him and his divine happiness!

She was kneeling, not moving, staring wildly down at the carpet. Then, in the oppressive silence of the room, she spoke in a mournful, tremulous voice:

"You're right, it's over. You don't believe me, so it's all over. You had better go. No one else will ever believe me. It's all over for me. I have no one else in the world. I'll leave tomorrow. I won't take anything with me. You'll have to give me time, though, to sort things out. What else is left for me, but to leave?"

Unable to contain her grief any longer, she fell to the floor, her arms outstretched, sobbing uncontrollably.

Carlos turned, wounded to the heart. Lying there in her dark dress, she looked already like some poor, abandoned, cast-out creature, alone in a corner, surrounded by the inclemencies of the world. Then respect, pride and domestic dignity were swept away as if by a great wind of pity. Suddenly, all he saw, blotting out her every weakness, were her beauty, her pain, her sublimely loving soul. A generous delirium, a grandiose kindness mingled with his love. And bending down, his arms open to her, he said softly:

"Maria, will you marry me?"

She looked up at him with uncomprehending eyes. But Carlos was standing there, arms wide, waiting to enfold her once again, his forever. She got to her feet, stumbling over the skirt of her dress, and fell upon his bosom, covering him with kisses, half-weeping, half-laughing, dizzy with amazement.

"Marry you? *Marry* you? Oh, Carlos . . . and live with you always? Oh, my love, my love! And look after you and serve you and adore you and be only yours? And poor Rosa too . . . No, don't marry me, it's impossible, I'm worthless! But, then, if that's what you want, why not? Let's go far away together, with Rosa and me in your heart! And you must be our friend, mine and hers, because we have no one else in the world. Oh, my God, my God!"

She turned pale and almost slipped from his arms in a faint, and her long, dishevelled hair, glinting gold in the light, brushed the floor.

: XV :

MARIA EDUARDA AND CARLOS — Carlos having spent that night in his rented cottage at Olivais—had just finished lunch. Domingos had served coffee, and, before leaving, had placed at Carlos' side a box of cigarettes and a copy of *Le Figaro*. The two windows stood open. Not a leaf was moving in the heavy air of that morning of overcast skies, made sadder still by the slow tolling of bells dying away over the distant fields. On the cork bench beneath the trees, Miss Sara was lazily sewing; Rosa, beside her, was playing on the grass. And Carlos—who had arrived wearing, as befitted their new conjugal intimacy, a simple silk shirt and a flannel jacket—brought his chair over to Maria Eduarda's, took her hand and slowly stroked it, playing with her rings.

"Now, my love, have you decided yet when you want to set off?"

The previous night, as they exchanged their first kisses as a betrothed couple, she had expressed a desire to leave unchanged their plan to go to Italy and find a romantic little house among the flowers of Isola Bela, except that there would now be no need to conceal the unease of a guilty happiness; they could enjoy instead the repose of an entirely legitimate contentment. And after all the uncertainties and torments that had troubled them since the day he first saw Maria Eduarda as she walked along the Aterro, Carlos longed, too, for the moment when he could settle, at last, into the comfort of a love free from doubts and unpleasant surprises.

"As for me, I would leave tomorrow like a shot. I'm hungry for peace. I'm even hungry for idleness! But tell me what *you* want."

Maria Eduarda did not respond; she merely looked at him with smiling eyes, grateful and loving. Then, without removing her hand, which Carlos was still stroking, she called through the window to Rosa, who replied:

"Wait, Mama, I'm coming! Can I have some crumbs, please? There are some sparrows who haven't had their lunch yet."

"No, come here."

When Rosa appeared at the door, all in white, her face flushed, with one of the last roses of summer tucked in her belt, Maria Eduarda told her to come closer, and she stood between them, resting against their knees. Retying a hair ribbon that had come undone, Maria Eduarda asked very seriously, very tenderly, if she would like Carlos to come and live with them in the Toca. The little girl's eyes lit up with surprise and laughter.

"You mean be here always, all the time, even at night, all night? And have your luggage here and all your things?"

They both murmured "Yes."

Rosa jumped up and down and clapped her hands, her face radiant, wanting Carlos to go at once to fetch his luggage and "all his things."

"Listen," Maria said to her very gravely, holding her close. "And would you like him to be your Papa, and to be always with us, and for us always to obey and love him?"

Rosa raised an earnest little face to her mother, from which all trace of a smile had been erased.

"But I can't love him more than I already do!"

They both kissed her, and their eyes filled with tears. And for the first time in Rosa's presence, Maria Eduarda bent over her and kissed Carlos lightly on the forehead. The little girl stared in astonishment, first at her friend and then at her mother. Then she seemed to understand everything; she slid off her mother's lap and leaned against Carlos and said with tender humility:

"Would you like me to call only you Papa, and no one else?"

"And no one else," he said, putting his arms about her.

Thus they obtained Rosa's consent, and she ran off, slamming the door, with her hands full of bread rolls for the sparrows.

Carlos got up, cupped Maria Eduarda's face in his hands and gazed at her profoundly, into her very soul, murmuring in rapt tones:

"You're perfect!"

She regretfully detached herself from this troubling adoration.

"Listen, there is, alas, still a great deal to tell. Let's go to our pavilion. You haven't anything else to do, have you? And even if you have, today you're mine. I'll be with you in a moment. Take your cigarettes."

On the steps down to the garden, Carlos paused to look up and feel the veiled sweetness of the grey sky. Wrapped in that soft mist in which nothing shone or sang, life seemed to him adorable, like fine, sad poetry, the perfect weather for two hearts—with no interest in the world and quite out of harmony with it—to abandon themselves to the continual enchantment of beating together in the silence and the shadows.

"It looks like rain, André," he said, when he passed the old gardener who was trimming the box hedge.

Startled, André pulled off his hat. They needed a good drop of water after the drought. The earth was really thirsty. And how was everyone in the house? The Senhora? The little girl?

"Very well, André, thank you."

And in his desire to see everyone around him as happy as he and the soon-to-be-consoled earth, Carlos placed a one-*libra* coin in André's hand, and André stared at it, dazzled, not even daring to close his fingers around that extraordinary piece of bright gold.

When Maria Eduarda came into the pavilion, she was carrying a small sandalwood box. She threw it down on the divan, comfortably installed Carlos among the cushions beside it, and lit his cigarette for him. Then she knelt at his feet, on the carpet, as if she were about to make a humble confession.

"Are you all right like that? Would you like Domingos to bring you a brandy and water? No? Then listen, because I want to tell you everything."

She wanted to tell him about her whole life. She had even thought of writing him a long, long letter, as heroines do in novels, but she had decided, instead, to spend the whole morning chattering away to him, nestled at his feet.

"Are you sure you're all right there?"

Carlos was waiting in some agitation, for he knew that her beloved lips were about to make revelations that would be wounding to his heart and bitter to his pride. However, this confiding to him of her whole life would complete his possession of her person; when he knew everything about her past, he would feel that she was more entirely his. And deep down, he felt an insatiable curiosity about these things that were sure to wound and humiliate him.

"Yes, go on. Then we'll forget all about it forever. But go on, tell me. Where were you really born?"

She had been born in Vienna, but she remembered little of her childhood and knew almost nothing of her father, except that he was very noble and very handsome. She had had a little sister, who had died aged two and whose name was Heloísa. Later on, when Maria Eduarda was older, her mother could not bear being questioned about her past, and she always said that poking about in the past was as harmful as shaking a bottle of old wine. Of Vienna Maria only a confused recollection of long avenues of trees, soldiers dressed in white, and a mirrored, gilded house where people danced; during quite long periods she stayed there alone with her grandfather, a sad, shy old man, who sat in the corners of rooms and told her stories about ships. Then they had gone to England, but of that she could only remember crossing a lot of very noisy streets on a rainy day, wrapped in furs, on a footman's lap. Her first clear memories dated from Paris; her Mama, who, by then, had been widowed, was also in mourning for that same grandfather; and she had an Italian nursemaid who took her every morning, with a hoop and a ball, to play in the Champs-Elysées. At night, she became used to seeing her mother wearing décolletée dresses, in a bedroom full of satins and lights; and a fair-haired man with a rather brusque manner, who used to lounge on the sofas, smoking, and would sometimes give her a doll as a present, and who addressed her always as "Mademoiselle Triste Coeur" because she looked so serious. In the end, Mama had sent her to a convent near Tours, because, although Maria Eduarda could sing the waltzes from *La Belle Hélène* and accompany herself on the piano, she still did not know how to spell. It had been in the convent gardens, with its beautiful lilac trees, that her mother had left her and wept bitterly as she did so; by her side, doubtless to console her, waited a very grave-faced gentleman with waxed moustaches, to whom the mother superior spoke with veneration.

At first, her mother had come to see her every month, staying in Tours for two or three days; she brought with her a profusion of presents, dolls, bonbons, embroidered handkerchiefs, and elaborate dresses which the severe convent rule did not allow her to wear. They would go for carriage rides in the countryside around Tours, and their calèche was always escorted by officers on horseback, who addressed her mother as "*tu*." Her teachers at the convent and the mother superior did not approve of these outings, nor did they like her mother disturbing the peace of their devout corridors with her laughter and the rustle of her silk dresses; at the same time, they appeared to be afraid of her, and addressed her as "Madame la Comtesse." Mama was a great friend of the general in charge of the barracks at Tours and even visited the Bishop. The Monsignor, when he came to the convent, would always make a point of stroking Maria Eduarda's cheek and referring with a smile to her "*excellente mère.*" Then Mama's visits to Tours became less frequent. She was away travelling in Germany for a whole year, during which she barely wrote; she returned one day, looking thinner and all dressed in black, and spent the whole morning clinging to her and weeping.

On her next visit, however, she appeared younger, lighter, more brilliant, and was accompanied by two large white greyhounds; she was planning a poetic pilgrimage to the Holy Land and to the whole of the Far East. By this time, Maria Eduarda was almost sixteen; with her diligent ways and her sweet, grave manner, she had won the affection of the mother superior, who would sometimes gaze at her sadly and stroke her hair—worn in two plaits as stipulated by the rules—and tell her that she would like to keep her always by her side. "*Le monde,*" she said, "*ne vous sera bon à rien, mon enfant!*" One day, however, a certain Madame Chavigny arrived to take her back to Paris and to Mama; she was an impoverished noblewoman, with white ringlets—the very image of stern virtue.

How Maria Eduarda had cried when she left the convent! She would have cried still more had she known what awaited her in Paris!

Mama's house, in Parc Monceaux, was, in fact, a gaming den with a veneer of sombre refined luxury. The footmen wore silk stockings; the guests, who bore the grand names of the French nobility, discussed bullfights, the Tuileries, and speeches made in the Senate; and the gambling tables were set up late each evening to provide a further piquant distraction. Maria Eduarda always went to her room at ten o'clock; Madame de Chavigny, who had stayed on as her companion, used to go out early with her to the Bois de Boulogne in a dowager's dark coupé. Gradually, however, the veneer began to crack. Poor Mama had fallen under the spell of Monsieur de Trevernnes, a man made dangerous both by his seductive powers and by his total lack of honour and good sense. The house soon descended into tawdry, noisy dissipation. When Maria Eduarda got up early, a healthy habit acquired at the convent, she would find men's overcoats abandoned on sofas; cigar butts lying in puddles of champagne on the marble-topped console tables; and, in one of the more private rooms, she would hear the clink of coins in a baccarat game still being played in the morning light. Then, one night, when she had already gone to bed, she heard shouting and the sound of feet running down the stairs; she came out of her room to find her mother lying on the carpet in a faint; all her mother would say, her face bathed in tears, was that some misfortune had occurred.

They moved to a third-floor apartment in Chaussée-d'Antin. Strange, suspicious people began to visit. Wallachians with large moustaches, Peruvians with fake diamonds, and Roman counts who were always tugging at their jacket sleeves in order to cover their filthy cuffs. Occasionally, in this rabble, a proper gentleman would appear, one who did not remove his overcoat as if he were at a *café-concert*. One such was a young Irishman, MacGren. Madame de Chavigny had left them when they had to give up the sombre, satin-lined coupé; and Maria Eduarda, alone with her mother, had, inevitably, unwittingly, begun to be drawn into that late-night life of drunkenness and baccarat.

Her mother used to call MacGren "the baby." And he was, in a way, a silly, happy child. He had immediately fallen in love with Maria Eduarda with all the ardor, effusiveness, and impetuosity of the Irish, and he promised to make her his wife as soon as he was free to do so, because MacGren, who was still a minor, lived largely on the generosity of a rich eccentric grandmother who adored him and who lived in Provence on a vast estate where she kept wild animals in cages. Meanwhile, he kept urging Maria Eduarda to run away with him, for he could not bear to see her surrounded by all those Wallachians who stank of gin. He wanted to take her to Fontainebleau, to a little ivy-grown cottage he was always telling her about, and to wait quietly there until he reached his majority, which would bring with it an income of two thousand *libras*. True, it would be a less than honest situation, but preferable to staying in that brutal, depraved atmosphere, which made her blush at every turn. At the time, her mother seemed agitated, almost irresponsible, and appeared to have taken leave of what little good sense she had. Her increasing financial difficulties left her dazed and stupid; she quarrelled with the maids; she drank champagne *pour s'étourdir*. To satisfy Monsieur de Trevernnes' demands, she had pawned her jewels and, nearly every day, wept jealous tears over him. Finally, an eviction order was issued, and that same night, they had to bundle some clothes into a bag and go to a hotel. And worse, far worse than all this, Monsieur de Trevernnes was starting to look at her in a way that frightened her.

"My poor love!" murmured a pale-faced Carlos, clutching her hands.

She sat for a moment, choked by sobs, her face buried in Carlos' lap. Then, wiping away the tears clouding her eyes, she went on:

"MacGren's letters are in this chest. I've always kept them in order somehow to justify myself to myself, if that were possible. In each and every one of them, he asks me to go to Fontainebleau; he calls me his wife; he swears that, as soon as we are together, we will go and kneel before his grandmother and beg her indulgence. He made me a thousand promises! And he meant it! What else can I say? My mother, one morning, set off to Baden with a crowd of ne'er-do-wells. I was left alone in Paris, in a hotel. I had the dreadful feeling that Trevernnes would appear at any moment. And I was all alone! I was so mad with anxiety that I even thought of buying a gun. But the person who appeared was MacGren.

And she had left with him, unhurriedly, as his wife, taking with her all her luggage. Her mother, back from Baden, had rushed to Fontainebleau, in tragic, hysterical mode, cursing MacGren and lashing out at him, threatening him with imprisonment; then she had burst into tears. MacGren, like a baby, had clung to her, kissing her and crying too. And her mother had ended up clutching them both to her bosom, having entirely accepted the situation and forgiven them for everything, calling them "her beloved children." She spent the rest of that day at Fontainebleau, radiantly happy, describing "the revels in Baden," and planning to move into the cottage herself and live with them in the calm noble role of grandmama. This was in May; that night, MacGren set off fireworks in the garden.

A quiet easy year began. Her one wish was for her mother to come and live peacefully with them at the cottage. When she begged her to do so, her mother would look very thoughtful and then say: "Yes, you're quite right! But let's see, shall we?" Then she would plunge back into the maelstrom of Paris, from which she emerged one morning, in a hired cab, distraught and barely having slept, wearing a fine fur coat over an old, worn skirt, and asking to borrow a hundred francs. Then Rosa was born. Her one concern then had been to make their union legal, but MacGren, with his childish fear of his grandmother, kept thoughtlessly postponing doing anything about it. He was such a baby! He spent the mornings catching birds with birdlime! At the same time, though, he was terribly stubborn, and, gradually, she lost all respect for him. One day in early spring, her mother turned up at Fontainebleau with her luggage, exhausted and tired of life. She had finally broken off her relationship with Trevernnes. Almost immediately, however, she cheered up, and started showering MacGren with effusive, occasionally embarrassing displays of affection, telling him how handsome he was. The two of them passed the days drinking cognac and playing bezique.

Then the war against Prussia broke out. MacGren, fired with enthusiasm, and despite Maria Eduarda's pleadings, immediately rushed off to enlist in Charette's Zouave battalion; his grandmother, for her part, approved of this display of love for France and sent him, in a letter written in verse in praise of Joan of Arc, a large remittance of money. Around this time, Rosa had the croup. Maria Eduarda rarely left her bedside and paid scant attention to what was happening in the war. She was only vaguely aware of the first defeats on the frontier. Then one morning, her mother, still in her nightdress, burst wildly into her room: the army had surrendered at Sédan, the emperor had been taken prisoner! "This is the end of everything, the end of everything!" her terrified mother kept saying. Maria Eduarda went to Paris in order to get news of MacGren; in Rue Royale, she had to take refuge in a doorway from a riotous, unruly crowd shouting slogans and singing the *Marseillaise* as they surrounded a calèche carrying a single passenger, a man, his face as pale as wax, and wearing a scarlet scarf around his neck. A terrified fellow beside her explained that the mob had gone to fetch Rochefort from prison and that the Republic had been proclaimed.

She could find no news of MacGren. Days of terrible anxiety followed. Fortunately, Rosa was getting better, but Maria Eduarda's poor mother was a source of great sadness; grown suddenly older, she sat slumped gloomily in a chair, muttering: "It's the end of everything, the end of everything!" And it really did seem like the end of France. Each day, another battle lost; whole regiments taken prisoner, piled into cattle-trucks and sped away to German jails; the Prussians marching on Paris ... They could not stay in Fontaineb-leau; a hard winter was beginning; and so, with the proceeds from whatever they could sell most easily and with the money MacGren had left behind, they set off for London.

That was her mother's idea. And in London, Maria Eduarda, lost and dis-oriented in that vast unfamiliar city, and ill too, bowed to her mother's foolish ideas. They rented an extremely expensive furnished house in a wealthy area near Mayfair. Her mother spoke of organising a centre of resistance there for Bonapartist refugees, but her real intention was to set up a gambling-house. The times, alas, had changed. The imperialists, stripped of their empire, no longer played baccarat. And she and her mother, with no income and with endless expenses, soon found themselves living in an extravagant house with three servants, huge bills and only a five-pound note in a drawer. Meanwhile, MacGren was somewhere in Paris, besieged by half a million Prussians. They were forced to sell their jewelry, their furs, and even their dresses, and to rent three barely furnished rooms in a poor part of Soho. These were London lodg-ings at their dingiest and most solitary; a single maid, as besmeared with grime as an old rag; a few damp pieces of coal that gave out more smoke than heat; and for supper, a little cold mutton and some beer from the tavern on the corner. In the end, they lacked even a shilling to pay the rent. Her mother, ill, dejected and weeping, never left her bed. Sometimes, at nightfall, swathed in a large waterproof cape, Maria Eduarda would take bundles of clothes down to the pawnshop (even underclothes, even nightshirts!) so that at least Rosa would not have to go without her cup of milk. The letters her mother wrote to former supper companions at the Maison d'Or went unanswered; others brought with them, wrapped in a screw of paper, the odd half *libra*, with the awful whiff of charity. One Saturday, a night of thick fog, on her way to pawn a lace peignoir belonging to her mother, she got lost and ended up wandering the huge city of London in that yellowish gloom, shivering and hungry, pursued by two brutes who stank of liquor. In order to shake them off, she jumped into a cab which took her home. However, she did not have even a penny for the fare, and her landlady was snoring in bed, dead drunk. The coachman got angry, and she, exhausted, burst into tears right there at the door. Concerned, the coachman got down from his seat and offered to take her to the pawnshop for free, and she could then pay him what she owed. She agreed, but then the poor man would only take a shilling from her, and, assuming she was French, he even aimed a few choice insults at the Prussians and insisted on buying her a drink.

She, meantime, looked for some kind of work—sewing, embroidery, translations, copying manuscripts . . . She found nothing. In that hard winter, work was scarce in London; a whole multitude of French people, as poor as she, had arrived in London, scrabbling to earn a crust. Her mother cried ceaselessly, and far more terrible than her tears were her constant remarks about the ease with which one could find money, comfort and luxury in London if one were young and pretty.

"What do you think of my life so far, my love?" Maria Eduarda exclaimed, bitterly wringing her hands.

Carlos kissed her silently, his eyes wet with tears.

"Anyway," Maria Eduarda went on, "the war finally came to an end. Peace was declared and the siege lifted. Paris was free again. The only difficulty was getting back."

"How *did* you get back?"

One day, by chance, in Regent Street, she met a friend of MacGren's, another Irishman, who had often dined with them at Fontainebleau. He came to visit them in Soho, and when he saw the wretched conditions in which they were living—the weak tea, the mutton bones being reheated over a few dying coals—he began, like any good Irishman, to blame the English government, and to swear a bloody revenge. Then, lips trembling, he promised to do all he could for them. The poor boy was also pounding the streets in his own desperate struggle to make a living, but he was Irish, and so, using every trick he knew, he immediately set off around London to scrape together the small amount of money they needed for their return to France. Indeed, he appeared that same night, exhausted and triumphant, brandishing three bank notes and a bottle of champagne. Her mother, after all those months of black tea, almost fainted with emotion when she saw the bottle of Veuve Clicquot with its gold foil top. They bundled up their few possessions. And at Charing Cross Station, as they were about to leave, the Irishman took Maria Eduarda to one side, and, barely able to speak, fiddling nervously with his moustache, told her that MacGren had died at the battle of St-Privat.

"Need I go on? In Paris, I started looking for work again, but everything was still in chaos. The Commune came into being almost immediately afterwards. Believe me, we often went hungry, but at least it wasn't London or winter or exile. We were in Paris, and we were suffering in the company of old friends. Things seemed less terrible somehow. With all these privations, though, poor Rosa began to grow weaker. It was a real torment to see her getting gradually paler and sadder, wearing ragged clothes, and living that garret life. My mother was already suffering from the heart complaint that eventually killed her. Any work I could find was poorly paid and provided only enough to pay the rent and to keep us from starving. I started to become ill too, out of anxiety and despair. I struggled on, though. It was painful to see the state my mother was in, and I feared that without a better diet, fresh air, and a little comfort Rosa might die. That was when I met Castro Gomes, at the house of a former friend of Mama's, who had lost nothing in the war, not even when the Prussians came, and who used to give me some sewing work to do. And the rest of the story you know. I can't even really remember what happened. I just drifted into it. Sometimes, I would see Rosa, poor little thing, wrapped in a shawl, sitting motionless in a corner, still hungry despite having eaten every scrap of food in her bowl . . ."

She could not go on; she burst into tears and fell forward into Carlos' lap. And he, greatly touched, could only say, as he stroked her hair with tremulous hands, that he would make up for all her past miseries.

"Listen," she murmured, wiping away her tears. "There is just one more thing I want to tell you. And it is God's truth, I swear to you on Rosa's soul! In those two relationships with men, my heart remained asleep. It was always asleep, always, never feeling anything, never wanting anything, until I saw you. And there's something else I want to say to you . . ."

She hesitated for a moment, blushing. She put her arms around Carlos, hanging about his neck, her eyes looking deep into his. Still more softly, she stammered one final, absolute confession.

"Not only my heart remained asleep, but my body too, it was always cold, cold as marble."

He clasped her passionately to him, and their lips met in a long silent kiss, completing, with a new and almost virgin emotion, the perfect communion of their souls.

A few days later, Carlos and Ega were driving along the road to Olivais on their way to the Toca.

All that morning, in Ramalhete, Carlos had, at last, been telling Ega about the passionate impulse which had, once more and forever, thrown him into Maria Eduarda's arms, this time as her husband; and given the absolute trust that bound him to Ega, he had even given him a detailed account of her painful story, which justified everything. Then, when the heat of the day had died down, he suggested they go to the Toca for supper. Ega took a turn about the room, unsure what to do. He started slowly brushing his overcoat, murmuring, as he had during Carlos' prolonged confidences: "Extraordinary. What a strange thing life is!"

And now, as they were travelling along, feeling the sweet breeze from the river, Carlos was still talking about Maria Eduarda, about life at the Toca, letting his overflowing heart sing the endless song of his happiness.

"It's true, Ega, I feel almost perfect happiness!"

"And no one at the Toca knows anything about it?"

No one—apart from Melanie, her confidante—suspected the profound change that had taken place in their relationship; and they had agreed that Miss Sara and Domingos, the first witnesses to their friendship, would be royally rewarded and then dismissed when he and Maria Eduarda left for Italy at the end of October.

"So you're going to get married in Rome?"

"Yes, wherever we can find an altar and a priest, not that there's any lack of either in Italy. And it is then, Ega, that the one obstacle to my happiness reappears, which is why I said 'almost perfect happiness'—the terrible obstacle of my grandfather!"

"Ah, of course—Afonso. Have you any idea how you're going to tell him about this whole affair?"

Carlos had no idea at all. He felt only that he entirely lacked the courage to say to his grandfather: "The woman I'm going to marry has made certain mistakes in her life." Besides, it seemed to him pointless. His grandfather would never understand the complicated, fatal, inevitable reasons that had dragged Maria Eduarda down. If he described them to him in detail, his grandfather would see only a tenuous, confused romance, entirely antipathetic to his own strong, candid nature. The ugliness of the sins committed would wound him and leave him unable to appreciate, calmly, the irresistible nature of the causes. Any real understanding of the case—a noble character caught up in an implacable web of misfortunes—would require a more flexible and more worldly spirit than his grandfather's. Old Afonso was a block of granite; one could not expect from him the subtle distinctions of a modern casuist. He would take only one tangible fact from Maria Eduarda's existence: she had, in quick succession, fallen into the arms of two different men. His entire attitude, as head of the household, would be based on that. Why then should he make a confession to his grandfather that would necessarily give rise to a conflict of feelings and an irreparable domestic schism?

"Don't you agree, Ega?"

"Speak more quietly, the coachman might be listening."

"He doesn't understand much Portuguese, especially not the way we speak. Anyway, don't you agree?"

Ega was striking matches on the sole of his shoe in order to light his cigar. He said rather irritably:

"Yes, old Afonso is certainly pretty granitic."

This was why Carlos had come up with another, more cautious plan; it consisted in concealing Maria Eduarda's past from his grandfather, and allowing him to get to know her as a person first. They would marry secretly in Italy. When they returned, she would go to Rua de São Francisco, and he to a filial existence in Ramalhete. Then Carlos would take his grandfather to visit the good friend whom he had met in Italy, Madame MacGren. He would be immediately won over by Maria Eduarda's charm, by the pleasures of a refined and serious household, by delightful little suppers, sensible ideas, Chopin, Beethoven, etc. And to complete the conquest of a man who so adored children, there was Rosa. Then, when his grandfather had fallen in love with Maria Eduarda, with Rosa and with everything, he would tell him frankly one morning: "This adorable, superior creature may have made mistakes in the past, but I married her, and since she is the person she is, did I not do well, despite all, in choosing her to be my wife?" And faced with the terrible irreversibility of an accomplished fact, and driven to defend Maria Eduarda with all the indulgence of a fond old man, he would be the first to think that, while this marriage might not be the best according to the rules of the world, it was certainly the best according to the dictates of the heart.

"Don't you agree, Ega?"

Ega, absorbed in thought, was flicking the ash off the end of his cigar. He was thinking that Carlos was basically planning to impose on his grandfather the same complicated stratagem that Maria Eduarda had tried to impose on him, and was even unwittingly imitating her subtle reasoning.

"And that will be that," Carlos went on. "If he, in his indulgence, accepts the situation, that's wonderful! We'll hold a big party at Ramalhete. If he doesn't, too bad! We'll live our separate lives, with each of us preaching the superiority of two excellent things: my grandfather the traditions of blood, and I the rights of the heart."

Seeing that Ega was still saying nothing, he asked:

"What do you think? Come on. You're not usually short of ideas!"

Ega shook his head, as if waking up.

"Do you really want me to tell you what I think? After all, we're two friends talking man to man! Well, here it is: your grandfather is nearly eighty, and you are twenty-seven or thereabouts. Now it's painful to say this, and no one could find it more painful than I, but, one day, your grandfather will die. Wait until he does. Don't get married. Imagine she has a very ancient, stubborn, crotchety old father who hates Carlos da Maia and his neat pointed beard. Simply wait, and continue your visits to the Toca in Mulato's carriage; that way you allow your grandfather to finish his old age calmly and with no great disappointments or griefs."

Carlos was silently twisting his moustache, but was now sitting comfortably back in the carriage seat. During all these anxious days, such a sensible, easy idea had never even occurred to him! Yes, that is what they would do, they would wait! What greater duty did he have than to save his poor grandfather all that suffering? Maria Eduarda, of course, being a woman, would be eagerly awaiting his transformation from lover into husband, by virtue of the priestly bond that purifies all and which no force can undo. However, she would also prefer the consecration of their marriage to be legal and public, rather than precipitate and secret. Besides, she was so fair, so generous, she would understand perfectly that he had a supreme obligation not to bring shame upon that saintly old man. And surely she knew that his loyalty was as hard and pure as a diamond? She had his word: from that moment on, they were married, not in a church or set down in the sacristy records, but in terms of honour and the unshakeable communion of their hearts.

"You're right!" he cried at last, slapping Ega's knee. "You are absolutely right! It's a brilliant idea. I must wait . . . And while I wait?"

"What do you mean, while you wait?" said Ega, laughing. "That's your business!"

Then more seriously, he added:

"While you're waiting, you still have plenty of the base metal that makes life pleasant. You install your wife, because as from today she is your wife, in Olivais or somewhere else, with all the taste, comfort, and dignity that befits a wife. And you simply let things happen. There's nothing to stop you making that nuptial journey to Italy. You come back, continue smoking your cigarettes and just let things happen. That's good sense; that's what the great Sancho Panza would advise. By the way, what the devil have you got in that package that smells so good?"

"A pineapple. Yes, that's it! Just wait and let things happen. It's an excellent idea!"

An excellent idea! And the one most suited to Carlos' temperament. Why get himself entangled in a lot of domestic bitterness, purely out of an excess of romantic chivalry? Maria Eduarda trusted him; he was rich; he was young; the world lay open before him, easy and indulgent. All he had to do was to let things happen.

"You're right, Ega! And Maria Eduarda will be the first to see the good sense and the rightness of the idea. I feel slightly sad at having to postpone setting myself up in my new life and new home, but that doesn't matter. The main thing is that my grandfather should be happy. And to celebrate the advent of this idea, let's just hope Maria Eduarda has a good supper for us!"

As they approached the Toca, Ega began to dread this first proper meeting with Maria Eduarda. The situation was so awkward; she would be sure to feel embarrassed, knowing that, as Carlos' confidant, he would be privy to her whole life, to her many misfortunes, and to her relationship with Castro Gomes. That's why he'd been reluctant to go there. Then again, not to go and see Maria Eduarda would indicate, with almost offensive clarity, a kind of charitable desire not to bruise her modesty. That is why he had decided "to plunge in." After all, who, if not he, should be the first to offer his hand to Carlos' bride? Apart from that, he felt an infinite curiosity to see this beautiful creature, endowed with all the noble grace of a modern goddess, at home and seated at her table! Nevertheless, he was feeling extremely nervous as he got out of the carriage.

In the end, everything passed off with ease and good humour. Maria Eduarda was sitting on the garden steps, sewing. She started and blushed scarlet when she first saw Ega, who was fumbling in his pocket for his monocle; they shook hands in diffident silence, but Carlos, by then, had gleefully removed the pineapple from its wrappings, and all awkwardness vanished in their admiration.

"Oh, it's magnificent!"

"What a wonderful rich colour!"

"And the smell! It's been perfuming the road all the way from Lisbon!"

Ega had not been back to the Toca since the fateful night of the Cohens' party, when he had got so outrageously drunk and angry. And he immediately reminded Carlos of the cab journey in the storm, Craft's hot toddy, the turkey supper ...

"I have already suffered enormously in this house, dear lady, dressed as Mephistopheles!"

"Because of Marguerite?"

"Who else would one suffer for in this world of love, dear lady, if not for Marguerite or for Faust?"

Carlos wanted him to admire the new splendours of the Toca. And Maria Eduarda led him through the rooms as if he were an old friend, regretting that he should have only come at the end of summer and the end of all the flowers. Ega was loud in his enthusiastic praise. The Toca had at last lost its sad, chilly, museum-like air! One felt that one could speak freely there now!

"We have here a complete barbarian, Maria," exclaimed Carlos, beaming. "He has a horror of art! He's an Iberian, a Semite!"

A Semite? Ega prided himself on being a fine example of an enlightened Aryan! And that was why he could not live in a house in which each chair had the grim solemnity of a bewigged ancestor.

"Yes," said Maria Eduarda, laughing, "but all these lovely eighteenth-century objects are more reminiscent of lightness, wit, and gracious manners."

"Do you really think so?" asked Ega. "As far as I'm concerned, the only thing that all this gilt, these garlands, and these rococos remind me of is a particular brand of futile, elitist vivacity. No, we live in a democracy! And what better to express the simple, solid, good-natured joy of democracy than a large armchair of morocco leather and varnished mahogany!"

Engaged thus in cheerful, frivolous conversation about bric-à-brac, they went out into the garden.

Miss Sara was walking among the box hedges, eyes lowered, a book in her hand. Ega, who knew all about her ardent nocturnal encounters, stared at her eagerly through his monocle; and while Maria Eduarda stooped to pick a geranium, he made plain to Carlos, with a silent gesture, his admiration for Miss Sara's small red mouth and round, pigeon-plump bosom. At the far end of the garden, next to the arbour, they found Rosa playing on the swing. Ega was astonished at her beauty, at her fresh complexion, smooth as the petal of a white camellia. He asked her for a kiss. She demanded very seriously that he first remove his monocle.

"But I need it in order to see you better!"

"Then why don't you wear one in each eye? With just the one, you can only see half of me."

"Charming! Charming!" murmured Ega. Deep down, however, he found the child precocious and impudent. Maria Eduarda glowed.

And over supper that happy intimacy grew. After they had eaten their soup, Carlos—apropos the countryside and a house he wanted to build in Sintra, near the Convento dos Capuchos—had pronounced the words "when we get married." And Ega alluded to that future in a way most guaranteed to please Maria Eduarda's heart. Now that Carlos was installed in a stable and happy state (he said), he must work! And he recalled his old idea of forming a club, to be represented by a journal that would shape literature, educate taste, elevate politics, create civilisation, and, in short, rejuvenate worm-eaten old Portugal. Carlos, given his intelligence and his money (even his good looks, added Ega, laughing), should be at the head of this movement. And what joy it would bring to Afonso da Maia!

Maria Eduarda was listening, attentive and serious. She sensed what a rehabilitating effect it would have on their union—providing evidence of its fecund and purifying influence—if Carlos' life were filled with intelligent activity.

"You're right, you're absolutely right!" she exclaimed ardently.

"And, though it goes without saying," Ega went on, "the country needs us! As our dear and oh-so-imbecilic friend Gouvarinho says, the country has no personnel. And how will it ever have the right personnel if we, who have all the right skills, do nothing but drive our dog-carts and write about the private lives of atoms? I, dear lady, am the one writing the biography of an atom! Such dilettantism is absurd. We are always complaining in bars and in books that 'the country is nothing but a rabble,' but damn it, why don't we work to reform it—to remake it according to our taste and remould it to fit our ideas? You don't know this country, Senhora. It's an admirable place! It's a little bit of top-quality wax. The question is, who will shape it? Up until now, the wax has been in brutish, commonplace, rough, vulgar, unimaginative hands. It needs to be placed in our hands, in the hands of artists. Let us make of that wax a jewel!"

Carlos was laughing as he prepared the pineapple on a dish, with the addition of some orange juice and Madeira wine. Maria Eduarda, however, scolded him for laughing. Ega's idea seemed to her a noble one, inspired by a lofty sense of duty. She almost felt guilty, she said, that Carlos had been so idle. But now that he would be living permanently surrounded by serene affection, she wanted to see him working, showing what he could do, taking charge.

"Yes," said Ega, leaning back and smiling, "the romance is over. Now..."

But Domingos was serving up the pineapple. Ega tasted it and burst forth with loud enthusiasm. It was marvellous! Delicious!

"What did you do to it? A little bit of Madeira wine..."

"And a touch of genius!" exclaimed Carlos. "It's delicious, isn't it? Now tell me, would anything that I could do for civilisation be worth as much as this dish of pineapple? These are the things I live for! I wasn't born to remake civilisation."

"You were born," said Ega, "to pluck the flowers from the plant of civilisation, which the masses water with their sweat! So was I!"

No, no, Maria Eduarda did not want them to talk like that!

"Such glib comments spoil everything. And you, Senhor Ega, should be inspiring Carlos, not corrupting him."

Ega protested, looking languidly about him. If Carlos needed an inspiring, beneficent muse, it was not Ega, a bearded graduate of law. No, Carlos' muse was *toute trouvée*!

"I mean, think of all the beautiful pages, the many noble ideas one could produce in a paradise like this!"

And with a gentle, caressing gesture, he indicated the Toca, the quiet trees, Maria Eduarda's beauty. Afterwards, in the drawing room, while Maria Eduarda was playing a nocturne by Chopin, and he and Carlos were finishing their cigars, standing by the door out into the garden, and watching the moon come up, Ega declared that ever since they had sat down to supper, he had been in the mood to get married himself. There really was nothing like marriage, the home, the nest...

"When I think, my friend," he murmured, sombrely chewing on his cigar, "that I devoted almost a whole year of my life to that licentious Israelite who enjoys being beaten..."

"What's she up to in Sintra?" asked Carlos.

"She's up to her neck in libertinism. She has clearly given her whole heart to Dâmaso. And you know what I mean when I say 'heart.' Such degradation! It's simply obscene."

"But you adore her," said Carlos.

Ega did not reply. Then, filled with a sudden hatred for bohemianism and romanticism, he loudly sang the praises of those two lofty human duties—family and work—meanwhile downing several glasses of cognac. At midnight, when he left, he stumbled twice as he walked along the avenue of acacias, already drunk and quoting from Proudhon. And when Carlos helped him into the victoria, where Ega demanded that the top be left down so that he could commune with the moon, he still kept grabbing Carlos' arm and talking about their journal, about the strong wind of spirituality and manly virtue that must blow over the land. At last, stretched out on the seat, taking off his hat in order to feel the night breeze, he said:

"And another thing, Carlos. See if you can sort something out for me with that Englishwoman. Some delicious vices lurk beneath those modestly lowered eyelashes. See what you can do. Come on, driver, off you go! God, it's a beautiful night!"

Carlos was delighted with that first friendly supper at the Toca. His intention had been only to introduce Maria Eduarda to his close friends once they were married and back from Italy. But in his mind, their "legal union" was now indefinitely postponed, remote, almost lost in some vague future. As Ega had said, he must wait and simply let things happen. Meanwhile, however, he and Maria Eduarda could not spend the whole long winter isolated in Olivais without the sociable warmth of a few friends around them. For this reason, when, one morning, he happened to meet Cruges, who had been Maria Eduarda's neighbour and used to bring him news of the "English lady," he asked him to come to supper at the Toca on the following Sunday.

The maestro arrived in a hired cab, in the late afternoon, wearing white tie and tails, and his feelings of uneasiness began as soon as he was met by Carlos and Ega, who were both wearing light-coloured country suits. Any woman, apart from Spanish whores like Lola and Concha, made him nervous and silent, and he found Maria Eduarda, with, as he put it, "her *grande dame* air," so intimidating that he stood before her dumbstruck and red-faced, fiddling with the linings of his pockets. Carlos decided to show him round the garden before supper. With the leaves from the bushes brushing his ill-fitting tailcoat, the poor maestro tried desperately hard to say something in praise of the beauty of the place, but, inexplicably, all he could come out with were commonplace, rather slangy comments: "Smashing view!" "Sweet little place you've got here!" Then he grew furious with himself and began to perspire, unable to comprehend how such hideous banalities, so contrary to his fine artist's taste, could dribble from his lips. By the time he sat down at the table, he had succumbed to an access of mute, black depression. Not even a discussion, kindly set up for him by Maria Eduarda, about Wagner and Verdi, could unclench his stubborn lips. Carlos made one last attempt to involve him in the cheerful table talk, recounting their trip to Sintra, when he had gone looking for Maria Eduarda at the Hotel Lawrence and found, instead, a large matronly woman with a moustache and a lapdog, roundly scolding her husband in Spanish. But every exclamation from Carlos—"You remember, don't you, Cruges?" "It's true, isn't it, Cruges?"—drew from the scarlet-faced maestro a reluctant, grunted "Yes." He ended up sitting at Maria Eduarda's side like some gloomy encumbrance. He ruined the whole evening.

It had been agreed that after coffee, they would go for a drive in the countryside, but when Carlos had already taken the reins and Maria Eduarda was sitting on the seat beside him, buttoning up her gloves, Ega, who feared the chill of the evening, jumped out and ran to fetch his overcoat. At that precise moment, they heard the sound of a horse trotting along the road, and the Marquis appeared.

This was a great surprise to Carlos, who had not seen him all summer. The Marquis stopped at once, doffing his broad-brimmed hat and bowing low as soon as he saw Maria Eduarda.

"I thought you were in Golegã," exclaimed Carlos. "In fact, Cruges told me you were. When did you get back?"

He had arrived the previous day. He had gone to Ramalhete and found the place deserted. He was on his way now to Olivais to see one of the two Vargas brothers who had recently got married and moved into a house there to spend the first few weeks of conjugal life.

"Which Vargas, the fat one who races horses?"

"No, the thin one who goes yachting."

Carlos leaned over to examine the Marquis' horse, a small, good-looking mare, a pretty dark chestnut.

"Is she new?"

"A little pony I got from Darque. Would you like to buy her off me? I'm a bit too heavy for her, and she'd be fine pulling a dog-cart."

"Ride around a little and let me see."

The Marquis rode around, sitting well in the saddle, showing off the horse. Carlos thought she had "a good action." Maria Eduarda murmured: "Very pretty, she's got a lovely head." Then Carlos introduced the Marquis de Sousela to Madame MacGren. The Marquis brought the horse closer and, with his hat off, shook Maria Eduarda's hand; and, while they waited for Ega, who was taking an age to return, they talked about the summer, about Santa Olávia, Olivais, the Toca. The Marquis had not been there for a long time. On the last occasion, he had fallen victim to Craft's eccentricity.

"Imagine, Senhora," he said to Maria Eduarda, "this fellow Craft invites me to lunch. I arrive, and the gardener informs me that Senhor Craft, along with his manservant and his cook, has left for Oporto, but that there is a message for me in the drawing room. I go in and see, hanging around the neck of a Japanese idol, a sheet of paper which says more or less: 'The God Tchi has the honour of inviting the Marquis, on behalf of his absent master, to go through to the dining room, where he will find, on the sideboard, cheese and wine—a fitting lunch for a strong man.' And that was my lunch! In order not to eat alone, I shared it with the gardener."

"I hope you had your revenge," exclaimed Maria Eduarda, laughing.

"Indeed, I did, Senhora. I invited him to supper, and when he arrived, having driven all the way from Olivais, my doorman told him that the Marquis had gone off on a trip and that there was neither bread nor cheese. The result: Craft sent me a dozen magnificent bottles of Chambertin. And I haven't seen the god Tchi since."

The god Tchi was still there, fat and ugly. Naturally, Carlos invited the Marquis to return that night, on his way back from Vargas' house, to revisit his old friend Tchi.

The Marquis arrived at ten o'clock, and they enjoyed a delightful evening. The Marquis immediately managed to get Cruges to shake off his melancholy by dragging him over to the piano; Maria Eduarda sang; and there was much witty conversation. The lights remained on in that lovers' hideaway until late into the night, for that first party with friends.

At first, these jolly gatherings were, as Ega called them, Sunday affairs, but the autumn was growing colder, and soon the trees at the Toca would be losing their leaves, and so Carlos made the meetings twice-weekly instead, on Sundays and Thursdays, which had been their traditional free days at university. He had found a wonderful cook from Alsace, brought up in the great traditions, and who had once served the Bishop of Strasbourg, but had ended up in Lisbon because of her son's extravagances and various other misfortunes. Maria Eduarda, for her part, applied a delicate knowledge to the composition of these suppers, and the days spent at the Toca were considered by the Marquis to be "days of civilisation."

The table glowed, and the tapestries, depicting dense leafy trees, created around it the shadowy gloom of a woodland retreat in which, out of mere caprice, silver candelabra had been lit. The wines came from Ramalhete's wonderful cellar. All things earthly and heavenly were discussed with great verve and imagination, everything except "Portuguese politics," which was considered an indecorous topic of conversation among people of taste.

When coffee was served, Rosa would appear, with her smile, her little bare arms, her white starched dresses over black silk stockings, everything about her exhaling the good healthy smell of flowers. The Marquis adored her, competing for her favours with Ega, who had already asked Maria Eduarda for Rosa's hand in marriage and who had, for some time now, been composing a sonnet in her honour. She preferred the Marquis; she found Ega "very . . ." and she would complete her thought by wiggling a finger in the air, as if to say that Ega was "very complicated."

"You see!" Ega would exclaim. "That's because I'm more civilised than the Marquis! It is a case of simplicity failing to understand refinement."

"No, it's not, you wretch!" everyone else around him exclaimed. "It's because you talk like a book, and Nature abhors artifice!"

They would drink to Maria Eduarda's health; and she would smile, happy to be with these newfound friends, and looking divinely beautiful, almost always dressed in black, with a modest décolletage that revealed the incomparable splendour of her throat and neck.

Then they began organising festivities. One Sunday, when they could hear bells ringing and, in the distance, rockets whistling through the air, Ega regretted that his austere philosophical principles prevented him from celebrating that village saint who, in life, had doubtless been gentleness itself, a delightful old stick-in-the-mud, full of dreams, but, he went on, would it not have been on just such a day, fine and dry, beneath a great sun-lit sky, that the Battle of Thermopylae took place? Why shouldn't they set off rockets in honour of Leonidas and the Three Hundred? And so they did, they set off rockets to the eternal glory of Sparta.

Then they celebrated other historical dates. The anniversary of the discovery of the Venus de Milo was commemorated with the release of a miniature hot air balloon. On another occasion, the Marquis brought from Lisbon a group of famous *fado*-singers, all crammed into one carriage: Pintado, Vira-Vira, and Gago; and, after dinner, until late in the night, with the moon shining on the river, five guitars had sobbed out the most plangent of Portuguese *fados*.

When they were alone, Carlos and Maria Eduarda spent their mornings in the Japanese pavilion, having grown fond of this first refuge of their love, small and cramped though it was, where their hearts could beat closer to each other. Carlos had replaced the straw mats with his own beautiful yellow and pearl-white Indian bedspreads. One of his greatest concerns now was to beautify the Toca; like a happy newlywed perfecting his nest, he never came back from Lisbon without bringing with him some Saxe figurine, an ivory carving, or a piece of faience-ware.

Maria Eduarda, meanwhile, was constantly reminding him of Ega's intellectual plans; she wanted Carlos to work and make a name for himself; this would make her so proud and would, above all, be a supreme joy to his grandfather. To please her (rather than to satisfy the needs of his own intellect), Carlos had gone back to writing his literary articles on medicine for the *Gazeta Médica*. He worked in the pavilion in the mornings. There he kept his first drafts, his books, and the famous manuscript of *Medicine Ancient and Modern*. And, in the end, he found it really delightful being there, wearing a light silk jacket, with his cigarettes beside him, the cool murmur of trees all around him, as he patiently chiselled out his sentences, while she sat silently embroidering. His ideas were more original, his style more colourful in the confined space of that satin-lined pavilion, which she perfumed with her presence. Maria Eduarda respected his work as something noble and sacred. Each morning, she herself brushed away any light dust that had blown in through the window onto the books; she made sure he had a supply of clean paper and new pens; and she was busily embroidering a satin cover for a down-filled cushion so that the worker would be more comfortable in his vast leather chair.

One day, she had offered to make a fair copy of one of his articles. And Carlos, who thought her handwriting very fine, almost comparable to Dâmaso's legendary hand, now kept her constantly at work as a copyist, feeling a greater love for any work with which she was associated. The pains the dear creature took! She used a special paper for the purpose, of a soft ivory white; and with her little finger crooked, she set about copying out Carlos' weighty thoughts on Vitalism and Transformism with as much delicacy as if she were making lace. A kiss was all the payment she required.

Sometimes, Carlos gave lessons to Rosa—history, which he told to her as familiarly as if it were a fairy tale, and geography, telling her about lands where dark-skinned people lived, and about ancient rivers that ran past ruined temples. For Maria Eduarda, this was the supreme pleasure. Serious, silent, with an almost religious awe, she would listen to her beloved Carlos teaching her daughter. Her work would fall from her hands, and Carlos' enthusiasm and Rosa's rapt attention as she sat at his feet, drinking in those beautiful stories about Joan of Arc or the caravels that sailed to India, filled Maria Eduarda's shining eyes with a mist of happy tears.

Afonso da Maia had been talking of leaving Santa Olávia since the middle of October, and his departure had only been delayed by some work he was having done in the old part of the house and in the stables; he had been filled, lately, with a passion for building; the rough touch of new wood and the sharp smell of paint made him feel younger, he said. Carlos and Maria Eduarda were also thinking about leaving Olivais. Carlos, out of domestic duty, would not be able to stay there all the time once his grandfather returned to Ramalhete. Besides, the late autumn was becoming dark and wild, and the Toca was rather less bucolic now, with its bare muddy garden, the mist over the river, and only one fire in the study, because the sumptuous fireplace in the dining room, flanked by glass-eyed Nubians, smoked appallingly whenever Domingos tried to light it.

On one such day, having stayed with Maria Eduarda until late and then having barely slept at all in his thin-walled "cottage" because of the rain and high winds that had started up in the early hours, Carlos rose at nine and went to the Toca. The windows of Maria Eduarda's room were still closed; the morning was brightening up; in the fine blue air, the garden, half-unclothed and washed clean, had the lovely silent grace of winter. Carlos was strolling about, looking at the pots full of chrysanthemums in flower, when the bell at the gate rang. It was the postman. He had written to Cruges only a few days before to ask if the apartment in Rua de São Francisco would be free for the first really cold snap in December; and, expecting a reply to this, he went down to open the gate, accompanied by Niniche. The post, that morning, however, consisted only of a letter from Ega and two rolled-up copies of newspapers—one addressed to him, the other to "Madame Castro Gomes, c/o Senhor Craft's house, Olivais."

Walking back beneath the acacias, Carlos opened Ega's letter first. It was dated the previous evening: "At night, in haste." It said: "Please read the superior piece of prose reminiscent of Tacitus in this rag I'm sending you. But don't worry. I have managed, by pecuniary means, to suppress the whole print-run, with the exception of two copies which were sent to the Toca and (thanks to the supreme logic of constitutional habit), to the Palace, to the Head of State! However, even that one won't reach its destination. I have an idea from which gutter this slime emerged and we need to take steps. Come quickly. I'll expect you at two. And, as Iago said to Cassius: 'Put money in thy purse.'"

Carlos anxiously unrolled the newspaper. It was called *The Devil's Trumpet*, and everything about it—the print, the paper, the abundance of italics, the worn type—bespoke filth and mischief. On the very first page, two crosses in pencil marked an article in which, as he saw at a glance, his name was mentioned over and over. And this is what he read: "'So, Senhor Maia, *Senhor Dandy*, you don't bother going to your consulting rooms any more, eh, you don't even have time to visit the sick?' —This remark, overheard in the Chiado, at the door of the Casa Havanesa, was directed at Maia, the Maia of the English horses, the very same Maia who lives in Ramalhete, and who fancies himself a regular *fashion-plate*; and then Father Paulino, *who keeps his eyes peeled* and who happened to be passing on this very occasion, heard a second *blast on the Trumpet*: 'Senhor Maia finds it *much warmer* clinging to the skirts of a *married Brazilian lady* who is neither Brazilian nor married, and whom the ninny has set up in a house near Olivais, in order, he says, *to enjoy the fresh air*! Good God, there's one born every minute! The man thinks he's nabbed himself a real prize, but the boys around here with real taste simply laugh, because what the trollop can't get enough of aren't his lovely eyes, but his lovely money. And this simpleton, who rides around on his *English* nags, as if he were a Marquis, no, *the* Marquis, imagined he'd got himself a really chic lady, from the Paris boulevards no less, and married, too, and with a title! And it turns out (and this is enough to make anyone burst their buttons laughing), it turns out that this *lady* was, in fact, a distinctly shop-worn *cocotte*, brought here by a Brazilian *who had grown tired of her* and wanted to pass her on to us handsome Lusitanians. And Maia, the poor dolt, fell for it! Worse still, he was only getting yet another man's leavings, because *she*, before Maia set his cap at her, had been playing fast and loose over there in Rua de São Francisco with a lad from one of Lisbon's very finest families, who also left her in the lurch, because the only women us Portuguese men really like are those *lovely ladies from Spain*. Fool he may be, but this doesn't mean Senhor Maia can't turn nasty! So just in case he does, he'd better be very careful indeed, because the Devil has his *Trumpet* ready to *trumpet* to the world at large any new exploits by *Maia the Conquistador*.' What do you say to that, Senhor Maia?"

Carlos stood stockstill beneath the acacias, the newspaper in his hand, wearing the same look of dumb, furious horror as a man whose face has suddenly been splattered with mud! It wasn't rage at seeing his love publicly ridiculed in a sordid rag like that, it was horror at hearing those words couched in the kind of thuggish, low-life slang in which Lisbon so excelled, splashing, as if with rancid grease, both Maria Eduarda and the splendour of their love. He felt dirty. And the sole idea that emerged out of his confusion was to kill the brute who had written these words.

Yes, kill him! Ega had suppressed this issue, and therefore must know the person responsible. It didn't matter that the copies in his hand were the only ones in print. His face had been spattered with mud. Whether the insult had been posted in every city square or hurled only at him, in secret, on one single sheet of paper, it didn't matter. The person who had dared to do this must be crushed!

He decided to go straight to Ramalhete. Domingos was at the kitchen window, cleaning the silver and whistling. However, when Carlos asked him to go into Olivais to find a cab, Domingos consulted the clock and said:

"Torto will be here at eleven o'clock to take the mistress to Lisbon."

Carlos then remembered that, the previous evening, Maria Eduarda had been planning a visit to the dressmaker's and to the bookshops. This was a nuisance on the one day when he—and his walking stick—needed to be free! Melanie happened to be passing carrying a jug of hot water, and she said that her mistress was not yet dressed and that she might not even go to Lisbon. Carlos continued pacing up and down the lawn between the walnut trees.

He sat down at last on the cork bench, unrolled the *Trumpet* that had been addressed to Maria Eduarda and slowly re-read the vile prose; and in that copy sent directly to her the coarse language seemed even more of an outrage, even more intolerable—one that must be punished by blood. It really was monstrous that someone should dare to hurl great handfuls of mud at a woman living quietly and inoffensively in her home! And his indignation grew to encompass not only the perpetrator of those filthy words, but also the rotten society that had produced the perpetrator. Every city had its vermin, but only Lisbon, ghastly Lisbon, with its moral putrefaction, its social degradation, its complete absence of good sense, its profound lack of taste, its lies and its vulgarity, could produce *The Devil's Trumpet*!

And yet even while he was in the grip of this high moral rage, a pang went through him, precise and piercing. It was true that, from his viewpoint, Lisbon society was nothing but a sordid dung-heap, but had the newspaper printed any actual calumny? No. It was Maria Eduarda's past, which she had ripped from herself like some shabby, ragged dress, and which he himself had buried deep down, covering it over with his love and his good name, and which someone was disinterring and holding up to the sunlight, revealing every tear and stain. And now this had become a permanent threat hanging over his life like a terrible cloud. In vain he had forgiven her, in vain he had forgotten. The world knew. And at any time, self-interest or malice could cause that article in *The Devil's Trumpet* to be rewritten.

He got to his feet, terribly shaken. And there, beneath the leafless trees, where, in the summer, when their murmuring leaves were filled with shade, he had walked with Maria, his chosen wife, Carlos wondered to himself for the first time if domestic and social honour, the purity of the men from whom he was descended and the dignity of his possible male descendants, really would allow him to marry her.

He could devote all his love and his whole fortune to her, yes, but marry her? And what if there was a child? His child, when he was a grown man, proud and pure, might one day read in some future equivalent of *The Devil's Trumpet* that his mother had been the mistress of a Brazilian, having first been the mistress of an Irishman. And his son would come to him, filled with indignation, and demand to know: "Is this a lie?" and he would have to bow his head and mutter: "No, it's true!" And his son would find himself forever tied to a mother of whose sufferings and charms the world knew nothing, but whose errors, very cruelly, were common knowledge.

She herself would agree! If he were to appeal to her reason, always so upright and honest, and show her the mockery and the insults to which a vile rag like that might one day expose any child born to them, she herself would happily release him from his vow, glad to enter Ramalhete by the velvet-lined back staircase, as long as a strong and constant love awaited her above. Throughout the summer, she had not once mentioned a union other than the one in which their hearts lived so loyally and so comfortably. No, Maria Eduarda was not a religious devotee, concerned about "mortal sin"! What did she care about a priest's blessing!

Yes, but could he, who had asked her to consecrate their union in that way, at the most dramatic point of their long love, could he say to her now: "Sorry, it was silly of me, let's forget about it, all right"? No, nor was that what his heart desired! He depended entirely on her, and he did so with a whole-hearted ardent love, while his reason argued with him, cautious and austere. He had found in that other soul his perfect religion; he had found in her arms a magnificent sensuality; outside of that there was no happiness; the only wise thing to do was to bind her to him by the strongest bond there was, his name, even if all *The Devil's Trumpets* in the world thundered forth their calumnies. And thus he would confront the world in an attitude of proud rebellion, affirming the omnipotence of Love, the all-conquering kingdom! But first, he would kill the man who had written that article! He paced up and down, trampling the grass. And all his thoughts reduced down to a sense of utter fury at the wretch who had sullied his love and, for a moment, introduced into his life such uncertainty and such torment!

Maria Eduarda opened the window nearby. She was wearing a dark outfit suitable for going to the city; and her bright tender smile and the warm full beauty of her shoulders beneath the close-fitting fabric of her dress, were enough for Carlos immediately to reject all the disloyal, cowardly doubts to which, under the leafless trees, he had momentarily succumbed. He ran to her. And the kiss he gave her, slow and silent, had the humility of someone imploring forgiveness.

"What's wrong? Why so serious?"

He smiled. He wasn't serious in the sense of solemn, perhaps just a little annoyed. He had received a letter from Ega, with another of Ega's endlessly complicated predicaments. And he had to go to Lisbon, and possibly spend the night there.

"Spend the night!" she exclaimed in disappointed tones, placing her hands on his shoulders.

"Yes, possibly. It's awful, I know, but with anything Ega gets involved in one must always expect the unexpected. Are you still going to Lisbon?"

"Now, most certainly . . . if you want me to, that is."

"It's a lovely day, but it will be cold on the road."

Maria Eduarda particularly liked these bright winter days, with a sharp, shivering breeze. They made her feel lighter, more intelligent.

"That's decided, then," said Carlos, throwing down his cigarette. "We'd better have some lunch, my love. Poor Ega will be positively howling with impatience."

While Maria Eduarda ran off to hurry Domingos along, Carlos walked slowly across the wet grass as far as the line of bushes that acted as a protective hedge for the house on that side. The land sloped down to reveal small houses, white walls, olive groves, and a large smoking factory chimney; beyond, lay the fine cold blue of the river, and beyond that, the hills, of a still deeper blue, and a group of white houses nestling by the water, clear and soft in the gentle, transparent air. He stopped for a moment, looking. And that village whose name he had never known, so still and happy in the light, filled Carlos with a sudden desire for peace and obscurity, in some similar corner of the world, by the water's edge, where no one would know him and where there would be no *Devil's Trumpets*, and he could enjoy the peace of a poor, simple man living under a humble roof in the bosom of the woman he loved.

Maria Eduarda called down to him from the dining-room window, where she had leaned out to pick the last climbing roses which were still in flower.

"It's a beautiful day for travelling, Maria!" said Carlos, walking across the grass towards her.

"And when it's sunny, Lisbon is lovely at this time of year."

"I know, but then there's the Chiado, the tittle-tattle, the politicking, the gossip-sheets and all the other horrors. I'm beginning to warm to the idea of a hut in Africa somewhere!"

Lunch took longer than intended, and it was nearly one o'clock when Torto's carriage set off down the road, still full of puddles from the night rain. As they headed downhill, just outside the village, a coupé came galloping past. Maria Eduarda was sure she had spotted Ega's white hat and monocle. They stopped. It *was* Ega, who had recognised their carriage too, and was already coming over to them, jumping over the muddy puddles on his long stork-like legs, calling out to Carlos.

When he saw Maria Eduarda, he looked embarrassed.

"What a lovely surprise! I was just coming to see you. It was such a beautiful day that I said to myself . . ."

"Well, pay off your cab and come with us," Carlos said, interrupting him and studying Ega with anxious eyes, wanting to know the reason for his sudden arrival at Olivais.

When he got into their carriage, having paid off his driver, Ega, feeling awkward and unable to talk about the article in *The Devil's Trumpet* in front of Maria Eduarda, started talking instead, under Carlos' constant watchful eye, about the winter and the floods in Ribatejo. Maria Eduarda had read about it. Such a tragedy, two children drowned in their cradles, cattle lost, awful! Finally, Carlos could contain himself no longer.

"I got your letter."

And Ega said:

"It can all be sorted out! It's all arranged. In fact, I really did come today purely out of bucolic nostalgia."

Very discreetly, Maria Eduarda looked out at the river. Ega made a rapid gesture with thumb and fingers indicating that it was merely a matter of money. Carlos felt easier, and Ega went back to discussing the victims of the floods in Ribatejo and the literary and artistic benefit evening which was going to be "perpetrated" in the Teatro da Trindade. It was to be a vast, official, solemn event. Parliamentary tenors, literary nightingales, pianists wearing the order of Santiago, and all the mellifluous and sentimental members of the Constitutionalist Party would be "on the front line." The King and Queen were to attend too, and garlands of camellias were already being woven for the occasion. Even he, despite being a democrat, had been invited to read a passage from his *Memoirs of an Atom*, but he had refused, out of modesty and because he could find nothing in the book stupid enough to please the Lisbon public. But he had suggested Cruges, and the maestro was going either to deafen them or lull them to sleep with one of his "meditations." There would also be a socially-minded poem by Alencar. In short, it promised to be a veritable orgy.

"You really should go," Ega said to Maria Eduarda. "It will be truly picturesque. It would give you the chance to see the whole of romantic, liberal Portugal in action, in white tie and tails, giving it their all."

"Yes, you really should," cried Carlos, laughing. "Besides, if Cruges is playing and Alencar is reciting, it will be just like one of our soirées."

"Of course!" exclaimed Ega, fumbling for his monocle and warming to his theme. "There are two things one must see in Lisbon: a procession following the stations of the Cross and an evening of poetry and music!"

They had reached Largo do Pelourinho by then. Carlos shouted to the driver to stop at the top of Rua do Alecrim; they would get out there and take the omnibus up to Ramalhete.

However, the carriage stopped shortly before, right by the pavement, opposite a tailor's shop. A tall man, with a large apostolic beard, and all dressed in heavy mourning, happened to be standing there, drawing on his black gloves. When he saw Maria Eduarda, who had leaned over towards the door, the man looked surprised; then, with a little colour in his long otherwise pale face, he gravely doffed his hat, a vast affair with a curved brim, of the type fashionable in 1830, and with a large black crêpe ribbon tied around it.

"Who's that?" asked Carlos.

"It's Dâmaso's uncle, Guimarães," said Maria Eduarda, who had also flushed slightly. "How odd that he should be here!"

Of course, it was the famous Monsieur Guimaran, the one who wrote for *Rappel* and who was a close friend of Gambetta! Carlos remembered having met this patriarch before at the circus with Alencar. He, in turn, greeted him, and the other man once more doffed his sombre Carbonari hat. Ega snatched up his monocle in order to examine this legendary uncle of Dâmaso's, who had helped govern France; and when they had said goodbye to Maria Eduarda, and the carriage was already proceeding up Rua de Alecrim and they were crossing the street to the Hotel Central, he turned round again, seduced by the patriarch's manner and by that magnificent revolutionary beard.

"What a fine-looking fellow, and what a magnificent hat, eh? How the devil does Senhora Dona Maria Eduarda know him?"

"From Paris. He was a great friend of her mother's. She's spoken to me about him before. He's a poor wretch apparently. He's not a close friend of Gambetta nor of anyone else important for that matter. He translates articles from the Spanish press for *Rappel* and just about keeps the wolf from the door."

"But Dâmaso said . . ."

"Dâmaso's a complete fraud. But let's get down to business. About that piece of filth you sent me from *The Devil's Trumpet* . . ."

As they walked slowly along the Aterro, Ega told him all about "that piece of filth." He had received a copy of *The Devil's Trumpet* the previous evening at Ramalhete. He was already familiar with the scurrilous rag, and even knew the owner and editor, Palma—known as "Big Palma," to distinguish him from another illustrious individual known as "Little Palma." He realised at once that, although the prose style was Palma's, the inspiration must have come from elsewhere. Palma knew nothing about Carlos or Maria Eduarda, or about the house in Rua de São Francisco or the Toca. It seemed unlikely that he would, purely for his own intellectual pleasure, write an article guaranteed to bring him only problems and beatings. The article must, therefore, have been commissioned and paid for. In the world of money, the person with the most always wins. Basing himself on this solid principle, he had gone straight to "Big Palma," to beard him in his den.

"You're not familiar with his den, too, are you?" asked Carlos, horrified.

"Not exactly. I went to the Ministry of Justice, to see a chap there who had worked with him once on some business involving 'religious almanacs.'"

Then he had gone to Palma's den. And he discovered that friendly Providence had taken a helping hand. First, the machine had broken down after printing only five or six copies, exhausted from churning out such defamatory rubbish. Second, Palma was furious with the gentleman who had commissioned the article because he had not played fair on the very serious matter of money. And so, no sooner had Ega proposed buying the whole print-run, than the journalist, trembling with hope and gratitude, had held out his large hand with its bitten fingernails. Ega had given him the five *libras* he had on him, and promised him another ten.

"It's expensive, but what can you do?" Ega went on. "I panicked slightly and didn't bargain him down. And as for him telling me the name of the gentleman who commissioned the article, Palma, poor thing, immediately launched into a litany of woes, saying that he had a Spanish mistress to support, that his landlord had raised his rent, that Lisbon is so terribly expensive, that the lot of literature in this unfortunate country, etc. etc."

"How much does he want?"

"One hundred *mil réis*, but if we threaten him with the police, he might come down to forty."

"Promise him a hundred, promise him the whole lot, as long as I get the name. Who do you think it might be?"

Ega shrugged and slowly drew a line on the ground with his walking stick. And more slowly still he listed the necessary attributes of the person who had inspired the article: someone who knew Castro Gomes; someone who had visited Rua de São Francisco; someone who knew about the Toca; someone who, for reasons of jealousy or vengeance, had a deep-seated desire to hurt Carlos; someone who knew Maria Eduarda's history; and, finally, someone who was a coward.

"You're describing Dâmaso," exclaimed Carlos, turning pale.

Ega shrugged again and drew another line on the ground.

"Possibly not . . . who knows! Anyway, we're going to find out for sure soon enough because, to bring this whole business to an end, I've arranged to meet Palma at three o'clock in the Lisbonense. You'd better come too. Have you got any money on you?"

"If it's Dâmaso, I'll kill him!" muttered Carlos.

He did not have enough money on him. They took a hired cab to go to Vilaça's office, but Vilaça had gone to Mafra for a christening. Carlos had to borrow a hundred *mil réis* from old Cortês, his grandfather's tailor. When, at around four o'clock, they arrived at the entrance to the Lisbonense in Largo de Santa Justa, Palma was standing in the doorway, wearing a worn velvet jacket and a pair of rather tight, pale trousers, and lighting a cigarette. He generously held out his hand to Carlos, who declined to take it. And "Big Palma," not in the least offended, his hand left hanging in the air, declared that he had been just about to leave, weary of waiting over a glass of cold grog. And also that he regretted having put Senhor Maia to the trouble of coming there in person.

"I had things all sorted out with friend Ega here, but, if you like, there's a room upstairs where we'll be more comfortable and where we can have a drink."

As they climbed the dismal stairs, Carlos remembered having seen those thick-lensed glasses and that flabby, sallow face before. Of course, in Sintra, with Eusèbiozinho and the two Spanish women, on the day when he had gone sniffing around the silent streets, like a stray dog, looking for Maria Eduarda! This only made Senhor Palma seem still more odious. Upstairs, they went into a small room, with a single barred window through which filtered the murky light from an inner courtyard. On the grease-and wine-spattered table-cloth stood a few plates and a cruet stand in which flies floated in the oil dispenser. Senhor Palma clapped his hands and ordered some gin. Then, with a bold tug at the waistband of his trousers, he said:

"Well, I hope I'm among gentlemen here. As I said to friend Ega, in this whole business . . ."

Carlos cut him short, significantly tapping the edge of the table with the tip of his walking stick.

"Let's get to the main point. How much do you want for telling me who commissioned that article?"

"Who commissioned it and proof of their identity!" added Ega, who was examining an engraving on the wall which depicted a group of naked women at the water's edge. "The name isn't enough. This is not to say that we don't trust you, of course, but obviously we'd be unlikely to believe it if you told us that the gentleman was the King himself!"

Palma shrugged. Of course he would provide proof. He might have other faults, but he was no fraud. When it came to business, he was all openness and honesty. And if they reached an agreement, he would immediately hand over all the proof he had right there in his pocket, conclusive and categorical. He had the letter from the friend who had commissioned the thing, the list of people to whom he was supposed to send *The Devil's Trumpet* and the first draft in pencil.

"And you're asking one hundred *mil reís* for all of that?" asked Carlos.

Palma hesitated for a moment, adjusting his spectacles with plump fingers. Then the waiter brought the bottle of gin, and the editor of *The Devil's Trumpet* generously offered the gentlemen a drink and even pulled up two chairs for them to sit on. Both refused—Carlos standing by the table where he had just placed his walking stick, Ega moving on to another engraving which showed two monks getting drunk. Then, when the waiter had left, Ega went over to Palma and familiarly patted the journalist's shoulder.

"A hundred *mil réis* is quite a sum of money, Palma! And we're being very kind in offering it to you. Because if someone were to take you to court over the kind of articles you publish in *The Devil's Trumpet*, you'd end up behind bars! Obviously, this is another matter entirely, you didn't mean to offend anyone, but, nevertheless, you could still end up behind bars. That's why Severino, if you remember, was sent off to Africa—stuck in the hold of a ship on sailor's rations and with the occasional lashing. Most unpleasant. That's why we wanted to sort this out here, gentleman to gentleman, in a friendly manner."

Palma, head bowed, was dissolving sugar lumps in his glass of gin. Then he sighed and said, rather glumly, that it was because they were all gentlemen and friends that he was accepting the hundred *mil réis*.

Carlos immediately produced a handful of *libras* from his trouser pocket, and, without a word, placed them one by one on a plate. And "Big Palma," roused by the clink of gold, unbuttoned his jacket and took out a wallet which bore an extravagant silver monogram beneath the coronet of a Viscount. His fingers were trembling, but he finally placed three pieces of paper on the table. Ega, who was waiting, watching eagerly through his monocle, gave a yelp of triumph. He had recognised Dâmaso's handwriting!

Carlos carefully examined the papers. There was a brief, slangy letter from Dâmaso to Palma, enclosing the article and recommending that he "spice it up a little." There was the draft of the article, laboriously produced by Dâmaso, with comments and corrections. There was the list, written by Dâmaso, of the people who should receive *The Devil's Trumpet*; these included the Countess de Gouvarinho, the Brazilian Ambassador, Dona Maria da Cunha, the King, all the friends who frequented Ramalhete, Cohen, various officials and the *prima donna* Fancelli.

Palma, meanwhile, was nervously drumming his fingers on the table-cloth, alongside the plate full of gleaming gold coins. It was Ega who, after glancing through the documents over Carlos' shoulder, said:

"Take the cash, friend Palma! Business is business, and you don't want your money to get cold!"

When he finally touched the money, "Big Palma" relaxed and grew loquacious. Damn it, if he'd realised the article was about a fine gentleman like Senhor Maia, he would never have accepted it. But there you are! It had been a friend of his, Eusèbiozinho Silveira, who first mentioned it to him. Then Salcede had joined in, soft-soaping him and saying it was all a joke and that Maia wouldn't mind, etc. etc., and full of promises. Anyway, he had succumbed to temptation. And both Salcede and Silveira had behaved like utter scoundrels.

"It was just lucky that the machine broke down! Otherwise, I'd have been in a fine mess, damn it! And I'm truly sorry about it, I really am! But what's done is done. No great harm's been caused, and you have to earn a living somehow."

He was gazing at the coins in his hand, mentally counting them; then in one relieved and noisy gulp, he drank what remained of his gin. Carlos had put away Dâmaso's letters in one of his pockets and was already opening the door. At the last moment, however, he turned to ask one more question.

"So my friend Eusèbiozinho Silveira was involved in the business too?"

Senhor Palma assured him that Eusébio had only spoken on Dâmaso's behalf.

"Eusébio, poor thing, was just the messenger. Dâmaso and I don't really have much to do with each other now. We haven't got on since we had a bit of set-to at Biscainha's place. Just between you and me, I threatened him with a smack in the face, and he backed down. After a while, though, we started talking to each other again when I was in charge of the society column in *A Verdade*. He came and asked me very nicely, on behalf of the Count de Landim, if I could say something flattering about the Count's birthday party. Then, when it was Dâmaso's birthday, I did the same thing. He took me out to supper, and we've been on better terms since, but he's not to be trusted, that one. As I say, though, poor Eusèbiozinho was just the messenger."

Without a word or a gesture to Palma, Carlos turned and left the room. The editor of *The Devil's Trumpet* nevertheless bowed in the direction of the door; then, quite unaffected, he returned cheerily to his gin and gave another tug at the waistband of his trousers. Ega, meanwhile, was slowly lighting a cigar.

"So are you in charge of the whole newspaper now, Palma?"

"No, there's Silvestre as well."

"Which Silvestre is that?"

"The one who works on *Pingada*. I don't think you know him. He's a skinny boy, not bad-looking. He's not the sharpest blade in the drawer, mind, and he writes a load of waffle, but he knows about society matters. He was with the Viscountess de Cabelas for a while, and refers to her as his 'vice-countess'. I mean sometimes he can be quite witty! And he really knows his society gossip: the dirty tricks the nobs get up to, who's having an affair with whom, all the frauds and swindles. Have you never read anything by him? Dull stuff. I always have to rewrite it. I was going to have one of my own articles in there this time, you know, a bit sophisticated, with just a touch of realism, which is the way I like it . . . Oh well, it'll have to wait till next time now. And another thing Ega, I owe you one. Any time you need us, me and the *Trumpet* are at your disposal!"

Ega held out his hand and said:

"Thank you, wise Palma! And *adiós*!"

"*Vaya usted con Dios, Don Juanito!*" exclaimed the worthy man with great panache.

Downstairs, Carlos was waiting in the cab.

"What now?" asked Ega, leaning in through the door.

"Jump in, and we'll go and sort out Dâmaso."

Carlos had already come up with a plan for this "sorting-out." He wanted to issue a challenge to Dâmaso, as the proven author of the insulting newspaper article. The duel must be fought either with swords or foils, that is, with one of those blades the mere glint of which used to make Dâmaso turn pale whenever he encountered them in the fencing gallery at Ramalhete. In the unlikely event of Dâmaso agreeing to fight, Carlos would wound him somewhere between his two chubby cheeks and his belly, a wound that would keep him confined to bed for months. If he refused, the only satisfaction Carlos would accept would be a document signed by Senhor Salcede in which he would write these simple words: "I, the undersigned, declare that I am a scoundrel." And he was counting on Ega's help in all this.

"Oh, yes please!" cried Ega, rubbing his hands, his whole face bright with glee. "When can we start?"

Meanwhile, he said, grim etiquette demanded another second; and he suggested Cruges, who was a passive, malleable fellow. However, it was impossible to find the maestro, because his maid invariably stated that Master Vitorino was not at home. They decided to go to the Grémio and, from there, send a note summoning him "to an urgent case involving friendship and art."

"Right," said Ega, still rubbing his hands, as the carriage trotted towards Rua de São Francisco, "so we're going to finish Dâmaso off, are we?"

"Yes, we have to put a stop to this persecution. It's becoming ridiculous. And with either a sword thrust or a letter, we can keep the vile creature out of action for a good long time. I'd prefer the sword thrust myself, but otherwise, I leave it to you to set out the terms in a strongly worded letter."

"Oh, you'll get a good letter, don't worry!" said Ega, baring his teeth in a fierce smile.

At the Grémio, once they had written the note to Cruges, they went and waited for him in the reading room. The Count de Gouvarinho and Steinbroken were standing by one of the windows, chatting. Both men were taken by surprise. Steinbroken opened his arms to *cher* Maia, whom he had not seen since Afonso's departure for Santa Olávia. Gouvarinho welcomed Ega with a smile, renewing a certain camaraderie that had grown up between them during the summer in Sintra; but he offered Carlos only the briefest and coldest of handshakes. Some days before, when they had met in Largo do Loreto, Gouvarinho had merely muttered in passing a curt "How are you, Maia?" in which Carlos had already sensed a new coolness. Gone were the effusive greetings and the affectionate slaps on the back, from the days when Carlos and the Countess used to lie in her aunt's bed in Santa Isabel, smoking cigarettes. Now that Carlos had abandoned the Countess, Rua de São Marçal, and the comfortable sofa onto which she would fall with a whisper of crumpled skirts, her husband appeared to be sulking, as if he had been abandoned too.

"I so miss the wonderful arguments we used to have in Sintra!" he said, giving Ega the warm slap on the back that once he would have given Maia. "First-rate they were!"

They had had some real "knock-down battles" in the garden of the Hotel Vítor, about literature, religion, morality. One evening, they had even fallen out over the divinity of Jesus.

"It's true!" said Ega. "You talked as if you'd joined the priesthood!"

The Count smiled. Joined the priesthood! Certainly not! No one knew better than he that there was a great deal of mythology in those sublime gospel stories, but it was a mythology that served to comfort the human soul. And that was what he had said to his friend Ega that night. Were philosophy and rationalism capable of consoling a grieving mother? No. Therefore ...

"At any rate, we had some brilliant arguments!" he concluded, looking at his watch. "And I confess that I love a good argument about religion or metaphysics. If politics would allow me a little time off, I would devote myself to philosophy. That's what I was really born to do, to worry away at philosophical problems."

Steinbroken, meanwhile, standing stiffly in his blue frock-coat, with a little sprig of rosemary in his buttonhole, had clasped Carlos' hands.

"*Mais vous êtes devenu encore plus fort! Et Afonso da Maia, toujours dans ses terres? Est-ce qu'on ne va pas le voir un peu cet hiver?*"

And he immediately regretted not having visited Santa Olávia. But what could he do? The royal family had decided to spend the summer in Sintra, and he had to go with them, as part of the court. Then he'd had to make a quick visit to England, from which he'd returned only a few days ago.

Carlos had read about this in the *Gazeta Ilustrada*.

"*Vous avez lu ça? Oh oui, on a été très aimable, très aimable avec moi à la* Gazette."

They had announced his departure and later his arrival with some particularly well-chosen words of friendship. Not that he would expect any less, given the genuine bond of affection between Portugal and Finland. "*Mais enfin on avait été charmant, charmant! Seulement,*" he added, with a sly smile, including Gouvarinho in his comment, "*on a fait une petite erreur ... On a dit que j'étais venu de Southampton par le Royal Mail ... Ce n'est pas vrai, non! Je me suis embarqué à Bordeaux, dans les Messageries. J'ai même pensé à écrire à M. Pinto, rédacteur de la* Gazette, *qui est un charmant garçon. Puis, j'ai reflechi, je me suis dit: 'Mon Dieu, on va croire que je veux donner une leçon d'exactitude à la* Gazette, *c'est très grave.' Alors, voilà, très prudemment, j'ai gardé le silence. Mais enfin c'est une erreur: je me suis embarqué à Bordeaux.*"

Ega muttered something about being sure that History would one day correct this error. The ambassador smiled modestly and made a gesture that seemed to be politely hoping that History would not put itself to any trouble. And then Gouvarinho, who had lit a cigar, glanced again at his watch and asked if his friends had heard anything about the ministerial crisis.

This came as a surprise to both men, who had not read the newspapers. What crisis could this be, exclaimed Ega, when everything was still so quiet, with both Houses in recess, and with this lovely autumn weather?

Gouvarinho merely shrugged knowingly. There had been a meeting of ministers yesterday evening, and this morning, the Prime Minister had donned his ceremonial dress and gone to the palace in order "to resign his post." That was all he knew. Gouvarinho had not spoken to his friends; he had not even gone to his party offices. As at other times of crisis, he had kept his distance and his peace and merely waited upon events. He had been there all morning, smoking cigars and reading the *Revue des Deux Mondes*.

This seemed to Carlos a distinctly unpatriotic stance to take.

"After all, Gouvarinho, if your friends go up in the world ..."

"Exactly," said the Count, his face flushing, "that is why I do not wish to make my presence obvious. I have my pride, and possibly good reason to have it too. If my experience, my words or my name are required, my fellow party members know where to find me and can come and ask me for any or all of those things."

He stopped talking and chewed nervously on his cigar. And Steinbroken, faced by these political matters, immediately withdrew further into the window bay, cleaning his spectacles, retreating, already impenetrable, into the great neutral modesty that befitted Finland. Ega, on the other hand, could not get over his shock. But why should a government fall, why should it fall when it had a majority in both Houses, peace in the country, the support of the army, the blessing of the church, and the protection of the Paris bank, Comptoir d'Escompte?

Gouvarinho slowly stroked his goatee beard and gave this reason:

"The government was burned out."

"What, like a tallow candle?" exclaimed Ega, laughing.

The Count hesitated. No, not like a tallow candle ... Tallow, which is made from fat, infers a certain obtuseness, and this particular government was overflowing with talent. Oh, yes, they had some really impressive talent.

"Oh, honestly!" cried Ega, throwing up his arms in disgust. "It's truly extraordinary! In this blessed country of ours all politicians are 'immensely talented.' The opposition is always happy to confess that the government ministers, upon whom they are constantly heaping insults, are possessed, regardless of whatever mistakes they may make, of 'tremendous talent'! The government is equally happy to admit that the opposition, whom it is endlessly reproaching for its *past* mistakes, is full of people 'of robust talent.' And yet everyone agrees that the country is a rabble. The ludicrous result is this: a country governed by people 'with immense talent,' and which has, by common consensus, the most stupid government in all Europe. My proposal is this: given that these immensely talented people always fail, why not try electing imbeciles instead?"

The Count smiled pleasantly and condescendingly at these ravings of a fantasist. And Carlos, trying to be friendly, asked, as he used the Count's cigar to light his:

"What post would you prefer, Gouvarinho, if your friends get promoted? Foreign Affairs, presumably."

The Count made a sweeping gesture, brushing aside any such possibility. It was unlikely that his friends would need his political experience. He had become more than anything an academic, a theoretician. Besides, he was not sure that his domestic duties, his health, and his habits would permit him to take on the burden of government. And the ministry of Foreign Affairs wouldn't attract him anyway.

"Oh, no!" he went on earnestly. "In order to be able to speak with any authority in Europe, as a minister for Foreign Affairs, you need an army of 200,000 men and the backing of a navy equipped with torpedos. We, alas, are weak. And I'm not prepared to take a subaltern position, so that a Bismarck or a Gladstone can come and tell me: 'Sorry, but that's the way it is!' Don't you agree, Steinbroken?"

The ambassador coughed and stammered out:

"*Certainement . . . C'est très grave . . . C'est excessivement grave . . .*"

Ega then declared that his friend Gouvarinho, with his geographical interest in Africa, would make a fine Minister of the Navy, pioneering, original, generous . . .

The Count's face glowed scarlet with pleasure.

"Yes, possibly. But I'll tell you this, my dear Ega, all the fine things, all the great things have already been done in the colonies. The slaves have been liberated; they've been given a reasonable knowledge of Christian morality; a Customs department has been set up . . . In short, the most important work has been done. Then again, there are still a few interesting final touches that could be made. For example, in Luanda—and I mention this merely as a detail, a further additional touch of progress—in Luanda, they really need a proper theatre, as a civilising influence!"

At that moment, a waiter came to tell Carlos that Senhor Cruges was waiting for him downstairs at the door. The two friends went to join him at once.

"He really is extraordinary, old Gouvarinho!" Ega said as they went down the stairs.

"And he," remarked Carlos, with immense worldly disdain, "is one of our best politicians. Or even, if one takes into account the quality of his underwear, *the* best!"

They found Cruges at the door, wearing a light jacket and rolling a cigarette. Carlos immediately asked him to go back home and put on a black frock-coat. The maestro opened his eyes wide.

"Are we going out to supper?"

"No, to a funeral."

And they quickly told the maestro, without alluding to Maria Eduarda, that Dâmaso had published in *The Devil's Trumpet* (the whole print-run of which they had suppressed, which was why they could not show him a copy of the vile rag) an article in which the kindest thing said about Carlos was that he was "a scoundrel." Therefore, he, that is Cruges, and Ega were going to go to Dâmaso's house to demand satisfaction or his life.

"That's all very well," grumbled the maestro. "But what am I supposed to do? I don't know anything about such matters."

"All you have to do," explained Ega, "is to put on a black frock-coat and frown. You come with me, say nothing, address Dâmaso as 'sir,' agree with all my suggestions, and never once stop frowning or take off your frock-coat."

Without another word, Cruges left to clothe himself in due ceremony and in black. As he crossed the street, he called back:

"Oh, Carlos, I asked about the apartment. The rooms on the second floor are free, and the walls have been newly papered."

"Thank you. Now go and make yourself look sombre, quickly!"

The maestro hurried off just as a calèche skittered to a halt outside the Grémio. Teles da Gama leaped out, and, even as he was opening the door, shouted to Carlos and Ega:

"Is Gouvarinho upstairs?"

"He is. Any news?"

"The Cabinet's been dissolved and Sá Nunes has been appointed!"

And with that, he ran across the courtyard. Carlos and Ega walked slowly along to Cruges' house. The curtainless windows on the second floor stood open. Carlos looked up at them and thought of that afternoon at the races when he had driven there in his phaeton, from Belém, just to gaze at those windows; it had been growing dark then, and a light had gone on behind the closed shutters, and he had contemplated it as if it were some inaccessible star . . . How things change!

They walked back again towards the Grémio, just as Gouvarinho and Teles were bundling themselves into the waiting calèche. Ega stopped and stood with his arms hanging loose by his side.

"There goes Gouvarinho racketing off into Power, and ordering *The Lady of the Camellias* to be performed in the middle of the African bush! God have mercy on us all!"

Cruges finally appeared wearing a top hat, buttoned into a solemn frock-coat and wearing new patent-leather boots. They all squashed into the narrow, uncomfortable cab. Carlos was going to take them to Dâmaso's house. And since he was hoping to be able to dine at Olivais that night, he would wait for them by the bandstand in the Jardim da Estrela in order to hear the result of "the fracas."

"Be quick and put the fear of God in him!"

Dâmaso lived in an old single-storey house with a vast green door, beside which dangled a long piece of wire which, when pulled, made what sounded like a sad convent bell echo and clang somewhere inside; the two friends had to wait for a long time before Dâmaso's rough-mannered Galician servant appeared, shuffling along in his slippers, no longer tortured (now that Dâmaso was free of Carlos and his ostentatious ways) by cruel, patent-leather boots. In one corner of the courtyard, a small door opened onto a bright garden, which appeared to be used as a dumping-ground for boxes, empty bottles, and other rubbish.

The servant, who recognised Senhor Ega, led them immediately up a narrow, carpeted staircase and along a broad, dark, musty corridor. Then he clattered ahead of them in his slippers towards the light issuing forth from a half-open door. Almost immediately, Dâmaso called out:

"Ega, is that you? Come in, man, I'm just getting dressed!"

Embarrassed by this effusive, friendly greeting, Ega replied gravely from the darkness of the corridor:

"That's all right, we'll wait."

Dâmaso insisted, standing at the door now in his shirtsleeves and adjusting his braces.

"Come in, man! I'm not ashamed, damn it, I've got my trousers on!"

"There's someone important here to see you," Ega shouted at last.

The door at the end of the corridor closed, and the servant came to open up the drawing room. The carpet was exactly the same as the one in Carlos' rooms at Ramalhete. And all around were abundant signs of his former friendship with Carlos: the portrait of Carlos on horseback in a showy frame of faience-ware flowers; one of the white and green Indian bedspreads bought from the Medeiros sisters and subsequently draped over the piano and pinned into position by Carlos; and on top of a Spanish chest of drawers, beneath a glass dome, a woman's small satin shoe, brand-new, which Dâmaso had bought in Serra after he had once heard Carlos say that "in every young man's room there should be some discreetly displayed relic of love."

Beneath these touches of chic, hastily added under Carlos' influence, stood the solid furniture that had belonged to Dâmaso's father, all massive mahogany and blue velvet; the marble console table and its gilt bronze clock with Diana stroking a greyhound; the large expensive mirror, with all kinds of visiting cards, portraits of singers and invitations to soirées stuck around the frame. Cruges was just about to examine these documents when Dâmaso's sprightly footsteps could be heard coming down the corridor. Clutching his top hat, the maestro scurried over to join Ega, who was standing firmly and confidently by the velvet-upholstered divan.

Dâmaso, who was buttoned up in a blue frock-coat, with a camellia in his buttonhole, laughed and threw up his hands when he saw Cruges.

"So this is the important person, is it? You and your jokes! And I put my frock-coat on especially. I very nearly wore my medal of the Order of Christ!"

Ega interrupted him gravely.

"Cruges may not be an important person, but the reason that brings us here, Dâmaso, is a grave and delicate one."

Dâmaso opened his eyes wide, finally noticing his friends' strange demeanour, unsmiling and solemn, and both dressed in black. He drew back, and the smile vanished from his face.

"What the devil is this about? Sit down, sit down!"

His voice was beginning to vanish too. Sitting on the edge of a low armchair, next to a table covered in richly bound books, his hands on his knees, he waited anxiously.

"We have come here," began Ega, "on behalf of our friend Carlos da Maia."

Dâmaso's chubby face suddenly flushed scarlet all the way to the parting of his carefully curled hair. He was dumbstruck, stunned, unable to breathe, and kept stupidly rubbing his knees.

Ega continued slowly talking, not moving from his position by the divan.

"Our friend Carlos da Maia's complaint is that Dâmaso published, or ordered to be published, in *The Devil's Trumpet*, an article which was extremely insulting to him and to a lady of his acquaintance."

"Me? In *The Trumpet*?" stammered Dâmaso. "*The Trumpet*? I've never written for the newspapers, thank God! And in *The Trumpet* of all places!"

Ega, very coldly, drew from his pocket the bundle of papers and placed them one by one beside Dâmaso on the table, on top of a magnificent edition of the Bible illustrated by Doré.

"Here is the letter that you wrote to 'Big Palma' enclosing the draft of the article. Here, again in your own hand, is the list of people to whom *The Trumpet* should be sent, from the King down to Fancelli. We also have Palma's own statements. You were not only the inspiration behind, but also the author of the article. Our friend Carlos da Maia, therefore, as the injured party, demands satisfaction by arms."

Dâmaso leapt out of his chair so violently that Ega involuntarily took a step back, fearing that he might attack him. Dâmaso, however, was standing in the middle of the room, wide-eyed and bewildered.

"Carlos wants to challenge me? Me? What have I ever done to him? He's the one who played a dirty trick on me! You know he did!"

And he unleashed a prodigiously loquacious flow of words, thumping his chest with the palm of his hand, his eyes brimming with tears. It had been Carlos who had insulted him, and mortally too! He had spent the whole winter pestering him to be introduced to a particularly chic Brazilian woman, who used to live in Paris and who had been giving Dâmaso the eye. And he, being a kind soul, promised that he would, saying: "Don't worry, I'll introduce you!" But what did Carlos do? He took advantage of a sacred occasion—a moment of bereavement, when Dâmaso had had to travel north for his uncle's funeral—and slipped into the Brazilian woman's house. And Carlos had so poisoned the woman's mind, that she, poor thing, had closed her door to him, to Dâmaso, a really close friend of her husband's! Damn it, he was the one who should have challenged Carlos! But no, he had been prudent, he had avoided any scandal out of consideration for Senhor Afonso da Maia. He had complained about Carlos, it's true, but only in the Grémio and in the Casa Havanesa, to his friends. And then Carlos goes and pulls a trick like this on him!

"Challenging me, *me*, whom everyone knows!"

He fell silent, exhausted. And Ega, holding out a hand to him, remarked placidly that Dâmaso was straying away from the nub of the matter. Dâmaso had conceived, drafted, and paid for the article in *The Trumpet*. This he did not and could not deny: the proof was there on the table; they also had Palma's own statement.

"The scoundrel!" cried Dâmaso, carried away on another wave of indignation that caused him to whirl round and bump clumsily into the furniture. "The shameless wretch! I'm going to have words with him! This business with Carlos is nothing, we can sort something out, we're gentlemen after all, but Palma is another matter entirely. I'll beat that traitor to a pulp. A man I've given money to, as much as seven *mil réis*! Not to mention suppers and hired carriages! The fellow's a thief! He once borrowed a watch from Zeferino in order, he said, to cut a fine figure at a christening, and he ended up pawning it! And he has the nerve to do this to me! I'll bury him! Where did you last see him, Ega? Tell me, man. I want to find him right now and beat the living daylights out of him! Treachery is one thing I won't take from anyone!"

Ega, with the patient calm of someone who knows the prey is his, commented again on the futility of all these ravings.

"We'll never get anywhere like this, Dâmaso. Our point is this: you insulted Carlos da Maia. You must either make a public retraction or give satisfaction by arms."

Dâmaso, however, was not listening and was appealing desperately to Cruges, immobile next to the velvet-upholstered sofa, and who, with a pained, pinched air, kept rubbing his new patent-leather shoes together.

"That Carlos! A man who was supposed to be my close friend! A man I would have done anything for! I even copied out his manuscripts. You know I did, Cruges! Say something, man! Don't *you* turn against me too! I even used to go to the customshouse sometimes to collect parcels for him."

The maestro lowered his eyes, red-faced, feeling infinitely uncomfortable. At last, Ega, who had had enough of all this, threw out one final demand:

"So what's it to be, Dâmaso, will you retract or will you fight?"

"Retract?" spluttered Dâmaso, drawing himself up in a painful attempt at dignity, but trembling all over. "Retract what? Huh, I like that! I'm not the kind of man to retract anything!"

"Fine, then, so you'll fight."

Dâmaso staggered backwards, aghast.

"What do you mean 'fight'? I'm not the sort to fight! If it was a fistfight, yes! You tell him to come up here, I'm not afraid of him, I'll knock him flat."

He was hopping plumply back and forth on the carpet, his fists clenched and ready. He wanted Carlos there, now, so that he could finish him off once and for all! But he wasn't going to fight a duel. Besides, duels in Portugal always ended in farce!

Ega, meanwhile, as if his mission were over, had buttoned up his overcoat and was picking up the papers that lay scattered over the Bible. Then he serenely made the final declaration with which he had been charged. Since Senhor Dâmaso Salcede refused to retract and also rejected any possibility of reparation by arms, Carlos da Maia warned him that if he met him henceforth, wherever it might be, in the street or in the theatre, he would spit in his face.

"Spit at me!" bawled Dâmaso, deathly pale and recoiling, as if the gob of spit were already hurtling towards him through the air.

And suddenly, terrified and perspiring, he hurled himself upon Ega, clutching his hands, and pleading pitifully:

"Oh, João, João, you who are my friend, please save me from this predicament!"

Ega was all generosity. He detached himself from Dâmaso's grip, pushed him gently back into his armchair, and soothed his anxiety by fraternally patting him on the shoulder. And he declared that since Dâmaso was appealing to his friendship, he would no longer be Carlos' necessarily demanding envoy, but Dâmaso's old comrade from the days of the Cohens and the Villa Balzac. Might he, in that capacity, offer Dâmaso some advice? He should sign a letter stating that everything he had ordered to be published in *The Devil's Trumpet* about Senhor Carlos da Maia and a certain lady had been false, an entirely gratuitous invention. This alone would save him. Otherwise, one day, in the Chiado or at the theatre, Carlos would have no option but to spit in his face. And should that disastrous thing happen, Dâmaso would have to fight him with either a sword or a pistol—unless he wanted the whole of Lisbon to label him an utter coward.

"In either case, you would be a dead man."

Dâmaso was listening, sitting crumpled in his velvet armchair, staring foolishly at Ega. He held out limp arms and murmured from the depths of his terror:

"All right, João, I'll sign, I'll sign."

"That would be the best thing to do. Find me some paper then. You're obviously too upset to compose it yourself, so I'll dictate."

Dâmaso got up, his legs still weak, casting a vacant glance about the room.

"Letter paper? It's for a letter, is it?"

"Yes, of course, a letter to Carlos!"

The wretch's footsteps, heavy and defeated, disappeared off down the corridor.

"Poor devil!" sighed Cruges and, wincing, once again gingerly touched one shoe.

Ega shot him a disapproving "*sh.*" Dâmaso returned, bearing his sumptuous writing paper with its monogram and coronet. In order to shroud that bitter moment in silence and secrecy, he drew the door curtain closed; and, as it unfurled, the ample velvet revealed the Salcede coat of arms, which showed a lion, a tower, an arm in armour and, underneath, in letters of gold, the formidable motto: "I am strong." Ega immediately pushed the books on the table aside, sat down and, with a flourish, wrote the date and Dâmaso's address.

"I'll draft the letter out and then you can copy it."

"All right," whimpered Dâmaso, who had collapsed once more into his armchair, wiping his face and neck with a handkerchief.

Ega was writing the letter very slowly and lovingly. And in that awkward silence, Cruges finally got up and limped over to the mirror to view the collection of cards and photographs stuck around the frame. These were Dâmaso's social glories, the documentary evidence of the passion of his life—the truly chic: notes bearing the names of aristocrats, photos of singers, invitations to balls, entrance tickets to the races, letters granting membership to the Yacht Club, the Jockey Club, the Pigeon-shooting Club, even newspaper cuttings announcing the birthdays, departures and arrivals of Senhor Salcede, "one of our most distinguished sportsmen."

Unlucky sportsman! He watched with dread as Ega scribbled away on the piece of paper. Good God, why so much fuss about a letter to Carlos, who was his friend? One line would be enough: "Dear Carlos, don't be angry, I'm sorry, it was just a bit of fun." But no, a whole page of tiny writing, full of crossings-out and corrections! Ega was even turning the sheet of paper over and dipping his pen in the inkwell, as if a ceaseless stream of humiliating words were about to flow from it! Dâmaso could not contain himself; he leaned over the table and looked at the letter.

"This isn't for publication, is it, Ega?"

Ega thought for a moment, his pen poised.

"Probably not. No, I'm certain it isn't. When Carlos sees how repentant you are, he will doubtless leave the letter in the bottom of a drawer somewhere."

Dâmaso gave a relieved sigh. Good, that seemed a decent way to behave among friends. After all, he really did want to show that he was sorry. It had been foolish of him to write that article, but then, when it came to women, he was like that, easily angered, a lion.

Somewhat reassured, he fanned himself with his handkerchief, beginning to feel that life once more had savour. He even lit a cigar, silently got to his feet and went over to Cruges, who, having hobbled past the various curios in the room, had finally alighted on the piano and was peering at the sheet-music there, with one painful foot in the air.

"Written anything new lately, Cruges?"

Cruges, blushing furiously, muttered something about not having written anything.

Dâmaso stayed there for a moment, chewing on his cigar. Then, after shooting an uneasy glance at the table where Ega was still interminably scribbling, he said quietly over the maestro's shoulder:

"Fancy, eh? What a predicament? I'm only doing this because of the people I know, otherwise, I wouldn't care! But things will sort themselves out, and then if Carlos just sticks it in a drawer somewhere . . ."

Ega had got up and was walking slowly over to the piano, holding the letter and quietly re-reading it to himself.

"Excellent! Just the job!" he exclaimed at last. "It's in the form of a letter to Carlos; it's more correct that way. You just have to copy it out and sign it. Listen: 'Dear Sir . . .' —obviously, since this is a matter of honour, we need to keep things formal—'Dear Sir, Since you have, through the intermediary of your friends João da Ega and Vitorino Cruges, expressed your indignation at a certain article in *The Devil's Trumpet*, of which I wrote the first draft and whose publication I also encouraged, I wish to declare frankly that this article, as I hereby recognise, contained nothing but falsehoods and nonsense, and my only excuse is that when I composed it and sent it to the editor of *The Devil's Trumpet*, I was in a state of complete inebriation . . .'"

He stopped. He did not even turn to Dâmaso, who was standing, stunned, his arms hanging limp by his side, having dropped his cigar on the carpet. It was Cruges whom Ega addressed, fixing his monocle more firmly in his eye.

"Is that a bit strong? I put it like that simply because it seemed the only way of salvaging our friend Dâmaso's dignity."

And he developed his idea, showing how clever and generous it was, while Dâmaso dazedly picked up his cigar. Neither he nor Carlos wanted Dâmaso (in a letter which could be made public), to declare that he had libelled Carlos because he was by nature a libellist. It was necessary, therefore, to attribute the libel to one of those fortuitous, uncontrollable causes which mean that one cannot be held responsible for one's actions. And what better excuse, given that they were dealing with a worldly-wise womaniser like Dâmaso, than that he was drunk? It wasn't a shameful thing to get drunk. Carlos himself, all of them, men of taste and honour, had at some time got drunk. Why go back as far as the Romans, who considered drunkenness both healthy and fashionable, when many great men in history were known to have drunk too much? In England, it was felt to be so chic that Pitt, Fox, and others never addressed the House of Commons unless they were three sheets in the wind. Musset, for example, was a terrible drunk! In short, History, Literature, and Politics were just one long drunken orgy. Now, if Dâmaso said he was drunk, his honour would be saved. He was a decent man who'd had one too many and committed an indiscretion. And that was all there was to it!

"Don't you agree, Cruges?"

"Yes, maybe he *was* drunk," the maestro murmured timidly.

"Don't you agree, Dâmaso?"

"Yes, yes, I was drunk," stammered the unfortunate man.

Ega immediately resumed his reading: "'Now that I have come to my senses, I recognise, as I have always recognised and proclaimed, that you are of completely noble character, and that the other people who, in that moment of drunkenness, I also dared to spatter with mud, deserve only my veneration and praise. I further declare that if, by any chance, I should happen to make other offensive comments about you, neither you nor anyone else who hears it should give it any more importance than one would to the meaningless ramblings of a drunk, for, due to a frequently recurring hereditary strain that runs in my family, I often find myself in a state of inebriation. I am, sir, yours respectfully, etc. etc.'" He spun round on his heels, replaced the letter on the table and, using Dâmaso's cigar to light his own, explained in a friendly, affectionate way what had made him determine upon that confession of incorrigible, garrulous drunkenness. It had been out of a desire to guarantee peace of mind to "our friend Dâmaso." By attributing any future imprudent actions to a hereditary tendency to intemperance, which wasn't his fault, just as it wasn't his fault that he was short and fat, Dâmaso would be safe "forever after" from any further challenges from Carlos.

"You, Dâmaso, have a quick temper and a sharp tongue. One day, in the Grémio, let's say, or chatting after the theatre, you might forget yourself and, quite unintentionally, let slip some critical comment about Carlos. Without such a precaution, the whole business—the spitting and the duel—might start up again. This way, Carlos would be unable to complain. There's your explanation, which covers everything: you've had a drop too much, a drop taken when in the grip of an inherited drunken impulse. You will thus achieve the state most desired in our century—total irresponsibility! And it cannot bring shame upon your family because you have none. What do you think?"

Poor Dâmaso was listening, crushed and exhausted, unable to understand these high-sounding words about heredity and "our century." He had but one desire: for this to be over and to have his easy peaceful life restored to him, free of foils and spit. He shrugged and said weakly:

"What else can I do? If it will avoid gossip . . ."

And he sat down, fitted the pen with a new nib, chose a piece of paper on which his monogram gleamed particularly brightly, and began to copy out the letter in his marvellous italic hand, as clear as an engraving on steel.

Ega, meanwhile, with his frock-coat unbuttoned and his cigar lit, prowled around the table, eagerly watching the lines traced by Dâmaso's earnest hand, a hand adorned with a large signet ring. For a moment, though, a pang of fear went through him. Dâmaso had stopped, his pen poised hesitantly over the paper. Oh no, was some remnant of dignity and revolt stirring inside all that flab and fat? Dâmaso looked up at him with dull eyes:

"Is 'inebriation' spelt 'b-r-i' or 'b-r-e'?"

"'b-r-i,' Dâmaso," replied Ega affectionately. "You're doing very well. You really do have lovely handwriting!"

And the poor wretch smiled at his own writing, his head on one side, genuinely proud of that great talent.

When he had finished copying it out, Ega checked it and put in the punctuation. The document had to be "chic" and perfect.

"Who's your notary, Dâmaso?"

"Nunes, in Rua do Ouro. Why?"

"Oh, no reason. It's something people always ask in these circumstances. A mere formality. Well, my friends, the letter, as regards paper, handwriting, and style, is a joy to behold!"

He put it straight into an envelope, on which gleamed the motto "I am strong," and slipped it carefully into the inside pocket of his frock-coat. Then, picking up his hat and patting Dâmaso's shoulder with light, playful familiarity, he said:

"Well, Dâmaso, I think we can congratulate ourselves! This could all have ended outside the city in a field somewhere, in a pool of blood! As it is, it's turned out very well indeed. Goodbye, then. No, don't get up. So, Monday's the big day, is it? Everyone will be there, I suppose. No, really, there's no need to show us out. Goodbye."

But Dâmaso walked with them along the corridor, dumb, crestfallen, head bowed. On the landing, he stopped Ega and gave voice to another anxiety that had assailed him:

"You won't show the letter to anyone else, will you, Ega?"

Ega shrugged. The document belonged to Carlos, but Carlos was such a good fellow, so kind!

This uncertainty, which continued to gnaw at Dâmaso, drew a sigh from him: "And to think I called that man 'my friend'!"

"Life's full of disappointments, Dâmaso!" remarked Ega, running gaily down the stairs.

When the carriage drew up outside the Jardim da Estrela, Carlos was already impatiently waiting at the wrought-iron gate, anxious not to miss supper at the Toca. He got in at once, stumbling over Cruges, and yelled to the driver to take them to Largo do Loreto.

"So, gentlemen, are we going to taste blood?"

"Better than that!" cried Ega above the noise of the wheels, brandishing the letter.

Carlos read Dâmaso's letter in utter amazement.

"This is incredible! It's almost an insult to the human race!"

"Dâmaso isn't human," said Ega. "What did you expect, that he would fight?"

"I don't know, but it pains one to read this. What am I supposed to do with it, anyway?"

According to Ega, it should not be published; that would only provoke gossip and curiosity about the article in *The Devil's Trumpet*, which had cost thirty *libras* to suppress. But it would be a good idea to keep it as a threat hanging over Dâmaso, thus rendering him null and inoffensive for many years to come.

"Well, I'm more than avenged," concluded Carlos. "You keep the letter; it's your work, so do with it as you will."

Ega gladly put it away, while Carlos, patting Cruges' knee, wanted to know how he had behaved himself during this affair of honour.

"Very badly!" shouted Ega. "Expressions of pity for Dâmaso; absolutely no dignity at all; hunched over the piano, clasping his shoe."

"What do you expect!" exclaimed Cruges, free to speak at last. "You tell me that formal clothes are required, and so I put on some new patent-leather shoes and spend the whole evening in agony!"

He could restrain himself no longer, and, looking very pale, he pulled off the offending shoe and uttered a great sigh of relief.

The following day after lunch, while heavy rain, caught up by a gusty south-west wind, was drenching the windows, Ega, in the smoking room, sunk in an armchair, with his feet to the fire, was re-reading Dâmaso's letter; and gradually there arose in him a feeling of regret that this monument to human cowardice, sure to prove of such interest to psychology and to art, should remain unseen in the darkness of a drawer! Imagine the impact, the tremendous impact if the confession of "our distinguished sportsman" should ever be published in the *Gazeta Ilustrada* or in the society columns of that new publication *A Tarde*, under the heading: "A Matter of Honour"! What a lesson that would be, what a worthy act of social justice!

Ega had spent all summer loathing Dâmaso, convinced, since his stay in Sintra, that Dâmaso was Madame Cohen's lover, and that because of that fat-buttocked imbecile, she had forgotten all about the Villa Balzac, the mornings spent on the black satin bedspread, their delicate kisses, the poetry by Musset he used to read to her, the partridge lunches, and so many other poetic delights. But what had made Dâmaso so utterly intolerable to him had been the smug radiant way he had paraded himself as the chosen man; the possessive air with which he, in his white flannel suits, would walk with Raquel along the streets of Sintra; the little secrets he always had to whisper to her over her shoulder; and the scornful, dismissive wave of the hand with which he would greet Ega when they passed. He was utterly odious! Ega hated him, and in his hatred of him, he had long cherished the desire for revenge—for Senhor Salcede to suffer a beating, dishonour, or to become the victim of some ridiculous act that would transform him, in Raquel's eyes, into a grotesque, despicable figure, as flat as a punctured balloon.

And now he had this providential letter, in which the man solemnly declared himself to be a drunk. "I'm a drunk, I'm always drunk!" That was what Dâmaso had written, on his own gold-monogrammed paper, as pathetically cowed as a mongrel dog putting its tail between its legs the moment it was threatened with a stick. No woman could stand that. Must he really hide this valuable document away in the back of a drawer?

For Carlos' sake, he could not, alas, publish it in the *Gazeta Ilustrada* or in *A Tarde*, but what prevented him showing it "in confidence," as a psychological curiosity, to Craft, to the Marquis, to Teles or Gouvarinho, to Cohen's cousin? He could even give a copy to Taveira, who still nursed feelings of resentment towards Dâmaso over that argument in Lola Gorda's house and would rush to read it aloud, again "in confidence," at the Casa Havanesa, in the billiard room at the Grémio, at Silva's, in the dressing-rooms of singers at the theatre. And within a week, Senhora Dona Raquel would be sure to know that her heart's delight was, by his own admission, a libellist and a drunk. Splendid!

Indeed, so splendid was this thought that he hesitated not a moment longer, and went up to his room to copy out Dâmaso's letter. Almost immediately, however, a servant brought him a telegram from Afonso da Maia, announcing that he would be arriving at Ramalhete the next day, and Ega had to go out at once to send a telegram to Olivais, warning Carlos.

Late that night, Carlos arrived at Ramalhete, chilled to the marrow and accompanied by a great mound of luggage, for he had left Olivais for good. Maria Eduarda was also returning to Lisbon, to the second-floor apartment in Rua de São Francisco, taken this time on a six-month lease, and which Cruges' mother had had newly carpeted. Carlos was clearly greatly saddened and filled with nostalgic thoughts of the Toca. After supper, beside the fire, finishing his cigar, he kept going over those happy days, the little cottage he had lived in, his morning bath taken in a great tub made for treading grapes, the party held in honour of the god Tchi, the Marquis' *fado* evening, the long talks over coffee with the windows open and the moths fluttering around the candle flames. Meanwhile, outside, in the mute black night, the rain, lashed by the winter wind, beat against the windows. Both men ended up sitting silent and thoughtful, staring into the fire.

"When I took a final stroll around the garden this afternoon," Carlos said at last, "there wasn't a single leaf on any of the trees. Don't you always feel a kind of terrible melancholy at the end of autumn?"

"Oh, yes, terrible!" murmured Ega gloomily.

The next day was dawning bright and pale when Ega and Carlos, fresh from their beds and still shivering, stepped down from the carriage at Santa Apolónia. The train had just arrived, and among the bustle of people flooding off the train, they immediately spotted Afonso in his old cape with the velvet collar, clutching his walking stick and pushing his way past the men in gold-braided caps, offering to take him to the Hotel Terreirense and to the Pomba d'Oiro. Behind him, Monsieur Antoine, the French chef, grave-faced and wearing a top hat, was carrying the basket in which the Reverend Boniface travelled.

Carlos and Ega both thought Afonso looked older and slower; however, as the first embraces were exchanged, they praised his robust, patriarchal appearance. Afonso shrugged and complained that, ever since the end of summer, he had been suffering from dizzy spells and a vague feeling of tiredness.

"Anyway, *you* both look wonderful!" he added, embracing Carlos again and smiling at Ega. "But what an ungrateful boy you are, João, not to have visited me once all summer. What have you been up to? What have both of you been up to?"

"Oh, a thousand things," said Ega cheerfully. "We have all kinds of plans, ideas, titles. Our main project is a magazine, an educational tool, that we're setting up now at the rate of a thousand horse-power. Anyway, we'll tell you all about it over lunch."

And over lunch, in order to justify their time in Lisbon, they spoke of the magazine as if it were already organised and the articles sent to press—such was the exactitude with which they described to Afonso the tendencies, the critical slant, and lines of thought on which the magazine would be based. Ega had already prepared something for the first issue: "The Portuguese Capital." Carlos was considering a series of essays in the English style, entitled: "Why the Constitutional System Has Failed in Portugal." And Afonso listened, delighted by these fine ambitions to enter the fray, eager himself to participate in the great work as a financial partner. Ega, however, felt that Senhor Afonso da Maia should step into the arena himself and offer the benefit of his knowledge and experience. Afonso laughed. Him? Write prose? Why, he even hesitated when it came to drafting a letter to his administrator! Besides, what he had to say to his country, as the fruit of his experience, could be reduced to three pieces of advice, three phrases—to the politicians: "less liberalism and more character"; to the men of letters: "less eloquence and more ideas"; to the citizenry in general: "less progress and more morality."

Ega thought this very fine! Those were the true characteristics of the spiritual reform that the magazine should be preaching! They should take them as their motto and print them in Gothic lettering on the frontispiece, because Ega wanted even that to look original. Then the conversation turned to the magazine cover, with Carlos proposing pale blue with a Renaissance typeface and Ega demanding that it should be an exact copy of the *Revue des Deux Mondes*, but using a slightly intenser canary yellow. And suddenly, carried away by their Southern European imaginations, they were no longer planning and shaping this confused plan merely to please Afonso da Maia.

His eyes bright with passion, Carlos exclaimed to Ega:

"This is serious now. The first thing we need to do is to set up an editorial office!"

Ega roared back:

"Of course! Not to mention furniture and machinery!"

All morning, in Afonso's study, they busied themselves with pencil and paper trying to establish a list of collaborators. However, difficulties began to emerge at once. Ega disliked almost all the writers suggested because they lacked the artistic, Parnassian elegance of style of which he wanted the magazine to be an impeccable model. And Carlos thought certain men of letters quite simply "impossible," although without wishing to confess that what mainly repelled him was their lack of manners and their appalling clothes.

They did decide on one thing, though: the editorial office. It would have to be luxuriously furnished, with sofas from Carlos' consulting rooms and a few antiques from the Toca; and above the door (adorned with a liveried doorman), would hang a highly polished black sign with *The Portuguese Review* in large gold letters. Carlos was smiling and rubbing his hands, thinking how pleased Maria Eduarda would be when she knew about this decision, which would, just as she so wanted, launch him into activity and into the fascinating battle of ideas. Ega, on the other hand, could already see the canary-coloured magazine piled up in the windows of bookshops, discussed at the Count de Gouvarinho's soirées, leafed through with horror by politicians in the Chamber ...

"We're really going to cause a stir in Lisbon this winter, sir!" he cried, making a sweeping gesture in the direction of the ceiling.

Afonso was the most contented of them all.

After supper, Carlos asked Ega to go with him to Rua de São Francisco (for Maria Eduarda had moved in there that morning) to bring her news of the great project. However, when they arrived, they found a cart at the front door from which trunks were still being unloaded, and, according to Domingos, his mistress was still eating her supper off one corner of the table and without the benefit of a table cloth. Ega preferred not to go up when the house was still in such a state of confusion.

"Goodbye, then," he said. "I'll perhaps go and find Simão Craveiro and talk to him about the magazine."

He walked slowly up the Chiado and read the latest news telegrams at the Casa Havanesa. Then, on the corner of Rua Nova da Trindade, a man with a hoarse voice and wearing a mammoth overcoat offered him a ticket. Other men, nearby, outside the Hotel Aliança, were shouting:

"Tickets for the Ginásio! Cheap tickets! Tickets for the Ginásio! Who'll buy a ticket?"

There was a lively confluence of carriages driven by liveried servants. The gas-lamps outside the Ginásio had a festive glow about them. Then Ega came face to face with Craft who was crossing over from the Largo do Loreto, wearing a white tie and with a flower in his buttonhole.

"What's all this about?"

"Some sort of benefit performance, I think," said Craft. "Organised by the good ladies of Lisbon; the Viscountess de Alvim sent me a ticket. Come and help me carry my charitable cross."

And in the hope of being able to flirt with the Viscountess, Ega immediately bought a ticket. In the foyer, they found Taveira, on his own, pacing up and down and smoking, waiting for the first play, *Forbidden Fruit*, to finish. Craft immediately proposed going to the bar and ordering some gin.

"So what's happening with the Cabinet?" he asked, as soon as they found a corner to sit down in.

Taveira had no idea. Desperate intriguing had been going on for the last few days. Gouvarinho wanted the post of Public Works, but so did Videira. And there were rumours of a terrible row at the Prime Minister's house over syndicates, when the Prime Minister, Sá Nunes, had thumped the table and bawled: "This isn't a den of thieves, you know!"

"The rabble!" grunted Ega scornfully.

Then they talked about Ramalhete, about the return of Afonso and the reappearance of Carlos. Craft thanked God that there would once more be a place that winter with a good fire where one could spend a civilised and intelligent hour or two.

Taveira added, with a glittering eye:

"They say there's going to be an even more interesting place to gather, in Rua de São Francisco! The Marquis told me. Madame MacGren, it seems, will be holding a regular soirée."

Craft did not even know that she had left the Toca.

"Yes, she came back today," said Ega. "Haven't you met her? She's charming."

"So it seems."

Taveira had glimpsed her in the Chiado. She had looked like a real beauty! And she had, altogether, a very pleasant air about her.

"Oh, yes, she's charming," said Ega again.

Forbidden Fruit had ended, and men lighting their cigars were slowly filling the foyer with talk and noise. Ega left Craft and Taveira drinking gin and hurried off down to the stalls in order to locate the Viscountess' box.

Scarcely had he lifted the curtain and affixed his monocle than he saw, in the very first tier of boxes, Madame Cohen, all in black, with a large white lace fan; behind her, he could see her husband's thick dark sideburns; and opposite her, leaning on the velvet-padded balustrade, wearing tails and with a huge pearl pinned to his shirtfront, stood Dâmaso, with his smiling, chubby face, Dâmaso, the drunk!

Ega sat limply down on the nearest seat; all thoughts of the Viscountess vanished from his mind, and he sat there in turmoil, staring blankly at the advertisements on the stage curtain, and smoothing his moustache with tremulous fingers.

Meanwhile, the bell was ringing, and people were drifting back into the stalls. A fat, ill-tempered man bumped against Ega's knee; another man, wearing light-coloured gloves, asked him very politely if he could come past. Ega heard neither of them, noticed nothing; his gaze, at first unfocused, now fixed on the Cohens' box and did not leave it, his whole being filled with emotions that drained the colour from his face.

He had not seen her since Sintra, where he had only caught distant glimpses, a pale dress beneath the green of the trees; but now, all in black, bareheaded, with a modest décolletage that revealed the white perfection of her throat and neck, she was once more *his* Raquel, from the divine days of Villa Balzac. This was how she had looked when, every night at the Teatro São Carlos, he used to contemplate her from Carlos' box, leaning his head back against the wall, saturated with happiness. She was wearing her gold-rimmed lorgnette, attached to her dress by a gold chain. She seemed paler, more delicate, but with that familiar languor in her heavy-lidded eyes, that air of romance, that look of a slightly faded lily; and then there was her magnificent heavy hair which fell onto her shoulders in a skilfully coiffed tangle that seemed somehow to hint at dishevelled nakedness. Little by little, amid the sound of violins tuning up and chairs scuffing the floor, Ega saw again, in a wave of memories that overwhelmed him, the big bed in Villa Balzac, certain kisses and certain smiles, and the partridge lunches they had eaten, as they sat, still only partly dressed, perched on the edge of the sofa; he felt again the delicious melancholy of those afternoons, when she would slip furtively away, her face thickly veiled, and he, weary, would sit on in the poetic twilight of the bedroom, humming tunes from *La Traviata*.

"If you wouldn't mind, Senhor Ega?"

A hollow-cheeked fellow with a sparse beard was reclaiming his seat. Ega stumbled to his feet, failing to recognise the gentleman as Senhor Sousa Neto. The curtain had risen again. At the front of the stage, a lackey with a duster under his arm was winking at the audience and talking confidentially about the mistress of the house. And Cohen, standing up now, dominating the centre of the box, was slowly stroking his sideburns with one beautifully manicured hand on which there glinted a single diamond.

In a proud show of indifference, Ega fixed his monocled gaze on the stage. The lackey had raced off in response to the furious ringing of a bell; and a sour old woman, in a green peignoir and with her hat awry, burst onto the stage, furiously fluttering her fan and arguing with an affected young woman who was stamping her foot and whining: "I'll always love him, I tell you! I'll always love him!"

Irresistibly, Ega cast a sideways glance up at the box: Raquel and Dâmaso were sitting with their heads close together, whispering and smiling, as they had in Sintra. And everything inside Ega fused into a feeling of immense hatred for Dâmaso! Leaning in the doorway, he ground his teeth, suppressing a desire to go upstairs and spit in Dâmaso's fat face.

And he could not take his eyes off him, eyes that darted fire. Onstage, a gouty, curmudgeonly old general was brandishing a newspaper and calling for his tapioca. The audience laughed; Cohen laughed. And at that moment, as Dâmaso leaned forward in the box, with his hands—in their pearl-grey gloves—resting on the balustrade, he spotted Ega, smiled and gave him that same casual, insolent little wave as he had in Sintra. This had the force of an insult for Ega. And to think that only the evening before, that coward had clasped his hands, trembling all over, and begged him to save him!

Suddenly, a thought occurred to him, and he patted his pocket to see if the wallet in which he had stored Dâmaso's letter the night before was still there. "I'll fix you!" he muttered. And he raced off down Rua da Trindade, bowled across Largo do Loreto and, on the far side of Praça de Camões, slipped in through a large door lit by a lantern. It was the office of *A Tarde*.

The courtyard occupied by this elegant newspaper stank to high heaven. On the unlit stone stairs, he passed a man with a heavy cold who told him that Neves was upstairs chatting. Years ago, during a long university vacation, Neves, now a member of parliament, a politician, and a newspaper editor, had shared a house with him in Largo do Carmo; and ever since that jolly summer, from which Neves still owed him three *moedas*, they'd been on familiar terms.

Ega found Neves in a vast room lit by bare gas-lamps; he was sitting on the edge of a table piled high with newspapers, his hat pushed back on his head, and was holding forth to some gentlemen from the provinces, who stood listening to him as respectfully as true believers. In the window bay, talking with two elderly gentlemen, a whippet-thin young man wearing a double-breasted jacket in pale wool and with such stiff, curly, untidy hair that he looked as if he had been caught in a gale, was whirling his arms about like a windmill on the crest of a hill. Another man, with almost no hair at all, was sitting at a desk, laboriously making notes on a strip of paper.

When Neves saw Ega (a close friend of Gouvarinho's) enter the office on that night of intrigue and crisis, he fixed him with such an urgent, enquiring look that Ega hastened to reassure him.

"It's nothing to do with politics, purely a personal matter. Carry on, please. We can talk later."

Neves concluded the insulting comment he was making about José Bento, "the great fool blurted out the whole story to the lady friend of Sousa de Sá, peer of the realm," and in his impatience, he jumped off the table, linked arms with Ega and drew him to one side.

"So, what is it?"

"Put very simply, Carlos da Maia has been insulted by a certain very well-known gentleman. Nothing very interesting, just a wretched little paragraph in *The Devil's Trumpet*, some dispute over horses. Maia demanded an apology, and the other fellow gave it in the baldest and most forthright terms in a letter which I would like you to publish."

Neves' curiosity was aroused.

"Who is it?"

"Dâmaso."

Neves drew back in surprise.

"Dâmaso! How extraordinary! Why, I had dinner with him only this evening. What does the letter say?"

"Everything. He begs forgiveness, declares that he was drunk and that he is by profession a drunkard."

Neves threw up his hands in horror.

"And you want me to publish that? About Dâmaso, our political ally? And even if he wasn't, it's not just a question of party loyalty, it's a question of decency! I couldn't do that. If it was something meriting a duel, a matter of honour, a proper dignified apology ... but a letter in which a man declares himself to be a drunkard! You must be joking!"

Ega was frowning furiously. But Neves, his face bright red, could still not accept the idea that Dâmaso would declare himself to be a drunkard!

"It's impossible! Absurd! There's something about all this that doesn't quite ring true. Let me see the letter."

And as soon as he laid eyes on the letter and on the florid signature, he roared:

"This isn't from Dâmaso, it's not even his handwriting. Salcede! Who the devil is Salcede? This isn't from *my* Dâmaso!"

"No, it's from *my* Dâmaso," said Ega. "Dâmaso Salcede, a fat fellow ..."

Neves again threw up his hands.

"Mine is Dâmaso Guedes! There is no other. Damn it, when someone says Dâmaso, they mean Dâmaso Guedes!"

He breathed a sigh of relief.

"God, you frightened me! I mean at a moment like this, with all this business about the Cabinet, a letter like that written by Guedes ... but if it's by Salcede, that's fine, no problem. Wait a minute, isn't he a great fat chap, a dandy with property in Sintra? A no-good rascal who played a dirty trick on us in the last election, and made Silvério spend more than three hundred *mil réis*. Oh, in that case, I'm happy to help. Pereirinha, look after Senhor Ega, will you? He has a letter which should appear tomorrow on the front page, in large print."

Senhor Pereirinha reminded him about Senhor Vieira da Costa's article on the reform of customs tariffs.

"We can run that later!" shouted Neves. "Matters of honour come first!"

And he returned to his group, where they were now discussing the Count de Gouvarinho; resuming his seat on the edge of the table, he unleashed his loud, commanding voice, affirming Gouvarinho's enormous gifts as a parliamentarian!

Ega lit a cigar and stood for a moment watching these men transfixed by Neves' eloquence. They were doubtless provincial members of parliament, whom the crisis had drawn to Lisbon, dragging them away from the tranquillity of their small towns and estates. The youngest, wearing a thin wool suit, was as round as a barrel and had an enormous red face, jocund and vulgar, which made one think of clean, healthy air and loin of pork. Another was very lean, his overcoat hanging loosely on his bowed shoulders, and with a hard, solid equine jaw; two of the other men were close-shaven, sunburnt priests, smoking cigarettes. All of them shared the same simultaneously cowed and distrustful air that marks out men from the provinces, disoriented among the carriages and the intrigues of the capital. They came there at night, to that party newspaper, to get the latest information, to be in the know, some with hopes of jobs, others with an eye on local interests, still others out of idleness. They all considered Neves to be "a man of robust talent"; they admired his fluency and his tactical skills; they would certainly enjoy quoting their friend Neves, the journalist from *A Tarde*, in the shops of their respective small towns. But alongside their admiration and the pleasure they took in rubbing shoulders with him, one could sense in them a slight fear that this "man of robust talent" might, at any moment, corner them by the window and ask for a loan. Neves, meanwhile, was celebrating Gouvarinho's oratorical skills. Not that he had José Clemente's brilliance, purity or gift for historical synthesis, nor the poetry of Rufino! But there was no one like him when it came to the wounding remark that stuck fast in the skin like a barb. And that was important in the Chamber, to have that barbed wit and to know how to use it!

"Gonçalo, do you remember that joke of Gouvarinho's about the trapeze?" he called, turning to the young man in the pale jacket standing by the window.

Gonçalo, whose dark eyes glittered with wit and malice, craned his scrawny neck above his loose collar and said:

"Oh, yes, the trapeze joke. Fantastic! Tell the boys here what it was!"

The "boys" turned to Neves wide-eyed, waiting for "the trapeze joke." It had been in the Chamber of Peers, in the debate on educational reform. Torres Valente was on the floor, that madman who wanted gymnastics to be taught in schools and for girls to be trained to jump over a vaulting horse. Gouvarinho got to his feet and said this: "Mr. President, I will say only one thing. Portugal will stray forever from the path of progress, along which she has proved such a guiding light, on the day that we legislators, with impious hand, replace the crucifix with the trapeze."

"Oh, very good," mumbled the two priests, much gratified.

And in the ensuing murmur of admiration, there was one shrill dissenting voice, that of the man as round as a barrel, who shrugged dismissively and said with a mocking smile on his plump, tomato-red face:

"Well, gentlemen, if you ask me, this Count de Gouvarinho is a bit of a sanctimonious old fool!"

There was an exchange of smiles among the smarter, more liberal provincial gentlemen, who thought the Count rather too fond of the crucifix. Neves, however, was on his feet, crying:

"Sanctimonious? How can our fat friend here call Gouvarinho sanctimonious? His mind has been formed by the century we live in; he's a rationalist, a positivist! But the point here is his gift for repartee, his use of parliamentary tactics! No sooner does that fellow from the majority party come out with his comment about the trapeze, than our friend Gouvarinho, even if he were as confirmed an atheist as Renan, immediately hurls the crucifix at him! That's what I call parliamentary strategy! Isn't that right, Ega?"

Ega murmured through the smoke of his cigar:

"Yes, of course, the crucifix does sometimes have its uses."

But at that moment, the bald man, who had thrown down his strip of paper and was stretching and yawning and leaning back in his chair, exhausted, asked

Senhor João da Ega if he was now too good to talk to the workers.

Ega immediately went over to the amusing, amiable, much-loved Melchior.

"Hard at work, Melchior?"

"I'm trying to come up with something to say about this book by Craveiro, *Songs of the Mountains*, but I can't think of anything. I just don't know what to put."

Ega, hands in pockets, smiling and friendly, joked:

"Don't say anything. You're just local journalists, news peddlers, advertisers. All you need to say about a book like Craveiro's—very respectfully of course—is where you can buy it and how much it costs."

Melchior looked at Ega ironically, his hands behind his head.

"But where else will books get reviewed? In the almanacs?"

No, in critical journals, or in newspapers that really are newspapers, rather than scandal-sheets with a kind of political poultice applied to the front page and written either in the language of the street or of the gutter, followed by a poor serial translation of some French novel, then a few birthday announcements, public appointments, police reports, and a list of the winners of the poor-house lottery. And since, in Portugal, there are no serious newspapers or critical journals, it would be best if nobody talked about books at all.

"You're right," murmured Melchior, "no one talks about anything, no one even seems to think about anything."

And just as well too, said Ega. Much of that silence comes from the natural desire of the mediocre not to mention the great. It's a matter of base, vulgar envy. In general, though, the silence of newspapers on the subject of books comes mainly from their having abdicated any lofty function of study and criticism, and having become, instead, low rags providing nothing but local, domestic information and all too aware of their own incompetence.

"Naturally, I don't mean you, Melchior; you're one of us and a first-rate journalist, but your colleagues, my friend, say nothing because they know they're incompetent."

Melchior gave a weary, sceptical shrug:

"The other reason they say nothing is because the public isn't interested, no one is."

Ega protested, warming to his theme. The public wasn't interested? That was odd. So the public wasn't interested in articles about books of which they bought three thousand or even six thousand copies? Given the population of Portugal, this was the equivalent of a major success in Paris or London. No, this silence was saying more clearly and loudly than any words: We are incompetent. We have become brutalised by gossip about which minister has arrived and which minister has departed, by the society columns, by descriptions of the charming hosts of such and such a soirée, by the slangy, insulting leader columns, by all the cheap prose in which we're mired. We don't know how to talk about a work of art or a history book, about a book of beautiful verse or a beautiful book about travel—we can no longer do it. We have neither the words nor the ideas. We may not quite be cretins, but we have become cretinised. Any work of literature flies by high above us, while, down here, we splash about in the mud.

"That, Melchior, is what lies behind the silence of the newspapers, a chorus of wailing journalists!"

Melchior was smiling, entranced, his head back, like someone enjoying a lovely aria. Then he thumped the desk with the palm of his hand and said:

"God, Ega, you talk well! Have you never thought of standing for parliament? I was only saying the other day to Neves: 'Ega would be the man for dazzling the Chamber with witticisms worthy of a Rochefort. He'd certainly set the cat among the pigeons!'"

And while Ega laughed contentedly and relit his cigar, Melchior threw down his pen.

"You're obviously in top form today! So tell me, dictate to me what I should say about this book by Craveiro!"

Ega asked what Melchior had already written. Only three lines: "We have just received a copy of the new book by our glorious poet Simão Craveiro. This delightful volume, in which the jewels of this prestigious author sparkle and shine, comes to us courtesy of that excellent publishing house . . ." And there Melchior had got stuck. He did not like the rather dull word "excellent." Ega suggested "popular." Melchior made the change and read it out again:

"'. . . comes to us courtesy of that popular publishing house . . .' No, too many *p*'s!"

He threw down his pen again in despair. He'd had enough! He just wasn't in the mood. Besides, it was late and his lady-friend was waiting for him.

"I'll leave it for tomorrow. The worst thing is I've been working on it for five days now! You're right, we *are* becoming brutalised. And it's really irritating me! Not because of the book as such, I don't care about the book, but because of Craveiro, who's a really nice fellow and, more importantly, a party member!"

He opened a drawer, took out a clothes-brush and started desperately brushing himself. And Ega was just about to help him get rid of the whitewash stains on the back of his jacket, when the gaunt, eager face of Gonçalo appeared between them, his hair caught in a permanent gale.

"And what's our Ega doing in this den of news-thieves?"

"Brushing down Sampaio, and listening to Neves recounting Gouvarinho's great witticism."

Gonçalo drew back, his dark bright eyes glinting with malice.

"The one about the crucifix? Amazing, eh! But there's an even better one than that!"

He linked arms with Ega and led him over to the window.

"We have to speak softly because of the boys from the provinces. There's another really funny one, too. I can't quite remember it, but Neves knows it.

Something about Liberty leading the racehorse of Progress . . . Some kind of equestrian image anyway. Freedom wearing a jockey's breeches and Progress with the bit between its teeth! Amazing! He's incredible that Gouvarinho! And there's more, my friend, there's more. Weren't you in the Chamber when they were debating that Tondela business? Extraordinary! The things they said! It was incredible, just incredible! The politicking and the eloquence and the talk just kill me. They're saying now that things are no worse here than they are in Bulgaria. Nonsense! There's never been a rabble like this since the world began!"

"A rabble you gleefully splash around with in the mud!" remarked Ega, laughing.

Gonçalo made a grand gesture of protest.

"Let us make one thing clear, I only splash around with the rabble because I'm a politician, but I also make fun of the whole thing because I'm an artist!"

Ega, however, thought that the country's incomparable misfortune lay precisely in that immoral clash of intelligence and character. There was Gonçalo, a man of intelligence, judging Gouvarinho to be an imbecile.

"An ass," Gonçalo corrected him.

"All right, an ass, and yet, as a politician, you want that ass to become a minister, and you'll support him with votes and speeches whenever he brays or kicks!"

Gonçalo ran his hand slowly over his brush of tousled hair, his face creased into a frown.

"I have to, for reasons of discipline and party solidarity. One has to make some compromises. The Prime Minister wants him, likes him even."

He glanced around and, standing very close to Ega, said:

"There's also talk of syndicates, bankers, and concessions in Mozambique. Money, my boy, all-powerful money!"

And when Ega bowed his head—defeated, but full of respect—Gonçalo, oozing cunning and cynicism, patted him on the back.

"Politics today, my friend, is a very different matter! We do the same as you, the literati. Literature used to be all about the imagination, fantasy, ideas. Nowadays, it's all about reality, experience, facts, documentation. Well, politics in Portugal has also joined the school of realism. In the days when the two main parties were the Regenerators and the Historicals, politics was about progress, road-building, liberty, chatter. We've changed all that. Nowadays, it's facts—money, money, money! Pelf! Lucre! The lucre of our souls, my friend! Marvellous money!"

And suddenly he stopped talking, aware of the silence in the room, in which his cry of "Money, money, money" seemed to vibrate in the hot air of the gas-lamps, like the ringing of a warning bell awakening the covetous and summoning the sly and the smooth-tongued from far and wide to plunder the helpless fatherland!

Neves had disappeared. The gentlemen from the provinces were gradually leaving too, some pulling on their overcoats, others casting a dull, leisurely eye over the newspapers on the table. Gonçalo said a brusque goodbye to Ega, turned on his heels and disappeared, embracing, as he left, one of the priests, whom he addressed as "You old rascal!"

It was midnight. Ega left. And in the cab that took him to Ramalhete, in his somewhat calmer state, it began to dawn on him that the effect of the publication of that letter would be to arouse Lisbon's voracious curiosity. The "dispute over horses" with which Neves had been so easily satisfied—distracted and absorbed as he was by that evening's political crisis—would convince no one else. If questioned, Dâmaso, in order to exculpate himself, would doubtless tell the most horrendous tales about Maria Eduarda and Carlos, and the terrible light of scandal would shine on things that should remain safely in the shadows. He was perhaps storing up problems and anxieties for Carlos, and all because of his irritation with Dâmaso. How could he have been so selfish and petty! And on his way up to his room, Ega decided to go straight to the offices of *A Tarde* tomorrow morning to stop the letter being published.

However, all that night, he dreamed of Raquel and Dâmaso. He saw them travelling along an endless road lined by apple orchards and vineyards, lying in a wooden cart, on a mattress covered with the lavish, lascivious, black satin coverlet from Villa Balzac; they were kissing, coiled immodestly about each other, beneath the cool shade of the trees, and accompanied by the slow squeak of the wheels. And in a cruel twist to the dream, he, Ega, without losing his human consciousness or pride, was one of the oxen pulling the cart! The horseflies stung him, the yoke weighed on him, and at the sound of each loud kiss coming from the cart behind, he raised his drooling snout, shook his horns and bellowed mournfully up to the heavens!

These agonised cries woke him, and his anger against Dâmaso revived, nourished by the incoherencies of the dream. Besides, it was raining. He decided not to go back to the newspaper offices and to allow the letter to be published. What did it matter, anyway, what Dâmaso said? The article in *The Devil's Trumpet* was dead, and Palma handsomely paid. And who would believe a man who declared himself, in print, to be a libellist and a drunkard?

Carlos agreed, when, after lunch, Ega told him what he had done after seeing Dâmaso in the Cohens' box eyeing him mockingly and whispering to Raquel.

"I saw quite clearly, with no room for doubt, that he was talking about you, about Dona Maria Eduarda, about all of us—the most hideous tittle-tattle. And so I didn't hesitate. We couldn't afford to wait for God's justice! We would have no peace until we had destroyed him!"

Yes, Carlos said, perhaps he was right. His one fear was that his grandfather might learn of the scandal and be upset to see his name mixed up with talk of drunkenness and the whole sordid business at *The Devil's Trumpet*.

"He doesn't read *A Tarde*," said Ega. "If he does hear the rumour, it will only be in a vague, distorted form."

Afonso did, indeed, glean only the confused impression that Dâmaso had

407

made a few unpleasant comments about Carlos at the Grémio, but had declared afterwards, in a newspaper, that he had been drunk at the time. And in Afonso's view, if Dâmaso was drunk (and why else would he have insulted his old friend, Carlos?) his declaration revealed great loyalty and an almost heroic love of the truth!

"Well, we certainly weren't expecting that!" Ega exclaimed later, in Carlos' room. "Dâmaso the Just!"

Their other friends, without having read the article in *The Devil's Trumpet*, approved of Dâmaso's downfall. Craft felt, however, that Carlos should have given him a few "quick blows with his stick" beforehand, and Taveira that they should have given the wretch an ultimatum, with a sword at his chest: "Your dignity or your life!"

A few days later, there was no further talk of the scandal. The Chiado and the Casa Havanesa had turned their interest elsewhere. A Cabinet had, at last, been formed! Gouvarinho was in charge of the Navy and Neves in charge of the Audit Office. The newspapers supporting the fallen government began, as was constitutional practice, to say that the country was irremediably lost and to make bitter comments about the King. And the last, faint echo of Dâmaso's letter came on the eve of the concert at the Teatro da Trindade, a paragraph in *A Tarde* itself, where these kind words were published:

"Our friend and distinguished 'sportsman,' Dâmaso Salcede, will be leaving shortly on a recreational tour of Italy. We wish our elegant *touriste* every happiness on this delightful excursion to the land of song and the arts."

: XVI :

AFTER SUPPER AT RUA de São Francisco, Ega, who had been out in the corridor, looking for his cigar-case in the pockets of his overcoat, went into the drawing room and asked Maria Eduarda, who was already seated at the piano:

"So you're definitely not coming to the concert, then?"

Effortlessly continuing the waltz she was playing, she turned to say languidly:

"No, I'm not interested, and besides, I'm really tired."

"It'll be a dreadful bore," muttered Carlos from the vast armchair in which he was lounging and smoking a cigar, his eyes closed.

Ega protested. It was an equally dreadful bore having to climb the pyramids of Egypt, and yet one had to suffer because it was not every day that a Christian got to climb a monument that had been in existence for five thousand years. At this concert, Dona Maria Eduarda, would, for a mere ten *tostões*, see something equally rare—the sentimental soul of a whole people displayed on stage, simultaneously naked and in tailcoats.

"Come now, be brave! A hat, a pair of gloves and off we go!"

She smiled and complained again of tiredness and indolence.

"Fine," said Ega, "but I don't want to miss Rufino. Come on, Carlos, move yourself!"

But Carlos, too, begged for clemency.

"Just a while longer, please! Let Maria play us a little from *Hamlet*. We've got plenty of time. Rufino and Alencar and all the really good people won't be on until later."

Succumbing to the warm, amiable cosiness of the evening, Ega sat down on the sofa with his cigar in order to listen to Ophelia's song, of which Maria Eduarda was already murmuring the sad, meditative words:

> *Pâle et blonde,*
> *Dort sous l'eau profonde...*

Ega adored this old Scandinavian ballad, and he found Maria Eduarda even more enchanting than the song, for she had never looked more beautiful; the close-fitting, pastel-coloured dress she was wearing that night lent her body the perfection of a marble statue; and as she sat between the candles on the piano—which drew a line of light around her pure profile and glinted golden on her hair—the incomparable ivory of her skin seemed to gain in splendour and delicacy. Everything about her was harmonious, healthy, perfect. And the very serenity of her person must make the ardour of her love utterly delicious!

Carlos was definitely the happiest man in the land, surrounded as he was by felicity and sweetness. He was rich, intelligent, and as strong as an ox; he spent his life adoring and being adored; he had precisely the correct number of enemies required to confirm his superiority; he had never suffered from dyspepsia; he was a skilful enough swordsman to inspire fear in his opponents; and his robust temperament meant that not even the folly of the general public irritated him. He was a truly fortunate being!

"Who is this fellow Rufino, anyway?" asked Carlos, stretching out his legs, when Maria Eduarda had finished the song.

Ega had no idea. He had heard that he was a member of parliament, a graduate, an inspired speaker.

Maria Eduarda, who was searching for the music of Chopin's *Nocturnes*, turned and asked:

"Is he the great orator you were all talking about once at the Toca?"

No, no, that was someone else, a truly great orator, a friend from Coimbra, José Clemente, a man who was both thoughtful and eloquent. This Rufino fellow was an eccentric with a large goatee beard, the member for Monção, and he had a sublime gift for that art which had once been a national talent, but which was now to be found only in the provinces—the art of combining sonorous words with a rich theatrical voice.

"I hate that sort of thing!" grumbled Carlos.

Maria Eduarda also hated the thought of someone trilling away without an idea in his head, like a bird on the branch of a tree.

"It depends on the occasion," remarked Ega, looking at his watch. "After all, a Strauss waltz has no ideas, but of an evening, with women in the room, nothing could be more delightful!"

No, no, Maria Eduarda felt that such rhetoric only demeaned language, which, by its very nature, should only serve to give form to our ideas. Music speaks to the nerves. If you hum a march to a child, it laughs and bounces up and down.

"And if you read it a page from Michelet," concluded Carlos, "the little angel gets bored and screams!"

"Yes, perhaps," said Ega. "It all depends on the latitude where you live and the customs it breeds. There is no Englishman, however cultivated and spiritual he may be, who does not have a weakness for physical strength, for athletes, for sports, for iron muscles. We Southerners, on the other hand, however critical we might be, love sweet words. During an evening spent with women, soft lights, a piano, and gentlemen wearing tails, even I long for a little rhetoric."

And so, with his appetite awakened, he immediately sprang to his feet to put on his overcoat and fly to the theatre, fearful that he might miss Rufino.

Carlos stopped him again, with a great idea:

"No, wait. I have another suggestion, we can have the concert here. Maria Eduarda will play Beethoven; you and I will recite Musset, Hugo, and the Parnassian poets, and, if you fancy a bit of eloquence, we have the complete works of Father Lacordaire. We will spend the night in a positive orgy of ideas!"

"Sitting in better chairs," added Maria Eduarda.

"And with better poets," said Carlos.

"And good cigars!"

"And good cognac!"

Ega threw up his arms in despair. This was how citizens were corrupted and prevented from supporting their nation's literature—with insidious promises of tobacco and drink! But his reasons for going to the concert were not purely literary. Cruges would be playing one of his *Autumn Meditations*, and he had to be there to applaud Cruges.

"Say no more!" cried Carlos, leaping up from his armchair. "I was forgetting about Cruges! It is a duty of honour! Let's go."

And shortly afterwards, having each kissed the hand of Maria Eduarda, who was staying behind at her piano, the two friends, surprised by the beauty of that winter night, so clear and sweet, walked slowly down the street, Carlos looking back twice at Maria Eduarda's lighted windows.

"I'm so glad," he exclaimed as he linked arms with Ega, "to have left Olivais! Here in Lisbon, we can at least all get together for some conversation and some literature."

He intended decorating the drawing room with more taste and comfort, converting the room next to it into a smoking-room hung with his Indian bed-spreads, and then arranging a particular day when friends could come to dine. Thus they would realise their old dream of establishing a group promoting dilettantism and art. They must also launch their magazine, which would be enormous intellectual fun. All of which promised a very chic winter, as the "late" Dâmaso used to say.

"And all of which," Ega said, summing up, "means bringing civilisation to the country. We're turning out to be worthy citizens, my friend!"

"Well, if they decide to put up a statue in my honour," said Carlos cheerily, "let it be here in Rua de São Francisco. God, it's a beautiful night!"

They reached the door of the Teatro da Trindade just as a man with an apos-tolic beard was stepping out of a hired cab; he was dressed in heavy mourning and wore a hat with a broad curved brim in a style fashionable in the 1830s. He walked past the two friends without noticing them, and was busy putting some change into his pocket. Ega, however, recognised him.

"It's Dâmaso's uncle, the democrat! Splendid-looking fellow!"

"And, according to Dâmaso, one of the family drunkards!" said Carlos, laughing.

From upstairs, in the auditorium, came a sudden burst of applause. Carlos, who was handing his overcoat to a doorman, feared that the applause might be for Cruges.

"No!" said Ega. "They're applauding rhetoric, not music!"

And indeed, when they reached the top of the staircase—which had been decorated with plants and flowers, and where two men in tails were tiptoeing up and down the lobby, whispering—they heard, coming from the stage, a loud booming voice, guttural and provincial, with long-drawn-out, sing-song vowels, summoning up "the religious soul of Lamartine"!

"It's Rufino, he's been superb!" murmured Teles da Gama, who was standing at the door, holding his cigar behind his back.

Carlos, who had little interest in the performance, stayed by Teles' side, but Ega, tall and thin, strode down the red-carpeted aisle. On both sides he saw rows of heads, absorbed and entranced, the wicker chairs packed with spectators all the way up to the stage, where ladies' hats, decorated with pale feathers or flowers, predominated. All around, leaning against the slender pillars supporting the gallery and reflected in the mirrors, stood the men from the Grémio, the Casa Havanesa, the Ministries, some in white tie, others in double-breasted jackets. Ega spotted Senhor Sousa Neto, looking thoughtful, resting his haggard face with its thin beard on the two fingers of one hand; in front of him was Gonçalo, with his usual windswept hairstyle; then the Marquis, well wrapped up in a white silk scarf; and in a group farther off, men from the Jockey Club, the two Vargas brothers, as well as Mendonça and Pinheiro, watching this rhetorical "sporting event" with a mixture of amazement and tedium. Up above, along the velvet balustrade of the gallery, was another line of ladies in pale dresses, languidly fanning themselves; behind them was a row of gentlemen, prominent among them Neves, the new minister, grave-faced, arms folded, wearing a camellia in the buttonhole of his ill-made tailcoat.

The heat from the gas-lamps was suffocating and their brash light illuminated the auditorium's faded canary-yellow walls, lined with glittering mirrors. Here and there, the silence was broken by a timid cough, swiftly muffled by a handkerchief. At the far end of the gallery, partitioned off and adorned with swags of cherry-red velvet, two gilt-backed chairs stood empty, solemn and royal in their scarlet damask.

Meanwhile, on the stage, Rufino, dark-complexioned and with a goatee beard, the orator from the remote region of Tras-os-Montes, was flinging wide his arms and speaking out in praise of "the Angel of Charity whom he had glimpsed up there in the blue, on wings of satin." Ega, squeezed between a very fat priest dripping with sweat and a corporal wearing tinted glasses, couldn't grasp what he was saying. Finally, he could contain himself no longer: "What *is* he talking about?" And the priest answered him, his gleaming face aflame with enthusiasm:

"It's all about charity and progress. He's been absolutely sublime. Unfortunately, he's nearly finished."

It was clearly some kind of peroration. Rufino seized his handkerchief and slowly mopped his brow; then he lunged towards the front of the stage, turning to the royal chairs with such an ardent, inspired gesture that his waistcoat rode up to reveal the top of his underwear. Then Ega understood. Rufino was praising a princess who had given 600 *mil-réis* to the flood victims in Ribatejo and was going to organise a bazaar in the park near the Palácio Real de Ajuda. However, it was not only this superb example of charity that had dazzled Rufino, for he, as he put it, "like all men trained in philosophy and attuned to the thinking of the times," could see in the great deeds of History not only their poetic beauty, but also their influence on society. The multitude would simply smile delightedly at the incomparable poetry of that finely gloved hand reaching out to the poor. He, however, as a philosopher, could already see, emerging from the delicate fingers of a princess, a far deeper, far finer consequence—the rebirth of Faith!

A fan, dropped from the gallery, elicited a yelp from a plump woman down below, followed by a great deal of shushing and a brief flutter of excitement. One of the masters of ceremonies, Dom José Sequeira, in his large red silk bow tie and his tails, immediately jumped onto the steps leading up to the stage and shot a stern, squint-eyed glance at that unruly section of the audience, whence came a cackle of laughter. Other men shouted indignantly: "Silence! Be quiet!" And from the chairs in the front row emerged the ministerial face of Gouvarinho, glasses glinting, concerned about the preservation of order. Ega looked for the Countess, expecting to find her next to the Count, but saw her at last, farther off, wearing a blue hat and seated between the Viscountess de Alvim—who was all in black—and a vast mauve satin back, belonging to the Baroness von Craben. The noise died down, and Rufino, who had meanwhile taken a sip of water, stepped forward, smiling, his white handkerchief in his hand.

"As I was saying, ladies and gentlemen, given this century's mental orientation..."

Ega was feeling crushed and suffocated; he had had enough of Rufino, and was sure that the priest next to him stank. He could stand it no longer and pushed his way through to the rear of the auditorium where he could unburden himself to Carlos.

"What an idiot, eh?"

"Dreadful!" muttered Carlos. "When is Cruges going to play?"

Ega did not know; the whole programme had been altered.

"The Countess de Gouvarinho is over there, in blue. Now there's an encounter I'd like to see!"

However, at this point, both men turned, hearing someone behind them whispering discreetly: "*Bonsoir, messieurs.*" It was Steinbroken and his secretary, who were tiptoeing towards them in their tails, looking very serious and clutching their crush hats. Steinbroken immediately regretted the absence of the royal family.

"*Monsieur de Cantanhede, qui est de service, m'avait cependant assuré que la reine viendrait... C'est bien sous sa protection, n'est-ce pas, toute cette musique, ces vers? Voilà pourquoi je suis venu. C'est très ennuyeux. Et Alphonse de Maia, toujours en bonne santé?"*

"Oui, merci."

An impressive silence filled the auditorium. Rufino, making the gesture of someone tracing slow, noble lines on a canvas, was describing the loveliness of a village at sunset, the village in which he had been born. And his booming voice grew soft, tender, fading to a crepuscular murmur. Steinbroken tapped Ega's shoulder. He wanted to know if this was the great orator of which people had told him. Ega declared patriotically that he was one of the finest orators in Europe!

"What kind of orator?"

"The sublime kind, like Demosthenes!"

Steinbroken raised his eyebrows in amazement and said something in Finnish to his secretary, who languidly put his monocle to his eye; crush hats under one arm, eyes closed, as respectfully attentive as if they were in church, the two Finnish diplomats stood listening, waiting for the sublime.

Rufino, meanwhile, his hands hanging by his side, confessed to a certain weakness of the soul! Despite the natural poetry surrounding his native village, where every violet in the meadow, every nightingale in the wood provided irrefutable proof of God's existence, he had been pierced by the thorn of unbelief! Yes, how often, as evening fell, and the bells in the old church tower tolled the last Hail Mary and the women in the fields were singing, had he walked past the cross outside the church and the cross in the cemetery, and glanced at them with the cruel, cold, casual smile of a Voltaire!

A ripple of emotion ran through the audience. Voices, overwhelmed by pleasure, could murmur only: "Oh, very fine, very fine."

It had been in just such a state of mind, devoured by doubt, that Rufino had heard a cry of horror echo throughout our nation, our Portugal. What had happened? Nature was attacking her own children. And waving his arms about, like someone floundering in a moment of crisis, Rufino described the floods. Here, a rustic house, once a flower-bedecked nest of love, was swept away; from down below, in the valley, came the mournful lowing of cattle; farther off, the black waters carried along on the current a rosebud and a cradle!

Deep, hoarse cries of "Bravo!" issued forth from heaving bosoms. And the men standing around Carlos and Ega turned passionately to each other, faces aglow, all feeling the same enthusiasm: "Such eloquence! Astonishing! Sublime!"

Rufino was smiling, drinking in his audience's excited response, created by his words alone. Then, respectfully, he turned to the royal chairs, empty and solemn.

Seeing Nature's implacable rage, he had raised his eyes to their natural refuge, to the exalted place from which salvation always comes—the Throne of

Portugal! And suddenly, to his amazement, he had seen the white wings of an angel spread out above him! It was the Angel of Charity, ladies and gentlemen! And where had it come from? Where had it found its inspiration? Where had that golden-haired angel come from? From science books? From chemistry laboratories? From dissection rooms where the soul is so cravenly denied? From the desiccated schools of philosophy that make of Jesus a precursor of Robespierre? No! Kneeling and submissive, he had dared to ask the Angel. And the Angel of Charity, pointing up to the heavens, had murmured: "I come from the beyond!"

A rapturous murmur ran through the packed stalls. It was as if the stucco-work on the ceiling had cracked open and angels were singing on high. A devout, poetic tremor shook the ladies' false hairpieces.

Rufino was drawing to a close, with a lofty certainty in his heart! Yes, ladies and gentlemen, from that moment on, his doubts had been like a mist which the sun, our radiant Portuguese sun, dissolves into air. And now, despite all the ironies of science, despite the proud and scornful remarks of Renan, Littré, and Spencer, he, who had been vouchsafed a divine confidence, could stand there, hand on heart, and declare to them all in a loud voice, that there *was* a Heaven!

"Hear, hear!" the grubby priest in the aisle called out.

And throughout the auditorium, in the crush and in the suffocating heat of the gas-lamps, the gentlemen from the Ministries, from the Praça do Comércio, from the Casa Havanesa, bellowed and applauded their proud affirmation of the existence of Heaven!

Ega, who was laughing, vastly amused by all this, heard beside him a snort of rage. It was Alencar, in overcoat and white tie, who was sombrely smoothing his moustaches.

"What do you think, Tomás?"

"Absolutely nauseating!" the poet said in a kind of suppressed roar.

He was shaking with disgust! On a night like that, a night of poetry, a night when men of letters should show themselves as they are, the sons of Liberty and Democracy, to see that excuse for a man licking the feet of the royal family... it was simply revolting!

At the front, by the steps of the stage, a tumult of embraces and compliments surrounded Rufino, who stood there gleaming with pride and sweat. And the men poured out of the door, fiery-faced and still greatly moved, all opening their cigar-cases. Then Alencar took Ega by the arm.

"I've been looking for you. Guimarães, Dâmaso's uncle, asked to be introduced to you. He says he has something very serious to tell you, very serious. He's downstairs in the bar."

Ega looked surprised. Something serious?

"Fine, let's go downstairs and join him in a drink. What are you going to recite, Alencar?"

"'Democracy,'" said the poet somewhat cautiously, as they went down the stairs. "It's a new thing I've written, you'll see. A few hard truths for this bourgeois audience."

They had just reached the door of the bar when Senhor Guimarães appeared, buttoning up his frock-coat, his hat pulled down over his eyes, and his cigar lit. Alencar, very gravely, introduced them.

"My friend, João da Ega . . . my old friend Guimarães, one of our finest, and a veteran of Democracy."

Ega went over to a table and politely pulled up a chair for that veteran of Democracy, and asked if he would prefer cognac or beer.

"I've had my usual tot, thank you very much," said Senhor Guimarães sharply, "and that's quite enough for me tonight."

A waiter was glumly wiping the marble table top. Ega ordered a beer. Then, Senhor Guimarães—putting down his cigar and smoothing his beard to ensure that his face bore an appropriately majestic look—said slowly and solemnly:

"I am Dâmaso Salcede's uncle, and I asked my old friend Alencar to introduce me to you so that I could ask you to take a good look at me and tell me if I strike you as a drunkard."

Ega understood at once and said in a frank and friendly manner:

"Ah, you're referring to a letter your nephew wrote."

"A letter that you dictated, a letter you forced him to sign!"

"Me?"

"He told me so, sir!"

Alencar intervened:

"Keep your voices down, confound it! This is a land of very inquisitive people!"

Senhor Guimarães coughed and drew his chair closer to the table. He had, he said, been out of Lisbon for some weeks dealing with his brother's inheritance. He had not seen his nephew because he only ever met the imbecile when it was absolutely necessary. The previous evening, at the house of an old friend, Vaz Forte, he had happened to notice a copy of *Futuro*, a Republican newspaper, not badly written, but rather short on ideas. And the first thing he saw on the very first page, in huge type, under the all-too-accurate heading *Society Tidbits*, was his nephew's letter. Senhor Ega could imagine his rage! He sat down right there, in Forte's house, and wrote to Dâmaso in more or less these terms: "I have read your infamous statement. If you do not issue another statement forthwith, to be published in all the newspapers, saying that you had no intention of including me among the family drunkards, I will come and find you and break every bone in your body, one by one. Well may you tremble, sir!" That's what he had written. And would Senhor João da Ega like to know what Senhor Dâmaso's reply had been?

"I have it here; it is, as our friend Zola puts it, *un document humain*. Here it is. Very grand writing paper, with a gold monogram and a count's coronet. Stupid ass! Would you like me to read it?"

In response to Ega's smiling gesture, Guimarães himself read it, slowly and emphatically:

My dear Uncle,

The letter you mention was written by Senhor João da Ega. I myself would be incapable of speaking so disrespectfully of our beloved family. He was the one who took my hand and forced me to sign; and I was in such a state, I hardly knew what I was doing and, in the end, I signed merely because I thought it would avoid further scandal. It was a trap set for me by my enemies. You know how fond I am of you, dear Uncle—indeed, last year, I had every intention of sending you half a barrel of Colares wine, but I did not have your address in Paris. Please do not be angry with me. I am unhappy enough as it is. If you care to, seek out the man who ruined me— João da Ega! Believe me when I say that I will, one day, wreak a revenge that will be the talk of Lisbon! I have not yet decided how, exactly; I am still in too great a state of confusion, but our family's name will once more be washed clean, because I allow no one to play fast and loose with my dignity. And the only reason I did not fight for my honour, before my departure for Italy, is that, what with all these upsets, and as if I did not have enough troubles already, I have had the most terrible dysentery, so bad I can barely stand . . .

"Are you laughing, Senhor Ega?"

"What else do you expect me to do?" Ega managed to stammer at last, barely able to speak for laughter and with tears in his eyes. "I'm laughing, Alencar is laughing, and you should be laughing too, sir. It's so utterly absurd. His dignity and his dysentery."

Crestfallen, Senhor Guimarães looked at Ega and looked at Alencar—who was snuffling into his moustaches—and said:

"Granted, the letter is clearly the work of a complete ass, but the fact remains . . ."

Ega appealed to Senhor Guimarães' good sense, to his experience of matters of honour. Would two gentlemen go and challenge a man in his house, grab him by the wrist and force him, under threat of violence, to sign a letter in which he declared himself to be drunk?

Senhor Guimarães, grateful for this deference to his tact and to his experience, admitted that, certainly in Paris, this would be most unusual.

"And in Lisbon too, sir! This isn't Kaffirland! And tell me something else, Senhor Guimarães, as gentleman to gentleman: would you say that your nephew was totally and unerringly truthful?"

Senhor Guimarães stroked his beard and declared roundly:

"No, the fellow's an out-and-out liar."

"Exactly!" cried Ega in triumph, throwing up his arms.

Alencar intervened again. The matter seemed to have been satisfactorily resolved. All that remained was for the two men to shake hands like brothers, like good democrats.

Standing up, Alencar knocked back his glass of gin. Ega was smiling and holding out his hand to Senhor Guimarães. However, there was still a frown on Guimarães' lined face; he wanted Senhor João da Ega (just in case there should be any shred of doubt) to state, in the presence of his friend Alencar, that he did not believe that he, Guimarães, looked like a drunkard.

"My dear sir!" exclaimed Ega, rapping a coin on the table to summon the waiter. "On the contrary! I have great pleasure in proclaiming to the four winds, with Alencar as my witness, that I think you have the face of a perfect gentleman and of a patriot!"

They shook hands warmly, while Senhor Guimarães declared his great satisfaction at meeting Senhor João da Ega, such a very liberal young man and so talented too. Should Ega ever need anything, political or literary, he should write to that well-known address: *Rédaction du Rappel, Paris*!

Alencar had rushed off. And Ega and Guimarães left the bar, exchanging impressions of the evening so far. Guimarães had been annoyed by the servility and sanctimoniousness of that man Rufino. When he had heard him talking about the princess' wings and the cross in the churchyard, he had almost yelled out from the back: "How much are they paying you to say this, you wretch?"

Suddenly, Ega stopped on the stairs, taking off his hat:

"Viscountess, are you leaving us already?"

It was the Viscountess de Alvim, who, accompanied by Joaninha Vilar, was coming slowly down the stairs, still tying up the long ribbons on her green plush cape. She complained of a terrible headache, although she had absolutely adored Rufino. But a whole night of literature, what a bore! And now, to make matters worse, there was a little man playing classical music.

"That's my friend Cruges!"

"Oh, he's your friend, is he? Well, you should have told him to play something a little more popular."

"Your disdain for the great masters wounds me, Viscountess. Would you like me to accompany you to your carriage? No? Goodnight, Senhora Dona Joaninha! Your servant, Viscountess. And may God rid you of that headache of yours!"

She turned, one foot on the step, threatening him with her fan and smiling.

"You impostor! You don't believe in God!"

"Forgive me, Viscountess. May the *Devil* rid you of your headache!"

Guimarães had discreetly disappeared. And from the door that opened into the auditorium, Ega could see Cruges on the distant stage, sitting on a stool so low that the tails of his coat brushed the floor and his pointed nose was almost pressed against the sheet music of the sonata he was so expertly playing. Ega tiptoed up the red-carpeted aisle, quite free of people now, almost empty; a cooler air was circulating; the ladies were yawning wearily behind their fans.

He stopped next to Dona Maria da Cunha, who was crammed into the same row as the Marchioness de Soutal, the two Pedroso sisters and Teresa Darque.

The good Dona Maria immediately touched his arm and asked the name of that extremely hirsute musician.

"He's a friend of mine," whispered Ega. "A great pianist, Cruges."

Cruges. The name passed among the ladies, who did not know it. And what was he playing, what was that sad tune?

"It's Beethoven, Senhora, the Sonata 'Pathétique.'"

One of the Pedroso sisters had not quite caught the name of the sonata, and the very serious, very beautiful Marchioness de Soutal, sniffing at a bottle of smelling salts, told her that it was the "Potato" sonata. The whole row dissolved into suppressed giggles. The "Potato" sonata! How funny! From the other end, Vargas, the fat man from the races, leaned forward with his vast, beardless, poppy-red face to say:

"Very good, Marchioness, very witty!"

And the joke passed to other ladies, who turned and smiled at the Marchioness, with a rustle of fans. Grave and beautiful, in an old dress of black velvet, she sat enjoying her triumph and sniffing her salts, while, in front of her, a grey-bearded music lover fixed the noisy party with large gold-rimmed spectacles that glittered with irritation.

Meanwhile, throughout the auditorium, the whispering was growing. Those members of the audience afflicted with colds were coughing freely. Two gentlemen had opened their newspapers. And bent over the keyboard, the collar of his tailcoat gaping at the back, poor Cruges, sweating and astonished by such a noisy lack of attention, rushed through the final notes.

"A complete fiasco," said Carlos, who had joined Ega and the party of women. Dona Maria da Cunha was thrilled and surprised to see him. So there at last was Senhor Carlos da Maia, Prince of Darkness! What *had* he been up to all summer? Everyone had been hoping to see him in Sintra, some more anxiously than others . . . A furious "Sh!" from the grey-bearded music lover silenced her. Just at that moment, Cruges, played two abrupt chords, pushed back the stool and crept off stage, wiping his hands on his handkerchief. There was some scattered applause, unenthusiastic and polite, and a great murmur of relief. Ega and Carlos ran to the door, where the Marquis, Craft, and Taveira were already waiting, in order to embrace and console poor Cruges, who was trembling all over, his eyes wild.

Immediately after this, in the attentive silence that followed, a very tall, very thin man went onto the stage, carrying a manuscript. Someone next to Ega said that the man's name was Prata and that he was going to talk about the "state of agriculture in the province of Minho." Behind him, a stage-hand appeared and placed a candelabra with two candles on the table; Prata, sideways to the light, peered at his notes; and emerging from between that sad profile and the large sheets of paper came a slow burble of words, like the sleepy murmur of someone reciting the novena, from which occasional phrases stood out like moans: "wealth of cattle," "the breaking up of property," "fertile and vulnerable region."

A silent, stealthy exodus began, one that not even the shushings of the master of ceremonies, standing vigilantly by the stage steps, could stop. Only the ladies remained and the odd aged bureaucrat, who bent forward zealously, one hand cupped to his ear, in order to catch Prata's prayerful murmurings.

Ega, who had also fled "the opulent paradise of the Minho," found himself just ahead of Guimarães.

"A bit of a bore, eh?"

Guimarães agreed that the current pontificator was not much fun. Then, more seriously, on another subject entirely, and clutching a button on Ega's tailcoat, he said:

"I hope you did not get the impression earlier on that I in any way support or care about my nephew."

No, of course he hadn't! Ega had seen at once that Senhor Guimarães had no family feeling for Dâmaso at all.

"Only disgust, sir, only disgust! When he went to Paris for the first time and found out that I was living in a garret, he never so much as came to visit me! The imbecile gives himself aristocratic airs, but, as you well know, he's the son of a usurer!"

He took out his cigar case and added gravely:

"His mother now, she was a different matter! My sister was from a good family. She made a most unfortunate marriage, but she was from a good family! Obviously, for a man of my principles, all this nonsense about nobility, parchments, and coats of arms is just a joke, nothing but a joke! But facts are facts, and there's no changing Portugal's history. And the Guimarães of Bairrada were of blue blood."

Ega smiled and nodded politely.

"Will you be leaving for Paris soon?"

"Tomorrow, via Bordeaux. Now that Maréchal MacMahon, the Duke de Broglie, Descazes and all that rabble are gone, one can breathe freely again."

Just then, Teles and Taveira, walking along arm-in-arm, turned and looked with some curiosity at the austere old man, all clad in black, who was talking loudly to Ega about French marshals and dukes. Ega noticed this; Guimarães was wearing a new cashmere frock-coat and a splendid, gleaming hat; and Ega liked being seen there talking with this correct and venerable gentleman who so impressed his friends.

"For a moment," he remarked, walking along beside Guimarães, "the Republic did appear to have been compromised."

"Lost! And I, believe it or not, sir, was about to be expelled for having spoken a few home truths at a meeting of anarchists. I was even told that in a cabinet meeting, Maréchal MacMahon, who is a vulgar devil, banged on the table and said: 'Ce sacré Guimaran, il nous embête, faut lui donner du pied dans le derrière!' I wasn't there, so I don't know if it's true, but that's what I was told. In Paris, since the French don't know how to pronounce Guimarães, and I hate my name being mangled, I sign myself Monsieur Guimaran. Two years ago, when I went to Italy, I was Monsieur Guimarini. And if I were to go to Russia for any reason, I'd be Monsieur Guimaroff. I do so hate people mangling my name."

They had returned to the door of the auditorium. The long, empty seats, in the heavy glare of the gas-lamps, gave the room a feeling of sad abandon and tedium; and on the stage, Prata talked on and on, one hand in his pocket, his nose stuck in his manuscript, and no one could now make out a single word that fell from the lips of this gaunt scarecrow. The Marquis, however, emerging from within, and wrapping himself in his silk scarf, said to Ega, in passing, that the little man was very practical, knew about pruning techniques and had even made some references to Proudhon.

Ega and Guimarães resumed their slow walk through the lobby, where, amid furtively smoked cigarettes, the whisper of muffled conversations was growing in volume, like voices in an echoing courtyard. Guimarães made fun of the man quoting Proudhon in a miserable little theatre like that, in the middle of a talk about manure in the Minho; it was nonsense!

"Oh, we're always quoting Proudhon," said Ega, laughing, "he's one of our classic monsters. Even ministers of state know that, according to Proudhon, property is theft and God is evil."

Guimarães shrugged.

"He was a great man, an immense man! They are the three great figures of the century: Proudhon, Garibaldi, and the *compadre*."

"The *compadre*?" exclaimed Ega, bewildered.

This was the affectionate name by which Guimarães used to call Gambetta in Paris. Gambetta never saw him without shouting out to him in Spanish: *Hombre, compadre!* And he, of course, would reply: *Compadre, caramba!* And the name had stuck, and it made Gambetta laugh. Because he was a good man and liked such Southern frankness, and he was a patriot to the hilt!

"An immense patriot, my friend. The greatest of them all!"

Ega had assumed that Senhor Guimarães, given that he worked for *Rappel*, would have been a worshipper at the temple of Victor Hugo.

"Hugo, sir, is not a man, he's a whole world!"

And Guimarães looked up and added in an infinitely grave tone:

"Yes, a world! And believe it or not, only three months ago, he said something to me that went straight to my heart!"

Delighted by Ega's interest and curiosity, Guimarães gave him a detailed account of this glorious episode, which still touched him.

"It was one night at the offices of the *Rappel*. I was sitting there writing, and he came into the room; he was already walking with some difficulty, but his eyes were alight, and he exuded kindness and majesty! I got up as if a king had come into the room. No, what am I saying? If he'd been a king, I'd have given him a kick in his backside. I got up as if he were a god. No, what am I talking about? No god would have made me get up out of my chair. Anyway, I got up!

And he looked at me and made a gesture with his hand, and said, smiling, with that aura of genius he always had about him: 'Bonsoir, mon ami!'"

And Guimarães took a few dignified steps in silence, as if remembering that bonsoir, that mon ami made him feel more keenly his importance in the world.

Suddenly Alencar, who'd been with another group of men, talking and gesticulating, rushed over to them, deathly pale, eyes blazing, and said:

"Isn't this a disgrace? That idiot's been going on and on for half an hour, reading from his notes, and everyone's leaving—there's not a soul left! By the time my turn comes, I'll be reciting to rows of empty seats!"

And he bustled off again, grinding his teeth, to vent his fury on others.

A weary round of applause inside the auditorium made Ega turn round. The stage was empty again, apart from the two candles burning in the candelabra. A sign placed on the piano by a stage-hand, announced in large letters "Ten minute interval," as if they were at the circus. And at that moment, the Countess de Gouvarinho emerged arm in arm with her husband, leaving behind her a long backwash of polite words, bent backs, and bureaucratic hats extravagantly raised. The master of ceremonies rushed around, looking for two chairs for them. The Countess, however, went over to join Dona Maria da Cunha, whom she had seen taking refuge in a window bay with the Pedroso sisters and the Marchioness de Soutal. Ega immediately went over to join the little party of intimate friends, waiting, first, for the ladies to finish planting loud kisses on one another's cheeks.

"So, Countess, are you still feeling deeply moved by Rufino's eloquence?"

"I'm certainly feeling very tired. It's so hot in there!"

"Dreadful. The Viscountess de Alvim left a little while ago, complaining of a headache."

The Countess, who had dark circles under her eyes and a little line at each corner of her mouth, murmured:

"I'm not surprised, this is no fun at all. However, we must carry our cross to Calvary."

"If only it were just a cross, Countess!" exclaimed Ega. "Unfortunately, it's a lyre!"

She laughed. And Dona Maria da Cunha, who was looking lively and quite rejuvenated that evening, beamed, full of affectionate admiration for Ega, who was one of her favourites.

"Ah, no one can ever get the better of you, can they, Ega? But tell me something, what's become of your friend Maia?"

Ega had seen how, only moments before in the auditorium, she had tugged at Carlos' sleeve and whispered to him. However, he maintained an air of innocence and said:

"He's over there somewhere, drinking in all this literature."

Suddenly, Dona Maria da Cunha's lovely, usually languid eyes lit up with a spark of mischief.

"Speak of the devil, or, should I say, angel. Here's our Prince of Darkness now!"

Carlos did, indeed, happen to be passing and was met by the Count de Gouvarinho's open arms, held out to him with an effusiveness which seemed to indicate a rebirth of his old affection. This was the first time Carlos had seen the Countess since that night in the Aterro, when he had abandoned her, furiously slamming shut the door of the carriage in which she sat weeping. They both looked down as they tentatively held out their hands to each other. In the end, she was the one who broke the embarrassed silence, opening her large ostrich-feather fan and exclaiming:

"It's terribly hot, isn't it?"

"Awful!" said Carlos. "Why don't you go and stand by the window and get some fresh air?"

She forced her pale lips into a smile:

"Are those doctor's orders?"

"No, Senhora, these are not my consulting hours. It was merely Christian charity."

Suddenly the Countess addressed Taveira—who was sharing a flirtatious joke with the Marchioness de Soutal—in order to scold him for failing to come to her last Tuesday soirée. Taken aback by such interest and familiarity, Taveira, red-faced and stammering, explained that he had not even known about it, that it had undoubtedly been his loss, that certain other things had come up.

"Besides, I didn't think you began to receive so early in the season. You never used to do so until halfway through Lent. In fact, I remember last year . . ."

He stopped. The Count de Gouvarinho had turned and placed a friendly hand on Carlos' shoulder, wanting his impressions of "our Rufino." He, the Count, was enchanted! Especially by the way Rufino "varied the tone," the way he negotiated the difficult art of shifting from the solemn to the light, descending from the emotional heights to the more playful plains of language. Extraordinary!

"I've heard many great parliamentarians, Rouher, Gladstone, Canovas, and many others, but they lacked those flights of fancy, that opulence of language. It was all very dry, nothing but ideas and facts. It didn't touch the heart! For example, that potent, reverent image of the Angel of Charity descending slowly on wings of satin. First-rate!"

Ega could contain himself no longer.

"I think that so-called 'genius' is a complete imbecile."

The Count smiled, as if at the foolish remark of a child.

"Well, we all have our opinions."

And he held out his hand to Sousa Neto, to Darque and Teles da Gama, and to others who had joined the inner circle, while his co-religionists, his colleagues from party headquarters and from the Chamber—Gonçalo, Neves,

423

Vieira da Costa—lurked in the background, unable to approach the minister they had created, now that he was talking and laughing with the young gentlemen and ladies from "society." Darque, who was a relative of Gouvarinho's, wanted to know how the Count was coping with the burdens of Power. The Count declared to those around him that he had, so far, done nothing more than review the means by which he hoped to tackle the problems. Otherwise, as regards work, the Cabinet was in a woeful state! The Prime Minister had a cold and would be laid up in bed for a whole week. And now his colleague in the Treasury had fallen prey to a fever.

"Is he better? Is he up and about yet?" people around him asked earnestly.

"He's pretty much the same, and tomorrow he's going to Dafundo. He hasn't been rendered entirely useless, mind. I was saying to him only yesterday: 'You go off to Dafundo and take your papers and your documents with you. Go for a little walk in the morning and breathe some good, fresh air. At night, after supper, by the light of the lamp, you can amuse yourself sorting out a few Treasury matters!'"

A bell rang. Dom José Sequeira, scarlet-faced and out of breath, came pushing his way through the crowds in order to announce to the Count the end of the interval and to offer his arm to the Countess. As she passed, she reminded Carlos about her "Tuesdays," with all the simplicity of someone delicately reminding another of an obligation. He gave a silent bow. It was as if all of the past—the fugitive sofa, her aunt's house in Santa Isabel, the carriages in which she had left her familiar smell of verbena—had been things that both of them had read about in a book and forgotten. Her husband followed behind, his head and his spectacles held high—the representative of Power at that festival of the Intelligence.

"Well," said Ega, as he and Carlos moved away, "the lady's certainly got spirit!"

"What the devil do you expect? She's had her hour of thoughtless passion and now she's calmly getting on with the routine of life."

"And the routine of life," concluded Ega, "involves constantly bumping into you, who have seen her in her shift! What a nice world this is!"

Just then, Alencar appeared at the top of the stairs, his overcoat draped over his arm, returning from the bar and the gin bottle with a brighter gleam in his hollow eyes, ready to perform. And the Marquis joined them, still well wrapped up in his white silk scarf, but sounding hoarse now and complaining that his throat was getting worse with each minute that passed. This wretched throat of his would be the death of him one day!

Then very seriously, looking at Alencar, he said:

"Listen, this poem you're going to recite, 'Democracy,' is it about politics or feelings? If it's politics, I'm off, but if it's about feelings and humanity and the blessed worker and fraternity, then I'll stay, because I like that kind of thing, and, who knows, it might even do me good."

The others assured him that it was about feelings. The poet removed his hat and ran his fingers through the limp curls of his inspired thatch.

"Let me tell you something, boys. One cannot have one without the other, just look at Danton. But why talk of such lions of the Revolution, you have only to look at our own Passos Manuel! Obviously, one needs logic, but I say to hell with a politics that has no heart and not even a tiny glimmer of the infinite!"

Suddenly, above the renewed silence in the auditorium, a booming voice even louder than Rufino's sent the great names of the explorers João de Castro and Afonso de Albuquerque echoing around the room. Filled with curiosity, they all went over to the door. A fat, burly fellow with a pointed beard and a camellia in his button-hole, was brandishing one clenched fist as if he were waving the flag, and loudly lamenting that we, the Portuguese, possessors of the noble estuary of the Tejo River and of a fine and glorious tradition, should allow the sublime legacy of our forefathers to be scattered on the winds of indifference!

"Oh God, patriotism," said Ega. "Let's leave!"

The Marquis stopped them, though, because he liked a bit of patriotism. And it was the poor Marquis whom the patriot appeared to be addressing, lifting his rotund barrel of a body onto the tips of his toes, and bellowing: "Who among you now, with a sword in one hand and the cross in the other, would be prepared to leap onto the deck of a caravel and carry the Portuguese name across uncharted seas? Who among us would have courage enough to imitate the great João de Castro, a man who tore up all the fruit trees in his garden in Sintra, such was the selfless nature of his poetic soul!"

"Now the wretch wants to deprive us of dessert?" exclaimed Ega.

Everyone around him laughed. The Marquis turned his back on the orator, disgusted by such cheap patriotism. Others concealed yawns behind their hands, utterly bored by "all our glories." And Carlos, his nerves on edge, trapped there by his duty to applaud Alencar, was just suggesting to Ega that they go downstairs to the bar to kill time, when he spotted Eusèbiozinho coming down the stairs, hurriedly pulling on his pale overcoat. He had not seen him since the infamous *Devil's Trumpet* episode, in which Eusèbiozinho had played the role of "messenger." And the anger that he had felt at the time revived at once in an irresistible desire to give him a sound beating. He said to Ega:

"While we're waiting for Alencar, I'm going to make good use of my time by giving that scoundrel a good thrashing!"

"Leave him," said Ega, "he wasn't the one responsible for the article!"

Carlos, however, was already running down the stairs. Ega followed anxiously behind, fearing violence. When they reached the door, Eusébio had headed off towards Carmo, and they only caught up with him in Largo da Abegoaria, silent and deserted at that time of night, with only two dim gas-lamps burning. When he saw Carlos bearing down on him, without his overcoat, his shirtfront pale in the dark night, Eusébio shrank back and stammered: "Fancy seeing you here . . ."

"You wretch," Carlos said in a low, threatening voice. "So you were involved in that disgusting business with *The Devil's Trumpet* too, were you? I should break every bone in your body!"

He had grabbed Eusèbiozinho's arm, not as yet with any violent intent; however, as soon as he felt his own strong hand close around that flabby, tremulous flesh, he was filled once more with the never-extinguished aversion which, as a boy, had made him leap on Eusèbiozinho and try to pound him to a pulp whenever the Silveira sisters brought him to his grandfather's house. And he shook him furiously, as he used to do, enjoying his own anger. The poor widower—his tinted glasses sent flying, his crêpe-banded hat rolling along the pavement—performed a skinny, disjointed dance. Finally, Carlos hurled him against the door of a coach house.

"Help! Help!" croaked the poor unfortunate. "Police!"

Carlos already had his hand around his throat, but Ega intervened:

"Stop! That's enough! Our dear friend here has had his dose of medicine!"

And Ega picked up the hat. Trembling and gasping for breath, lying face down on the ground, Eusèbiozinho was still groping for his umbrella. A venomous kick from Carlos' boot sent it rolling across the paving stones into a gutter full of filth and still-fresh horse dung.

The square remained empty, with the gas flames slumbering in the dim lamps. Carlos and Ega walked calmly back to the concert. In the foyer, full of lights and pot plants, they passed the bearded patriot, who, surrounded by friends, was on his way to the bar, wiping the sweat from his face and neck with his handkerchief and exclaiming with the weary radiance of one who has triumphed:

"By God, that was hard work, but I think I struck a chord!"

Alencar would already be in full song! The two friends bounded up the stairs. And there was Alencar, on stage, where the two candles in the candelabra still burned.

Tall and thin, and cutting a sombre figure against that canary-yellow backdrop, the poet cast a slow, pensive, hollow eye over the stalls and the gallery; and in the face of such melancholy and such solemnity, the audience sat in heavy rapt silence.

"'Democracy!'" announced the author of "Elvira," as grandly as if he were announcing a great revelation.

Twice he wiped his moustaches with his white handkerchief, which he then threw down on the table. And raising his hand in a large lingering gesture, he began:

> It happened in a garden.
> Moonlight falling on vast trees
> Full of love and secrets . . .

426

"What did I tell you?" exclaimed Ega, touching the Marquis' elbow. "It *is* about feelings. I bet you it's the banquet!"

It was indeed the banquet, already described in *Flower of Martyrdom*, a romantic banquet, set in a shadowy garden where Cyprus wines are drunk, where the brocade trains of dresses brush the lawns between the magnolia trees, and where songs accompanied by cellos rise up from the waters of the lake. However, the stern social ideal of Poetry would soon reveal itself, for while beneath the trees radiant with moonlight, everything is "laughter, the drinking of toasts, and lascivious murmurings," outside, by the golden railings surrounding the garden, a pale gaunt woman in rags weeps, frightened by the dogs' barking and clutching to her scrawny bosom a child crying for food. And the poet, tossing back his hair, asked why, in this proud century, were people still going hungry? What had been the point, from Spartacus onwards, of man's desperate struggle to achieve Justice and Equality? What had been the point of the cross of the great Martyr up there on the hill where, among the fir-trees,

> *The sun's rays disappear,*
> *The sad wind falls silent,*
> *And the eagles wheeling*
> *Among the clouds watch*
> *As the Son of Man dies!*

The auditorium remained mute and suspicious. And Alencar, gesturing with his two hands, bemoaned the fact that all the genius of all the generations was impotent when faced by that most simple of things—giving food to a crying child!

> *It is a torment to the heart,*
> *A stain upon the conscience,*
> *That for all our human knowledge*
> *We cannot resolve this one black question!*
> *The ages roll by, and still no dawning light;*
> *Still, on one side I see hunger*
> *And on the other indigestion!*

Ega squirmed and spluttered into his handkerchief, convinced he would burst. "Indigestion!" It was the most extraordinary word ever proclaimed from the heights of lyricism! Serious men round about smiled at such grubby "realism." One joker said that the cure for indigestion was bicarbonate of soda.

"Not for my indigestion," grumbled a man with a greenish face, who was unbuckling his waistcoat.

They were silenced by a fearsome "Sh!" from the Marquis, who had loosened his scarf a little, greatly moved, as he always was, by such poetic, humanitarian sentiments. Meanwhile, onstage, Alencar had found the solution to human suffering! It had been taught him by a voice, a voice that spoke from the depths of the centuries and which, though always suppressed, had been growing irresistibly louder from Golgotha to the Bastille! And then, taking up a more solemn stance behind the table, with the boldness of a pioneer and the courage of a soldier, as if that honest piece of furniture were a pulpit or a barricade, Alencar raised his forehead with Dantonesque audacity and uttered a fearful cry. What Alencar wanted was a Republic!

Yes, a Republic! Not a Republic of terror and hatred, but of gentleness and love! A Republic in which the millionaire smilingly opens his arms to the worker! A Republic that was dawn, consolation, refuge, mystical star, and dove.

> *The Dove of Fraternity,*
> *Reaching out snow-white wings*
> *Above our human murk and mud,*
> *Wraps its children, yes, every one,*
> *In the same holy Equality!*

From up above, in the gallery, came a passionate "Bravo." And immediately, to crush such enthusiasm, various stern members of the audience turned round and said: "Sh! Silence!" Then Ega held up his skinny hands to applaud, roaring out, loud and clear:

"Bravo! Excellent! Bravo!"

Then, quite pale from his own daring, he adjusted his monocle and said to those beside him:

"Alencar's ideas about democracy may be absurd, but I refuse to support bourgeois repression! That's why I applauded."

And he again held up his thin hands, this time alongside those of the Marquis, whose hands thundered together like steam-hammers. Others around them, not wishing to appear less democratic than Ega and that nobleman of ancient lineage, immediately joined in with ardent cries of "Bravo." People glanced uneasily at this revolutionary sector of the audience. Then silence fell, a more sombre and emotional silence, as Alencar (who had, very cleverly, foreseen those expressions of bourgeois intolerance) asked in furious verses what it was that they hated or feared about the sublime advent of the Republic? Was it the food given lovingly to the child? Was it the hand of justice held out to the proletariat? Was it the proffered hope? Was it the dawn?

> *Is it the great light you fear?*
> *Or is it merely the ABC?*
> *Then punish those who read,*
> *And return the masses to obscurity!*
> *Go backwards, never forwards,*
> *Extinguish the gas that lights the streets,*
> *Let children dispense with clothes,*
> *And, yes, bring back the gallows!*

More applause, sincere this time, broke out in the auditorium; they were succumbing at last to the repetitious charm of that sonorous, humanitarian lyricism. All the dangers of a Republic no longer mattered. The lines rolled forth, clear and incantatory; and the more positive spirits in the audience were swept along on the wave. In that sympathetic glow, Alencar was smiling, his arms outstretched, as he listed one by one, as if unthreading pearls, all the gifts the Republic would bring. Beneath its flag, not red, but white, he saw the land covered with wheat fields, all hungers satisfied, the nation singing in the valleys beneath the smiling eyes of God. For Alencar did not want a Republic without God! Democracy and Christianity, like a lily and an ear of corn, completed each other and should fold each other in a fond embrace. The hill of Golgotha would be the platform for the Convention. And for this sweetest of ideals to become reality there was no need for cardinals or missals or novenas or churches. The Republic, made solely of purity and faith, prays in the fields; the full moon is the blessed host; and, among the laurel bushes, nightingales intone the *Tantum ergo*. And everything prospers, everything glows—instead of a world of Conflict, there is a world of Love . . .

> The ploughshare replaces the sword,
> Justice laughs at Death.
> Schools are free and strong,
> And the Bastille lies broken.
> The tiara rolls in the mud,
> The lily of equality springs up,
> And a whole new humanity
> Plants the cross on the barricade!

A heartfelt, generous round of "Bravos" made the flames in the gas-lamps tremble! That Southern passion for verse, sonority, and romantic liberalism, for the image that crackles in the air with the brief brilliance of a rocket, carrying all before it, made every heart beat faster, and caused heads of government departments to lean over the ladies in front of them and shout out their enthusiasm for that Republic inhabited by nightingales! And when Alencar, raising his hands to the ceiling, and modulating his slightly hoarse voice almost as if he were reciting a prayer, summoned down to Earth that dove of Democracy—which had first taken flight from Calvary, and which returned now, streaming light—then tender emotion bathed every soul, and a deep shudder of ecstasy ran through everyone present. The ladies softened in their seats, their faces half-turned to Heaven. The stifling auditorium was filled with the cool air of the chapel. The poetry became more like a murmured litany, as if it were addressed to an image draped in satin folds and crowned by stars of gold. And it was hard now to tell if the thing evoked and expected was the Goddess of Liberty or Our Lady of Sorrows.

Alencar, meanwhile, watched her descend, spreading her perfume. She was already touching our human valleys with her divine feet. Her fecund bosom was already overflowing with universal abundance. Everything was blossoming and growing young again.

> *Roses smell more sweetly!*
> *Fruit is more succulent to the tongue!*
> *The soul shines out bright and pure,*
> *Free now from shadows and from veils . . .*
> *Pain, in terror, runs away,*
> *And Hunger flees and War too.*
> *Man sings on the good Earth,*
> *And Christ smiles in the Heavens!*

Raucous voices burst forth to acclaim him, so loudly that the canary-yellow walls shook. Excited young men climbed onto their chairs; a couple of white handkerchiefs fluttered in the air. And the poet, shaking and exhausted, stumbled down the stairs into the eager arms reaching out to him. He kept repeating breathlessly: "Boys! Boys!" When Ega ran down from the back of the theatre with Carlos, shouting: "You were wonderful, Tomás!" Alencar was overcome by emotion, and his eyes filled with tears.

The ovation continued as he progressed down the aisle; people slapped him on the back, more serious people shook his hand, others congratulated him. Gradually, he raised his head in a proud smile revealing rotten teeth, and he truly felt himself to be the poet of Democracy, consecrated and anointed by this triumph, and charged with the unexpected mission of liberating souls! Dona Maria da Cunha tugged at his sleeve as he passed and murmured delightedly that she had thought it "beautiful, quite beautiful." The poet, overwhelmed, exclaimed: "What we need, Maria, is light!" Teles da Gama came and clapped him on the shoulder, telling him that "he had trilled most splendidly." Alencar, completely overcome by now, stammered: "*Sursum corda*, Teles, my friend, *sursum corda!*"

Ega, meanwhile, above the tumult, was looking everywhere for Carlos, who had disappeared once he had embraced Alencar. Taveira assured him that Carlos had gone down to the bar. Then, downstairs, a boy swore that Senhor Dom Carlos had taken a cab and was already setting off up the Chiado.

Ega stood at the door, uncertain whether or not he could survive the rest of the concert. At that moment, the Count de Gouvarinho, with the Countess on his arm, came marching down the stairs, looking angry and sombre. The Count's groom raced off to summon the coupé. And when Ega approached, smiling, to ask what effect Alencar's great democratic triumph had had on them, Gouvarinho gave expression to his deep, barely contained irritation, muttering through clenched teeth:

"Admirable poetry, but utterly indecent!"

The coupé arrived. He just had time, as he shook Ega's hand, to growl quietly:

"To speak of barricades and make extravagant promises to the working class at a society event, under the protection of the Queen, and in the presence of a Minister of the Crown, is perfectly indecent!"

The Countess had already climbed into the carriage, picking up her long silk train as she did so. The Count followed, plunging furiously into the darkness of the coupé. A courier in braided uniform trotted alongside on a white nag.

Ega was about to go upstairs again, but the Marquis appeared, swathed in a greatcoat, fleeing a poet with large moustaches who was upstairs reciting some adorable little verses dedicated to a pair of adorable little eyes; the Marquis loathed poetry addressed to parts of the human body. Then Cruges came out of the bar, buttoning up his overcoat. Confronted by this general exodus of friends, Ega decided to leave as well and to go and have a drink with the maestro at the Grémio.

They put the Marquis in a hired cab, and he and Cruges walked slowly down Rua Nova da Trindade, enjoying the strange charm of that starless winter night, so mild that a stray May breeze seemed to be blowing.

They were passing the door of the Hotel Aliança when Ega heard someone hurrying along behind him, calling: "Senhor Ega! One moment, please, Senhor Ega!" He stopped and recognised the broad-brimmed hat and the white beard of Senhor Guimarães.

"Forgive me, sir!" exclaimed Guimarães, struggling to catch his breath. "I saw you leaving, and I just wanted to have a word with you before my departure tomorrow."

"Of course. Cruges, you go on, and I'll catch up!"

Cruges stationed himself on the corner of the Chiado. Senhor Guimarães again apologised, but it really would be just a word or two.

"I've been told that you are Senhor Carlos da Maia's great friend, that you're like brothers."

"Yes, we're very good friends."

The street was deserted, with just a few urchins hanging about the brightly-lit door of the theatre. In the dark night, the high façade of the Hotel Aliança cast a long shadow over Ega and Guimarães. Senhor Guimarães cautiously lowered his voice.

"Well, the thing is . . . as you know, or maybe you don't, I was a close friend in Paris of Senhor Carlos da Maia's mother. You're in a hurry, and that particular story is irrelevant now, but years ago, she placed in my safe-keeping a box which, she said, contained certain important papers. At the time, of course, we both had many other things to think about, and the years passed, and she died. In a word, since you clearly are in a hurry, I still have that box in my possession, and, just in case, I brought it with me when I came to Portugal this time to sort out my brother's legacy. Today, in the theatre, I was thinking that it would be best to hand it over to the family."

Cruges was growing impatient.

"Are you going to be much longer?"

431

"Just a moment," called Ega, intrigued by the box and the papers it contained. "Do go on."

Senhor Guimarães quickly summed up his request. Knowing how close Senhor João da Ega and Carlos da Maia were, it had occurred to him that perhaps he could give the box to Ega so that he could restore it to the family.

"Of course!" said Ega. "I'm staying at the Maias' house, at Ramalhete."

"Excellent! Maybe you could send a trustworthy servant to fetch it tomorrow. I'm staying at the Hotel Paris, in Pelourinho. Or better still, I can bring it myself, I wouldn't mind at all, even though I am leaving tomorrow."

"No, no, I'll send a servant," insisted Ega, holding out his hand to Guimarães, who shook it warmly.

"Thank you so much! I'll attach a note and then, if you could give it, on my behalf, to Carlos da Maia or to his sister . . ."

Ega looked startled.

"To his sister? What sister?"

Senhor Guimarães stared at Ega, equally amazed. And slowly letting go of his hand, he said:

"What do you mean 'what sister?' Why, the only one he has, Maria Eduarda!"

Cruges, who was now stamping his feet impatiently, called from the corner:

"I'll go on ahead to the Grémio."

"Fine—see you there."

Senhor Guimarães, meanwhile, was stroking his long beard with his black-gloved hands and gazing at Ega, as if trying to penetrate his mind. When Ega linked arms with him, asking if they could walk as far as the Loreto together in order to talk a bit more, Guimarães, at first, took only a few slow, uncertain steps.

"I think," said Ega, smiling but nervous, "that there must be some confusion. I've known Maia since he was young, I'm even living in his house at the moment, and I can assure you that he has no sister."

Senhor Guimarães began to mutter a few embarrassed excuses, which only unnerved and tortured Ega all the more. Senhor Guimarães had assumed it was no secret, that the whole business about his sister's past life had been forgotten, now that they were reconciled.

"And since, only a few days ago, I saw Senhor Carlos da Maia with his sister and yourself in the same carriage, on the Cais do Sodré . . ."

"The lady who was in the carriage?"

"Of course!" cried Senhor Guimarães, rather irritated now and weary of all this strange confusion. "The very same, Maria Eduarda Monforte, or Maria Eduarda Maia, if you like, whom I've known since she was a child, and who often sat upon my knee, who ran away with MacGren, and, later on, lived with that awful fellow Castro Gomes—the very same!"

They were standing in the middle of Largo do Loreto, beneath a streetlamp.

Senhor Guimarães suddenly stopped, seeing Ega's eyes wide with horror and a terrible pallor covering his face.

"You knew nothing about it, then?"

Ega took a deep breath and pushed back his hat on his head. Guimarães, dumbstruck, merely shrugged. He had obviously made a terrible blunder! One should never interfere in other people's affairs! But there it was. Senhor Ega must think this some kind of nightmare, especially after that dire evening of poetry they had just suffered through. He apologised most sincerely and wished Senhor João da Ega a very good night.

As if in one illuminating flash, Ega had understood the whole catastrophe, and he eagerly grasped Senhor Guimarães' arm, terrified that he might leave, disappear, taking with him his evidence, the papers, the box left behind by the Monforte woman, and, with them, the certainty he now so desperately wanted. And as they walked across the square, he began vaguely and hesitantly to justify his reaction, in order to reassure the man and coax out of him everything he knew, the proof, the entire truth.

"I'm sure you'll understand, Senhor Guimarães, that these are very delicate matters, which I assumed no one else knew about. That is why I was struck dumb, made speechless, when I heard you suddenly speak of them so openly. You see, and I say this in strictest confidence, the lady is not known in Lisbon as Carlos' sister."

Senhor Guimarães made a broad gesture with his hand. Ah, so Senhor Ega had merely been keeping him in the dark? And quite right too. These were very serious matters, which required all kinds of veils and concealments. He understood, yes, he understood perfectly. Indeed, given the Maias' position in Lisbon society, the lady was hardly a presentable sister.

"Not that it was her fault at all, sir! It was her mother, that extraordinary mother chosen by the Devil himself!"

They were walking down the Chiado. Ega stopped for a moment, staring at Guimarães with feverish, devouring eyes.

"Did you know that lady, Madame Monforte, well?"

Intimately! He had first known of her in Lisbon, but only from afar, as the wife of Pedro da Maia. Then tragedy had struck, and she had eloped with the Italian. He himself had run away to Paris that same year, with one Clemence, a seamstress from Levaillant, and what with one thing and another, business affairs and other misfortunes, he had ended up staying there for good! But it wasn't his life story that he was there to tell. He had finally met Madame Monforte one night at the Bal Laborde, and their friendship dated from that meeting. By then, the Italian had died in a duel, and a bladder complaint had seen off old Monforte, her father. She was living at the time in grand style, with a young man called Trevernnes, in a lovely house in Parc Monceaux. She was an extraordinary woman, and he confessed unashamedly that he owed her a great deal. When the delightful Clemence became ill with tuberculosis,

Madame Monforte used to bring her flowers, fruit, and wine, and keep her company and watch over her like an angel, for she was nothing if not generous! Her daughter, Maria, was seven or eight at the time, and as pretty as a picture. Madame Monforte had had another daughter by the Italian, another pretty little creature, but she'd died in London.

"The times I used to sit Maria Eduarda on my knee, sir! She may not remember, but I once gave her a talking doll that could say 'Napoleon.' That was at the height of the Empire, when even the wretched dolls were imperialists! Then, when she was in Tours, at the convent, I went there twice with her mother. At the time, my principles did not allow me to enter such dens of religiosity, but I went in order to keep her mother company. And when Maria Eduarda ran away with the Irishman, with MacGren, her furious mother turned up at my door, demanding that I call out the police commissioner so that they could arrest MacGren. In the end, she hired a carriage and went to Fontainebleau, where the three of them made their peace and even lived together. In short, it was one long chain of disasters."

A weary sigh escaped Ega, who was walking along, dragging his feet, sunk in gloom.

"And Maria Eduarda, of course, had no idea whose daughter she was."

Senhor Guimarães shrugged.

"She didn't even know the Maia family existed! Madame Monforte had always told her that her father was an Austrian nobleman, whom she had married in Madeira. A terrible mess, my dear sir—a terrible mess!"

"Dreadful!" murmured Ega.

But, Senhor Guimarães went on, what else could Madame Monforte have done? "It would have been damnably hard to say to her daughter: 'I ran away from your father, and that's why he killed himself!' Not so much out of any feeling of shame—because the girl must have realised that her mother had lovers, and she herself, poor thing, took a lover when she was eighteen—but because of the gunshot, the corpse, the blood.

"She never even spoke to me about all that," exclaimed Senhor Guimarães, stopping, and throwing his arms wide to the deserted street, "no, she never spoke to me about her husband, or about Lisbon, or about Portugal, not once. I remember on one occasion, when we were at Clemence's house, I mentioned a sorrel horse that had belonged to Pedro da Maia and which she used to ride. A superb beast! I didn't say anything about her husband, mind, only the horse. But she struck the table with the edge of her fan and said in the shrill tones of a fishwife: *'Dites donc, mon cher, vous m'embêtez avec ces histoires de l'autre monde!'* And she was quite right really, they *were* tales from another world! Anyway, to cut a long story short, I think that, later on in life, even she believed that Pedro da Maia had never existed. She was a silly woman, and, in the end, she took to drink, but there we are, she had a generous heart and was very kind to Clemence. *Parce sepultis!*"

"Dreadful," murmured Ega again, taking off his hat and running one tremulous hand over his head.

Now his one desire was to keep accumulating evidence, details. He brought up the subject of the papers again, Madame Monforte's box. Senhor Guimarães had no idea what was in it, and it wouldn't surprise him at all if it contained only dressmaker's bills or old cuttings from *Le Figaro* in which she was mentioned.

"It's just a small box that she gave me on the eve of her departure to London with her daughter. It was during the war. Maria was already living with the Irishman, and even had a little girl, Rosa. Then came the Commune, and all the ensuing horrors. When Madame Monforte returned from London, I was in Marseilles. That was when poor Maria Eduarda moved in with Castro Gomes, simply, I think, in order not to die of hunger. I went back to Paris, but I didn't see Madame Monforte again. Well, by that time, she was very ill. Nor did I ever again speak to Maria Eduarda, who, by then, was living with that ghastly impostor Castro Gomes, a *rastaquouère* ripe for the guillotine. If I ever did meet her, it was only to greet her from afar, as when I saw her in the carriage the other day, with you and with her brother. And so I kept the papers. And to be perfectly honest, what with my various political commitments, I never even gave them a thought. But now they're here for the family to dispose of as they wish."

"If it's no bother," said Ega, "I could come to your hotel now and take them away with me."

"No bother at all! If it's on your way, then that will be one job done."

They walked on for a while in silence. The concert had doubtless ended. A line of carriages came thundering down the Chiado. Then two women and a young man passed by, the young man was gesticulating and talking loudly about Alencar. Senhor Guimarães had slowly taken his cigar case out of his pocket, then, stopping to strike a match, he asked:

"So, Dona Maria Eduarda is simply regarded as a relative, is she? And how did she find out? How did that happen?"

Ega, who was walking along, head bowed, started, as if he had just woken up. He began telling some garbled story at which he himself blushed in the darkness. Yes, Maria Eduarda was regarded as a relative. The family administrator had been the one to discover the connection. She had broken entirely with Castro Gomes and with her past. The Maias gave her an allowance, and she lived very quietly in Olivais, as the daughter of a member of the Maia family who had died in Italy. Everyone was very fond of her, and Afonso da Maia had a special affection for the little girl . . .

Then, suddenly, when he found himself dragging in the name of that noble old man, he could stand these inventions no longer and blurted out:

"Anyway, all in all, it's a dreadful business!"

"A real drama," Senhor Guimarães said gravely.

And since they had now reached the hotel, he asked Ega to wait for a moment while he ran upstairs to fetch the papers.

Alone in the square, Ega reached out his hands to the heavens, in a silent unburdening of all the anguish he had been feeling as he had sleepwalked his way from Loreto. And his one clear feeling was of the indestructible truth of Guimarães' story, perfect, complete, with not a single flaw that might cause it to crack and break into a thousand pieces. The man had known Maria Monforte in Lisbon, when she was still Pedro da Maia's wife and a dazzling sight on her sorrel horse; he had met her again in Paris, after her elopement, when her first lover had died, and subsequently too, when she had lived with other lovers; Maria Eduarda had sat on his knee, and he had given her dolls ... And he'd kept track of Maria Eduarda ever since: in Paris, in the convent at Tours, in Fontainebleau with the Irishman, in the arms of Castro Gomes, and, finally, only a few days ago, in a hired carriage with him and Carlos da Maia, in Cais de Sodré! It all fitted and agreed entirely with the story told by Maria Eduarda. Out of it all emerged one monstrous certainty: Carlos was his own sister's lover!

Guimarães had not yet returned. On the second floor, a bright light in an open window had just come on. Ega began walking slowly across the square. And now, gradually, a feeling of incredulity rose up in him, rebelling against that whole catastrophe, worthy of some cheap melodrama. Was it likely that such a thing could happen to a friend of his, in Lisbon, in an apartment rented from Cruges' mother? It was impossible! Such horrors only happened in the social confusion and tumult of the Middle Ages! But in a well-policed, well-run bourgeois society, guaranteed by a plethora of laws, and documented by another plethora of baptismal records and marriage certificates, it was impossible! In modern life, it was simply not within the bounds of possibility that two children, separated by the folly of their mother, after only briefly sharing the same cradle, should grow up in different countries, be brought up and educated, only to follow the remote parabolas of their two separate destinies in order to do what? To sleep once again in the same bed, this time illicitly! No, it was impossible. Such things belong only in books, in which they appear as the subtle inventions of art, purely in order to give the human soul a new horror to contemplate. Then he looked up at the lighted window, where Senhor Guimarães was probably searching through the papers in his trunk. Yes—that man with his unshakeable story devoid of discrepancies! And gradually, that bright light shining on high seemed to Ega to penetrate and illuminate the whole intricate misfortune, and to reveal to him its slow evolution. Yes, it was all perfectly possible! A child, the daughter of a woman who took her away with her, grows up, becomes the mistress of a Brazilian man, comes to Lisbon and stays in Lisbon. In a neighbouring area lives the son of that same woman, whom she did not take with her; he too grows up and becomes a man. With his fine appearance and sophisticated clothes, he stands out in this provincial, ill-dressed city. She, for her part, is fair and tall and imposing, the flower of a superior civilisation, wearing clothes designed by Laferrière—highly conspicuous in this multitude of small, dark women. In the narrow little world of the Baixa and the Aterro, where everyone rubs shoulders with everyone else, it is inevitable that the two will meet and, given their great personal beauty, be fatally drawn to each other. What could be more natural? If she were ugly and wearing some cheap confection from the Loja da América, if he were a round-shouldered fellow in a bowler hat, they would never notice each other and would follow their respective diverse destinies. As it was, though, it was inevitable that they would meet and very probable that they would fall in love. And then, one day, a Senhor Guimarães happens by, and the terrible truth bursts forth!

The hotel door creaked in the darkness, and Senhor Guimarães came over to him, wearing a silk cap and carrying a package.

"Do forgive me, I couldn't find the key to the trunk. It's always the same when one is in a hurry. Anyway, here is the famous box!"

"Thank you, thank you!"

It resembled a cigar box and Guimarães had wrapped it in an old copy of *Rappel*. Ega put it in the large pocket of his overcoat; and immediately, as if there were nothing more to be said between them, held out his hand to Senhor Guimarães. However, the latter insisted on walking with him as far as the corner of Rua do Arsenal, even though he only had his silk cap on rather than a proper hat. For someone who lived in Paris, the night had an oriental sweetness to it, and he, with his journalistic habits, never normally went to bed until late, until two or three in the morning.

Walking slowly along, his hands in his pockets and a cigar in his mouth, Senhor Guimarães returned to the subject of politics and that evening's concert. Alencar's poem (the title of which, "Democracy," had given him such high hopes) had turned out to be pretty feeble stuff.

"A lot of flowers, a lot of talk, a lot of waffle about liberty, but there was no real thrust to it, no focused attack on this rabble of a monarchy and its court. Don't you agree?"

"Oh, definitely," murmured Ega, scanning the horizon, hoping desperately for a cab to appear.

"It's the same with the Republican newspapers here. They're full of pretentious verbiage. I say to them: 'You infernal cowards, why don't you deal with the genuine social questions?'"

Fortunately, a cab appeared, approaching slowly from the direction of Terreiro do Paço. Ega hurriedly shook Senhor Guimarães' hand, wished him a good journey, and told the driver to take him to Ramalhete. Senhor Guimarães, however, still had hold of the door, telling Ega to be sure to visit him in Paris. Now that they were friends, he wanted to introduce him to everyone he knew there. Senhor Ega would see then that Paris is not, as Lisbon is, full of imbecilic poseurs and pretentious scarecrows twirling their moustaches. There, in the first nation of the world, everything is joy and fraternity and wit galore.

"You can write to me care of the editor of *Rappel*. Everyone knows it. And I'm very relieved about that box."

"I'll take good care of it."

"Your servant, sir! And please give my compliments to Senhora Dona Maria Eduarda!"

As the carriage rolled along the Aterro, Ega was anxiously asking himself: "What shall I do?" Dear God, what should he do with the terrible secret in his possession, of which he was sole owner, now that Senhor Guimarães was leaving, this time for good? And when he imagined, with horror, the anguish into which this revelation would throw the man he loved best in the world, his instinct was to keep the secret and let it die with him. He would say nothing; Guimarães would be absorbed back into Parisian life, and those who loved each other could continue to love each other! He would not then have to create any terrible crisis in Carlos' life, nor would he, as his friend, suffer his part in those afflictions. What could be crueller than to ruin the lives of two adorable, innocent creatures by presenting them with proof of incest!

However, at the word "incest," all the consequences of that silence rose up before him like fearful, living things, flickering before him in the darkness. Could he calmly bear witness to the lives of these two people, knowing that their relationship was an incestuous one? Could he go to Rua de São Francisco, and sit down happily at the table, and glimpse, in the next room, the bed in which they slept, and know that this awful depravity was the work of his silence? No, it was impossible. But would he likewise have the courage to go into Carlos' room the next day and say to his face: "Excuse me, Carlos, but your lover is actually your sister"?

The carriage had stopped outside Ramalhete. Ega went in, as he usually did, by Carlos' private staircase. Everything was dark and silent. He lit a candle and drew aside the curtain at the door that led into Carlos' rooms; he took a few timid steps across the rug, footsteps that already seemed to have a sad echo. A mirror glinted palely in the shadows. And the candle light fell on the untouched bed with its broad smooth bedspread and silk drapes. The idea that in Rua de São Francisco, Carlos would, at that moment, be sleeping with a woman who was his sister, pierced him then with such painful clarity, like a physical image, so vivid and so real, that he could see them clearly: naked, their arms about each other. All of Maria Eduarda's beauty, all of Carlos' sophistication vanished. They were merely two animals, born of the same womb, copulating in a corner like dogs, driven by the brute impulse of lust!

He ran to his room, fleeing from this vision, which was only accentuated by the darkness in the corridor, hardly dissipated by the single tremulous flame of his candle. He bolted the door and, hand shaking, hurriedly lit, one after the other, the six candles in the candelabra on the dressing table. It now seemed to him urgent, inevitable and necessary to tell Carlos *everything*. At the same time, though, he felt less and less capable of speaking to Carlos face to face and destroying his happiness and his life with this revelation of incest. He could not do it! Let someone else tell him! He would be there afterwards, loyal and loving, to console him and to share his pain. But the supreme sorrow of Carlos' life would not come from words uttered by his lips! Let someone else tell him! But who? A thousand incoherent, foolish ideas passed through his poor head. He could ask Maria Eduarda to run away, to disappear. He could write an anonymous letter to Carlos, detailing the story told him by Guimarães. And all this confusion, this anxiety, gradually resolved itself into a hatred of Senhor Guimarães. Why had the imbecile spoken to him in the first place? Why had he insisted on giving him papers that belonged to someone else? Why had Alencar introduced him? Ah, if it hadn't been for Dâmaso's letter. Yes, the cause of it all was that wretch Dâmaso!

As he paced up and down in his room, still with his hat on, he suddenly noticed an envelope on the bedside table. He recognised Vilaça's handwriting. He did not even open it. An idea had suddenly occurred to him. Why not tell everything to Vilaça? He was, after all, the Maias' administrator. The household had never kept any secrets from him. And who better to sort out this singularly complex situation, involving a female member of the family thought to be dead, but who had now unexpectedly reappeared, than the family's faithful administrator, their old confidant, the man who, by inheritance and by destiny, had always been party to the family secrets and to its domestic problems? And giving it no further thought, without studying the possibility in any more depth, he fixed immediately on this decision as a means of salvation, one that at least provided solace, and lifted from his heart that leaden weight, suffocating and unbearable.

He would have to get up early and go to Vilaça's house. He wrote on a piece of paper: "Wake me at seven." He went downstairs, to the long stone corridor where the servants had their rooms, and hung this message on the key to the footman's door.

When he went back upstairs, feeling calmer, he opened Vilaça's letter. It was a brief note, reminding him that a loan of two hundred *mil réis* from the Banco Popular fell due in two days' time.

"God, it's just one thing after another!" cried Ega angrily, crumpling up the letter and hurling it to the floor.

: XVII :

THE FOOTMAN WOKE EGA promptly at seven. At the sound of the door opening, Ega sat bolt upright in bed, and all the black anxieties of the previous night—Carlos, his sister, the ruined happiness of the Maia family—rose up suddenly in his soul, as if they too had been startled awake. The balcony door had been left open; a silent, grey, dawn light filtered in through the opaque white blind. For a moment, Ega looked around him with a shudder, then, all courage gone, he plunged back beneath the covers, savouring that small sense of warmth and comfort before having to confront the bitter events of the day.

And gradually, as he lay snuggled beneath the blankets, he began to think that his planned early-morning visit to Vilaça's house was perhaps not as urgent or as useful as he had thought. What was the point of seeking out Vilaça? This had nothing to do with money or lawsuits or legalities, with things that required an administrator's experience. It would simply mean bringing another person in on the secret, a secret of such awful delicacy that even he was terrified by it. And he muttered to himself as he huddled farther under the covers, with only his nose exposed to the cold: "It would be nonsense to go and see Vilaça!"

Besides, couldn't he muster enough courage to tell everything to Carlos that very morning, clearly and manfully? Was the matter as horrifying as it had seemed to him the night before? Would it inevitably ruin the man's life? There had been a similar case near his mother's estate in Celorico, in the village of Vouzeias, when a brother and a sister had, quite innocently, been planning to get married. When the papers for the banns were brought together, their true relationship was revealed. For a few days, the betrothed couple were, as Father Serafim put it, "flabbergasted," but, later on, as the best of friends, they used to laugh about it, vastly amused at having to address each other as "brother" and "sister." The groom, a handsome, strapping young man, told people simply that "there'd been a bit of a mix-up in the family." In the case of Carlos and Maria Eduarda, the matter had gone a step further, there were more sophisticated emotions in play, but their hearts remained totally innocent and free of all guilt. Why, then, should Carlos' existence be blighted? His initial ignorance of the true situation should be an impediment to any feelings of remorse, and once he had got over the first horror, what reason was there for his suffering to last indefinitely? It would mean an end to pleasure, of course, but that would be the same with any romantic disappointment. It would be far less painful than if Maria Eduarda had betrayed him with Dâmaso.

Suddenly, the door opened and Carlos burst in, exclaiming:

"Why the early start? Baptista told me about it downstairs. What is it, an affair, a duel perhaps?"

He was still in his overcoat, with the collar turned up, concealing the white tie he had been wearing the night before; he had doubtless just returned from Rua de São Francisco in the carriage Ega had heard outside in the street, only moments before.

Ega immediately sat up in bed and, reaching for his cigarettes on the bedside table, said, with a yawn, that the previous evening he had arranged with Taveira to go to Sintra this morning, and, just in case, had asked for an early call. But he wasn't sure now, he had woken feeling rather tired.

"What kind of day is it?"

Carlos had gone over to the window to open the blind. There, on the desk, in the full light of day, lay Madame Monforte's box, wrapped in a copy of *Rappel*. And Ega's first thought was: "If he notices and asks me about it, I'll tell him everything!" Horrified by this decision, his poor heart began beating frantically. The blind was somewhat stiff, but when Carlos finally managed to raise it, a broad ray of sun bathed the desk in light; to Ega's immense relief, however, Carlos did not notice the box.

"So what's this about Sintra, then?" said Carlos, sitting down on the end of the bed. "It's not a bad idea, actually. In fact, Maria Eduarda was talking only yesterday about going to Sintra. I know—why not make it a joint outing? We could go as a foursome in the break!"

He was already looking at his watch, calculating how much time it would take to harness the horses and warn Maria Eduarda.

"The trouble is," began Ega, embarrassed, picking up his monocle, "Taveira was talking about us going with a couple of women."

Carlos cringed in mock horror. How sordid, going to Sintra with women in broad daylight! At night, in the dark, in order to get drunk, fine! But in full view of the Lord's good light! Was it Lola Gorda they were going with?

Polishing his monocle on a corner of the sheet, Ega launched into some complicated tale. They weren't Spanish women; on the contrary, they were seamstresses, decent girls. He had promised ages ago to take one of them, the daughter of Simões, the upholsterer who had died recently . . . They really were very decent folk!

In the face of such long-standing promises and such out-and-out decency, Carlos immediately gave up any idea of a trip to Sintra.

"Fine, then, that's that. I'm going to have a bath and then down to business.

If you do go, bring me some cheese pastries back for Rosa, will you? She loves them!"

As soon as Carlos had left the room, Ega folded his arms, downcast and dispirited, realising that he would never have the courage to tell Carlos "everything." What should he do? Once more, he found himself taking refuge in the idea of going to see Vilaça and handing Madame Monforte's box over to him. There was no more honest, more practical man alive, and, given the very mediocrity of his bourgeois spirit, who better to deal with such a catastrophe calmly and unemotionally? Vilaça's "lack of emotion" decided him.

He leaped out of bed and impatiently rang the bell. And while he waited for the servant to come, he put his dressing-gown over his shoulders and went to have another look at Madame Monforte's box. It did, indeed, resemble an old cigar box, wrapped in newspaper, its corners soiled and worn, and still bearing the remains of a wax seal on which one could make out what had doubtless been Madame Monforte's motto—*Pro amore*. On the lid was written, in a somewhat uneducated female hand: "*Monsieur Guimaran, à Paris.*" When he heard the servant's footsteps, he covered the box with a towel that had been left draped over a nearby chair. Half an hour later, he was rolling down the Aterro in an open carriage, feeling more cheerful, and taking deep breaths of the fine fresh morning air he so rarely enjoyed.

The day did not get off to a good start. Vilaça had already gone out, and his maid did not know whether he had gone straight to the office, or to inspect a property in Alfeite over which there was some dispute. Ega set off for Vilaça's office in Rua da Prata. Senhor Vilaça had not yet arrived.

"What time will he be back?"

The clerk, a thin, pale young man, who kept fiddling nervously with a coral chain on his waistcoat, said that Senhor Vilaça should not be long, unless, of course, he had taken the nine o'clock boat across to Alfeite. Ega left in despair.

"Right," he called to the driver, "to the Café Tavares."

In the Tavares, which was still deserted at that hour, a waiter was sprinkling sand on the floor. While Ega waited for his meal to be served, he read through the newspapers. There were brief comments about the concert, with a promise of more detailed criticism of this brilliant artistic event later on. Only the *Gazeta* was more expansive, full of lofty phrases, describing Rufino as "noble" and Cruges as "promising"; as regards Alencar, they distinguished the philosopher from the poet; the *Gazeta* reminded the philosopher that not all of philosophy's ideal aspirations, as lovely as mirages in the desert, can be put into practice in society; but to the poet, the creator of those splendid images, those inspired stanzas, the *Gazeta* cried unreservedly: "Bravo! Bravo!" There were other equally stupid remarks. A list followed of all the people whom the *Gazeta* remembered having seen, the most prominent among them being João da Ega, always so witty and vivacious, with his monocle and his fine profile. Ega smiled and stroked his moustache. At that precise moment, his steak arrived, smoking and spitting straight from the pan. Ega put the *Gazeta* to one side, saying to himself: "Hm, not such a bad newspaper after all!"

The steak was excellent, and after a little cold partridge, some pineapple dessert, and a strong coffee, Ega felt a gradual lifting of the gloom that had been oppressing his soul since the previous night. After all, he thought, lighting a cigar and checking his watch, from a purely practical point of view, this disaster meant only that Carlos would lose a beautiful mistress. And although that loss would be a source of anguish to him now, it might, subsequently, have its compensations. Up until then, a shadow had lain across Carlos' future— that promise of marriage which would irreparably bind him by his honour to an admittedly very interesting woman, but a woman whose past, alas, was rather too full of Brazilians and Irishmen. Her beauty made it all seem very poetic, but how long would it last, that charm, that glow of a goddess descending to Earth? Perhaps Guimarães' revelation would turn out to be a providential liberation? In a few years' time, Carlos would have recovered and would feel as serene as if he had never suffered; he would be free and rich, and with the whole wide world before him!

The café clock struck ten. "Right," thought Ega, "to business."

His carriage rattled its way back to Rua da Prata. Senhor Vilaça had still not arrived, and the clerk concluded that Senhor Vilaça must have gone to Alfeite. Faced by this uncertainty, Ega felt suddenly utterly dispirited again; all his courage drained away. He dismissed the cab, and with the package in one hand, he wandered along Rua do Ouro as far as the Rossio, stopping distractedly outside a goldsmith's or studying the contents of a bookshop window. The previous night's gloom, briefly banished, grew still heavier and again filled his soul. He could see no "liberations" now, no "compensations." All he could feel around him, as if floating in the air, was that one horror—Carlos sleeping with his own sister.

He returned to Rua da Prata, again climbed the dingy stone stairs, and there on the landing, outside the green baize door, he bumped into Vilaça, who was just rushing out, pulling on his gloves.

"At last!"

"Ah, so you're the friend who has been looking for me! Well, I'm afraid the Viscount do Torral is expecting me, so you'll have to be patient . . ."

Ega almost grabbed him by the lapels. A Viscount! But his was a matter of the utmost urgency and seriousness! Vilaça would not budge, however, and finished pulling on his gloves with the same brisk business-like air.

"But as you see, my friend, the man is waiting for me. I have an appointment at eleven!"

Ega, furious now, clung to his sleeve and, with his face very close to Vilaça's, he murmured in tragic tones that what he had to say involved Carlos— and it was a matter of life and death. Vilaça looked shocked and immediately strode back into the office, ushering Ega into a small side room, as narrow as a corridor, furnished with a wicker sofa, a desk piled high with dusty books and, at the far end, a cupboard. Vilaça closed the door, pushed back his hat and asked:

"What is it?"

Ega, with a gesture, indicated that the clerk outside could hear. Vilaça opened the door and yelled at the boy to hurry over to the Hotel Pelicano as fast as he could and ask the Viscount do Torral if he would be so kind as to wait for half an hour. Then, with the door bolted, he repeated the same anxious question:

"What is it?"

"It's terrible, Vilaça, awful. I don't even know where to begin."

Vilaça, looking very pale now, slowly put his umbrella down on the desk.

"A duel?"

"No, no, it's not that. You know that Carlos is involved with a Mrs. Mac-Gren, who arrived in Portugal last winter and has been here ever since?"

A Brazilian woman, or, rather, the wife of a Brazilian, who had spent the summer in Olivais? Yes, Vilaça knew about her. He had even discussed the matter with Eusèbiozinho.

"With Eusébio? Well, she's not Brazilian. She's Portuguese, and she's his *sister*!"

Vilaça fell back onto the sofa, clapping his hands in astonishment.

"Eusébio's sister!"

"No, not Eusébio's sister! Carlos' sister!"

Vilaça was dumbstruck, uncomprehending, his eyes unnaturally wide and fixed on Ega, who was pacing the room and repeating: "His sister, his own sister!" Ega finally sat down on the wicker sofa; and quietly, very quietly, despite the fact that the office was empty, he told Vilaça about his encounter with Guimarães at the concert and how the terrible truth had, quite by chance, burst upon him, in that single word, outside the Hotel Aliança. However, when he mentioned the papers that Madame Monforte had given to Guimarães and never reclaimed, and which Guimarães had kept all those years until seized by an urgent desire to restore them to the Maia family, Vilaça, who had been sitting hunched and stupefied, suddenly came to and sprang into angry life.

"This is some plot! It's all a trick to get money!"

"What do you mean 'get money'? Who?"

"Who?!" exclaimed Vilaça wildly, on his feet now. "Why, that woman, Guimarães, the whole lot of them! Don't you see, if Carlos' genuine and legitimate sister were to appear, she would have a right to more than four hundred *contos*!"

The two men stood staring at each other, shocked by this unexpected idea, which had shaken Ega, despite himself. However, when Vilaça, trembling, returned to the subject of that vast sum of four hundred *contos* and the possibility of a plot, Ega merely shrugged.

"That's simply impossible. She's incapable, absolutely incapable of such an intrigue. Besides, if it's a matter of money, what reason would she have to pass herself off as his sister, when Carlos has promised to marry her?"

Marry her! Vilaça threw up his hands in disbelief. Senhor Carlos da Maia was going to give his hand and his name to that creature, to the mistress of a Brazilian? Good God! But even in his astonishment, his suspicions grew, and he saw in all this further proof of dirty work afoot.

"No, Vilaça, no!" insisted Ega, impatient now. "If it were all a matter of documents and she had those documents, whether they're genuine or not, she would have presented them straight away—not slept with her brother first!"

Vilaça stared down at the floor. He was filled by an awful feeling of dread that this great house and family, his pride and joy, might be torn in two, plundered by an adventuress. But as Ega, greatly upset, was reminding him, it wasn't merely a matter of documents or legality or fortunes, Vilaça's face lit up again, and he cried:

"Wait, there's another thing! Perhaps she's the daughter of the Italian!"

"What if she is? It still comes to the same thing."

"Not so fast!" roared Vilaça, thumping the desk with his fist. "In that case, she would have no right to her father's inheritance, and would not get one *real* from the family! *That* is the point!"

Ega made a despairing gesture. Alas, no! She was the daughter of Pedro da Maia. Guimarães knew her; she had sat on his lap as a child, and he had given her dolls when she was just seven years old, only four or five years after the Italian's sojourn in Arroios, where he was laid up with a gunshot wound. The Italian's daughter had died in London when still only a baby.

Vilaça fell back again on the sofa, defeated.

"Four hundred *contos*—a fortune!"

Ega summed up the situation. There might not, as yet, be any legal certainty, but there was a very strong suspicion. And, of course, Carlos could not be allowed to continue innocently splashing around in this whole sordid mess. It was vital that Carlos should be told everything that same night.

"And you, Vilaça, are the one who must tell him."

Vilaça jumped so violently that the sofa bumped against the wall.

"*Me?*"

"Yes, you're the family administrator!"

And what was this if not a question of filiation, and therefore of inheritance? Who, if not the administrator was in possession of all the legal details?

Vilaça, who had turned bright red, muttered:

"Well, you're putting me in a damnably awkward spot!"

No, Ega was merely putting him in the spot where Vilaça, as administrator, logically and professionally belonged.

Vilaça protested, almost stuttering in his agitation. Damnation! He was not trying to shirk his duties; he simply knew nothing about the affair! What could he say to Carlos? "Your friend Ega told me this story, which was told to him, in turn, by a certain Guimarães last night in Largo do Loreto . . ." That was all he had to say!

"Well, tell him that."

Vilaça faced Ega, eyes blazing:

"Tell him that, you say, tell him that! It would take some nerve, sir!"

He tugged desperately at his waistcoat and strode furiously down to the end of the room, where he collided with the cupboard. He walked back and again stood facing Ega.

"You can't go to a man and say something like that without proof. Where is the proof?"

"I'm sorry,Vilaça, but you really are being obtuse! Why else do you think I came here, if not to bring you what proof there is—good or bad—Guimarães' story and this box containing Madame Monforte's papers?"

Vilaça, who was muttering under his breath, went over and examined the box, turning it round in his hands, reading the motto on the wax seal: *Pro Amore.*

"So, shall we open it?"

Ega had already drawn a chair up to the desk. Vilaça cut the paper, worn at the corners, in which the box was wrapped. And it was, in fact, an old cigar box, held shut with two tacks and crammed with papers, some in bundles tied together with ribbon, others loose inside open envelopes which bore the Monforte monogram, beneath a Marquis' coronet. Ega undid the first bundle. They were letters in German, which he did not understand, sent from Budapest and Karlsruhe.

"This isn't much help. What else is there?"

Another package, whose pink knot Vilaça carefully untied, contained an oval box, which bore a miniature of a man with ginger moustaches and sideburns and wearing a white uniform with a high golden collar. Vilaça thought the painting "quite beautiful."

"Some Austrian officer," snorted Ega. "Another lover. *Ça marche.*"

They removed the papers in order, with the tips of their fingers, as if they were relics. One large envelope stuffed with dressmakers' accounts, some paid, others with no receipt attached, proved of great interest to Vilaça, who pored over the various items, amazed at the prices of sophisticated fashion and its infinite inventiveness—bills for six thousand francs! A single dress costing two thousand francs! Another bundle contained a further surprise. They were the letters that Maria Eduarda had written to her mother from the convent, in a careful, round, artistic hand, full of grave devout phrases, doubtless dictated by the good sisters; and in these compositions, as virtuous and cold as school exercises, the little girl's honest heart shone through only in the occasional, now desiccated flower affixed to one corner with a pin.

"We'll put those to one side," murmured Vilaça.

Then Ega, impatient now, emptied all the contents onto the table and spread the papers out. And among the letters, bills and visiting cards, was a large envelope, bearing these words in blue ink: "For my daughter Maria Eduarda." Vilaça glanced over the expensive, legalistic piece of paper it contained and which bore the same gold monogram beneath the coronet of a Marquis. Passing it in silence into Ega's hand, he seemed almost unable to breathe, his ears scarlet.

Ega slowly read it out. It said:

Since you, Maria, have just had your baby and are still very weak, and I myself am not at all well, with stabbing pains in my side, it seems to me prudent, given what might happen in the future, to write a statement which is for you alone, my dear daughter, and the substance of which is known only to Father Talloux (Monsieur l'Abbé Talloux, coadjutor at Saint-Roch) because I told him about it two years ago when I had pneumonia. It is as follows: I hereby declare that my daughter, Maria Eduarda, who usually signs herself Maria Calzaski, believing this to be her father's name, is Portuguese and the daughter of my husband, Pedro da Maia, from whom I voluntarily separated, and that I took her with me first to Vienna and then to Paris, and that she now lives in Fontainebleau with Patrick MacGren, to whom she is to be married. My husband's father was Afonso da Maia, widower, who lived in Benfica and also in Santa Olávia, near the river Douro. These facts can be verified in Lisbon, where all the necessary documents will, I am sure, be found; and my mistakes, of which I now see the consequences, should not prevent you, my dear daughter, from enjoying the position and fortune which rightfully belong to you. And that is why I am making this signed declaration, in case I do not have the opportunity to do so before a notary, as I intend to do as soon as I am better. And, if I should die first, which pray God I do not, I ask my daughter to forgive me for everything. I sign below with my married name—Maria Monforte da Maia.

Ega sat looking at Vilaça. The latter, his hands folded on the table, could only murmur:

"A fortune! A fortune!"

Then Ega stood up. Right! Everything was much simpler now. They had merely to hand this document to Carlos, with no further explanation. Vilaça, however, was scratching his head, seized by another doubt.

"I'm not sure if this bit of paper would stand up in court."

"Who cares about the courts!" Ega exclaimed angrily. "What matters is that he doesn't sleep with her again!"

A timid tapping outside silenced him. Suddenly uneasy, he opened the door. It was the clerk, who whispered through the crack.

"Senhor Carlos da Maia is downstairs in his dog-cart; when I came in, he asked for Senhor Vilaça."

There was panic! Ega, all flustered, picked up Vilaça's hat by mistake, and

Vilaça threw all the Monforte papers into a drawer.

"Perhaps I'd better say you're not in," said the clerk.

"Yes, tell him we're not in," Ega and Vilaça said urgently.

They stood listening, still pale. Carlos' dog-cart rolled off down the road, and they both breathed a sigh of relief. Except that now Ega was regretting not having invited Carlos to come up in order to reveal everything to him, there and then, boldly and with no more vacillation or shillyshallying, with the papers on the table before them. Then they would have cleared the ditch in one leap!

"No," Vilaça said, mopping his brow with his handkerchief, "we need to do things slowly and methodically. We need to prepare ourselves, to take a deep breath before we plunge in."

At any rate, Ega concluded, further talk was useless. The other papers in the box were of no interest, now that they had found Madame Monforte's confession. All that remained was for Vilaça to turn up that evening at Ramalhete, at half past eight or nine, before Carlos left for Rua de São Francisco.

"But you'll be there too, won't you?" said Vilaça, terrified.

Ega promised. Vilaça gave a small sigh. Then, accompanying Ega out onto the landing, he added:

"What a mess! And there I was, happily dining at Ramalhete."

"And me too, dining with them in Rua de São Francisco."

"See you later, then!"

"Yes, see you later!"

Ega didn't dare return to Ramalhete that day, to dine with Carlos and see him so happy and at peace, knowing that black misfortune was about to descend on him like the night. He went to beg some food from the Marquis, who, ever since the concert, had been confined to his house, with a poultice on his throat. Then, at around half past eight, when Ega calculated that Vilaça must already have arrived at Ramalhete, he left the Marquis deep in a game of draughts with his chaplain.

The lovely day, which had become overcast during the afternoon, had ended in a fine freezing drizzle. Ega took a cab. And he had just drawn up outside Ramalhete, feeling terribly nervous, when he saw Vilaça standing in the doorway, his umbrella under his arm, rolling up his trouser bottoms, ready to leave.

"What happened?" shouted Ega.

Vilaça opened his umbrella and murmured very softly and secretively:

"I couldn't do it. He said he was in a hurry and didn't have time to talk to me."

Ega stamped his foot in despair.

"Oh, really, man!"

"What did you expect me to do? Keep him here by force? We've arranged to meet tomorrow, at eleven o'clock."

Ega raced up the stairs, muttering between gritted teeth: "God, at this rate, we're never going to get ourselves out of this mess!" He went as far as Afonso's study, but did not go in. The curtain was slightly drawn back, and through the gap, he had a glimpse of one warm cosy corner of the room, its damask furnishings bathed in a tender rose-pink light: the cards lay waiting on the whist table; on the sofa embroidered in subtle silks, a languid, thoughtful Dom Diogo was gazing into the fire and stroking his moustaches. And he could hear Craft, pacing up and down, pipe in hand, engaged in some discussion, his voice intermingled with the more measured tones of Afonso, who was sitting calmly in his armchair, and then both voices were drowned out by Sequeira, who was declaring angrily: "But if there were a revolt tomorrow, the same army which you gentlemen want to do away with because, you say, they're a load of wastrels, would be the very ones who would guard your backs. Talking and philosophising are all well and good, but when things turn nasty, if there aren't half a dozen bayonets fixed and ready, then there'll be trouble!"

Ega went from there to Carlos' rooms. The candles were still burning in the candelabra; a vague perfume of eau de Lubin and cigar smoke filled the air; and Baptista told him that Senhor Dom Carlos had left ten minutes before. He had obviously gone to Rua de São Francisco! He would be sleeping there! With his nerves frayed and the prospect of a long sad night ahead of him, Ega felt a need to deaden his feelings and dissipate all these tormenting ideas with some strong sensation. He had not as yet dismissed the cab, and so he set off in it to the Teatro São Carlos. He ended up having supper at Augusto's with Taveira and two Spanish girls, Paca and Carmen Filósofa, and drinking far too much champagne. By four o'clock in the morning, he was drunk and lying sprawled on the sofa, intoning sentimentally, purely for his own benefit, the lines Musset had dedicated to Malibran. Taveira and Paca, cuddled up together on the same chair—he looking every inch the attentive lady's man and she equally amorous—were eating spoonfuls of jelly from little bowls. Carmen Filósofa—who, having over-eaten, had already loosened her clothing, removed her corset and rolled it up in a copy of that day's newspaper—was beating time on the edge of her plate with her knife, gazing up at the gaslights and singing:

> Señor alcalde mayor,
> No prenda usted los ladrones . . .

The next day, Ega woke at nine o'clock beside Carmen Filósofa, in a room with large, generous windows, through which poured all the melancholy of a dark rainy morning. And, while he waited for the closed carriage which the servant had rushed off to summon, poor Ega, angry and ashamed, thick-tongued and padding about barefoot on the carpet as he gathered together his scattered clothing, had only one clear idea—to escape from there and take a long, cool, perfumed bath, where he could purify himself of Carmen's sticky presence and of the previous night's orgy, the thought of which now made him shudder.

He went to the Hotel Bragança for that purifying bath, so that he would be washed and ready to meet Carlos and Vilaça at eleven o'clock. However, he had to wait for the underwear which the coachman, with a note for Baptista, had raced off to fetch from Ramalhete; then he had some lunch, and it was gone midday when he finally stepped out of the carriage and went in through the private door to Carlos' rooms, carrying his dirty clothes in a bundle.

Baptista was crossing the landing with some camellias arranged in a wicker basket.

"Has Vilaça arrived?" asked Ega softly, tiptoeing in.

"Senhor Vilaça has been here for a while now. Did you get the underwear, sir? I sent a suit as well because it always makes one feel so much fresher."

"Yes, Baptista, thank you, thank you very much!"

And Ega was thinking: "Good, Carlos knows everything now, the ditch has been leapt!" But he delayed further, removing his gloves and his overcoat with pusillanimous slowness. Finally, aware that his heart was beating hard, he drew aside the velvet curtain at the door. A heavy silence hung in the hallway; large drops of rain beat against the French windows, through which one could see the trees in the garden blurred by mist. Ega lifted the next curtain, which bore an embroidered version of the Maia coat of arms.

"Ah, it's you!" cried Carlos, getting up from his desk, clutching some papers in his hand.

He appeared to have responded to the news with a firm, manly attitude of mind; only his eyes glittered with a dry fire, anxious and seemingly larger in his pale face. Sitting opposite him, Vilaça was slowly, wearily mopping his forehead with his Indian silk handkerchief. The Monforte papers lay scattered on the desk.

"What is this nonsense that Vilaça has been telling me?" Carlos demanded, his voice trembling only very slightly as he stood before him, arms folded.

Ega stammered out:

"I . . . I didn't have the courage to tell you . . ."

"Well, I have the courage to hear! What the devil did the man say?"

Vilaça immediately got up. He did so with the alacrity of a nervous young recruit being relieved from a particularly dangerous position, and asked permission, if they no longer needed him, to go back to his office. Carlos and Ega, he said, would doubtless prefer to speak freely. Besides, all the papers from Madame Monforte would remain there. And if they did need him, he could be found at Rua da Prata or at home.

"As I'm sure you'll understand, sir," he added, twisting his handkerchief about in his hands, "I took the initiative of coming to talk to you because I believed it to be my duty as the confidential friend of the family. This was our friend Ega's opinion too."

"Of course, Vilaça, thank you!" said Carlos. "If necessary, I'll send for you."

Vilaça, still holding his handkerchief, looked slowly about him. Then he peered under the desk. He seemed bemused. With some impatience, Carlos observed Vilaça's timid steps as he searched the room.

"What is it, man?"

"My hat. I thought I'd put it down in here, but it must be outside . . . Anyway, if there's anything you need . . ."

Still peering uneasily into the corners of the room, he finally left, and Carlos violently drew the curtain shut. Turning to Ega and sitting down heavily in a chair, he said:

"Right, what did he say?"

Seated on the sofa, Ega began by describing his meeting with Senhor Guimarães in the downstairs bar in the theatre, after Rufino had said his piece. The man had demanded an explanation for Dâmaso's letter, on the subject of hereditary alcoholism. Once they cleared the matter up, they became quite friendly.

The curtain stirred again, and Vilaça's face reappeared.

"I'm terribly sorry, but I can't find my hat, and I could swear I left it in here . . ."

Carlos bit back a curse. Then Ega, too, joined in the search, first, behind the sofa, then, in the bay of the window. Carlos, in despair, and in an attempt to bring the matter to a close, went and looked behind the curtains round his bed. Vilaça, scarlet-faced and anxious, even checked the bathroom.

"How can it have vanished like that? Perhaps I left it in the hall! I'll have another look. I do apologise."

The two friends were left alone again. And Ega resumed his story, describing how Guimarães had spoken to him two or three times during the various intervals about this and that, the concert, politics, Victor Hugo, etc. Then he, Ega, had looked for Carlos so that they could go on together to the Grémio, and had ended up leaving the theatre with Cruges. And as they were passing the Hotel Aliança . . .

Again the curtain was drawn aside, and this time Baptista apologised, saying:

"Forgive me, gentlemen, but Senhor Vilaça can't find his hat and he's sure he left it in here . . ."

Carlos leapt furiously to his feet, picking up the chair he had been sitting on as if to break it over Baptista's head: "You and Senhor Vilaça can go to the devil! Tell him to leave without his hat, or else give him one of mine!"

Baptista withdrew, a grave look on his face.

"Go on," exclaimed Carlos, falling back in his seat, looking paler now.

And Ega gave him a detailed account of his long and terrible conversation with Guimarães, from the moment when the man, quite by chance, just as he was holding out his hand to say goodbye, had mentioned "Maia's sister." And how later, at the door of the Hotel Paris, in Largo do Pelourinho, he had given him Madame Monforte's papers.

"And that's it, that's all I know. You can imagine the kind of night I had! But I just didn't have the courage to tell you. I went to Vilaça, I suppose, in the hope that he would know something or possess some document that would demolish Guimarães' whole story. But he knew nothing and had no such document. He was as shocked as I was."

In the brief ensuing silence, a heavier shower of rain fell, dousing the trees in the garden and beating against the windowpanes. Carlos sprang suddenly to his feet, as if every fibre in his being rebelled against the facts.

"And do you believe it's possible? Do you believe that it could happen to a man like me, like you, in Lisbon? I see a woman, look at her, get to know her, sleep with her, and, of all the women in the world, she turns out to be my sister! It's impossible. No Guimarães, no papers, and no documents can ever persuade me otherwise."

And when Ega remained sitting silently at the end of the sofa, his eyes cast down, Carlos cried:

"Say something! Say that you, like me, have your doubts! It's too extraordinary! You both seem to accept it as if it were the most natural thing in the world, as if Lisbon were full of brothers and sisters sleeping together!"

Ega murmured:

"Well, there was a similar case in Celorico, near my mother's estate . . ."

At that moment, without any noise to forewarn them, Afonso da Maia drew the curtain aside; he was leaning on his stick and smiling broadly at some idea which he plainly found very amusing. It was still the matter of Vilaça's hat.

"What the devil have you two done with Vilaça's hat? The poor man was in a terrible state. He had to wear one of my hats in the end. It came too far down on his head, though, and so we padded it out with handkerchiefs . . ."

Then he noticed his grandson's distraught face and Ega's evident distress. He noticed how Ega, avoiding his gaze, glanced anxiously at Carlos. The smile on his face died, and he took one slow step forward into the room.

"What is it? What's wrong? Has something happened?"

Then Carlos, in the ardent egotism of his love, not even thinking about the cruel shock he was about to give his poor grandfather, filled only by the hope that he, as a witness of the past, might know some fact, possess some certain truth that would contradict Guimarães' whole story as well as the papers left behind by Madame Monforte, went towards him and burst out with:

"It's the most extraordinary thing, grandfather! Maybe you know something . . . you *must* know something that will help us out of this predicament! I'll tell you very briefly what's happened. I met a lady who arrived in Lisbon some time ago and who lives in Rua de São Francisco. Now, suddenly, I'm told that she's my own sister! A man who has known her since she was a child and who is in possession of some papers has turned up . . . The papers are over there. They're letters, a declaration made by my mother . . . A whole jumble of things, all kinds of evidence . . . What does all this mean? Didn't my sister, the one my mother took with her, didn't she die? Surely you know!"

Afonso da Maia, beginning to shake, leaned hard for a moment on his stick, then sat down heavily in an armchair by the door. He remained there, staring at his grandson and at Ega, his eyes wild and uncomprehending.

"The man," went on Carlos, "is someone called Guimarães, an uncle of Dâmaso's. He talked to Ega and gave Ega the papers. Ega, tell my grandfather—tell him everything from the beginning!"

With a sigh, Ega summarised his long story. He concluded by saying that the important thing, the decisive point was that this man Guimarães, who had no reason to lie and who had spoken of these things purely by chance, had known this lady, ever since she was a little girl, as the daughter of Pedro da Maia and Maria Monforte. And he had never lost track of her. He had watched her grow up in Paris, she had sat on his knee as a child, he had given her dolls to play with. He had gone with her mother to visit her at the convent. He had been to the house where she lived in Fontainebleau, as the wife of . . ."

"Anyway," Carlos broke in, "he saw her a few days ago, in a carriage, with me and with Ega. What do you think, Grandfather?"

With a great effort, as if the words he was speaking were torn from his heart, the old man murmured:

"This lady, of course, knows nothing . . ."

Ega and Carlos simultaneously cried: "No, nothing!" According to Guimarães, the mother had always concealed the truth from her. She thought she was the daughter of an Austrian man. She always signed herself Calzaski.

Carlos, who was rummaging about on the desk, held out a piece of paper.

"Here's my mother's declaration."

Afonso, his poor fingers trembling, took a long time fumbling for and finding his spectacles in his waistcoat pocket; he slowly read what was on the paper, growing paler with each line and breathing hard; when he had finished, he let his hands, still holding the paper, fall limply onto his lap, and he sat there slumped, all his strength apparently gone. Words finally came to him, dully, slowly. He knew nothing. He could deny nothing that was in Madame Monforte's declaration. The lady living in Rua de São Francisco might well be his granddaughter. He knew no more than that.

Carlos' shoulders drooped as he stood before his grandfather, as overwhelmed as Afonso by the certainty of his misfortune. His grandfather, that witness of the past, knew nothing! The declaration, the whole of Guimarães' story, remained entire and irrefutable. There was nothing, no memory, no written document, that could shake it. Then Maria Eduarda was his sister! And grandfather and grandson seemed bowed down by the same sorrow—born of the same thought.

At last, Afonso got to his feet and, still leaning on his stick, walked over to the desk and placed on it Madame Monforte's declaration. He glanced at, but did not touch, the papers scattered round the cigar box. Then, slowly, drawing one hand across his forehead, he said:

"That's all I know. We always thought the child had died. Thorough investigations were made. She herself said that her daughter had died, and even showed someone or other a portrait."

"That was another, younger child, the daughter she had by the Italian," said Ega. "Guimarães told me about her. But this is the daughter who survived. She was already seven or eight at the time—four or five years after that Italian fellow first came to Lisbon. It's her."

"Yes, it's her," murmured the old man.

He made a vague, resigned gesture and, after taking a deep breath, said:

"Well, we need to think carefully about all this. I think we should talk to Vilaça again. He may have to go to Paris. But, first of all, we need to calm down. After all, no one has died . . . no one has died . . ."

His voice trailed tremulously away. He held out his hand to Carlos, who kissed it, unable to speak; and Afonso, pulling his grandson to him, planted a kiss on his forehead. Then he took two steps towards the door, so slowly and hesitantly that Ega ran over to him: "Take my arm, sir."

Afonso did so, resting his whole weight on him. They crossed the hallway, silent except for the rain still lashing the windows. The curtain fell in folds behind them, the curtain bearing the Maia coat of arms. And then Afonso, letting go of Ega's arm, put his face close to Ega's and in words filled with grief, whispered: "I've heard about this woman! She lives in Rua de São Francisco. She spent the whole summer in Olivais! She's his mistress!"

Ega managed to say: "No, sir, no!" but Afonso placed a finger to his lips, indicating that Carlos might hear. And then he moved off, bent over his walking-stick, overcome at last by that implacable fate which, having wounded him before, when he was still young and strong, with his son's misfortune, was now destroying him in late old age with his grandson's misfortune.

Weary and exhausted, Ega went back into the room where Carlos had resumed the agitated pacing that shook the floorboards and set the glasses on the marble console tinkling. Sitting silently at the desk, Ega began to go through some of the other papers left by Madame Monforte: letters, a little Morocco leather address book, visiting cards from members of the Jockey Club and from senators of the Empire. Suddenly, Carlos stopped in front of him, wringing his hands in despair.

"There we were, two people in seventh heaven, and then some nobody comes along, an idiot, a Guimarães, who with only two words and some documents destroys those two people's lives forever! It's just awful, Ega!"

Ega risked offering a trite word of consolation:

"It would have been worse if she'd died!"

"Worse?" cried Carlos. "Why? If she'd died, or if I had, the reason for this love would be over, and all that would remain would be grief and longing; that would be something quite different. Like this, though, we're both alive, but dead to one another, even though the passion that binds us lives on! Do you really think that just because you've come here and proved to me that she's my sister that I love her less than I did yesterday—or in a different way? Of course I don't! My love isn't going to accommodate itself to these new circumstances as simply as that, and transform itself into friendship. Never! And I don't want it to!"

This was brute rebellion, his love defending itself, not wanting to die merely because of the revelations of a Guimarães and a cigar box full of old documents declaring his love to be impossible and ordering it to die!

There was a melancholy silence. Ega lit a cigarette and sat down again, sunk in one corner of the sofa. Weariness was overwhelming him, after all the emotion, the late supper at Augusto's, that early awakening beside Carmen. The whole room was growing sad, in the still sadder light of the declining winter afternoon. Ega finally closed his eyes. However, he was soon shaken awake by another exclamation from Carlos, who was again standing before him and again wringing his hands in despair.

"And that isn't the worst thing, Ega! The worst thing is that we have to tell her everything, tell her the whole story, her!"

Ega had already considered this. It was important that she be told at once, without delay.

"I'll go and tell her myself," murmured Carlos.

"You?!"

"Who else? Would you prefer Vilaça to go?"

Ega frowned and said:

"What you should do is take the train tonight and go straight to Santa Olávia. You could write to her from there and tell her everything. That would be safer."

Carlos flung himself down in an armchair with a great weary sigh.

"Yes, perhaps tomorrow, on the night train. I'd thought of that too, it seems the best idea. Now, though, I just feel so exhausted!"

"Me too," said Ega, stretching and yawning. "And we're not going to get any further today; we'll only become more confused and more stuck. We need to rest. I'm going to lie down for a while."

"See you later, then."

Ega went up to his room and lay down on the bedcovers; and given his immense tiredness, he quickly fell asleep. He woke up late to the sound of his door opening. It was Carlos coming in and striking a match. Night had fallen; downstairs the supper bell rang.

"And now there's this wretched supper to get through!" said Carlos, lighting the candles on the dressing table. "If only we could come up with an excuse to slip out to a tavern and talk in peace! Worse still, yesterday I invited Stein-broken."

Then, turning round, he asked:

"Ega, do you think my grandfather knows everything?"

Ega jumped off the bed and stood by the wash-basin, rolling up his sleeves.

"Well, to be honest, I think he suspects something. He did react to the whole business as if it were a real catastrophe. If he didn't suspect anything, he would have felt only the surprise of someone discovering a long-lost grand-daughter."

Carlos gave a long sigh. A moment later, they were going downstairs to supper.

As well as Steinbroken and Dom Diogo, Craft had also arrived "asking to be fed." The quiet conversation about various ailments—Sequeira's rheumatism, the poor Marquis' worsening state—created an air of melancholy that seemed to hover over the table, normally so cheerful, and decorated as always with flowers and lights.

Afonso, in his study, had complained of a bad headache, thus justifying his gaunt pale appearance. Carlos, upon whose sickly pallor Steinbroken had already commented, explained that he'd slept very badly the night before. And Ega, in an attempt to brighten up the supper, asked Steinbroken for his impressions of the great orator at the benefit evening, Rufino. The diplomat hesitated. He had been somewhat surprised to learn that Rufino was a politician, a parliamentarian. The gesticulations, the bit of shirt sticking out at the front between waistcoat and trousers, the goatee beard, the mop of hair, the boots—none of these seemed the attributes of a statesman.

"*Mais cependant, cependant ... Dans ce genre là, dans le genre sublime, dans le genre de Demosthènes, il m'a paru très fort ... Oh, il m'a paru excessivement fort!*"

"What about you, Craft?"

At the concert, Craft had liked only Alencar. Ega made an incredulous gesture. Oh, really! What could be more comical than Alencar's romantic version of Democracy, of the Republic as a sweet fair-haired girl, all dressed in white like Ophelia, praying in the field, beneath God's watchful eye? Craft, however, had found it excellent precisely because it was sincere. After all, wasn't it exactly the scandalous lack of sincerity which they found so distasteful in Portuguese literature? No one, in verse or prose, ever seemed to believe in what they were so ardently declaiming and beating their breast about. And that's how it had been at the concert. Not even Rufino seemed actually to believe in the influence of religion; just as the man with the pointed beard didn't truly believe in the heroism of the Castros and the Albuquerques of this world; even the poet who spoke about those adorable little eyes didn't wholeheartedly believe in the adorability of those little eyes. It was all counterfeit and false! What a difference with Alencar! He had real faith in what he was talking about, in fraternity among nations, in a Republican Christ, in a devout Democracy crowned with stars.

"He must be getting on a bit, old Alencar," remarked Dom Diogo, who was rolling bits of bread between his long, pale fingers.

Carlos, beside him, finally emerged from his silence.

"He must be well into his fifties."

Ega swore that he was at least sixty. Alencar had already published some pretty wild poetry in 1836, filled with remorse for deflowering so many virgins and calling upon death to come.

"Yes," murmured Afonso, "I first heard his name years ago now."

Dom Diogo, taking a sip of wine, turned to Carlos and said:

"Alencar is the same age as your father would have been. They were close friends, part of the distinguished social circle of the time. Alencar often used to go to Arroios with poor Dom João da Cunha—God rest his soul—and the others, their generation's cream of society. But that's all gone now, all gone!"

Carlos lowered his eyes; in fact, everyone fell silent; an air of sadness passed among the flowers and the candles, as if issuing forth from the depths of that past, full of graves and griefs.

"And poor Cruges, the poor man, what a fiasco!" exclaimed Ega, in order to dispel that gloomy mist.

Craft thought the fiasco perfectly justified. Why offer Beethoven to people brought up on Offenbach's vulgar music? Ega, however, could not permit such scorn for Offenbach, one of the finest modern manifestations of scepticism and irony! Steinbroken accused Offenbach of knowing nothing about counterpoint. And, for a moment, they discussed music. Ega ended by declaring that there was nothing in art as beautiful as the *fado*. And he appealed to Afonso, hoping to rouse him a little.

"It's true, isn't it, sir? You, like me, are one of the faithful supporters of *fado*, our great national creation."

"Oh yes," murmured Afonso, raising a hand to his head, as if to justify his glum lack of interest. "There is a great deal of poetry in *fado*."

Craft, on the other hand, attacked *fado*, *malagueñas*, *peteneras*, and all such "Southern" music, which seemed to him nothing but a lot of guttural moaning made up entirely of the fruitless lazy repetition of "Ay-ay-ay." He had heard a *malagueña*, one of those famous *malagueñas*, sung one night, in perfect style, by a lady from Málaga itself. It was in Madrid, in the house of the Villa-Rubia family. The lady had stood by the piano, mumbled something about "stone" and "tomb," then launched into one of those never-ending moans: *Ay-ay-ay-ay-ay*. Well, he got so bored that he escaped into the next room, watched a rubber of whist, leafed through a vast album of photographs, discussed the Carlist war with General Jovellos, and when he went back, there the woman was, carnations in her hair and eyes fixed on the ceiling, still wailing out that same *Ay-ay-ay*!

Everyone laughed. Ega protested vigorously, enjoying himself now. Craft was nothing but a desiccated Englishman, suckled on the flat bosom of Political Economics, incapable of understanding the world of poetry that could be contained in an "Ay." Ega wasn't talking about *malagueñas*, though, it wasn't his responsibility to defend Spain. Spain had quite enough spirit and quite enough knives of its own to convince Craft and other Britishers of the error of their ways. He was talking about *fado*!

"Where have you heard *fado*? In drawing rooms, with a piano accompaniment, I bet. Well, there I agree, it is pretty dull stuff. But if you were to hear it played by three or four guitarists, one night in the country, with a lovely moon in the sky. Just as we did in Olivais this summer, when the Marquis brought "Vira-Vira" along. Do you remember, Carlos?"

And he stopped, as if embarrassed, regretting having stirred up memories of the Toca, however glancingly evoked. Carlos said nothing, but a shadow seemed to pass over his face. Craft was muttering that, on a fine moonlit night, all country sounds were beautiful, even the croaking of frogs. Again, a strange cheerlessness filled the room; the footmen served dessert.

Then, in the silence, Dom Diogo said thoughtfully, with that majestic look of his, like a nostalgic lion recalling a glorious past:

"One particularly distinguished piece of music, years ago now, was that serenade called 'Monastery Bells.' It really was just like hearing bells. They don't write things like that any more."

The supper ended on a gloomy note. Steinbroken returned to the subject of the Royal Family's absence from the concert, which had been troubling him ever since. However, no one else there was interested in the Palace. Then, Dom Diogo brought up some tedious story about the Infanta Dona Isabel. It was a relief when the footman brought round the silver bowl and the jug of perfumed water.

After coffee, served in the billiard room, Steinbroken and Craft embarked on a game with a stake of fifteen *tostões* to add interest. Afonso and Dom Diogo had retired to the study. Ega installed himself in an armchair with *Le Figaro*. He soon let it slip to the floor, though, and his eyes closed. Carlos, who was pensively pacing up and down, smoking, regarded the sleeping Ega for a moment, then pushed aside the curtain and vanished.

He was going to Rua de São Francisco.

But he did not hurry; he strolled along the Aterro, wrapped up in a fur coat and finishing his cigar. The night sky had cleared, and a crescent moon could be seen among scraps of white cloud driven along by a keen north wind.

That afternoon, alone in his room, Carlos had made a decision to go and speak to Maria Eduarda himself, for reasons of dignity and justice, reasons of his own making and which he repeated to himself incessantly in order to justify his actions. He and Maria Eduarda were not weak-willed children dependent on Ega or Vilaça to resolve or sort out the worst crisis of their lives; they were two strong-minded people, resolute and sensible enough to find a fair and dignified way out of this catastrophe destroying their existence. That is why he and only he should go to Rua de São Francisco.

Now that he knew she was his sister, it would, of course, be terrible to see her in that room, still warm from their love . . . but, on the other hand, why shouldn't he? Were they two religious fanatics, obsessed with the Devil, terrified by the sin into which they had unconsciously plunged, and eager to hide their carnal horror of each other in some distant convent or monastery? No! Did they need to set between them the leagues that separated Lisbon from Santa Olávia, terrified of succumbing to their former frailty should their eyes meet again, still burning with the old flame? No! Both of them had suffcient strength to bury their hearts beneath reason, as if beneath a cold, hard stone, so completely that they would feel neither the heart's rebellion nor its grief. And so he could now return with an easy mind to that room still warm from their love.

Besides, why call on reason, strength and courage? He wasn't going to reveal the whole truth to Maria Eduarda all at once and then bid her a tragic theatrical farewell and risk facing a crisis of passion and grief. On the contrary! All that evening, immersed in his own torment, he had searched desperately for a way of softening and mitigating the horror of the revelation he had to make to the poor woman! And he had, at last, found one, a very complicated and cowardly one, it's true, but what else could he do? It was the only way, through a process of slow, charitable preparation, to save her from a brutal, fulminating grief. And it would only work if he himself went, coolly and calmly, to Rua de São Francisco.

That is why he was going there—and as he walked along the Aterro, dragging his feet, he kept summarising and retouching the plan, rehearsing quietly to himself the words he would say to her. He would go into the drawing room, looking as if he were in a terrible hurry, and tell her that some business with the house, a mix-up by the administrators there, meant that he had to leave for Santa Olávia in a matter of days. And he would leave her apartment at once, saying that he had to go directly to Vilaça's house. He could even add: "It won't take a moment, I won't be long." One thing worried him. What if she kissed him? He decided that he would exaggerate his haste, and keep his cigar in his mouth, and not even take off his hat. And then he would leave. And not come back. She, poor love, would sit up late, listening to each carriage that came down the street! The following night, he would leave for Santa Olávia with Ega, writing her a letter announcing that he had, alas, received a telegram and had been obliged to take the first train he could. He might even add: "I'll be back in two or three days." And there he would stay, far from her forever. He would write from Santa Olávia at once, a hesitant confused letter, mentioning the unexpected discovery of certain family documents, proving them to be closely related. He would do all this in a muddled, brief, hasty fashion. Finally, in another letter, he would reveal the *whole* truth, enclosing her mother's declaration, thus demonstrating the need for a complete separation until all doubts had been resolved, and asking her to depart at once for Paris. Vilaça would be charged with the matter of money, giving her, for the journey, three hundred or four hundred *libras*. Yes, it was all very complicated, all very cowardly, but there was no other way. And who but he could carry this business out with the necessary kindness and tact?

And caught up in the tumult of these thoughts, he suddenly found himself in Travessa da Parreirinha, opposite Maria Eduarda's house. A dim light from the drawing room shone through the curtains. The rest of the house—the window of her narrow dressing-room and her bedroom balcony with its pots of chrysanthemums—was in darkness.

And that dumb façade, from which there emerged only the languid glow from a sleepy corner bedroom, gradually filled him with a strange unease and doubt. It was fear of the soft darkness he could sense inside, full of warmth and perfume, mingled with the scent of jasmine. He did not go in; he continued slowly along the opposite pavement, thinking about certain details of the house—the broad generous sofa with its silk cushions, the lace on the dressing table, the white curtains around her bed . . . Then he paused by the long strip of light spilling out from the door of the Grémio and went mechanically in, attracted by the simplicity and reassuring safety of that stone-paved courtyard, lit by large bright gaslights, with no darkness and no perfume.

In the room downstairs, he glanced uncomprehendingly at the various news telegrams on the table. A waiter passed, and he ordered a cognac. Teles da Gama, who strolled in from another room, whistling, his hands in his overcoat pocket, stopped for a moment to ask if he was going to the Gouvarinhos on Tuesday.

"Possibly," murmured Carlos.

"Oh, do come! I'm trying to round up a few people. More to the point, it's Charlie's birthday. Everyone will be there, and there's supper too."

The waiter came in with a tray, and Carlos, standing by the table, stirring the sugar in his glass, remembered, for some strange reason, the afternoon when the Countess, putting a rose in his button-hole, had given him that first kiss; he recalled the sofa onto which she had fallen with a whisper of crumpled silk. How vague and remote all that seemed to him now.

As soon as he had finished his cognac, he left. Now, walking along close to the houses, he could no longer see that troubling façade with its bedroom brightness dim behind the glass. The street door was closed, the gaslight burned on the landing. He went up, more aware, as he mounted the stone stairs, of the beating of his heart than of the sound of his own footsteps. Melanie, who opened the door, told him that her mistress had felt a little tired and had gone to lie down in her room, and the drawing room did, in fact, look as if it had been abandoned for the night, with the candles extinguished, the embroidery rolled up in its basket, the books lined up primly on the table edge, where, beneath its yellow lace shade, the oil-lamp spread a tenuous light.

Carlos slowly took off his gloves, again made uneasy by that sleepy air of quiet contemplation. Suddenly Rosa ran in, laughing and skipping, her long hair loose on her shoulders, her arms held out to him. Carlos lifted her into the air, saying as he always did: "There's my little goat!"

But then, as he held her there, her small feet kicking, it occurred to him that the child was his own niece and bore his name! He put her down, almost dropping her, and stared at her, as if seeing for the first time that fine ivory-complexioned face in which his own blood flowed.

Drawing back and smiling, her hands clasped behind her back, over her starched skirts, she asked softly: "Why are you looking at me?"

He didn't know why, but she seemed like a very different Rosa; and his disquiet was mingled with a longing for the old Rosa—the other Rosa, the daughter of Madame MacGren—to whom he told stories about Joan of Arc and whom he used to push on the swing at the Toca, beneath the acacias in flower. She, meanwhile, seeing him so grave and silent, only smiled more broadly, her neat teeth shining, a tender look in her lovely blue eyes, imagining he was about to play a trick on her and put on the booming voice of Charlemagne. She had her mother's smile, the same dimple in her chin. Carlos suddenly saw in her all of Maria Eduarda's grace and charm. And he picked her up again, so violently this time—kissing her so hard on her hair and cheeks—that Rosa, frightened, kicked and screamed. He let her go, afraid he had acted improperly. Then, very gravely, he asked:

"Where's Mama?"

Rosa was rubbing her arm and frowning: "You hurt me."

Carlos smoothed her hair with his still trembling hand.

"Don't be silly, now, Mama doesn't like it. Where is she?"

The little girl, placated and happy again, was skipping round and round, holding onto Carlos' wrists, to make him skip too.

"Mama went to lie down. She says she's really tired—and she calls *me* lazy. Come on, skip! Don't be mean!"

At that moment, out in the corridor, Miss Sara called: "Mademoiselle!"

Rosa lay one finger on her laughing lips: "Tell her I'm not here! Go on, just to annoy her. Tell her."

Miss Sara had come in through the door and spotted Rosa at once, standing on tiptoe behind Carlos, yet trying to make herself really small. She smiled kindly and murmured: "Good evening, sir." Then she said that it was almost half past nine and that Mademoiselle had a slight cold and ought to go to bed. Carlos tugged gently on Rosa's arm, and stroked her hair to encourage her to obey Miss Sara.

Rosa repelled him, indignant at such a betrayal.

"You're no help, you rotten thing! Well, I'm not even going to say goodnight to you, so there!"

She stalked angrily across the room, pushed aside the governess who was smiling and offering her hand, and then, once out in the corridor, burst into vexed, stubborn tears. Miss Sara smilingly apologised for Mademoiselle. It was her cold making her so impertinent. She wouldn't do that if her Mama was there.

461

"Goodnight, sir."

"Goodnight, Miss Sara."

Left alone, Carlos wandered about for a few moments in the drawing room. Finally, he raised the tapestry curtain that gave onto the small area used by Maria Eduarda as a dressing room. There, in the darkness, caught by a long ray of light from the streetlamp, the pale glow of a mirror trembled. Very quietly, he pushed open the bedroom door.

"Maria, are you asleep?"

There was no light, but the same streetlamp, through the raised blind, picked out from the shadows the vague whiteness of the curtains around the bed. It was from there that she murmured sleepily:

"Come in! I was so tired, I had to lie down. What time is it?"

Carlos didn't move, his hand still on the door handle.

"It's late, and I need to go and find Vilaça. I came to tell you that I might have to go to Santa Olávia the day after tomorrow, for two or three days."

A movement beyond the curtains made the bed creak.

"To Santa Olávia? But why? And so suddenly too. Come in! Come here!"

Carlos took a soundless step across the carpet. He could still hear the soft creaking of the bed. And that perfume of hers, which he knew so well, and which hung in the warm dark air, wrapped around him and entered his soul with the unexpected seduction of a new, strangely troubling caress. He stumbled on, insisting that he had to talk to Vilaça urgently, that very night.

"It's a dreadful bore, something to do with administrators and some claim about water rights . . ."

He touched the bed, and sat right on the very edge, filled by a sudden weariness that coiled about him and sapped him of all the energy required to continue inventing lies about water rights and administrators, as if these lies were mountains of iron to be shifted.

Maria Eduarda's large, beautiful body, swathed in a white silk dressing-gown, stirred and stretched languidly on the soft bed.

"I felt so tired after supper, so lazy. But do you really have to leave so suddenly? What a nuisance! Give me your hand!"

He felt for her hand among the whiteness of the bedclothes; he found a knee instead and became aware of its shape and soft warmth through the light silk; he left his hand there, open and limp, as if dead, in a torpor that engulfed every ounce of will and consciousness, leaving him only the feeling of that warm smooth skin on which his palm was resting. A sigh, a tiny child-like sigh, escaped Maria Eduarda's lips and died in the shadows. Emanating from her, Carlos felt the heat of desire, as dizzying and terrifying as the hot breath issuing forth from an abyss opening up in the earth beneath his feet. He was still mumbling: "No, no . . ." But she held out her arms to him, put her arms about his neck, drawing him to her, in a murmur—a continuation of that first sigh in which the words "my love" whispered and trembled. Unresistingly, like a dead thing blown by the wind, he fell upon her breast. Their dry lips met in a moist open-mouthed kiss, and Carlos grasped her furiously to him, crushing her and consuming her, in a fit of passion and despair that shook the bed.

At that hour, Ega was just waking up in the billiard room, still stretched out in the armchair where he had lain prostrated by tiredness. Yawning and sleepy, he shuffled into Afonso's study.

A bright fire was burning, and Reverend Boniface was toasting himself, curled up on the bearskin rug. Along with Steinbroken and Vilaça, Afonso was playing a game of whist, but he was so distracted and confused that, twice now, an unhappy, irritated Dom Diogo had grumbled that if his headache was that bad, it would be best to stop the game altogether. When Ega came in, Afonso looked up at him anxiously.

"Where's Carlos? Has he gone out?"

"Yes, I think he left with Craft," said Ega. "They mentioned something about visiting the Marquis."

Vilaça, who was cutting the cards with his usual meticulous slowness, shot Ega an acute, enquiring glance, but Dom Diogo was already drumming his fingers on the table, mumbling: "Come on, come on . . . Who cares where the others are?" Ega stayed for a moment, yawning distractedly, following the slow fall of the cards. At last, indolent and bored, he decided to go upstairs and read in bed; he lingered for a moment by the bookshelves, then left, taking with him an old copy of *Panorama*.

The next day, at lunchtime, he went into Carlos' bedroom, and was astonished when Baptista—still unhappy after the previous night's events and sensing some misfortune—told him that Carlos had gone out early to the Tapada, on horseback.

"Really? And he left no orders, made no mention of going to Santa Olávia?"

Baptista looked at Ega in amazement.

"To Santa Olávia? No, sir, he mentioned no such thing. But he left a letter for you to read. I think it's from the Marquis. And he says he'll see you there later, at six. I believe it's a supper invitation."

On a visiting card, the Marquis informed them that it was "that most fortunate of days," his birthday, and that he was expecting Carlos and Ega at six o'clock to help him eat his prescribed chicken.

"Well," murmured Ega, going out into the garden, "we'll meet there, then."

It seemed to him extraordinary. Carlos going riding, Carlos dining with the Marquis, as if nothing had disrupted his easy life as a fortunate and happy young man! Now he was certain that, the night before, Carlos had gone to Rua de São Francisco. Good God! What could have happened there? As he went upstairs, he heard the bell for lunch. The footman told him that Senhor Afonso da Maia was having tea in his room and would not be down. Everyone had vanished! For the first time at Ramalhete, Ega lunched alone at the big table, reading the *Gazeta Ilustrada*.

That evening at six, in the Marquis' apartment (the Marquis was wearing a lady's sable boa about his neck), he found Carlos, Darque and Craft sitting in a circle round a plump young man playing a guitar, while in the next room, the Marquis' administrator, a handsome fellow with a black beard, was engaged in a game of draughts with Teles.

"Did you see my grandfather?" asked Carlos, when Ega shook his hand.

"No, I lunched alone."

The supper, which was served shortly afterwards, was a jolly affair, generously washed down with some of the Marquis' superb wines. And no one drank more or laughed more than Carlos, who had emerged, almost suddenly, from sombre gloom into a rather high-strung gaiety, which worried Ega, who heard in it a false note, something like the sound of a cracked glass. In the end, though, over dessert, Ega himself grew quite lively, thanks to a splendid 1815 port. Then they had a game of baccarat in which Carlos—sombre again and constantly glancing at his watch—had the most extraordinary luck, "a cuckold's luck," as an indignant Darque put it, handing over his last twenty *mil-réis* note. At midnight, however, the Marquis was reminded by his administrator of doctor's orders: the time-limit on his birthday celebrations. There was a general putting on of overcoats and complaints from Darque and Craft, who were leaving with their pockets empty and not even enough change for the omnibus. A charitable collection was made, with them passing round their hats, mumbling blessings upon their benefactors.

In the cab that took Carlos and Ega back to Ramalhete, they sat for a long time in their respective corners, silently smoking. Only when they were half-way down the Aterro did Ega seem to wake up.

"So what's it to be? Are you still going to Santa Olávia or what?"

Carlos shifted in the darkness of the cab. Then slowly and wearily he said:

"Possibly tomorrow. I haven't said or done anything yet. I decided to give myself forty-eight hours to calm down and reflect. But we can't talk now over the noise of the wheels."

Each one again retreated into his corner and into silence.

At home, as they went up the velvet-lined staircase, Carlos declared that he was exhausted and had an appalling headache.

"We'll talk tomorrow, Ega. Goodnight."

"Yes, see you tomorrow."

Ega woke in the early hours with a terrible thirst. He leapt out of bed and was gulping down the jug of water on the dressing table, when he thought he heard a door bang downstairs, in Carlos' room. He listened. Then, shivering, he plunged back between the sheets. But he was wide-awake now, unable to rid himself of a strange, foolish idea, which had assailed him for no reason, but which worried him and made his heart beat loudly in the great silence of the night. He heard a clock strike three. The door banged again, then a window; it was probably the wind getting up. Nevertheless, he could not go back to sleep, but kept tossing and turning, the victim of a terrible unease, a tormenting idea fixed in his imagination. Then, in despair, he got out of bed, pulled on his overcoat, and, his hand shielding the light, stole down to Carlos' room on the tips of his slippered feet. In the hallway, he paused, trembling, his ear to the door curtain, hoping to hear the sound of steady breathing. The silence was heavy and absolute. Gingerly, he went in. The bed was still made and empty. Carlos had gone out.

He stood staring foolishly at the smooth bedspread, at the top of the lace sheet so neatly turned down by Baptista. There was no doubt about it now. Carlos had gone to spend the rest of the night in Rua de São Francisco. He was there now, he was sleeping there! And only one idea emerged out of his horror—to escape, to run away to Celorico and not witness this incomparable infamy!

And the following day, Tuesday, was equally desolating for poor Ega. Embarrassed, and terrified of meeting either Carlos or Afonso, he rose early, slipped down the stairs as cautiously as a thief, and went and had lunch at the Tavares. Later, in Rua do Ouro, he saw Carlos pass by in his break with Cruges and Taveira, whom he had doubtless recruited so as not to find himself alone at table with his grandfather. Ega ate a melancholy dinner at the Hotel Universal. He only returned to Ramalhete at nine to get dressed for the Countess de Gouvarinho's soirée, for that morning in Largo do Loreto, she had stopped her carriage in order to remind him to come, saying that it was Charlie's birthday party. And it was in an overcoat and with his crush hat in hand that he finally appeared in Ramalhete's small Louis XV drawing room where Cruges was playing Chopin, and where Carlos had settled down to a game of bezique with Craft. He asked if his friends wanted him to pass any message on to the noble Count and Countess.

"Have fun!"

"Be fascinating!"

"I'll be there for supper," promised Taveira, lounging in an armchair with *Le Figaro*.

It was two o'clock in the morning when Ega returned from the soirée, where he had, in the end, amused himself by initiating a desperate flirtation with the Viscountess de Alvim, who, at supper, after the champagne, and overcome by so much wit and so much boldness, had given him two roses. As he lit the candle outside Carlos' room, Ega hesitated, gripped by curiosity. Would Carlos be there? However, ashamed of such espionage, he continued up the stairs, determined, as he had been the night before, to run away to Celorico. In his room, he carefully placed the Viscountess' two roses in a glass in front of the mirror. And he was just beginning to get undressed when he heard slow heavy footsteps advancing down the dark corridor and stopping outside his door, waiting and silent. Frightened, Ega shouted: "Who is it?"

The door creaked open, and Afonso da Maia appeared, looking terribly pale, a jacket over his nightshirt, and carrying a candlestick in which the candle was almost burning out. He did not come in. In a hoarse, shaky voice, he said:

"What about Carlos? Was he at the Gouvarinhos?"

Greatly shaken, and still in his shirtsleeves, Ega stammered out some excuse. He wasn't sure. He had only been briefly at the Gouvarinhos' party. Carlos had probably gone there later with Taveira, for supper.

Afonso had closed his eyes, as if about to faint, reaching out a hand to support himself. Ega ran to him.

"Don't upset yourself, sir!"

"What do you expect? Where is he? He's with that woman. You don't have to tell me, I know. I had him followed—yes, I've stooped that low, but I had to put an end to this anguish. He was there yesterday until morning, and he's there now, at this very moment. Was it for this horror that God had me live so long?"

He made a wild gesture of disgust and grief. Then his footsteps, still heavier, still slower, disappeared off down the corridor.

Ega stood by the door, stunned. Then he slowly got undressed, determined quite simply to tell Carlos the next day, before he left for Celorico, that his infamous behaviour was killing his grandfather as well as forcing him, his best friend, to run away so as not to have to be a witness to it any longer.

As soon as he woke up, he dragged his trunk into the middle of the room and threw onto the bed, in armfuls, the clothes he was going to pack. And for half an hour, in his shirtsleeves, he busied himself with this task, weaving into his angry thoughts memories of last night's soirée, certain looks the Viscountess had given him, certain hopes that made him regret his departure. A cheerful sun was filling the balcony with golden light. In the end, he flung open a window to breathe in the air and to gaze up at the beautiful blue winter sky. Such weather certainly made Lisbon very alluring. Celorico, the house and Father Serafim were already casting a long shadow over his soul. When he looked down, he saw Carlos' dog-cart with Tunante in the harness, pawing the pavement, excited by the cool air. Carlos was obviously going out early, so as to avoid him and his grandfather!

Afraid that he wouldn't manage to speak to him all day, Ega ran downstairs. Carlos had locked himself in the bathroom. Ega called to him, but Carlos gave no sign of life. In the end, Ega knocked on the door and shouted through it, making no attempt to conceal his irritation.

"Would you please listen to me! Are you going to Santa Olávia or not?"

After a moment, over the sound of running water, Carlos shouted back:

"I'm not sure. Possibly. I'll let you know."

Ega could contain his anger no longer.

"Things can't continue like this forever. I've received a letter from my mother, and if you're not leaving for Santa Olávia, then I'm going to Celorico. It's absurd! This has been going on for three days now!"

And he almost repented of his violence when Carlos' imploring voice emerged from within, humble and weary:

"Please, Ega, be patient with me. I'll let you know."

Filled by one of those sudden emotions that afflict the highly-strung, Ega was touched by these words, and tears filled his eyes. He stammered a response:

"All right, all right—I was only shouting so you could hear me in there—there's no rush!"

And with that, he fled to his own room, feeling only compassion and tenderness, his eyelashes wet with tears. He understood now the torments that poor Carlos must be going through, in the despotic grip of a passion which had, until then, been legitimate, and which, in one bitter moment, had become, instead, monstrous, but without in any way losing its charm or its intensity. Frail and human, Carlos could not stop the violent impulse of love and desire carrying him along like a whirlwind! Giving in, time and again, he kept being driven into those arms, which innocently continued to call to him. And there he was now, terrified, exiled, slipping secretly out of the house, spending the day in tragic wanderings, far from family and friends, like an excommunicate who fears meeting in a pair of pure eyes the horror of his own sin. And meanwhile, there was poor Afonso, knowing everything and dying from the grief of it! Could he, the beloved guest from happier times, possibly leave now that this wave of misfortune had broken over the house, a house where he had been welcomed more generously and more affectionately than in his own? That would be ignoble! He immediately unpacked his trunk, and still, in his selfishness, furious with all these calamities battering him, he put his clothes back in the chest of drawers, as angrily as he had taken them out, snarling:

"Damn women, damn life, damn the lot!"

When he went downstairs, already dressed, Carlos had vanished! Baptista, glum and frowning, certain now that some major catastrophe had occurred, stopped him to murmur: "You were right, sir. We leave tomorrow for Santa Olávia, and we're taking enough clothes for some weeks. The winter's getting off to a bad start!"

At four o'clock that morning, when it was still pitch-black outside, Carlos softly closed the street door in Rua de São Francisco. And in the cold of the street, he was overwhelmed more painfully still by the fear that had already touched him as he got dressed in the half-dark of the bedroom, beside a sleeping Maria Eduarda—the fear of going back to Ramalhete! It was that same fear which, the previous day, had made him spend every hour out in his dog-cart and end up dining lugubriously with Cruges in one of the private rooms at the Café Augusto. It was fear of his grandfather, fear of Ega, fear of Vilaça, fear of the dinner bell summoning them all together; fear of his bedroom, where, at any moment, any one of them might draw aside the curtain and fix their eyes upon his soul and his secret. He was sure now that *they knew everything*. And even if he fled to Santa Olávia, placing between himself and Maria Eduarda a distance as high as a cloister wall, the memory and pain of the infamy into which he had plunged would never leave the minds of those men, his best friends. His moral life was in ruins. Then why leave, if, even by abandoning his passion, he would not find peace? Wouldn't it be more logical to trample desperately on all laws, human and divine, and carry the innocent Maria Eduarda far away from there and hurl himself for all eternity into the crime which had become his grim lot on Earth?

That is what he had thought yesterday, that is what he had thought . . . but then he had foreseen another horror, a supreme punishment, waiting for him in the solitude in which he was burying himself. He had already noticed it coming nearer; the other night, it had sent a premonitory shudder through him, and tonight, lying beside Maria Eduarda, who had fallen, exhausted, into sleep, he had sensed it tightening its grasp on him, like the first chill of a death agony.

Arising out of the depths of his being, it was as yet very tenuous, but nonetheless perceptible, a feeling of satiety, of repugnance, ever since he had known she was of the same blood as him. A sudden, physical, carnal repugnance that came like a shiver. It was, more than anything, the perfume that wrapped about her, which hung among the bed curtains and clung to his skin and his clothes, and which had once so excited and now so enervated him—the previous night, he had drenched himself in eau-de-cologne to get rid of it. And then it was her body, which he had always adored as if it were some ideal marble statue, but which suddenly seemed to him, as it was in reality, too large and muscular, with the thick limbs of some barbarous Amazon, with all the copious beauties of some animal made for pleasure. Her soft lustrous hair now, unexpectedly, had for him the coarseness of a lion's mane. The way she moved in bed, yes, even tonight, had frightened him, as if hers were the movements of a wild beast, slow and careful, tensed and ready to pounce. When her arms enfolded him and crushed him to her firm, full breasts, she now filled his veins with a fire that was entirely bestial. And yet, as soon as the last sigh had died on her lips, he would begin to retreat imperceptibly to the edge of the bed, feeling strangely frightened. Huddled in the sheets, lost in the depths of an infinite sadness, he would escape into thoughts of another possible life, far from there, in a simple, sunny house, with his wife, his legitimate wife, a flower of domestic grace, small and shy and modest, who would not utter such lascivious cries or use such intoxicating perfume. And, alas, he had no doubts now—if he ran away with her, he would find himself struggling against the indescribable horror of physical disgust. And once the passion that had been the justification for the crime was dead, what would be left for him then, bound to a woman whose presence sickened him—what would be left but to kill himself!

But having slept with her once, fully aware of the bond of kinship between them, could he ever calmly recommence his life? Even if he could summon up the necessary indifference and strength to extinguish that memory in himself, it would not die in his grandfather's heart or in his friends." That foul secret would remain between them, spoiling and besmirching everything. Life henceforth offered him only unbearable bitterness. What should he do, dear God, what should he do! Ah, if only someone could counsel and console him!

When he reached the door of his house, his only desire was to throw himself at the feet of a priest, at the feet of a saint, and confess all the miseries of his soul, and beg for the sweetness of his mercy! But where would he find a saint?

Opposite Ramalhete, the streetlamps were still on. He quietly opened the door. Cautiously, on tiptoe, he went up the stairs, his footsteps muffled by the cherry-red velvet. On the landing, he was just feeling for a candle, when, through the half-open curtain, he saw a light moving in the room. Frightened, he drew back. The light was coming closer, growing brighter; slow heavy steps were approaching dully across the carpet; the light emerged onto the landing, and with it his grandfather, in his shirtsleeves, looking pale, dumb, tall, and spectral. Carlos did not move, unable to breathe; and the old man's wide, reddened, horrified eyes fell on him and lingered on him, piercing him to the very depths of his soul, reading in those depths his secret. Then, without a word, his white head shaking, Afonso walked across the landing, where the light falling on the velvet stained it the colour of blood, and his steps disappeared off into the house, slow, muted, ever quieter, as if they were the last steps he would take in this life!

Carlos went into the dark room and bumped into a sofa. He fell onto it, his head buried in his arms, not thinking, not feeling, seeing only his grandfather's pale face pass and repass before him like a tall ghost, carrying the reddish light in his hand. Gradually, he was overcome by tiredness, inertia, and by an infinite lassitude of will, in which only one desire remained and grew, the desire to rest endlessly in some great silence, some great darkness. And so his thoughts slipped towards death. That would be the perfect cure, a certain refuge. Why didn't he go to meet it? A few grains of laudanum tonight and he would enter a state of absolute peace . . .

He lay for a long time, immersed in this idea, which brought him relief and consolation, as if, battered by a noisy storm, he saw ahead of him an open door, emanating warmth and silence. A murmur, the whistling of a bird at the window, made him conscious of the sun and the day. He got up and, filled by an immense lethargy, very slowly got undressed. He plunged between the sheets and buried his head in the pillow to recapture the sweetness of that inertia, of that foretaste of death, and, in the hours that remained to him, desired only to be oblivious of any light or any earthly thing.

The sun was already up, when there came a noise, and Baptista burst into the bedroom.

"Oh, sir, master! Your grandfather's been taken ill in the garden, he's unconscious!"

Carlos leapt out of bed, grabbed an overcoat and pulled it on. In the hallway, the distraught housekeeper was leaning over the banister, shouting: "Go on, quick, next to the baker's, Dr. Azevedo!" And Carlos collided with a boy running down the corridor, who said without stopping:

"At the end of the garden, near the fountain, sir, at the stone table!"

Afonso da Maia was there, in the corner of the garden beneath the branches of the cedar tree, still sitting on the cork bench, but sprawled forward on the rough table, his head between his arms. His broad-brimmed hat had rolled onto the ground; around his shoulders, with the collar up, he still wore his old blue greatcoat. All about him, on the leaves of the camellias, along the sandy paths, shone a clear, golden winter sun. Bubbling up among the shells in the fountain, a thread of water kept up its slow, mournful song.

Carlos immediately lifted his grandfather's head, the face already stiff and waxen, the eyes closed, a trickle of blood at either corner of his long white beard. Then he fell on his knees on the damp ground and seized his grandfather's hands, murmuring: "Oh Grandpa, Grandpa!" He ran to the pool and sprinkled him with water.

"Call someone! Call someone!"

He felt his grandfather's heart, but he was dead. It was dead and cold, that body, which, older than the century, had, like a great oak, so gallantly withstood the years and the storms. He had died there alone, with the sun already up, at that rough stone table on which he rested his weary head.

When Carlos got to his feet, Ega was there, dishevelled and wrapped in a dressing-gown. Carlos embraced him, trembling all over and crying helplessly. The servants stood around watching, terrified. And the housekeeper, beside herself, was pacing up and down between the rosebushes, clutching her head and moaning: "Oh, my dear master! Oh, my dear master!"

The porter arrived, panting, with Dr. Azevedo, whom he had very fortunately met in the street. The doctor was a young man, barely out of medical school, thin and nervous, with the ends of his moustache carefully curled. Rather awkwardly, he greeted first the servants and then Ega and Carlos, the latter still struggling to calm himself, his face bathed in tears. Then, having removed his gloves, the doctor, aware of the attentive, anxious gaze of all those tear-filled eyes, studied Afonso's body with a slow exaggerated meticulousness. Finally, nervously twirling one curled end of his moustache, he muttered a few technical terms to Carlos. Otherwise, he said only: As his colleague would already have realised, there was, alas, nothing further to be done. He proffered his heartfelt sympathy and said that if there was anything more he could do, he would be glad to help.

"Thank you, sir," stammered Carlos.

Ega, in his slippers, went with the doctor to show him the way out through the garden gate.

Carlos, meanwhile, remained standing by the old man, not crying now, but absorbed in the horror of that abrupt end! Images of his grandfather full of life and vigour—smoking his pipe by the fire, watering the roses in the morning—crowded into his heart, leaving it ever sadder and blacker. And he wished his life could end as well, that he could simply lie down and rest, like his grandfather, on that stone table, and effortlessly, painlessly, fall like him into eternal peace. A flickering ray of sunlight fell through the dense branches of the cedar tree onto Afonso's dead face. In the silence, the birds, startled for a moment, now resumed their chattering. Ega came over to Carlos and touched his arm.

"We must take him upstairs."

Carlos kissed his grandfather's cold limp hand. And slowly, lips trembling, he tenderly lifted his grandfather up by the shoulders. Baptista ran to help him; Ega, stumbling over his long dressing-gown, took the old man's feet. Through the garden, across the sun-filled terrace, through the study where his armchair waited in front of the lit fire, they carried him in a silence broken only by the scuffling footsteps of the servants, as they ran to open doors or to help when the distraught Carlos or Ega staggered beneath the weight of the large body. The housekeeper was already in Afonso's room with a silk bedspread to place over the simple, uncurtained iron bedstead. And there they lay him, at last, on the bright embroidered sprigs of the blue silk.

Ega had lit two silver candlesticks; the housekeeper, kneeling by the bed, was saying the rosary; and Monsieur Antoine, his white cook's hat in his hands, stood in the doorway with the basket he had brought, full of camellias and palm fronds. Carlos, meanwhile, kept moving about the room, his body shaken by long sobs, and, still gripped by one final, absurd hope, he repeatedly went over to the bed to feel the old man's hands or heart. In his velvet jacket and large white shoes, Afonso seemed stronger and larger as he lay there, rigid, on the narrow bed; in contrast to his short white hair and his long untidy beard, his skin had taken on the colour of old ivory, the lines on his face as hard as if they had been chiselled; the stiff eyelids, with their white lashes, had the solace and serenity of one who has finally found rest; as they lay him on the bed, one of his hands had remained open and pressed to his heart, in the simple, natural attitude of someone who had always lived according to his heart!

Carlos stood immersed in painful contemplation. What filled him with despair was the thought that his grandfather had departed like that without their having said goodbye, without a tender word being exchanged. Nothing! Only that anguished look, when he had passed him on the landing, holding a lit candle. He had already been walking towards death then. His grandfather had known everything—and that's what killed him! And this certainty beat ceaselessly in his soul, like a long, repeated, sombre note. His grandfather had known everything—and that's what killed him!

Ega came to him and indicated with a gesture their state of dress—he still in his dressing-gown, Carlos with an overcoat over his nightshirt.

"We must go downstairs and get dressed."

Carlos stammered:

"Yes, yes, we must get dressed . . ."

But he stayed where he was. Ega led him gently by the arm. Carlos was moving like a sleepwalker, slowly wiping his head and beard with his handkerchief.

And suddenly, in the corridor, desperately wringing his hands, his face once more wet with tears, he gave agonised vent to his feelings of guilt.

"Oh, Ega, dear Ega, my grandfather saw me this morning when I came in! And he walked straight past me and said nothing. He knew everything—and that's what killed him!"

Ega drew him along, consoling him, dismissing such an idea. What nonsense! His grandfather was nearly eighty and had a weak heart. How often, ever since Afonso had come back from Santa Olávia, had they talked with dread about precisely that! It was absurd now to make himself even more miserable with such imaginings!

With his eyes fixed on the ground, Carlos mumbled slowly, as if to himself:

"No, that's not it. It's odd, I know, but I'm not trying to make myself more miserable. I accept it as a punishment. I want it to be a punishment. I simply feel very small and very humble before the person meting out that punishment. This morning, I considered killing myself, but not now! My punishment is to live, crushed forever. What hurts me most is that he didn't say goodbye to me!"

Once more his tears flowed, but gently now, less desperately. Ega led him into his room, as if he were a child. And he left him there, on the sofa, his face buried in his handkerchief, as he wept quietly and continuously, washing himself clean and relieving his heart of all the confused and nameless anxieties that had been tormenting him during those last few days.

At midday, upstairs in his room, Ega was just getting dressed when Vilaça irrupted into his room, his arms flung wide.

"How did it happen? How did it happen?"

Baptista had sent the groom to fetch him, but the boy had been able to tell him very little. Downstairs, Carlos, the poor man, had embraced him, bathed in tears, unable to say anything except that Ega would explain everything. And so there he was.

"But what happened? Was it very sudden?"

Ega told him briefly how they had found Afonso that morning in the garden, slumped over the stone table. Dr. Azevedo had come, but it was too late.

Vilaça raised his hands to his head.

"Oh, how dreadful! You know, my friend, it was that woman who killed him, turning up like that out of the blue! He was never the same after that shock! That's what it was!"

Ega said quietly, absent-mindedly putting a few drops of eau-de-cologne on his handkerchief:

"Yes, possibly, the shock of that, plus his age and not taking good enough care of himself, and of course his weak heart."

They spoke then about the funeral, which would be a simple affair as befitted that simple man. They needed somewhere to leave the body until it could be taken to Santa Olávia, and Ega had thought of asking the Marquis if they could use his family vault.

Vilaça was scratching his chin, hesitating.

"I have a vault too: Senhor Afonso da Maia himself had it built for my father, God rest his soul. He could stay there for a few days. That way, there would be no need to ask anyone else, and, besides, I would consider it a great honour."

Ega agreed. Then they sorted out further details regarding who else should be informed, the timing, the key to the vault. Finally, Vilaça, glancing at his watch, got to his feet with a great sigh.

"Right, I'll go and deal with this sad business now! But I'll be back later. I want to see him one last time, when they've dressed him. Who would have thought! Why, only the night before last, I was playing cards with him. I even won three *mil-réis* from him, poor man!"

A wave of sadness choked him, and he fled, his handkerchief pressed to his eyes.

When Ega went downstairs, Carlos, dressed now in heavy mourning, was sitting at his desk before a piece of paper. He immediately got up and flung down the pen.

"I can't do it! You write to her, will you, just a brief note."

Without a word, Ega picked up the pen and wrote a very short letter. It said: "Dear Madam: Senhor Afonso da Maia died this morning, very suddenly, of an apoplexy. You will understand that, for the moment, Carlos can do nothing other than ask me to inform you of this tragic news. Yours, etc." He did not read the letter to Carlos. And when Baptista came in, all in black, with their lunch on a tray, Ega asked him to have the groom take the note to Rua de São Francisco. Baptista whispered over Ega's shoulder:

"We mustn't forget the mourning clothes for the servants, sir."

"Yes, Senhor Vilaça is dealing with it."

They ate and drank quickly from the tray itself. Then Ega wrote notes to Dom Diogo and to Sequeira, Afonso's oldest friends; and the clock was striking two when the undertakers arrived with the coffin, to prepare the body. Carlos, however, would not allow mercenary hands to touch his grandfather. It was he and Ega, aided by Baptista, who—very bravely, and subordinating emotion to duty—washed him and dressed him and placed him in the great oak coffin lined with pale satin; Carlos added a miniature of his grandmother. In the afternoon, with the help of Vilaça, who had returned "to have one last look at his master," they carried him down to the study, which Ega had chosen not to change or adorn in any way, and which, with its scarlet damasks, carved shelves and rosewood desk crowded with books, preserved its austere air of studious peace. The only change they made, in order to have somewhere to put the coffin, was to push together two large tables; they draped them in a black velvet cloth bearing the family's gold-embroidered coat of arms, which they'd found in the house. Above, Rubens' *Christ* opened his arms against the red sky of the setting sun. Beside the coffin, on each side of the tables, burned twelve candles in silver candlesticks. Broad, overlapping palm fronds had been

473

arranged at the head of the coffin, among bunches of camellias. And Ega had placed a little incense in two bronze holders.

That night, the first of Afonso's old friends to appear was Dom Diogo, solemnly dressed in a tailcoat. Leaning on Ega, terrified by the sight of the coffin, he could only murmur: "And he was seven months younger than me!" The Marquis came later, swathed in blankets, and carrying a great basket of flowers. Craft and Cruges knew nothing about it; they had chanced to meet at Rampa de Santos, and only got their first inkling of what had happened when they found the street door to Ramalhete closed. The last to arrive was Sequeira, who had spent the day at his country house, and who embraced Carlos, and then, in his bewilderment, Craft; with his bloodshot eyes full of tears, he stammered: "I've lost a friend of many years, and I won't be far behind him!"

And so the night of vigil and mourning began, slow and silent. The twelve tall flames from the candles burned with funereal solemnity. The friends exchanged the occasional murmured comment, their chairs drawn up close together. Eventually, the heat, the smell of incense, and the perfume from the flowers obliged Baptista to open the windows onto the terrace. The sky was full of stars. A soft breeze whispered through the trees in the garden.

Later, Sequeira, who had been sitting, unmoving, arms folded, in his chair, suffered a slight dizzy spell. Ega led him into the dining room and gave him a restoring glass of brandy. A cold supper had been set out there, with wines and sweetmeats. Craft joined them, along with Taveira, who had learned of the sad event at the offices of *A Tarde* and gone straight there, barely stopping to have supper. With a little Bordeaux wine and a sandwich, Sequeira grew more animated, remembering the past, the glory days, when he and Afonso were young. However, he fell silent when Carlos came in, as pale and slow as a sleepwalker, muttering: "Yes, eat something, please, eat."

He picked up a plate, walked round the table and left again. He wandered into the hallway, where all the candelabra had been lit. A dark slender figure appeared at the top of the stairs. Two arms embraced him. It was Alencar.

"I never came here during the happy times, but here I am at this hour of sadness!"

And the poet tiptoed down the corridor as if through the nave of a cathedral.

Carlos, meanwhile, took a further few steps around the hallway. At one end of a divan sat a large basket and a wreath of flowers, on which lay a letter. He recognised Maria Eduarda's writing. He did not even touch it, but went back into the study. Alencar, standing before the coffin, his hand on Ega's shoulder, was saying softly: "The soul of a hero has departed!"

The candles were burning low. There was a general air of weariness. Baptista arranged for coffee to be served in the billiard room. And there, as soon as he had been given a cup, Alencar, surrounded by Cruges, Taveira, and Vilaça, also began talking about the past, about the brilliant days in Arroios, about the passionate young men of the time.

"You won't find people like those Maias now, my boys—lion-hearted, generous, valiant! Everything seems to be dying in this wretched country of ours! The spark has died and the passion with it. Afonso da Maia! I can see him now, standing at the window in the palace of Benfica, with his great satin cravat, and that noble face of his, the face of a Portuguese hero of yesteryear. And he's gone! Along with my poor Pedro. My soul is quite overwhelmed with grief."

His eyes grew dark, and he took a long drink of brandy.

Ega, after only a sip of coffee, returned to the study, where the smell of incense created a chapel-like melancholy. Dom Diogo was lying on the sofa, snoring. Sequeira, opposite him, was dozing too, head drooping, arms still folded, face flushed. Ega gently woke them both. The two old friends, having embraced Carlos, left in the same carriage, their cigars lit. Gradually, the other men all went over and embraced Carlos too, then donned their overcoats. The last to leave was Alencar, who, out in the courtyard, on an emotional impulse, kissed Ega on the cheek, still bemoaning the past and his vanished companions.

"I'll have to rely on you youngsters now. So don't abandon me! If you do, why, when I want to visit someone, I'll have to go to the cemetery. Goodbye now, and don't catch cold!"

The funeral took place the following day, at one o'clock. Ega, the Marquis, Craft, and Sequeira carried the coffin to the door, followed by their friends, prominent among them the Count de Gouvarinho at his most solemn and wearing his Grand Cross. Steinbroken, accompanied as always by his secretary, carried a wreath of violets. The long line of carriages filled the narrow road and disappeared from view as it snaked its way along the neighbouring side streets; people leaned out of every window; policemen shouted at drivers. At last, the hearse, a very simple affair, set off, followed by two carriages from the house, empty and with their lamps draped in long black crêpe veils. Behind, one by one, came the hired cabs carrying the guests, who were buttoning up their overcoats and closing the windows against the cold misty day. Darque and Vargas travelled in the same coupé. Gouvarinho's courier trotted by on his white horse. And in the deserted street, the great door of Ramalhete finally closed for a long period of mourning.

When Ega returned from the cemetery, he found Carlos in his room, tearing up papers, while Baptista, kneeling on the carpet, was hurriedly fastening a leather trunk. And seeing Ega, pale, shivering, and rubbing his hands, Carlos shut the drawer full of letters and suggested they go into the smoking room, where there was a fire.

As soon as they went in, Carlos drew the curtain and looked at Ega.

"Would you mind going to talk to her?"

"No. But why? To tell her what?"

"Everything."

Ega dragged an armchair over to the fire and stirred the coals. And Carlos, beside him, staring into the flames, went on:

"Besides, I want her to leave, to leave for Paris at once. It would be absurd for her to stay on in Lisbon. Until we sort out what money is due to her, I'll set up a monthly allowance for her, a very generous one. Vilaça will be here shortly to discuss the details. But, anyway, I want you to take her five hundred *libras* tomorrow, so that she can leave."

Ega said quietly:

"Perhaps, if it's a matter of money, it would be best if Vilaça went instead."

"Dear God, no! Why make the poor creature blush before Vilaça?"

There was a silence. They were both gazing at the bright, dancing flames.

"Would it be very hard for you, my poor friend?"

"No. I'm beginning to go numb. It's just a matter of closing my eyes, getting through one more painful hour, and then resting. When will you be back from Santa Olávia?"

Carlos wasn't sure. He had been hoping that Ega would come and idle away a few days with him, once his mission to Rua de São Francisco was over. Later on, they would have to take his grandfather's body there.

"And after that, I'm going to travel. I'll go to America, to Japan, I'll do that stupid but very effective thing—amuse myself."

He shrugged and went slowly over to the window, where a pale ray of sunlight was dying in the now clear afternoon. Then, turning to Ega, who was again stirring the coals into life, he said:

"I don't dare ask you to come with me, Ega. I'd like to, but I don't dare."

Ega put down the tongs, straightened up and, greatly moved, opened his arms wide to Carlos and said:

"Go on, damn it, dare, why don't you?"

"Then come with me!"

Carlos put his whole soul into these words, and when he embraced Ega, two large tears rolled down his cheeks.

Ega then reviewed the situation. Before going to Santa Olávia, he needed to make a pilgrimage to Celorico. The Orient was an expensive place. He therefore needed to wheedle a few letters of credit out of his mother. And when Carlos assured him that he was rich enough to pay for the luxuries of both of them, Ega said very gravely:

"No, no! My mother's rich too. A trip to America and to Japan is a form of education, and my mother has a duty to complete my education. I will, however, accept one of your leather trunks."

When, that night, Carlos and Ega, accompanied by Vilaça, reached Santa Apolónia station, the train was just about to leave. Carlos barely had time to jump into his reserved compartment, while Baptista, clutching their travel rugs, was thrust roughly into another compartment by the guard, to the protests of the people already packed inside. The train set off at once. Carlos leaned out of the window and shouted to Ega: "Send me a telegram tomorrow and tell me what happened!"

Driving back to Ramalhete with Vilaça, who was going to collate and seal up Afonso da Maia's papers, Ega immediately mentioned the five hundred *libras* that he was supposed to give Maria Eduarda the following morning. Vilaça had, indeed, received such an order from Carlos. But frankly, between themselves, didn't it seem a somewhat excessive amount for a journey? Carlos had also spoken of setting up a monthly allowance for this lady of four thousand francs—one hundred and sixty *libras*! Didn't Ega find that equally disproportionate? For a woman, a mere woman.

Ega reminded him that this mere woman had a legal right to much more.

"Yes, yes," he grumbled, "but all that legal business requires very close scrutiny. I'd rather not talk about it, if you don't mind!"

Then, when Ega referred to the fortune left by Afonso da Maia, Vilaça gave him details. Theirs was certainly one of the wealthiest families in Portugal. The inheritance from Sebastião da Maia alone represented an income of a good fifteen *contos*. The properties in the Alentejo, with the improvements Vilaça's father had made, had tripled in value, although Santa Olávia remained a bit of a drain on expenses. The estates near Lamego, though, were worth a fortune.

"There's a lot of money!" he said with satisfaction, slapping Ega's knee. "And let them say what they like, but that makes up for everything."

"It certainly makes up for a lot."

As they entered Ramalhete, Ega felt a great wave of nostalgia, thinking of the happy loving home it once had been and never would be again. In the hallway, his steps already echoed sadly, like footsteps in an abandoned house. There was still a faint smell of incense and phenol. On the chandelier in the corridor, only one dim light was lit.

"The house already feels like a ruin."

"A very comfortable one, though!" replied Vilaça, looking around at the tapestries and the divans, rubbing his hands and shivering in the cold night.

They went into Afonso's study, where for a moment they stood warming themselves by the fire. The Louis XV clock struck nine, and the silvery minuet of its chime rang out for a moment, then died. Vilaça prepared himself for his task. Ega announced that he was going to his room to sort out his papers too, and make a clean sweep of two years of his youth.

He went upstairs. And no sooner had he put the candle down on the chest of drawers than he heard outside, in the silence of the corridor, a long desolate moan, infinitely sad. His scalp pricked with fear. Whatever it was, that thing moaning in the dark, it was outside Afonso da Maia's room. At last, reminding himself that the whole house was awake and full of servants and lights, Ega finally dared to take a few nervous steps along the corridor, a candlestick grasped in one tremulous hand.

It was the cat! It was the Reverend Boniface, scratching at the closed door of Afonso's bedroom, miaowing mournfully. Ega, furious, drove him away. Poor Boniface fled, plump and slow, his soft tail brushing the floor, but he returned at once, and, alternately scratching at the door and rubbing against

Ega's legs, began to miaow again, a piercing lament, as plangent as any human grief, weeping for the lost master who used to stroke him and let him sit on his lap and who had gone away.

Ega ran back to the study and asked Vilaça if he would mind staying at Ramalhete that night. Vilaça agreed, rather shocked by Ega's fear of the stricken cat. He had left the pile of papers on the desk in order to warm his feet again by the dying fire. Then, turning to Ega, who, still terribly pale, had sat down on the sofa where Dom Diogo always used to sit, he said softly and gravely:

"Three years ago, when Senhor Afonso ordered me to begin renovation work on this house, I reminded him that, according to ancient legend, the walls of Ramalhete have always proved fatal to the Maia family. Senhor Afonso da Maia laughed at such omens and legends, but fatal they've proved to be!"

The following day, carrying the Monforte papers and the money—in the form of bills of exchange and *libras*—which Vilaça had handed over to him at the door of the Bank of Portugal, Ega, heart pounding, but determined to be strong and to confront the crisis calmly, went up the stairs to the second-floor apartment in Rua de São Francisco. Domingos, wearing a black tie, tiptoed down the corridor ahead of him and drew back the curtain to the drawing room. Ega had barely put the cigar box down on the sofa when Maria Eduarda, looking very pale and dressed entirely in black, entered the room, holding out both her hands to him.

"How is Carlos?"

Ega stammered:

"As you can imagine at a time like this. It was such a terrible shock . . ."

A tear trembled in Maria Eduarda's sad eyes. She had not known Senhor Afonso da Maia, nor ever seen him, but she suffered because she could so keenly feel Carlos' suffering. How he had loved his grandfather!

"It happened very suddenly, then?"

Ega went into a long, detailed description. He thanked her for the wreath she had sent. He recounted the cries and grief of poor Boniface.

"And Carlos?"

"Carlos has left for Santa Olávia."

She clasped her hands together, shocked and saddened. Gone to Santa Olávia! Without so much as a note or a word? She grew paler still, terrified by this hasty departure, almost as if he were running away. Then, with an air of resignation and confidence which she did not feel, she said softly:

"Of course, at moments like this one doesn't always think of others."

Two tears rolled slowly down her cheek. And in the face of such mute, humble grief, Ega did not know what to say. For a moment, nervously fingering his moustache, he watched Maria Eduarda weeping in silence. Finally, he got up, went over to the window, then came back, his arms open in a gesture of great affliction.

"No, it isn't that, my dear lady! There's something else! These have been terrible days for us, days of great anguish!"

Something else? She waited, her large eyes gazing at Ega, her whole soul in suspense.

Ega took a deep breath.

"Do you remember a man called Guimarães, who lives in Paris, Dâmaso's uncle?"

Maria Eduarda, taken aback, nodded slowly.

"This man Guimarães was a great friend of your mother's, is that correct?"

She nodded, again without saying anything. Poor Ega still held back, his face white and strained, in a torment of embarrassment.

"I'm telling you all this, dear lady, because Carlos asked me to. God knows I find it very hard. It's so dreadful I don't even know where to begin . . ."

She put her hands together, pleading and anguished: "For God's sake, tell me!"

And at that moment, very quietly, Rosa pushed aside the curtain and came in, holding her doll in her arms and with Niniche at her side. Her mother cried abruptly: "Leave the room! Go away!"

Frightened, the little girl advanced no further, her lovely eyes suddenly full of tears. The curtain fell, and from the far end of the corridor came the sound of bitter, wounded crying.

Ega had but one desire then, a desperate longing to bring the business to a close.

"You would, I imagine, recognise your mother's handwriting . . . well, I have here a declaration which she made in your regard. That man Guimarães was in possession of this document, as well as other papers with which your mother entrusted him in 1871, on the eve of the war. He had kept them until now, intending to restore them to you, but he had no idea where you lived. Then, a few days ago, he saw you with me and Carlos in a carriage. It was near the Aterro, you probably remember, opposite a tailor's shop, when we drove in from the Toca. Anyway, this man Guimarães went straight to the Maia family's administrator and gave him these papers to give to you. You can imagine our surprise when we realised that you were a relative of Carlos, a very close relative."

He had cobbled together this story on the spot and blurted it out almost in one breath, gesturing nervously. She, deathly pale now, and in the grip of some indefinable terror, barely understood what he was saying. She could only murmur feebly: "But . . ." And then she fell silent again, overwhelmed, watching Ega's every move, as he bent over the sofa and, with trembling hands, began unwrapping Madame Monforte's cigar box. Finally, he turned to her, holding a piece of paper and gabbling an explanation:

"Your mother never told you . . . And there was a very grave reason for this . . . She had run away from Lisbon, she had run away from her husband . . . Forgive me for speaking so bluntly, but this is not the moment to mince words.

479

Here it is! You know your mother's handwriting. It is her handwriting, isn't it?"

"Yes, it is!" cried Maria Eduarda, making as if to grab the piece of paper.

"I'm sorry!" said Ega, snatching it away from her: "I'm not a family member, and it would be improper for me to be here when you read it."

This was a providential inspiration of the moment, which saved him from having to witness the terrible shock, the horror of the things she was about to find out. He would leave her all the papers that had belonged to her mother. She could read them once he had gone, and then she would understand the whole dreadful truth. Taking out of his pocket the two heavy rolls of coins and the envelope containing the promissory note on a bank in Paris, he placed everything on the table along with the statement by Madame Monforte.

"Only a few words more. Carlos thinks that it would be best if you were to leave at once for Paris. You have a right, as will your daughter, to part of the Maia family fortune, since it is now your family too. In the bundle of things I am leaving you is a draft on a Paris bank to cover immediate expenses. Carlos' administrator, Vilaça, has already reserved you a private compartment on the train. When you are ready to leave, please send a note to me at Ramalhete, so that I can be there at the station. I think that is all. Now I must leave you."

He picked up his hat and took her cold lifeless hand.

"I know how terrible this all is, but you are young, and you will still have many joys in your life; you have your daughter to console you for everything. I don't really know what else to say!"

Choking back his tears, he kissed the hand which she, very erect in her dark dress, and as still and pale as a marble statue, unconsciously, wordlessly held out to him. Then he fled.

"To the telegraph office!" he called to the driver when he got downstairs.

He only began to calm down a little as they drove down Rua do Ouro, and he took off his hat and gave a long sigh. And he kept repeating to himself all the consoling words he could have said to Maria Eduarda: she was young and beautiful; her sin had been committed entirely unwittingly; time heals all wounds; and one day soon, reconciled to these events, she would find herself the member of a respected family with a large fortune, living in the wonderful city of Paris, where a pair of lovely eyes and a few thousand-franc notes are a guarantee of a safe future.

"She'll be in the position of a pretty and very wealthy widow," he said out loud to himself in the carriage. "There are worse things in life."

When he left the telegraph office, he dismissed the carriage. He walked back through the consoling winter light to Ramalhete, where he wrote Carlos the long letter he had promised. Vilaça was already installed there, wearing his velvet beret, still collating Afonso's papers and sorting out the servants' wages. They dined late. And they were sitting by the fire, in the Louis XV room, smoking their cigars, when the footman came to tell them that there was a lady downstairs in a carriage, asking for Senhor Ega. They were terrified, immediately imagining that it would be Maria Eduarda, having made some drastic decision. Vilaça still clung to the hope that she might bring some new revelation, which would change everything and save them from that vast unnecessary expense. Ega was trembling as he went down the stairs. There he found a hired cab in which sat Melanie, wrapped in a voluminous coat and bearing a letter from Madame.

By the light of the lamp, Ega opened the envelope, which contained only a white card with the pencilled words: "I have decided to leave for Paris tomorrow."

Ega suppressed a desire to ask how Madame was. He raced up the stairs, and, followed by Vilaça, who had waited in the hallway, listening, he ran to Afonso's study in order to write a note to Maria Eduarda. On a sheet of black-edged paper he informed her (along with details regarding luggage) that a carriage had been reserved for her as far as Paris, and that he would have the honour of seeing her at Santa Apolónia station. Then, when it came to addressing the envelope, he sat with his pen poised, not knowing what to write. Should he put Madame MacGren or Dona Maria Eduarda da Maia? Vilaça thought it preferable to use her old name, because legally she wasn't yet a Maia. But, said Ega, embarrassed, she wasn't Madame MacGren either.

"I won't put any name. She'll just assume I forgot."

He took the letter downstairs in its blank envelope. Melanie slipped it inside her muff. And leaning out of the window, she enquired sadly, on behalf of her mistress, where Senhor Carlos' grandfather was buried.

Ega stared at her through his monocle, unsure whether Maria Eduarda's curiosity on the subject was indiscreet or touching. Finally, he told her where to find him. He was in the Prazeres cemetery, on the right at the back, where she would see an angel bearing a torch. It would be best to ask the gatekeeper for the Vilaça family vault.

"*Merci, monsieur, bien le bonsoir.*"

"*Bonsoir, Melanie!*"

The following day, at Santa Apolónia station, Ega, who had arrived early with Vilaça, had just despatched his luggage to the Douro, when he saw Maria Eduarda walking along, holding Rosa's hand. She was wearing a vast dark fur coat, with a double veil over her face, as thick as a mask; a gauze veil covered the little girl's face and was tied in a bow on top of her hat. Miss Sara, in a pale check overcoat, was carrying a bundle of books. Behind, came Domingos, red-eyed and clutching a roll of blankets, beside Melanie, who was also dressed in heavy mourning and holding Niniche in her arms. Ega ran over to Maria Eduarda, took her arm and led her in silence to the carriage, in which all the curtains were drawn. Before she got in, she slowly removed one glove and silently held out her hand to him.

"We'll see each other again at Entroncamento," murmured Ega. "I'm going north as well."

A few men stopped out of curiosity to see, disappearing into that closed mysterious first-class carriage, an apparently beautiful lady, all swathed in black and with an air of terrible sadness. Indeed, no sooner had Ega closed the door than Neves, from *A Tarde* and the audit office, left a group of other men, grabbed him by the arm and said earnestly:

"Who's that?"

Ega dragged him along the platform only to whisper tragically in his ear: "Cleopatra!"

Neves, furious, was left snorting: "Stupid ass!" Ega, meanwhile, had left. Vilaça was waiting for him by Ega's reserved compartment, still dazzled by the melancholy noble figure of Maria Eduarda. He had never seen her before, and she seemed to him like a queen out of a novel.

"I mean it, my friend, she really made an impression on me. God, she's a beautiful woman! She's costing us a small fortune, but she's a superb piece!"

The train chugged out of the station. Domingos was left sniffling on the platform, his colourful handkerchief pressed to his face. And Neves, still furious, spotted Ega at the door of his carriage and surreptitiously made an obscene gesture as he passed.

At Entroncamento station, Ega knocked on the windows of the private compartment, which had remained closed and secret. Maria Eduarda opened the door. Rosa was asleep. Miss Sara was reading in one corner, her head resting on a pillow. And Niniche, startled, began barking.

"Would you like anything to eat or drink, Senhora?"

"No, thank you."

They stood in silence, while Ega, with one foot on the step, slowly took out his cigar case. In the ill-lit station, various country folk walked past them, swathed in blankets. A guard was pushing a cart laden with parcels. Up ahead, the engine huffed and puffed in the shadows. Two men prowled around outside the compartment, casting inquisitive, languid glances at this magnificent woman, so grave and sombre, wrapped in her dark fur coat.

"Are you going to Oporto?" she asked softly.

"No, to Santa Olávia."

"Ah!"

Then his lips trembling, Ega managed to say: "Goodbye!"

Too overcome to speak, she said nothing, but squeezed his hand.

Ega walked slowly back through groups of soldiers, military coats slung over their shoulders, who were hurrying off to get a drink at the cantina. At the door of the station buffet, he turned again and raised his hat. She waved her arm in slow farewell. And that was the last time he saw Maria Eduarda, a large silent black figure against the glaring station lights, standing at the door of that carriage carrying her away forever.

: XVIII :

WEEKS LATER, in the first few days of the New Year, the *Gazeta Ilustrada* announced in its society column: "That distinguished and brilliant sportsman, Senhor Carlos da Maia, and our friend and collaborator, João da Ega, departed yesterday for London, whence, shortly, they will travel to North America and continue their fascinating journey onwards to Japan. Many friends went on board the *Tamar* to say goodbye to these two charming *touristes*. Among them were the Finnish ambassador and his secretary, the Marquis de Sousela, the Count de Gouvarinho, the Viscount de Darque, Guilherme Craft, Teles da Gama, Cruges, Taveira, Vilaça, General Sequeira, our glorious poet Tomás de Alencar, etc., etc. As we shook hands for the last time with our friend and collaborator, João da Ega, he promised to send us a few letters with his impressions of Japan, that wonderful land from which we receive both the Sun and so many of our fashions. This is excellent news for all those who appreciate acute observation and wit. *Au revoir!*"

After these affectionate lines (on which Alencar had collaborated), the first news of the "travellers" came in a letter from Ega to Vilaça from New York. It was short and business-like; however, he added a postscript entitled: "General information for friends." There he described the dreadful crossing from Liverpool, Carlos' persistent sadness, a snow-covered New York in brilliant sunshine. And he added: "The intoxication of travel is beginning to take hold of us, and we are determined to trudge this narrow universe until our griefs grow tired. We are planning to go to Peking, to visit the Great Wall and then cross Central Asia, via the oasis-city of Merv, then Khiva and on into Russia; from there, we will go to Armenia and Syria, then down into Egypt to purify ourselves in the sacred Nile; then up to Athens to send a greeting to Minerva from the Acropolis, and on to Naples, followed by a quick glance at Algeria and Morocco, after which we will finally collapse in Santa Olávia around the middle of 1879, to rest our weary limbs. I will write no more for now because it's late, and we're off to the opera to see Patti in *The Barber of Seville*. Warm good wishes to all our dear friends."

Vilaça copied out this paragraph and put it in his wallet to show the faithful friends of Ramalhete. They all admiringly approved of such fine adventurous plans. Only Cruges, terrified by the vastness of the universe, murmured sadly: "They'll never come back!"

However, after a year and a half, on a lovely March day, Ega reappeared in the Chiado. He caused a sensation! He looked splendid, strong and tanned, bursting with wit, exquisitely dressed, and full of stories and adventures from the Orient, unwilling to tolerate anything in art or poetry that did not come either from Japan or China, and announcing his plans for a great book, "his book," which would bear the grave title of some heroic chronicle: *Travels in Asia*.

"And how's Carlos?"

"Oh, he's in splendid form! He's installed in Paris, in a delightful apartment in the Champs-Elysées, living the extravagant life of an artist-prince from the Renaissance."

To Vilaça, though, who knew all their secrets, Ega confessed that Carlos was still very "shaken." He lived, laughed, drove his phaeton around the Bois de Boulogne, but there remained in the depths of his heart the heavy dark memory of that "terrible week."

"But the years pass, Vilaça," Ega added, "and with the years, everything on Earth, with the exception of China, passes too."

And that year passed. People were born and people died. Wheat fields ripened, the leaves of trees fell. More years passed.

Towards the end of 1886, Carlos went to spend Christmas near Seville, in the house of a friend of his from Paris, the Marquis de Villa Medina. And from the Villa Medina estate, called *La Soledad*, he wrote to Ega in Lisbon, announcing that, after an exile of nearly ten years, he had decided to visit old Portugal, to see the trees in Santa Olávia and the marvels of the new Avenue in Lisbon. Besides, he had some amazing news, which would astonish Ega; if curiosity got the better of him, he should come and meet him with Vilaça to eat pork in Santa Olávia.

"He's going to get married," thought Ega.

He had not seen Carlos for three years (not since his last stay in Paris). Alas, he was unable to rush to Santa Olávia, because he was laid up in a room in the Hotel Bragança with a bad sore throat after spending a prodigiously amusing Epiphany supper with friends at Silva's. Vilaça, however, did go to Santa Olávia, taking a letter from Ega, explaining about the sore throat and begging him not to linger too long over that pork in the craggy landscape of the Douro, but to fly to the great capital with his great news.

Carlos did not, in fact, stay long in Resende. And one mild luminous January morning in 1887, the two friends, together at last, were having lunch in a room in the Hotel Bragança, with the two windows that gave onto the river flung wide.

Ega, cured now, and radiant with irrepressible excitement, downing coffee after coffee, kept putting his monocle to his eye in order to admire Carlos and his "immutability."

"Not a single white hair or a wrinkle, nor even a hint of fatigue! That's Paris for you, my boy! Lisbon wears a man down. I mean, look at me, look at this!"

With one thin finger he pointed at his gaunt face, at the two deep lines on either side of his nose. What most terrified him was his bald patch, which had started two years ago and had since spread and was already a gleaming spot on top of his head.

"Look at this dreadful thing! Science, it seems, can find a cure for everything except baldness! Whole civilisations are transformed, but baldness never goes away! My head's starting to look like a billiard ball, isn't it? What causes it, do you think?"

"Idleness," said Carlos, laughing.

"Idleness! What about you, then?"

Besides, what else could he do in a country like Portugal? When he had returned from France, he had considered entering the diplomatic service. He had always had the gift of the gab, and now that his Mama, poor thing, was lying in her great vault in Celorico, he also had money. Then he had changed his mind. After all, what was Portuguese diplomacy but another form of idleness? An idleness spent abroad, where one was constantly aware of one's own insignificance. He would rather be idle in Lisbon!

And when Carlos mentioned politics, the traditional occupation of the feckless, Ega thundered back: "*Politics!*" The world of politics had become morally and physically repellent to him ever since business had attacked constitutionalism like a form of phylloxera! Politicians nowadays were just like marionettes, who made gestures and struck poses because two or three financiers were behind them, pulling the strings. If they were, at least, well-made, well-varnished marionettes—but no, that was the worst of it. They had no style, no manners; they never washed or cleaned their nails. This extraordinary phenomenon occurred nowhere else, not even in Romania or Bulgaria! The three or four salons in Lisbon which welcomed anyone, whoever they were, excluded most politicians. And why? Because the ladies found them too revolting!

"Look at Gouvarinho! He certainly doesn't welcome his co-religionists at his Tuesday salons."

Carlos, who was smiling, enjoying Ega's acerbic wit, suddenly started in his chair.

"Of course, I forgot to ask! How is the Countess, our good Countess de Gouvarinho?"

Ega, pacing the room, told him the latest news about the Gouvarinhos. The Countess had inherited about sixty *contos* from an eccentric aunt who lived in Santa Isabel, and she now rode around in superior carriages and received every Tuesday. However, she was suffering from some grave illness, which affected her lungs, or was it her liver? She was still very elegant, but had also grown very serious, a perfect flower of prudery. The Count continued much the same, a talkative scribbler, a vain minor politician, but he was grey-haired now, had twice been a minister, and was positively bristling with Grand Crosses.

"Didn't you see the Gouvarinhos when they were in Paris recently?"

"No. By the time I found out they were there and went to leave my card, they had departed for Vichy the night before."

The door opened, and a resonant voice bellowed:

"So here you are at last, my boy!"

"Alencar!" cried Carlos, throwing down his cigar.

And they exchanged a long embrace, with loud, mutual slaps on the back and a resounding kiss on the cheek—a fatherly kiss from Alencar, who was trembling with emotion. Ega brought over another chair and called for the waiter.

"What are you having, Tomás? Brandy? Curaçao? At any rate, more coffee! More coffee, and very strong, for Senhor Alencar!"

The poet, meanwhile, was immersed in contemplation of Carlos, still clasping his hands and smiling broadly, thus revealing his ever more ruined teeth. He thought Carlos looked magnificent, a superb specimen, an honour to the race. Ah, yes, Paris—with its wit and its ardently lived life—definitely preserved a man!

"And Lisbon wears a man down," added Ega. "That's my phrase. Come on, take a seat, there's your coffee and there's your drink!"

It was now Carlos' turn to study Alencar. He seemed to him more handsome, more poetic, with his wild inspired mop of white hair, and those deep lines in his dark face, carved like cart-tracks by the tumultuous passage of emotions.

"You look every inch the poet, Alencar! You would make the perfect subject for an engraving or a statue!"

The poet smiled, smugly stroking his long romantic moustache, grown white with age and yellow with nicotine. Well, old age had to have some compensations! His stomach wasn't too bad, and he kept pretty well, and he still had a good heart.

"Which is not to say, dear Carlos, that things here aren't going from bad to worse, but enough of that. People always complain about their own country, it's human nature. Even Horace complained. And, as you superior intelligences know all too well, in the days of Augustus . . . not to mention, of course, the fall of the Republic, the collapse of the old institutions. Anyway, let's not talk about the Romans. What's in that bottle? Chablis . . . Hm, not unpleasant in the autumn, with oysters . . . Let's have some Chablis, then. To your return, Carlos! And to your good health, dear João, and may God give you the glories you both deserve, boys!"

He drank and mumbled something about it being a good Chablis with a fine bouquet. Then, flicking back his white mane, he finally, noisily, drew up a chair.

"Ah, Tomás!" cried Ega, placing one hand affectionately on his shoulder. "There's no one like him, he's unique! The Good Lord made him on a day when he was at his most imaginative, and then he broke the mold."

"Nonsense!" murmured the poet, beaming. There were other poets as good as him. All humanity came from the same clay, as the Bible said, or from the same monkey, as Darwin believed.

"Because, as far as I'm concerned, this evolution business, the origin of the species, the development of the cell and all that . . . I mean, obviously Darwin, Lamarck, Spencer, Claude Bernard, and Littré are first-rate people, but for a few thousand years now, man has proved, and quite sublimely too, that he has a soul!"

"Drink your coffee, Tomás!" advised Ega, pushing his cup towards him. "Drink your coffee!"

"Thank you! Oh, and before I forget, João, I gave the little one your doll. She immediately started to kiss and cradle it, with that deep-seated maternal instinct, that divine essence, which all girls have. She's a niece of mine, Carlos. She was left without a mother, poor thing, and so I'm bringing her up and trying to make a woman of her. You must come and see her. Besides, I'd like you to dine with me one day, so that I can serve you partridges *a la española*. Are you staying long, Carlos?"

"Yes, for a week or two, long enough to get a good deep breath of Portuguese air."

"Quite right, too, my boy!" exclaimed the poet, reaching now for the bottle of brandy. "This place isn't as bad as they say, you know. Just look at the sky, look at the river!"

"Yes, it really is lovely!"

And all three of them sat for a moment staring out at the incomparable beauty of the river—vast, lustrous, serene, the same blue as the splendid sun-filled sky.

"And what about your poetry?" Carlos said suddenly, turning to the poet. "Or have you abandoned the divine language?"

Alencar shook his head sadly. Who now understood that divine language? The only language the new Portugal understood was that of money, of filthy lucre. Now it was all about banking syndicates!

"But the occasional poem still surfaces from within, and the old me trembles. Have you read the newspapers? No, of course not. You wouldn't read the rags that pass for newspapers here. Well, I did have one little thing published, dedicated to João here. I'll recite it to you if I can remember it."

He ran his hand over his gaunt face and launched into the poem in mournful tones:

> *Ah, light of hope, light of love,*
> *What wild wind has unleaved thee,*
> *Abandoning your companion soul*
> *Never again to find thee?*

Carlos murmured: "Beautiful!" Ega murmured: "Exquisite!" And the poet, warming to his theme, and moved by his own words, made a gesture as of a wing flying off into the distance:

> *Time was, in the moonlight hour,*
> *When my soul, like a nightingale stirring,*
> *Would burst, unthinking, into song.*
> *Ah, then, every thought was a flower*
> *Which the soft May winds, all in a throng . . .*

"Senhor Cruges!" announced the waiter at the door. Carlos opened wide his arms, and the maestro, tightly buttoned up in a light overcoat, abandoned himself to Carlos' embrace, stammering:

"I only found out yesterday that you were arriving. I wanted to come and meet you at the station, but they didn't wake me in time . . ."

"Still as disorganised as ever, I see," cried Carlos gaily. "Do they *ever* wake you in time?"

Cruges shrugged, red-faced and shy after their long separation. Carlos made him sit down at his side, touched to see the maestro again, still as tall and thin as ever, although his nose seemed sharper and his tangle of shoulder-length hair curlier.

"Allow me to congratulate you! I read about your triumph in the newspapers, a lovely comic opera, I understand, *The Flower of Seville . . .*"

". . . *of Granada*," the maestro said, correcting him. "Yes, it's not a bad little piece, and people seem to like it."

"A wonderful work!" exclaimed Alencar, refilling his glass with brandy. "The music's so full of the South, so full of light, you can smell the orange blossom! But as I said to him the other day: 'Forget operettas, my boy, fly higher, and write a grand historical symphony!' I gave him an idea for one just the other day. The departure of Dom Sebastião for Africa. Sea shanties, drums, the tears of the people, the waves beating. Sublime! And no castanets this time. He has enormous talent, this boy, and besides, given how many trousers of mine he soiled when he was young and used to sit on my knee, why, he's almost like a son to me!"

Cruges was uneasily running his fingers through his hair. Finally, he confessed to Carlos that he couldn't stay long, he had a *rendez-vous*.

"With a lover?"

"No, with Barradas. He's doing a portrait of me in oils."

"Holding a lyre?"

"No," replied the maestro gravely, "my baton. And I'm in tails."

He unbuttoned his overcoat and revealed himself in all his glory, with two coral buttons in his shirtfront, and his ivory baton tucked in the top of his waistcoat.

"You look magnificent!" agreed Carlos. "But why not come and have dinner with us later. You too, Alencar. I want to hear those beautiful lines of yours properly. At six o'clock on the dot, without fail. I've ordered a little Portuguese supper, with stew, baked rice, chickpeas, etc., to make me feel at home."

Alencar made a gesture of utter scorn. The miserable francophile cook at the Bragança would never be up to creating the noble delicacies of old Portugal; nevertheless, he would be there at six on the dot, to toast the health of his Carlos!

"Are you leaving now, boys?"

Carlos and Ega were going to Ramalhete to visit the great house.

The poet immediately declared this to be a sacred pilgrimage, and so he left with Cruges. He was going in the same direction, towards Barradas' house. A talented boy, that Barradas. His paintings tended to be somewhat on the dark side, sketchy and unfinished, but there was a real spark there.

"And he had an aunt, my boys—Leonor Barradas! What eyes, what a body! But it wasn't just her body! She had soul, poetry, a sense of sacrifice! You just don't get women like that anymore. Never mind. At six, then!"

"At six on the dot, without fail!"

Alencar and the maestro left, having first stocked up on cigars. And shortly afterwards, Carlos and Ega were strolling, arm-in-arm, along Rua do Tesouro Velho.

They were talking about Paris, about the young men and women whom Ega had met four years before, when he had spent a delightful winter there in Carlos' apartments. And Ega was surprised, with each name evoked, to learn of the brief splendor, the abrupt end met by all that carefree youth. Lucy Gray, dead. Conrad, dead. And Marie Blond? She had grown fat and bourgeois and was married to a manufacturer of tallow candles. And the fair-haired young Pole? He had vanished, disappeared. And that Don Juan, Monsieur de Menant? He was now the sub-prefect of the Département of Doubs. And the young man who lived next door, the Belgian? He had lost all his money on the stock exchange. And still others—dead or lost or drowned in the mud of Paris!

"Well, all in all," remarked Ega, "this little Lisbon life of ours, simple, peaceful and easy, is infinitely preferable."

They were in Largo do Loreto, and Carlos paused, looking around him, reacquainting himself with the old heart of the capital. Nothing had changed. The same guard patrolled sleepily round and round the sad statue of Camões. The same red curtains, bearing ecclesiastical arms, hung in the doorways of the two churches. The Hotel Aliança had the same silent deserted air. A lovely sun gilded the street; coachmen, hats pushed back on their heads, came riding by, whipping their scrawny horses; three fishwives, with baskets on their head, walked past, swaying strong agile hips in the bright daylight. On one corner, some ragged idlers stood smoking; and on the opposite corner, in the Havanesa, more idlers, this time wearing frock-coats, were also smoking and talking politics.

"It's quite hideous for anyone coming from outside!" exclaimed Carlos.

"It isn't the city, it's the people. Such ugly people—sallow, sluggish, vulgar, pinched, and cowed!"

"But Lisbon's changed," said Ega seriously. "It's changed a lot. You must go and see the new Avenue, yes, before we go to Ramalhete, let's take a stroll along the Avenida!"

They walked down the Chiado. On the other side of the street, the shop awnings cast a dark, jagged shadow. And Carlos recognised men he had seen ten years before, leaning in the same doorways, in exactly the same melancholy pose. They had wrinkles now and their hair was greying. But there they were, spent and faded, propping up the same shop windows, and wearing fashionable collars. Then, outside the Livraria Bertrand, Ega, laughing, touched Carlos' arm.

"Look who's over there, at Baltreschi's!"

It was Dâmaso, a fatter, sleeker, stouter Dâmaso, with a flower in his buttonhole, sucking on a large cigar, and gawping at the scene around him, with the wide, brutish stare of a well-fed, contented ruminant. When he saw his two former friends coming towards him, he made as if to escape and take refuge in the shop. However, inevitably, irresistibly, he found himself face to face with Carlos; he held out his hand, with a smile on his scarlet chubby-cheeked countenance.

"Fancy seeing you here! What a surprise!"

Carlos offered him a limp hand and reciprocated Dâmaso's greeting with an indifferent, absent-minded smile.

"It is, indeed, Dâmaso. How are things?"

"Oh, you know, much the same. Are you staying long?"

"A few weeks."

"Are you staying at Ramalhete?"

"No, at the Bragança, but don't bother to call, I'm always out."

"Yes, of course. I was in Paris three months ago, staying at the Continental."

"Really. Well, it's been nice to see you, goodbye!"

"Goodbye, my friends. You look in fine fettle, Carlos, very well indeed!"

"It's all in the eye of the beholder, Dâmaso."

And in Dâmaso's wide eyes the old admiration really did seem to revive as he followed Carlos with his gaze, studying from behind his frock-coat, his hat, his way of walking, as he used to in the days when Carlos da Maia was, for him, the supreme example of his beloved chic, "of the kind one only ever sees abroad."

"Did you know that Dâmaso had got married?" said Ega, after they had walked a little distance, and again taking Carlos' arm.

Carlos was amazed. What! Our Dâmaso! Married! Yes, he had married one of the daughters of the Count and Countess of Águeda, an impoverished family with a whole troupe of daughters of marriageable age. It had fallen to him to marry the youngest. And the excellent Dâmaso, who was a real find for that distinguished family, now paid for the dresses of all the older girls too.

"Is she pretty?"

"Fairly . . . and she makes a strapping young fellow called Barroso very happy indeed."

"Poor Dâmaso!"

"Oh, yes, poor, poor, poor little Dâmaso! But, as you see, he's immensely happy and has even grown fat on perfidy!"

Carlos had stopped. He was staring up in astonishment at some extraordinary second-floor balconies, festooned with monogrammed banners as if for a holy day procession. He was about to point this out, when, from among a group gathered in the doorway of that festive building, a mischievous-looking youth, with a beardless, pimply face, ran across the road, calling to Ega and laughing hysterically.

"If you're quick, you'll catch up with her down there, go on, run!"

"Catch up with whom?"

"Adosinda! She's wearing a blue dress and white feathers in her hat. Go on, quickly! João Eliseu tripped her up with his walking-stick and sent her flying. God, it was funny. Quick!"

The young man strode back on skinny legs to rejoin his friends, who had fallen silent now, examining with provincial curiosity the tall elegant man accompanying Ega, and whom no one knew. Ega, meanwhile, was explaining to Carlos about the balconies and the group of young men.

"They're boys from the Turf Club. It's a new place, the former Jockey Club that used to be in Travessa da Palha. You can play cards there for very low stakes, and they're nice people. And, as you see, they're always prepared, with banners and everything, in case a procession should happen to pass by."

Then, going down Rua Nova do Almada, he told Carlos about Adosinda. Two weeks or so ago, he had been having supper at Silva's with a few friends after the theatre, when this extraordinary-looking woman all dressed in red turned up; for some reason, she rolled her r's excessively and even added r's to words that had none—anyway, she kept asking to speak to the "Viscrount." Which "Viscrount?" She didn't quite know. A viscrount she had met at the Croliseum. She sat down, they offered her champagne, and Dona Adosinda began to reveal herself to be a truly astonishing creature. They were talking about politics, about the government and the deficit. Dona Adosinda immediately announced that she knew the deficit very well, and that he was a lovely fellow. The deficit "a lovely fellow"—well, everyone roared with laughter. Dona Adosinda became annoyed and declared that she had been to Sintra with him, and that he was a perfect gentleman and worked for the Bank of England. The deficit employed by the Bank of England—howls and screams and wails of laughter! And they didn't stop laughing, endlessly, wildly and frenetically, until five o'clock in the morning, when Dona Adosinda was raffled off and won by Teles! Oh, it had been a splendid night!

"Indeed," said Carlos, smiling, "a grand orgy reminiscent of Heliogabalus or the Count d'Orsay."

Ega then energetically defended his orgy. Where in Europe or in any civilisation would one find a better one? Where in Paris, in the desolating banality of the Grand-Treize, could one hope to spend a more amusing night, or in London, for that matter, in the dull and proper tedium of the Bristol Club? What made life bearable was the opportunity now and then to have a good laugh. In Europe, men of refinement did not laugh, they merely smiled coolly, wanly. Only the Portuguese, in that barbarous corner of the world, still preserved that supreme gift, that blessed and consoling thing—the belly-laugh!

"What the devil are you staring at?"

It was Carlos' old consulting room, which was now apparently, according to the sign, a small dressmaker's shop. The two friends relapsed at once into memories of the past. What futile hours Carlos had spent there, reading the *Revue des Deux Mondes*, waiting in vain for patients to come, still full of faith in the joys of work! And the morning that Ega had appeared there in his splendid fur coat, preparing to transform, in a single winter, the whole of stick-in-the-mud old Portugal!

"And it all came to naught!"

"Yes, it all came to naught, but we laughed a lot. Do you remember that night when the poor Marquis wanted to take Paca to the consulting room, so that he could finally make use of that divan, that piece of furniture worthy of a seraglio?"

Carlos gave a sad sigh. The poor Marquis! The death of the Marquis had been one of the most upsetting events of recent years, and he had learned about it over lunch, in a prosaic item in the newspaper. As they ambled across the Rossio, they recalled other disappearances: Dona Maria da Cunha, poor thing, who had succumbed to dropsy; Dom Diogo, who had finally married his cook; good old Sequeira, who had died one night in a cab after a visit to the circus.

"Changing the subject," said Ega, "did you see Craft in London?"

"I did," replied Carlos. "He's found a lovely house near Richmond, but he's aged considerably and complains a lot about his liver. And, alas, he drinks too much. It's such a shame!"

Then he asked after Taveira. This well-dressed young man, according to Ega, had endured another ten years of working for the government and of life in the Chiado. But he was still never less than beautifully turned out, albeit going slightly grey, still always involved with some Spanish woman or other, still bossing everyone around at the Teatro de São Carlos, and spending every evening at the Casa Havanesa muttering sweetly and contentedly: "This country's going to rack and ruin." He was, in short, a typical example of the Lisbon dandy.

"And what about that fool Steinbroken?"

"He's Ambassador to Athens," exclaimed Ega, "in the middle of all those other classical ruins!"

The idea of Steinbroken in ancient Greece amused them no end. Ega imagined the good Steinbroken, very stiff in his high collars, commenting sagely about Socrates: "*Oh, il est très fort, il est excessivement fort!*" Or else, apropos the battle of Thermopylae, fearful of committing himself: "*C'est très grave, c'est excessivement grave!*" It would be worth going to Greece just to see him!

Suddenly, Ega stopped:

"There's the new Avenida! Not bad, eh?"

Carlos had emerged out of the peaceful, leafy Passeio Público into a wide open space, in which an obelisk, with bronze lettering on the pedestal, rose up, white as sugar, into the glittering winter light; and the large globes of the streetlamps surrounding it glinted in the sun, gleaming and transparent, like great soap bubbles suspended in the air. On either side stood massive buildings of varying heights, sleek and elegant and newly painted, with decorated zinc urns on the cornices, and black-and-white tiled courtyards, where doormen stood, smoking cigarettes; these two stiff ranks of dandified houses reminded Carlos of the families who used to sit in immobile rows on either side of the Passeio Público after the one o'clock mass, listening to the band, in their Sunday-best cashmeres and silks. The paving stones dazzled like fresh whitewash. Here and there, a pale sparse bush shrank from the breeze. And at the far end, the green hill, with its scattering of trees, and the fields of Vale de Pereiro, lent an unexpectedly rustic touch to that sudden burst of cheap sophistication, which had set out to transform the old city, but had swiftly run out of breath and ground to an almost immediate halt among piles of gravel.

There was, however, a fresh clean breeze blowing; the abandoned rubble gleamed gold in the sunlight; and the divine over-arching serenity of the incomparable blue sky sweetened everything. The two friends sat down on a bench, next to a grassy area surrounding the stagnant greenish water of a pond.

In the shade strolled young men, in pairs, with flowers in their buttonholes, wearing well-cut trousers and pale-coloured gloves with bold black stitching. This was a whole new generation unknown to Carlos. Ega would sometimes murmur a "Hello" and raise his walking-stick in greeting. And the men would continue strolling up and down, looking slightly shy and awkward, as if unaccustomed to that vast space, to all that light, and to their own chic clothes. Carlos was astonished. What were they doing there, during working hours, these sad young men in their narrow trousers? There were no women, apart from a sickly-looking creature in scarf and shawl, enjoying the sun on a bench farther along, and two matrons wearing short beaded capes, the landladies of guesthouses, taking their small shaggy dog for a walk. What was it that attracted these pale-faced youths to this place? What alarmed Carlos most were their inordinately long boots, which protruded below their trouser bottoms and had curved, pointed tips like the prows of boats.

"This is unbelievable, Ega!"

Ega was rubbing his hands. Yes, and it was significant too. The shape of those boots explained everything about contemporary Portugal. It showed how things really were. Having abandoned the ways of the old King, ways that had suited it very well, poor wretched Portugal had decided to become modern, and, lacking the originality, energy, and character to create a style and fashion of its own, it had imported models from abroad—models of ideas, trousers, customs, laws, art, cuisine. However, since it had no sense of proportion, and was, at the same time, dominated by an impatient desire to appear very modern and very civilised, all these models were immediately exaggerated and twisted and distorted into caricatures. The original model for the boot, which had come from abroad, was slightly narrow in the toe, and so the local Portuguese dandy had made it narrower still and as sharp as the point of a needle. Writers, for their part, read the precise chiselled style of a Goncourt or a Verlaine and immediately tortured and tangled and mangled their own poor sentences until they descended into the crazed or the burlesque. Legislators, hearing that their counterparts abroad were raising the standard of education, immediately introduced into the primary school curriculum metaphysics, astronomy, philology, Egyptology, chrematistics, comparative religion, and an infinite number of other horrors. And it was the same with everything else, in all classes and professions, from the orator to the photographer, from the jurist to the sportsman. It was exactly what happens with the blacks in colonial Africa who see Europeans wearing spectacles and imagine that this is what it means to be civilised and white. So what do they do? In their eagerness for progress and whiteness, they place on their noses three or four pairs of spectacles, with clear lenses, tinted lenses, and even coloured lenses. And thus adorned, they stumble about town in their loincloths, noses in the air, desperately balancing these multiple pairs of spectacles, and all in the name of being immensely civilised and immensely white.

Carlos was laughing.

"So things here are going from bad to worse!"

"Oh, it's frightful! It's so vulgar and so false—above all, false. There's nothing genuine in this wretched country now, not even the bread that we eat!"

Carlos, leaning back on the bench, pointed with his walking-stick.

"There's still that, which *is* genuine."

And he indicated the upper parts of the city, the old hills of Graça and Penha, with their ancient houses clinging to slopes parched and blackened by the sun. Above, sat ponderous convents and churches and other squat ecclesiastical dwellings, reminding one of plump slow friars, devout ladies in mantillas, processions, surplice-clad members of fraternities crowding the churchyards, bunches of anise hung in the streets, lupin seeds and fava bean stew sold on every corner, and fireworks set off in praise of Jesus. Higher still, its ruined walls silhouetted against the radiant blue, was the Castle, shabby and commonplace, where once, to the sound of the national anthem played on bassoons, white-trousered soldiers marched down into town with a call to insurrection. And in its shelter, in the gloomy quarter occupied by São Vicente and the cathedral, stood the crumbling mansions, with their wistful views out over the estuary and their enormous coats of arms on dilapidated walls, where, amid gossip, church-going, and card-games, the old Lisbon nobility, decrepit and stubborn, dragged out its last days.

Ega looked at it for a moment pensively.

"Yes, that is perhaps more genuine, but so unintelligent, so down-at-the-heels! People don't know which way to turn, and if we turn to ourselves, it's worse still!"

He suddenly tapped Carlos on the knee, his face alight.

"Wait! Look who comes!"

It was a victoria, very correct and beautifully turned out, advancing slowly and with style, to the steady trot of two English mares. It proved a disappointment though. Reclining languidly in it was only a very fair young man, as white as a camellia, with a little down on his upper lip. He waved to Ega, and gave a lovely virginal smile. The victoria passed.

"Didn't you recognise him?"

Carlos struggled to remember.

"Your former patient! Charlie!"

Carlos clapped his hands. Charlie, *his* Charlie! It made him feel quite old. But he was a pretty young thing!

"Yes, very pretty. He's friendly with an older man and is nearly always to be seen out and about with him. But I bet he came with his mother, who has probably gone for a walk somewhere around here. Shall we go and see?"

They searched the length of the Avenida, but the person they saw at once was Eusébiozinho. He looked gloomier than ever and more tubercular, arm in arm with a very stout lady with a high colour, who was bursting out of a very tight red silk dress. The couple were walking sedately along, taking the sun. Eusébio, downcast and submissive, didn't even notice Carlos and Ega, absorbed as he was in watching through his thick dark glasses the slow march of his own shadow.

"That monster is his wife," said Ega. "After various brothel romances, our Eusébio fell in love with her. The woman's father, who owns a pawnshop, caught them one night on the stairs enjoying a bit of illicit pleasure. All hell broke loose, and he was forced to marry her. He disappeared after that, and I haven't seen him since. They say his wife beats him regularly."

"May God preserve her!"

"Amen!"

Then Carlos, remembering the beating he had given Eusébio and the whole business of *The Devil's Trumpet*, asked after "Big Palma." Was that illustrious man still dishonouring the universe with his presence? He was, said Ega. However, he had abandoned literature and become the factotum of a one-time minister, Carneiro; he took Carneiro's Spanish mistress to the theatre for him and was now an influential friend to have in the world of politics.

"He'll be a member of parliament one of these days," said Ega. "And the way things are going, he might even make it to minister. But it's getting late, Carlos. Shall we hail this cab and go straight to Ramalhete?"

It was four o'clock, and the brief winter sun was already turning pale.

They took the cab. In Rossio, Alencar, who happened to be passing, saw them and waved enthusiastically. And then Carlos gave expression to the surprise he had felt that morning at the Hotel Bragança.

"You know, Ega, you seem awfully close to Alencar these days! What brought about this transformation?"

Ega admitted that he now felt huge admiration for Alencar. Firstly, because, in the midst of that entirely false Lisbon, Alencar was the only genuine Portuguese left. Secondly, in the midst of all that contagion of spite and deceit, Alencar remained steadfastly honest. Thirdly, he was so loyal, kind, and generous. The way he had taken in his niece was truly touching. He was more courteous and had better manners than other younger men. Even his liking for the bottle fit well with his poetic nature. And lastly, given the downhill slide of literature in general, Alencar's poetry stood out for its precision, simplicity, and for its remnant of real emotion. He was, in short, a most estimable bard.

"And there you have it, Carlos; see how we have fallen. Nothing, in fact, better exemplifies Portugal's awful state of decline in the last thirty years than this simple fact: so low has Portuguese character and talent sunk that suddenly old Tomás, the man who wrote *Flower of Martyrdom*, the Alencar of Alenquer, now takes on the proportions of a genius and a man of justice."

They were still talking about Portugal and its ills when the cab stopped. It was with great emotion that Carlos looked out at Ramalhete's severe façade, the small windows sheltering under the roof, the great bunch of sunflowers in place of a coat of arms! At the sound of the carriage, Vilaça appeared at the door, drawing on a pair of yellow gloves. Vilaça had grown fatter, and everything about him, from his new hat to the silver handle on his walking-stick, revealed his importance as administrator—almost master, during Carlos' long exile—of the vast Maia estate. He immediately introduced the gardener, an old man, who lived there with his wife and son, guarding the deserted mansion. Then he said how glad he was to see Carlos and Ega together again at last. And slapping Carlos on the back with fond familiarity, he added:

"You know, after we parted in Santa Apolónia this morning, I went and had a bath at the Hotel Central, and I didn't even need to have a nap. That's the great advantage of the sleeping-car! When it comes to progress, Portugal doesn't lag behind anyone! Do you need me now, sir?"

"No, thank you, Vilaça. We're just going to walk around the rooms. Come and dine with us. At six! At six o'clock on the dot, mind, because we've got some special dishes on the menu."

And the two friends walked through the entrance hall. The carved oak benches, as solemn as cathedral choir stalls, were still there. Beyond, however, the hallway was a sad sight, stripped bare of furniture and hangings, revealing the flaking whitewash on the walls. All the oriental rugs, displayed as if in a shop, all the glinting Moorish copper dishes, the statue of the young girl, in her marble nakedness, shivering with cold and laughing as she dipped a toe in the water—all of these now filled Carlos' rooms in Paris; and boxes were piled in one corner, ready to be dispatched, taking with them all the best faience-ware from the Toca. In the broad carpetless corridor, their footsteps echoed as if in an abandoned cloister. Here and there, in the dim light, the scrawny shoulder of a hermit or the ghastly white of a skull stood out against the darker tones in some of the religious paintings. An icy draught chilled the rooms. Ega turned up his coat collar.

In the main room, the green brocade furniture was draped in cotton sheets, as if in shrouds, giving off a mummy-like whiff of turpentine and camphor. And on the floor, in the Constable portrait leaning against the wall, the Countess de Runa, lifting the hem of her scarlet English hunting costume, seemed about to step out of the gilt frame and escape as well, to complete the scattering of her race.

"Let's go," said Ega. "This is really macabre!"

Carlos, however, pale and silent, opened the door to the billiard room. All the finest pieces from the Toca, in a confusion of styles and centuries, had recently been stored there, in what was the largest room in Ramalhete, as if it were an antiques warehouse. At the far end, obscuring the fireplace, its majestic architecture dominating everything, loomed the famous wooden cabinet dating from the time of the Hanseatic League, with its warriors armed like Mars, the bas-relief carvings on the doors, and preaching at each corner the four Evangelists, swathed in wind-ruffled garments as if caught in some prophetic gale. Carlos immediately noticed that a catastrophe had occurred on the cornice, to the two fauns defiant among the agricultural trophies. The cloven foot of one had been broken, and the other had lost his bucolic panpipes.

"How could they be so clumsy!" he cried angrily, his love of art wounded. "With a wonderful piece like this too!"

He climbed onto a chair to examine the damage. Ega, meanwhile, was looking at the other items of furniture—wedding chests, Spanish cabinets, Italian Renaissance sideboards—remembering the happy house in Olivais that they had adorned, the delightful nights spent talking, the suppers, the fireworks set off in honour of Leonidas . . . How everything passed! Suddenly he stubbed his toe on a lidless hat-box crammed with miscellaneous items—a veil, unmatched pairs of gloves, a silk stocking, ribbons, artificial flowers. They were things that had belonged to Maria Eduarda and been found in some corner of the Toca, then deposited here when they were emptying the house. And even more regrettably, mixed up with these odds and ends, all bundled together in the promiscuity of detritus, he found an embroidered velvet slipper, Afonso da Maia's old slipper! He quickly hid the box beneath a piece of tapestry. Then, as Carlos was jumping down from the chair, dusting off his hands and still indignant, Ega hastened to end this pilgrimage, which was threatening to spoil the happiness of the day.

"Let's go out onto the terrace, have a quick look at the garden and then leave!"

However, they had yet to broach the saddest memory of all—Afonso da Maia's study. The door-handle resisted. In his efforts to open it, Carlos' hand shook. And in his imagination, Ega, equally moved, saw the room as it once had been, with its Carcel oil-lamps casting their rose-pink light, the crackling fire, the Reverend Boniface ensconced on the bearskin rug, Afonso in his velvet smoking jacket, sitting in his old armchair and knocking out the ashes from his pipe into the palm of his hand. The door opened, and all these feelings vanished in the grotesque, absurd, desperate sneezing fit that seized them both, choked by the acrid dust stinging their eyes and leaving them dazed. Vilaça, following advice given in an almanac, had ordered handfuls of white pepper to be sprinkled in a thick protective layer over the furniture and the enveloping sheets. Unable to breathe or see, their eyes misted with tears, the two friends faced each other, convulsed by the most violent of sneezes.

Carlos finally managed to fling open the doors of the French window. On the terrace, a remnant of sunlight was slowly fading to nothing. The two friends, reviving slightly in the pure air, stood in silence, wiping their streaming eyes, still shaken by the occasional belated sneeze.

"What a ridiculous thing to do!" cried Carlos indignantly.

Ega, as he fled the room with his handkerchief pressed to his face, had stumbled and collided with a sofa, grazing his shin.

"God, how stupid! I really cracked my shin hard against that sofa!"

He looked back at the room, where all the furniture had disappeared beneath vast white shrouds. And he realised that what he had bumped against had been old Boniface's velvet stool. Poor Boniface! What had become of him?

Carlos, who'd sat down on the terrace's low parapet, among the empty flower pots, described the end of the Reverend Boniface. He had died in Santa Olávia, resigned and so fat he couldn't move. And Vilaça had had the poetic idea—the only one in his entire life as administrator—of ordering a tomb to be made, a simple white marble slab and with it he had a rose-tree planted underneath the windows of Afonso's bedroom.

Ega joined Carlos on the parapet, and they both sat absorbed in thought. Below them, the garden, with its sandy paths, clean and cold in its winter bareness, had the melancholy of a forgotten retreat no one cared for any more: green algae covered Aphrodite's large limbs; the cypress and the cedar were growing old together, like two friends in a wilderness; and the weeping fountain wept more slowly, just a thread of water drip-dripping into the marble basin. At the bottom of the garden, framed like a seascape by the walls of the two tall buildings opposite, Ramalhete's brief vista—a fragment of river and hill—had taken on a sad and pensive note that late afternoon; on the strip of river, a steamship, ready for its voyage, was heading slowly downstream, disappearing at once, as if swallowed up by the uncertain sea; on the top of the hill, the windmill had stopped, frozen in the icy air; and in the windows of the houses on the farther shore, a ray of sun was gradually dying, faint in the first grey of evening, like a glimmer of hope on a face gradually clouding with despair.

Then, in that mute scene of solitude and neglect, Ega, gazing off into the distance, said slowly: "So you had no idea she was getting married, not the slightest suspicion?"

"No, none. The first I knew about it was the letter I received in Seville."

This was the amazing news Carlos had promised and which he had announced that morning to Ega at the station, after they had exchanged their first greetings and embraces. Maria Eduarda was going to marry.

She had announced this to Carlos in a very simple letter, which he had received when staying at the estate of his friends, the Villa Medinas. She was going to marry. This did not seem to be a romantic impulse, a decision taken hastily, but one that had been some time in the ripening. She referred in the letter to having "thought long and hard." Besides, the groom was close to fifty. And Carlos, therefore, saw in that marriage a union of two souls disappointed and bruised by life, weary of or else frightened by their isolation, and who, sensing in each other the same seriousness of heart and mind, had decided to share what remained of their warmth, joy, and courage facing old age together.

"How old is she?"

Carlos thought she must be forty-one or forty-two. She said in her letter that she was only six years and three months younger than her fiancé. His name was Monsieur de Trelain. He was obviously a man of generous spirit, free of prejudices, almost merciful in his benevolence, because, even though he knew of Maria Eduarda's past mistakes, he clearly loved her.

"He doesn't know everything, does he?" asked Ega, jumping to his feet.

"No, not everything. She says that Monsieur de Trelain knows of all those errors into which she had fallen unknowingly, which I understand to mean that he doesn't know everything. Come on, we'd better get moving, I still want to see my old rooms."

They went down into the garden. For a moment, they said nothing as they walked along the path where Afonso's roses had once grown. The cork bench was still there beneath the two Judas trees; Maria Eduarda had sat on that bench during her one visit to Ramalhete, making up a little posy of flowers to take with her as a relic. As he passed, Ega plucked a small marguerite, which was flowering all alone.

"She's still living in Orléans, then?"

Yes, said Carlos, she lived in a house she had bought there called Les Rosières. Her fiancé must live nearby in some small chateau. She described him as a neighbour, so he must be a country gentleman, from a good family, and with a decent fortune.

"Of course, she only has the money you send to her."

"Yes, I thought I wrote to tell you all that," murmured Carlos. "In the end, she refused to have any part of her inheritance. And Vilaça arranged things through a gift I made to her, equivalent to an income of twelve *contos de réis*."

"Good. Does she mention Rosa in the letter?"

"Yes, in passing, just to say that she's fine. She must be a young woman now."

"And a very pretty one too!"

They were walking up the wrought-iron staircase that led from the garden to Carlos' rooms. Grasping the handle of the glass-paned door, Ega stopped again to ask one last question: "And how do you feel about it all?"

Carlos was lighting a cigar. Then, throwing the match over the wrought-iron handrail, around which a climbing plant entwined, he said: "It gives me a feeling of conclusion, a sense that finally it's all over. It's as if she had died, and with her all the past, only to be reborn in another form. She's no longer Maria Eduarda, she's a French lady called Madame de Trelain. Everything that happened vanishes beneath that name, is buried a thousand leagues deep, finished and done with, without leaving so much as a memory. That's how I feel about it."

"Did you never meet up with Senhor Guimarães in Paris?"

"Never. And, of course, now he's dead."

They went into the room. Vilaça, assuming that Carlos would stay at Ramalhete, had ordered it to be made ready; and yet everything had a chill about it—the marble tops of the chests of drawers dusted and empty, a candle intact in a solitary candlestick, a fustian coverlet carefully folded on the curtainless bedstead. Carlos put his hat and his walking-stick down on his old desk. Then, as if summing things up, he said:

"That's life for you, Ega! For several nights, in this very room, I felt certain that the world had ended for me. I considered killing myself. I considered joining the Trappists. And I did so coldly, as if that were the only logical conclusion. Now, ten years have passed, and here I am again."

He stopped in front of the long mirror suspended between two columns of carved oak, smoothed his moustache and concluded with a melancholy smile: "Hm, and fatter too!"

Ega also looked thoughtfully around the room.

"Do you remember the night I turned up here in emotional agony and dressed as Mephistopheles?"

Carlos uttered a cry. Of course, Raquel! What about Raquel? What had happened to that lily of Israel?

Ega shrugged.

"Oh, she's still around, but she's quite lost her looks!"

Carlos murmured: "Poor thing!" And that was all they said about Ega's grand romantic passion.

Carlos, meanwhile, went over to examine a picture that had been left on the floor near the window, forgotten and turned to the wall. It was the portrait of his father, Pedro da Maia, with his kidskin gloves in his hand, and with those great Arab eyes in the sad pale face which time had only turned still more yellow. He placed it on top of a chest of drawers. And wiping it over with a handkerchief, he said:

"The thing that really saddens me is not having a portrait of Grandfather! But I'll definitely take this back with me to Paris."

Then, from the sofa on which he had set himself down, Ega asked if, during the last few years, Carlos had ever considered the idea or even nursed a vague desire to return to Portugal.

Carlos regarded Ega with horror. Why would he return? In order to troop glumly from the Grémio to the Casa Havanesa? No! Paris was the only place on Earth that suited the definitive type he had now become: "the rich gentleman who lives well." Riding in the Bois de Boulogne; lunch at Bignon's; a stroll along the boulevard; an hour at the club reading the newspapers; a bit of fencing in the fencing gallery; the Comédie Française or a soirée in the evening; Trouville in the summer, and hare-shooting in the winter; and throughout the year women, bullfights, some scientific dabbling, antiques, and a certain amount of witty banter. What could be more inoffensive, more insignificant, or more pleasant?

"And there you have one man's existence! In ten years nothing has happened to me, apart from when my phaeton collapsed on the road to Saint-Cloud . . . It was even reported in *Le Figaro*."

Ega got up and made a desolate gesture: "We have failed in life, my friend!"

"Yes, I think we have, but everyone fails to some degree. That is, the life you plan in your imagination always fails in reality. You tell yourself: 'I'm going to be this way, because therein beauty lies.' But, as the poor Marquis used to say, when it's a matter of one thing or t'other, it's always 't'other' that wins. It might sometimes be better, but it's always different."

Ega agreed with a silent sigh, starting to pull on his gloves.

The room was growing dark in the cold and melancholy winter twilight. Carlos put on his hat, and they went down the stairs lined in cherry-red velvet, and past the panoply of ancient weapons, now grown dull and tarnished. Out in the street, Carlos stopped to take a long look at the sombre mansion, which, in the early darkness, looked more than ever like an ecclesiastical residence, already taking on the grim look of a ruin, silent and uninhabited, with its severe walls, its row of small closed windows, and the grilles on the ground-floor windows full of shadows.

A shudder ran through his soul, and taking Ega's arm, he said softly:

"It's odd, you know, I only spent two years in this house, and yet it seems to contain my whole life!"

Ega was not surprised. Only there, in Ramalhete, had he experienced the one thing that gives savour and significance to life—passion.

"That's an idea worthy of an old romantic, Ega! A lot of other things give value to life as well."

"And what are we, if not romantics?" exclaimed Ega. "What have we been since we were at school, since we were sitting for our Latin exam? Romantics, which is to say, inferior individuals ruled in life by feelings and not by reason."

Carlos wanted to know if, deep down, they really were so much happier, those people who were guided solely by reason, never deviating from it, determined to toe that inflexible line—dry, rigid, logical and emotionless to the last—and putting themselves through torments.

"I don't think so," said Ega. "From the outside, at least, they're an unconsoling sight, and inside, too, they are perhaps unconsoled as well. Which just goes to show that in this pretty world of ours it's best to be either foolish or dull."

"In short, it's not worth living."

"That depends entirely upon how strong a stomach you have!" added Ega.

They both laughed. Then Carlos, serious again, offered his theory of life, the definitive theory he had drawn from experience and which was now his guide. It was a Muslim fatalism. Desire nothing and fear nothing. Succumb neither to hope nor to disappointment. Accept everything, what comes and what escapes one, with the same tranquillity with which one accepts the natural changes from stormy days to mild. And in that placid state of mind, allow that piece of organised matter called the "I" gradually to deteriorate and decompose until it re-enters and is lost in the infinite universe. Above all, have no appetites, and, still more importantly, no discontentment.

Ega broadly agreed. What he was principally persuaded of, in these narrow years of life, was the futility of all effort. There was no point in trying to achieve anything on this Earth, because, as the wise author of Ecclesiastes taught, everything ends in disillusion and dust.

"If someone were to tell me that down there the fortune of a Rothschild or the imperial crown of Carlos V were just waiting for me, and that it could be mine if I ran to grab it, I wouldn't so much as quicken my step. No! I would maintain this slow, prudent, proper step, which is the only pace at which one should walk anywhere in life."

"Oh, I agree!" said Carlos with great conviction.

And they slowed their step as they went down the Rampa de Santos, as if that really were the road of life, along which one should always walk slowly and scornfully, certain, as they were, of finding at the end only disillusion and dust. They could already see the Aterro, with its long line of lights. Suddenly Carlos stopped, as if annoyed with himself.

"Oh, really! I came from Paris with such an appetite, and yet what I forgot to order for tonight's supper was a large dish of pork sausages and peas!"

And it was too late now, remarked Ega. Then Carlos, who had been immersed until then in memories of the past and theories about the meaning of